THE 13TH REALITY

BOOKS 1 & 2

DON'T MISS THE REST OF
THE 13TH REALITY
SERIES!

✳

The 13th Reality
Books 3 & 4

The Blade of Shattered Hope
The Void of Mist and Thunder

THE 13TH REALITY

BOOKS 1 & 2

THE JOURNAL
OF CURIOUS LETTERS

———— ✳ ————

THE HUNT FOR
DARK INFINITY

JAMES DASHNER

ILLUSTRATED BY BRYAN BEUS

Simon Pulse

New York London Toronto Sydney New Delhi

SIMON PULSE

An imprint of Simon & Schuster Children's Publishing Division

1230 Avenue of the Americas, New York, New York 10020

This Simon Pulse paperback edition July 2015

The Journal of Curious Letters text copyright © 2008 by James Dashner

The Journal of Curious Letters interior illustrations copyright © 2008 by Bryan Beus

Originally published in hardcover in 2008 by Deseret Book Company

The Hunt for Dark Infinity text copyright © 2009 by James Dashner

The Hunt for Dark Infinity interior illustrations copyright © 2009 by Bryan Beus

Originally published in hardcover in 2009 by Deseret Book Company

Cover photograph copyright © 2015 by Miguel Sobreira/Arcangel Images

All rights reserved, including the right of reproduction in whole or in part in any form.

SIMON PULSE and colophon are registered trademarks of Simon & Schuster, Inc.

For information about special discounts for bulk purchases, please contact Simon & Schuster Special Sales at 1-866-506-1949 or business@simonandschuster.com.

The Simon & Schuster Speakers Bureau can bring authors to your live event. For more information or to book an event contact the Simon & Schuster Speakers Bureau at 1-866-248-3049 or visit our website at www.simonspeakers.com.

Cover designed by Gail Ghezzi

Interior designed by Tom Daly

The text of this book was set in Adobe Garamond.

Manufactured in the United States of America 0615 OFF

2 4 6 8 10 9 7 5 3

Library of Congress Control Number 2015938658

ISBN 978-1-4814-5315-8 (pbk)

These titles were previously published individually by Aladdin.

CONTENTS

✸

THE JOURNAL
OF CURIOUS LETTERS

This book is dedicated to my wife, Lynette,

and to our mothers,

Linda Dashner and Patti Anderson.

Thank you for making my life so far

a wonderful thing to have lived.

ACKNOWLEDGMENTS

✳

I used to think this section was major lame. Why on earth, as a reader, would I give a flying tahooty about the people who helped the author? Well, I'm here to tell you that you should be very interested. Because without the awesome people I mention below, this book wouldn't be in your hands.

Before anyone else, I need to thank Chris Schoebinger and Lisa Mangum at Shadow Mountain. Despite being an author, I can't come up with words great enough to express how much they've changed my life. Fabulicious. Astoundendicularly whammy. Terrificaliwondershonks. (See, told ya.) Thank you, Chris and Lisa.

Thanks to my wife, Lynette. Always my first reader,

she's not afraid to tell me when something sounds like a two-year-old blurted it out while sitting on the potty.

Thanks to my sister, Sarah Kiesche, for keeping up my Web site during the Jimmy Fincher books and being my number one fan.

Thanks to my agent, Jenny Rappaport, for her work on my behalf.

Thanks to J. Scott Savage. His keen and almost eerie understanding of how to weave a good story has helped me greatly. And our regular lunches to "talk shop" have been invaluable. I do wish he'd use a little more deodorant, though.

Thanks to Annette Lyon, Heather Moore, Michele Holmes, Lu Ann Staheli, Lynda Keith, and Stephanni Hicken. These crazy ladies all read the manuscript and gave excellent feedback.

A huge thanks to the younger folks, whose advice was perhaps most relevant: Jacob Savage, Alyssa Holmes, and Daniel Lyon.

Thanks to Shirley Bahlmann (and her kids), Danyelle Ferguson, and Anne Bradshaw. Shirley is the only one besides my wife who has helped me with every book I've written.

Thanks to Crystal Hardman, Tony and Rachel Benjamin, Pam Anderton, and Julie Sasagawa. Eating at Jim's Restaurant will never be the same.

ACKNOWLEDGMENTS

Thanks to Peter Jackson for making the *Lord of the Rings* movies.

Thanks to the dude who invented football.

Thanks to the many chickens that provided me with spicy buffalo wings over the years.

And last, but certainly not least, thanks to all the Jimmy Fincher fans. Without your loyal following, Atticus Higginbottom would have never been born.

PART 1

---✳---

THE FIRE

CHAPTER 1

MASTER GEORGE AND MISTRESS JANE

Norbert Johnson had never met such strange people in all of his life, much less two on the same day—within the same *hour* even. Odd. Very odd indeed.

Norbert, with his scraggly gray hair and his rumpled gray pants and his wrinkly gray shirt, had worked at the post office in Macadamia, Alaska, for twenty-three years, seven months, twelve days, and—he looked at his watch—just a hair short of four hours. In those long, cold, lonesome years he'd met just about every type of human being you could imagine. Nice people and mean people. Ugly people and pretty people. Lawyers, doctors, accountants, cops. Crazies and convicts. Old hags and young whippersnappers. Oh, and lots of celebrities, too.

Why, if you believed his highfalutin stories (which most people quit doing about twenty-three years, seven months, twelve days, and *three* hours ago), you'd think he'd met every movie and music star in America. Though exactly *why* these famous folks were up in Alaska dropping off mail was anybody's guess, so it may have been a slight exaggeration of the truth.

But today's visitors were different, and Norbert knew he'd have to convince the town that this time he was telling the truth and nothing but the truth. Something scary was afoot in Macadamia.

The first stranger, a man, entered the small, cramped post office at precisely 11:15 A.M., quickly shutting the door against the blustery wind and swirling snowflakes. In doing so, he almost dropped a cardboard box full of letters clutched in his white-knuckled hands.

He was a short, anxious-looking person, shuffling his feet and twitching his nose, with a balding red scalp and round spectacles perched on his ruddy, puffy face. He wore a regal black suit: all pinstripes and silk and gold cuff links.

When the man plopped the box of letters onto the post office counter with a loud flump, a cloud of dust billowed out; Norbert coughed for several seconds. Then, to top everything off, the stranger spoke with a heavy English accent like he'd just walked out of a Bill Shakespeare play.

"Good day, sir," he said, the faintest attempt at a smile creasing his face into something that looked like pain. "I do hope you would be so kind as to offer me some assistance in an important matter." He pulled a lace-edged handkerchief from within the dark recesses of his fancy suit and wiped his brow, beads of sweat having formed there despite the arctic temperatures outside. It was, after all, the middle of November.

"Yessir," Norbert answered, ready to fulfill his duty as Postal Worker Number Three. "Mighty glad to help."

The man pointed outside. "Simply dreadful, isn't it?"

Norbert looked through the frosted glass of the front door, but saw only the snow-swept streets and a few pedestrians bundled up and hurrying to get out of the cold. "What's dreadful, sir?"

The man huffed. "By the Wand, man, this place, this *place*!" He put away his hanky and folded his arms, exaggerating a shiver up and down his body. "How can you chaps stand it—the bitter cold, the short daylight, the biting wind?"

Norbert laughed. "I take it you're just a-visiting?"

"Visiting?" The sharply dressed man barked something between a laugh and a snort. "There'll be no visiting from me, my good man. The instant these letters are off, I'll be heading back to the ocean. The very *instant*, I assure you."

The ocean? Norbert eyed the man, a little offended by the stranger's dislike of the only town where Norbert had ever set foot. "Well, sir, how long you been here?"

"How long?" The man looked at his golden pocket watch. "How *long*? Approximately seven minutes, I'd say, and that's far too long already. I'm, er, eager to be on my way, if you don't mind." He scratched his flaky red scalp. "Which reminds me—is there a cemetery closer than the one down by the frozen riverside?"

"A cemetery?"

"Yes, yes, a cemetery. You know, where they bury poor chaps with unbeating hearts?" When Norbert only stared, the man sighed. "Oh, never mind."

Norbert remembered hearing the word *befuddled* once on television. He had never been quite sure what it meant, but something told him it explained exactly how he felt at that moment. He scratched his chin, squinting at the odd little man. "Sir, may I ask your name?"

"No, you may not, Mister Postman. But if you must call me something, you may call me Master George."

"Alrighty then," Norbert said, his tone wary. "Uh, Master George, you're a-telling me you just arrived here in Macadamia seven minutes ago?"

"That's right. Please—"

Norbert ignored him. "And you're a-telling me you

come all this way just to mail these here letters, and then you're a-going to up and leave again?"

"Egads, yes!" Master George squeezed his hands together and rocked back and forth on his heels. "That is, if you'd be so kind as to . . ." He motioned to the box of letters, raising his thin eyebrows.

Norbert shook his head. "Well, how'd you get here?"

"By . . . er, plane, if you must know. Now, really, why so many questions?"

"You got yourself your own plane?"

Master George slammed his hand against the counter. "Yes! Is this a post office or a trial by jury? Now, please, I'm in a great hurry!"

Norbert whistled through his teeth, not taking his eyes off Master George as he slid the box closer to him. Then, reluctantly, Norbert looked down, a little worried the stranger might disappear once they broke eye contact.

The box was filled to the rim with hundreds of envelopes, yellowed and crumpled like they'd been trampled by a herd of buffalo, the addresses scrawled across the wrinkly paper in messy blue ink. Each frumpy envelope also bore a unique stamp—some of which looked to be rare and worth serious money: an Amelia Earhart, a Yankee Stadium, a Wright Brothers.

Norbert looked back up at the man. "So, you flew

in your own plane to the middle of Alaska in the middle of November to deliver these letters . . . and then you're heading back home?"

"Yes, and I'll be sure to tell Scotland Yard that if they're in need of a detective to ring you straight away. Now, good sir, is there anything else I have to do? I want to make absolutely sure there will be no problem in the delivery of these letters."

Norbert shrugged, then shuffled through the stack of envelopes, verifying they all had stamps and proper addresses. The letters were destined to go everywhere from Maine to California, from France to South Africa. Japan. China. Mexico. They were headed all over the world. And by the looks of it, the man had estimated the required postage to perfection.

"Well, I'll have to weigh each one and type the location into the computer, but they look all right to me on first glance. You wantin' to stick around while I check them all?"

Master George slipped a fat wallet out of his jacket pocket. "Oh, I assure you the necessary postage is there, but I must be certain. Here." He pulled out several hundred-dollar bills and placed them on the counter. "If you find that additional postage is required, this should be more than sufficient to pay in full. Consider the rest as a tip for your valuable service."

Norbert swallowed the huge lump in his throat.

"Uh, sir, I can tell you right now it won't take nearly that much. Not even close."

"Well, then, I will return home feeling very satisfied indeed." He squinted at Norbert's name tag before tipping his head in a formal bow. "I bid you farewell, Norbert, and wish you the very best."

And with that, Master George slipped back out into the frigid air.

Norbert had a sneaking suspicion he'd never see the man again.

Norbert had just placed the box of odd letters on a shelf under the front desk when an even stranger character than the finely appareled English gentleman stepped into the quiet post office. When the woman walked in the door, Norbert's mouth dropped open.

She wore nothing but yellow—her floor-length dress, her heavy overcoat, her pointy-toed shoes, her tightly fitted gloves. She pushed back the hood of her coat, revealing a bald head that shone as bright as a chrome ball, a pair of horn-rimmed glasses perched on her steep ridge of a nose, and eyes the color of burning emeralds.

She looked like a lemon that had been turned into an evil sorceress; Norbert surprised himself when he chuckled out loud before she said a word. By the way her

eyes narrowed into green laser points, Norbert figured that wasn't the smartest thing he'd done in a while.

"Something funny, mailman?" she asked, her voice soft and seductive, yet somehow filled with a subtle hint of warning. Unlike Master George, she had no accent Norbert recognized—she could've been from any city in Alaska. Well, except for the fact that she looked like a walking banana.

After a long moment with no response, she continued, "You'll find that Mistress Jane doesn't react kindly to those who mock her."

"Um," Norbert stuttered. "Uh, who . . . who is Mistress Jane?" As soon as he said it, he knew he must sound like an idiot.

"Me, you blubbering fool. Are you daft?"

"No, ma'am, I can hear just fine."

"Not *deaf*, you moronic stack of soiled snow, daft— *daft*. Oh, never mind." She took a step closer, placing her gloved hands on the counter right in front of Norbert. Her eyes seemed to have tracking beams focused on his own, pulling his gaze into a trance. "Now listen to me, mailman, and listen to me well. Understand?"

Norbert tried to utter agreement, but managed only a small squeak. He nodded instead.

"Good." She straightened and folded her arms. "I'm looking for a little stuff-bucket of a man—red-faced, ugly, more annoying than a ravenous mouse in a cheese factory. I know he came here just minutes ago, but I *don't* know if I'm in the correct Reality. Have you seen him?"

Norbert called upon every ounce of willpower in his feeble little body to hold his face still, hiding all expression. He forced his eyes to focus on the Lemon Lady's bald head and to not let them wander to the box of letters on the shelf at his feet. He didn't have a single clue what was going on with these two strangers, but every instinct told him Master George equaled good, Mistress Jane equaled bald—he blinked—uh, *bad*.

What does she mean about being in the correct reality, *anyway?* Norbert marveled that two such interesting people could enter his tiny post office within a half hour of each other.

"Polar bear got your tongue—?" Mistress Jane asked with a sneer, glancing down at his name badge. "Norbie? Anybody in there?"

Norbert ignored his racing heart and simply said, "No."

"No what?" the yellow woman snapped. "No, you're not in there, or no, the man I'm looking for didn't come here?"

"Ma'am, you're my first customer of the day, and no, I've a-never seen any such person as you described in my life."

Mistress Jane frowned, held a finger up to her chin.

"Do you know what Mistress Jane does with liars, Norbie?"

"I'm not a-lying, ma'am," Norbert answered, trying his best to look calm. He didn't like fibbing to such a scary woman—and crossing his fingers under the counter wouldn't amount to a hill of beans if she found out—but somehow he just knew that if this evil lady wanted to stop Master George from doing whatever he was trying to do, then those letters needed to get in the mail, no matter what. And it was all up to Norbert Johnson.

The lady looked away as if lost in deep thought over what she should do next. "I know he's up to something," she whispered, barely audible and not really speaking to Norbert anymore. "But which Reality . . . I don't have time to look in them all . . ."

"Miss Jane?" Norbert asked. "May I—"

"It's *Mistress* Jane, you Alaskan ice head."

"Oh, uh, I'm awfully sorry—I just wanted to know if there's any postal service you'll be a-needing today."

The nasty woman looked at him for a long time, saying nothing. Finally, "If you're lying to me, I'll find out and I'll come back for you, *Norbie*." She reached into the pocket of her overcoat, fidgeting with something hidden and heavy. "And you won't like the consequences, I can promise you that."

"No, ma'am, I'm sure—"

Before he could finish his sentence, though, the last and by far *most* bizarre thing of the day occurred.

Mistress Jane disappeared.

She vanished—into thin air, as they say. *Poof,* like a magic trick. One second there, the next second gone.

Norbert stared at the empty space on the other side of the counter, knowing he needed a much stronger word than *befuddled* to explain how he felt now. Finally, shaking his head, he reached down and grabbed the box containing Master George's letters.

"These are going out *tonight,*" he said, though no one was in the room to hear him.

CHAPTER 2

A VERY
STRANGE LETTER

Atticus Higginbottom—nicknamed "Tick" since his first day of kindergarten—stood inside the darkness of his own locker, cramped and claustrophobic. He desperately wanted to unlatch the handle and step out, but he knew he had to wait five more minutes. The edict had been decreed by the Big Boss of Jackson Middle School in Deer Park, Washington. And what Billy "The Goat" Cooper commanded must be obeyed; Tick didn't dare do otherwise.

He peeked through the metal slats of the door, annoyed at how they slanted down so he could only see the dirty white tiles of the hallway. The bell ending the school day had rung ages ago and Tick knew that by now most of the students would be outside, waiting for their buses or already walking home. A few stragglers still roamed the hallways, though, and one of them stopped in front of Tick's jail cell, snickering.

"Hope you get out before suppertime, Icky Ticky Stinkbottom," the boy said. Then he kicked the locker, sending a terrible *bang* of rattled metal echoing through Tick's ears. "The Goat sent me to make sure you hadn't escaped yet—good thing you're still in there. I can see your beady little eyes." Another kick. "You're not *crying* are you? Careful, you might get snot on your Barf Scarf."

Tick squeezed his eyes shut, steeled himself to ignore the idiot. Eventually, the bullies always moved on if he just stayed silent. Talking back, on the other hand . . .

The boy laughed again, then walked away.

In fact, Tick was *not* crying and hadn't done so in a long time. Once he'd learned to accept his fate in life as the kid everyone liked to pick on, his life had become a whole lot easier. Although Tick's attitude seemed to annoy Billy to no end. *Maybe I should fake a cry next time,* Tick thought. *Make the Goat feel like a big bad king.*

When the hall had grown completely still and silent, Tick reached down and flicked the latch of the door. It swung open with a loud *pop* and slammed against the locker next to it. Tick stepped out and stretched his cramped legs and arms. He couldn't have cared less about Billy and his gang of dumb bullies right then— it was Friday, his mom and dad had bought him the latest gaming system for his thirteenth birthday, and the Thanksgiving holidays were just around the corner. He felt perfectly happy.

Glancing around to make sure no one had hung around to torture him some more, Tick adjusted the red-and-black striped scarf he always wore to hide the hideous purple blotch on his neck—an irregular, rusty-looking birthmark the size of a drink coaster. It was the one thing he hated most about his body, and no matter how much his parents tried to convince him to lose the scarf, he wore it every hour of every day—even in the summer, sweat soaking through in dark blotches. Now, with winter settling in with a vengeance, people had quit giving him strange looks about the security blanket wrapped around his neck. Well, except for the jerks who called it the Barf Scarf.

He set out down the hall, heading for the door closest to the street that led to his house; he lived within walking distance of the school, which was lucky for him because the buses were long gone. He rounded the corner and saw Mr. Chu, his science teacher, step out of the teacher's lounge, briefcase in hand.

"Well, if it isn't Mr. Higginbottom," the lanky man said, a huge smile on his face. "What are you still doing around here? Anxious for more homework?" His straight black hair fell almost to his shoulders. Tick knew his mom would say Mr. Chu needed a haircut, but Tick thought he looked cool.

Tick gave a quick laugh. "No, I think you gave us plenty—I'll be lucky to get half of it done by Monday."

"Hmmm," Mr. Chu replied. He reached out and swatted Tick on the back. "If I know you, it was done by the end of lunchtime today."

Tick swallowed, for some reason embarrassed to admit his teacher was exactly right. *So, I'm a nerd*, he thought. *One day it'll make me filthy dirty rotten rich*. Tick was grateful that at least he didn't really look the part of a brainy nerd. His brown hair wasn't greasy; he didn't wear glasses; he had a solid build. His only real blemish was the birthmark. And maybe the fact that he was as clumsy as a one-legged drunk. But, as his dad always said, he was no different from any other kid his age and would grow out of the clumsiness in a few years.

Whatever the reason, Tick just didn't get along with people his own age. He found it hard to talk to them, much less be friends. Though he did *want* friends. Badly. *Poor little me*, he thought.

"I'll take your lack of a smart-aleck response—and the fact you aren't holding any books—as proof I'm right," Mr. Chu said. "You're too smart for the seventh grade, Tick. We should really bump you up."

"Yeah, so I can get picked on even *more*? No, thanks."

Mr. Chu's face melted into a frown. He looked at the floor. "I hate what those kids do to you. If I could . . ."

"I know, Mr. Chu. You'd beat 'em up if it weren't for those pesky lawsuits." Tick felt relieved when a smile returned to his teacher's face.

"That's right, Tick. I'd put every one of those slackers in the hospital if I could get away with it. Bunch of no-good louses—that's what they are. In fifteen years, they'll all be calling you *boss*. Remember that, okay?"

"Yes, sir."

"Good. Why don't you run on home, then. I bet your mom's got some cookies in the oven. See you Monday."

"Okay. See ya, Mr. Chu." Tick waved, then hurried down the hall toward home.

He only tripped and fell once.

⌒

"I'm home!" Tick yelled as he shut the front door. His four-year-old sister, Kayla, was playing with her tea set in the front room, her curly blonde hair bouncing with every move. She sat right next to the piano, where their older sister Lisa banged out some horrific song that she'd surely blame on the piano being out of tune. Tick dropped his backpack on the floor and hung his coat on the wooden rack next to the door.

"What's up, Tiger?" his mom said as she shuffled into the hallway, pushing a string of brown hair behind her ear. The cheeks of her thin face were red from her efforts in the kitchen, small beads of sweat hanging on for dear life along her forehead. Lorena Higginbottom loved—absolutely *loved*—to cook and everyone in Deer Park knew it. "I just put some cookies in the oven."

Righto, Mr. Chu.

"Mom," Tick said, "people stopped calling each other 'Tiger' a long time before I was born. Why don't you just call me 'Tick'? Everyone else does."

His mom let out an exaggerated sigh. "That's the worst nickname I've ever heard. Do you even know what a tick *does*?"

"Yeah, it sucks your blood right before you squish it dead." Tick pressed his thumb against his pant leg, twisting it with a vicious scowl on his face. Kayla looked up from her tea set, giggling.

"Lovely," Mom said. "And you have no problem being named after such a creature?"

Tick shrugged. "Anything's better than Atticus. I'd rather be called . . . *Wilbur* than Atticus."

His mom laughed, even though he could tell she tried not to.

"When's Dad gonna be home?" Tick asked.

"The usual, I'd guess," Mom replied. "Why?"

"He owes me a rematch in Football 3000."

Mom threw her arms up in mock desperation. "Oh, well, in that case, I'll call and tell him it's an emergency and to get his tail right home."

Lisa stopped playing her music, much to Tick's relief, and, he suspected, to the relief of every ear within a quarter mile. She turned around on the piano bench to look at Tick, her perfect teeth shining in an evil grin. Wavy brown hair framed a slightly pudgy face, like she'd never quite escaped her baby fat. "Dad whipped you by five touchdowns last time," she said sweetly, folding her arms. "Why don't you give up, already?"

"Will do, once you give up beating that poor piano with a hatchet every day. Sounds like an armless gorilla is playing in there."

Instead of responding, Lisa stood up from the piano bench and walked over to Tick. She leaned forward and gave him a big kiss on the cheek. "I wuv you, wittle brother."

"I think I'm gonna be sick, Mom," Tick groaned, wiping his cheek. "Could you get me something to clean my face?"

Lisa folded her arms and shook her head, her eyes

set in a disapproving stare. "And to think I used to change your diaper."

Tick barked a fake laugh. "Uh, sis, you're two years older than me—pretty sure you never changed my diaper."

"I was very advanced for my age. Skilled beyond my years."

"Yeah, you're a regular Mozart—well, except for the whole music thing."

Mom put her hands on her hips. "You two are just about the silliest kids I've ever—" A loud buzz from the kitchen cut her off. "Ah, the cookies are done." She turned and scuttled off toward the kitchen.

Kayla screamed something unintelligible, then ran after her mom with a huge smile planted on her face, dropping tea cups all over the floor and hallway.

Tick looked at Lisa and shrugged. "At least she's not burning things." Kayla had been caught several times at the living room fireplace, laughing with glee as she destroyed important objects in the flames. Tick headed for the staircase. "I'll be back in a minute—gotta use the bathroom."

"Thanks for sharing *that* bit of exciting news," Lisa quipped as she followed Kayla toward the kitchen.

Tick had his hand on the banister when his mom called back for him. "Oh, I almost forgot. You got a letter in the mail today. It's on your bed."

"Ooh, maybe it's a *love* letter," Lisa said, blowing a kiss at Tick.

Tick ignored her and ran up the stairs.

~

The bed squeaked as Tick flopped down next to his pillow where a tattered yellow envelope rested, his full name—Atticus Higginbottom—and address scrawled across it in messy handwriting. The stamp was an old picture of the Eiffel Tower but the postmark smeared on top of it said, "Macadamia, Alaska." The upper left corner of the envelope had no return address. He picked up the envelope and flipped it over—nothing there either. Curious, he stared at the mysterious letter for a moment, racking his brain. Who could possibly have written him from the state of Alaska? No one came to mind.

He wedged his finger under the sealed flap on the back and ripped the envelope open. A simple rectangle of white cardstock that barely fit in the envelope held a long message on one side, typed by what appeared to be an old-fashioned typewriter. Baffled, Tick pulled the card out and began to read.

```
Dear Master Atticus,
    I am writing to you in hopes that
you will have the courage of heart
```

and the strength of mind to help
me in a most dreadful time of need.
Things are literally splitting apart
at the seams, as it were, and I must
find those who can assist me in some
very serious matters.

Beginning today (the fifteenth of
November), I am sending out a sequence
of special messages and clues that
will lead you to an important,
albeit dangerous, destiny if you so
choose. No, dangerous may not be a
strong enough word. Indubitably and
despicably <u>deadly</u>—yes, that's better.

I will say nothing further. Oh,
except several more things. If ever
you want the madness to stop, you need
only to burn this letter. I'll know
when you do and shall immediately
cease and desist.

However, if this letter remains
intact for one week after you receive
it, I will know you have chosen to
help me, and you will begin receiving
the Twelve Clues.

Know this before you decide, my
friend: Many, many lives are at stake.

Many. And they depend entirely on
this choice that you must make. Will
you have the courage to choose the
difficult path?

Do be careful. Because of this
letter, very frightening things are
coming your way.

Most faithfully yours,
M.G.

P.S. I recognize that, like most
young people, you probably love
sweetened milk and peppermint sticks.
Unfortunately, I have neither the time
nor practical means to send you any
as a welcoming gift. Please do not
think me unkind. Good day.

Tick stared at the letter for ten minutes, reading
it over and over, wondering who could've played such
a trick. His sister Lisa? No—he couldn't see her using
words like "despicably" and "indubitably." His mom
or dad? Certainly not. What would be the point? Tick
had no true friends to speak of, so the only other option
was that it was a trick from the bullies at school. But
again, such an idea made no sense. Plus, how would

anyone he knew manage to get an Alaskan postmark on the envelope?

His dad did have an old aunt who lived up there somewhere, but Tick had never even met the lady as far as he could remember, and doubted she even knew he existed. Plus, Tick didn't think her initials were M.G.

A knock at the door snapped his attention away— his mom wondering why he hadn't come down for cookies. Tick mumbled something about not feeling well, which was far truer than he liked to admit.

It couldn't be for real. It had to be a scam or a joke. It *had* to be.

And yet, as the purple and orange glow of twilight faded into black darkness, Tick still lay on his bed, contemplating the letter, ignoring his growing hunger. He felt hypnotized by M.G.'s message. Eventually, no closer to understanding or believing, he fell asleep to the soft hum of the central heating.

But in his dreams, he kept seeing the same words over and over, like a buzzing neon sign on a haunted hotel:

Very frightening things are coming your way.

CHAPTER 3

A KID'S WORST NIGHTMARE

Tick woke up to the wonderful sound and smell of sizzling bacon, coupled with the uncomfortable sensation of sliding down a mountain. By the time he shook his head and burned the cobwebs of sleep away, he realized his dad had taken a seat on the edge of the bed, making the mattress lean considerably in that direction.

Tick tried not to smile. Edgar Higginbottom was a tad on the heavy side. Certainly with his pale skin, scraggly hair, and a nose the size of Rhode Island, he didn't qualify as the most handsome man on the planet, but whatever the big guy lacked in looks, he more than made up for in kindness and humor. Tick thought his dad was the coolest person on the planet.

"Morning, Professor," Dad said in his gravelly voice. Everyone in the family joked that Tick might be the smartest one living in the house, so his dad had taken to calling him *Professor* a long time ago. "Gee, I came home last night all ready to take you down in Football 3000 again, but you're up here dead to the world. I even brought a movie home for us to watch. You sick?"

"No, I just didn't feel that great last night." Tick rolled over, slyly pushing the envelope and mysterious letter farther under his pillow. Luckily, his dad hadn't seen it. Tick didn't know what he was going to do when his mom asked about it. In the brightness of the morning, it almost felt like the letter had been a dream or a prank after all, though he couldn't wait to read it again.

"Well, you look like three days of rough road if you want to know the truth," his dad said. "You sure you're okay?"

"Yeah, I'm fine. What time is it?"

"Ten-thirty."

Tick sat up in bed. "Serious?" He couldn't remember the last time he'd slept in so long. "It's really ten-thirty?"

"No."

"Oh." Tick fell back on the bed.

"It's ten-thirty-*six*," Dad said with his patented wink.

Tick groaned and pressed his hands over his eyes. It didn't seem like it should be a big deal, but for some reason it bothered him that the letter from Alaska had drained his brain so much that he'd slept for more than twelve hours.

"Son, what on earth is wrong with you?" Dad put his hand on Tick's shoulder and squeezed. "I'm pretty close to calling the Feds and telling them an alien's kidnapped my son and replaced him with a half-baked clone."

"Dad, you watch way too many sci-fi movies. I'm fine, I promise."

"It's been at least seven years since I've seen a movie without *you*, big guy."

"Good point." Tick looked over at his window, where a fresh batch of snow curtained the bottom edges. The sight made him shiver.

Dad stood and held out a hand. "Come on, it's not too late for breakfast. Mom made her famous puffed-oven-pancakes. Let's get down there before Kayla tries to throw them in the fireplace again."

Tick nodded and let his dad help him up, then followed him out of the room, the whole time thinking about the letter and wanting desperately to tell someone about it.

Not yet, he thought. *They might think I'm crazy.*

"So what was that letter all about?" his mom asked. The whole family sat at the kitchen table, little Kayla next to Tick, her hands already sticky after only one bite.

Tick's hand froze halfway on its journey to put the first chunk of puffy pancake, dripping with hot syrup, into his hungry mouth. He'd hoped his mom had somehow forgotten about the mystery letter; he'd failed to come up with a plan on what to say.

"Oh, it's nothing," he said, then stalled for time by popping the bite into his mouth and chewing. He lifted his glass of cold milk and took a long drink, his mind spinning for an answer. "You know that Pen Pal Web site I subscribed to a while back?"

"Oh, yeah!" Mom replied, lowering her own fork. "You never told us how that went—did you finally find someone?" The Pen Pal site took a bunch of data from kids all around the world and then matched them up as writing buddies with others kids their same age and with the same interests. A parent had to approve it, of course, and Tick's mom had done just that, giving the company all kinds of information and filling out a million forms. Maybe it wasn't too far of a stretch to think one of the pen pals might want to send a letter via regular mail instead of e-mail. It was Tick's only chance.

"Maybe," Tick mumbled through another huge bite. He stared at his plate, hoping she'd move on to grill one of his sisters about something else. She didn't.

"All the way from Alaska," she continued. "Is it a boy or a girl?"

"Uh . . . I don't know actually. Whoever it was just signed it M.G."

"Alaska, huh?" Dad said. "Hey, maybe your pen pal knows old Aunt Mabel up in Anchorage. Wouldn't that be something?"

"I highly doubt it," Mom answered. "That woman probably hasn't set foot out of her house in ten years."

Dad gave her a disapproving stare.

Lisa chimed in, her plate already empty. "Tick, how can you *not* know who it is? Didn't you have to give them your address?"

"We told you not to do that unless we checked it out first," Dad said, his brow creased in concern. "You know what the world's like these days. Is this from someone we've already approved?"

Tick suddenly lost every ounce of his appetite. "I don't know, Dad—yeah, I think so. It didn't say much. It was kind of dumb, actually." He wanted to tell them the truth, but something about the letter made him nervous, and he bit his tongue instead.

He forced the rest of his pancake down, anxiously waiting to see where the conversation went. For several moments the only sounds were the soft clanks of silverware against plates, drinks being put back on the table,

Kayla babbling about her favorite cartoon. Finally, his dad mentioned the big game between the Huskies and the Trojans, opening up the morning paper to read about it.

Relief washed through Tick. When he stood to take his dishes to the sink, his mom put her hand on his arm.

"Would you mind taking Kayla out to play in the snow? She's been asking for it all morning."

"Uh . . . sure," Tick replied, smiling at his sister even though his thoughts were a million miles away. "Come on, kid."

Late that night, after watching the movie Dad had brought home—a creepy sci-fi flick where the hero had to travel between dimensions to fight different versions of the same monster—Tick lay on his bed, alone, reading the letter once again. Night had fallen hours earlier and the darkness seemed to creep through the frosted window, devouring the faint light coming from his small bedside lamp. Everything lay in shadow, and Tick's mind ran wild imagining all the spooky things that could be hiding in the darkness.

Why are you even doing this? he asked himself. *This whole thing has to be a joke.*

But he couldn't stop himself. He read through the

words for the hundredth time. The same ones jumped out at him without fail.

> *Dreadful time of need.*
> *Indubitably and despicably deadly.*
> *Very frightening things are coming.*
> *Lives are at stake.*
> *Courage to choose the difficult path.*

Who would send him such a—

A noise from the other side of the room cut him out of his thoughts. He leaned on his elbow to look, a quick shiver running down his spine. It had sounded like the clank of metal against wood, followed by a quick burst of *whirring*—almost like the hum of a computer fan, but sharper, stronger—and it had only lasted a second or two before stopping.

What in the world . . .

He stared at the dark shadow that arrowed across the floor between his dresser and the closet. He reached for his lamp to point it at the spot, but froze when he heard the noise again—the same mechanical whirr, but this time followed by a series of soft thumps that pattered along the carpet toward him. He looked down from the lamp too late to see anything. Tick froze. It sounded like a small animal had just run across the room and under his bed.

Tick pulled his legs to his body with both arms, holding himself in a ball, squeezing. *What was it? A squirrel? A rat? What had that weird sound been?*

He closed his eyes, knowing he was acting like the biggest baby on the planet but not caring. Every kid's nightmare had just come true for him. Some . . . *thing* was under his bed. Probably something hideous. Something crouching, ready to spring at him as soon as he got the nerve to peek.

He waited, scared to open his eyes. Straining his ears, he heard nothing. A minute went by, then two. He hoped an ounce of courage would magically well up inside him from somewhere, but no such luck. He was thoroughly and completely creeped out.

A sudden image from an old movie popped in his head: a horrible, monstrous gremlin eating through the bottom of his bed, straight through to the mattress, biting and chewing and snarling. It was all Tick needed.

Moving faster than he'd thought possible, Tick jumped off the bed and sprinted for the door, ripping it open even as he heard the sound of small feet scampering across the carpet behind him. He bolted out of his room and quickly closed the door.

Something slammed into it from the other side with a loud clunk.

CHAPTER 4

EDGAR THE BRAVE

Five minutes later, Tick's dad stood next to him in front of the closed door to his room, robed and slippered, flashlight in hand. "Are you sure?" he asked, his voice still deep and rough from having woken up. "Did you see it?"

"No, but I heard it loud and clear." Tick shuddered at the memory.

"Was it a rat?"

"I don't know. It . . . It sounded like a machine or something." Tick winced, sure his dad would finally send him to an insane asylum—first his bizarre behavior at breakfast that morning, now this.

"A *machine*? Tick, what book were you reading

before you went to bed? Stephen King or something?"

"No."

"Was it the movie we watched?"

"No, Dad. I promise I didn't imagine it. The thing had to have been huge—more like a . . . a dog or something." Tick felt stupid and resolved to quit babbling.

"Well, I guess opening the door is all there is to it, then."

Tick looked up at his dad, whose face wore a scared, tense expression, and felt oddly relieved that his old man was just as spooked as he was. "Let's do it, Dad."

Dad smiled, flicking on the flashlight. The hallway light was on as well, but Tick thought you could never have too much light when searching for mechanical demons that ate through the bottom of a bed before gobbling up the child who slept on it.

Several seconds passed, the two of them staring down at the brass doorknob.

"Well?" Tick asked.

"Oh . . . yeah." Somewhat sheepish, Dad reached forward and twisted the handle, pushed, then pulled his hand back like he expected a troll to jump out and bite it off.

As the door swung open with a long, groaning creak that echoed through the house, a wave of light from the hallway spread over the carpet like a rising tide. Tick tensed, sure the strange something would dart at them the second it had a chance, scuttling across the floor like a possessed badger. But he saw nothing unusual.

Dad reached around the edge of the doorframe and turned on the bedroom light. In an instant, every last shadow in the room disappeared, bringing a completely different feel to everything.

Tick felt his fear go down a notch. Just a notch. "Maybe it went under the bed again."

Letting out a big sigh, Dad walked over and knelt down next to the bed, where a heavy quilt draped nearly to the floor, hiding the space underneath. "Listen, Tick, I'm not gonna lie to you—you've got me just as freaked out as you."

"Really?"

"Let's just say if something runs out at me, I'm going to scream like a little girl and run to your mom."

Tick laughed. "Me, too."

Dad quickly pulled up the quilt and beamed the flashlight under the bed, sweeping it back and forth like a sword of sunshine. Nothing but a few random books scattered across the dusty carpet. "Not under there," he said with relief. He leaned against the bed to push himself to his feet—no small effort for a man the size of Edgar Higginbottom.

"The closet?" Tick said, licking his dry lips.

"Yeah, the closet. Where every monster that's ever eaten a child dwells. Just great."

They edged across the room, which now seemed as wide as the Sahara Desert. Tick noticed his dad tiptoeing, which for some reason made him laugh, though it came out sounding like a panicked hyena cornered by three starving lions.

"What?" Dad asked, settling back down onto his heels.

"Nothing. Go for it." Tick gestured to the closet door, which stood ajar a couple of inches.

Dad reached out and flung it open, then took a quick step back. Nothing moved in the cluttered pile of dirty clothes, sports balls, Frisbees, and other junk. There didn't seem to be enough space for a mechanical dog-sized monster to hide.

Tick stepped forward and nudged a pile of clothes with his foot. No response. They spent the next ten minutes searching the room from top to bottom, their initial fear having almost completely melted away, but found nothing.

"It has to be here somewhere, Dad. I'm telling you, there's no way I imagined that thing. It scared me half to death."

"Don't worry, son, I believe you. But sometimes we wake from dreams and they seem very . . . *real*. You know?"

Tick wanted to argue, but he was smart enough to consider the possibility, even though it kind of made him want to kick his dad in the shins for suggesting it. Tick *had* been on the bed for a long time—maybe he'd fallen asleep without realizing it. But then the thing that clunked against the door . . . ?

No, he was convinced it'd been real. But why worry his poor dad any longer? He nodded. "Yeah, maybe."

"Come on," Dad said, flicking off the flashlight and putting his arm around Tick's shoulders. "You can sleep on the little couch in our bedroom. It'll be like old times when the branch outside your window used to give you the heebie-jeebies on a windy night. It's been years since we've had a sleepover."

Tick felt dumb and embarrassed, but he didn't hesitate, grabbing his pillow and blanket before following his dad out of the room. In the hallway, they shared a glance, then Dad shut Tick's bedroom door, pulling on the knob until they both heard the comforting click of the latch taking hold.

CHAPTER 5

A MOST UNWELCOME PATCH OF SMOKE

The next Saturday afternoon, still in the bliss of Thanksgiving vacation and full from leftover turkey sandwiches, Tick sat in the front room, staring out the window at the falling snow. His family lived in a heavily wooded area and the east side of the state of Washington made for lots of snow in the wintertime. Many people in town grumbled about it, but Tick never did.

He loved the cold, he loved the snow, and he loved what came with it—Thanksgiving, then Christmas vacation, then the football play-offs, then the annual Jackson County Chess Tournament—where he'd won his age bracket three straight years. But even more than any of that, Tick loved the look of the cold white powder resting in soft clumps on the dozens of evergreen trees outside his house.

He heard a rumble coming down the street and saw the mailman's truck slugging through the thick snow with chained tires. Tick watched as it pulled up to their mailbox; he saw the mailman reach out and put a stack of letters inside. A flash of yellow in the bunch made Tick's heart jump-start to super speed. He leaned forward for a better view but it was too late. The truck lumbered away, sending twin sprays of snow shooting out behind the tires.

Tick jumped up from the couch and ran to the front door, where he quickly put on his coat and snow boots. The rest of his family seemed busy with their own thing so no one noticed his nervous reaction to seeing the golden piece of mail.

It had been a full week since receiving the letter from Alaska, and he'd thought seriously of burning it every single day. He knew the weird thing in his closet had to be related to the "very frightening things" he'd been warned about. It seemed so simple to throw the letter into the fire to make sure nothing else happened.

But the part of Tick that loved chess and brain-teasers and science desperately wanted to see what the "Twelve Clues" were all about, so he hadn't burned the letter and the week had dragged on worse than the one right before Christmas.

And now, it looked like his choice *not* to burn the letter may have paid off.

He trudged his way through the few inches of snow to the mailbox. His dad had cleared everything with the blower earlier that morning, grumbling about how early winter had set in this year, but now Tick could barely tell he'd done anything at all. The storm was one of those that just kept on coming. The world lay bathed in white, a wintry wonderland that Tick knew would put even the scroogiest Scrooge in the holiday spirit.

He reached the brick mailbox and opened it up, pulling out the stack left moments earlier. He shuffled through the stack, taking each piece off the top and placing it on the bottom—a JC Penney catalog; power bill; an early Christmas card from Aunt Liz; junk mail; junk mail; junk mail.

And then there it was, the envelope, crinkled and golden, with Tick's name and address written messily in blue ink across the front; no return address; the stamp an exotic temple perched high on a mountain. As promised, his next message had arrived.

And this time it was postmarked from Kitami, Japan.

Tick couldn't believe his luck—no one had to know about this second letter. Something inside of him still itched to tell his parents, but he couldn't bring himself to do it. Not until he knew more, *understood* more. Not until he'd figured out the puzzle. With a crazy mix of excitement and panic, he locked the door to his room and sat on the bed, the yellow envelope in his sweaty hands.

He paused, considering the creepy thing from his closet one last time. He could still stop, burn both letters, and never look back.

Yeah, right.

Tick tore open the letter. He pulled out a single piece of the same white cardstock that had been used the first time, though this time it was only about half the size of the first one. As before, one side was blank while the other contained a typed message:

Mark your calendar. One week from the day before the day after the yesterday that comes three weeks before six months from six weeks from now minus forty-nine days plus five tomorrows and a next week, it will happen. A day that could very well change the course of your life as you know it.

I must say, I hope to see you there.

Scribbled directly below the last line were the initials "M.G." and a note that said "This is clue 1 of 12."

Tick sat back against the wall, his head swimming in confusion and awe.

He no longer doubted the messages represented a very serious matter—clues to something extremely important. He was sure the phrase in the first letter that said many lives were at stake wasn't a joke and it scared him. No matter the source, Tick knew he had to get to the bottom of it.

And he felt an overwhelming itch to figure out the first clue. He looked over at his calendar and started running through the words of the message, trying to mentally pinpoint the special day it referred to, but his mind kept spinning in too many directions for him to think straight. *Let's see . . . one week from today . . . six weeks before . . . six months . . . minus forty-nine days . . . ARGH!*

Shaking his head, Tick grabbed the first letter from M.G., folded it up with the second, then stuffed them both into the back pocket of his jeans and ran downstairs. It was time to get serious. First things first.

"Mom, I'm running over to the library!" he yelled as he quickly put on his coat and gloves. He was out the door before she could respond.

By the time Tick left his neighborhood, the snow had let up, the air around him brightening as the sun fought its way through the thinning clouds.

Deer Park was a small town and since the city center was only a couple of miles from Tick's house, he walked there all the time. And, being a bookworm and study bug, the library often ended up as Tick's destination of choice. Especially when he wanted to use the Internet. His family had it at home, but it wasn't as fast as at the library, and Kayla always seemed to want to play her Winnie the Pooh game the second he sat down at the computer, bugging him until he gave in.

He crossed over the town square where, during the summer, a huge fountain usually sprayed. Now the square lay as a flat expanse of whiteness, countless footsteps in the snow crisscrossing it as people bustled around the town.

The library was one of the oldest buildings around, a gray bundle of granite built decades ago. To get there, Tick always took a shortcut between the fire station and the drugstore, a thin alley the width of his shoulders. The stone walls that towered over him as he walked along the alley made him think of old medieval castles.

He had almost reached the end of the alley when a quick breeze whipped past his left ear, followed by an eerie, haunting moan that rose up behind him like the last call of a lonely ghost before heading back to its grave. Tick spun around, stumbling backward when he saw what was there.

A swirling, rippling cloud of gray smoke floated in the alley, surging and receding, billowing out then shrinking back again every two or three seconds. Like it was . . . *breathing*.

And then the smoke turned into a face.

The wispy smoke coalesced and hardened, forming into unmistakable facial features. Dark eyes under bushy gray eyebrows. A crooked nose with black, gaping holes for nostrils. Thin lips pulled back into a wicked grin, exposing an abyss of a mouth with no teeth. Wild, unkempt hair and beard.

Tick willed himself to move, but he could only stare in amazement at the impossible thing floating in front of him.

The moaning sound returned—a deep, low groan filled with grief and pain. It came from every direction, amplified by the narrow stone walls, growing louder and creepier. Tick felt goose bumps break out all over him, chills washing across his skin in waves.

"What . . . who are you?" he asked, amazed that he had found the courage to speak.

Instead of answering, the smoky face groaned louder, its eyes flaring wider.

Then it lunged toward Tick, who turned and ran for his life.

CHAPTER 6

THE LADY
IN THE TREES

Tick shot out of the alley at a full run and slammed into a man walking past, both of them tumbling to the ground in a chaotic jumble of arms and legs.

"I'm sorry, I'm sorry!" Tick yelled, helping the man to his feet as he looked back at the alley, expecting the smoky apparition to appear. But nothing came out and the creepy sound had stopped completely.

"It's okay," the man replied as he brushed himself off. "What's the rush?"

Tick finally focused on the man he'd tackled and saw it was Mr. Wilkinson, the school custodian. "Oh, just going to the library. Sorry." Tick took three hesitant steps so he could see clearly down the alley. It was empty, no sign of a spooky ghost-face anywhere. "Well, gotta run. Don't want to waste any study time!"

Not waiting for an answer, Tick took off for the old library building, wondering if somehow Mr. Wilkinson had saved him from a terrible fate.

~

Five minutes later, Tick stood doubled over in the lobby of the library, hands on his knees, gasping like each breath might be his last. Even though the thing in the alley had disappeared and not chased him, Tick had run as hard as he could until he was safe inside the musty-smelling entryway of the old building.

Maybe I am imagining things, he thought. *There's no way I just saw what I think I saw.*

The librarian behind the desk gave him an evil stare as Tick caught his breath. If he'd been in a better mood he would've laughed at how she fulfilled every cliché in the book: hair up in a bun; glasses perched on the tip of her nose with a linked chain drooped around her neck; beady eyes that told small children they'd never reach adulthood if they didn't read thirty books a day. This librarian must be new; the rest of the staff knew him like a mother knew her own kids.

He spotted Ms. Sears over by the non-fiction section and quickly walked toward the computers, trying to avoid her; the last thing he needed right now was some nice chitchat about the weather.

She saw him anyway.

"Hi there, Tick," she called out to him, her beaming smile managing to calm his nerves a bit. Ms. Sears had gray, tightly curled hair that looked like a cleaning pad permanently glued atop her freckled head. "What are you up to today? Here to study up on your chess strategy? Or maybe look for a pen pal?"

Tick shook his head, trying to dislodge the heavy feeling that clung to his bones like an oily sludge. "Nah, I just wanted to poke around on the Internet. Got a little boring over at my house."

"Your dad didn't break out the karaoke set again, did he? If so, I hope all your windows were closed." She gave him a wink.

"No, I think he finally figured out he sounds like a wounded goat when he sings." He knew his voice sounded tight and he hoped Ms. Sears didn't notice. So many questions bounced around inside his head he felt like he'd need surgery to relieve the swelling.

"Oh, Tick, you better hope I don't tell your father you just said that," she replied. "By the way, I hear you're no match for him in that silly football video game."

Tick forced a laugh. "How in the world did you know that?"

"Small town, kiddo. Small town."

"Yeah . . . guess so." An awkward silence followed, and he shrugged his shoulders. "Well, I better get to a computer."

"Have fun. Let me know if you need any help." She turned and pushed her book cart down another aisle.

Relieved, Tick jogged to the long row of computer desks and found an empty one, glad to sit down and rest. As he pulled out his library card, he nervously glanced around, though he had no idea what he was looking for. *Getting a little paranoid, aren't you?* he chided himself. *There has to be a perfectly reasonable explanation for all of this. Something.*

He slid the card into the electronic reader, then typed his password when the prompt appeared on the screen. A few seconds later a window opened for him, connecting him to the Internet. Peeking around the library stacks like a top-level CIA agent searching for spies, Tick pulled out the two mystery letters and unfolded them, pressing them flat on the desk next to the keyboard.

He read through them both again, even though he already knew the first thing he wanted to try on the Internet search engine. He hoped other people had received similar letters and were talking about them in blogs or message boards. Holding his breath, wishing like crazy he'd find something useful, Tick typed "M.G." and clicked SEARCH. An instant later, the computer screen told him how many hits: 2,333,117.

Great.

Web sites about MG Cars, Madagascar, Magnesium, MG Financial Group were listed, but nothing that gave any kind of hint about who had sent the two letters. He tried other phrases: "frightening things"; "despicably deadly"; "forty-nine days plus five tomorrows."

Nothing useful popped up.

Discouraged, he sat back and stared at the screen. He'd been afraid to admit how much he really wanted there to be others like him. He didn't want to be alone in this crazy stuff. The first letter had been addressed to "Dear Master Atticus," but the wording of the message made Tick think more than one letter had been sent out, a plea for help from anyone willing to give it.

Well, maybe he'd have to be the first one to put some clues out there for other people to find.

Rejuvenated by the thought, he typed in the address for the Pen Pal site, then logged into his own section and personal profile. He briefly described the situation, listed some of the key phrases from both letters, then asked if anyone out there had received something similar. He clicked SUBMIT and sat back in the chair again, folding his arms. Hopefully, if anyone else in the world searched for the same things as he'd just done, they would somehow get linked up with his Pen Pal information and e-mail him.

It was a start.

The snow had started up again, big fluffy flakes swirling in the wind. Tick pulled his red-and-black scarf up around his ears and mouth as he left the library and headed for home. He walked in the opposite direction from where he'd come earlier, perfectly willing to take the long way around in order to avoid the haunted alleyway. He shivered, not sure if it was from the cold weather or the memory of the spooky smoke-ghost.

He walked all the way around the downtown area, doing his best to stay in the most public of places. The sky had melted into a dull gray, flakes of white dancing around him like a shaken snow globe. *Maybe that's where I am,* he thought. *I've been sucked from the real world and placed in some alien's giant coffee table knickknack.*

A shot of relief splashed through his nerves when he finally made it to the small section of forest that lined the road to his neighborhood. All he wanted was to go home and warm up, maybe play his dad in Football 3000 . . .

From the corner of his eye, Tick saw something move in the trees just to the left of the road. Something huge, like a moose or a bear. He turned and looked more intently, curious. Though he lived in a small town, big animals rarely ventured into the woods this close to his neighborhood. Just a few feet away from him, a shadow loomed behind a thick tree frosted with snow, its owner obviously trying to hide from him. *Animals don't hide,* Tick thought, warning alarms clanging in his mind as he readied himself to run.

But then the thing stepped out from behind the tree and Tick's feet froze to the ground.

Despite its enormous size and odd appearance, it wasn't an "it" at all.

It was a person. A lady.

And she was eight feet tall.

CHAPTER 7

MOTHBALL

The sight of a giant, skinny woman coming out of the forest didn't help Tick's anxiety much after his experiences with the freaky thing in his bedroom and the ghost-face in the alley. He yelped and started to run down the street toward his home, only making it two steps before he tripped over a chunk of ice that had fallen off the back of someone's tire well. His face slammed into the fresh snow, which was, to his relief, powdery and soft.

By the time he scrambled up from the ground, the enormous woman was beside him, helping him to his feet instead of ripping out his throat. Her face fell into a frown, as though saddened to see him so afraid. Her expression somehow made Tick feel guilty for running away so quickly.

"'Ello," she said, her voice husky and thick with a strange accent. "Pardon me looks. Been a bit of tough journey, it has." She stepped back, towering over Tick. Her eyes were anxious and hesitant and the way she fiddled with her huge hands made him think of Kayla when she was nervous. The gesture made the giant lady seem so . . . *innocent*, and Tick relaxed, feeling oddly at ease.

She had thick black hair that cascaded across her shoulders like a shawl, her face square and homely with bright blue eyes. Her gray clothes were wet and worn, hanging on her impossibly thin body like droopy sheets on a wooden laundry rack. The poor woman looked miserable in the cold, and the slight hunch to her shoulders only added to the effect. But then she swept away that impression with a huge smile, revealing an enormous set of yellow teeth.

Tick knew he was staring, but he couldn't look away. "You're . . . huge," he said before he could stop himself.

The woman flinched, her smile faltering just a bit. "I'm a bit lanky, I'll admit it," she said. "No reason for the little man to poke fun, now is it?"

"No . . . I didn't mean it that way," he stammered. "It's just . . . you're so *tall*."

"Yeah, methinks we established that."

"And . . ."

"Lanky. Come to an understanding now, have we?" She pointed down at him. "The little man is short and ugly. Mothball is tall and lanky."

Tick wasn't sure he'd heard her right. "Mothball?"

The woman shrugged her bony shoulders. "It's me name. A bit unfortunate, I'll admit it. Me dad didn't have much time to think when I popped out me mum's belly, what with all the nasty Bugaboo soldiers tryin' to break in and all. Fared better than me twin sis, I did. Like to see you go through life with a name like Toejam."

Tick had the strangest urge to laugh. There was something incredibly likable about this giant of a person. "Buga-*what* soldiers? Where are you from?"

"Born in the Fifth, I was, but lived in the Eleventh for a season. Ruddy rotten time that turned out to be. Nothin' but midgets stepping on me toes and punching me knees. Not fun, I can promise ya that. At least I met me friend Rutger there."

Every word that flew out of the woman's mouth only confused Tick even more. As hard as it was to believe the sheer size of the lady standing in front of him, the conversation was just as bizarre.

"The Fifth?" he asked. "What's that, an address? Where is it? Where's the Eleventh?"

Mothball put her gigantic hands on her hips. "By

my count, you've done asked me several questions in a row, little man, and none time to answer them. Me brain may be bigger than yers, but you're workin' it a bit much, don't ya think?"

"Okay, then," Tick said. "Just answer one."

"Ain't it in the Prime where they say 'Patience is a virtue'? Looks like you missed out on that bit of clever advice."

Tick laughed despite the craziness of it all. "Mothball, I'm more confused every time you speak. How about you just tell me whatever you want, and I'll shut up and listen." He rubbed his neck, which hurt from looking up at her so much. His scarf was crusted in snow.

"Now that's more like it, though I must admit I don't know what to say now." Mothball folded her arms, her face scrunching up into a serious frown as she stared down at Tick. "No harm in tellin' that you're from the Prime, I reckon, and that I'm from the Fifth, and me friend Rutger's from the Eleventh I told you about just now. Wee little gent, old Rutger—looks a little like a ball of bread dough, he does. The poor bloke is short as a field swine and twice as fat. You'll be meetin' him, too, ya know, right directly if he's about his business."

"Wait," Tick said, forgetting his promise to be quiet, at which Mothball rolled her eyes. "You sound like you know who I am. This is somehow related to the letters I got in the mail, isn't it?"

"What else, little man? Did ya ever see an eight-foot woman *before* you got the notes from the Master?"

"Mast—" Tick paused, his mind churning like the snowflakes that swirled around his body. This giant woman had obviously come to talk to him specifically, for a purpose, and yet he'd learned nothing. "Look, Mothball, maybe you could explain everything, from the beginning?"

She shook her head vigorously. "Can't do that, little man. Can't do that at'all."

"Then why did you come here? Why did you step out of the woods to talk to me?"

"To rub ya a little, give ya a bit of confidence, ya know. Me boss sent me. Sendin' me all over the place, he is, just to help where I can."

"Help with what?"

"Not sure to be quite frank. I know I can't talk about the messages, and I can't tell you anything about the Master or the Barrier Wand or the Realities or the Kyoopy or the Chi'karda or anythin' else to do with 'em." She held out a finger as she said each of the strange items as though she'd been given a list beforehand. "Other than that, feel free to ask your questions, since I have no idea anymore what to talk to ya about."

Tick rubbed his eyes, frustrated. He tried his best to memorize each of the odd words Mothball had said, burning them into his mind for later analysis. "Miss

Mothball, it's official. This is the craziest conversation I've ever had."

"Sorry, little man. Truly I am." She kicked the snow at her feet, making a huge divot. "'Simportant you figure things out for yourself. It won't work otherwise. But, er, maybe you've seen something, er, *strange* since you got those letters?"

Tick's interest perked up considerably. "Yeah, I have. Just a couple of hours ago I saw this smoky, wispy thing that formed into a face and made a freaky sound. Can you tell me about that?"

Mothball's face lit up despite the scary subject matter of his question. "Ah! Tingle Wraiths! That's what you've seen, I'd bet me left shoe. Scary fellas, them. Now *that* I can talk about."

"You know what they are? Where they come from?"

"I ruddy well should! They almost killed me friend Rutger just last winter. 'Ere, did you get a little tingle down your spine when the Death Siren started? Ya know that's where they get the name from." She paused. "Ya know, *tingle*. Down your spine. Tingle Wraith. Get it?"

"Yeah . . . I get it." If she noticed his sarcasm, she didn't show it. "But what are they?"

"That awful sound you 'eard is the Death Siren and it only gets louder and louder, I'm afraid. They can't move more than a few feet or so once their face is formed, but there's no need as long as you can hear that terrible cry of theirs. Thirty seconds, once it starts— that's all you've got."

"What do you mean?"

Mothball's brow furrowed as she wagged a finger at him. "If any man, woman, or child hears the Death Siren for thirty seconds straight, their brain turns right to mush. Nasty death, that. Seen it happen to an old bloke once. His body flopped around like a chicken with its ruddy noggin lopped off. The poor wife finally let 'im out of 'is misery. Bludgeoned him over the head with a teapot, she did."

"You're serious?"

"Do I look like the kind of person who'd make funnies about an old woman knocking 'er own sweet husband over the head with a teapot?"

"Well . . . no, I guess."

"Sad, it was." She stared at an empty spot past Tick's shoulder for a few seconds, then looked him in the eyes. "You'll be all right. S'long as you can run, they'll never catch you. Just avoid 'em if you can."

"Don't worry, I will."

A long pause followed, and Tick began to panic that Mothball would leave without telling him anything else. "So . . . what do I do? What are the messages *for*? Who is M.G.? What's supposed to happen on the day he talked about in the first clue?" The questions poured out, even though he knew what her answer would be before she said it.

"Sorry, can't speak about it. Master's orders."

Tick wanted to scream. "Well, then I guess there's not much more for us to talk about, is there?"

"Not much, you thought right there, little man."

Tick shivered, staring absently at the world of white surrounding them. "O . . . kay. So, what do we do now?"

"Best be on me way, then." Mothball bowed her head, as if she felt just as awkward as he did. A few seconds later she snapped her fingers and looked up. "Ah, me brain must've shut off there for a moment. I forgot something." She pulled out a small writing pad and a pencil from her pocket. "What's yer name—if you don't mind me asking?"

Her question surprised Tick. "You don't know? How did you find me if—"

"Just be needin' to verify, I do." She held her pencil at the ready, waiting for his answer.

"Atticus Higginbottom. But everyone calls me Tick."

She scanned the pad with the tip of her pencil. "Ah, there you are." She wrote a big checkmark where the pencil had stopped, then reached into a different pocket and pulled out a crumpled yellow envelope. She held it out for Tick. "'Ere ya go, little man. Congrats to ya on makin' a very wise and brave choice not to burn the Master's first letter. Now this should keep you occupied for a spell."

Nothing was written on the front of the envelope, but Tick took it, knowing it had to be the second clue. He didn't know why he felt so surprised. M.G. never said *all* the messages would come through the mail. But it did seem odd to receive two on the same day. Maybe M.G. was sending another kind of message altogether: *Never assume anything, expect the unexpected.*

He folded the envelope and put it in his pocket, anxious to go home and read it. "Thanks. I guess I won't bother asking you any questions about it."

"Shapin' up right nicely, you are." Mothball smiled. "Very well, until next time, then. Best of luck to you and yours and all that."

Tick felt an overwhelming feeling that if she left, he'd never understand anything that was going on. He desperately wanted her to stay, to talk, to help. But having just met her, he didn't know what to do or say. "You really have to go?" he asked, like a small child begging Grandma to stay just a little while longer.

Mothball's face softened into the nicest, kindest expression Tick had ever seen. "'Fraid so, little man. Got others to visit, ya know. Quite weary on me legs, it is, but not much choice in the matter. You'll do well— me bones tell me as much."

"Will I ever see you again?"

"I hopes ya do, Master Tick. I certainly hopes ya do."

And with that, the tall woman turned and walked back into the thick copse of trees, her large shoulders sending an avalanche of snow off the limbs where she brushed them.

Tick stared for a while, half-expecting to see a magic poof of smoke or the fiery blastoff of an alien spaceship, but nothing happened. Mothball had simply vanished into the trees.

His life had turned completely crazy and for some reason it made him more excited than he'd felt in a very long time.

He set off for home with a smile on his face.

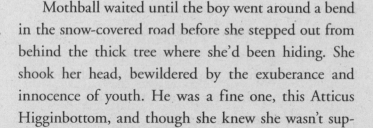

Mothball waited until the boy went around a bend in the snow-covered road before she stepped out from behind the thick tree where she'd been hiding. She shook her head, bewildered by the exuberance and innocence of youth. He was a fine one, this Atticus Higginbottom, and though she knew she wasn't supposed to do it, she'd settled on the one she'd be rooting for in this whole mess.

She walked the half-mile to the designated spot that lay deeper in the forest. No one in these parts probably remembered that this place had once been a burial ground, its wooden grave markers long since decayed and crumbled to dust.

Poor deadies, she thought. *No one comin' to pay respects and such.*

She triggered the nanolocator signal for Master George, then waited for her boss to work his navigation skills. Funny little man, he was. A *good* man, really. As nervous as a midge bug caught in a toad paddy, but a kind and gentle soul when you dug down deep. Why, he'd saved her life, he did, and she owed him for it.

Several long moments passed. Mothball fidgeted back and forth on her feet, wondering if the restless man had messed up a thingamajig or whatchamacallit on the Barrier Wand. He was a very *precise* old chap, and usually responded in a matter of seconds, especially when expecting the nanolocator signal, as he should be now. Mothball had been right on schedule.

A small deer bounced along nearby, leaving delicate little footprints in the thick layer of snow. To Mothball's delight, it stopped to examine the unusually tall visitor. She was so used to scaring creatures away, it felt nice for a change to see something not turn and take flight.

"Watch out for the little man, won't you?" she said, glad no one was around to see her talking to a deer. "Tough times ahead, he's got. Could use a friend like you."

The animal didn't respond, and Mothball laughed.

A few seconds later, she felt the familiar tickle at the back of her neck. As she *winked* away from the forest, vanishing in an instant, she couldn't help but wonder what the deer would think of such a sight.

CHAPTER 8

A VERY
IMPORTANT DATE

Tick tore open the envelope from Mothball the second he'd left the odd woman's line of vision. He had to pull his gloves off to do it, and the cold bit into them with tiny frozen pinpricks. With no surprise, he pulled out a single piece of cardstock that looked exactly like the others. His fingers growing stiff in the frigid air, he read the single paragraph.

> At the appropriate time, you must
> say the magic words with your eyes
> closed. If you can't speak and close
> your eyes at the same time, you
> belong in a hospital. As for what

> the magic words are, I can't tell you
> and I never will. Examine the first
> letter carefully and you will work
> them out.

He read it again three times, then stuffed the letter and the envelope into his coat pocket. Shivering as he put his gloves back on, he couldn't help but feel a mixture of excitement and wariness.

Magic words? Eyes closed? What is this, Oz?

Things were getting just plain weird. Pulling his scarf tighter, Tick rubbed his arms, trudging through the snow toward home.

He got to his house just in time for dinner, which he wolfed down like a kid determined to eat all the Halloween candy before a sibling stole it. He barely heard the conversation around the table and excused himself after stuffing the last three bites' worth of spaghetti into his mouth all at once.

He leapt up the stairs to his room, determined to finally put some major thought into figuring out the clues. Something about seeing an eight-foot-tall woman appear out of the woods on a snowy day made everything seem *real*. Though he had no idea about the whys or hows or whats, he was now committed to the game.

Tick unfolded the original letter and both clues and put them on his desk, pointing his lamp to shine directly on their stark black words. He reread the first letter from M.G., which seemed to be mostly an introduction to set things up. The most recent message said the first letter would reveal "magic words" he'd need to say on a special day, but he'd get to that later. One thing at a time.

The first clue obviously told him the date of that special day—the day when he'd have to have solved the ultimate puzzle spelled out by the coming clues. He focused on the paragraph, reading it several times.

```
Mark your calendar. One week from
the day before the day after the
yesterday that comes three weeks
before six months from six weeks from
now minus forty-nine days plus five
tomorrows and a next week, it will
happen. A day that could very well
change the course of your life as you
know it.
     I must say, I hope to see you
there.
```

As he read through it, he tried to visualize in his mind the stated time periods, adding and subtracting as he went. But by the time he got to the end, the words always jumbled up and fell apart inside his thoughts. He realized he needed to treat it like a math problem, solving it in sections until everything could be added together.

He pulled out a pencil and drew parentheses around phrases that were easy to identify as a stand-alone period of time. Then he assigned letters to them to help him solve them in the most logical order. All the while, he knew he must be the biggest dork this side of the Pacific Ocean, but he didn't care. He was just starting to have fun.

He first attempted to figure out the clue from beginning to end, adding and subtracting time with each new phrase as it came in order. But he kept hitting a snag because of the words "before" and "six weeks from now" in the middle of the paragraph. The phrases seemed to split the timeline into two pieces and he realized he needed to work around them, not from first word to last word.

After a half hour and lots of erasing and starting over, he copied the phrases and their assigned letters to a different sheet of paper. Then, using the Seattle Seahawks calendar that hung next to his bed (which also had a one page, year-at-a-glance section for this year and the next), he penciled in the dates as he figured them out. When he finished, he leaned back in his chair and took a look:

Beginning Date: Today, November 26.
A. 6 weeks from now = January 7
B. 6 months from A = July 7
C. the day before the day after the
   yesterday that comes 3 weeks before B
   = 3 weeks plus 1 day before B = 22 days
   before B = June 15
D. 1 week from C = June 22
E. D minus 49 days = May 4
F. E plus 5 tomorrows and a next week =
   E plus 12 days = <u>May 16</u>

He went over his math again to make sure he'd
done it right, and was just about to put the calendar
away, quite satisfied with himself, when he realized
he'd missed the easiest and most important part of the
clue. The beginning date.

You idiot, he thought.

Whoever M.G. was, he or she would have no way
of knowing when people received the cryptic letters,
much less when they would test out the first clue to
figure out the all-important date. Tick reread one of
the lines from the first letter:

```
Beginning today (the fifteenth of
November), I am sending out a sequence
of special messages . . .
```

November the fifteenth. Even before officially starting the messages, M.G. had provided the mystery's first hint: the start date needed to solve Clue Number One.

Tick quickly went through the calendar again, calculating three times what the date should be based on the new starting date, erasing and rewriting. Finally, confident that he'd solved it, his paper showed a different result:

May 6

At first, he worried that the results were only *ten* days apart when the beginning dates had been off by *eleven*, but after looking at the calendar three times, he determined it had to do with June only having thirty days.

May sixth. The all-important date. Just over five months from now.

Tick wrote the date in big letters on the bottom of the first clue, then ripped out the one-page calendar and stapled it to the back of the cardstock. He examined the second clue for a while, which really did nothing but refer him to the first letter he'd received as a code or something to figure out the "magic words." After an hour of staring at the typed message, his brain exhausted, he gave up. He folded everything up together and stuck the stack in his desk drawer.

For the rest of the evening, Tick couldn't quit thinking about the first clue. According to the stranger known as M.G., something very important was to happen on May sixth of the next year.

But what?

Much later that night, after playing Scrabble with his mom and Lisa (Tick's best word: galaxy, 34 points on a double-word score), eating two-thirds of a bag of Doritos while watching *SportsCenter* with his dad (swearing on his life he'd never eat another chip—a promise he knew wouldn't last past tomorrow), analyzing the clues for a while (still no luck with the magic words), then reading for an hour in bed (the latest seven-inch-thick fantasy novel he'd checked out from the library), Tick finally went to sleep.

In the middle of the night, ripping him from a dream in which he'd just received the very prestigious Best Chess Player in the World trophy, crowds chanting his name and cheering wildly, Tick heard the *sounds* again: the metallic whirring, the scraping, the patter of tiny footsteps. All coming from inside the closet, where the door was closed.

Something bumped against the door.

Tick sat up, suddenly very, very awake.

CHAPTER 9

THE GNAT RAT

Tick's first instinct was to run and get his dad again, the creepy chills of the night he'd first heard the noises returning in full force. But he steeled himself, resolving not to go running off like a baby again until he knew it was all for real. Whatever was moving around in his closet couldn't be very big, and it had to have a reasonable explanation. Maybe it was just a squirrel that had chewed a hole through the wall—too small for them to have noticed that night when he and his dad had searched the room.

What about the mechanical fan sound? he thought. He told himself that maybe the little squirrel had accidentally eaten his dad's electric shaver, but then realized he was probably one step away from the mental hospital talking to himself like this, and telling jokes at that. *Just go check it out,* he told himself sternly.

He reached up to his headboard, keeping his eyes riveted on the closet, and flicked on the lamp. The warm glow banished the dark shadows, illuminating fully the door with its many posters and sports banners taped haphazardly across it. Encouraged and braver with the light on, Tick swung his legs around and stood up from his bed, hoping the closet door didn't burst open when he did so. Nothing moved. The sound had completely stopped.

Maybe I just imagined it. I haven't heard it since it woke me up.

Think it all he wanted, he couldn't convince himself. A slice of fear cut through his heart, making it pound even harder, sending a pulse of heat through his veins. His hands were sweaty and his shoulders and back tingled, making him remember what Mothball had said about the smoke-ghost he'd seen in the alley. The Tingle Wraith. But its sound had been totally different, and Tick didn't really expect to see one in his closet.

No, this was something different, if anything at all.

He crept over to the door with ginger steps, staring at the thin sliver of space between the floor and the bottom of the door. If anything shot out from that crack, Tick knew he'd die of a heart attack on the spot.

He stopped a couple of feet away and paused, clenching and unclenching his fists.

Just open it, you sissy.

He reached forward and twisted the handle, knowing his dad had done the exact same thing just over a week ago, remembering that there had been nothing there then.

He pulled the door open and stepped back.

Something very odd rested on top of a pile of dirty clothes.

Something Tick had never seen before in his life.

Edgar Higginbottom was a light sleeper, which he hated. Anything and everything woke him up. Cars outside, dogs barking, a child crying. When his kids had been babies, Edgar had woken up the instant any of them fussed. Often he'd lain there, wishing against all hope that Lorena would somehow hear and offer to take a turn checking on them or feeding them. But he always got up after a few seconds, feeling guilty for being so selfish after all his wife had gone through to bring those kids into the world in the first place.

This time, though, it had been a sudden light that snapped him awake, followed by the slight creak of someone walking in the house. He pushed himself up onto one elbow and looked at the door to his room, which stood slightly ajar. Judging from the angle of the shadows caused by the light, and the direction from which the sound had come, he guessed Tick had gotten out of bed for some reason.

What's he doing up at—Edgar looked at his clock—*three in the morning?*

He flopped back down onto his side, then rolled his big body onto his back, rubbing his eyes and yawning as he stared at the ceiling. Then, with a grunt, he threw off the covers and sat up on the edge of the bed, searching for his slippers with his toes.

He found them, put them on, and stood up.

Tick's mind seemed to split into two factions as he stared at the object. One side wanted him to run because anything that magically appeared in a closet had to be bad. The other side wanted to investigate because the thing looked completely harmless. The latter won the battle, his curiosity once again victorious over common sense.

He stepped closer and dropped to his knees, leaning forward.

It was a strange metal contraption, about a foot long, five or six inches wide, and maybe eight or nine inches tall. Its shiny gray surface had no blemishes, sparkling and clean, with round, gear-looking things attached to the side. A thin handle was attached to the top of the box and a small snout-like nose and a sinuous metallic tail were attached to either end. Along the bottom edges a series of ten evenly spaced rods poked out from the box and curved toward the floor, ending in a flat piece of metal about the size of a quarter. The first thought that popped into Tick's mind was the thing looked like a stainless steel accordion, ready to march away.

But it didn't move or make a sound.

Tick noticed some writing on the side of the box, shadowed by the light coming from the room. He shifted his position closer and squinted his eyes. It took a few seconds, but he finally made out what it said:

GNAT RAT
Manufactured by Chu Industries

What in the world . . .

Tick thought of Mr. Chu, his science teacher, but he obviously had nothing to do with this. Tick would know if his favorite instructor had his own company or was affiliated with one. It had to be a coincidence.

But . . .

His mind was blank, churning to come up with an explanation for the weird thing sitting in his closet. It had to be related to the letters from M.G., the Tingle

Wraith, and Mothball, but how or why . . . ? No clue.

And what in the world is a Gnat Rat? He reached out a finger and brushed the back of the smooth gray metal box.

The thing jumped.

Tick gasped and fell backward, even though the Gnat Rat had barely moved—an inch at most—before coming to rest again. A slight buzzing came from it like the distant sound of his mom's oven timer from downstairs. Whatever the thing was, it had just turned on or powered up.

A mechanized clicking sound sprung up and the ten pairs of metal legs started moving back and forth, slowly marching the Gnat Rat off the pile of clothes and out of the closet, toward Tick. His eyes wide and focused on the toy-like thing coming at him, Tick stood up, unsure what to do. It seemed totally harmless, a cheap robot you could buy at any discount store.

But then he remembered it slamming into his door when he'd closed it from the hallway that night. He thought about its name: Gnat Rat. And finally, he thought about how it had somehow *disappeared* and come back, magically. All of these things led to one conclusion.

A Gnat Rat is bad.

Tick was about to bolt away when he heard a loud click like the sound of a gun being cocked. He looked

in shock at the ominous toy. A small door slowly swung open on the Rat's back side.

Then little *things* started flying out of it.

Light or no light, a son suffering from insomnia or not, Edgar couldn't ignore the call of nature. He finished washing his hands in the bathroom, flicked off the light, and stepped back into his bedroom. Trying his best to be quiet so Lorena could sleep—though he probably could've danced around the room with cymbals on his knees and blowing on a trumpet and she would've remained dead to the world—Edgar walked through the room and into the hallway.

Sure enough, it was Tick's room with a light on, and an odd mechanical hum echoed out his door and down the hall. *Did he get some new gizmo I don't know about?*

Edgar had taken only one step forward when he heard the boy scream.

Tick shrieked as dozens of winged, buzzing little drones flew out of the Gnat Rat in a torrent like a pack of raving mad hornets. Without exception they came directly at him, swarming around his body before he could react, attacking, biting, *stinging.*

Tick swatted at them, slapping and hitting his own body, dancing and kicking, yelling for help. Pinpricks of pain stabbed every inch of his skin, under his clothes, in his hair; the mechanical gnats were hungry and Tick must've looked awfully delicious. Panic shot through him in a rush of adrenaline, his mind shutting down, offering no ideas on what he should do.

He heard his bedroom door slam against the wall.

"Atticus!" his dad yelled.

But Tick couldn't look at him. He'd squeezed his eyes closed, scared the gnats would blind him. They were relentless, attacking him over and over again, their sharp stingers finding fresh spots to hurt him with a frightening ease. Overwhelmed by pain and fear, he fell to the ground.

He felt his dad gripping his arms, dragging him across the floor and out of his room. Down the hall, into the bathroom. He heard the rush of water in the bathtub.

Dad, he thought, wanting to warn him, but afraid to open his mouth. *They'll eat you alive, too.*

It hurt too much to cry. Tick felt like he'd been taken to an acupuncture school and the overanxious students had given up on the little needles and decided to use knives instead. His whole world had turned into one big ouch. He'd never felt so hopeless.

His dad heaved Tick off the floor and plopped him

into the tub, splashing the cold water all over his paja-mas, his skin, his hair. Though his whole body felt racked with pain, Tick sensed the gnats leaving him in hordes even before he'd landed in the shallow pool of water.

They're machines, he thought distantly. *They run on electricity. The water would kill them.*

An angry buzz filled the bathroom, but Tick couldn't bring himself to open his eyes. He heard a towel whipping through the air. His dad must be trying to chase the gnats away and out of the room. Horror filled Tick's stomach as he realized the vicious gnats might be going for his sisters, his mom.

"Dad!" he yelled with a slur, his mouth swollen. "Kayla! Lisa! Mom!"

And then he passed out.

⟋

"What were they?" the doctor asked. "Where did they come from?"

Edgar didn't feel like talking. Even if he did, he had no answer for the man.

They stood in a curtained-off section of the emer-gency room, surrounded by the sounds of medical machines beeping, the murmur of voices, the squeak of gurneys rolling along the hallway; a child cried in the distance. Everything smelled of ammonia and disinfec-tant. It was all extremely depressing.

Edgar stared down at his son lying on the bed, eyes closed. Every inch of the boy's body looked red and puffy, pockmarked with hundreds of black dots. Lorena and Lisa cried in the corner, clutching little Kayla in a three-way hug. Edgar felt certain his heart had broken into two pieces and was slowly sinking to his stomach.

Tick had always been a lucky kid. Edgar liked to joke that Tick had been born clutching a rabbit's foot. When Tick had been only five years old, the family had taken a shopping trip to Spokane and Tick had darted for the middle of a busy road, already two steps past the curb before Edgar even noticed. Even as Edgar had sprinted to save his boy, he watched in utter horror as a huge truck, blaring its horn and screeching its brakes, seemingly ran right over Tick. Edgar would never forget the scream that erupted from his own throat at that moment, an alien sound that still haunted his dreams sometimes.

But when the truck passed, Tick stood there in the street, untouched, his hair not so much as ruffled. It had been nothing short of a miracle.

Then, a few years later, the family had gone to the coast for a summer trip, enjoying a rare hot and sunny day on the Washington beach. Tick, showing off his newly discovered body-surfing talent, had been swept away by a sudden and enormous wave, sucking him out to sea. The current pulled the poor boy from the soft sands directly into an area of jagged, vicious rocks nearby. Edgar and Lorena barely had time to register the shock and terror of what was happening before they saw Tick standing on a jutting shoulder of stone, waving with a huge smile on his face.

Or the time he fell off the big waterslide tower at Water World Park, only to land on a pile of slip 'n slide tubes left there by a family eating lunch.

The stories went on and on. They never talked about it; Edgar was afraid to jinx the whole thing, and he had no idea if Tick even realized anything out of the ordinary was happening. Kids rarely do—life is life, and they know nothing different until much later.

But despite all that he'd seen of Tick's narrow escapes, Edgar couldn't help but feel the panic rising in his chest. Had the boy's streak of luck finally run out? Would he survive this—

"What *happened*?" the doctor repeated.

"I don't know," Edgar mumbled. "A bunch of bugs, or bees, or gnats, or something attacked him. I threw him in the bathtub, shooed the things away with a towel. They stayed in a tight pack, and when I opened a window, they flew right out."

The doctor looked at Edgar, his expression full of doubt and concern, eyebrows raised. "*You* shooed them away?"

"Yes, I did." Edgar knew the man's concern before he said it.

"But you—"

"I know, Doctor, I know." He paused. "I didn't get stung. Not once."

CHAPTER 10

THE TEMPTATION OF THE FLAMES

Tick could think of a million things he'd rather do than get stung all over his body by mechanical gnats that popped out of a demon lunch box with legs. It was a long list and included being dropped in a boiling vat of vinegar and having his toenails removed with hot pincers. Two days after the attack, he'd returned home from the hospital feeling and looking much better, but the experience remained vivid in his mind, playing itself out over and over again. Without any doubt, he knew the Gnat Rat and its stinging bugs had been the single worst thing that had ever happened to him. And that included the time Billy "The Goat" Cooper had almost broken Tick's arm in front of the girls' locker room.

Despite the lingering horror he felt, Tick was madly curious to know where the Gnat Rat had come from. And where it had gone. The boxy contraption must have disappeared right after releasing the bugs because his dad said he never saw it and saw no signs of a nest or a hole anywhere in the walls or floorboard. The Rat would've been impossible to miss since Tick had collapsed right next to it in his room. The thing had simply vanished—or run away to whatever magical hole it lived in. Either way, Tick knew he could never look at the world in the same way again, and the knowledge made him feel sick, fascinated, and scared, all at the same time.

The doctors had probed him over and over, not bothering to hide their suspicion that some serious child abuse had occurred. But they found dozens of stingers, just like the ones that came from a normal yellow jacket common to the area. That finding, coupled with the obvious fact that Edgar and Lorena Higginbottom were perhaps the two nicest people to ever live in Deer Park, and quite possibly the world, quickly dissolved the distrust of the doctors toward the parents.

Though they said no fewer than a hundred times how impossible it seemed that the bees targeted Tick and no one else, let alone the fact that bees rarely attacked during the middle of winter, the doctors eventually let the matter drop and sent Tick home.

I must have some seriously sweet blood, Tick thought, picking at the bandages covering his arms.

The only thing more baffling than the lone victim and the Gnat Rat disappearing was how quickly Tick healed. He almost felt disappointed he wouldn't miss more than a couple of days of school. Almost.

Now, lying in bed, staring at the ceiling late the next Tuesday night, he couldn't sleep. More than ever before in his life, Tick felt terribly *afraid*. His life was at risk, and for what?

He'd put on a show for his family, acting brave and cracking jokes, but he knew he did it more for himself than anyone else. He didn't want to accept the horror of what he'd experienced, didn't want to accept the potential for worse things to come. But the fear crashed down on him after dinner and he'd never felt so hopeless.

Sighing, he sat up in bed and retrieved the letter and clues from his desk drawer, staring at them for a long moment. As he did, he felt the last ounce of bravery drain from his spirit. Quietly, he crept from his room and took the letters downstairs to the living room.

It was the only room in the house with a fireplace.

~~~

Twenty minutes later, the gas-log fire had heated the entire room, its blower wafting warm and comforting air across Tick's face as he sat directly in front of it, staring at the licking flames. The rest of his family had long since fallen asleep, and he had been extra, extra careful not to wake his freakishly light-sleeping dad. This was Tick's moment of truth and he needed to be alone.

He gripped the first letter tightly in his right hand, clenching a fist around the wrinkled cardstock. He didn't know how it worked, but he trusted the instruction told to him by the mystery-person, M.G. If ever he wanted it to stop, just burn the letter and everything would "cease and desist." Tick had no doubt it was true, just as he had no doubt that Gnat Rats, Tingle Wraiths, and an eight-foot-tall woman named Mothball really and truly existed.

Burn the letter, stop the madness.

The thought had run through his mind a thousand times since he'd first come to consciousness after the brutal gnat attack. Only two clues in—ten to go—and he wanted to quit. *Desperately* wanted to quit. How could he keep going, when things worse than the Gnat Rat might attack him? How could he, Atticus Higginbottom, a kid with a pretty decent brain but the body of a thirteen year old, fight the forces that some unknown enemy threw at him? How could he do it?

He sat up, crossing his legs under him, facing the fire. He thought about the tremendous ease of simply throwing the letter into the fire not two feet in front of him, of watching it crinkle and shrivel into a crispy ball of black flakes, of returning his life back to normal. He could do it and be done. Forever.

And then it hit him—an odd feeling that started somewhere deep down in his stomach and swelled into his chest, spreading through his fingers and toes.

The first letter said many lives were at stake. Whether that meant ten or ten thousand, Tick didn't know. Neither did he have any idea how twelve clues, written to him in cryptic messages from some stranger, had anything to do with saving people's lives. But could he really risk that? Could Tick really be a coward and throw this challenge to the flames, when so much might be on the line? When so many people's lives were on the line?

Even if it were just *one* person?

What if that one person was Kayla and her life was in the hands of someone else? The thought gripped Tick's heart, squeezed it hard. He pictured Kayla's big-toothed smile, her cute look of concentration when she played on the computer, her giggle fits when Tick tickled her under her arms. Tick's eyes rimmed with tears. The thought of anything bad happening to his little sister made him feel a sadness that was heavy and bleak.

In that moment, in the darkness of deepest night,

sitting in the warmth of a flickering fire and thinking about things far beyond what any kid should have to contemplate, Tick made his decision, committing to himself that he would never waver from it, no matter what.

In that moment, he answered the question posed to him by the one known as M.G.

Will you have the courage to choose the difficult path?

"Yes," Tick whispered to the flames. "The answer is yes."

He folded up the letter and turned his back on the fire.

In a place very far from the home of Atticus Higginbottom, Master George awoke with a start. Exactly what had jolted him from sleep, he wasn't sure, but it didn't make him very happy. He rather liked the act of blissful slumber and believed very strongly in the old adage about beauty sleep. (Though he knew if Mothball or Rutger were around they'd say something persnickety about him needing to sleep for the next forty years to gain a single ounce of beauty.)

He looked down at his toes, poking out from his red crocheted socks like little mice searching for food. He'd pulled his blanket up too far, exposing his feet, and wondered if the chill of the night had awakened him.

No, he thought. *I don't feel cold. This was something much more. Something* shook *me.*

And then he shot up into a sitting position, any remnant of sleep completely quashed. He threw the covers off, put on his velvet slippers, and shuffled to the next room where all kinds of buzzing machinery and humming trinkets blinked and clinked and chirped. A large computer screen took up the entire left wall. Several hundred names were listed in alphabetical order, their letters glowing green, a variety of symbols and colors to the right of each name.

One of the names had a flashing purple checkmark next to it, which made Master George gasp and sit down in his specially-ordered, magnetically adjustable, ergonomically sophisticated swivel chair. He spun in three complete circles, moving himself with the tips of his toes, almost as though he were dancing. And then he laughed. He laughed loud and long and hard, his heart bursting with pride and joy.

After many disappointments, someone had finally made a Pick, one so powerful it had shaken the very foundation of the Command Center. *The ramifications could be enormous,* he thought, giddy and still chuckling.

And then, to his utter and complete astonishment, defying every sense of rational thought in his bones, two more purple checkmarks appeared on the screen, almost at the same time.

Three? So close together? Impossible!

He stood up, rocketing the chair backward with the backs of his knees, squinting to make sure it hadn't been a trick of his eyes. There they were—three purple marks.

While dancing an old Irish jig he'd learned from his great-grandpapa, Master George went in search of his tabby cat, Muffintops. He found her snoozing behind the milk cupboard in the kitchen and yanked her into his arms, hugging her fiercely.

"Dearest Muffintops," he said, petting her. "We must celebrate right away with some peppermint tea and biscuits!" He set her down and began rummaging through his pots and pans to find a clean teapot. Once he'd set some water on the stove, he straightened and put his hands on his hips, staring down at his whiskered friend.

"My goodness gracious me," he said. "Three Picks within a few minutes of each other? I daresay we have a lot of work to do."

❧

Upstairs in his room, Tick was wide awake, despite the late hour.

He studied the first letter from M.G. until the sky

outside faded from black to bruised purple and the first traces of dawn cast a pallid glow outside his window. The wind had picked up, the infamous branch that used to haunt his dreams as a kid taking up its age-long duty, scraping the side of the house with its creepy claws of leafless wood. But Tick kept reading, searching, *thinking*.

The magic words.

He didn't know what they were, why he needed them, or what would happen on May sixth when he was supposed to say them, but he knew they were vital and he had to figure them out. And the first letter supposedly told him everything necessary to do just that.

Nothing came to him. He searched the sentences, the paragraphs, the words for clues. He tried rearranging letters, looked for words that were perhaps spelled vertically, sought the word "magic" to see if it lay hidden anywhere. Nothing.

He remembered the famous riddle from *Lord of the Rings* where the entrance to the Mines of Moria said "Speak friend, and enter." It had literally meant for the person to *speak* the word "friend" in the Elven language and the doors would open. But nothing like that seemed to jump out at Tick as he sought for clues.

Figuring out the date of the special day from the first clue had been a piece of cake compared to this, and he grew frustrated. He also felt the effects of staying up all night and a sudden surge of fatigue pressed his head down to the pillow, pulled his eyelids closed.

When his mom poked her head in to wake him up for school, he begged for one more day, knowing she'd have a hard time arguing with a kid who'd been eaten alive just a few days earlier.

After his mom tucked him back into bed and patted his head like a sick three year old, Tick pondered the pledge he'd made by the fireplace the night before—to keep going, to fight the fear, to solve the puzzle. No matter what.

I'm either really, really brave or really, really stupid.

Finally, despite the light of sunrise streaming through his window, he fell asleep.

PART 2

---✳---

THE
JOURNAL

CHAPTER 11

OLD AND DUSTY

That Friday, completely healed and caught up on the work he'd missed at school, Tick sat in his science class, trying to pay attention to Mr. Chu as he talked about the vast mysteries that still awaited discovery in the field of physics. Usually, Tick enjoyed this class more than most, but he couldn't get his mind off the second clue, frustrated that he wasn't able to crack the code of the first letter.

"Mr. Higginbottom?" Mr. Chu asked.

Tick's attention whipped back to the real world, and he stared at his teacher, suddenly panicked because he had no clue why Mr. Chu had said his name. "Sorry, what was the question?"

"I didn't ask you a question," his teacher answered, folding his arms. "I was just wondering why you're staring out the window like there's a parade out there. Am I boring you?" He raised his eyebrows.

"No, I was just . . . pondering the physics of the tetherball outside."

Several snickers broke out in the room, though Tick knew it wasn't in appreciation for his joke. Some of the kids in his class didn't even listen to what he said anymore; they automatically laughed at him whenever he spoke because they assumed the others would think they were cool for poking fun at the nerdy Stinkbottom with the Barf Scarf. The laughter didn't faze Tick in the least; in his mind, those people had ceased to exist a long time ago.

"Well," Mr. Chu said. "Maybe you'd like to come up to the board and give us a diagram of what you're thinking about?" Tick knew the man had to give him a hard time every now and then or it would be overwhelmingly obvious that he favored the smart kid with the red-and-black scarf.

"No, sir," Tick replied. "Haven't figured it out yet."

"Let me know when you do. And in the meantime, grace me with your attention."

Tick nodded and resettled himself in his seat, looking toward the front of the classroom. Someone behind him threw a wad of paper at his head; he ignored it as it ricocheted and fell to the floor. Mr. Chu continued his lecture, but faltered a few minutes later when someone grumbled about how boring science was.

"Oh, really?" Mr. Chu asked, his tone almost sarcastic. "Don't you realize all this stuff leads to things that are much, much more fascinating? We need to build a solid foundation so you can have a lot of fun later."

He only received blank stares in answer.

"I mean it! Here's an example. How many of you have heard of quantum physics?"

Along with a few others, Tick raised his hand. He'd once watched a really cool show on the Discovery Channel with his dad about the subject. Both of them had agreed afterward that quantum physics must have been something *Star Trek* fans invented so they'd have another topic to discuss instead of debating the average number of times Mr. Spock visited the toilet every day.

"Who'd like to take a stab and tell us what it's about?" Mr. Chu asked.

Trying to make up for his earlier daydreaming, Tick was the only one who offered. Mr. Chu nodded toward him.

"It's about the really, really small stuff—stuff smaller than atoms even—and they have a lot of properties that don't seem to follow the same rules as normal physics."

"Wow, you're smart, SpongeBob," someone whispered from the back. He thought it was Billy the Goat, but couldn't be sure. Tick ignored him.

"Such as?" Mr. Chu prodded, either not hearing the smart-aleck remark or disregarding it.

"Well, I don't remember a whole lot of the show I saw on T.V., but the thing that really seemed cool was they've basically proven that something can literally be in two or more places at once."

"Very good, Tick, that's part of it." Mr. Chu paced back and forth in front of the students, hands clasped behind his back, trying his best to fit the mold of Very Smart Professor. "We can't get into it very much in this class, but I think many of you will be excited to learn about it as you study more advanced classes in high school. My favorite aspect of the Q.P., as we used to call it in my peer study groups, is the fact they've also proven you can affect the *location* of an object simply by observing it. In other words, how you study it changes the outcome, which means there must be more than one outcome occurring simultaneously. Does that make sense?"

Tick nodded, fascinated, wishing they could drop the easy stuff and dig deeper into this subject. He didn't bother to look around the room, knowing that the rest of his classmates would once again return nothing but blank stares.

"Basically," Mr. Chu continued, "it means alternate versions of the present could exist at any moment, and that your actions, your observations, your *choices* can determine which of those you see. In other words, we're living in one of maybe a million different versions of the universe. Some people call it the multiverse." He folded his arms and shook his head slightly while staring at the floor, a small smile on his face, as if recalling a fond memory. "Nothing in all my studies has ever fascinated me as much as quantum physics."

He paused, looking around the room, and his face drooped into a scowl of disappointment like a kid who'd just told his parents he'd seen a dragonfly, only to get back a "Who cares? Go wash your hands for dinner" in return.

"Uh . . . anyway, I guess that's enough on that subject. The bell's about to ring. Don't forget your monthly research report is due Monday."

Tick gathered his things and put them in his backpack, not worried about the assignment; his had been done since before the Gnat Rat attack.

Mr. Chu came up to him and put a hand on his shoulder. "Tick, you should think about studying quantum physics in more detail when you get a chance. It's right up your alley. Pretty crazy world we live in, don't you think?"

"Tell me about it," Tick muttered. "Hey, Mr. Chu?"

"Yes?"

"Does your family . . . I mean . . . have you ever heard of a company called Chu Industries?"

Mr. Chu's face wrinkled into a look of confusion. "No, never heard of it before. But there are a lot of Chus in the world. Why?"

"Oh . . . nothing. Just an ad I saw somewhere. Made me wonder if you had anything to do with it."

"I wish. Sounds like it could've made me rich."

"Yeah, maybe. Well, see ya Monday." Tick swung his backpack over his shoulder and walked to his next class.

❦

That night, Tick decided he needed a better way to organize the letters and clues he'd received from M.G. and Mothball, especially knowing that because of his decision not to burn the first letter, more and more would be coming.

He went down to the basement and rummaged through a couple of boxes labeled with his name and last year's date. Every year or two, Lorena Higginbottom insisted on a full top-to-bottom cleaning of the entire house, and her number one rule was that if you hadn't used something in more than a year, it needed to be thrown away or put into storage. These boxes were the result of last spring's mine sweep through Tick's closet.

He remembered he'd been given a journal for Christmas two or three years ago from his Grandma Mary. He'd vowed to write in it every day, chronicling the many adventures of the genius from Jackson Middle School, but the night he'd sat down to complete his first official entry, he hadn't been able to think of one thing that sounded interesting. He had managed to write his name on the front cover before he'd put it aside, hoping Grandma Mary would never find out. She'd have been devastated if she knew what had happened to her gift.

But he'd never forgotten how cool his name looked on the cover, and the journal would be the perfect thing for him now. Tick's life was no longer boring or uninteresting.

He found the journal lying beneath a stack of Hardy Boys books. Tick had read each of them several times before they'd made way for bigger and better novels. He pulled the journal out and stared at the cover. It had a marble-brown hardcover, its edges purposely worn and slightly burnt to make it look like the old record-book of an international explorer on the high seas. The pages inside were slightly yellowed for an aged appearance, lined from top to bottom, just waiting for him to record his thoughts and notes and scribbles.

It was perfect.

In the center of the front cover was a three-inch wide rectangle of burnt orange where he'd written his name a couple of years ago. Using the permanent black marker he'd brought downstairs with him, he added a few more words to the title. Finished, he held the journal up and took a prideful look:

TICK HIGGINBOTTOM'S
JOURNAL OF CURIOUS LETTERS

He then took out the glue from his mom's scrapbooking case and pasted the first letter from M.G. onto the first page of the journal, centering it as best he could. He left a few blank pages for notes and calculations, then glued in the first clue, along with his solution and the ripped-out calendar with the special date of May sixth circled. Finally, he attached the second clue. He made sure everything was dry, then closed the book.

Satisfied with his efforts, and glad to have everything he needed in one portable book, he took his journal and went back upstairs.

The next day, almost as though the mysterious M.G. knew Tick was organized and ready to go, the third clue came in the mail.

CHAPTER 12

THE VOICE OF M.G.

It was Saturday, and just as he had done a couple of weeks earlier, Tick spied on the mailbox, waiting for the mailman to show up. The day was clear and crisp, the sun almost blinding as it reflected off the snow still covering the ground. Tick sipped hot chocolate and watched countless little drops of water fall from the trees in the yard as clinging icicles dripped away the last remnants of their lives. His mom and dad had gone Christmas shopping, Lisa was upstairs playing house with Kayla, and the soft melody of Bing Crosby crooning "White Christmas" echoed through the house. Tick didn't know if life could be any better.

The truck finally rumbled up to his house around

noon, and Tick didn't bother looking to see if there was any sign of a yellow envelope. He had his boots and coat on and was out the door before the mailman had even left for the next house. By the time the truck drove off, Tick had already pulled out the stack of letters.

Sitting right on top was a crumpled yellow envelope with the same messy handwriting, postmarked from South Africa. Other than a strange lump in one corner, the rest of the envelope was flimsy and flat. Intrigued, a shiver of excitement rattling his nerves, Tick sprinted back to the house and up to his room in no time, where the *Journal of Curious Letters* lay resting on his bed.

He ripped open the envelope and peered inside, seeing nothing at first. He billowed it out, turning it upside down and shaking it until a little, flashy square fell out and tumbled off the bed. Tick picked it up off the floor. It was a tiny cassette tape, the kind his dad used when he made everyone talk about themselves for a tape to send to Grandma and Grandpa in Georgia. (A couple of years ago, his dad had finally switched to a video camera, but he still occasionally used the tape recorder, too.)

Nothing had been written on the tape label, but it didn't take a rocket scientist to figure out what M.G. intended the recipients of this clue to do. It took Tick ten minutes to dig out his dad's little tape machine, hidden behind some socket wrenches in his dad's infamous "junk drawer." Tick could hardly contain himself as he went back to his room, locked the door, popped in the tape, and pushed PLAY.

He heard a few seconds of scratchy background noise, then a loud clank. Tick, pencil in hand, planned to transcribe every word into his journal, but once the message started, he could only listen, fascinated.

A man spoke, his voice quirky and heavy with a British accent. Not like Mothball's accent; no, this man's voice sounded much more sophisticated and tight, like the head butler at an English manor who has just realized his entire staff is stricken with the flu on the night of the big Christmas party to which hundreds of very important people are invited.

Well, one mystery had been solved: M.G. was a man.

When the short message ended, Tick laughed out loud, then rewound it to listen again. Then he quickly fast forwarded through the rest of the tape to make sure there were no other messages. On the fourth time, he wrote every single word into his journal:

Say the magic words when the day arrives,
then hit the ground below you ten times, as
hard as you can, with a very specific object.
It's a bit of a quandary because I can't tell
you what the object is. Let's just say, I hope

your soul is stronger than mine because there
are no exceptions to this requirement. Also,
the object must be the opposite of wrong but
not correct.

Whew, glad to have that bit done. I really
need to use the lavatory before I . . . oh,
sorry, . . . meant to turn the recorder off.
Where is that confounded button . . . ? Ah!
There we are—

Click.

Tick hit the STOP button, shaking his head at how
crazy this M.G. guy seemed. Ever since he'd mentioned
peppermint sticks and sweetened milk in the first letter, Tick had sensed a subtle sense of humor in the
man, a contrast to the message of doom that seemed to
be laced throughout the clues and warnings. He wondered if he'd ever get to meet M.G. He'd already begun
to feel a sense of trust toward him.

Tick stared at his own handwriting, rereading the
words, committing them to memory. Something in the
back of his mind told him this one was simple, an itch
he couldn't quite scratch. The mystery lay in figuring
out what the object must be. Once he knew that, it
seemed pretty obvious what he needed to do: hit the
ground ten times after saying the magic words.

Tick decided it really came down to two phrases:

Let's just say, I hope your soul is stronger
than mine

and

the object must be the opposite of wrong but
not correct

Thinking, Tick flipped to a blank page in the journal to see if jotting down notes could whip up his brain functions into a frenzy. Staring at the empty lines on the page made him suddenly remember that he'd never written down the odd words Mothball had said that day by the woods when she'd been listing the things she wasn't allowed to mention. Mad at himself for not doing it sooner, Tick squeezed his eyes shut and searched the darkness of his vision, hoping bright neon words would jump out and remind him of what she'd said. One or two did almost immediately, and after a few minutes he'd remembered four and wrote them in a list on the left side of the page.

The Master
The Barrier Wand
The Realities
The Kyoopy

There'd been another weird word that he couldn't quite recall. Nothing else came to him, and he realized his eyes were getting droopy, his brain nice and ready for an afternoon nap. Wanting to check his e-mail—and needing some fresh, cold air to wake him up—he threw his new journal into his backpack and headed off for the library, telling Lisa he'd be back in a couple of hours.

~~~

"Tick, don't you ever take that scarf off?" Ms. Sears asked, stopping Tick before he could make it to the library computers. He'd spent some time studying his *Journal of Curious Letters*, as well as finishing up the last bit of homework for the weekend, and wanted to check his e-mail account, though he'd yet to receive anything since leaving the hint phrases on the Pen Pal site.

"I guess my neck gets cold pretty easily," he said, shrugging while he faked a shiver. Of course Ms. Sears knew about his birthmark, but he wanted to avoid a lecture on not being ashamed of who you are. "Any cool books come in lately?"

Her brow furrowed as she thought, making her entire weave of hair shift like a jittery land mass triggered by an earthquake. "There's a new one by Savage, but I think he's too scary for you," she said, trying to hold back a smile.

Tick rolled his eyes. "I'll take my chances."

"Okay, but if you have nightmares, tell your mom that I warned you." She smiled. "I'll hold it up at the counter for you."

"Thanks, Ms. Sears." He inched toward the computers, and she got the message.

"Okay, then," she said. "Have fun."

He nodded, then sat down at a computer as soon as she walked away. His mind still spun, the clues of M.G. bouncing around his brain like renegade alphabet soup. He knew several things for sure, and he also knew what he still needed to figure out. For some reason, on May sixth he needed to close his eyes, say some magic words that he didn't know, and hit the ground ten times with an object still left to be determined. Piece of cake.

After logging into his e-mail Web site, he hesitated a second before hitting the INBOX button. He'd checked his e-mail almost every day for weeks, and he was always disappointed to find nothing there. *But what are the odds?* he thought. Who knew if anyone else out there had received anything, much less went searching the Internet for others. But Tick felt like he'd explode if he didn't find someone with whom to swap ideas and thoughts.

He clicked the mouse.

The INBOX page only took a couple of seconds to load and a subject line written all in capital letters caught his eye the instant it appeared. His breath caught in his throat. He stood up in excitement, his chair tipping backward to the ground with a ringing metallic clang. He noticed a few scowls from the other library patrons as he righted the chair and sat down, the skin of his face on fire. Once settled, he looked at the screen again, hoping his eyes hadn't been lying to his brain.

But there it was, in black capital letters, bold against the white background:

From: SOFIA PACINI
Subject: MESSAGES FROM M.G.

CHAPTER 13

TALKING TO SOFIA

As he opened the e-mail, Tick's heart pounded so much he felt like he was trying to breathe underwater. He could hardly believe it; to receive an e-mail from another person experiencing the same mysteries as he was would validate everything once and for all—even more than meeting Mothball or being attacked by the Gnat Rat.

Forcing his eyes to slow down and take in each word, Tick read the e-mail.

Dear Atticus Higginbottom,

I'll write to you in English, since I know you must be a typical American who can only speak

Americanese, and my English is, well, brilliant.
My name is Sofia Pacini and I live in the pretty
Alps in the country of Italy. Do you know where
Italy is? Probably not. You're too busy studying
the Big Mac and the Spider-Man and not world
geography. Maybe you can learn from Sofia
and be smart. I'm just teasing you, so please
don't cry. :)

I saw your post on the Pen Pal Web site and almost
swallowed my shoe. No, I didn't have a shoe in
my mouth, it just sounds like something a funny
Americanese boy would say.

Tick paused, trying to hold in a laugh since he'd
already embarrassed himself enough in front of the
library crowd. But this Italian girl . . . *was she for real?*
He continued reading.

I got a letter from a person named M.G. in
November. You too? At first I laughed and thought
it was my friend Tony, but the letter came from
Alaska, so I don't know. Then more came, and I
met a really tall lady called Mothball. Did you meet
her? She's like a walking tree with clothes, but I
like her.

So what do you think? Is this for real? What will
happen on the day? Did you figure everything out?
Find anyone else? Write me back.

Your new friend,
Sofia

P.S. You have a weird name, btw.

Tick hated when the e-mail ended, wishing she'd
written him pages and pages of what she thought
and felt and if she'd figured out the magic words or
anything else. He clicked the REPLY TO SENDER
button.

Dear Sofia,

He paused, wondering what in the world he should
write to her. The chilling thought hit him that maybe
he shouldn't trust her. Maybe she was on the side of
whoever or whatever had sent the Tingle Wraith and
Gnat Rat. Maybe she was a spy, ready to feed him
information leading him away from the solution, not
toward it.

That's just a chance I'll have to take, he thought.
Shrugging the worry away, he began typing his message.

I know I have a weird name. Everyone calls me Tick,
so you can, too.

Sounds like we're in the same boat. I've received
three clues now, one of them on a tape. How about
you? I met Mothball, too. She gave me the second
clue. Maybe we can help each other?

He almost started telling her the things he'd figured
out and which ones had him stumped, but decided to
wait to see if she would write him back. One more e-mail
from her ought to help him know for sure if she was okay.
After thinking for a minute, he finished his letter.

I wonder how many others like us are out there.
I hope someone else writes me. Let me know if
anyone writes to you, OK?

Have you seen anything like a ghost made out of
smoke that turns into a grandpa face? What about
a Gnat Rat? That thing put me in the hospital, but
I'm OK now. How old are you? I'm thirteen, and I
live in Washington, though you already know that
because I guess you saw my Pen Pal account.

You're from Italy? That's way awesome. I wish we
could meet and talk face to face about this stuff.

I'm keeping all my notes in a book called Tick
Higginbottom's Journal of Curious Letters. Pretty
cool, huh?

Talk to you later,
Tick

He clicked SEND, knowing Sofia probably wouldn't
read the e-mail until tomorrow because it was already
past bedtime in Italy. His initial excitement tempered
by the thought that he wouldn't hear back from Sofia
for at least a day, he logged off the computer and
grabbed his backpack.

On his way out, Ms. Sears reminded him of the
book she had held for him and he checked it out just
to be nice. With everything going on in his life, reading a new book suddenly seemed dull in comparison.
Tick shook his head; he never would've thought he'd
say *that*.

The book tucked safely in his backpack next to his
journal, Tick exited the library and headed home.

Halfway there, he figured out the answer to the
third clue.

It came to him when he tripped over a big stick in
the middle of the sidewalk. As he rubbed his knee while

sitting on the cold ground, he looked at the soles of his shoes, which were caked with chunky black sludge. He wondered where they'd gotten so dirty and had just had the thought that it must've been from the mud caused by the melting snow when both of the important phrases from the third clue seemed to solve themselves simultaneously, several words flashing across his mind's eye in a rush of understanding.

Opposite of wrong but not correct.

Opposite of wrong but not the word *correct. The word* right*!*

Soul is stronger than mine.

Sole *is stronger than mine.*

Sole of his shoe.

Sole of his right *shoe.*

Not bothering to get up from the sidewalk, Tick whipped out his journal and turned to the page where he'd written the words from the audio tape. He'd misunderstood when M.G. said he hoped Tick's soul was stronger than his. The real word was *sole*, not soul, meaning M.G. hoped the sole of his shoe was strong enough to protect his foot, his *right* foot, as he hit the ground with it ten times.

Tick scribbled his thoughts down then stood up, his blood surging through his veins. Though he still felt so clueless it was ridiculous, he'd taken another small step. On May sixth, Tick needed to say magic words that he didn't know then stomp the ground with his right foot ten times.

As he ran the rest of the way home, he couldn't help but marvel at how completely stupid that sounded.

Three days passed with no reply from Sofia, and though he'd never met her, Tick felt worried sick that something terrible had happened to her. Or that maybe she'd given up and burned the letter from M.G., surrendering once and for all. Tick could barely think of anything else, losing his focus in school; he actually got a B on a test, shocking his English teacher beyond words. Every morning and night he checked his e-mail at home, and he swung by the library every chance he got.

When an entire week had passed in silence, his heart felt completely ill and he didn't know what else to do but give up on her.

The Thursday before Christmas vacation started, he walked home from school, his head down, staring at his feet through the falling snow. They'd had a couple of weeks' break from the white stuff, but it had come back with a fury the night before and hadn't let up. Tick didn't complain, of course, he loved the heavy snow. But he couldn't cheer up, feeling sad about Sofia and the lack of any more clues from his mysterious stranger.

He was just passing the patch of woods where he'd met Mothball when something caught his eye on the other side of the road. A wooden sign had been hastily nailed to a sharpened stick and hammered into the ground. Some words were painted on it in messy blue paint, the letters dripping like blood. He couldn't tell what most of the sign said from his position, but two of the words stood out like a pair of leprechauns in a hamster cage.

Atticus Higginbottom

CHAPTER 14

SHOES AND MITTENS

Tick ran over to the sign, squinting his eyes through the swirling snow to read the smaller words underneath his name. His brow crinkled in confusion. He read the sign over again, almost expecting the words to change the second time. Just when he thought he was used to how bizarre his life had become, he received a message that seemed to make no sense.

Atticus Higginbottom
Meet me when night is a backwards dim
Don't look for a her 'cause I am a him
The steps of your porch will do just fine
But don't bring snakes, spiders, or swine

For you I have important news
In return I ask for children's shoes
One more thing, or see me spittin'
Be sure to bring two nice soft mittens

If Tick had woken up that morning and guessed one thousand things a special sign made just for him might have said, a request for children's shoes and mittens would not have made the list. Not knowing what else to do, and not real keen on anyone else seeing the sign, he yanked it up out of the ground and carried it home with him, trying to sort out the message. There didn't really seem to be too many clues in the poem, just a request to meet on the steps of his porch.

Meet me when night is a backwards dim

Tick figured that one out almost instantly. "Dim" spelled backward was "mid," which meant the stranger wanted him to be waiting on his porch at midnight—presumably tonight. The now familiar shiver of excitement tickled Tick's spine as he looked at his watch and saw he still had almost seven hours to wait.

Bummer, he thought. It was going to be a long evening.

At dinner that night, Tick sat with his whole family eating meatloaf, the one thing in the universe his mom cooked that disgusted him like fried toenails. If given the choice, it would've been a tough decision between the two. He absolutely hated, despised, and loathed meatloaf. Yuck.

He forced down a bite or two, then did his best to smash the gray-green blobs of meat into a little ball so it looked like he'd eaten more than he really had. Kayla devoured hers, though she put just as much on the floor as she did in her mouth.

"What's the latest at school?" Dad asked, reaching for the bowl of mashed potatoes.

"Not much. I'm doing okay." Tick realized he'd let his mind get too occupied lately, spending less time with his family. He resolved to do better. They were, after all, just about the only friends he had in the world, besides Mr. Chu.

And Mothball, he thought. *And Sofia. Maybe.*

"Just okay?" Lisa said. "What? Did Einstein Junior get a bad grade or something?"

"Oh, please," his mom said through a snicker as though the idea was the funniest thing that had ever been spoken aloud.

"Well . . . I did get a B on my last English test."

Dead silence settled around the table like he'd just announced he was an alien and was about to have a baby because on Mars the men were the ones who got pregnant. Even Kayla had dropped her wad of meatloaf, staring at him with blank eyes.

"What?" Tick asked, knowing very well what the answer would be.

"Son," his dad said, "you haven't gotten a B on anything since I've known you. And I've known you since the day you were born."

"Yeah," Lisa agreed. "I think the world has stopped spinning."

Tick shrugged, scooping up a mouthful of green beans. "Ah, it's nothing. Maybe I had bad gas that day."

Kayla laughed out loud, then yelled in a sing-songy voice, "Tick had tooty-buns! Tick had tooty-buns!"

That broke everyone up, and dinner continued like normal.

"Anything happen lately with your Pen Pal account?" Mom asked.

Tick almost choked on his potatoes, for a split second worried that somehow his mom had logged into his account and seen the e-mail from Sofia. But then he realized he was just being a worrywart, her question totally innocent. He'd been doing the Pen Pal thing for a couple of years, still having never really connected with anyone for more than a few letters here and there. No one had ever seemed interesting enough for him to want to stay in touch—or maybe it was the other way around.

"Not really. I got an e-mail from some girl in Italy, but she seems kind of psycho."

"Psycho?" Dad asked. "Why, what did she say?"

"She called me an Americanese boy and asked me a million dumb questions."

Mom tsked. "Last time I checked, not speaking English well and being curious did not make someone a psycho. Give her a chance. Maybe she likes chess."

"Maybe she's cute," Lisa added. "You could marry her and join the mafia."

"Sweetheart," Dad said. "I don't think everyone from Italy is in the mob."

"Yeah, it's probably only like half," Tick said. He expected Lisa to laugh at his joke, but was disappointed to see she thought he'd been serious.

"Really?" she asked.

"It was a joke, sis."

"Oh. Yeah, I knew that."

"Well, anyway," Dad said, moving on. "I think this weekend we should all go see a movie, go bowling or something. Who's in?"

By habit, everyone around the table raised their hand. Kayla shrieked as she waved both arms in the air.

"All right, plan on it. Everyone meet right here at noon on Saturday."

For some reason, right at that moment, the thought hit Tick that he should tell his dad about everything.

Keeping the secret was eating away at his insides and now with nothing but silence from Sofia, the feeling was getting worse, not better. Just thinking about telling someone seemed to take a thirty-pound dumbbell off his shoulders.

Next time Mom's out shopping, he thought, *I'll tell him. Maybe he can help me figure everything out. If he believes me.*

Tick put his dishes away, then watched some ridiculous game show on TV with his family. The whole time, he thought of one thing and one thing only.

Midnight.

It was time for bed, but Tick wanted to check his e-mail one more time. He felt obsessed, checking it constantly in hopes that Sofia would finally write him back.

He sipped a cup of hot chocolate as he logged into the computer in the living room, almost spilling his drink when he saw Sofia's name in the INBOX. He put his cup down and leaned forward, clicking on her e-mail.

Dear Tick,

Someone needs to teach you how to answer a stinking question. I asked you many and all you did was write back asking me more. If I lived in the USA, I would smack your head with a pogo stick. I am a good, smart Italian girl, and so I will actually answer your questions.

First, I have to tell you that I had a very hard week. Something is chasing me, and I'm very scared. I almost burned the letter five times. Well, not really. When a Pacini makes a decision, a Pacini never goes back. I made my choice, and I'll stick to it like butter on a peanut, or whatever you crazy Americans say.

Anyway, I will now answer your questions.

I have four clues now. I got the last one last night. Maybe you did, too. It's about dead people, which doesn't sound good.

We should definitely help each other.

Saw the ghost thing, but not the rat thing. Don't want to talk about it.

I'm twelve years old, almost thirteen.

I like your journal idea. I made one, too. Hope it's okay to steal your name. Mine is called Sofia Pacini's Journal of Curious Letters. I even used English to make it seem like yours.

I joke a lot, and if we meet you will think I'm crazy.
Last summer I beat up seventeen boys. Glad we can
be friends.

Ciao (that's Italiano, smart boy)
Sofia

He'd just finished reading the e-mail when his dad told him to log off and go up to bed. Grumbling, he obeyed, hating that he'd have to wait until tomorrow to write Sofia back. He thought about sneaking downstairs after his parents were asleep, but he knew Edgar "Light Sleeper" Higginbottom would catch him as soon as he heard the buzz of the computer fan. It was going to be hard enough to tiptoe through the house and open the door to the front porch at midnight without waking him.

He brushed his teeth and said good night to everyone, then got into bed, his lamp on for reading. He decided to take a break from the fantasy novel he had been reading and pulled out the book by Savage, flipping to Chapter One.

Twenty minutes later, he did the worst thing he could possibly do.

He fell asleep.

CHAPTER 15

LITTLE BALL OF
BREAD DOUGH

Tick snapped awake a half-hour after midnight. His alarm clock glowed with evil red numbers, as if they wanted to make sure he knew his mistake was unforgivable.

Jumping out of bed with a groan, he ran to his window and looked outside for any sign of the supposed visitor. He couldn't see the entire porch from his angle, but the steps were visible in the bright moonlight that poked through a break in the clouds. No one was there, and Tick felt his heart sink.

I'm such an idiot!

Maybe he'd messed the whole thing up and lost the trust of M.G. He didn't know who'd painted the sign, but he had no doubt it was related to the M.G. mystery, and he even suspected it was Mothball or maybe her friend Rutger. She'd said he might come visit him. Sofia mentioned in her e-mail that she'd received the fourth clue, but Tick hadn't seen his yet. What if the midnight meeting was supposed to provide it?

Hardly able to stand the frustration and worry, Tick put on some warm clothes, determined to go outside and search for his visitor.

Stepping only on quiet spots in the house, avoiding the most obvious creaks and groans he knew from years of experience, he crept down the stairs and to the front door. After quietly slipping into his coat and boots, then wrapping his scarf tightly around his neck, he very carefully unlocked the deadbolt, then turned the handle. Knowing if he opened the door slowly, it would let out a creak that would wake the dead, he jerked it open in one quick motion, preventing almost any sound at all.

His heart pounding, he stepped out into the bitterly cold night, quietly shutting the door behind him.

After searching the whole yard and finding nothing, he sat on the front porch and put his head into his cupped hands, squeezing his eyes shut in anger at himself. How could he have been so stupid? He should never have lain down to read—everyone knew that was the number one way in the world to make yourself fall asleep. He blew out an exasperated sigh as he leaned back and folded his arms, looking up at the sky. Dark, churning clouds, their edges softly illuminated by the moon hiding behind them, seemed to move across the sky at an unnatural pace like something from a horror movie in fast forward.

Tick shivered, and he knew it wasn't the cold alone that caused it.

He leaned forward to stand up when something hit him on his right temple, followed by the soft clatter of a rock tumbling down the steps. He looked just in time to see a pebble the size of a walnut come to a rest a few feet away.

Belatedly, he said, "Ow" as he looked around to discover where the rock had come from. Nothing stirred in the darkness, the only sound a slight breeze whispering through the leafless trees in the front yard and sighing over the snow-covered bushes lining the front of the house. He thought one bush may have moved more than the others, and he was just about to investigate when another rock hit him, this time in the right shoulder. Sure enough, the rock came from the suspected bush, the powdery layer of snow almost completely knocked off.

"Who's over there?" he asked, surprised he didn't

feel more scared. "Quit throwing rocks like a baby and come out."

The bush rustled again, then a small figure stepped out from behind the branches. It was impossible to make out details in the scant light, but the person looked like a little kid, maybe six or seven years old, bundled up in layers and layers of clothes. He or she resembled nothing so much as a big round ball with little bumps for arms and legs and a head.

"Who are you?" Tick asked, standing up and stepping closer. "Are you the one who left me the note on the sign?"

The little person walked toward him, waddling like an overweight duck. A shaft of moonlight broke through the clouds just as the visitor reached a spot a few feet in front of Tick, revealing in vivid detail what he'd thought was a child.

It was a man. A very short and very fat man.

He was dressed all in black—black sweat pants and sweatshirt, black tennis shoes, black coat, black hat pulled over his ears. Tick's dad had once made a joke that sweat suits were made for people to exercise in, but the only people who seemed to wear them were fat people like himself.

Knowing all too well what it felt like to be made fun of, Tick always tried never to do it to anyone else. As the strange little round man walked up to him, Tick promised himself he would do his best to refrain from all known fat jokes.

"I'm *large*, okay?" the man said, though he barely came to Tick's waist. His voice was normal with no accent or strange pitch. Tick didn't know why that surprised him so much, but then he realized he'd been expecting the guy to sound like one of the Munchkins from *The Wizard of Oz*.

So much for not judging others on their looks.

The short man continued, "And I must be the dumbest fat guy you'll ever meet, because I wore all black to camouflage myself in a place that is covered in *snow*."

Tick stared, with no idea how to respond.

"My name is Rutger," the stranger said, holding a hand up toward Tick. "My hand might be the size of your big toe, but don't be scared to shake it. Nice to meet you."

Tick reached down and clasped Rutger's hand, shaking it very gently.

"What's that?" Rutger asked. "Feels like I'm grabbing a floppy fish. You think I'm made of porcelain or something? Shake my hand if you're gonna shake my hand!"

Tick gripped harder and shook, completely amazed by this new person. He finally spoke back. "Sorry. I'm just a little surprised. I didn't know . . ."

"What? That I'd look like a shrunken Sumo wrestler? Come on, let's sit and talk awhile. This weight is killer on my tiny legs." Rutger didn't wait for a response, walking over to the porch steps and taking a seat on the bottom step. Even then, his feet barely touched the ground in front of him.

Tick smiled, finally feeling at ease, and joined Rutger on the steps. "So, you're friends with Mothball, right?"

Rutger slapped his round belly. "You betcha I am! That tall stack of sticks is the best friend a man can have, even if she *is* three times my size. Well, up and down, anyway, if you know what I mean." He raised his hand vertically, as if guessing the height of something. "Ah, Mothball's a funny one if you get her going. Word to the wise though. Don't ever ask her about the day she and her twin sis were born unless you have about seven days with nothing else to do but sit and listen."

Tick grinned. "I'll remember that. Why'd you throw those rocks at me?"

"Why were you late?"

"I . . . uh, good point. Slept in."

Rutger looked at Tick intently, searching for something. "Looks like you forgot your assignment, too."

"I did? What—" Then Tick remembered the poem and what it had asked for. He'd meant to scrounge around in the basement to find some old shoes and mittens. "Oh, never mind—you're right, I forgot. Sorry."

Rutger slapped Tick on the shoulder. "It's okay, I can wait."

"Huh? You mean . . ."

"That's right, big fella. Come back with what I asked for and maybe I'll talk."

Tick paused before responding, hopeful that Rutger would wink and say he'd only been kidding. "You're . . . serious?"

Rutger leaned closer like a giant rubber ball rolling forward. "I've been to more places in the last two weeks than you've seen in your whole life, boy. My shoes are just about ready to call it a day and walk off my feet— no pun intended, though that was a pretty good one. And my hands—cold, young man, *cold*."

"You mean, the shoes and mittens are for *you*?"

"Who else, boy? Do you think I'd be traipsing around the Realities with a little child stuck to my hip? Of course they're for me!" His voice had risen considerably, and Tick worried his dad would hear.

"Don't talk so loud. You'll wake the whole neighborhood."

Rutger answered in an exaggerated whisper. "You won't hear another peep from me until I'm holding a nice new pair of shoes and a warm-as-muffins pair of mittens." He nodded curtly and folded his arms.

Tick stood up. "I'll go—but what did you mean when you said the *Realities*?"

"Oh, come on, boy. It's all about the kyoopy—science, Chi'karda, Barrier Wands!"

Tick stared, wondering if anyone in history had ever answered a question as poorly as Rutger just had. "What are you talking about?"

Rutger put two fingers together and swiped them across his lips, the age-old sign for zipping one's mouth shut.

"Fine," Tick muttered. "Be back in a minute."

He walked up the porch steps and opened the front door. Just before he stepped into the house, Tick heard Rutger say something creepy.

"Good. Because when you get back, we need to talk about dead people."

CHAPTER 16

NOWHERE IN BETWEEN

Tick wasted five minutes searching for the box in the basement where his old clothes were stored—the ones his mom couldn't bear to part with. He finally spotted it and pulled almost everything out before he found a pile of shoes of varying sizes. He chose three pairs that seemed the closest to Rutger's size, then rummaged through everything else again, searching for mittens or gloves. He found nothing.

He walked back upstairs, still doing his best to keep quiet, and dove into the closet holding all of their winter clothing. He finally came across a pair of yellow mittens his grandma in Georgia had knitted out of yarn a long time ago. They'd been his once, but Kayla had been wearing them ever since she destroyed her own pair in the fireplace. Tick tried not to laugh at the thought that they should fit Rutger just perfectly.

I can't believe I have a Hobbit in my own front yard. Holding in a snicker, he went outside.

~~~~~

"Oh, those will do just fine. Just fine! Thank you." Rutger hurriedly pulled on the mittens, then replaced his worn shoes with a pair of sneakers that Tick must've grown out of very quickly because they still looked relatively new.

"Glad to be of service," Tick said, settling on the step beside his new friend. He shivered from the cold and tightened his scarf around his neck. "Now I think you had a lot to tell me? What was that about dead people?"

The little man rubbed his newly wrapped hands together and leaned against the step behind him. "Ah, yes, dead people. There's a phrase that Mas—" He caught himself before saying anything else, looking at Tick with guilt written all over his face.

"What?" Tick asked.

"Oh, nothing . . . nothing. I was just going to say that there's something a good friend of mine always says: 'Nothing in this world better reflects the difference between life and death than the power of choice.' Says that all the time, my friend does."

"What does that have to do with me?"

Rutger looked at him intently. "What's your name, son?"

"Atticus Higginbottom. Or Tick."

"Yes, that's right." Rutger pulled out a notepad and pencil from his pocket, then started scanning it, much like Mothball had done. "There you are, and there we go." He wrote a checkmark next to Tick's name, then put the pad and pencil back into his pocket. When he pulled his hand out, this time he was holding a yellow envelope. "I believe you've been expecting this."

"The fourth clue?"

"You got it."

He handed the envelope to Tick, who immediately ripped it open then pulled out the cardstock containing the next message from M.G. Before he could read it, Rutger placed a pudgy hand on top of the clue.

"Remember what I said about dead people, young man."

"What exactly *did* you say?"

"Well, nothing really, now that you mention it. Wasn't supposed to say much, anyhow. It's for you to figure out."

"You've really cleared things up for me, Rutger, thank you."

The round man's eyes narrowed. "Do I sense a hint of sarcasm?"

Tick laughed. "Not just a hint." He pulled the message out from under Rutger's hand. "May I please read this now?"

Rutger waved a hand. "Read to your heart's delight."

Squinting to see in the patchy moonlight, Tick did just that.

The place is for you to determine and can be in your hometown. I only ask that the name of the place begin with a letter coming <u>after</u> A and <u>before</u> Z but nowhere in between. You are allowed to have people there with you, as many as you like, as long as they are dead by the time you say the magic words. But, by the Wand, make sure that <u>you</u> are not dead, of course. That would truly throw a wrinkle into our plans.

Tick looked over at Rutger. "I can bring people with me, as long as they're dead before I say the magic words? That doesn't make any sense."

The short man smiled and shrugged his shoulders. "Hey, I didn't write the clues."

"And how can a letter come after A, before Z, but

nowhere in between? Wouldn't that exclude all twenty-six letters?"

"Who am I, Sherlicken Holmestotter? You figure it out, kid." He rubbed his arms and shoulders with his mittened hands.

"Sherlicken who? Do you mean Sherlock Holmes?"

Rutger gave him a blank stare. "No, I mean Sherlicken Holmestotter, the greatest detective who ever lived."

Tick didn't know what to think of that answer. "So are you going to tell me anything worthwhile or not?"

"I'm leaning toward the *not*, actually."

"Boy, you and Mothball sure are a lot of help. Why didn't M.G. just send me letters in the mail like he did with the other stuff?" Tick shivered again, and realized his warm clothes and scarf weren't enough to block out the freezing cold.

"Nice to meet you, too." Rutger looked down at the ground, no small feat with his huge belly. "I guess you didn't want me to come, did you?"

"Hey, I was just kidding." Tick tried to keep from laughing as he reached out and patted the man's shoulder. Maybe it was the guy's size, but Tick felt like he was consoling a little kid. "I'm glad we met. I just wish you could tell me a little more about what's going on."

"Trust me, I'm dying to tell everything, but that would defeat the whole point, now wouldn't it?"

Tick threw his hands up in frustration. "What *is* the point?"

Rutger grew serious. "I think you know, Tick. You've made a choice to pursue this endeavor, and no matter what, you must see it to the end. By the very act of making it to the special day, and solving the riddles of what will happen at that time, you will be properly prepared for . . ." He paused, fidgeting with the buttons on his coat.

"For what?"

"I can't tell you."

"What a surprise." Tick wanted to be angry, but instead felt torn between disappointment and eagerness to solve everything at once. He'd always been that way; he wanted to know things right then and now, which was probably one reason why he did so well in school. He often read ahead in his books, curiosity lighting the fire of his impatience, which only added to his status as Nerd-Boy of the Universe.

"I will say this," Rutger said. "I truly hope you make it, Tick. I want to see you when it all comes down to the boiling point." He turned his squat little body and looked Tick in the eye. "You'll be there, I'm sure of it."

"I'll try."

Rutger snorted. "*Try* is for dingbats with no heart. You will *do*, young man, *do*."

"Who are you—Yoda?"

"Huh?"

"Never mind."

Rutger stood up with a loud groan, seeming to barely rise in height even though he had his legs straight under him. "Well, must be off to the wild blue yonder. Feels like I haven't eaten in three weeks." He patted his stomach. "Boy, I sure do enjoy a lovely meal now and then." He cleared his throat loudly, as if trying to give a hint.

"Where are you from, anyway?" Tick asked, trying his best to avoid any subject that dealt with the man's weight.

"I, young man, am from the Eleventh—the finest place you could ever visit."

"The Eleventh?"

"Things developed a little differently there, if you know what I mean."

"No, I don't know what you mean."

"Oh. Yes. Well, someday you will."

Tick sighed. "What were those words you said earlier? Kyoopy, Barrier Wands, chika-something?"

Rutger only raised his eyebrows in reply.

"Let me guess, you can't tell me."

"That's my boy, getting smarter by the minute." Rutger stretched and let out a big yawn. "Well, it was very nice to meet you, Tick. I expected someone a little more generous with treats and goodies, but what can you do?"

Tick rolled his eyes. "Do you want something—"

"No, no, maybe *next* time you can be a good host," Rutger replied with no subtlety. "You go on inside and stuff yourself with turkey and beans while little old Rutger walks his long journey home. At least I have new shoes, I guess."

Little? Tick thought, but wisely didn't say. "Oh, hang on a minute. You're a pathetic actor." He slipped inside the house and grabbed some bread, a bag of cookies, and a couple of bananas, throwing them all into a grocery bag, trying his best to be quiet. He forced himself to take extra precautions with every trip through the front door. He didn't need his dad waking up to find him giving out free food to a weird little fat guy in the middle of the night.

When he handed the bag to Rutger, the man beamed with joy. "Oh, thank you seven times over, my good man! Thank you, indeed!"

Tick smiled. "You're welcome. When will I see you again?"

Rutger started down the sidewalk, looking over his shoulder as best he could. "Many tomorrows, I expect, many tomorrows. Good-bye, Master Atticus!"

"Bye." Tick waved, feeling a pang of sadness as he watched Rutger set off down the road.

Edgar watched from the upstairs window in the hallway, his emotions torn between fascination at the miniature fat man that seemed to have struck up a friendship with his son, and his sadness that Tick was involved in something very strange and had failed to tell his own father about it. He and Tick had always had a special bond, sharing anything and everything. Had things changed so much? Had his boy grown up, leaving his poor father behind to wallow in ignorance?

It all made sense now. Tick had been acting so bizarre lately and the reasons behind it could very well change the way Edgar viewed the world in which he lived. As he'd watched the two speak together on the steps of the porch, he'd readied himself to run outside at the first sign of danger. But the man seemed to be a friend, and Edgar decided to wait a while before he confronted Tick about it.

He told himself he didn't know why he wanted to wait, but his heart knew the truth. Deep inside, he hoped his son would decide to tell him on his own what was going on. Edgar could hold out just a little bit longer—maybe a day or two—watching his son's every move.

Down below, Tick waved as his short friend disappeared down the dark road.

Quickly, Edgar turned and went back to his room.

CHAPTER 17

SMOKY BATHROOM

The next day was Friday, the last day of school for two weeks, and Tick thought it would never end. Having enjoyed a grand total of four hours of sleep the night before, he nodded off in class constantly, waking with an unpleasant string of drool on his chin more than once. Mr. Chu was the only teacher who gave him a hard time about it, but Tick survived.

Finally, the last bell of the day rang.

Tick was at his locker, the excitement of the coming vacation days perking him up a bit, when disaster struck in the form of a tap on his shoulder. He turned to see Billy "The Goat" Cooper sneering at him with arms folded, his goons gathered behind his massive body.

Just wait it out, Tick, just wait it out.

"Well, looky here," Billy said, his voice the sound of marbles being crushed in a vice. "Looks like Ticky Stinkbottom and his pet Barf Scarf are excited to go home and wait for Santy Claus. Whatcha getting this year, Atticus? A new teddy bear?"

"Yes," Tick said, stone faced, knowing it would throw the Goat off track.

Billy faltered, surely having expected Tick to adamantly say no or try to walk away. "Well, then . . . I hope . . . it smells bad."

Tick really wanted to say something sarcastic—*It's a teddy bear, not a Billy the Goat doll*—but his common sense won out. "It probably will, with my luck," he said instead.

"Yeah, it will. Just like your feet." Billy snorted out a laugh, and his cronies joined in.

Tick couldn't believe how idiotic this guy was, but held his face still and said nothing.

"Here's an early Christmas present for you, Ticky Stinkbottom," Billy said, and his cronies' forced laughter ended abruptly. "Stay in your locker for three minutes, instead of the usual ten. Then, go into the bathroom and stick your head in a toilet. Do that and we won't bother you until we get back from Christmas break. Deal?"

Tick felt his stomach drop because he knew Billy

would send a spy to make sure he did what he'd been ordered to do. "With my hair wet, I might catch a cold on the way home."

Billy reached out and slammed Tick up against the locker, sending a metallic clang echoing down the hallway. "Then I guess it's a good thing we don't have school for two weeks, now isn't it?" He let go and stood back. "Come on, guys, let's go."

As they walked off, Tick lowered his head and stepped into his locker, closing the door behind him.

⁓

A few minutes later, he stood alone in the boys' bathroom, staring at his distorted image in a moldy, warped mirror. He pulled down his scarf with two fingers and examined his birthmark, which looked just as ugly as ever. He felt himself sliding into that state of depression he'd visited so often before he had resolved to quit letting the bullies rule his life.

But then he thought of Mothball and Rutger, the letters and clues, and the way they all made him feel *important*. He snapped out of the gloom and doom, and smiled at himself in the mirror.

Forget those morons. I'm not sticking my head in the toilet, spy or no spy.

A moving smudge suddenly appeared on the reflection of his face, like black moss growing across the mirror. Startled, Tick reached out and touched it with his finger, but only felt the cool hardness of the glass. In a matter of seconds, the entire mirror was dark, blacking out everything. Tick took a step back, a shot of panic shooting through him.

The blackness grew, enveloping the wall and the sink, moving outward in all directions. It took on substance, puffing out like black cotton, devouring the entire bathroom wall. Tick spun to see that all the walls and the ceiling were covered now, dark smoke everywhere. The room looked like the result of a five-alarm fire, but Tick couldn't see flames and felt no urge to cough.

Then, with a great whooshing sound, every bit of the strange smoky substance rushed to the exit of the bathroom in streaks of wispy darkness, coalescing there into a big ball of black smoke. Tick's heart stuttered to a stop as he realized what hovered between him and the exit.

A Tingle Wraith.

Tick moved to run, but stopped instantly. He had nowhere to go. The Wraith completely blocked the one and only exit out of the bathroom, its dark smoke already forming into the same ancient, bearded face he'd seen in the alley a few weeks ago. Mothball's words about the creature came back to him, sending a sickening lurch through his body.

If any man, woman, or child hears the Death Siren for thirty seconds straight, their brain turns right to mush. Nasty death, that.

Tick turned to look for another way out. A tiny window let some daylight in, but other than that, there were only stalls and urinals. He ran to the thin slat of a window and grabbed the metal crank bar to open the window. He twisted the bar clockwise and a horrible screech of metal on metal boomed through the room as the glass slowly tilted outward.

Somewhere in the back of his mind, he knew the Wraith would start its deathly cry soon. He looked over his shoulder and saw the mouth forming into a wide, black abyss.

Tick quickened his pace, cranking the window as hard as he could. It jammed when it reached the half-way point. He pushed and pulled but the lever wouldn't budge. He beat against the glass with both fists, but ended up with bruised knuckles, leaving the dirty glass unbroken. Desperate, he tried to squeeze through the window anyway, pushing one arm through. It didn't take long to see it was hopeless. The crack was too thin.

He ran to the stalls, jumping up on one of the toilets to see if he could lift a ceiling tile and climb up. But it was too far above his head.

And then he heard it, the worst sound to ever beat

his eardrums, a cacophony of nightmarish wails. The sound of dying men on a battlefield. The sound of a mom screaming for a lost child. The sound of criminals at the gallows, waiting to drop into their nooses. All mixed together into one horribly terrifying hum.

The Death Siren.

Thirty seconds.

As the Wraith's cry increased in volume with every passing second, Tick squirmed his way onto the top of the stall siding, balancing as it creaked and groaned below him. He held on with one hand and reached up with the other, stretching to see if he could touch the tiles. His fingertip brushed it, but that was all.

Frantic, he jumped back down to the floor and ran out of the stall, spinning in a wide circle, looking for ideas, for a way out.

The Death Siren rose in pitch and volume, growing more horrible by the second. Tick covered his ears with both hands, hoping to quell the noise, but the stifled groan he heard was worse. Spookier. Creepier. He knew it was almost over, that he only had a few more breaths until his brain turned to mush from the loud, haunting cry.

He looked directly at the Tingle Wraith. As he stared at its wispy black face, long and old and sad, its mouth bellowing out the terrible sound, Tick realized he had only one choice.

He dropped his hands from his ears, closed his eyes, and ran straight toward the smoky ghost.

Tick held both arms out in front of him, stiffening them like a battering ram, and charged. He crossed the floor in two seconds, his clenched fists the first thing to make contact. Not knowing what to expect, and his mind half insane knowing the thirty seconds were almost up, Tick threw himself forward with every bit of strength in his legs and feet.

A cold, biting tingle enveloped his hands and arms and then his whole body as he ran straight through the black smoke of the Wraith. The Death Siren took on a different pitch—lower, gloomy. Tick felt like he'd dived into a pool of arctic water, everything muffled and frigid and dark.

But then he was through the Wraith's body, slamming into the wall on the other side. His mind sliding into shock, Tick flung open the bathroom door and threw his body out into the hallway, banging the door shut behind him.

Silence filled the school, but he could still hear a muted ringing in his ears, like the tolling of death bells.

CHAPTER 18

EDGAR THE WISE

Tick crouched on the floor of the hallway, panting for several minutes, exhausted and unable to move another inch. He kept looking at the crack under the bathroom door, sure the Tingle Wraith would follow him, but nothing came out. Mothball had told him the Wraiths couldn't move very much once they were positioned and formed. Their weapon was the Death Siren.

He finally stood, his nerves and heart settling back to normalcy, filled with relief. Tick felt sure the creature had gone away. Shaking his head as he remembered the horrible feeling of running *through* the Wraith, he set off for home, knowing what he had to do.

It was time to have a little chat with Dad.

The next few hours seemed to take days. Tick did his best to act normal: showering to wash away the icky feel of the Tingle Wraith, joking around with Mom and Lisa, playing with Kayla, reading. When his dad finally came home from work, Tick wanted to take him up to his room right that minute and spill the whole story. He couldn't do this alone anymore. He needed support, and Sofia was just too far away.

But Tick had to wait even longer because after dinner, Dad challenged Tick to a game of Scrabble, which he usually loved, but tonight seemed to drag on longer than ever before. To liven things up, he put down the word "kyoopy," at which his dad had a fit, demanding a challenge. Tick held in a snicker as he lost the challenge and had to remove the word, losing his turn. He still won by forty-three points.

Finally, as they were cleaning up the game, Tick managed to casually ask his dad to come up to his room for a minute.

"What's going on, son?" his dad asked, sitting on Tick's bed, one leg folded up under the other. "You've been acting a little strange lately."

Tick paused, running through the decision one last time in his head. This was it, no turning back. He couldn't tell his dad about everything tonight and then say he was kidding tomorrow.

All or nothing, now or never.

He chose *all* and *now*.

"Dad, there's a good reason I've been acting so crazy." Tick leaned down and pulled his *Journal of Curious Letters* from underneath the bed where he'd stowed it away that morning. "Remember that letter I got a few weeks ago? The one from Alaska?"

"Yeah. Let me guess—it wasn't from a nice Pen Pal buddy?"

"No, it was from a stranger, saying he was going to send me a bunch of clues in hopes I could figure out something important that could end up saving a bunch of people." He paused, expecting his dad to say something, but he only got a blank look, ready to hear more. "I thought it was a joke at first, but then weird things started happening—like the Gnat Rat—and I started receiving the clues and I've met some very interesting people and I believe it's true, Dad. I *know* it's true."

Tick expected a laugh, a chastisement, a lecture on not playing make-believe when you're thirteen years old. But his heart lifted at his dad's next words.

"Tell me everything, from the beginning."

And Tick did.

It took thirty minutes, and Tick showed his dad every page and note of his journal, hiding nothing, repeating every word he could remember of his conversations with Mothball and Rutger. He told it all, and when he finished, he felt like three loads of concrete had been lifted from his chest.

His dad held the journal in his hands, staring at the front cover for a long minute. Tick waited anxiously, hoping with all his heart that his dad would believe him and offer help.

"Tick, you're my son, and I love you more than anything in this world. This family is the only thing in the universe I give a crying hoot about and I'd do anything for any one of you guys. But I need some time to digest this, okay?"

Tick nodded.

"I'm going to take your journal. I'm going to study it tonight. And I'm going to think long and hard about everything you've told me. Tomorrow night, we'll meet again right here in this very spot. And if anything weird or dangerous happens, you find me, you call me, whatever you have to do. Deal?"

"Deal. Just let me copy down the fourth clue so I can work on it while you have my book."

When he was finished, the two hugged, his dad left the room, and Tick fell asleep with no problem at all.

The next night, Tick sat at his desk in the soft golden glow of his lamp, studying the fourth clue he'd scribbled on a piece of paper, waiting for his dad to come. Something about this riddle made him think it wasn't as hard as it first seemed, and he read it again, thinking carefully about each word.

> The place is for you to determine
> and can be in your hometown. I only ask
> that the name of the place begin with a
> letter coming after A and before Z but
> nowhere in between. You are allowed to
> have people there with you, as many as
> you like, as long as they are dead by
> the time you say the magic words. But,
> by the Wand, make sure that you are not
> dead, of course. That would truly throw
> a wrinkle into our plans.

Tick closed his eyes and thought.

It really came down to two hints: the letter the place begins with and the thing about dead people. The word that kept popping into his mind when he thought about the latter was *cemetery*. It matched the clue perfectly—a lot of people would be there and they'd all be dead. The way M.G. worded it made it sound like Tick would have to kill people or something, but he obviously didn't mean that, it was just a clever twist of language. The place where he was supposed to go on May sixth had to be a cemetery.

And yet, what about the letter it begins with? *After* A and *before* Z, but nowhere in between . . .

"Son?"

Tick snapped back to reality and turned to see his dad standing in the doorway. "Hi, Dad." He stood from his desk chair and went over to sit on the bed, in the same position as last night. A surge of anxiety swelled in his chest, hope and fear battling over his emotions as he awaited the verdict.

His dad joined him, a somber look on his face, his eyes staring at the *Journal of Curious Letters* gripped in both of his hands. "Tick, I've read through this a million times and thought about it all day." He finally looked at his son.

"And you think I'm psycho." Tick was amazed that at the same time he could both want and not want his dad to tell him what he thought of everything.

"No, not at all. I believe it. All of it."

Tick couldn't suppress the huge grin that shot across his face. "Really?"

His dad nodded. "There's something I didn't tell you last night. I, uh, saw you talking to the little man you called Rutger. I saw for myself he was real. And the whole thing about those gnats. I can't get that out of my mind. Then there's the letter from Alaska. I know you don't know anyone up there." He shook his head. "It's a lot of evidence, son. A lot."

"So you—"

His dad held up a hand, cutting off Tick. "But that's not why I'm convinced."

"It's not?"

"No." His dad leaned forward and put his elbows on his knees. "Tick, I've known you for thirteen years, and I can't think of a time when you've ever lied to me. You're too smart to lie, too good of a person. I trust you, and as I looked into your eyes as you told me this crazy story, I knew it was true. Now, I wanted some time to think about it and such, but I knew."

Tick wanted to say something cheesy and profound, but all that came out was, "Cool."

His dad laughed. "Yeah, cool. I can feel it deep down that this is important and that you were chosen to help because you're a special kid. There's always been something almost magical about you, Tick, and I think I knew that someday your life would take a turn for the unique. We've never really talked about it, but I've always felt like you had a guardian angel or some kind of special gift. These letters and clues and all this weird stuff has to be related somehow."

Tick didn't really know what his dad was talking about, and didn't care—he was too excited about finally having someone nearby who knew what was going on. "So you'll help me figure it out?"

"Now, maybe I can help a little here and there with the riddles but"—he pointed a finger at Tick—"you better believe I'm going to be the toughest bodyguard anyone's ever had. All this dangerous stuff scares me too, you know?" He reached out and gave his patented bear hug, then leaned back. "So where do we go from here?"

Tick shrugged. "I guess we just keep getting the clues and hope we can figure everything out by May sixth."

His dad scratched his chin, deep in thought. "Yeah . . ." He seemed doubtful or troubled.

"What?"

"I was thinking maybe this M.G. guy expects you to be a little more proactive. You know, dig a little deeper to find out what's going on."

"Dad, I can tell you're thinking really hard 'cause it looks like you might bust a vein."

His dad ignored the joke. "You have two weeks off from school for Christmas, right?"

"Right."

"And I have plenty of vacation time . . ." He paused. "But what would we do about your mom? I don't want her involved in this. She'd worry herself to the deathbed quicker than she can make a batch of peanut-butter cookies."

"Dad, what are you talking about?"

His dad's eyes focused on Tick. "I think we should do a little investigating."

"Investigating?"

"Yeah." He reached out and squeezed Tick's shoulder. "In Alaska."

By the next evening, Edgar had it all arranged, in no small part due to his clever and cunning mind, he kept telling himself. After using the Internet to discover that Macadamia, Alaska, was only three hours' drive from where his Aunt Mabel lived in Anchorage, everything fell into place. Edgar hadn't seen his aunt in years, and his mother had told him awhile back that Mabel's health wasn't doing so well. She'd stayed in Alaska even after her fisherman husband died over a decade ago, insisting that her failing heart, hemorrhoids, and severely bunion-infested feet would make a move impossible.

The plan was set, the tickets purchased, the rental car reserved.

In ten days, just after Christmas, Edgar and Tick would fly to Anchorage, Alaska, for a three-day visit with Aunt Mabel.

Lorena had grilled Edgar on how crazy it sounded to go on vacation on such short notice, but Edgar played it cool, claiming he'd been thinking about his aunt ever since Tick had gotten the letter from Alaska. And the winter break gave them the perfect opportunity.

He also used the excuse that because the tickets were expensive, only two people could afford to go. Plus Tick had been a baby the last time he had seen his great-aunt, so he didn't know her at all. Kayla was too young to appreciate the trip, and Lorena and Lisa seemed more than pleased to not have to go to a bitterly cold land of ice and snow in the middle of winter when the sun would only peek above the horizon for a couple of hours a day. Finally, Edgar pulled out all the stops, asking Lorena if she really was in the mood to hear Mabel tell her the fifty top things she'd done wrong in her life.

Lorena kissed Edgar and told him to have a good time.

When Edgar told the news to his aunt over the phone, she almost blew up his left eardrum with her shrieks of excitement. Of course, she soon settled down and told him to be sure and bring lots of warm clothes, to remember his toothbrush, to have earmuffs for baby Atticus, and about one hundred other pieces of advice.

All in all, the plan fell into place quite nicely.

Edgar only hoped that once they got to Alaska, Mabel would quit talking long enough to allow them to investigate the town of Macadamia.

Someone had sent that first letter.

And Edgar meant to find out who.

CHAPTER 19

AN ODD
CHRISTMAS PRESENT

Tick had felt so relieved that his dad believed his story and wanted to help, the whole Alaska expedition didn't really hit him until the next day when his dad told him he'd bought airline tickets. His dad seemed to think they could find out who mailed the original letter and get more information from him or her. Tick thought a trip to Alaska seemed plenty exciting all by itself, and he could barely stand having to wait ten more days.

Every day of Christmas vacation, Tick and Sofia exchanged e-mails, finally getting into a consistent groove of answering questions and learning more about each other. Tick could tell Sofia was feisty and confident—not someone to mess with unless you wanted a nice kick to the shin, or worse. She was also very smart, and Tick rarely noticed a language barrier. He felt like they were similar in many ways and he found himself liking her very much. They even played chess online, though it took almost a week to finish one game because of the time difference.

Sofia was the first to figure out the last piece of the fourth clue—the first letter of the special place. At first, Tick worried they were violating some rule by helping each other with the clues, but Sofia pointed out that none of the letters said they couldn't. In her opinion, the guy in charge should be impressed they'd had the initiative to seek out others and collaborate.

Tick felt dumb when Sofia told him the answer.

    I only ask that the name of the
    place begin with a letter coming
    after A and before Z but nowhere in
    between.

Tick already suspected the clue pointed them to a cemetery, but it was Sofia who explained that cemetery began with a "C," a letter that was certainly after A and before Z in the alphabet. *Also, the letter was nowhere to be found in the word "between."* That's what the sentence had meant, which now seemed painfully obvious to Tick.

They wondered about *which* cemetery to go to, since any decent-sized town had more than one. But the wording of the clue made it clear that the particular place they went to didn't matter, as long as it was a cemetery. Sofia would choose one in her hometown at the appointed time, and Tick would do likewise.

Of course, both of them recognized how strange it was that they had to go to a graveyard but that it didn't matter which one. But everything about the whole mess was odd, so they were getting used to it.

Tick was really happy to have found Sofia; for the first time in a long while he felt like he had a friend. Yeah, she lived in Italy and liked to beat up boys, but beggars couldn't be choosers. He couldn't wait to get the next clue and talk to her about it.

On Christmas Day, he got his wish.

It had been a perfect couple of days. Snow fell in billions of soft, fluffy flakes, blanketing the yard and the house in pure white, covering up the dirt and grime that had begun to show up after a couple of weeks without a fresh snowstorm. The classic songs of Bing Crosby and Frank Sinatra floated through the house like warm air from the fire. Tick's mom went all out in the kitchen, cooking up everything from honey-baked ham to stuffed bell peppers, cheesy potatoes to fruit salad, chocolate-covered peanut butter balls to her famous Christmas cookies, which were full of coconut, butterscotch, pecans, walnuts, and several other yummy surprises.

Tick was stuffed and happy, remembering once again why the holiday season had always been his favorite time of year. And it only helped matters that he'd be heading to Alaska in a couple of days. Life was sweet.

After the hustle and buzz and laughter of Christmas morning, tattered wrapping paper lying about in big colorful piles, Tick sat back on the couch, staring at the new goodies he'd received: three video games, some new books, a couple of gift certificates, lots of candy. He usually felt a twinge of sadness once all the presents had been opened, knowing it would be 365 long days until the next Christmas. But today he felt none of that. He felt content and warm, excited and happy.

The mystery of M.G. and his Twelve Clues had brought a new light to Tick's life and, despite the dangers that came with the letters, he'd never felt more alive.

He looked up at the decorated tree, its dozens of white lights sparkling their reflection in the red metallic balls and silver tinsel. Something square and bulky tucked behind a large nutcracker ornament caught his attention. He'd looked at this seven-foot tree a thousand times in the last month, and he knew the thing buried in the branches hadn't been there before this morning.

Instantly alert, he looked around to see what his

family was doing. His mom had her nose in a book, his dad was in the kitchen, Lisa had earphones on listening to her new CDs, and Kayla played with her kitchen set, making pretend pancakes and eggs. Trying to look nonchalant, Tick got up from the couch and walked over to the tree, staring at the spot that had caught his eyes.

A box, wrapped in an odd paper with pictures of fairies and dwarves and dragons, was snuggled between two branches, held up by a string of lights. The words "From M.G." were clearly scrawled across the box in blue ink. Tick looked around one more time before he snatched the unopened present and stealthily placed it with his other things. Then, grabbing a big armful of stuff, including the mystery box, he headed upstairs to his room.

He sat on his bed and stared at the strange wrapping paper. The present itself was very light and he felt certain the next clue must lie inside. But who had put it there, and when? He ripped the paper off a plain white cardboard box. After flipping open the lid, Tick saw exactly what he'd expected.

The fifth clue. He pulled out the cardstock paper and read the message.

```
Everything will fail unless you
say the magic words exactly correct.
It behooves me to remind you that
```

```
I cannot tell you the words, nor
will I in the face of any amount of
undue pressure you may apply toward
me. Which, of course, would be quite
difficult for you to do since you
don't know who I am and since I live
in a place you cannot go.
      Best of luck, old chap.
```

Tick read the clue a couple more times, then glued the cardstock into his journal. He thought about the trick used in the fourth clue with the word *between*. Something similar could be happening here.

```
    Everything will fail unless you
say the magic words exactly correct.
```

Say the magic words exactly correct. Could "exactly correct" be the magic words? Tick thought it would be really dumb if that were the answer; plus, he'd been told the first letter from M.G. would reveal the special words, not one of the later clues.

Tick closed the book, frustrated. This new message told him nothing he didn't already know, only that he had to say something specific when the day came, something *magic*. Other than that, M.G. just seemed to be rubbing it in that he wouldn't tell Tick what the words were—neener, neener, neener.

Disappointed, wondering if he was missing something obvious, and still baffled at how the present had gotten into his family's Christmas tree, Tick went downstairs and e-mailed Sofia about the fifth clue. Knowing she probably wouldn't respond for a while, he joined his dad in the kitchen, sharing the news as he started snacking on everything in sight.

Sofia wrote him back that night, which would have been early the next morning her time. His heart lifted when he saw her name in the INBOX and he quickly clicked on the message.

Dear Tick,

I got the Fifth Clue, too. Doesn't say much, does it? I think your idea that the magic words are "exactly correct" is just what you say. Stupid. No way, too easy.

I'm sure you're excited for the big trip to Alaska with your dad. You'll probably get lost and eaten by a polar bear. Your funeral will have the coffin closed because all that will be left is your right pinky

finger. Just kidding. I hope you escape alive.
I thought I saw a man spying on me yesterday. He
looked mean, but disappeared before I got a look.
Not good.

Have fun in Ice Land. Write me as soon as you
return.

Ciao,
Sofia

Tick reread the sentences about the man spying on
her. Sofia threw that in like she was telling him she'd
bought a new pair of socks. If some creepy-looking
dude was watching her, chances were he'd be coming
after Tick next. Unless someone was already spying
on Tick and he hadn't noticed? He felt the familiar
shiver of fear run up and down his spine, once again
reminded that this M.G. mystery business wasn't all
fun and games.

He wrote a quick note back to Sofia, telling her
to be careful and that he'd write her again the second
he got back from Alaska. He was just about to log off
when he heard the chime of his e-mail program. When
the new e-mail message popped up, Tick felt like an icy
fist had smashed his heart into pulp.

From: DEATH
Subject: (no subject)

His stomach turning sour, Tick clicked on the e-mail. It only had one line of text.

See you in Alaska.

CHAPTER 20

THE LAND
OF ICE AND SNOW

Two days later, Tick and Edgar sat in their seats on the airplane, thirty thousand feet in the air, soda and stale pretzels making them look forward to a much better meal once they landed in Anchorage. Tick sat by the window, his dad's oversized body wedged into the aisle seat like a Macy's Thanksgiving Day Parade balloon stuffed into the back of a pickup truck. The steady roar of the plane's engines made Tick feel like his ears were stuffed with cotton.

The two of them had discussed the fifth clue and the strange e-mail from "Death" many times over, with no progress. Tick didn't know who was more determined to figure everything out—him or his dad.

They'd gotten much braver—or dumber—with every passing day, to the point they were willing to ignore an obvious and outright warning like the one received in the e-mail. They were going, and that was final.

"We need to keep a sharp lookout," his dad said through a mouthful of pretzels. "If either one of us sees something suspicious, yell it out quickly. When in doubt, run. And we need to stay in public as much as possible."

"Dad, I'd say you sound like a paranoid freak, but I agree one hundred percent." Tick took a sip of his drink. "I think I'm half excited and half scared to death."

"Hey, we're committed, right? There's no turning back now."

"Cheers." They clicked their plastic cups together.

In two hours, they'd be in Alaska.

Seven rows back, a tall man with black hair and razor-thin eyebrows crouched in his tiny seat as best he could, reading the ridiculous in-flight magazine, which was full of nothing but advertisements and stupid articles about places he'd never care to visit. This spying business was deathly boring, and he hated it. No action, no results, boring, boring, boring.

But all of that would change very soon. The Spy would become the Hunter.

His name was Frazier Gunn, and he'd worked more than twenty years for Mistress Jane. He despised the woman, *loathed* her, in fact. She was the cruelest, most selfish, despicable, horrifying creature he'd ever met, and yet, his devotion to her was absolute. An odd mixture of feelings, but that's how it had to be when you served someone who planned to take over the Realities. They needed a leader like her, ruthless and without conscience. He didn't have to like her—he only needed to *pretend* to like her.

Because someday he planned to replace her.

Of course, if he ever failed even one of his assigned missions, she'd feed him to the Croc Loch near the Lemon Fortress with no remorse. But he was safe for now and had been promised a great reward if he could unlock the secret behind the bizarre series of letters Master George had sent out to kids all over the world. He had only recently discovered the identities of several recipients, enabling him to further his investigation with stealth and caution. But finally, the time for intimidation and action was at hand.

It'd been a fun trick sending the "Death" e-mail to the boy named Atticus, quite clever in fact. It was the dumb kid's own fault for putting his information about the letters on the Internet for anyone to find. There'd been a slight risk that Atticus might've chickened out and not gone to Alaska, thereby ruining a chance to learn more for Mistress Jane, but Frazier couldn't resist the calculated threat.

He reached into his pocket to feel the reassuring lump of the special *thing* he'd brought along to perform the important task he planned. He couldn't wait to activate it; the devices they'd retrieved from the Fourth Reality were so much fun, futuristic and deadly. The spectacle would make all the hours of spying on the brats around the world worth every minute.

And if it didn't work, there was always Plan B. Or C. Or D.

Giving up on the magazine, Frazier Gunn leaned back and closed his eyes. The boy and his father couldn't very well disappear on an airplane, now could they?

Tick felt so relieved when he and his dad were finally in the rental car, bags safely stowed away in the trunk, heading down the frozen freeway to Aunt Mabel's house. Even though it was still mid-afternoon, the land around them had grown dark, the sun's brief journey above the horizon having ended an hour ago.

Tick held a map in his lap, navigating for his dad. Mabel lived on the outskirts of Anchorage in a small suburb that seemed pretty easy to find. Most of the way followed one main road that stretched endlessly before them, the faded yellow lines of the lane markers seeming to flash then disappear beneath the car.

"Well, Professor," Dad said. "Prepare yourself for Aunt Mabel. She's quite the character and full of more ideas on how to save your life than you'll probably care to hear. Just know that she means well and do a lot of nodding."

"I'm excited to meet her."

His dad laughed. "You should be, you should be. Trust me, if you want entertainment, we're going to the right place."

They'd eaten at a fast food restaurant before heading out from the airport, and Tick still had his soda, from which he took a big long swallow. "You think she'll mind when we go exploring out to Macadamia?"

"You can bet your life savings she'll mind, all right, but, oh well. We'll tell her we didn't want to waste such a good opportunity to see the sights of this beautiful land she calls home. That'll get her, I hope."

"When do you think we'll drive out there? Tomorrow morning?"

"Sounds good to me. That'll give us the whole evening with Mabel tonight, and breakfast tomorrow— she makes a mean plate of eggs, bacon, the works. Hopefully, we can figure some things out and return to her place tomorrow night."

"I just hope Macadamia isn't a dead end."

His dad reached over and patted Tick on the leg.

"No, we'll find something. It couldn't have been a ghost that sent that letter, now could it?"

"Judging by what I've seen lately? Maybe."

"Good point."

Tick studied the map. "Looks like you turn into her neighborhood up there to the right."

Edgar flipped on the blinker as he slowed the car.

———

A mile or so behind, Frazier Gunn pulled off the road and stopped, not wanting to take any chances of being spotted. He'd wait an hour or so, then find himself a discreet parking space where he could watch the house. The boy and his father would probably spend the night, saving their planned expedition to Macadamia for tomorrow.

Frazier wanted to see what they discovered there before he put his plan into action. Every little bit of information on what Master George was up to might help Mistress Jane's cause, and Frazier meant to find out everything he could. When the two adventurers drove back to Anchorage after their investigation, he'd implement the device that sat in his pocket, ready and hungry to get to work.

He grinned at the thought.

———

Tick and his dad stood in front of the door to Aunt Mabel's home, staring at the plastic flowered wreath that must've hung there for two or three decades— its every surface covered in dust. The house itself was a cold and weary pile of white bricks, but the warm light shining through colorful curtains in the windows made it seem like the coziest place on Earth. However, neither of the Higginbottoms moved to push the doorbell just yet.

"Well, here we are," Dad said. A thick layer of snow and ice covered the yard around them; it looked like a miserably frigid wasteland that hadn't seen the full sun in years.

"Here we are," Tick repeated, gripping his suitcase.

"Now, one last warning." Dad looked at his son. "Aunt Mabel is at least one hundred and fifty years old, she laughs like a hyena, and she smells like three tubes of freshly squeezed muscle ointment."

Tick grinned. "Good enough for me. I love ancient history and watching nature shows, and I don't mind the smell of peppermint."

His dad nodded. "That's the spirit. Let's do this thing." He reached out and pushed the doorbell button.

Three seconds later, Aunt Mabel pulled the door open.

CHAPTER 21

OLD, FUNNY, AND SMELLY

L ittle Edgar!" she yelled, a shriek that sounded like fighting cats. The intense smells of peppermint and homemade cooking wafted out of the house with the warm air, and Tick had to suppress a laugh.

Aunt Mabel looked as ancient as Tick's dad had indicated, her heavily wrinkled but thin face covered in at least three pounds of makeup, capped off by bright red lipstick covering a lot more than her lips, as if she'd been jumping rope when she applied it that morning. Her small body seemed too frail to support the loud burst of excited salutations that came from her lungs as she hugged both Edgar and Tick.

"So good to see you! So glad you made it safe!

About time you came to visit your poor old Auntie!"

Tick returned the hug, suddenly feeling very relieved and at home. She was family after all, and this trip obviously meant the world to an old widow who lived alone. Despite the icy cold weather, Tick felt warm inside and looked forward to getting to know his great-aunt Mabel—though he had to admit she did scare him a *little*.

"Well, come in, come in!" she said, her fake teeth sparkling as her face lit up like a giddy clown. "I need to sit these bones down—my bunions are inflamed like you wouldn't believe. Take off your coats and such—especially that hideous scarf, young man." She gestured to the side of the foyer where they put their coats and bags—Tick left his scarf on by habit, despite what she'd said—then Mabel led them into a small living room where a couple of couches covered in orange velvet beckoned for them to sit. A dusty lamp with beads hanging from the shade glowed a dull yellow from its stand on a chipped wooden end table. The entire house looked like it had been decorated with props from a really old TV show.

Once they were settled, Aunt Mabel brought in three steaming hot cups of herbal tea; it tasted like boiled cardboard but warmed Tick very quickly. He leaned back on the soft couch and put his foot up on his knee, eager to see Mabel in action.

"Well, land's sake, it's a delight to see you boys," she

started. "Living up here at the North Pole with noth-ing but seventeen quilts and a couple of icicles to keep you company makes a woman grow old quicker than she should. And let me tell you, when you were born before any of your neighbor's *grandparents*, you can forget having friends come over to play pinochle and watch reruns of *Andy Griffith*." Mabel paused, but only long enough to take in a huge gasping breath. "There's this boy that lives down the corner—mean as a snake, I tell you. He came over to shovel my driveway after the last storm, but he *didn't* put salt on the sidewalk to melt the ice. The nerve of that young troublemaker . . ."

After coming from the wintry air into a nice warm house, and after a long day of busy travel, Tick felt his eyelids dropping as Aunt Mabel continued to rant about each of her neighbors and their various faults and crimes. He tensed his muscles in an attempt to wake himself up.

". . . and Missus Johnson down the road—I'm pretty sure she's a *spy* for the Homeland Security International Espionage and Intelligence Spy Division. Always snooping, asking questions, you know. Just the other day, I was taking my garbage out to the road as she was walking by. Do you know what she said to me?"—Mabel didn't pause long enough for anyone to answer—"She had the nerve to ask me how my *health* was doing. I tell you right here and now I bet she wants to set up a sting operation from this house once I'm dead and gone, buried like a sack of dirty clothes in the town dump. And Mr. King up by the corner—did you know he has *thirteen* children? And every last one of them the spawn of the devil or my name isn't Mabel Ruth Gertrude Higginbottom Fredrickson."

And so it went for at least another twenty minutes, Tick finally having to pinch himself to stay awake. His dad seemed pleased as could be, smiling and nodding the entire time, throwing out a few "Hmms" and "Uh-huhs" every now and then. Finally, as though she'd exhausted her capacity to use her frail body's vocal cords, Mabel stopped talking and leaned back in her seat.

"Uh, wow," Dad mumbled, caught off guard that his aunt had actually quit yapping. "Sounds like your life is a lot more interesting than you let on, Aunt Mabel. We're sure glad we could come and visit you." He looked over at Tick, raising his eyebrows.

Tick straightened in his seat. "Yeah, I'm really excited I finally got to meet you." He raised his cup as if saluting, and immediately felt like an idiot.

"You boys aren't mocking me, are you?" Mabel asked, her eyes narrowing.

"No!" Tick and his dad said in unison.

"Good. Let's eat some supper." She squirmed in her seat, but couldn't move an inch. "Atticus, dear boy, be a gentleman and assist your elders." She held out a hand.

Tick jumped up and gently helped her stand, then escorted her into the cramped but cozy kitchen.

A wave of mouth-watering smells bombarded them when they entered, and Tick proceeded to eat the most scrumptious meal he'd had in a long time, which was saying a lot considering how good of a cook his mom was. There were freshly baked rolls soaked in butter, grilled chicken with lemon sauce, corn on the cob, mashed potatoes with chunks of garlic—all of it delicious.

Aunt Mabel talked the entire time they ate, covering every topic from her ingrown toenail to how she'd finally lost her last tooth to decay, but Tick barely heard her, enjoying three more helpings of the fantastic dinner.

Frazier crept up to the car of his prey, his eyes flickering to the house of the old woman. He'd watched their shadows leave the front room and head deeper into the house, probably to the kitchen for dinner. The thought made his stomach rumble and he resolved to bag this place and find something to eat as soon as he'd accomplished his task. Even expert spies like himself had to chow down every once in a while.

He crouched behind the left front tire, making sure the body of the car stayed between him and the house. He reached into his pocket and pulled out the special device—an oval-shaped metal container, about eight inches long and three inches wide, a seam wrapped around the middle. On one side of the seam, several buttons and dials poked out. Frazier looked at the familiar label on the other side—the label that marked items taken from the Fourth Reality:

Manufactured by Chu Industries

He split the little machine into two pieces along the seam, slipping the part with the controls back into his pocket. The other half, with its dozens of wires and clamps coiled inside like poisonous snakes ready to wreak havoc, didn't look nearly as menacing as it should, considering what Frazier knew it could do to something like a car. More precisely, what it would do, indirectly, to the people *inside* the car.

Frazier snickered, then reached underneath the tire well to place the Chu device as far and as deep as he could toward the engine. He pushed the small button in the middle and heard a hiss followed by a metallic clunk as the gadget reached out with tiny claws and adhered itself to the car. A spattering of tiny clicks rang out as the machine crawled its way to where it needed to go.

Smart little devices, these things. In a matter of moments, the beautiful but deadly trinket would find exactly what it needed.

Once in place, it only needed Frazier's signal to come alive.

~⁓~

Aunt Mabel must think I'm three years old, Tick thought.

It all started at bedtime. Mabel followed Tick into the bathroom and pulled a container of floss from a dusty cabinet. She yanked off a three-foot long piece and handed it to Tick.

"Now, catch every nook and cranny," she said as Tick started threading the minty string between his two front teeth. "You never can tell what nasty little monsters are having a nice meal of your gums."

Tick finished and threw the used floss into a small wastebasket, wishing Mabel would leave him alone. When she didn't move an inch, hovering behind him as he stared into the mirror, Tick reached over and grabbed his toothbrush and toothpaste. Warily glancing back at Mabel, he finally turned on the water and started brushing.

"Here, let me take a turn," Mabel said a few seconds later. To Tick's horror, she reached around his shoulder and grabbed the toothbrush from his hand

and began vigorously scrubbing his teeth, pushing his head down lower with her other hand. Tick never would've thought such an old and frail woman could have so much strength in her arms. "Gotta get those molars!" she yelled with enthusiasm.

Next came pajama time. Tick had brought a pair of flannel pants and a T-shirt to sleep in, but that was not good enough for Aunt Mabel. She went to the basement and dug through some boxes before returning with a musty old pair of long johns that were as red as her lipstick and looked like Santa's underwear. Tick begrudgingly put them on, heeding his dad's pleas that they do everything humanly possible to make the old woman happy so nothing jeopardized their trek the next day. He almost broke his promise when Mabel topped everything off by twisting a scratchy wool stocking cap onto his head. Instead, he forced a grin and followed her to the bed she'd prepared for him.

After tucking him in with no fewer than seven thick quilts, Mabel kissed him on the forehead and sang him a bedtime song, which sounded like a half-dead vulture warning its brothers that the chickenhawk he'd just eaten was poisonous. Tick closed his eyes, hoping that if Mabel thought he was asleep, he could avoid an encore. Satisfied, Aunt Mabel tiptoed out of the room—making sure before she closed the door that the night-light she'd plugged in worked properly.

Tick rolled over, wondering if his great-aunt would do the same routine with his dad. When he finally quit laughing at the image of Mabel brushing his dad's teeth, Tick fell asleep.

The next morning, after a wonderful meal of eggs, bacon, sausage, cheese biscuits, and freshly-squeezed orange juice, and after a long lecture on how important it was not to talk to strangers, especially those holding guns or missing any teeth, Tick and his dad were able to escape for a day of "exploring the wonders of Alaska." Aunt Mabel seemed exhausted from her efforts and couldn't hide the fact that she was almost relieved to get some rest from taking care of the boys.

After filling up the car with gas and junk food, Tick and his dad began their three-hour journey, the *Journal of Curious Letters* sitting on the seat between them.

Next stop: Macadamia, Alaska.

CHAPTER 22

GOING POSTAL

After driving down the straightest road Tick had ever seen—with nothing but huge piles of snow and ice on either side—they pulled into the small town of Macadamia right around noon. The first thing they did was stop at a gas station to fill up the car for the drive back so they wouldn't have to do it later. The cracked and frozen streets were deserted, with only a few cars parked along the main road in front of various dilapidated shops and dirty service centers.

"Well, I figure we have about six hours until we need to head back," Tick's dad said as he started the car again. "Or, if we don't discover anything today, we can always call Aunt Mabel and tell her we got stuck somewhere for the night and that we'll come back tomorrow. She won't want us taking any risks."

"Yeah," Tick said. "But she'll be spitting nails if I'm stranded at some nasty hotel without her there to brush my teeth for me."

His dad laughed. "You're a good sport, Professor. Now you know why your mom and Lisa were just fine letting the two of us come up here alone." He put the car into gear and drove away from the gas station. "The lady in the gas station said the post office was just up here on Main Street. That'll be our first stop."

⁓

Five minutes later, Tick followed his dad through the frosted glass door of the post office, loosening his scarf, not sure what to expect. But he did have an odd sensation in his stomach, knowing the original mysterious letter from M.G. had been mailed from this very building. It was almost like seeing the hospital room where you'd been born, or a house your ancestor had built. Despite how he felt, this was where any investigation would have to begin—he just hoped it didn't end here as well.

The place was boring, nothing but gray walls and gray floors and gray counters—the only thing breaking the monotony was a tiny faded Christmas tree in a corner with six or seven ornaments hanging from the sparse branches. No worker was in sight.

"Hello?" Dad called into the emptiness. A little bell sat on the main counter; he gave it a ring.

A few seconds later, an old man with bushy eyebrows and white stubble on his cheeks and chin appeared from the back, looking none too happy that he actually had to serve a customer. "What can I do for you?" he asked in a gruff voice before his feeble attempt at a smile.

"Uh, yes, we have a question for you." Dad stumbled on his words, as if not sure of himself now that the investigation had officially begun. "We received a letter—postmarked from this town—in the middle of last month. In November. And, we're, uh, trying to find the person who sent it to us, and, um, so here we are." He rubbed his eyes with both hands and groaned. "Tick, your turn."

"Oh. Yeah." Tick pulled the original envelope from his journal, where he'd stuck it between two pages, then placed it on the counter. "Here it is. Does this look familiar to you at all, or the handwriting?"

The man leaned forward and for some reason sniffed the envelope. "Doesn't mean a thing to me. Good day." He turned and took a step toward the back of the office.

Tick felt his heart sinking toward his stomach. His dad gave him a worried look, then quickly said to the man, "Wait! Does anyone else work here? Could we speak to them?"

The old man turned and gave them an evil glare. "This is a small town, you hear me? I retired a long time ago, until I was forced to come back last month because one of the workers decided he was a psycho and up and quit. Good riddance. If you want to talk to him, be my guest."

"What was his name?" Tick asked. "Where does he live?"

The formerly retired postal worker sighed. "Norbert Johnson. Lives north of here, the very last house on Main Street. Don't tell him I sent you."

The man left the room without another word or a good-bye.

They pulled up in their car at the dead end of Main Street, staring at a small house that seemed to huddle in the cold, miserable and heartbroken. Tick didn't know if it officially approached haunted-house status, but it was close—two stories, broken shutters hanging on for dear life, peeling white paint. A couple of dim lights shone through the windows like dying fires. Two wilted trees, looking as though they hadn't sprouted leaves in decades, stood like undernourished sentinels on either side of the short and broken driveway.

"Son," his dad said, "maybe this time you should do the talking."

"Dad, you're supposed to be the grown-up in this group."

"Well, that's why I'll provide the muscle and protect you from harm. You're the brains of this outfit; you do the talking." He winked at his son then climbed out of the car.

Tick grabbed his journal and followed him down the icy driveway, up the creaky wooden stairs of the snow-covered porch, then to the sad-looking front door, brown and sagging on its hinges. His dad knocked without hesitating.

A long moment passed with no answer or noise from inside. Tick shivered in the biting cold and rubbed his arms. His dad knocked again, then found a barely visible doorbell and pushed it, though it didn't work. Another half-minute went by without so much as a creak from the house.

Dad moaned. "Don't tell me we came all this way and the man we need to talk to is on vacation in sunny Florida."

Tick craned his neck to look at a window on the second floor. "There're lights on inside. Someone has to be home."

"I don't know—we always leave a light on when we go on vacation—scares the burglars away." He knocked again, half-heartedly. "Come on, let's go."

With slumped shoulders, they started down the

porch steps. They were halfway down the sidewalk when they heard a scraping sound from behind and above them, then a low, tired voice. "What do you folks a-want?"

Tick turned to see a disheveled, gray-haired man peeking out of an upstairs window, his eyes darting back and forth around the yard, looking for anything and everything.

"We're trying to find Norbert Johnson," Tick shouted up to the window. "We have some questions about a letter mailed from here."

The man muttered something unintelligible before letting out a little shriek. "Do . . . do you work for Master George or Mistress Jane?"

Tick and his dad exchanged a baffled look. "Master George . . ." Dad said under his breath, then looked back up toward the man at the window. "Never heard of either one of them, but my son got a letter from someone named M.G. Could be the same person, I guess."

The man paused, his squinty eyes scrutinizing the man and boy below him for signs of trouble. "Do you swear you've a-never heard of a woman named Mistress Jane in your life?"

"Never," Tick and his dad said in unison.

"You've a-never seen or worked for a lady dressed all in yellow who's as bald as Bigfoot is hairy?"

Tick couldn't believe how weird this whole conversation had become. "Never."

The man slammed his window shut without saying another word, leaving Tick to wonder if this Norbert guy really had gone bonkers like the old postal worker had suggested.

The front door popped open and Norbert stuck his head out, smoothing his thin gray hair. "Come on in," he said in a quick, tight voice, looking around the yard again. "I've got something for you."

Frazier had pulled to the side of the road two houses down from the one at the end of the street, curious as to what Tick and his dad would learn from the man who lived there. It seemed they merely wanted to discover if the postal workers knew who had mailed the letter they had received, but something about the whole thing seemed fishy.

With his spy equipment—conical sound trapper, thermo-magnetically heightened microphones, and molded earpieces—Frazier had heard every word exchanged in the post office and had found it quite interesting.

Norbert Johnson. The name didn't ring a bell, but Mistress Jane certainly didn't tell him about every person she came across in her travels. Maybe she'd interrogated Johnson about the whole affair. That would have been enough to drive any man crazy. The way Norbert had acted at his own house—all nervous and paranoid before finally letting the two strangers in—sure seemed to support the "crazy" theory.

Frazier picked up his eavesdropping gadget and pointed it at the house, then reinserted his earpieces. It took a few seconds to pinpoint the murmurs of the conversation before he locked it in place as best he could, settling back to have a listen. The first thing he heard made his eyes widen. It was the voice of the man named Norbert.

"Here you go. The big lady told me it's called the sixth clue."

CHAPTER 23

BONDING WITH NORBERT

Big lady?" Tick asked, holding the yellow envelope like his life depended on it. "Who gave this to you?"

They sat in a messy living room, not a single piece of furniture matching any of the others. *At least it's warm,* Tick thought. He and his dad sat on a frumpy couch that leaned toward the middle, facing Norbert on his rickety old chair, where he wrung his hands and rocked back and forth.

"Big ol' tall woman. Looked like ugly on a stick," Norbert answered in almost a whisper. "Just about scared me out of my pants, what with her a-coming out of the old graveyard behind my house."

The mention of a cemetery made Tick's ears perk

up. *It can't be a coincidence* . . . It must be related some-how to the fourth clue and where he was supposed to go on May sixth.

"Did she say anything else to you?" Dad asked. "Talk to you at all?"

"Not much." Norbert's fidgeting made Tick's head dizzy. "Told me some real smart kids would come a-looking for me, and I should give that there letter to 'em. Gave me several copies. Don't know about you fellas, but when an eight-foot monster lady tells me to do some-thing, I'm gonna pretty much do it. So there you go."

Tick inserted his thumb under the flap and started ripping open the envelope as Norbert kept talking.

"Since that piece of parcel looked just like the ones from the British fella, and since I figured the British fella was an enemy of the Banana Lady, I reckoned I'd be a-doing a good task."

Tick stopped just before pulling out the white card-stock of the sixth clue. "British? Who was British?"

His dad leaned forward, a surprisingly difficult task that made the pitiful couch groan like a captured wol-verine. "Mr. Johnson, I'm more confused than the Easter Bunny at a Christmas party. Could you please tell us everything you know about the letter we got from Alaska and who sent it? Maybe start from the beginning?"

"The Easter Bunny at a—" Tick began, a question-ing smirk on his face.

"Quiet, son."

Norbert finally settled back in his chair and began his story, seemingly relieved that he'd been given direction on how to go about this conversation. Though Tick desperately wanted to read the next clue, he slipped it inside his journal and listened to the strange man from Alaska.

"I'd worked there at the post office in Macadamia for twenty-plus years, and I was just as happy as can be. Well, as happy as a single man in his fifties who smells a little like boiled cabbage can be." Tick involuntarily sniffed at this point, then tried to cover it up by scratching his nose. Norbert continued without noticing.

"Then *they* had to come along and ruin my life. It was a cold day in November—of course, every day is cold in November when you live up here, if you know what I mean. Anyway, first this busy little British gent named Master George, dressed all fancy-like, comes walking into my shop holding a box of letters that looked just like the one I gave you." He pointed at the journal in Tick's lap. "Goes off about how they need to get out right away, do-da, do-da."

Tick decided that last part was Norbert's way of saying "etcetera" and held in a laugh.

"I assured the fella I'd take care of it and he left. Wasn't a half-hour later when the scariest woman I've ever laid eyes upon came a-stomping in, dressed from head to toe in nothing but yellow. And she was bald—not a hair on her noggin to be found. Called herself Mistress Jane, and she was mean. I'm telling you, *mean*. You could feel it coming off her in waves." Norbert shivered.

"What did she want?" Dad asked.

"She was a-looking for Master George, which told me right away that the British gent must be a good guy, because Lemony Jane surely wasn't."

Tick felt like the final mystery of a great book had been revealed to him. The source of the letters suddenly had a name, a description. He was no longer a couple of initials and a blurred image. M.G. had become Master George. From England. And he was the good guy.

"She threatened me," Norbert continued. "She was cruel. And I couldn't get her out of my mind. Still can't. She's been in my dreams ever since, telling me she's gonna find out I lied to her."

"Lied to her?" Dad repeated.

"Yes, sir. Told her I'd never met anybody named Master George, and I hid the letters under the counter before she could see them. Flat out lied to her, and she told me bad things would happen if she ever found I'd a-done it. And done it, I did."

"So . . ." Tick started, "you quit your job because you were scared of her?"

Norbert looked down at his feet as if ashamed of

himself. "You got me all figured out, boy. Poor Norbert Johnson hasn't been the same since the day I met that golden devil. Quit my job, went on welfare, borrowed money. I been hiding in this house ever since. Only reason I met the tall lady who gave me the letters is because I heard a noise out in the backyard."

"I thought you said she came out of a graveyard," Dad said.

"She did. Like I said, back behind my house is an old, old cemetery. Got too old, I reckon, so they built another one closer to downtown."

"Mothball," Tick said quietly.

"Huh?" Norbert replied.

"Her name is Mothball. The lady who gave you this letter." Tick slipped it from his journal and held it in his hand.

Norbert looked perplexed. "Well what in the Sears-and-Roebuck kind of name is that?"

"She said her dad was in a hurry when he named her, something about soldiers trying to kidnap them."

Norbert did nothing but blink.

"Never mind." Tick turned to his dad. "Why in the world would she have given *him* the sixth clue?"

His dad furrowed his brow for a moment, deep in thought. "Well, maybe it's like I said—I think they wanted us to be proactive and seek out information, not just wait around to find it. Maybe they went back to all the towns they mailed the letters from and gave copies of the clues to the postal workers who would cooperate. They knew if we did some investigating, going to the source would be the most logical step."

Tick thought for a second. "Dad, I think you nailed it."

"I'm brilliant, my son. Brilliant." He winked.

Norbert cleared his throat. "Excuse me for interrupting, folks, but what in the name of Kermit the Frog are you guys a-talking about? You came here asking me questions, but it sounds like you know a lot more than I do."

Dad leaned over and patted Tick on the shoulder. "My boy here, the one who's receiving these letters, is trying to figure out the big mystery behind them. We think it was a test of sorts to see if we'd seek you out, which is why you were given the sixth clue to give to us."

Norbert nodded. "Ah. I see." He rolled his eyes and shrugged his shoulders.

"Look," Tick said. "Do you know anything else about Master George, Mistress Jane, Mothball, anything?"

Norbert shook his head in response.

"Well, then," Tick said. "I think we've got what we came for. Dad, maybe we should get going. I can read the clue while you drive." Tick tried his best to hint that he didn't feel very comfortable in Norbert's house.

"Just a minute." His dad looked at their host. "Mr. Johnson, you've done a great service for us and we'd like to return the favor. Is there, uh, anything we can do to help you, uh, get your nerve back and go back to work?"

Norbert didn't reply for a long time. Then, "I don't know. It's awfully kind of you to offer. I guess I'm just too scared that woman is gonna come back for me and string me up like a fresh catch of salmon."

"Well, let me tell you what I think," Dad said, holding up a finger. "I agree with you one hundred percent. I think this Mistress Jane person must be evil, because we wholeheartedly believe what M.G.—Master George—is doing must be a noble cause because he wants my son's help. And we've committed to that cause heart and soul, as you can tell."

"I reckon I can see that. What's your point?"

"Well, if this . . . yellow-dressed, bald, nasty woman made you quit your job, shun society, and hole up in a house all by yourself, then I think she's won a mighty victory over the world. She's beaten the great Norbert Johnson once and for all, and will move on to her next prey."

Tick liked seeing his dad try and help this poor man and decided to do his part. "Yeah, Norbert, you're doing exactly what she wanted you to do—give up and be miserable. Go back to work, show her you're the boss of your own life."

Norbert looked back and forth between Tick and his dad, his face a mask of uncertainty. "And if she does come back? What then?"

"Then by golly," Dad said, "stand up to her. Show her who's in charge."

"And call us," Tick chimed in. "By then, maybe we'll have figured everything out and know how to help you."

Norbert scratched his head. "Well, I don't know. I'm a-gonna have to think about this."

Dad smiled. "Listen, we'll exchange phone numbers and keep in touch, okay? How's that sound?"

Norbert didn't answer for a very long time, and Tick wondered if something was wrong. But then he saw moisture rimming on the bottom of the man's eyes and realized the guy was all choked up.

Finally, their new friend spoke. "I can't tell you how much it means to me that you folks care enough to give me your phone number. I just wished you a-lived up here in Alaska. I could use a friend."

"Well, hey," Dad said. "In this world, with the Internet and all that, we can keep in touch just fine."

And with that, their new friendship was sealed and Tick felt mighty proud of himself.

Frazier watched as Tick and his dad stepped out of the house, then shook hands and embraced their new little buddy. They said a few more sappy words, just like they had inside, and headed for their vehicle.

What is this, a soap opera? I might need a tissue for my weepy eyes.

He snickered at his own joke, then put the car into drive, ready to follow, the twilight of midday having long faded into the full darkness of late afternoon.

Frazier pulled out his half of the special device, fingered the big button in the middle of its shiny gray surface.

In just a few minutes, he thought. *Just a few minutes and the show begins.*

CHAPTER 24

PEDAL TO THE METAL

Norbert stared out his frosty window, watching the boy Tick and his father climb into their rental car, warm it up, then begin their long trek back to Anchorage. Norbert hadn't felt this good in weeks, like he was doing something *right*, finally taking a stand against the yellow witch who haunted his dreams. He couldn't explain it—the boy and his dad seemed to pulse with some invisible force, strong and magnetic. Norbert felt like a new person, as if powerful batteries had replaced his old junky ones, revved him up to face the world like he'd never done before.

The new year could bring a new life. He'd go back to work . . .

His thoughts petered out when he noticed another car pull out into the road just moments after Edgar had driven past it. The black Honda had been parked on the sidewalk, idling, and wasn't in front of a house, just a blank lot of snow-covered weeds and brush. Something about that didn't seem right. Not at all.

Then it hit Norbert.

The person in the black car was *following* his new friends. That couldn't be a good thing. *No sir, that couldn't be good one bit.*

The new Norbert acted before the old Norbert could talk himself out of it. He threw on some warm clothes, a wool cap, and his faded, weather-beaten shoes. He frantically searched for his keys, forgetting where he'd put them since his last venture to town. They weren't on his dresser, weren't on his kitchen counter—he couldn't find them anywhere. After five minutes of hunting, he was just about to give up when he saw them on the floor under the table; he grabbed them and turned toward the garage.

The doorbell rang, freezing his blood solid.

Trying to stay brave, he ran up the stairs to his usual spying window and took a peek. Relieved, he saw it was just a kid girl with a man who looked an awful lot like Master George—dressed in a fancy suit, shiny shoes, the works. But this guy stood a lot taller and had plenty of hair, shiny blond hair slicked back against his skull.

Must be another one of those smart kids looking for their letter.

He bolted back down the stairs, grabbed another copy of Mothball's golden envelopes (could that *really* be her name?) and tore open the door. He held out the letter and was just about to drop it into the girl's hand and close the door when he caught a glimpse of his visitor's car parked in the driveway. It was much nicer and . . . faster than his. An idea popped in his head.

"You folks lookin' for a clue from M.G.?" he asked.

The befuddled (Norbert's new favorite word) strangers nodded in unison.

"Someone's in a whole lot of trouble—friends of Mothball," he said, then shook the envelope in front of them. "This is the sixth clue. If you want it, you've gotta help me save them."

Driving slowly down Main Street, with a full tank of gas in the car, Edgar settled his bones for the long drive back to Aunt Mabel's. He looked over at Tick, who was just pulling the sixth clue from its envelope.

"Read it, boy!" he shouted cheerfully. "I can hardly wait. What a trip, huh? What a trip!" He felt so good they'd accomplished something—not just getting the next clue, but perhaps helping poor Norbert get his life back together. Though he'd dared not admit it, Edgar had been scared to death their trip to Alaska would prove a waste, thereby nullifying his value to Tick, who'd had the courage to tell him about everything.

Tick put the white piece of cardstock down in his lap. "Nah, let's just wait 'til we get back to Washington. What's the rush?" Tick let out a fake yawn and stretched.

"Professor, these windows *do* roll down, and I *am* strong enough to throw you out of one."

"Okay, okay, if you insist." Tick read the words out loud, holding the paper up so Edgar could glance at it and follow along as he drove.

Recite the magic words at exactly seventeen minutes past the quarter hour following the six-hour mark before midnight plus one hundred and sixty-six minutes minus seven quarter-hours plus a minute times seven, rounded to the nearest half-hour plus three. Neither a second before nor three seconds after.

(Yes, I'm fully aware it will take you a second or two to say the magic words, but I'm talking about the precise time you begin to say it. Quit being so snooty.)

"Oh, boy," Edgar said. "Can't say my head's in the mood to figure that one out. Glad it's your problem."

Tick laid the clue down onto his lap, already scrutinizing its every word. "I'll have it figured out by the time we stop for you to use the bathroom and buy more Doritos." He opened up his journal and started jotting down thoughts and calculations from the clue.

"Very funny," Edgar replied, elbowing his son. "You know, I was so worried about that 'death' e-mail you got, but now I'm feeling pretty fat and happy."

"Better than skinny and sad, I guess," Tick said.

Edgar laughed. *What a great kid I have,* he thought. *What a great kid.*

⁓

Frazier waited until he and his prey were well out of town, cruising down the long and straight two-lane highway that headed back to Anchorage. He hated how short the days were this far north. It wouldn't be as fun to watch the coming mayhem in the darkness. He looked in his rearview mirror and saw some lights in the distance, but they seemed too far back for him to be worried. Once he engaged the device, it wouldn't take long to have his fun and be done with it.

He gripped the Chu controller in his palm, put the tip of his thumb on the button.

Then he pushed it.

Tick stared ahead at the long blank road, lost in thought about the sixth clue. The headlights revealed nothing but cracked asphalt and dirty piles of plowed ice, swallowed up in darkness on both sides. *There must not be a moon out,* he thought. Even the snow seemed black tonight.

"Uh-oh," his dad said in a worried whisper.

Tick looked over and saw the tight cowl of panic on his dad's face. He felt something shudder in his chest. "What?"

His dad had both hands gripped tightly on the steering wheel, trying to squeeze the inner lining out of it. "The wheel's frozen!" His legs moved up and down, alternately pumping the gas and brakes as the frightening, plastic-springy sound of the pedal filled the car.

"Dad, what's wrong?"

His dad kept yanking on the wheel, pushing on the brakes. "It's not responding—it's not doing anything. I can't *do* anything!"

"What do you—"

"Son, the car's out of control—it won't let me . . ." His voice faded as he tried everything again, his look of disbelief overcoming the panic. "What in the . . ."

Tick could only watch, bile building in his throat and stomach. Something was horribly wrong, and it had to have something to do with their new enemies. "You can't get it to stop?"

Dad looked over at him, exasperated. "Son, I can't do *anything!*"

In unison, they looked forward. The road remained straight for as far as they could see, but it ended in blackness. Anything could be hiding in the darkness, waiting for an out-of-control car to smash into it.

"The steering wheel won't move?" Tick asked, knowing the answer anyway.

His dad unsnapped his seatbelt, squirming in his chair to turn around.

"What are you doing?" Tick yelled.

Dad reached over and unbuckled Tick's belt as well. "Someone's got to us, kid. We've gotta get out of here."

❦

From the backseat, Norbert stared at the two cars in front of him as they gained ground, knowing deep inside that something terrible was happening. He sensed frantic movement in Tick's car—dark shadows bobbing and jerking around—and saw the calm demeanor of the person sitting in the one following them, barely revealed by the headlights of the car in which Norbert sat. They were almost on the stranger.

"It's now or never," Norbert said, then tapped the

shoulder of the man driving. "Put the pedal to the metal, pal."

"Do whatever he says," the girl said to the driver like she was his mother.

~⁓~

Frazier laughed as he saw the man and the boy squirming inside their car, desperate for a way out of this little predicament. He looked down at his controller, trying to find the dial that would make the car ahead go even faster. He finally found it and turned it up just a little, loving every minute of this game.

When he finally glanced back up to the road, he yelped as a car zoomed past him on the left, then swerved to the right to cut him off. Overreacting, Frazier slammed on his brakes and twisted the steering wheel, shooting off the road with a horrible squeal of brakes before slamming into a massive snowbank.

His airbag exploded open, scorching his forearms and catapulting the Chu device into the backseat.

~⁓~

Tick felt like a sailor going down with a submarine. The front doors wouldn't open; some kind of permanent locking mechanism kept them sealed.

"What could possibly be doing this?" Dad yelled, struggling to lean his huge girth over the back of the seat to check the rear doors. From the click of the handle being yanked and released, Tick knew they were locked, too. His dad groaned as he dropped back into the driver's seat.

The car had inexplicably sped up just a few moments earlier, rocketing them faster and faster toward the unknown. The car remained on a straight path for now—the steep piles of snow on the roadside nudging the wheels back onto the road if they began to stray—but it couldn't last much longer. Tick knew if they hit a turn, they'd be in a whole heap of trouble.

Tick felt a block of ice in the pit of his stomach; they probably had only a minute or two before they'd crash. "We need to break a window!" he yelled.

"Right!" Dad replied. "Plant your back on the seat and kick the windshield with both feet on my signal, okay?"

Desperation swept away Tick's fear, clearing his mind. "Okay," he said as he got into position, tucking his journal down the seat of his pants as far as it would go.

When they were both ready, feet stuck up above them, coiled for the kick, Edgar grabbed Tick's hand. "On three—one . . . two . . . three!"

With synchronized screams, they both kicked the windshield with all their might.

It didn't budge.

Screaming his frustration into the frigid air, a plume of frozen vapor shooting from his mouth, Frazier Gunn tried to open the buckled back door. When it stubbornly refused, he leaned over to look through the window, searching for the Chu controller. He couldn't see a thing.

How could this have all fallen apart? How?

He shot a quick glance down the road to see the fading red glow of two cars' taillights. The device would be out of range in a matter of seconds and once that happened, he'd have no more power over the car's operations. It would continue to drive like a maniacal machine until it ran out of gas or smashed into something.

Of course, without being able to turn, the latter is *exactly* what would happen. Crash, boom, bang. The thought made him pause, then smile. Chances were, he'd still complete his task, one way or the other. Mistress Jane didn't need to know all the details.

Not caring anymore about the controller or his banged up car, Frazier turned and headed back toward town.

He needed to find a cemetery.

On Tick and his dad's fifth synchronized kick, a huge crack shot across the wide glass with the sound of breaking glaciers. Tick's heart leapt to his throat and the next kick seemed to have twice the power from his adrenaline rush. Several more cracks splintered through the windshield like an icy spider web. Tick was crouched too far down in the seat to see up ahead, but his mind assured him they were probably shooting toward a bend in the road with brutal speed. One way or another, it would all be over very soon.

"One more ought to do it!" his dad yelled, gasping in breaths. "One . . . two . . . THREE!"

Tick kicked with both legs again, and almost slipped to the floor of the car when his feet kept going, crashing through the windshield with the horrible clinking and crackling sound of shattered glass. Several tiny shards flew back into the car from the onrushing wind, but the bulk of the windshield, held together by a strong film of clear plastic, flew up into the air and tumbled away behind them.

"Come on!" Dad yelled, helping Tick back into a sitting position.

The air ripped at their hair and clothes, so cold that Tick's skin felt like frozen rubber. Squinting his eyes, he saw a big turn in the road a couple of miles directly ahead. He couldn't tell what waited there, be it a cliff or a field or a towering barn; he saw only darkness, a wall of black tar.

"We've gotta hurry!" his dad screamed over the wind. "Together now, come on!"

Summoning every last trace of courage left in his body, Tick followed his dad over the dashboard and through the gaping, wind-pummeled hole that led to the hood of the car.

⟞⟝

"There they are!" Norbert screamed, his voice squeaky with panic. "Pull up there, right to the front! If those guys jump, they're dead!"

"Hurry!" the girl yelled.

The blond, fancy-dressed driver obeyed without a word, gunning the engine until their vehicle pulled even with the out-of-control car. Just a few feet away, to Norbert's right, Tick and his dad had climbed halfway onto the hood of the car, the wind trying to rip them to pieces.

"Okay, get as close as you can," Norbert said, rolling down the window. "I wanna see every scratch on that there paint job!"

Once again, like a soldier following orders, the driver did as he was told.

⟞⟝

Tick couldn't believe his eyes. Out of nowhere, a car had appeared to their left, just a few feet away. His first thought was that whoever had caused this whole mess had pulled up to finish them off. But then the backseat window rolled down, and his heart lifted when he saw the ridiculous face of Norbert Johnson, who was somehow smiling and yelling and crying at the same time.

"Norbert's come to save you!" he screamed over the howling, rushing wind. "I'll pull you through the window!"

Tick's dad immediately scooted back into the car to gain solid footing, then grabbed Tick by both arms, yanking him over to his side and toward Norbert's open window. "You first!" he yelled.

With no time to lose, Tick carefully inched across the hood, gripping the metal with the tips of his icy cold fingers, his dad helping him along with a firm hold. The other car was literally a foot away from theirs, running side by side like insane drag racers. Before Tick knew it, Norbert had reached out and grabbed him, pulling him through the window and into his car. He groaned and grunted as he rolled past Norbert and fell onto the floor of the backseat, suddenly safe and warm, feeling the sharp corners of his journal poking him in his side.

He scrambled up and onto the seat, looking toward his dad with a sudden burst of terror. His dad had half-crawled onto the hood, gripping the edge of the door bar with one arm and reaching out for Norbert with the other. The look on his dad's face made Tick hurt inside. He had never seen anything close to the fear and panic and sheer horror that now masked his favorite person's normally cheerful and bright demeanor. The man looked as terrified as any kid would be, and it scared Tick.

"Get my dad!" he cried. "Please save my dad!"

But Norbert didn't need any further instruction. He was on his knees, leaning out the window, grabbing at the large man with both hands. Tick knew his dad had to weigh three times what he did, and it wouldn't be easy to pull him off the other car and into this one. Not able to breathe, he looked ahead.

The road curved sharply to the right, just a hundred feet from where they were.

"Hurry!" he yelled.

Norbert suddenly jerked back into the car, his arms gripped tightly, pulling on Tick's dad as best he could. Tick watched as his dad's hands, then arms, then head, then shoulders squeezed through the open window, Norbert screaming with the effort.

"I'm stuck!" Dad yelled. "My big fat tubby body is stuck!"

"No!" Tick yelled. He reached forward and grabbed his dad's shirt, yanking and pulling as hard as he could.

"You can do it, Dad. Suck in your breath!"

"Son, I . . . can't, I'm stuck!"

Norbert and Tick kept working, gripping and regripping, heaving and reheaving. Though he couldn't bear to look, Tick knew they only had precious seconds left until it was all over.

"Pull away from the other car and slow down!" Norbert yelled to the driver. "Don't you worry, Mr. Higginbottom. We won't let go of you. Keep your feet up!"

The driver veered to the left as he slowly applied the brakes, though it seemed like the worst roller coaster ride in history to Tick. His dad would be roadkill if he slipped out of the window.

"Don't let go of Big Bear," Dad whispered to Tick, actually breaking a smile. "Please, don't let go of me."

Tick couldn't talk, he just squeezed his grip even tighter.

Just as the car slowed to a snail's pace, they heard a horrendous screeching and metallic crunch as the other car slammed into something they couldn't see. A bright flash lit the night around them as a terrible explosion rocked the air.

Even when they finally came to a complete standstill, and cheers erupted from everyone, including his dad, Tick couldn't let go. He scrambled around

Norbert and hugged his dad's arms and shoulders and head like he hadn't seen him in ten years, bursting into tears. After a very long moment, his dad finally spoke up.

"Professor, do you think you could give me a push now? I'm, uh, kind of stuck."

CHAPTER 25

THE GIRL
WITH BLACK HAIR

Frazier stood in the snow-swept graveyard, shivering and rubbing his hands together as he waited for Mistress Jane to wink him back to the Thirteenth Reality. He'd sent the nanolocator signal several minutes ago, but she often took her time about these things. She always wanted to make sure people knew the Mistress was in charge; she helped others at *her* convenience, not theirs.

A crunch in the snow behind him made Frazier spin around to see who had intruded on his waiting ground. He almost lost his lunch when he saw what stood there.

Where did she *come from? She must be—*

He didn't have time to finish his thought before the gigantic woman covered his nose and mouth with a foul-smelling piece of cloth, gripping it in place with her huge hand.

As he faded into blackness, he couldn't help but wonder if Mistress Jane would even miss him.

Tick, his journal now clasped in his right hand, stared in disbelief at what could've been his death.

Next to him, his dad shook his head, arms folded as he stared down into the gully. "Boy, I'm sure glad I paid ten bucks for insurance. The rental company can pay for that mess."

They stood with Norbert on the side of the road, watching the licking flames as the once out-of-control car burned. When it ran off the road, the car had shot off a steep embankment and crashed into a rocky ditch, crumpling into a mass of metal and broken glass, consumed by gasoline fire.

Despite the cold, Tick was still sweating from the intensity of their last-second escape. As soon as their rescue car had come to a stop and they'd managed to dislodge his dad, they'd run to this spot, unable to believe that if Norbert had shown up only a few seconds later, Tick and his dad might be buried somewhere in the wreckage below.

"Norbert, I don't know how we can ever—" Dad said.

The postal worker waved his hand like swatting at flies. "Not another word, Mr. Higginbottom, not another word. I just a-did what any good upstanding citizen would've done in the circumstances. You folks made me feel like myself again. That's thanks enough."

Tick finally broke his stare from the burning car and looked at Norbert. "How did you know we needed help? And who are those people in the car back there?" The driver and his daughter had not gotten out yet, probably still in shock over what they'd just seen. "Why would they want to save us?"

Norbert smiled, a barely noticeable crack in his still-panicked face. "Those are some good questions you're a-spouting out, boy, good questions indeed. I reckon they're in the same boat as you and your daddy, here. Back at the house, I'd just noticed a suspicious car pull onto the road to follow you folks when this fancy man and his little girl showed up, a-looking for the same stuff as you. Let's go talk to them." He gestured to the destroyed car. "Gazing down there won't fix a thing. What's done is done. Come on."

They walked back to the car and to the people who had saved their lives. The driver's side door popped open when they were still a few feet away; a tall, nicely dressed man stepped out, smoothing his greased blond hair back as he did so.

He bowed slightly as they approached, closing his eyes for a long second. "Good evening, sirs." His accent was thick, maybe German. "I apologize that we have not formally made acquaintance—if you'll excuse me."

Tick's dad had moved forward to shake the man's hand, but stepped back in surprise as the stranger hurriedly walked around the car and opened the passenger-side door, bowing in deference to the person inside. Baffled, Tick stared as a girl about his age got out of the car and waved at them. Even though they'd been a couple of feet apart during the few crazy seconds it took to save his dad, Tick had not gotten a good look at the girl until now, thanks to the car's headlights that were still shining brightly in the darkness.

She had an olive complexion and long dark hair framing her brown eyes and thin face. She was maybe an inch or two shorter than Tick and wore clothes that seemed like nothing special—he'd almost expected a princess the way her blond companion acted toward her.

"Hi there," she said, her gaze focused on Tick.

She also had an accent, but very subtle. "Hi," he answered. "Uh, thanks for saving us—to you and your . . . dad."

The girl laughed. "Oh, he's not my dad. He's my butler."

The man jerked his head stiffly in another bow. "It is a pleasure. My name is Fruppenschneiger, but you may call me Frupey."

It took every ounce of willpower for Tick not to laugh. *Frupey?*

His dad lumbered forward, his legs obviously sore from the car ordeal, and vigorously shook the hands of Frupey and the girl. "Thank you, thank you so much. I still can't believe how all this happened. Thank you for saving us."

Frupey answered in his formal voice. "It was our pleasure, so that Miss Pacini may receive the sixth clue."

Tick felt his stomach lift off from its normal position and lodge itself in his throat. "What?" he croaked. "Did you just say . . ." He looked at the dark-haired girl, who was smiling like she'd just been crowned Miss Universe.

"Hello, Americanese Boy," she said, holding her hand out. "It's about time we finally met face to face, huh?"

Tick couldn't believe it.

Sofia.

CHAPTER 26

TIME CONSTRAINTS

It took only a few seconds for Tick and Sofia to break past the thin wall of awkwardness; they did, after all, know each other very well from their e-mail exchanges. They sat in the back of the car and talked nonstop during the drive back to Norbert's home. Tick's dad squeezed in the backseat next to them, butting in every now and then to ask a question or two.

Sofia had never given Tick a hint in her e-mails that she was from a wealthy family, and nothing about her screamed it out, either. She said she'd planned all along to surprise Tick in Alaska, figuring she might as well go along, too. The cost of the trip was no problem for her family, and as long as Frupey the Butler went with her, Sofia's parents pretty much let her do whatever she wanted.

"So how in the world did you get so rich?" Tick asked when they reached the town.

"My ancestors invented spaghetti."

Tick laughed, but cut it short when Sofia looked at him with a stone-dead face. "Wait . . . you're serious?"

Sofia finally let out a chuckle and slapped Tick on the shoulder. Hard. "No, but I got you good, didn't I? Actually, my grandfather would say his father *did* invent it, or at least made it perfect. Ever heard of Pacini Spaghetti?"

"Uh . . . no. Sorry."

Sofia huffed. "Americans. All you eat are hamburgers and French fries." She pinched all five fingers of her right hand together in a single point, shaking it with each word; it was just like something Tick had seen once in a mafia movie about an Italian mob boss. Sofia even made a small "uh" sound after her words sometimes, like "and-uh" and "French-uh."

"Hey, I eat spaghetti all the time," Tick argued. "With authentic Ragu Sauce."

"Authentic . . ." Sofia pursed her lips. "Then I guess you've *also* never heard of Pacini Sauce. What is this . . . Rag-oo? It sounds like some kind of disease."

"It tastes pretty good, but, I tell you what," Tick said, "you send me some of your stuff and I'll try it."

"Frupey!" she barked at her butler, driving the car.

"Yes, Miss Pacini?" he said, looking into the rearview mirror.

"Please send three cases of our noodles and sauce to these poor Americans."

"I'll do it the second we return, Miss."

"Thank you." She looked back at Tick. "He's such a good butler. You really should get one."

"Yeah, right," Tick said, sharing a laugh with his dad. "The only thing my family's invented is Edgar Stew, and trust me"—he lowered his voice into a pretend whisper—"it wouldn't sell."

"At least your mom's a good cook," his dad chimed in, ignoring Tick's insult. "I bet we could get rich off her if we knew how."

"What," Sofia teased, "does she make a good hamburger and French fry?"

"Do you really think that's all we eat?" Tick asked.

"Oh, sorry, I forgot. She makes a good hot dog, too?"

Even as they laughed, Tick couldn't get over the craziness of it all. Here he was, joking around with a girl from Italy in the back of a butler-driven car, in the state of Alaska, having just escaped from a runaway Oldsmobile.

His life had certainly changed forever.

Once they got back to Norbert's, Tick's dad called Aunt Mabel and told her they wouldn't be back until the next day, then he called the police and began the long process of dealing with the car accident. Frupey and Norbert scrounged around in the kitchen, trying to find food for everyone. *Car chases evidently make people hungry,* Tick thought as his own stomach rumbled.

Tick and Sofia sat together on the pitiful couch in the front room, discussing the latest clue they'd received. They had to use Sofia's copy because Tick's bit the bullet along with the rental car—he'd failed to slip it back into his journal during the frantic rush of excitement. The only light in the room came from a junky old lamp without a shade, its bare lightbulb blinding if you looked at it directly.

"Well, it's obviously just like the first clue," Tick said as Sofia scanned the words again. "Except this one tells us the time instead of the day."

"You Americans are so smart," she replied. "How did you ever figure *that* out?"

"Man, you sure are smart-alecky for a rich Italian girl."

"Girl?" she asked, her eyes narrowing. "Do I look like a little baby doll to you?"

Tick laughed. "I never would've guessed you'd actually be *scarier* in real life than in the e-mail."

Sofia elbowed him hard in the stomach. "Just

remember what I told you—I beat up seventeen boys last summer. No one messes with a Pacini."

"It's okay, I don't usually go around picking fights with gi—, I mean . . . young women . . . who own spaghetti companies."

"That's better, Americanese Boy. Now let's figure this out, huh?"

"Sounds good, Italian . . . ese . . . Woman." Tick didn't understand why she could call him *boy*, but he couldn't call her *girl*. He wanted to laugh again—for some odd reason, he felt really comfortable around her—but he didn't particularly want another jab to the stomach. He took the sixth clue from her instead and read through it again while she stared into space for a minute, thinking.

Recite the magic words at exactly
seventeen minutes past the quarter
hour following the six-hour mark
before midnight plus one hundred
and sixty-six minutes minus seven
quarter-hours plus a minute times
seven, rounded to the nearest
half-hour plus three. Neither a second
before nor three seconds after.

(Yes, I'm fully aware it will take
you a second or two to say the magic

```
words, but I'm talking about the
precise time you begin to say it. Quit
being so snooty.)
```

Once again, M.G.'s sense of humor leaked through the message, and Tick found himself eager to meet the man Norbert had already met. At least now they knew his real name.

Master George. *Sounds like something from Star Wars.*

"How long did it take you to figure out the first clue?" Tick asked.

"How long it take you?" Sofia responded. Every once in a while, she messed up her English, but for the most part, she knew it perfectly.

"Once I sat down to do it, maybe an hour."

"Then it took me *half* an hour."

"Yeah, right."

Sofia gave him an evil grin and raised her eyebrows. "Should we race on this one? Like a . . . Master George Olympics."

Tick had assumed they'd work together to solve it, but her idea suddenly sounded very fun. *If I was a nerd before, I've hit rock-bottom geek stature by now,* he thought.

"You're on," he said, ready for the challenge.

"I'm on what?" she asked. "Speak English, please."

Tick rolled his eyes. "Here, we'll put the clue on this little coffee table, where we can both see it, okay? Neither one of us are allowed to touch it. I'll run and get some paper and a pencil from Norbert so you can have something to write on." He stood up.

"What about you?" she asked.

Tick held his journal out. "I'll write in this—why didn't you bring yours?"

Sofia shrugged. "I got tired of carrying it around. Who needs it?" She tapped her head with a finger. "It's all stored up here anyway. So, what about a prize? What does the winner get?"

"Hmm, good question." Tick scratched his neck, faltering when he realized he wasn't wearing his scarf—he must've lost it in the wind after they busted the windshield.

"What's wrong?" Sofia asked.

"Huh? Oh, nothing." He paused. His scarf was gone, and Sofia hadn't said a thing about his birthmark—maybe he could actually survive without . . . no. He had an extra one at home, and deep down, Tick knew it would be around his neck when he returned to school.

"Tick," Sofia said, staring up at him, "did your brain freeze?"

"No, no . . . it's just . . . never mind." He snapped his fingers. "I've got it—the winner gets to visit the house of the loser next summer. But, uh, you have to pay for it either way because you're rich."

"Wow, what a deal."

"I'll be back in a sec with the stuff."

A couple of minutes later, pencils in hand, the race began.

⟨⟩

Just as he'd done with the first clue, Tick jotted down the phrases from the sixth clue that seemed to go together logically. Once he'd done that, he assigned letters to them to indicate the order they should be calculated. It seemed easy now that he'd gone through the process before.

The biggest problem was determining which midnight the clue referred to—the one that *began* the day of May sixth or the one at the end of it? Then he realized whatever time he ended up with probably wouldn't be midnight, so it really didn't matter.

He nervously glanced over at Sofia, who was doing a lot more thinking than writing, tapping her pencil against her forehead, staring at the clue.

I'm way ahead of her, he thought, then continued his scribbles.

A couple of minutes later, the page in his journal looked like this:

Beginning Time: Midnight.
A. six-hour mark before midnight = 6:00 P.M.
B. quarter hour following A = 6:15 P.M.
C. seventeen minutes past B = 6:32 P.M.
D. C plus 166 minutes = 9:18 P.M.
E. D minus 7 quarter hours = 7:33 P.M.
F. E plus a minute times 7 = 7:40 P.M.
G. F rounded to nearest half-hour = 7:30 P.M.
H. G plus three half-hours = 9:00 P.M. on
    May 6

"Bingo!" he yelled, turning to say his time out loud. His words died somewhere in his throat when he saw Sofia looking at him with a smirk, holding up her paper with the answer scrawled across it:

9:00 P.M.

"Dang," Tick muttered. "But you didn't even take notes or anything!"

"I've got brains—I don't need notes."

Tick folded his arms. "I take it back—you're not a woman. You're a *girl*. And I hate spaghetti."

"I believe Americans call this a . . . sore loser, right?"

"Something like that."

Sofia put her hands behind her head and looked up

at the ceiling, letting out a big sigh, relishing her win. "I can't wait to visit your little house in Washington. Will your mother make me a hot dog?"

Tick snapped up the sixth clue from the table and stood up. "If you're lucky. And what makes you think our house is *little*, rich girl?"

Sofia lowered her arms to her lap and eyed Tick up and down. "I looked at your clothes and I said to myself, he must live in a little house." She winked, then punched Tick in the leg, hard.

"Ow!" he yelled, rubbing the spot. "What's that for?"

"To let you know I'm kidding."

Tick shook his head. "You are one weird kid."

"Ah, yes. That's the kettle calling the papa black."

Tick burst out laughing, falling back on the couch holding his stomach.

"What's so funny?"

"Well, for one thing, you said it backwards. And it's *pot*, not *papa*."

"Whatever. When I come to visit you, I will teach you Italian so we can talk like intelligent people."

"I think spaghetti is just about the only Italian word I need to know, thank you very much. That, and pizza."

Sofia tried to punch him again, but this time Tick was too fast; he jumped up and ran out of the room, the sounds of pursuit close behind. Luckily, dinner was ready in the kitchen—ramen noodles and peanut butter sandwiches.

~

The next day, Tick's heart hurt when he had to say good-bye to Norbert, then Frupey and Sofia after they dropped him and his dad off at a car rental agency— the rich girl and her butler had a flight to catch. In just one day, they'd become like close family, and he hated to think he may never see them again. At least he knew he could expect an e-mail from Sofia, and he hoped she really would come visit him next summer.

Of course, by then, the magic day would have come and gone, and who knew what might change after that.

After another couple of fun-filled days being pampered by Aunt Mabel and having his life mapped out for him in detail, Tick and his dad headed back to Washington.

Once there, Tick began the longest three months of his life.

PART 3

---*---

THE MAGIC WORDS

CHAPTER 27

APRIL FOOL

Tick stared at his own reflection in the dark puddle of grimy water only inches away from his face, dismayed at how pitiful he looked. Like a scaredy-cat kid, eyes full of fear. Both ends of his scarf hung down, the flattened tips floating on the nasty sludge like dead fish. He winced when Billy "The Goat" Cooper yanked his arm behind him again, ratcheting it another notch higher along his back until the pain was almost unbearable.

Tick refused to say a word.

"Come on, Barf Scarf Man," the Goat growled, digging his knee into Tick's spine, wedging it below his twisted arm. "All you have to say is, 'Happy April Fool's Day. Please get me wet.' You can do it, you're a big boy."

Tick remained silent, despite the pain, despite the mounting humiliation as more school kids gathered around the scene. A few months ago, he would've given in and said the words, done as the Goat commanded. He would've let it end quickly and moved on. But not now. Never again.

Billy pushed Tick's face into the water, holding it there for several seconds. Tick remained calm, knowing he could hold his breath much longer than the Goat would dare keep him down. When he finally removed his hand from the back of Tick's head, Tick slowly raised himself out of the water, spit, then took a deep breath.

"Say it, boy!" Billy yelled, unable to hide the frustration in his voice. If he couldn't get Tick to obey, the tables would turn and *he'd* be the one suffering a humiliating defeat. "Say it or I'll wrap your sorry scarf around your head and dunk you 'til you quit breathing."

Tick felt a sudden surge of confidence and he spoke before he could stop himself. "Go ahead, Billy Boy. At least then I'd never have to look at your Frankenstein goat face again."

His spirits soared when the crowd around them laughed. A few kids clapped and whistled.

"Frankenstein goat face!" one kid called out. "Billy the Frankenstein Goat Face!"

This created more laughs, followed by murmurs

of conversation and shuffling of feet as people moved away, evidently having had enough.

"Leave him alone, Goat Face," a girl yelled over her shoulder.

Tick closed his eyes and took a gulp of air, knowing Billy would push him down at least one more time, would hold him under longer than ever before. But to his shock, he felt his arm released; the pressure of Billy's knee against his spine disappeared. As Tick's entire right side lit up with tingles and pressure from the blood rushing back to where it belonged, he scooted away from the pool of water and turned to sit on his rear end, staring up at Billy.

The Goat looked down on him with an odd expression. It wasn't anger or hate. He seemed . . . surprised.

"You're weird, man," Billy said. "I'm sick of you anyway. Go home and cuddle with your Barf Scarf." He kicked Tick's leg, then turned to walk away with his hoodlum friends.

Tick didn't totally understand the storm of emotions that swelled within him at that moment, but he surprised himself when he laughed out loud right before the tears came.

⌇⌇⌇

As Tick walked home, he put Billy out of his mind and thought of the long three months he'd just endured.

After the thrill and excitement, the life-threatening danger and escapades of Alaska, he'd expected to come home and barely rest, clue after clue and stranger after stranger showing up at his doorstep, delivering one adventure after another.

But nothing had happened. Nothing.

He and Sofia e-mailed back and forth, never failing to ask the other if they'd seen something or met someone. The answer was always a frustrated *NO!*

Where were the clues? What had happened to Mothball and Rutger? Did something get lost in the mail? Had they somehow proven themselves unworthy? Had the man in charge moved on to other, more deserving, kids? The questions poured out of their minds and into their e-mails, but no answer ever came back.

Tick was sick with discouragement.

All he could do was watch the snow pile up in his front yard all through January and February. The weathermen loved reminding their viewers that it had been the worst winter on record, revealing snow tallies in fancy charts with as much enthusiasm as if they were announcing the lottery winners. It was March before the snow finally started to melt, revealing patches of deadened grass that desperately longed for spring.

Tick hadn't missed a single day of school during

the three months, trying his best to keep focused while he worried about not hearing from Master George. But even competing in the Jackson County Chess Tournament in the middle of March hadn't been the same and Tick had placed fifth in his age bracket. His family seemed shocked that he'd lost the top spot, but his mind had been somewhere else, and the three-year winning streak ended with a dull thump instead of a big bang.

His dad constantly tried to cheer him up, encouraging him that something would come soon, but after a couple of months, even his dad seemed disheartened. Like a wounded snail limping to its next meal, Tick lived out each day hoping for a letter from Master George.

Tick did receive one exciting thing in the mail: a package of free spaghetti and sauce from Frupey the Butler. True to Sofia's word, it had tasted wonderful, and Tick knew he could never eat the cheap stuff again.

But even in the depths of the three-month doldrums, Tick and Sofia had never given up. They made a commitment to study their own journals every day, even if only for a few minutes, to keep their minds fresh, hoping something new might pop out and surprise them. They forced themselves to stay active in the game, even if the other side offered no help. And every day, no matter what, they sent an e-mail to each other.

Tick felt sure he'd hit rock bottom when he got home and checked his e-mail, clicking on a new one from Sofia.

Tick,

Hello from Italy.

Ciao.
Sofia

Tick groaned and wrote his own quick reply:

Sofia,

Howdy from America.

Later.
Tick

Depressed, Tick shut off the computer and slumped his way up the stairs to wait for dinner. A few minutes later, he fell asleep with the *Journal of Curious Letters* clasped in his arms like a teddy bear.

April sixth was a Saturday, and the sun seemed to melt away any remnants of clouds, beating down with a warmth that hadn't been felt in months. Tick made his usual trek to check the mail, basking in the golden light, his spirits lifted despite the circumstances. The sounds of trickling water came from everywhere as the massive amounts of snow increased their melting pace, disappearing by inches a day now. It wouldn't be long before hundreds of tulips stood like fancy-hat-wearing soldiers all over the yard, the result of painstaking pre-winter planting by his mom over the years.

Even Tick, not exactly a flower expert, enjoyed his mom's ridiculous amount of tulips every spring.

As he made his way down the steaming sidewalk, Tick took a deep breath, loving the strong smells of the forest that returned with the melting snow. The scents of moist dirt and bark and rotting leaves that had lain beneath the white stuff all winter filled his nostrils, and he felt better than he had in months. Spring tended to do that to people.

His good mood was short-lived, though. When he saw that the mailman hadn't brought anything from Master George, he slipped right back into poor-little-Tick mode and went back inside the house.

Later that afternoon, Tick sat at the desk in his bedroom, working on the math homework he'd been too depressed to finish the day before. He'd opened up his window, grateful that he was able to do so without freezing to death; the winter had seemed to last for ten years. He was just finishing up his last problem when he heard the phone ring, followed by the sound of footsteps coming up the stairs and down the hall toward his room.

"Tick, it's your girlfriend."

He turned to see his sister Lisa at the door, holding out the phone.

"What?"

"Phone's for you. It's a girl."

Tick's first thought was that it must be Sofia—who else would call him? He jumped up from his desk and walked over to grab the phone. At the last second, Lisa put it behind her back, smirking at Tick.

"Wow, you seem awfully excited," she said, eyebrows raised. "Are we having a little love affair that we haven't shared with Sis?"

"Give it—it's probably my, uh, science project partner."

Lisa chuckled. "You're gullible, kid—it's actually a man." She handed him the phone and left.

Tick closed the door and sat on his bed, putting the receiver to his ear. "Hello?"

At first, all he could hear was static and the sounds

of . . . beeping . . . or some kind of machinery in the background. Then came a loud clonk, followed by a soft boink and then a rolling series of metal clicks, like someone cranking up a thick chain into a holding wheel. Finally, surprising him, he heard the distinct *meow* of a cat.

"Hello?" he repeated. "Anybody there?"

From the other end came a rattling sound as the person picked the phone back up. A voice spoke through the scratchy static, a man with the one accent Tick could identify—British. "Is this . . . let me see . . . ah, yes, is this Mister Atticus Higginbottom?"

"Yes . . . this is Atticus."

"Uh, dear sir, you were supposed to be walking about today. I mean, er—it's a nice day to go for a walk, don't you think? Simply smashing, really, from what I hear." The man coughed. Tick heard the cat meow again, followed by some muffled words as the stranger covered up his end with his hand. "In a *minute*, Muffintops. Patience, dear feline!"

"Sir, do I know you?"

"No, no, no, not yet, anyway. But we certainly have some common acquaintances, if you get my meaning. In fact, I'm on instruction from them, old chap."

"On . . . instruction?"

"Yes, yes, quite right. They need you to go for a *walk*, good man. Asked me to call you."

"A walk? Where?"

"The usual, I suppose. What's a young master like yourself sitting inside all day for anyhow? Got a bit of the flu, do you?"

"No, I was just . . ." But the stranger had a point. Tick should be outside on the first beautiful day of the year so far.

"Well, off you go. Not a moment to waste."

"But . . . where am I supposed to go? Who—"

"Cheers, old boy. Only a month to go—I mean, er, a month or two, yes, that's right."

"Wait," Tick urged.

The phone clicked and went silent.

CHAPTER 28

A MEETING
IN THE WOODS

Tick told his mom he had to go to the library, then headed out the door. Though he didn't need a jacket, he'd instinctively put on his scarf, which began to scratch and make him too warm before he'd made it past the driveway.

Stupid scarf. He loosened it, but he couldn't bring himself to take it off.

The cloudless sky was like a deep blue blanket draped across the world, not a blemish in sight. As much as Tick loved the winter and snow, even he had to admit it was about time for some warm weather.

As he left his neighborhood and started down the

road that led through the woods to town, Tick thought about the phone call he'd received. Every instinct in his mind told him it had to be Master George—in fact, he realized he'd heard the voice once before. On the tape of the third clue.

Wow, he thought. *I just spoke with Master George.* Master George!

Tick felt a shiver of excitement and a sudden bounce lifted his steps. After three grueling months, things seemed to be rolling again. He just hoped he had chosen the right direction to take a walk, though he couldn't think of another way that could possibly be classified as "the usual."

He was almost to the spot where he'd seen the wooden sign with Rutger's silly poem scrawled across it when he felt something hit him in the right shoulder. A rock rattled across the pavement, and Tick looked into the woods across the street. The last time someone had thrown a rock at him—

Another one flew out of the trees, missing him badly.

"Rutger, is that you?" Tick said, cupping his hands around his mouth to amplify his voice.

No reply came, but a few seconds later another rock shot out, this time smacking him in the forehead. "Ow!" he yelled. "Do you really have to do that?"

"Yes!" a male voice said from within the thick trees.

Grinning, Tick crossed the street and stepped into the forest.

It didn't take long to find them. Rutger, his stomach sucked in as far as it would go—which wasn't much— hid behind a tall, thin tree with no branches, his body jutting out on both sides. Mothball, on the other hand, was trying her best to squat behind a short, leafy bush, her head poking at least two feet above its top, her eyes closed as if that would somehow make her invisible.

It was one of the most ridiculous things Tick had ever seen.

"Uh, you guys really stink at hide-and-seek," he said. Both of them stepped out from their hiding places, faking disgust.

They looked the same as the first time he'd met them. Rutger, incredibly short and round as a bowling ball, still wore his black clothes and the shoes and mittens Tick had given him months ago, though it seemed too warm for the outfit. Mothball had different clothes on, but they were still gray and hung on her eight-foot-tall frame like flags with no wind. The forest floor was mushy and wet and water dripped on them from the branches above.

"'Ello, little sir," the giant woman said, a huge smile crossing her wide face.

"Looks like you're a lot smarter than we thought," the tiny Rutger added—well, tiny in terms of height. If anything, he looked even *fatter* than the last time Tick had seen him. "But . . . I don't suppose you brought any *food*?"

"Man, am I glad to see you guys again," Tick said, ignoring Rutger's plea for something to eat. "What took you so long?"

"'Tis all part of the plan, it is," Mothball said in her thick accent, folding her huge arms together. "Master George—he's a smart old chap—reckoned he'd take a long wait and see who stuck it out. You know, weed out the ninnies with no patience."

"Last time you guys wouldn't tell me M.G.'s name," Tick said.

Rutger reached out and lightly slapped Tick on the leg. "Well, you figured it out yourself, now didn't you? Wouldn't it seem silly for us to not say his name when you already know what it is? Good job, old boy, good job!"

Tick knew he probably had little time available to him and wished he'd sat down to organize all of his questions before going out. He had a million things he wanted to ask, but his mind felt like soup in a blender. "So . . . how many kids like me are left? How many are still getting the clues?"

Rutger stared up at the sky as he slowly counted on his fingers. When he got to ten, he quit and looked at Tick. "Can't tell you."

"Thanks."

Mothball shifted her large body and leaned back against a tree. "Master George sends his regrets on the bit of trouble you had in the northern parts. Never meant that to happen, he didn't."

Tick squinted his eyes in confusion. "Wait a minute, what do you mean by that?" He couldn't put his finger on it, but something about her statement struck him as odd.

Rutger cleared his throat, trying to take the attention away from Mothball, whose face suddenly revealed she'd said something she wasn't supposed to.

"All my good friend means," Rutger said, "is that we never expected our, uh, enemy to catch up with you so quickly. Don't worry, though, we've, uh, taken care of the problem for now." He rolled his eyes and turned around, whistling.

"Didn't help matters much there, now did ya, my short friend?" Mothball muttered.

A swarm of confusion buzzed inside Tick's head, and he felt like the answer was somewhere right in the middle if he could just get to it. "But . . . what about the Gnat Rat thing, and the Tingle Wraith? You make it sound like—"

"Come on, now," Mothball said, straightening back to her full height. "Time's a-wasting, little sir. Got a lot to talk about, we do."

"But—"

"Mister Higginbottom!" Rutger interjected, spinning his wide body around to look at Tick once again. "I immediately demand you cease these questions, uh, immediately!"

Mothball snorted. "You just said *immediately* two times in the same sentence, you lug. Methinks he gets the point without you blowin' a lung and all."

Rutger fidgeted back and forth on his short legs, as if he'd only spouted off to save themselves from getting deeper into trouble. "Just trying to . . . teach the young master some patience and, uh, other . . . things like patience."

"You two are without a doubt the strangest people I've ever met," Tick said.

"Try living with a million Rutgers in one city," Mothball said. "That'll give you weak knees." She paused, then laughed. "Quite literally, actually, if the little folks are in the punching mood."

"Very funny, Flagpole," Rutger said.

"Thanks much, Bread Dough," she countered.

Tick thought it was fun watching the two friends argue, but he was hoping for answers. "Did you guys get me out here for a reason or what? And what's up with the phone call from Master George?"

"Been sittin' here all ruddy day, we 'ave," Mothball said. "'Ad to spur you a bit, burn your bottoms to get a move on."

"Couldn't you have just knocked on my door?"

"What, and get the detectives called in? Spend the rest of me life in a Reality Prime zoo?"

Tick held up a hand. "Whoa, time out—what does that mean?"

"What?" Mothball asked, looking at her finger-nails as though considering a manicure.

"What's 'Reality Prime'?" His mind spun, the word *reality* jarring something in his brain.

Mothball looked over at Rutger, shrugging her bony shoulders. "Methinks the little sir's gotten hit over the head, he has. Did *you* 'ear me say that?"

"Say what?" Rutger asked, his face a mask of exaggerated innocence.

"I've already forgotten."

Tick groaned as loud as he could. "I'm not an idiot, guys."

Rutger reached up and grabbed Tick by the arm. "We know, kid, we know. So quit acting like one. We'll tell you what you need to know when you're ready, not a second before."

"So what, I can't ask questions?"

"Bet yer best buttons you can—ask away," Mothball

said. "Just don't complain like a Rutger when we say mum's the word."

"Now wait just one minute . . ." Rutger said, letting go of Tick and pointing a finger at Mothball.

"I get it, I get it," Tick said before Rutger could continue. He thought about the list of words in his journal he'd heard from these two, framing questions inside his mind. "Okay, what's a kyoopy? Can you answer that?"

Mothball and Rutger exchanged a long look, signifying to Tick that this was no longer a black-and-white issue—which would be to his advantage. "Come on," he urged. "As long as you don't tell me how to figure out the clues, what does it matter if I know a little bit about what's behind all this?"

"Fair enough, methinks," Mothball said. "Master George does seem a bit more willing to let on. I mean, he called you on the telly, didn't he?" She gestured toward Rutger. "Go on, little man, tell him 'bout the kyoopy."

Rutger scowled. "Do I look like Hans Schtiggen-schlubberheimer to you?"

"Hans *who*?" Mothball and Tick asked in unison.

Rutger looked like someone had just asked him what gravity was. "Excuse me? Hans Schtiggen-schlubberheimer? The man who started the Scientific Revolution in the Fourth Reality? If it weren't for him, Reginald Chu would never have—" He stopped, looking uncertainly at Tick. "This is impossible, not knowing what we can and can't say in front of you. Blast it all, I can't wait until the special day gets here."

Of course, right then Tick thought of his teacher, Mr. Chu, just as he had when he saw "Chu Industries" on the Gnat Rat. But just like before, he didn't think it could have anything to do with his science instructor— it had to be a coincidence. "Who is Reginald Chu?" he asked. "And what kind of awful name is *Reginald*?"

"It's not a very fortunate name," Rutger agreed. "Downright stinky if you ask me. Fits the man, though, considering what he's done. Started out with good intentions, I'm sure, but he and his company have done awful, awful things."

"Well, what's he done? And what is the Fourth Reality? What are *any* of the realities? Are there other versions of the universe or something?"

Mothball sighed. "This is balderdash, really." She leaned over and put a hand on Tick's shoulder. "Rutger's spot on, he is. We just don't know what to talk about with you. Methinks Master George will explain everything— if you make it that far."

"Listen to me," Rutger said. "Focus your mind on the clues for now. Don't worry about all this other stuff. You can do it, and it will all be worth it—when the *day* comes. You'll be taken to a very important place."

Tick felt incredibly frustrated. "Fine, but at least . . . Can you just answer one question? Just one."

Rutger nodded.

"Can you tell me, in one sentence each, the definition of a kyoopy and the definition of a . . . a reality. No details, and I won't ask any more questions about it."

Rutger looked up at Mothball, who shrugged her shoulders. "Blimey, just do it. The poor lad's mind might explode if we don't."

"All right." Rutger took a deep breath. "Kyoopy is a nickname for the theory of science that explains the background of everything we're about." He paused. "And a Reality is a place, uh, or a *version* of a place, if you will, that comes about *because* of the kyoopy." He looked up at Mothball. "Wow, that was good."

Right at that very second, something clicked for Tick and he felt like an idiot for missing it before. "Wait a second . . . kyoopy. You mean . . . Q . . . P . . . right? Q.P.?"

Rutger looked confused. "Was I saying it wrong before? Yes, yes! Q.P."

"Looks like the little sir is on to something," Mothball said, a satisfied smile on her lips, but Tick's mind was in another world at that moment. Q.P. He'd heard that phrase before from Mr. Chu, and he couldn't wait to ask him about it again.

Kyoopy. Q.P.

Quantum physics.

"Now," Rutger said, clearing his throat, "could we *please* move on? I believe you'll be wanting the next clue."

CHAPTER 29

A BUNDLE OF CLUES

The air had grown cooler as the sun made its way across the sky and toward the horizon. The drip-drip-drip of the melting snow slowed considerably, and Tick shivered as he eagerly waited to see the next clue.

Mothball pulled out a familiar yellow envelope, though this one seemed thicker than the others, and a separate piece of white paper had been stapled to the upper left corner, its edges flapping loosely as she handled it. After a long look at Rutger, Mothball handed the package over to Tick, who snapped it out of her hand without meaning to look so anxious.

"Thanks," he said, fingering the note attached to the envelope. "What's this?"

"Flip it over and read it," Rutger answered. "Thought you could at least figure *that* out by yourself."

"Very funny," Tick muttered as he did what he was told, lifting the paper to read the few sentences typed on the back:

> Within you will find the next four
> clues in the sequence, numbers 7, 8, 9,
> and 10. Now, most certainly you will
> read these and conclude to yourself
> that I, your humble servant, have gone
> batty because they don't seem like
> clues at all. I will only say this:
> EVERYTHING you receive is a clue.

Tick looked up at Mothball, then down at Rutger, whose folded arms were resting on his huge belly. "Four clues at once?"

"He's a bit hasty," Mothball said. "You see, has to be *twelve* clues, there does, and we've only got a short time to go, ya know."

"Why does there have to be twelve?"

"'Tis part of the riddle, Master Tick." She winked at him. "There you are, I've just given you my own bit of a clue. Quite clever, I am."

"Yeah," Rutger grumbled. "A regular Hans Schtig-genschlubberheimer."

Mothball snapped her fingers as her face brightened with recognition. "Ah, I remember that name now! Yeah, me dad taught my sis and me all about him, he did. That bloke invented the very first version of the Barrier Wand."

Rutger shushed Mothball. "Are you crazy? I thought we were done giving out secrets the boy doesn't need to know yet."

Mothball shrugged as she winked at Tick again. "It's got nothing to do with the clues, little man. Give the sir somethin' to think about, it will."

"Barrier Wand?" Tick had heard those words before from Mothball. "I won't even bother asking."

Rutger turned to Tick, rolling his eyes as he nodded toward Mothball, as if he were shrugging off the escapades of a little kid. "Solve the riddle of Master George, be where you're supposed to be on the special day, do what you're supposed to do, go where you're supposed to go—then you'll know very well what a Barrier Wand is, trust me."

"Sounds good . . . I guess." Tick couldn't wait to tear open the envelope of clues, but he also wanted to stand there all day and ask them questions. "Isn't there anything else you can tell me? Anything?"

"Done opened our mouths quite enough, we have," Mothball said. "Master George will probably step on his cat he's so nervous about it all."

"You mean . . . he can hear us? Do you have a microphone or something?"

Rutger laughed, a guffaw that echoed through the trees, like he'd just been told the funniest joke of the century. "You have much to learn, kid, much to learn."

Tick looked down with mixed confusion and anger. "What's so funny?"

Rutger stuttered his laugh to a stop, wiping his eyes with pudgy hands. "Oh, nothing, sorry. Nothing at all." He cleared his throat.

"Well, off we go, then," Mothball said. "Best of luck, Master Atticus."

"Yes, yes, indeed," Rutger added, reaching up to shake Tick's hand vigorously. "Please, don't take anything the wrong way. I'm a little funny in the head sometimes."

"Yeah," Tick said. "I noticed."

Rutger's face grew very serious. "Mothball and I . . . well, we're rooting for you, kid, a great deal. You'll make it, and we'll meet you again very soon. Okay?"

"It's in one month," Tick blurted before he knew what he was saying. "May sixth. I have to go to a cemetery and stomp my right foot on the ground, at nine o'clock at night, and say certain words and close my eyes. I just have to figure out *what* to say, and—"

Rutger held up a hand. "Sounds like you're on the

right track." He and Mothball exchanged a look, and there was no doubting the huge smiles of pride that spread across their faces.

So far, so good, Tick thought. *I just need to know the magic words.*

"We really must be going, now," Rutger said. "Good luck to you, and be strong."

He and Mothball folded their arms in unison, staring at Tick.

"Okay, see ya," he said, then paused, waiting for them to turn and go. They didn't move. "Aren't you leaving?"

"Better we wait for you to be off," Mothball said. "Just tryin' to be proper and all."

"Man, you guys are weird." Tick smiled then, hoping they knew they had become two of his favorite people on the planet. He felt the familiar pang of goodbye, then gave a simple wave. "See ya later, I guess. Will you be there if I . . . make it—whatever that means?"

"We'll be right there waitin' on ya, we will," Mothball said. "Be the grandest day of yer life, bet yer best buttons."

Tick nodded, wishing he could think of a way to extend the visit, but knowing it was time to go. "Right. Okay. Bye." He turned and walked away, heading back through the trees toward the road.

Tick ran all the way home, his sadness at saying good-bye to Mothball and Rutger quickly melting into anticipation of opening the next four clues.

He closed the door to his room and sat at his desk, wishing he could somehow transport Sofia from Italy so they could rip this thing open together. The thought made him want to kick himself for not asking Mothball and Rutger about their interactions with Sofia or any other kids. He wondered if Sofia had received this package yet. He'd have to e-mail her as soon as he was done taking a look.

He opened up the envelope and pulled out four pieces of cardstock, exactly the same as all the other clues. Each card had its own message typed in the middle of the page, with a number written in blue ink directly above it with a big circle around it, indicating its place in the sequence—seven through ten. Tick wondered about the significance of the order as he spread everything out on his desk in front of him, then read the first one, the seventh clue:

```
Go to the place you have chosen
wearing nothing but your underwear.
Oh, calm yourself, I'm only giving you
a bit of rubbish. Don't want you to
think I'm without a sense of humor.
No, quite the contrary—you must dress
```

```
warmly because you never know where
you'll end up.
```

Tick paused, thinking. The first line had made his stomach turn over before he realized Master George was just kidding around. That's all Tick needed was to go running across town in his undies to hang out at a graveyard in the middle of the night.

Nothing else about the clue seemed mysterious or riddle-like at all, giving weight to the little note that had been stapled to the front of the envelope. This one seemed like nothing more than a warning to dress warmly. But according to the attached note, *everything* was a clue, so it had to have some kind of hidden message.

Just when I think I'm getting the hang of it, he thought, shaking his head. He moved on to the next one, the eighth clue:

```
Eventually you will fail. I say
this because the vast majority of
those who receive these letters will
do so, utterly. For those extreme
few of you who may succeed, I will
conveniently explain away this clue
as a small typing error. For you, it
was meant to say, "Eventually you will
not fail."
```

Tick surprised himself by chuckling out loud. This Master George guy had quite the sense of humor and sounded like he was as quirky as an elf in Santa's workshop. Tick couldn't wait to meet him.

As for the clue itself, there was nothing to figure out, no mysteries—not even any advice this time. More and more, Tick was beginning to think he'd missed something important he was supposed to get from these messages.

He moved on to the ninth clue:

```
Ordinary kids would've given up
by now. I know what is haunting you,
what is chasing you, what is making
your life miserable. Cheer up, friend,
much worse lies ahead.
```

This one made Tick sit back in his chair and pause for a very long time. It was the shortest clue yet, but packed with so much. The kindness of Master George showing empathy for what Tick was going through and the terrible things he'd seen. The encouragement that Tick wasn't just an ordinary kid. The pride knowing he'd stood up and endured. And finally, the almost humorous warning that he'd only seen the beginning and "much worse" was still to come.

Tick felt like three starving warthogs had been

unleashed inside his brain, grunting and thrashing to find food. He wanted to know the truth, to know *every-thing*, so badly it made his head hurt, and he felt frustrated to no end. He'd just read the next *three* clues, and yet seemed no closer to discovering the magic words. If his family hadn't been downstairs, Tick would've screamed at the top of his lungs.

Almost reluctantly—almost—he read the final piece of paper from the envelope, the tenth clue:

Remember to bring two items with you, stowed carefully away in your pockets, while you say the magic words. Sadly, I must refrain from telling you what the items are. I can only say this: they must be impossible to pick up, no matter how strong you are, but small enough to fit in your pockets, since that is where they must be, on penalty of death (or at least a particularly nasty rash). I realize this riddle is very easy, but my cat just messed on the Peruvian rug in my parlor, so I haven't much time to think of a better one. Good day.

Messed on the Peruvian rug in his parlor? Tick was beginning to like Master George more and more every second.

And the man was right—this one was too easy. Tick got up from his desk, excited to e-mail Sofia. Then he would show all the new clues to his dad.

It took him ten minutes to finally persuade Kayla to quit playing her Winnie the Pooh computer game, and another couple minutes to clean the sticky spots off the keyboard from her fingers. She'd broken the no-food-at-the-computer rule and helped herself to a Popsicle while maneuvering Pooh and Piglet through the horrible dangers of the Hundred Acre Wood.

He finally logged in to his e-mail and opened up the INBOX, hoping that Sofia had sent him something as well. His hand froze in midair, hovering over the mouse like a cloud when he saw what waited for him.

An e-mail from someone named "shadowka2056."

The subject line said, "Master George is crazy."

CHAPTER 30

THE THIRD MUSKETEER

Tick clicked open the e-mail, his heart pounding.

Dude, what's up with all this stuff, man? I couldn't
believe it when I was finally non-stupid enough to
search the Internet to see if there were any others like
me. Can you believe all this is for real? Actually, I guess
I should ask first if you're still doing this whole mess.
For all I know you burned the letter a long time ago.

My name's Paul Rogers and I live in Florida.
Ever been here? I can see that you're from
Washington—man, we're like on opposite corners
of America. How cool is that?

I don't know what to say until I know more about
what you're up to. Have you gotten everything?
Have you met Mothball and Rutger? They kept
telling me I needed to go to one of the postmarked
places to get another clue. I said, what do I look
like, King Henry the Eighth? I ain't made of money,
dude. I finally talked the little fat man into giving
me the clue anyway. Looks like there's more than
one way to skin a cat in this game.

Anyway, I'm up to Number Ten, how about you? If
you don't have a clue what I'm talking about and
think I'm totally bonkers, go ahead and delete this
e-mail. Trust me, you don't wanna know.

Laters,
Paul

Tick, excited, immediately hit REPLY and typed
out his answer.

Dear Paul,

I'm really glad you wrote me. I'm totally still in it,
and I'm up to the tenth clue as well. Pretty easy
one, right? Hands. Our hands. You can't really
pick up your own hands, but they can fit in your

pockets nice and easy. It's about time we had one that was simple, huh?

I actually did go to Alaska—it was my dad's idea. We almost got killed, but it wasn't too bad. We met a funny guy named Norbert who's met Master George! And he also met some crazy lady named Mistress Jane. From what Norbert said, I don't think I want to meet her.

There's another one of us—Sofia. She's from Italy and she was there, too. She didn't almost get killed though. But she did help save us.

Man, this e-mail sounds so stupid. By the way, you can call me Tick.

Have you figured out the magic words? I just don't get it—I've studied that first letter backward and forward and I don't see anything. I'm really hoping you know something I don't.

I don't really know what else to say. It's good to know there are at least three of us now. May 6th is coming soon.

Your new friend,
Tick

Feeling kind of dumb because he didn't say much worthwhile, but not knowing what else to do until he knew the guy better, Tick hit the SEND button, hoping Paul would reply quickly since he lived in the same country.

Tick then sent another e-mail to Sofia, telling her everything and asking her if she received the package of four clues.

On Monday, Tick sat in Mr. Chu's class, anxious for it to be over. Tick wanted to ask him about quantum physics, see if he could learn anything new that would give him a hint about what the "kyoopy" had to do with Master George. A warm sun beat on the windows, making the room hot and stuffy. Several kids had given up long ago, their heads making ridiculous jerking motions as they kept falling asleep and waking up.

Tick had yet to hear back from either the new kid Paul or Sofia. He must've checked his e-mail at least twenty times on Sunday, with no luck. He didn't get it—every time *he* got an e-mail, he responded in a second, excited to keep the conversation going. Oh, well.

The bell finally rang and the students filed out of the room, at least three of them bumping into Tick's desk and knocking off his things. Each time, he picked them up without a word and put them back on his desk. The bully stuff seemed so silly now compared to the other things he was dealing with that nothing bothered him anymore. He defiantly adjusted his scarf and waited for the classroom to empty.

"Tick?" Mr. Chu asked as he finished erasing the whiteboard. "Aren't you going to your next class?"

Tick stood up. "Yes, sir. I just wanted to know if you'd have any time after school to talk about . . . something."

"Sure," Mr. Chu replied, raising his eyebrows in concern. "Is anything—"

"No, no, nothing's wrong. I'm just wondering about a subject we talked a little about a while back and I want to know more about it."

"What is it?"

Tick paused, nervous that somehow saying the two words would reveal everything about Master George and his mysteries. "Quantum physics," he finally sputtered out, as if ashamed of the topic.

"Oh, really?" Mr. Chu's face brightened at the prospect of sharing information on his favorite science subject. "What's sparked your interest?"

"I don't know—just curious I guess."

"Well, okay, I'd be happy to talk about it. Come by after school, okay?"

"Okay. Thanks." Tick gathered his things and headed off to his next class.

❦

Long after the last bell had rung, Tick and Mr. Chu sat at his desk, discussing the many theories—all of them confusing—of quantum physics. The stale smells of dried coffee and old books filled the air as Tick leaned forward, his elbows resting on top of several messy piles of papers that needed grading. Through the window over his teacher's shoulder, Tick could see the long shadows of late afternoon creeping across the parking lot, where only a few cars remained.

"It's basically the study of everything that's teensy tiny," Mr. Chu was saying. "Now that doesn't sound like a very technical term, but that's what it's all about. Forget about the atom—that thing's huge. We're talking about electrons and protons and neutrons. And stuff that's even smaller—quarks and gluons. Sound like fun?"

"Well . . . yeah, actually," Tick answered.

"The basic thing you need to know is that all the stuff you *think* you know about the laws of physics—like, what goes up must come down—goes right out the window when you get down to particles that small. It's been proven those rules don't apply. Everything is different. And did you know that light has properties of both waves *and* particles . . ."

Mr. Chu went on to talk for at least a half hour straight, telling Tick all the basics of quantum physics and the experiments scientists had done to establish theories. What it really sounded like, though, was all a fancy way to say no one had a clue how it worked or why it was different from the big world.

"... and so by *observing* an electron, you are actually *deciding* where it is, what position it's in, what speed it's moving. And another person could be doing an alternate experiment at the same time, observing the same electron, but in a totally different position. Now, this is getting on the fringe of what the real experts say, but some people think an electron and other particles can literally be in more than one place at once—an infinite number of places!"

Tick felt like he was a pretty smart kid, but some of Mr. Chu's words made as much sense to him as an opera sung in pig latin. But that last sentence really made him think. "Wait a minute," he said, stopping his teacher. "You keep talking about these little guys like they're in a different universe. But aren't those tiny things inside my body, inside this chair, inside this desk? Isn't the big world you talked about just a whole bunch of the little worlds?"

Mr. Chu clapped his hands. "Brilliant!"

"Huh?"

"You nailed it, Tick, exactly." Mr. Chu stood up

and paced around the room in excitement as he continued talking. "They're not really separate sciences—they have to be related because *one* is made of the *other*. An atom is a bunch of tiny particles, and you, my friend, are nothing but a bunch of atoms."

"Right."

"This is where all the crazy, crazy theories come in—the ones that are so fascinating. One theory is that time travel is possible because of quantum physics. I don't buy that one at all because I think time is too linear for time travel to work."

Tick's head hurt. "Are there any you do believe in?"

"I don't know if *believe* is the right word, but there are some I sure love to think about." He paused, then sat back down at his desk and leaned forward on his elbows, looking into Tick's eyes. "One theory says there are different versions of the world we live in—alternate realities. An infinite number of them. If it can happen on the teensy-tiny level, why not on the big fat level too? All it would take is some vast manipulation of all those little particles that make up the *big* particles. Who knows—there might be some force in the universe, some law we don't know about, that can control quantum physics and even create or destroy different versions of our own world."

Mr. Chu had talked nonstop without breathing and finally took a big gulp of air.

"Sounds like it'd make a sweet movie," Tick said, trying to act like a normal kid with simple interests. But the truth was his thoughts were spinning out of control. Different versions of the world! Though he couldn't quite piece it all together, he knew this might explain where Mothball and Rutger came from.

"Oh, trust me, it's been done," Mr. Chu replied. "Especially the time travel part of it—but nothing I've seen that I like yet." He yawned. "I've talked your poor ear off for long enough, big guy. If you're really serious about studying Q.P., you should get a book or two from the library. It's fun stuff, especially for nerds like you, I mean, me." He smiled as he stood up and held out his hand. "Nice talking to you, Tick. It's always great to have students who actually *care* about what they're learning."

"Yeah, thanks," Tick said as he stood to leave. "See you tomorrow." He slung his backpack onto his shoulder and headed for the door. At the last second before leaving, another teacher—Ms. Myers—poked her head in from the hallway.

"Reginald, do you have a moment?" she asked. "I need to talk about parent-teacher conferences."

"Sure," Mr. Chu replied. "Come on in. Tick, we'll see you later. Thanks for coming by."

Tick almost dropped his books at the word *Reginald,* the coolness of their entire conversation fading into a disturbing, eerie feeling in his stomach. He forced out a good-bye, then quickly exited into the hallway.

He couldn't believe it, but he knew he'd never heard his favorite teacher's first name before. *It was Reginald? His name was* Reginald *Chu?*

Tick suddenly felt very, very ill.

CHAPTER 31

PAUL'S LITTLE SECRET

Tick lay on his back, staring up at the ceiling of his room as the last rays of the sun faded from the day, casting a darkly golden glow to the air. His stomach felt like someone had jacked up an industrial hose and pumped in five tons of raw sewage.

Reginald Chu.

He had thought it was all just a coincidence, but that was before he'd learned Mr. Chu's first name. Rutger said the founder and owner of Chu Industries, the ones who manufactured the Gnat Rat and had done "awful, awful things," was a man named Reginald Chu. Could there really be two people with that name in the world, much less two who both loved science? And who had both crossed paths with a kid named Atticus Higginbottom?

No way.

But then . . . how could his favorite teacher be someone who owned a major company the world had never heard of? Tick had looked up Chu Industries several times on the Internet, only to find nothing. Of course, he hadn't looked up the *name* Reginald Chu yet.

He got up from bed and headed downstairs, hoping a search might reveal something. As he passed Kayla on the stairs, clutching no fewer than five dolls in her small arms, Tick thought about the things he and Mr. Chu had discussed after school. One thing popped in his mind that seemed the most obvious answer to this dilemma.

Time travel. Mr. Chu created this horribly powerful company in the future and sent things back in time to haunt his old students.

Tick almost laughed out loud—talk about hokey and ridiculous. Despite the crazy stuff he'd seen the last few months, it didn't make him think any more than before that time travel was possible. Even Mr. Chu said it was a dumb theory. *Of course, if he was a bad guy . . .*

But what about the idea of alternate versions of the universe? Maybe his teacher had an alter ego in another reality. Just as nuts, but for some reason not *quite* as nuts. Tick shook his head, unable to believe he was actually having this conversation with himself.

He logged onto the Internet, then did a search for the name "Reginald Chu."

Three hits.

One obscure reference to a presentation Mr. Chu did at Gonzaga University with some other teachers, and a couple of unrelated hits about a guy in China. That was it. Just for fun, Tick typed in Chu Industries again, with the same result.

Nothing.

Trying his best to move his mind on to brighter things, he logged into his e-mail. He almost jumped out of his chair with joy when he saw replies from both Sofia and the new guy in Florida.

He froze for a second, not knowing which one to open first.

He clicked on Sofia's.

Tick,

Wow, another kid! Why did it have to be another American? That's all I need, running around with two boys who do nothing but eat hot dogs and belch and talk about stupid American football.

Yeah, I figured out the riddle about hands, too. BEFORE I got your e-mail, just in case you're wondering.

Next time you write this Paul boy, make sure to put my name in the address, too. That way we can all talk together.

Time is running out! We need to figure out the Magic Words!

Ciao,
Sofia

Oh, please, Tick thought. *She just has to make sure I know she figured it out on her own.*

He was about to hit REPLY on instinct, but remembered the e-mail from Paul. Tick quickly closed the one from Sofia and clicked on the other.

Tick,

Dude, are you serious about the whole Alaska thing? Man, I need to hear that story from the beginning. Try to do a better job of it next time— I couldn't understand a single thing you said about it. :)

I must be the dumbest person this side of the Mississippi because I didn't get the hands thing at first. Now it seems really obvious.

But that's okay. I'm one up on you, big time.

I figured out the magic words.

See ya later, Northern Dude.

Paul

P.S. No way I'm telling so don't ask. Rutger said I'm not allowed to. We can talk about anything else, but each person has to figure out the magic words for themselves. Good luck.

P.P.S. I'm fourteen years old, six feet tall (yes, six feet), African-American, and drop-dead handsome. I love to surf, I play the piano like freaking Mozart, and I currently have three girls who call me every day, but my mom always tells them I'm in the bathroom. Let me know a little about you, too. Later.

What!

Tick sat back, unable to believe his eyes. He couldn't care less about Paul's little introduction at the moment—the guy knew what the magic words were! It was finally right there for the taking, but he wouldn't—*couldn't*—share.

That stupid little Rutger . . .

Tick hit the REPLY button, then added Sofia's e-mail address right after Paul's. From now on, hopefully they could stay connected as a trio and make their way toward the special day together. After pausing to think about what he wanted to say, Tick started typing.

Paul (and Sofia),

Okay, this e-mail has both of your addresses on it, so be sure and do that from now on so we can keep in touch. Paul, this is Sofia. Sofia, this is Paul. I'll forward the different e-mails to everyone later. Sofia needs to know that Paul seems to think he's something special. :)

Paul, did you really figure out the magic words? Are you serious? You really can't tell us? I've looked at that first letter over and over and over and I can't find the answer! Sofia, Rutger told Paul we're allowed to share and help each other, BUT NOT ABOUT THE MAGIC WORDS.

(If I ever get my hands on that guy . . .)

Sofia and I will just have to start figuring out a way to get you to tell us anyway.

Tick went on to write a very long e-mail, telling the story of Alaska and a little about himself and Sofia. When he finally finished and turned off the computer, Tick's eyes hurt. He was just standing when his mom called everyone in for dinner.

⁓

Frazier Gunn sat in his little prison cell and brooded.

How had it come to this? He'd been having a dandy of a time in Alaska, pulling off his plan to take care of *two* of the bratty kids George was scheming with—and poof. Everything fell to pieces.

After being knocked out in the freezing cold cemetery, Frazier had awakened in this teeny little room, which was barred and chained with enough locks to hold the Great Houdini. The walls of his cell were made of metal, lines of rivets and bolts all over the place. He felt like a grenade locked in an old World War II ammunition box.

And he'd been here for over *three months*. His captor had obviously injected him with a shockpulse because his nanolocator was dead, not responding whenever he tried to send a signal to Mistress Jane. Plus, if it had been working, she would've winked him away a long time ago. Of course, that fate might be worse than his current one. The woman had a nasty temper and low tolerance for failure.

At least he had a comfortable bed in which to sleep. And delicious food slipped through a small slot on the bottom of the door three times a day without fail. He'd been given books to read and a small TV with a DVD player and lots of movies. Mostly about cats, oddly enough, but still, it was enough to keep him occupied for a while.

But three *months*. He felt his mind slipping into an abyss of insanity.

To make matters worse, the room *swayed*. Not very much and not very often, but he could feel it. It was like a gigantic robot trying to put her cute little metal box to bed. He kept telling himself it was all in his imagination, but it sure seemed real enough when he leaned over the toilet and threw up.

Frazier was a miserable, miserable man, and it only poured salt in his wounds that he didn't know *why* he was here, or who had captured him.

It had to have something to do with that nuisance of all nuisances, George. *Master* George. *Please. What kind of man has the audacity to refer to himself as Master anything?*

The sound of scraping metal jolted him from his moping. He looked up to see a small slot had slid open in the center of the main door, only a couple of inches tall and wide and about waist-high from the floor.

This is new. He stood and walked over to the opening, peeking through. He yelped and fell backward onto his bed when a cat's face suddenly appeared, baring its fangs and hissing.

"Who's there!" he yelled, his voice echoing off the walls with a hollow, creepy boom. He recovered his wits and righted himself, staring at the small open space. The cat had already disappeared, replaced by a mouth with an old ruddy pair of chapped lips.

"Hello in there?" the mouth spoke, the voice heavy with an English accent.

"Yeah, who is it?" Frazier grunted back at his captor, though he already knew who was behind the door.

"Quite sorry about the inconvenience," Master George said. "Won't be long now before we send you on your way."

"Inconvenience?" Frazier snarled. "That's what you call locking up a man for three months?"

"Come on, old chap. Can you blame us after what you did to those poor children?"

"Just following orders, old man." Frazier sniffed and folded his arms, pouting like a little kid. "I never meant any true harm. I was, uh, just playing around with the car to scare them. No big deal."

"I must say," George countered, "I disagree quite strongly with your assessment of the situation. Mistress Jane has gotten too dangerous. She's gone too far. I mustn't allow you to return to her until . . . we've taken care of something."

"Taken care of what?"

"Just one more month or so, my good man," George replied, ignoring the question. "Then we'll send you off to the Thirteenth where we won't have to worry about you coming back."

Intense alarms jangled in Frazier's head. What the old man had just said made no sense. Unless . . .

"What do you—"

His words died in the metallic echo of the small door sliding shut.

CHAPTER 32

SHATTERED GLASS

A week went by with Tick, Sofia, and Paul e-mailing each other almost every day. They talked about their lives, their families, their schools. Though Tick had never met Paul and had met Sofia only once, he felt like they'd all become great friends.

Tick and Sofia used every ounce of persuasive skills they possessed to convince Paul to tell them the magic words. On more than one occasion, Sofia even threatened bodily harm, never mind that she lived on another continent. But Paul stubbornly refused, not budging an inch. Finally, the other two gave up and reluctantly admitted he was right, anyway. Better to follow the rules in this whole mess than risk jeopardizing their chances of achieving the goal all together.

The goal. What *was* the goal? Yeah, they pretty much knew that on the special day they had to perform a silly ritual in a certain place—probably to show their ability to follow instructions and obey orders as much as to show they could solve the riddles of the clues. But then what would happen?

Tick felt strongly that if they did everything correctly, they would *travel* to another place. Somehow Mothball and Rutger were doing it. Somehow Master George was traipsing about the world to all kinds of strange places, mailing letters. Tick always felt a surge of excitement when he considered the possibilities of what may happen on the special day, only to have it come crashing down when he remembered he hadn't figured out the magic words.

After dinner one night, Tick sat at his desk, his *Journal of Curious Letters* open before him, while his dad lounged on the bed with his hands clasped behind his head. Tick had told him everything, but his dad hadn't been much help, falling back on his normal Dad capacity of offering encouragement and rally cries. Tick suspected his dad knew more than he let on, but that he felt much like Paul did—it was up to Tick to solve the puzzle.

"Go through your list again," his dad said. "Everything we know needs to happen on May sixth."

Tick groaned. "Dad, we've gone over this a million times."

"Then once more won't hurt. Come on, give it to me."

Tick flipped to the page where he'd accumulated his conclusions. "Okay, on May sixth, I need to be in a cemetery—any cemetery—with no one else there but all the dead people."

"That excludes me, unfortunately." His dad let out an exaggerated sigh. "I still don't know if I'm going to let you do this."

"Dad, it'll be fine. It's probably a good thing you won't be there, anyway—I'm sure I'll be abducted by aliens or something."

"Whoa, now *that's* a dream come true."

Tick rubbed his eyes, then kept reading. "I need to be dressed warmly, and at nine o'clock on the nose I need to say the magic words, with my eyes closed, then stomp on the ground with my right foot ten times—all while keeping both of my hands in my pockets."

"Is that it?"

"That's it."

His dad rolled into a sitting position on the bed with a loud grunt. "All that's pretty easy, don't you think?"

"Well . . . yeah, except for one tiny thing."

"The magic words."

Tick nodded. "The magic words. At this rate, Paul

will be the only one of the three of us who gets to . . . do whatever it is that's gonna happen."

His dad scratched his chin, doing his best Sherlock Holmes impression. "Son, it can't be that hard. I mean, all the other clues have been challenging and fun, but not really *hard*, you know what I mean?"

"Maybe this is Master George's last way of weeding out those who aren't willing to stick with it. Maybe I'm one of those last schmoes who ends up losing. The seventh clue said most people would fail."

"Listen to me," his dad said, unusually serious. "I don't care what happens, and I don't care who this Master George fancy lad from England is. You're not a *schmoe*, and you never will be. You hear me?"

"Yeah, but . . ." Tick's eyes suddenly teared up and his heart seemed to swell and grow warm, like his veins had brought in steaming hot soup instead of the usual blood. It hit him then that he was worried—no, scared—that he wasn't going to solve the riddle of the magic words. He'd analyzed the first letter from M.G. more times than he could count, and nothing had come to him.

His dad got up and knelt next to his son, pulling him into his arms. "I love you, kid. You mean more to me than you can ever know, and that's all that matters to me."

"Dad, no offense, but . . . I mean, I really appreciate all your help." He pulled back from the hug and looked at his dad. "I want this so bad. I know it sounds dumb, but I *want* this. I've never really done anything important before, and Master George said I might be able to save peoples' lives."

"Then by golly we'll figure it out, okay? Give me that jour—"

His words cut off when a thunderclap of broken glass shattered the silence, followed by the tinkle of falling shards and a loud thump on the floor. Dad fell onto his back with a yelp and Tick's hand went to his chest, clutching his shirt like an old woman shocked by the spectacle of kids skateboarding in a church parking lot.

Someone had wrapped a note around a rock and then thrown it through the window.

While his dad went for the rock, Tick ran to the window to see if he could get a look at who had thrown it. He just caught a glimpse of a figure leaving the front yard and disappearing into the thicker trees of the neighboring woods.

A very short, very fat, figure.

Snickering, Rutger waddled along on his short legs through the dark trees and back to the main road. The thrill of throwing the rock had been a great boon to his

spirits, and he had enjoyed every second of it. Now he just had to get away before Tick caught him.

As he thought about it more while escaping, he realized that breaking one of the Higginbottoms' windows maybe hadn't been the smartest thing to do, or the nicest. But it sure was funny.

He crossed the road and entered the forest on the other side, trying to remember the best way back to the old abandoned graveyard. He could've stuck to the road for a while longer, but he was worried he'd be caught. As he paused behind an enormous bush—it had to be big to hide *him*—he heard Tick's voice from a distance.

"Did you really have to break my window, Rutger!" the kid yelled.

Rutger laughed, then set off again, feeling his way in the darkness.

Tick and his dad walked up and down the road a few times, trying to spot the eccentric little man, but he was nowhere in sight, the darkness too deep. A slight breeze picked up, making Tick shiver.

"I can't believe he broke my window," he said, but then he laughed.

"You think it's funny, huh?" Dad said.

"Actually . . . yeah. That guy's crazy."

"Well, young man," Dad said in his best attempt at a stern voice, "maybe you won't laugh so much when I tell you it's coming out of your allowance. Come on, let's go see what the note said."

⌒

Tick picked up the rock, which was about the size of his fist, and carefully pulled the pieces of tape off the white cardstock that had been wrapped around the hard, cold surface. When he finally got it off safe and sound, he turned it over to see that it was the next clue—number eleven—from Master George.

"Read it, read it," his dad urged.

Tick read it out loud as he devoured each word with his eyes.

Given that the day is almost here, I will issue a final warning. If you succeed in this current endeavor, your life will be forever altered, becoming dangerous and frightful. If you do not, very bad things will happen to people you may never meet or know. The choice to continue is yours.

"Dang it," Tick said.
"What?"

"I was hoping he'd give us another hint on how to come up with the magic words. This isn't a clue." Tick waved the paper in the air, then dropped it on the desk next to his journal. "It's just a warning. No different from the stuff he said in the very first letter."

"But remember," his dad pointed out, "he said *everything* you receive is a clue."

"Yeah, well right now I'm kind of sick of it." Tick flopped onto his bed and rolled over toward the wall.

After a long pause, his dad spoke quietly. "Sleep on it, Professor. You'll feel better in the morning, I promise."

The floor creaked as his dad walked toward the hallway; then the light went off and he heard the soft thump of his dad gently closing the door.

Despite the tornado of thoughts churning inside his mind, Tick fell asleep.

⁓

Tick knows he's dreaming, but it's still creepy.

He's in the forest, moonlight breaking the darkness just enough to make the trees look like twisted old trolls, their limbs reaching out to grab him, choke him.

Leaves and snow swirl around his body like fairies on too much pixie dust. A huge tree looms at his back. Tick watches the leaves spinning in the air, mesmerized.

He jumps to catch one, and some unseen force holds him in the air . . .

311

And then the leaves turn into letters.

One by one the letters pass in front of Tick, glowing briefly, teasing him with their riddles, reminding him that he can't solve the biggest one of all. The first letter.

The first letter.

The first letter . . .

CHAPTER 33

THE FINAL CLUE

The last yellow envelope from Master George came on the third of May, only three days before the Big Day. Tick came home from school on a warm and rainy afternoon to find it on his pillow, addressed to him and postmarked from Brisbane, Australia.

Until then, he'd been in a foul mood, with good reason. Two days earlier, Sofia had announced she was pretty sure she'd solved the riddle of the magic words. Positive, in fact. Tick knew he should be happy for her, but instead felt jealous and angry. Especially since he knew she couldn't tell him; in his mind it was like Paul and Sofia had this secret about Tick and kept giggling about it behind his back.

With each passing day May sixth grew closer and closer and Tick became more dejected, moping around like an old man searching for his lost soul in an Edgar Allan Poe story. He just didn't get it—he was smart. He'd always thought he was way smarter than anyone his own age, and many who were older. Yet for some reason he couldn't figure out those stupid magic words! Paul and Sofia did it, why couldn't he?

As Tick opened the last letter, hoping against hope it somehow held the final link to the magic words, he thought again about how odd it was that Master George traveled around the world to mail his messages. And how Mothball and Rutger got around the world so quickly. It had to be something magical, and Tick sure hoped he'd find out all about it in three days.

He pulled out the white cardstock. The last clue. Scared to death he'd finish it and be no better off than before, he almost reluctantly read its words:

Everything you need to determine
the magic words is in the first
letter. Quit struggling so much and
read them, won't you? Listen to the
words of Master George—they've been
there all along! This is the last
clue. I shall never see or speak to

> you again. Unless I do. Good-bye, and
> may the Realities have mercy on you.

Tick slumped down on his bed, groaning out loud. It seemed like the last few clues had been a complete . . .

Wait a minute.

He sat back up and put the paper in his lap, reading through the clue again. Had Master George made a mistake while typing it? The second sentence made no sense.

> Quit struggling so much and read
> them, won't you?

Read *them*? Why would he say *them* when referring to the first letter he'd sent out? There'd been only one piece of paper in that original envelope, so why would he use the plural word *them* when telling Tick to read it? The first letter . . .

Tick stopped. He felt like the Earth had stopped spinning and the air had frozen around him in an invisible block of ice; his mind and spirit seemed to step out of his body and turn around to look at him, not believing he could've missed something so obvious.

The first letter.

He grabbed his journal, ripping it open to find

the clue that had first revealed he needed to discover magic words to say on May sixth. It had been the second clue, telling him that at the appointed time, he would need to say the words with his eyes closed. Master George couldn't tell him what the words were, but the last sentence told him how he could figure it out himself:

```
    Examine the first letter carefully
and you will work them out.
```

Old M.G. had been purposefully tricky with his language to throw his readers off the trail. When Tick read that clue the first time, his mind had immediately interpreted it as referring to the very first letter he'd received in the mail from Master George. And once that had been set in his mind, he'd never even considered the possibility of a different meaning. But what the mysterious man really meant *was* something entirely different.

The first letter.

Not the first envelope. Not the first paper. Not the first message.

The first letter.

M.G. meant that Tick needed to literally examine the first *letter* of something. And only one possibility made sense. Even though some of the Twelve Clues had not seemed like clues at all, Master George had been very clear.

Everything is a clue.

His blood racing through his veins like he'd just done windsprints, setting his heart into a thumpity-thump that he could feel and hear in his ears, Tick went through his *Journal of Curious Letters* page by page, clue by clue. He kept a finger on the last page of the dusty old book, flipping back there after seeing each of the twelve riddles in turn, jotting down a letter, then going back again.

One by one, Tick wrote down the first letter of each clue, twelve letters in all. When he finished, he sat back and stared at the result, wanting to laugh and cry and scream at the same time.

MASTERGEORGE

CHAPTER 34

THE MIRACLE OF SCREAMING

Tick took his journal downstairs with him, eager to e-mail Sofia and Paul and let them know he'd finally—*finally*—figured it out. He placed his precious book on the desk and quickly logged in and sent off the messages, his excitement building by the second. He couldn't wait until his dad got home from work so he could tell him, too.

It's all in place now, he thought. *Just three days and it's really going to happen!*

Of course, he didn't know what "it" was, but that was beside the point.

Tick stood up from the computer desk and stretched, suddenly happier than he'd been in weeks. He felt stupid for all the jealous feelings he'd had toward his new friends and the whole thing in general; he'd acted like a little baby, at least within his own mind.

But that was all in the past, now. *Three days.*

So bottled up with energy he could hardly stand it, he decided to run over to the library and hang out like he didn't have a care in the world. Maybe he'd check out a book and read it as a reward. He'd probably have just enough time to finish it before the Big Day came. He told his mom he'd be back in time for dinner and headed out the door.

Halfway to the library, the sun finally breaking through the storm clouds that had hung over the world all day, he realized he'd left his journal sitting on the computer desk back home and wondered if he should go back and put it away. *No, I won't be gone that long.* As he ran on, he hoped he didn't look as ridiculously happy as he felt.

⟳

Kayla noticed the ugly old book sitting on the computer desk, wondering where it had come from. It looked like something from her favorite Disney cartoon. Maybe it was a book of pirate treasure maps! She was a very young girl, but she knew one thing for certain.

Pirate treasure maps equal fun.

She looked around to make sure no one was around,

then grabbed the book from the desk, pulling it down onto her lap as she sat on the floor. Words were written in a little box in the center of the cover, but she recognized the first one right away.

Tick.

Uh-oh, she thought. *He doesn't like me to mess with his things.*

Well, just a peek couldn't hurt, could it?

She opened the book up and flipped through the pages, seeing lots of pieces of paper that had been glued to the ones already there. No pirate maps though. Maybe this was an art project her brother had been putting together as a surprise for her, though it wasn't very pretty. All it had were a bunch of words that looked funny.

Kayla quickly grew bored, sad the book didn't have anything to do with pirates. She was flipping through it one last time when one of the pieces of paper slipped into the air like it had been shot out of a cannon and dropped to the floor in front of her. She picked it up and saw that this one had more words than any of the others—a *lot* more.

The glue must've cracked, letting the boring old paper escape.

Well, Kayla thought, *now I'm in a pickle.* Her mom wouldn't let her use glue without a grown-up around and if she asked for help, her mom might be mad that she'd broken Tick's book. Plus, she couldn't remember exactly where the piece of paper had been inside the book.

Maybe, just maybe, Tick wouldn't notice it was missing since so many other papers were glued throughout. And if she just stuck it somewhere or threw it away, he might find it and then he'd know for sure she'd been messing with his stuff.

Kayla put the book back on the desk, then clutched the loose paper in her hands. With devious eyes, she looked over at the fireplace, focusing on the little knob that started up the gas and flame.

It'd been awhile since she'd had fun with fire . . .

Tick walked down the road of his neighborhood, holding the nice, thick book he'd checked out at the library. The sun slowly fell toward the horizon, the first glowing fingers of twilight creeping through the trees. Tomorrow was Saturday and after months and months of thinking and solving and worrying and running, he couldn't wait to spend a couple of days relaxing.

On instinct, he checked the mailbox when he got to his house, even though he already knew his mom had gotten it earlier—hence the twelfth clue. Tick couldn't help but hope absolutely nothing else happened until

Monday night, the Big Day. He needed a break from all the stress.

Easy to say when you have it all figured out, he thought. He'd sure not enjoyed the three-month-long "break" he'd had after Christmas.

He walked down the driveway toward his front door.

⌒

Kayla knew she didn't have much time. The warm fire licked the air with an almost silent whooshing sound, reminding her of how much she loved watching things burn. Now that it was mostly warm outside, they never had the flames going, and if her mom walked in, there'd be a certain favorite doll that would get locked away for a whole week. She needed to hurry.

She threw the stupid piece of paper into the flames.

A wave of ugly black stuff, rimmed with a fiery line of glowing orange, traveled across the paper from both of the short sides as the whole thing slowly curled up into a ball. A little line of smoke escaped into the room, and in a few seconds, all that remained was a crispy sheet of ash.

"Kayla, what are you doing!"

She jumped at her brother's voice, letting out a little shriek as she turned around to see him standing right behind her. Without meaning to, her eyes immediately looked over at the book sitting on the computer desk.

Tick followed her gaze, then practically leaped over to grab the book. He flipped it open, his eyes showing he already knew what had happened. His face reddened, his hands began to shake. He almost dropped the book. Then a *tear* fell out of his right eye. Kayla didn't understand; why would such a dumb old—

Tick's shout, full of rage, cut off her thoughts. "Bad girl, Kayla! You're a very bad, bad, naughty, stupid, naughty girl!" Then he ran out of the room and out the front door, slamming it closed behind him.

Kayla bawled.

Tick ran.

Clutching the journal in both arms, he didn't know where he was going, or how long it would last, but all he could do was run, his loosened scarf flapping in the wind. His heart wanted to explode out of his chest, panic and anger and disappointment crushing his feelings like someone had injected a full-sized elephant into his bloodstream. It hurt, and tears flowed down his face as he pounded the pavement with his clumsy feet. He fell twice, only to get up and keep running.

How could Kayla have done something so *stupid!* Everything had just fallen into place, everything was perfect. But now the message had been sent. Tick didn't know how, but he *knew* it had been sent.

Burn the letter, stop the madness.

Tick had been cut off. Even though he'd figured out all the clues, and was ready to perform the silly ritual in three days—he'd been cut off. Somehow Master George would know the first letter had been burned, which meant he'd think Tick had given up and was out of the game.

After everything, after all that work and sweat and danger, it was all over.

Tick was in the forest now, still running, dodging trees and brush, tripping and getting back up again, ignoring the scratches. He sucked at the air around him, forcing it into his lungs so his heart wouldn't give up and die.

But then it finally became too much. He stopped, doubling over to take in huge, gulping breaths. Sunset had arrived and the woods had grown very dark, the trees standing as monuments of shadow all around him. When he finally caught his breath, he straightened and folded his arms around the *Journal of Curious Letters*.

There had to be a way to fix this. There had to be.

Tick knew that Master George somehow tracked what all of his subjects were doing. Tick didn't know what kind of magic or futuristic device accomplished the task, but he knew his actions had been monitored.

How else did Mothball and Rutger always know where and how to find him? Even in Alaska! Based on what Paul had said, they went *there* to give him a clue, not the other way around.

Surely Master George cared more about Tick's intent than the mistake of Kayla burning the letter. And Tick's intent was stronger than anything he had felt in his entire life. He wanted to see this through. He wanted to reach the end of the mystery.

He wanted it very, very badly.

Not sure if he'd finally flipped his lid once and for all, Tick screamed at the top of his lungs, belting out several words as loudly as his body could handle.

"MASTER GEORGE, I DIDN'T BURN THE LETTER!"

It hurt his throat and made him cough, but he shouted it a second time anyway.

Drawing in a deep breath through his torn throat, Tick concentrated. He had to do something. He had made his choice long ago to *not* burn the letter. That choice still had to mean something, didn't it? If only he had chosen to take his journal with him to the library instead of leaving it where Kayla could find it.

He felt a funny tickle growing in the pit of his stomach, a reserve of energy he hadn't known was there. A wave of warmth spread up from his stomach into his chest. The air in the woods stilled around him, as if the whole world hushed, waiting for him to make his move.

Tick gritted his teeth. He tapped into that quiet pool of energy, channeling the heat that filled his body and forcing it through his shredded voice box, yelling out for the third time:

"MASTER GEORGE! I . . . DID . . . NOT . . . BURN . . . THE . . . LETTER!"

The woods swallowed up his words, returning only silence. The fire in his belly flickered and then went out, leaving Tick feeling weak and shaky.

He waited, hoping he would see some kind of sign that Master George had heard him. Nothing.

Dejected, throat burning, and not knowing what else he could possibly do, not knowing if what he had done had changed anything at all, he headed for home.

$\sim$

Kayla sat in the middle of the living room, hosting a tea party for her three favorite dolls. Humming to herself, she passed out cups of steaming hot tea.

The front door swung open, followed by her very sad-looking brother. His clothes looked dirty, his hair was all messed up, and he was sweating.

What happened to him? she wondered. *He was supposed to be at the library.*

He came into the living room and knelt down

beside her, pulling her into a fiercely tight hug. Kayla thought Tick was acting really weird but she finally squeezed back, wondering if he was okay.

"I'm sorry, Kayla," he said. "I'm really, really sorry I yelled at you like that." He leaned back from her; his eyes were all wet. "You're a good girl, you know that? Come here." He hugged her again, then stood up and headed for the stairs, his head hung low, that strange-looking book with his name on the cover gripped in his right hand.

Halfway up the stairs, he leaned over the railing and repeated himself. "You're a good girl, Kayla. I'm sorry I yelled at you, okay? I know you didn't mean to mess up my book."

Kayla was confused. When had Tick yelled at her? Earlier, he'd been talking to his friends on the computer while she played with her dolls but he hadn't said anything to her. And she hadn't touched his book at all. How could she? He had taken it with him when he left for the library.

She and her dollies laughed at the silliness of boys and she poured herself another cup of invisible tea.

~

Tick flopped down on his bed with a groan. How could he know if screaming in the woods had done any good? Was he really going to have to agonize all weekend, waiting, then head to the cemetery on Monday night and hope for the best? Was it really all over?

With a heavy heart he opened up his *Journal of Curious Letters* to torture himself by studying the spot where Master George's first letter had once been glued, safe and sound. When the front cover flipped over and fell in his lap, Tick looked at something he couldn't understand. He stared for a very long time at the page before him, his mind shifting into overdrive trying to comprehend the message his eyes were frantically sending down the nerve wires to his brain. A message that was impossible.

The first letter was *there*, glued to the page like it had always been, not a burn mark or blemish to be found. It was there! How . . . ?

Master George—or *someone*—had just pulled off the coolest magic trick Tick had ever seen.

Kayla had just poured the last cup when she heard loud thumps from upstairs—was somebody *jumping* up there?—followed by happy screams of joy. It was Tick, and he sounded like he'd just received a personal letter from Santa Claus.

What a weirdo, she thought, taking a sip of her tea.

Far away, Master George sat upright in his ergo-nomic chair, staring at the flashing lights of his Command Center. He shook his head, feeling a bit dazed. He'd just been readying himself to . . . do something.

He couldn't remember what exactly.

He'd been thinking about . . . Atticus Higgin-bottom.

But why? It was as if a bubble in his brain had popped, taking the last few minutes of his life with it. It was downright maddening—he couldn't remember anything. Why was he even sitting in the chair? He only sat here when someone had made a Pick—or if someone had burned their letter. He shook his head. *Had* someone burned their letter? Had *Atticus* burned his letter?

He looked up at the computer screen, counting the purple check marks. No. Everyone was accounted for, the mark by Atticus's name glowing bright and steady. That was good. The special day was coming up quickly and Master George couldn't afford to lose a single member of the group. Especially not Atticus.

I really must be getting old.

Bewildered, he stood up, calling for Muffintops, and thinking how much he'd like a nice pot of pepper-mint tea.

CHAPTER 35

THE FINAL
PREPARATION

By Sunday night, Tick had heard back from Paul and Sofia about the strange incident with the burned letter and its miraculous reappearance. They were as shocked and clueless as he was about how or why it happened. Paul wasn't shy about expressing his doubt that it had occurred at all. His theory was Tick had been so stressed out about the magic words that he'd experienced one whopper of a bizarre dream.

But Tick knew it was real. He'd even asked Kayla about it and she didn't remember anything about burning the letter. No, Tick knew something magical had happened. Something supernatural. Something miraculous. And he couldn't wait to ask Master George what it might mean.

He sat at the desk in his room, waiting for his dad. The lamp on the desk provided the only light, failing miserably to push back the gloom. They'd planned all weekend to meet at eight o'clock Sunday evening to discuss the Big Day, and to run through the clues one final time. Though they didn't really know what they were planning for, it seemed they'd have only one shot at this. Or rather, *Tick* would have only one shot. The clues had been very clear—he must go alone, unless his dad wanted to drop dead of a heart attack right before the special time.

Tick had just pulled out the *Journal of Curious Letters* when he heard a soft knock at the door. "Come in," he called out.

His dad opened the door and shut it behind him. "Twenty-five hours to go, kiddo."

Tick groaned. "I know. I've been dying for this day to come and now that it's here, I wish we had a week or two more. I'm scared to death."

"Well, at least you're honest." Dad came in and sat on the bed, ignoring the loud creak of the bedsprings, which sounded as if they were about to break. "Most kids would act all tough and say they weren't scared at all."

"Then most kids would be faking it."

His dad clapped his hands together. "Well, we won't have much time to talk tomorrow night before you go, so let's run through everything."

Tick wasn't ready for that yet. "Dad?"

"Yeah?"

"What if . . . whatever I do *takes* me somewhere? Something tells me it will. What if I'm gone a long time?"

His dad's face melted into a look of deep sadness, all droopy eyes and frowns. "Professor, trust me, I've been so worried about all this I can't sleep at night. How could any good father let his son go off to who-knows-where to do who-knows-what and for who-knows how long? *Especially* after the dangerous things we've been through." He paused, rubbing his hands together. "But what can I say—I'm nuts? It's hard to believe in all this—but I believe in *you*. I'm taking a huge leap of faith, but I'm gonna let you walk out of this house and down that road"—he pointed out the window—"and off to wherever or whatever it is you've been called to do. It's going to *kill* me, but I'm gonna do it. I'm either the best or the worst dad in history."

A long silence followed. Tick felt something stir within him, a new appreciation for his parents and what they went through worrying about their kids. It couldn't be easy. And now Tick was going to do the worst thing possible to his dad—make him let him go without having a clue what might happen to his only son.

"What about Mom?" Tick finally asked.

His dad looked up from the spot he'd been staring at on the floor. "Now *that* could be a battle."

"What are you going to do? She'd never let me go."

His dad laughed. "That's exactly why you're going to go tomorrow night, and leave the explaining-to-Mom bit to me. Once you're gone, I'll sit her down and spill the beans, every little morsel, from beginning to end. Your mom and I have loved each other for many years, son, and eventually she'll understand why you're doing this, and why you and I feel so strongly about it."

Tick snorted. "Yeah, sometime after she tries to kill you for letting me go."

His dad nodded. "You're probably right, there. Just try to not be gone *too* long and maybe I'll survive."

Tick suddenly had a horrible thought. "What if . . . what if I never—"

His dad held up a hand and shushed Tick loudly. "Stop. Stop, Atticus."

"But—"

"No!" He shook his head vigorously. "You're coming back to me, you hear? These people know what they're doing, and you *will* come back to me. And there won't be another word said about it, is that understood?"

Tick couldn't remember the last time his dad had looked so stern. "Yes, sir."

"Good. Now let's run through those clues."

It took a half hour, but they read through each and every one of the Twelve Clues, studying their words one last time to make sure they hadn't missed anything. But it all seemed to be there, straightforward and solved. Looking back, it had all been pretty easy in a way. The real test seemed to be the endurance and the bravery to keep going.

And, of course, figuring out the magic words, which seemed to be the most important piece of the puzzle. No matter what else he'd done, without those words to say, he felt sure everything would fail.

When they read the twelfth clue, they realized they'd perhaps missed something—a little phrase their mysterious friend had thrown in to verify they'd decoded the magic words correctly.

```
Listen to the words of Master
George—they've been there all along!
```

And they really *had* been there. If Tick had just known to look at the first letter of the individual clues, he probably would've figured out "Master George" the second they'd learned the name from Norbert up in Alaska.

And so, after thoroughly examining the entire *Journal of Curious Letters* with his dad, Tick felt ready to go.

Tomorrow night, in the cemetery close to downtown, at nine o'clock, he'd show up, alone, in warm clothing, say the words "Master George" with his eyes closed, hands in pockets, then stomp the ground with his right foot ten times.

After that, who knew *what* might happen.

Tick went downstairs to check his e-mail before bed, realizing this might be the last chance he had to see if his friends had sent anything. It was already approaching early morning on Monday for Sofia because of the time difference, and Paul was probably already in bed.

What would happen to the others between their turns and his? If they were being taken somewhere, would they just wait around all day until he arrived? Was the staggered time difference on purpose—so Master George wouldn't have to do . . . whatever he was going to do to everyone all at once?

There I go again, Tick thought. Asking a billion questions even though he knew the answer was out of his reach for now. One more day. Twenty-four hours. Then, hopefully, he'd know everything at last.

He logged in to his e-mail and was excited to see messages from both Sofia and Paul. He opened Sofia's, who'd sent hers hours before Paul.

Tick and Paul,

Not much to say now, huh? Don't think Sofia Pacini is in love with two American boys, but I really hope I see you both tomorrow. I'm sure somehow they're going to bring us magically together. Right?

Good luck. I wish we knew what to expect.

Ciao,
Sofia

For some reason, Tick felt a pang of sadness in his heart, realizing the possibility he might never hear from Sofia again. What if something terrible happened tomorrow? What if only *some* of the people who performed the ritual made it to wherever they were going? Tick told himself to shut up and clicked on Paul's e-mail.

My little buddies,

Hot diggity dog, tomorrow's the day. Let's don't jinx anything.

Hope you're right about us meeting. If so, see ya tomorrow.

Out.
Paul

Tick hit REPLY TO ALL and typed a quick message, knowing his friends might not see it anyway.

Paul and Sofia,

Good luck tomorrow. See you soon. I hope.

Tick

He turned off the computer and stood up, looking over at the fireplace. He thought back to the two events that had happened in the last few months related to the pile of stacked brick, now cold and dark. First, the commitment he'd made to not burn the first letter, to stay in the game—made while kneeling before a fire that could've ended it all. And then the bizarre incident with Kayla and the letter—something that either proved miracles really did happen or Tick had serious mental issues.

With a swarm of butterflies in his belly, Tick finally turned out the lights and headed up the stairs to his room, ready for one last night before the Big Day he'd been preparing for since November.

It took him over two hours to fall asleep.

PART 4

✦

THE BARRIER WAND

CHAPTER 36

AMONG THE DEAD

The next evening—Monday night, May sixth—Tick stood on the front porch with his dad, looking at his digital watch every ten seconds as the sun sank deeper and deeper behind the tree-hidden horizon. The last remnants of twilight turned the sky into an ugly black bruise, a few streaks of clouds looking like jagged scars. It had just turned seven-thirty, and the temperature couldn't possibly be any more perfect for a romp in the town cemetery. Warm, with a slight breeze bearing the strong scents of honeysuckle and pine.

"Are you ready for this?" Dad asked for the fifth time in the last half hour.

"I guess," Tick replied, tugging at the scarf around

his neck, in no mood to offer any smart-aleck response. He felt like he should have done more to prepare, but there was nothing he could think of to *do*. The only real instruction he'd been given in the Twelve Clues was to show up and do a couple of ridiculous cartoon actions.

He did have a backpack full of warm clothing, some granola bars and water, a flashlight, some matches, and—most important—his *Journal of Curious Letters*. He didn't know if he'd be stranded somewhere and suddenly realize he needed to search for clues he'd missed before. Or maybe he needed it to enter the realm of Master George—kind of like a ticket.

Tick was as ready as he possibly could be. He looked at his dad, who seemed ten times more nervous than Tick did, wringing his hands, rocking back and forth on his feet, sweat pouring off his face. "Dad, are you okay?"

"No." He didn't offer anything else.

"Well . . . there's nothing to worry about. I mean, it's not like I'm going off to war or something. Mothball and Rutger will probably *be* there in the cemetery waiting for me. I'll be fine."

"How do you know?" Dad asked, almost in a whisper.

"How do I know what?"

"That you're not going off to war?"

"I . . . I don't know." Tick couldn't *believe* how the minutes dragged by.

"*Many lives are at stake.* That's what the man said, right?"

His dad's voice shook, worrying Tick. But he had no idea what to say. "I promise I'll come back, Dad. No matter what, I promise to come back."

"I don't know what scares me more," Dad said. "Letting you run off on your adventure or knowing I have to somehow tell your mom tonight that you may not come back for a while. Can you imagine how much that woman's going to *worry*? I may be strung up on a pole when you return."

"Dad, how long have you guys been married?"

"Almost twenty years. Why?"

"Don't you think she trusts you?"

"Well . . . yeah. What are you, a psychologist now?"

Tick shrugged. "No, I just think Mom will understand, that's all. She's always taught me right from wrong, hasn't she? And to make sacrifices for other people—to *serve* other people. I'm just obeying orders, right?"

His dad shook his head in mock disbelief. "Professor, I can't *believe* you're only thirteen years old."

"Thirteen and a half."

His dad barked a laugh, then pulled Tick into a hug, squeezing him tight. "You better be off now, son. Don't want to take any chances of being late, now do you?"

"Nope." Tick returned the hug, trying to fight off tears.

"I love you, Atticus. I'm so proud of what you're doing." His dad pulled back, still holding Tick by both shoulders as he looked into his eyes. "You go and make the Higginbottom family proud, okay? You go out there and fight for what's right, and fight for those who need your help."

"I love you, too, Dad," Tick said, hating how simple and stupid it sounded, but feeling the truth of it in his heart. They hugged again, for a very long minute.

Finally, without any need for additional words, Tick turned from his dad, walked down the stairs of the porch, waved one last time, then headed for his destiny.

He only wished he knew what it was.

⁓

Yeah, right, Edgar thought as Tick disappeared down the dark road. *Like I'm going to let my only son run off to who-knows-what all alone.*

Edgar turned and hurried back inside where he grabbed the flashlight and binoculars he'd hidden in the closet. Though he really did believe in the whole Master George affair, he was also a father, and he couldn't just let Tick go on his adventure without a little . . . supervision. After all, the clues hadn't banned anyone from being *near* the cemetery, now had they?

"Honey, Tick and I are going for a walk!" he yelled upstairs.

"This late?" her muffled voice called from the bedroom. "Why?"

"Don't worry . . . I'll explain everything when we get back!" He groaned at the prospect.

Before she could reply, Edgar was out the front door and down the porch steps. He'd have to be quick if he wanted to keep up with Tick.

One thing, Edgar vowed as he walked down the driveway. *I see one suspicious thing and I'm ending this.*

By the time Tick reached the forest-lined road that led to town, the sun had made its last glimmer upon the world and gone to bed for the night. Now past eight o'clock, darkness settled on the town of Deer Park, Washington, and Tick felt himself shiver despite the warm and comfortable air.

He couldn't believe it was here. The Big Day. The Big *Night*.

As he walked down the lonely road, the constant buzz of the forest insects broken only occasionally by a passing car, he ran through everything he needed to do in his mind. Even though it seemed so simple, he knew he only had one shot at this and didn't want to mess everything up. Dual feelings of excitement and apprehension battled over his emotional state, making him nauseated and anxious for it to be over, one way or another.

He arrived at the town square and passed the fountain area, where the shooting display of water had been turned off for the night, and made his way down the small one-way lane that led to the old city cemetery. A few people walked about the square, but it mostly seemed vacant and silent, like a premonition that something very bad was about to happen to this quiet and unassuming town.

Quit freaking yourself out, Tick told himself. *Everything's going to be fine.*

The entrance to the Deer Park Cemetery was a simple stone archway, both sides connected to a cast-iron fence encircling the entire compound. There was no gate, as though those in charge figured if some psycho wanted to visit dead people in the middle of the night, more power to them. As for grave digging, that had gone out of style with Dr. Frankenstein a couple of hundred years ago.

Tick paused below the chipped granite of the arch and looked at his watch, clicking the little light button on the side to see the big digital numbers: 8:37. Just over twenty minutes to go.

The moon, almost full, finally slipped above the horizon, casting a pale radiance upon the hundreds of old-fashioned tombstones; they seemed to glow in the dark around the chiseled letters declaring the names and dates of the dead. Barely defined shadows littered the ground, like holes had opened up throughout the graveyard, zombies having escaped to wreak their nightly havoc.

Once again, Tick shivered. No doubt about it, this was plain creepy.

Hoping it didn't matter exactly *where* he stood when he performed his little song and dance as long as he was inside the cemetery, Tick stayed close to the entrance, near a tight pack of graves reserved for young children. Tick pulled out his flashlight and flicked it on, examining some of the names while he waited for the last few minutes to pass. Most of the names he didn't know, but he did recognize a few that had been much-publicized tragedies over the last few years. A car accident. Cancer.

Despite his youth, Tick knew there must be nothing in the world so bad as losing one of your kids. Like he'd just swallowed a bag of sand, it hit him then that if anything happened to him tonight, his mom would be devastated. His poor mom. Of course, she'd be so busy yelling at his dad for letting him go in the first place that maybe she wouldn't have the time or energy to hurt properly.

He turned off his flashlight and returned it to his

bag. He pulled out the jacket and gloves and put them on, not wanting to take any chances that the instructions to dress warmly had been anything but literal. He tightened his scarf and glanced at his watch. He could see the numbers perfectly in the moonlight.

Five minutes to go.

He put his backpack on the ground, then thought better of it, swinging it back onto his shoulders. If he were about to magically travel somewhere, much better to have everything . . . *attached*.

For the millionth time, he wondered which was stranger—the things he'd been through or the fact that he actually believed there was something *true* behind it all. That he wasn't crazy.

One minute to go.

Tick stared at his watch now, clicking the button that made it show the ticking seconds as well as the hour and minute. As the appointed time grew closer and closer, his heart picked up; sweat beaded all over his body; he felt himself on the verge of throwing up.

Ten seconds.

He quickly put his hands deep into the pockets of his jeans, counting down the last few seconds inside his mind.

Five . . . four . . . three . . . two . . . one . . .

Tick closed his eyes and shouted out the words, "MASTER GEORGE!" He stomped the ground below him ten times with his right foot and a quick and cold shiver of excitement went up and down his back.

Tick waited, holding his breath for a long minute. He finally opened his eyes and looked around, but saw that he stood in the exact same spot as when he began. Everything was the same. He waited longer still, hoping something would change around him. Several more minutes passed. Then a half hour. Then an hour. Then two. Desperate, he went through the entire ritual again.

Nothing happened.

Absolutely nothing.

CHAPTER 37

A FAMILIAR NAME

Knowing for a fact he'd never felt so depressed in all his life, Tick began the long walk back home. He wished he had a cell phone so he could prevent his dad from telling his mom about everything—now that it was all moot. Now that Tick had failed, and wouldn't be going anywhere after all. At least then he could enjoy the one saving grace of Mom not thinking her husband and only son had gone bonkers.

If the town had been quiet before, it now seemed completely devoid of any life whatsoever. Tick didn't see one person as he walked past the fountain area, and there wasn't a light to be seen anywhere. Even the street-lamps had been extinguished, or they'd burned out.

Only the moon shone its pale milky brilliance around the square, making everything look like a much bigger version of the graveyard he'd just left.

Dead and quiet. Full of shadows.

Tick picked up his pace.

When he left the town behind him and started down the long road leading to his house, the creepiness increased. He couldn't explain it, but Tick felt a constant chill in his bones, like something very big and very hungry watched him from the woods. He looked back and forth, scanning both sides of the road, but saw only the tall shadows of the trees, black on black. This time, Tick threw all reservations out the window and simply ran, resolving not to stop until he lay in his bed where he could cry himself to sleep.

As he jostled down the road, concentrating on his feet so he wouldn't trip, Tick had to consciously ignore the feeling that an enormous ghost was right behind him, ready to tap him on the shoulder. Goose bumps broke out all over his body, slick with sweat. He kept running.

He made it to his neighborhood and finally to his house, not slowing until he reached the porch. He stopped, bending over with his hands on his knees as he gulped in air to catch his breath. He didn't want to walk back inside panting like a chased dog. But then the feeling he'd had near the forest returned full force and he ran up the steps to the front door.

The handle rattled when he gripped it, but didn't turn. Locked. He glanced at his watch where he could barely see it was just past eleven o'clock. Tick stepped back, looking for the first time at all the windows on the bottom floor. He should've noticed before—everything was dark, not a single light was on in the house. Yes, it was late, but his dad was supposed to be telling a very long story to his mom, so surely his parents were still up. They would stay up and watch for him, wouldn't they?

Tick knew his dad kept a spare key to the house hidden in a fake rock placed behind the bushes. He walked back down the porch steps and searched for it, even getting down on his knees to feel around with his hands. But they came up empty, even after scouring the usual area several times.

He couldn't find the key anywhere.

Tick sat back on his heels. *What in the world?*

Frustrated, Tick gave up and walked back to the front door, where he reluctantly pushed the doorbell.

A long moment passed. No one answered. Not a sound came from within the house. Tick, getting more worried by the second, pushed the doorbell again.

Still no response.

Finally, in a panic, he pushed the bell over and over again, hearing the loud ring through the wood of the door. He stopped when he heard a booming shout;

it sounded like it came from one of the upstairs bed-rooms. The shout was followed by a quick series of loud thumps—someone running down the stairs. Then the door jerked open, revealing a man Tick had never seen before in his life.

"What do you want!" the stranger screamed at the top of his lungs, spittle flying out of his mouth. The man was pale and sickly, so thin he looked like he'd crumble into a pile of sticks at any moment. His ruffled black hair stood up in patches on his head, his face covered in a scraggly beard. Dark, sleep-worn eyes stared at Tick, full of fire and anger. "Who are *you*, you little brat? What do you want?"

Tick felt a sick fear swell inside his stomach. "I'm . . . I'm . . . Atticus Higginbottom. I . . . I live here."

"*Live* here? What are you, one of those no-good townies? Get out of here!" The man kicked out, miss-ing Tick badly. "Get!" He slammed the door closed.

Tick, his world crashing down around him, turned and ran, the darkness weighing on his shoulders like black stone.

⁓

Edgar stood in the dark cemetery, his chest rising and falling with heavy breaths. He'd searched everywhere—behind every tombstone, tree, and bush in sight. He didn't know how it could be possible, but what he'd seen from his hiding spot across the road must not have been a trick of his mind.

It had really happened.

What he'd seen had *really* happened.

Tick had disappeared. Like a Las Vegas magic show, Edgar's only son had vanished from sight. There one second, gone the next. No smoke, no sound, nothing.

His son had *disappeared*.

Panicked, Edgar started searching all over again, even though he knew it was useless. Deep down inside, he tried to convince himself Tick was okay, that they'd known something like this would happen. This was what they'd been preparing for all along! Edgar told himself that Tick was safe now, in some other world or realm, learning how he could help save the lives that were depending on him. Where had all the good feelings about this whole mess gone to? He and Tick had devoted themselves to this cause, believing in its purpose.

But it hadn't seemed real until the moment he'd seen his son vanish. And now Edgar didn't know if he could ever forgive himself for letting Tick go. If something happened to his boy . . .

Dejected, a sinking weight of despair filling his stomach, Edgar finally gave up and headed for home. He was about to have a very long night explaining things to his wife.

Tick didn't know what else to do—where else to go—except back to the cemetery. Something *must* have happened when he'd performed the ritual—something horrible. He'd messed it up somehow, sending him to the wrong place or time. He thought back to the crazy things Mr. Chu had told him about quantum physics. Where *was* he?

Once he left his neighborhood, he couldn't run another step. He slowed to a walk, breathing heavily, constantly looking behind to make sure no one was following him—especially the creepy man who'd answered the door at his house.

It was a weird feeling to suddenly feel like the only place you've ever lived is no longer yours, occupied instead by some monster of a man willing to kick a little kid. Tick had run the gamut of emotions in the last hour— excitement that the special day was here, disappointment when seemingly nothing had happened, dejection and despair, panic and fear that his home wasn't his home anymore. Now he just felt numb as he slowly made his way back to town. To the cemetery. It was the only place where he could hope to find some answers.

He tried to take in his surroundings as he walked, searching for signs that other things about his home-town were different than what he was used to. But the darkness was too great and all he saw were shadows hiding other shadows. He almost pulled out his flashlight, but thought better of it—who knew what lurked in this new nightmare. He wanted to remain as hidden as possible.

As he entered the town square for the third time that night, he realized the lack of lights couldn't be a coincidence—the place was a haven for nothing but ghosts and ghouls. Where was he? What had happened to this place that should feel so familiar but instead seemed so alien? His heart hurting, his body exhausted, Tick picked up the pace again and quickly ran across the waterless fountain area and down the small road until he reached the entrance to the cemetery.

He didn't know how he'd missed it before, but Tick saw that more than half of one side of the stone archway had crumbled and fallen to the ground into a pile of dusty rubble. Dozens of rods from the iron fence were missing or bent, looking like the mangled teeth of a horrific robot. The moon vanished entirely behind a large bank of clouds, casting everything into sinister shadows. The tombstones seemed bigger, less defined, leaning at odd angles.

Tick rubbed his hands over his arms, standing in the same place where he'd performed the magic-words-

and-foot-stomping ritual. He finally realized what he was feeling.

Terror. Absolute, shrill, make-your-hair-stand-on-end terror.

Out of the corner of his eye, he saw a light come on.

He sucked in a quick intake of air as he turned to see a small spotlight shining on a single tombstone, about thirty yards deeper into the cemetery grounds. Compared to the heavy darkness around him, it seemed like the sun itself had changed its mind and come back for a nighttime visit. Realizing he hadn't seen a spark of electricity since leaving for his house and returning, Tick felt like he was witnessing some kind of magic trick.

Curious, he walked toward the light, ignoring the fear constricting his chest.

He stepped around several large graves, almost tripping on a stone border around a particularly wide one. He kept his eyes riveted on the bright spot, scared it might be a trap, but not knowing where else to go. As he got closer, he saw that the light came from a large flashlight, sitting alone in front of a grave. He looked around the area, squinting his eyes to see if any monsters or zombies were hiding in the shadows, readying themselves to jump out and eat him.

The light hurt his vision, and he knew if someone was out there, he wouldn't be able to see them.

He focused on the brightly displayed tombstone, now close enough that he could read the etched words, dusty indentations on an old black-gray slab of granite.

> **HERE LIES**
>
> **ATTICUS HIGGINBOTTOM**
>
> **BELOVED SON OF EDGAR AND LORENA**
>
> **GOD REST HIS SOUL**

Everything in his mind immediately vanished, all fear and thoughts washed away in the disbelief of what he saw before him. Tick fell to his knees, unable to take his eyes away from the words on the grave marker.

Tick looked at the dates.

According to the tombstone, he'd been dead for three years.

CHAPTER 38

SITTING DOWN

Before Tick could completely process the fact he was looking at his own grave, he heard a noise behind him. He twisted around, still on his knees, and for a split second thought he saw the reincarnation of Frankenstein's Monster. A scream formed in the back of Tick's throat. But it quickly fell mute when he realized the figure was someone very familiar, standing just a few feet away, towering over him.

Mothball.

Tick quickly stood up, relieved to see a familiar face, the questions flying out of his mouth before he had his feet under him. "Mothball, what's happening? Where am I? How did—"

The tall woman held up a hand. "Best the little sir keep quiet for a moment, let yer tall friend do the talkin' for a bit." She stepped forward and bent over to pick up her flashlight, grunting with the effort. "Not every day ya get to see yer own tombstone, now is it? Downright spooky, it is."

"Mothball, what's going on?" Tick felt tears forming in his eyes now that the initial shock of seeing his name on the granite slab had settled into a stark reality.

"What's going on?" Mothball repeated. "I'll tell ya what's going on. The little sir did it, he did. Solved Master George's riddles, made it quite nicely. Got lots of learnin' to do now, ya do. Hope yer mind's still got some empty spots."

Tick couldn't shake the sick feeling in his stomach. "Mothball, why does this grave have my name on it? Who's that crazy guy living in my house? Where is my family?" His voice broke on that last word, and he suddenly wondered if he really wanted to know the answer.

"One question at a time, if yer wantin' any answers." She pointed down at the tombstone. "There's a fine reason that there piece of rock has yer name on it." She paused. "Yer dead here, little sir. Dead as a mouse that's got no heart, you are. Smell worse than Rutger's feet I'd wager." She offered Tick a smile, but he was in no mood to laugh.

"What are you talking about? How can I be . . . dead? I'm standing here talking to you."

"I take it back, then. Yer *Alterant* is dead—that's what I meant." Mothball sighed and fidgeted, looking as uncomfortable as a vampire in a cathedral.

"An Alter-what? Mothball, *please* just tell me what's going on."

Mothball stepped closer to Tick, put one of her huge arms around his shoulder. Her flashlight was pointed at the ground, but it still illuminated her face enough to show creases of concern in her temples and brow, her eyes full of something indescribable—sorrow or compassion. "Perk yer ears, Master Tick, methinks I need to tell ya something."

Tick stared up at her, waiting. "What is it?"

"Life's a bit harder than you've ever known, it is. *Different*, too. When ya finally meet Master George, yer going to learn things that'd be a mighty bit hard for a grown-up to hear, much less a young'un like yourself. How it all works—the whys and hows and whatnot—better be leaving to me boss, I will. But I can tell ya one thing before we shove off." She paused, looking away from Tick into the darkness of the graveyard.

"Yeah?" Tick prodded.

"This . . . place. If things had been different for you, Tick—if different choices had been chosen, different paths taken—well, that really could be yer little self under this here pile of dirt. This version of the world is fragmented, as Master George calls it. It's weak, splintering, *fading*. All words I don't use much, I'll admit it. But we wanted ya to see it, to feel what it's like to see yer own self dead as a stump."

Tick shook his head. "But I don't get it, Mothball. Are you saying this is another version of our world? That I did something here that ended up with me dead?"

"No, no, no, you've got it all wrong. I'm not saying yer dead because of anything ya did directly—at least, not for sure. Probably never know, we will." She took her arm away, throwing it up in the air, frustrated. "Oh, this is rubbish—need to get a move on, we do."

"Wait!" Tick reached out and grabbed Mothball's shirt. "What about my family. Are they okay?"

Mothball knelt down on the ground, bringing her eyes level with Tick's. "They're right as rain, little sir. You don't have to worry about them at'all. See what I'm tryin' to tell ya is that the choices we make in this life can lead to things we'd never s'pect to have anything to do with us. Realities can be created and destroyed." She gestured with her head to Tick's tombstone. "That little feller might ruddy well be you for sure, he could. But ya just might have the power within yer beatin' heart to make sure it doesn't happen. That's what it's all about, really."

Some of Tick's anxiety and fear had vanished. Though he didn't have a clue what Mothball was talking about, he felt . . . *moved*, which made him feel very adult. "Mothball, when do I get to actually understand what it is you're talking about?"

Mothball smiled as she stood back on her feet. "Not much for speeches, I'll admit it. By the looks of it, you'd rather listen to a croakin' toad than hear me go on a bit. Righto, off we go." She moved away from the tombstone and walked deeper into the scattered graves of the cemetery, the beam of her flashlight bobbing up and down with each step.

Tick fell in line behind her, having to take two steps for every one of hers, adjusting his scarf and backpack as he went. "When you say 'off we go,' where exactly are we off-we-going *to*?"

"Ah, Master Tick," she said over her shoulder, "glad we got the bologna-and-cheese talk out the way, I am. Now's time for the fun part. Hope yer excited."

"I am, trust me. Anything to get away from this place."

Mothball laughed, a booming chuckle that seemed sure to wake up a few dead people. "Don't like the deadies, do ya? That'll change, it will. Most times it takes a place like this to go off winking, it does."

"Winking? What's that?"

"Find out soon enough, ya will. Ah, here we are." Mothball stopped, then turned around to face Tick. She shone her flashlight on a small patch of unmarked grass.

"Have a nice sit-down, we will." When Tick didn't move, she gestured for him to sit. "Right here, chop-chop."

"Why do we have to sit down?" Tick asked as he sat cross-legged in the exact spot where she'd shone the light.

Mothball sat across from him, folding up her huge legs underneath her. "No offense, lad, but methinks I've had enough of yer questions for now. Save them for Master George, and we'll all be a mite happier indeed."

Tick knew something amazing was about to happen, and his insides swelled with butterflies, like the last moment before a roller coaster shoots down its first gigantic hill. "Whatever you say, Mothball. I'll shut up."

"Now there's a line I'd wish old Rutger'd learn to say. That wee little fat man could talk the ears off a mammoth, he could."

Tick laughed, but didn't say anything, keeping his promise.

"All right, that about does it, I'd say," Mothball said to herself as she settled her body, growing still. "Just keep yourself nice and comfy there, lad, and good old Master George will wink us away any minute."

There was that word again. *Wink.* Tick almost asked about it, but kept quiet, nervously pulling on his scarf.

"Feel a little tingle on yer neck and back, you will," Mothball whispered. "Things'll change then, right quick. Try to keep yer pants on straight and don't go screamin' like a baby or you might just drown. Come to an understanding, have we?"

Tick nodded, his thrill of anticipation suddenly turning a little sour. *Drown?*

Before he could dwell on what she meant, he felt cold pinpricks along the back of his spine, a quick wave that he might not have noticed if he hadn't been waiting for it.

Then, as promised, everything changed.

In less time than it took to form a single conscious thought, Tick found himself thousands of miles from the graveyard. He sat in the same position as before, but now he was sitting inside a small raft, bobbing up and down in the middle of a dark and choppy sea of black water.

And it was raining.

CHAPTER 39

A LOT OF WATER

Nothing happened to mark their transportation from one place to another. No booming alarm, no bright flash of light, no movement of any kind. Tick and Mothball simply went from sitting across from each other on a small patch of grass in the middle of a cemetery to sitting across from each other on a raft in the middle of the ocean.

Heavy, cold rain fell from a sky Tick couldn't see, pelting his entire body, sluicing down the inward sides of the small boat and forming a standing pool of water. Mothball still had her flashlight fully ablaze; the light cast an eerie cone of radiance revealing countless pellets of rain and a small circle of angrily churning waters just a few feet from where they floated. The raft rocked back and forth, up and down, already making Tick's stomach ill.

Mothball shifted her body until she was on her knees, then shone the flashlight somewhere behind her. Tick leaned to his right to catch a glimpse of what she was looking at and saw a huge structure floating nearby, rigid and unmoved by the uneasy sea. He couldn't make out much as Mothball scanned the area with her light, but it appeared to be a building of some sort, a huge square made out of silvery metal walls, rivets and bolts scattered all over its slick and shiny surface. It seemed impossible that it could be a large boat or ship. It was just there, solid, like its foundation went all the way to the ocean bottom.

"Won't be but a moment!" Mothball yelled over her shoulder, working at something with her large arms and hands.

"Where are we?" Tick screamed back, several drops of heavy rain flying into his mouth, almost gagging him.

Mothball turned and looked at him, her hair and face soaked. "Middle of the ocean, we are!"

"Thanks a lot—figured that one out on my own!" Tick slicked his rain-soaked hair out of his eyes.

Instead of replying, Mothball set her right foot against the edge of the raft and pulled on something, grunting with the effort. After a second of hesitation, a bright light suddenly flared against the darkness of the storm, accompanied by the heavy groan of bending metal and the scrape of rusty hinges. Mothball had opened an enormous door of solid steel that led inside the boxy structure. Tick caught a glimpse of a long hallway lined with cables and wiring and thick ductwork.

"Made it, you did!" Mothball yelled into his ear as she grabbed him by the shoulders, helping him across the unstable raft and toward the opening. "You'll be speaking directly with Master George in a moment. Up ya go!" With a playful roar she picked Tick up and halfthrew him through the open doorway.

He landed with a squishy flump, scrambling to stand up. Every inch of his body drenched, Tick rubbed at his arms, shivering from the uncomfortable, cold feeling of wearing wet clothes. His scarf drooped off his neck, soggy and seeming like it weighed a hundred pounds. He swung his backpack off his shoulders and placed it on the metal grid that made up the hallway floor.

Mothball crawled inside and closed the heavy door behind her. It slammed shut with a loud boom that rattled the entire structure. "Nasty business, that," she muttered as she climbed to her feet, stooping to avoid hitting her head on the low obstacles that ran along the ceiling. "Don't you worry, Master George is sure to have a roaring fire lit. Come on, now."

She started down the hallway and Tick followed,

barely able to contain his anticipation of meeting the man behind all the mystery.

Mothball rounded a corner and came upon a stout wooden door. Tick thought it seemed out of place inside a huge metal box floating on the ocean. She paused, then rapped three times with her large knuckles. "Got the last one, I did!" she yelled through the dark oak.

Muffled footsteps sounded from the other side, then the click of a latch. The door swung wide open and Tick's five senses almost crashed and burned trying to take in everything at once.

Beyond the open doorway was an enormous room that looked like it had been plucked out of an ancient king's castle and magically transported inside the metal building. Fancy, fluffy, *comfortable*-looking furniture sat atop lush carpets and rugs; the walls were covered in dark wooden bookshelves, complete with hundreds of leather-bound books; a massive brick fireplace cast a warm and flickering glow upon the whole room as the fire within it roared and crackled and spit. Several people were in the room, scattered amongst the plush furniture.

Tick recognized Sofia at once, sitting on an over-stuffed chair next to the fire; when their eyes met, she stood and waved. Next to her was a couch where a tall, dark-skinned boy sat, grinning from ear to ear. That had to be Paul. An Asian boy sat next to him, short dark hair framing his angry, scrunched-up face. Tick thought he looked like he'd just been told he hadn't passed a single one of his classes at school. Rutger was there, too, his little round body perched atop a pile of cushions. He leaned back, clasping his stubby hands behind his head like he owned the place.

And finally, standing by the door, his hand still on the inside handle, was a man dressed in the fanciest suit Tick had ever seen, black and pinstriped, a long golden chain marking where his pocket watch hid for the moment. His face was puffy and red, like he'd just walked ten miles through a freezing wind. A round pair of glasses perched on his nose, making his dark eyes seem two times bigger than they were. His balding scalp was red and slightly flaky. Tick thought he looked a little odd and a little anxious, but somehow nice all the same.

"Master George?" he said, wincing when it came out more as a croaky whisper than anything else.

The man smiled, revealing slightly crooked teeth. "Indeed, my good man. Master George, at your service." He bowed his head and held out a hand, which Tick accepted and shook, his confidence and ease growing by the second.

"Nice to meet you," Tick said, remembering his manners.

"Likewise, boy, likewise." He stepped back and swept

his arm in a wide gesture, as if revealing the warm room as the grand prize on a game show. "Welcome to our first meeting with new members in more than twenty years."

"Members?" Tick asked.

"Why, yes, old chap—or, should I say, *young* chap?" Master George chuckled, then turned it into a cough when no one else laughed. "Ah, yes, well—welcome to your future, my dear boy. Welcome to the Realitant Headquarters."

Tick entered the room, knowing he would never, ever be the same.

CHAPTER 40

MASTER GEORGE

"Have a sit-down," Master George said as he ushered Tick toward a chair between the fire and where Rutger rested on top of his pile of cushions. "The fire should dry your clothing in no time. We're simply delighted you could make it. We were beginning to worry a bit. The rest of these poor chaps had to listen to Rutger's interminable stories and recollections all day—quite a tasking thing to do, I assure you." He winked at Tick as he gestured for him to sit.

Tick sat down with a squish, looking over at Sofia. She waved again, then shrugged her shoulders as if to say, "What in the world have we gotten ourselves into?" Tick smiled back at her, wishing they could talk, but it seemed as though their host had a specific agenda and was eager to begin.

Master George stepped in front of the blazing fire, rubbing his hands together as he took in each person there with a lingering gaze. "We've got quite a lot to do in the next few hours, and more explaining than I daresay I look forward to. I haven't the faintest idea where to start." He pulled out a silk handkerchief and wiped his brow. "Look at that, would you? Already sweating and I've yet to say anything of importance."

"Maybe that's because you're standing in front of a *fire*," Rutger quipped, the simple effort of talking throwing his balance off. He tumbled off the pillows and flopped to the floor. "Ouch."

"'Tis going to be a long night, it is," Mothball muttered from where she stood in the back, arms folded.

"Rutger, *behave* yourself," Master George commanded, his face reddening for just a second before he replaced his irritation with a forced smile. "Now, let us begin, shall we? First things first—a quick go around the room for introductions." He motioned to Sofia. "Ladies first?"

"Okay," she said, seemingly pleased by the attention. She stood up and waved at everyone staring at her. "My name is Sofia Pacini, and I'm from Italy. I'm almost thirteen years old, and my family is famous for making spaghetti and several sauces. It's the best in the world, and if you haven't heard of us, you've got real problems." She looked at Master George. "Anything else?"

"Oh, no, that's very nice, thank you very much. Next?" He motioned with his eyes to the boy who must be Paul.

"Uh, yeah . . . do I really have to stand up?"

Master George said nothing, but shook his head.

"Great. My name is Paul Rogers, and I'm from the U.S. of A.—Florida to be exact. I've been chatting with Sofia and Tick on the Internet, so it's good to finally see you guys in person. I love surfing and playing the piano. I don't have a clue why I'm here, but I'm busting to find out. Oh, and I'm fourteen years old—way older than these kids." He pointed at Tick and Sofia.

"A delight, Paul, thank you. Mister Sato?" Master George nodded toward the Asian boy sitting next to Paul.

"I will say nothing," the boy answered in a curt voice, folding his arms for dramatic effect.

"Pardon me?" Master George asked, then exchanged looks with Mothball and Rutger. Something about his expression told Tick that Sato's actions weren't exactly a surprise.

"I trust no one," Sato replied. He looked around the room, pointing at each person in turn. "Not you, not you, not you, none of you. Until I know everything, I will say nothing." He nodded as if proud of himself for being such a jerk.

Tick glanced at Sofia, who made a pig face, pushing her nose up with her index finger and sticking out her tongue. Tick had to cover his mouth to keep from laughing out loud.

"Well," Master George struggled for words, "that's . . . splendid." He rubbed his hands together again. "I believe we all know my trusted friends Mothball and Rutger quite well by now, so Mister Higginbottom, please—tell us a bit about yourself before we begin our very long discussion."

Tick shifted in his seat. "Uh, yeah, I'm Atticus Higginbottom, but everyone calls me Tick. I'm from the east side of Washington state, I'm thirteen years old, I like science and chess"—he winced inside at how nerdy that made him sound—"and I'm excited to find out why we've been . . . brought here."

"Amen," Paul chimed in.

"You better talk fast," Sato said. "I want to know right now why you kidnapped me and brought me here."

"Kidnap?" Mothball asked, almost spitting. "What, left yer brain in Japan, 'ave you?"

"I only followed the instructions out of curiosity. Then you kidnapped me. I demand to be taken home."

What a jerk. He's going to ruin everything, Tick

thought. He looked at Sofia and rolled his eyes. She nodded, frowning in Sato's direction.

"Well, then," Master George said, his enthusiasm dampened. "Jolly good beginning this is."

"Just ignore the kid," Rutger said to Master George. He turned toward the disgruntled Japanese boy. "Sato, hear him out. If you don't like it, we'll send you right back where you came from. Now stick a sock in it."

Sato's face reddened, but he didn't say anything, huffing as he leaned back in his seat.

"And on that note," Master George said, trying his best to regain his composure, smiling broadly. "We shall begin. Rutger, would you please bring some victuals from the pantry? These good people must be famished."

Paul clapped loudly and whistled. Sofia, then Tick, joined him.

Master George waited until Rutger had scuttled out a side door. "Let me begin by saying how proud each of you should be of your accomplishment of simply being here today. I sent letters to hundreds of young people, and you four are the only ones who made it this far. Quite an accomplishment indeed. Especially considering the dreadful things I sent to test your mettle."

Tick perked up at this, remembering his conversation with Mothball and Rutger about how sorry Master

George had been about the Alaska incident, which made it seem like he *wasn't* as sorry about the other scary things that had happened—like the Gnat Rat and the Tingle Wraith. "You mean . . ." Tick began, but then stopped, wondering if he was out of line.

"Yes, Mister Higginbottom," Master George answered, seemingly not bothered by the interruption. "It was I, er, *we* who sent some of the things that must've scared you greatly. Objects like the Gnat Rat and Tingle Wraith are much easier to wink to and fro than humans, fortunately. But none of them could or would have hurt you beyond any easy repair, mind you. But the man in Alaska—the one sent by Mistress Jane—now that was an entirely different affair, I assure you. I do apologize for that bit of trouble."

"Wait a minute," Paul said. "Mothball here told me my brain would turn to mush if I heard the Tingle Wraith's Death Siren for more than thirty seconds."

"A slight exaggeration on her part," Master George answered with a look of chagrin. "Because of your still-developing brains, you would've recovered in no more than three or four weeks—albeit with a lingering headache and blurred vision. And a certain bodily odor we can't quite figure out . . ."

"*You* sent those awful things to attack us?" Sofia asked. "But why?"

"Yeah, man," Paul chimed in. "That's just not right."

"Finally," Sato said. "You people are starting to see why I am so angry."

"Why would you want to hurt us?" Tick asked, glaring at Master George, sudden confusion and hurt constricting his chest.

Paul's face looked like someone had just kicked him in both shins. "Dude, how can we trust you now?"

"Now please," Master George pleaded, holding up both hands in front of him. "We haven't even been about our business yet, and already we lose our focus!" His voice rose with every word. "Must I treat you like children? Are you no different from the hundreds who didn't make it nearly as far as you? If so, you may all leave this instant! If you can't handle a couple of cheap tricks like the Gnat Rat, then you've no place being here!"

Tick stared at Master George, surprised he could change from a nice old Englishman to an angry ogre so quickly. The others seemed as dead silent and awestruck as he felt.

"This is no *game*," Master George continued, his face more flushed than before, though Tick would've thought it impossible. "Everything I've done was meant to bring to me the strongest, the bravest, the cleverest. I let no excuses lie on the table—none at all. If you couldn't persuade your mum and dad to let you come, then you'd be off. If you couldn't bring yourself to follow such silly instructions, then you'd be off. If you let a little thing like two days of horrendous bee stings bother you, then you'd be off. Now, you're here and I'm ready to begin instruction. Have I made a *mistake?*"

Master George shouted the last word, folding his arms and staring around the room, daring someone to respond. A full minute passed, the crackling fire the only sound in the room. Even Sato seemed impressed. Tick felt scared to swallow or breathe, afraid of how Master George would take it.

"All right, then," the Englishman finally said. "If from this point forward you'd be so kind as to act like the brave souls I meant to gather, we can move on." He paused, pretending to brush unseen dust off his suit jacket. "Now, you may be wondering why I sent letters only to young people such as yourself. Am I correct?"

No one said a word, afraid to rock the boat again.

"Come on, now," Master George said. "Only *children* would be afraid to speak up."

Everyone spoke at once at this remark, but Paul drowned out the others. "Never thought about it, actually. But now you mention it, that's a good question that I think I'd like to know the answer to very much. Uh, sir. Master." He cleared his throat. "Master George."

"Much better, much better. I knew you blokes from America were smart. Now—"

He was interrupted by a loud noise from the side.

Rutger shuffled through the door balancing two silver trays stacked with enormous plates of steaming hot food in his arms.

"Who's hungry?" he announced loudly. "I've prepared generous portions for everyone." Wonderful smells wafted across the room.

He started handing out plates and utensils, almost dropping the entire load with every step. "We've got roasted duck, thrice-baked potatoes, succulent legs of lamb with basil and—my favorite—roast beef. Plus a slice of cherry cheesecake." Panting, he put down a plate for himself then handed the last one to Tick. "Eat up!"

Tick needed no urging. After a quickly muttered thank you, he dug in as he balanced the plate on his lap. The food was tender and hot, juicy and rich. It may have been his hunger, but everything on the plate seemed the most delicious stuff he'd ever put in his mouth. By the sounds of smacking lips and slurping fingers from around the room, he wasn't alone in that regard.

"Well," Master George said, "I'm glad to see we still have our appetites. Now, if I may, I will continue our discussion. About the letters—the reason I wrote only to youngsters is because what you're about to hear would never be believed by a cantankerous old grownup. They're far too set in their ways, thinking they're all smart and such. No, I needed to bring in a new batch of recruits, and I knew they must be young and spry, ready to take on the world, as it were."

"Uh, Master George?" Rutger said through a large mouthful of food.

"Yes, Rutger?"

"Don't you think we should, uh, move on and tell them *why* they're here? Time's a wasting."

Master George snapped his fingers and waved his hands in the air. "Yes, yes, you're right, of course. Thank you, on we go." He folded his hands in front of him and looked down at the floor. "I shall now tell you everything, from beginning to end."

And so Master George began his story, the craziest, wackiest, most bizarre thing Tick had ever heard. And he loved every minute of it.

CHAPTER 41

THE TALE OF
THE REALITIES

What each of you considers the world in which you have always lived and breathed," Master George began, "is not exactly what you may think. It is in fact much, much more. Your world, the place where you were born, is what we call Reality Prime. It is the first and greatest version of the universe with which you are familiar. However, several decades ago, a group of scientists discovered great mysteries in the field of study we affectionately call the *kyoopy*."

Kyoopy! Tick thought. *The Q.P.! Quantum physics.*

"Now," Master George continued, "we haven't the time or need to explore the deep scientific mumbo-jumbo, but suffice it to say the scientists discovered that alternate versions of the universe exist in harmony and congruity with the world in which we grew up. The reality we all know so well is not alone—there are *other* Realities. Parallel universes that have evolved and developed differently from Reality Prime because of vastly significant events that literally broke them apart from ours."

"Master George," Paul interrupted. "I consider myself one smart dude, but this seems crazy."

Just let him talk, Tick thought as he took his last bite. He set the empty plate on the floor at his feet.

"Don't worry, Mister Rogers. Give me time, and all will become as clear as my mum's fine crystal."

"Sounds like a bunch of lies so far," Sato said, almost under his breath, but loud enough for everyone to hear.

Master George ignored him. "There is an energy force in the universe that binds and controls all the Realities, a greater force than any the laws of physics have ever attempted to define. This power is the lifeblood of the kyoopy, and only a handful of scientists even knows it exists. We call this power the Chi'karda, and everything we'll be about depends on it. Everything."

"What is it?" Tick asked, remembering that Mothball had once said the word to him.

"Rutger?" Master George asked. "What do I always say about the Chi'karda?"

Everyone turned to look at the short man, lounging on his pillows. "You always say, 'When it comes to individual destiny, there is no power greater in the universe than the conviction of the human soul to make a choice.'" He rolled his eyes as if he didn't want to be bothered anymore.

"Precisely," Master George said in a loud whisper, holding up his index finger. "Choice. Conviction. Determination. Belief. *That* is the true power within us, and its name is Chi'karda. It is the immeasurable force that controls what most scientists of the world do not yet understand. Quantum physics."

"So what does this . . . Chi'karda thing have to do with the alternate universes?" Sofia asked.

"It's what *creates* them, my dear girl," Master George answered. "It's happened throughout history, when choices have been made of such magnitude they literally shake the world and split apart the fabric of space and time, creating two worlds where there used to be only one, running parallel to each other within the complex intricacies of the kyoopy. What do you think causes earthquakes?"

"Wow," Paul breathed. "Serious?"

"Quite right, sir, quite right. The creation and destruction of alternate worlds through the power of the Chi'karda has been known to trigger great and terrible quakes. *Wow*, indeed. Allow me to give you an example that will explain it much better, so you can throw out the hard words and difficult phrases. Everyone, close your eyes, please." He motioned with his hands, urging Tick and the others to obey.

Tick closed his eyes.

"I want you to picture in your mind an enormous tree," Master George said. "Its trunk is ten feet wide, with twelve thick branches, er, branching off, breaking up into tinier and tinier limbs until they are barely measurable. Can you picture it?"

A scatter of mumbled yeses sounded across the room, even from Mothball and Rutger.

"The trunk of that tree is Reality Prime, the version of the world in which you were born and have lived your whole lives. The main branches of the tree are very established *alternate* Realities that have stood the test of time and survived, each one different from Reality Prime in significant ways. From there, the smaller and smaller branches are weak and crumbling Realities, *fragmented* Realities, most of them heading for the day when they will vanish altogether or be absorbed into another Reality. We had each of you visit one of those fragmented Realities before you came here, to give you a bit of understanding at what they can be like.

"The Realitants are a group of explorers devoted to charting and documenting the main branches of this tree for the sake of science and in hopes that one day we can better understand the makeup of the universe and how it works. And to, er, protect Reality Prime from potential, er, unforeseen dangers."

Master George cleared his throat loudly, and Tick's eyes flew open. Master George's hands gave the slightest twitch at his sides. "Until recently, we had fully charted twelve main Realities, and everything was going just splendid—there'd even been talk that perhaps some-day we'd discover the perfect Reality—a utopia if you will. But the reason you are here today is because quite the opposite has occurred. One of our own, a trai-tor like the world has never known, has discovered a Thirteenth Reality, and very bad things are about to happen. Very bad things indeed."

"I knew it," Sato grumbled.

"What's in the Thirteenth Reality?" Tick asked. "What's so bad about it?"

"Oh, Mister Higginbottom, it is quite a hard thing to talk about. With every other Reality, we've had mostly positive, fascinating experiences. For example, there's the Fifth Reality, home of our dearest Mothball. There, circumstances somehow led to a drastic change in the gene pool, where everyone became taller and stronger, evolving into a much different society than the one you know so well. Then, of course, there's the Eleventh, where Rutger was born. As you can see, they, er, had quite the, er, *opposite* effect in their Reality."

Everyone looked at Rutger, who patted his big belly as if it were his most prized possession.

Master George cleared his throat again and moved on quickly. "There's the Fourth, perhaps the most fascinating Reality of them all. Their world is much more advanced than ours, the technology revolution occurring much sooner there than it did in Reality Prime. Going there is much like traveling to the future—quite fascinating indeed. It's where I acquired the Gnat Rat and the Tingle Wraiths."

Tick's jaw dropped open.

The Gnat Rat. Manufactured by Chu Industries.

That explains it, he thought. *No wonder I couldn't find anything on them.* Mr. Chu couldn't have had anything to do with the company after all—it was in another Reality.

"But I haven't answered your question, have I?" Master George said, looking uncomfortable. "You most clearly asked me about the *Thirteenth* Reality, and here I am, doing everything in my power to avoid answering you."

"Well?" Sofia asked.

"What? Ah, yes, the question. The Thirteenth Reality. I'm afraid this new place is . . . quite extraordinary. You see, for the first time, a Reality has been discovered in which . . . oh, poppycock, this is difficult to say."

"Go ahead and say it," Mothball urged from the back. "These kids can take it, they can."

"Yes, yes, you're quite right, Mothball." Master George straightened his shoulders. "The Thirteenth Reality has a mutated and frightening version of the Chi'karda that simply chills my bones to think about. It is most certainly the source of every frightening myth, dangerous legend, or terrifying nightmare that has ever leaked into the stories and tales of the human race."

"A . . . *mutated* version of the Chi'karda?" Paul repeated. "What in the world does that mean?"

Master George's brow creased as he frowned. "Remember what Rutger told all of you about the sheer power of the Chi'karda? The Thirteenth has somehow turned that power of pure creation into something completely different. Something frightening."

"But why?" Paul pushed. "What does that *mean*?"

Master George's face paled. "It means that we have discovered a Reality that contains the closest thing to—oh, I hate to even utter the word—but it contains the closest thing to *magic* we have ever seen. And not the good kind of magic like in your storybooks. No, this is a very real, very *dark* power. And if it isn't contained, if it somehow escapes from the Thirteenth Reality, everything will be lost."

CHAPTER 42

THE DOOHICKEY

Magic?" Sofia said. "That sounds fun."

"You're talking, like, abracadabra and all that stuff?" Paul chimed in. "Wizards and broomsticks?"

"No, no, no, nothing of the sort," Master George replied, his face scrunched up in annoyance. "This is real—perfectly real—and it's all explained by the laws of science, particularly the kyoopy, quantum physics. It's all a matter of unique Chi'karda manipulation. In the Thirteenth Reality, though, it's been mutated into something far more powerful and horrific. And it can be controlled by someone who understands the nature of it."

"What can it do?" Tick asked.

"Well, it can make things fly, create horrible beasts,

the like. What all of you would consider magic, which is why I used the word—though any scientist would despise such ridiculous nomenclature. This is real, this is *science*. And while it's not unique to the Thirteenth, it is there that they've learned how to twist it, how to use it much more powerfully."

"What do you mean?" Paul asked. "The same power exists in other places?"

"Why, yes, of course. It's even here in Reality Prime—though thankfully not the dark and sinister version that exists in the Thirteenth. Ever heard of *luck*?"

Master George continued, excited, not bothering to wait for anyone to answer. "The Chi'karda is essentially the power of conviction, of belief, of strong choices. There have been instances where wonderful things have occurred, where the tiny world of quantum physics has fundamentally *changed* because of an overwhelming, powerful display of Chi'karda. Some call it a lucky break, good fortune, a windfall, a crazy coincidence. Oh, it's happened plenty, but in the Thirteenth, the Chi'karda has mutated into something hideous."

"Man," Paul said. "That is just plain awesome."

"*Awesome?*" Master George asked, his tone suggesting he felt exactly the opposite. "I assure you, there's nothing awesome about it once you know what Mistress Jane intends to do with this dark Chi'karda."

"Who is this Mistress Jane?" Sofia asked, glancing at

Tick then at Master George. "Norbert told us she went looking for you in Alaska. He said she threatened him."

Master George's face grew dark. "Mistress Jane is the most foul, despicable, wretched creature to ever walk the folds of the Realities. She was once one of us, someone who worked toward understanding and unity. But she betrayed us for hopes of glory and power. We have many spies in her camp, and we're certain she plans to annihilate the Reality system in its entirety. You have no idea the ramifications of her twisted plans."

"The tree," Rutger said through a yawn.

"Pardon me?" Master George replied.

"The tree, the tree! Use your analogy to explain what she wants to do."

"Ah, yes." Master George turned his attention back to the kids. "Imagine the tree for me again, if you will. One of the big branches we talked about—one of the main Realities that shoots off from the trunk of Reality Prime—is now under the control of Mistress Jane. Using the dark Chi'karda of the Thirteenth Reality, Mistress Jane plans to sever the other branches from the trunk, if you will, destroying them entirely. Then she can conquer Reality Prime and rule the known universe. If that happens, she'd be able to create her own twisted Realities at will, essentially recreating the tree for her own purposes."

If the other kids in the group were anything like

Tick, all Master George saw at that moment were wide-eyed stares. Tick had a feeling they underestimated the horrible intentions of Mistress Jane.

"Oh, poppycock, we're getting too deep into all of this," Master George complained as he paced back and forth in front of the fire. "All you need to know is there are different versions of the world we live in called Realities and all of them are important in their own way. Mistress Jane plans to use her newly discovered powers to destroy life as we know it. And we, the Realitants—and I mean *we*—must stop her."

"How?" Tick and Paul asked in unison.

Master George smiled. "Ah, yes, *how* indeed. It's time for the fun part, my good people. I have something to show you." He walked through a small door in the far corner of the room, reappearing a few seconds later. In his hand he held a long golden rod, at least three feet in length and several inches in diameter; it shone and sparkled in the firelight, polished to perfection. Up and down one entire side were a series of dials and knobs and switches, a small label below each one. Once he returned to his lecture spot, Master George held the rod high for everyone to see.

"This, my friends," he said proudly, "is a Barrier Wand."

Oohs and ahs sounded across the room.

"This instrument—and the Chi'karda Drive within

its inner chamber—is the single most important invention in the history of mankind. I say this without the slightest pause, *knowing* it's true. It is the *only* way a person can travel from one Reality to another. It harnesses and controls the power of the Chi'karda—manipulates it, bends it, wields it, shapes it."

Master George ran his hand down the length of the device. "*This* is how we control travel between the barriers of the Realities—what we call winking, because it literally happens in the blink of an eye. Without this Barrier Wand, and the few others like it, there would be no study of the Realities, no travel between them, no . . . Mistress Jane problem, actually. If we can remove her Barrier Wand from the Thirteenth Reality, she and her twisted powers will be trapped there for a very long time. Enough time for us to devise a more permanent solution to the problem."

"How does the Barrier Wand work?" Paul asked.

"Oh, yes, thank you for asking." Master George held the golden rod up so everyone could clearly see as he pointed out the controls running down the near side. "You simply adjust the doohickey here, then the thingamajig here, then the whatchamacallit here, and so forth and so on. It's simple really. Trust me—it *does* work. With this Wand, you can control the Chi'karda to such a degree that it will transport you between Realities."

"Ooh, can I see it?" Sofia asked, her hands twitching with curiosity to hold the Wand.

"Of course. Come on up, all of you. Have a look!"

Tick shot out of his chair, grimacing at the coldness of his still-damp pants, and got to Master George first. He laughed out loud when he was close enough to read the labels on the instrument. "I thought you were joking."

"Joking about what?" Master George asked.

"The most important scientific discovery of all time, and the first dial is called the Doohickey?" Tick pointed to a neatly printed label on the Wand.

Sofia chuckled as she pointed at a small switch. "And there's the Thingamajig."

"That's for a very important reason, thank you very much," Master George said, momentarily pulling the Barrier Wand away from the kids. "It's so spying eyes can't figure out how it works. We've labeled them that way on purpose."

"Ingenious," Paul snickered.

Tick looked over at Sato, still sitting on the couch, arms folded in defiance. "Don't you want to see it?"

Sato stared at the floor. "Leave me alone."

Tick shrugged, then surprised himself when he let out a huge yawn. He glanced at his watch, surprised to see it was almost three o'clock in the morning.

Master George seemed to sense Tick's thoughts.

"It's grown very late indeed, my good associates. It's almost morning here. I think we should all be off to bed. We can finish our discussion tomorrow. There is still much to learn—and much to prepare for."

"Wait a minute—" Paul began.

"No, no, no," Master George said, waving his Wand like a great magician. "We must have fresh minds to continue. To bed it is—no arguments. No need to worry about the dirty plates; I'll be happy to clean up."

A hand grabbed Tick's shoulder and he turned to see Mothball.

"Come on," she said. "Off we go. I'll be showin' ya to yer sleepin' quarters. Methinks we could all use a good night's rest, I do. Come on."

She moved toward the side door. Tick, Sofia, and Paul fell in line behind her, grumbling like two-year-olds who didn't want to go to bed.

Sato didn't move a muscle.

"Looks like Mr. Happy will be sleeping on the couch," Paul whispered to Tick as they stepped through the door.

~⁓~

Sato fumed on the inside as he sat alone in the big room, the fire spitting, slowly fading to ashes. Master George hadn't so much as given him a glance, completely ignoring Sato's obvious distrust and unhappiness. They *all* ignored him for the most part, thinking they were so smart and so funny. *Better* than Sato.

Little did they know he'd listened intently to every single word that came out of the old man's mouth, storing them away inside his computer of a mind, learning every morsel. He had to know every piece of the puzzle if he hoped to accomplish what he'd planned to do from the very first day he'd received the letter from M.G.

He had to make things right. To quench the thirst for revenge that consumed him. To avenge the death of his family.

I need to stay sharp, he thought. *Befriend no one.* He couldn't trust anyone, precisely for the very reason his family died.

No, Sato would never make the same fatal mistake his parents had. And he'd never trust another person ever again.

Especially Master George.

CHAPTER 43

A BUMP IN THE NIGHT

*T*hese are our digs?" Paul asked.

"I miss my mansion," Sofia moaned.

Tick agreed. Their "sleeping quarters" didn't look very inviting. They stood in a small rectangular room in which six cots had been set up, three along each of the longer walls. Folded gray and black blankets and pillows lay stacked on top of each cot. The only other furniture in the room was a desk and a three-drawer wooden dresser. The floor of the room was a flat metallic gray.

"Would you rather sleep out in the raft?" Rutger asked. "We can arrange it."

"Mister Tick," Mothball said, nudging him. "There's

some dry clothes in the chest of drawers there. Better be changin' out of yer soppies, ya should."

"Oh, thanks."

Tick walked over to the dresser as everyone else chose a cot and started spreading out their blankets. After a full minute of rummaging through the drawers, the only thing Tick found that was close to wearable was an enormous one-piece nightshirt. "This thing looks like a dress," he said to Mothball.

"If ya'd rather soak in yer wet undies all night, fine by me," she replied.

"Where's the bathroom?"

She nodded toward a short metal door. Sighing, Tick went and changed into his ridiculous pajamas.

⁓

Frazier Gunn had listened to the muffled murmurs of people talking all night. His captor had *guests*, apparently. Almost insane from the months of isolation, Frazier felt like chewing through the metal and killing every last one of them.

I'd need stronger teeth, he thought.

He knew he was going crazy, and he didn't care. He curled up on the floor like a dog and tried to go back to sleep.

Frazier longed to hear more clearly through the cold metal walls of his terrible prison. The only word he felt confident he'd understood in all these months was *Annika*. George had mentioned the name several times, and for some reason it resonated through the metal without being distorted beyond recognition.

Annika. An unusual name for sure. Frazier had only known one person in his life named Annika. She was one of Mistress Jane's closest servants and one of several people, including Frazier, who intensely competed for Jane's favor.

Was it a coincidence? Did George somehow know Annika? There'd always been rumors of spies in Jane's camp. Had Frazier discovered a gold nugget of information?

If only he could escape. If only he could warn Mistress Jane . . .

~~~

"Hey, looky!" Paul laughed when Tick walked out in his long nightshirt, which hung all the way to the floor. "If it's not Ebenezer Scrooge himself! Where's your stocking cap, Grandpa?"

"Very funny," Tick said as he walked to an empty cot and started setting up his bed.

"I think you look right handsome, I do," Mothball said.

"Uh-oh, looks like someone's got a crush," Paul said.

Sofia huffed as she settled under her blanket. "Paul,

you're almost as annoying in person as you were on the e-mail. Keep smarting off and you'll get a Pacini fist in the nose."

"Oh, come on, you know you love me." He leaned back against the wall with his hands clasped behind his head. "Man, this is the life—no chores, no one yelling at me to brush my teeth. I love living in the middle of the ocean."

"Ha!" Rutger barked from the doorway. "You'll be wishing for chores once we send you on your initiation mission."

Tick froze, his pillow still in his hands. "Initiation mission?"

Rutger nodded with a wicked smile. "You didn't think Master George was kidding about retrieving Mistress Jane's Barrier Wand, did you?"

"You can't possibly mean *we* have to do it," Sofia said.

"You'll find out tomorrow. Get some sleep."

"Oh, that'll be nice and easy after telling us something like that," Tick said, straightening his blankets and getting into bed.

"Dude," Paul yawned, "where in the world *are* we anyway?"

"That's an easy one," Mothball said. "Middle of the ocean, we are."

"But *where*? Which ocean?"

Mothball and Rutger exchanged a wary look. "Go on, you tell 'em," Mothball finally said.

"This is the headquarters of the Realitants, you see," Rutger began, "and there's a reason we're here. Master George has to do a lot of *winking*, a lot of working with the Chi'karda. And this is the one place in the world where it's the most concentrated, the easiest to penetrate and control. It's by far the strongest link between all of the Realities."

"But where *are* we?" Sofia insisted.

Rutger rocked back and forth on his feet. "You're going to laugh when I tell you."

"Blimey, just tell 'em, fat man," Mothball said, rolling her eyes.

"Yeah, tell us," Paul added.

Rutger folded his hands and rested them on his belly. "We're smack dab in the middle of the Bermuda Triangle."

Master George let out a long, blissful sigh as he stuck his sore feet into a tub full of salt and warm water. Muffintops jumped onto his lap, purring as she licked his hands.

"Hello there, little friend," he said, petting her soft fur. "Quite the day, we've had—busy, busy, busy. Never knew it would be so difficult explaining all the many things we know. Those poor little chaps. They've no idea what lies ahead of them. None at all."

Master George leaned back and closed his eyes, wiggling his toes in the hot water. "Dear Muffintops, can we really do it? Can we really send them to that dreadful place? There's a mighty good chance everything will fall to pieces, you know. They could be attacked or captured. I don't know if the Sound Slicers will be enough . . ."

The cat looked up at Master George, as if it wanted to answer but couldn't.

"Ah, yes, I know, I know. We've no choice really. Must let them *prove* themselves, mustn't we?" He paused, thinking about the three eager children and how different they were from the boy Sato. Of course, Master George had expected nothing different from the troubled son of his former friend.

Master George smiled. When he really thought about the potential of the four kids he had gathered together, he didn't know who he felt sorrier for in the coming days, weeks, and years.

His new batch of Realitants or Mistress Jane.

⁓

"The Bermuda Triangle?" Paul asked, sounding like he'd just been told they were living inside an alien's big toe on Mars. "I feel like I'm in a bad made-for-TV movie."

Rutger answered. "For some reason this area by far has the biggest concentration of Chi'karda in the world. Something tremendous must've happened here a long,

long time ago, but we haven't been able to figure it out. There's certainly nothing recorded in the history books."

"Why's it such a big deal that there's more Chi'karda here than anywhere else?" Tick asked, stumbling only a little over the unfamiliar word.

"Why's it a big deal?" Rutger repeated, throwing up his arms like Tick had just asked him why he needed oxygen to breathe. "Do you have an unreasonable level of earwax, boy? Didn't you listen to a word Master George said tonight?"

"Hey, be nice," Sofia warned. "Unless you want a punch in the nose, too."

Rutger ignored her. "Everything having to do with the Realities revolves around the Chi'karda. Because it's so powerful here, it's the easiest place to *wink* to and from the other Realities. It's also the best place for Master George to monitor Chi'karda levels around the world. That's how he's watched all of you from day one so closely."

"How?" Paul asked.

"By using another invention from Chu Industries in the Fourth Reality. It's called a nanolocator."

"Sounds fancy," Sofia said. "Maybe Pacinis should make them."

"I assure, you, Miss Pacini, there's a big difference between making nanolocators and *spaghetti* sauce." Sofia leaned forward like she was ready to get out of bed and attack Rutger, but he held up his hands in reconciliation, then hurried to continue. "A nanolocator is basically a microscopic robot, but it's so tiny you can't see it with the naked eye. It crawls into your skin and sends various signals back here to the Command Center."

"What kind of signals?" Tick asked, shifting on his cot to get more comfortable. He wasn't sure he liked the idea of a tiny robot crawling under his skin.

"Signals that monitor your Chi'karda levels, your global position, your body temperature—all kinds of things. Our fearless leader had to have some way to keep tabs on you, don't you think? The nanolocators also told us where to send the Gnat Rats and Tingle Wraiths, which were programmed to find you and no one else."

"Ah, man, I feel so . . . violated," Paul said in a deadpan voice, then barked a laugh.

"How did he get it inside our bodies?" Tick asked.

"That's easy," Mothball said. "The little fella was on the first letter he sent you."

"Serious?" Paul asked.

"When each one of you opened the envelope and pulled out the letter, the nanolocator quickly sought a heat source—your hand—and slipped right between your skin cells." Rutger grinned. "Brilliant, don't you think?"

"Dude, that just seems *wrong*," Paul said, shaking his head.

"Oh, boo hoo," Rutger replied, rubbing his eyes in a mock cry. "How else were we supposed to know when or if you burned the first letter. Or when you made your Pick?"

"Pick?" all three kids asked at once.

"I'll take that one," Mothball said. "A Pick's what Master George calls a ruddy big decision. Your Chi'karda level spikes like a rocket shootin' off to space, it does. Showed up on his big monitor and let him know when yer were truly committed to the job he offered, when you really promised yourself there was no turning back. Smart old chap, don't you think?"

"Master George watched his big screen every day," Rutger said, "so he'd know when you made your Pick. Word is he just about suffocated his cat hugging the poor thing when you three made your Pick at almost the same time. That was uncanny."

Tick thought of that night he knelt in front of the fireplace and the decision he'd made to not burn the letter in his hand. He remembered the sensation of warmth that had spread throughout his whole body. *That was my Pick,* he realized. He'd felt that same sensation again later, when he screamed out in the dark woods and managed to somehow change reality. *Is that what using the Chi'karda feels like?* Tick shivered. It was a lot to think about.

"What are we in, anyway?" Paul asked, looking

above and around him. "Is this a boat or what?"

"No, it's a building, firmly rooted in the ocean floor far below us," Rutger said. "Master George used a little trick he learned from the Eighth Reality, where it's mostly ocean. They developed some amazing cabling technology that allows them to build entire cities on the ocean. We're perfectly safe and stable. You can barely feel the waves unless we have a real doozy of a storm."

Mothball yawned, a booming roar that made Tick jump. "Master George will have our hides, he will, if he finds out we kept you up so late. Come on, now, we need—"

"Wait," Tick interrupted her. "Just one more question, okay?"

"Be quick about it. Me bones hurt I'm so tired."

"What's the deal with cemeteries? Rutger said something once about the difference between life and death . . . I can't remember."

"It was another famous Master George quote," Rutger replied. " '*Nothing in this world better reflects the difference between life and death than the power of choice.*' Chi'karda levels are very high in cemeteries. Master George says it has to do with the lingering effects of the life-changing choices those people made. One way or another, their choices led them to their fates, whether good or bad."

"And so we needed to go there because . . ." Tick

started but stopped, worried his answer would be wrong.

"So we could *wink* easier," Sofia said. "The stronger the levels of Chi'karda, the easier it is to travel between Realities."

"Exactly," Rutger agreed. "Not only can you travel between the barriers, you can travel between different locations of heavy Chi'karda spots within the *same* Reality. That's how Master George could wink you from your towns to this place. He simply honed in on your nanolocator signals and winked you away!"

"My head hurts," Paul groaned, falling onto his back as he rubbed his forehead.

"That's because you Americans aren't smart enough to get it," Sofia said. "I'll be happy to tutor you on everything tomorrow."

"Methinks I've had enough for one day," Mothball said. "Good night, all."

She and Rutger left the room, flicking off the light as they went.

A few more words were said after they'd left, but sheer exhaustion soon pulled the three of them into a deep sleep.

⁓

Something jolted Frazier out of his dreamless slumber.

He swatted at the dark air around him, scrambling

into a sitting position. What had it been? Was he—

He heard a loud thump against the wall by his cot. Then another, a clang of metal against metal that echoed throughout the small cell. Then another, this time *louder*.

What was that?

He scurried over to the light switch and flipped it on, squinting in the brightness. To his shock, a small dent, about three inches wide, bent the wall inward just above his bed. The bolts connecting the wall to the surrounding metal had loosened slightly, rattling as another big thump sounded. The wall bent even farther.

One final boom sounded through the room, and the entire piece of metal fell onto his bed, its bolts cracking like whips as they broke in half. Frazier stared past the hole in the wall, seeing the endless ocean in front of him, the first traces of dawn casting a purple glow over the deep waters. Then, inexplicably, a face appeared from below—someone he'd never seen before. It was a man with scraggly black hair and an unshaven face.

"Come on, Mister Gunn, we don't have much time!"

"What . . . who . . . what . . ." Frazier couldn't find any words after such a long time in confinement.

"Mistress Jane sent us to rescue you," the man yelled.

"Rescue me?" Frazier could hardly believe it.

"Yes!" the man replied. "And then we're going to destroy this place once and for all."

CHAPTER 44

ESCALATION OF PLANS

Tick woke to the awful smell of fish breath and an annoying scratchy feeling on his right cheek. From somewhere in the distance, he thought he heard a loud boom like an underground explosion. He opened his eyes to see two yellow orbs staring at him. It was a cat, pawing at his face to . . . wake him?

Tick sat up, accidentally knocking the cat to the floor. "Oh, sorry." The sleek feline hissed in annoyance, then padded over to Paul's cot to wake him as well.

That's one smart cat, Tick thought.

Sofia was already awake, rubbing her eyes and stretching. Tick looked at his watch to see only a few hours had passed since they went to bed. The thought made him twice as tired; all he wanted to do was go back to sleep.

But then the whole world seemed to go crazy at once.

Another boom, this time much louder, shook the building as it echoed off the walls. The door to the room flew open and banged against the wall, rebounding back and knocking Master George to the floor, who was wearing a bright red nightshirt even more ridiculous than the one Tick wore. He grunted and scrambled back to his feet.

"Good job, Muffintops, jolly good job!" Master George picked up his cat and petted its back. "You three, we must hurry! Our plans have been . . . escalated."

The others had slept in their clothes, but Tick still wore his horrible pajamas. As Paul and Sofia moved to follow Master George, Tick quickly went into the bathroom where he'd hung his clothes to finish drying. They were still damp, but he changed into them as fast as he could. He'd just pulled on his second shoe when someone pounded on the door.

"Mister Higginbottom!" came the muffled voice of Master George. "What part of 'we must hurry' did you not understand?"

"Sorry!" Tick called as he wrapped his scarf around his neck. He opened the door and followed the old man, who was already across the room. Another boom sounded, and Tick felt like he was in a bunker, taking heavy artillery from the enemy. He tried to fight the panic that surged up his chest and into his throat.

They gathered back in the main room with the fireplace. Sato sat in the exact same spot where they'd left him only a few hours before, though his puffy eyes showed he'd just woken up as well. Rutger and Mothball were there too; the tall woman had an enormous backpack perched on her shoulders.

Master George stood in front of the now-cold fireplace, holding the shiny Barrier Wand in both hands, his cat curled on the ground at his feet. "My friends, we are officially under siege."

"What're you talking about?" Sofia asked as another boom sounded in the building. "Is someone *bombing* us?"

"I'd hardly call them bombs, my good lady, but we haven't any more time to talk about it. Jane's power over the mutated Chi'karda must be growing if she has enough daring to attack us here. I must send you off on your mission immediately." He started adjusting the seven dials and switches of the Barrier Wand, his tongue pressed between his lips.

"Whoa, dude," Paul said. "I don't like the sound of this."

"We don't have time to argue," Rutger said from where he leaned against the door. "Master George and I will stay here and protect the Command Center as best we can; we have a few tricks up our sleeve that Mistress Jane doesn't know about. You four are going with Mothball to the Thirteenth Reality."

"The Thirteenth—" Tick started, his stomach falling into a pit of cold ice.

"Don't waste another moment of my time with complaints or questions!" Master George finished his flipping and turning of the Wand's controls and looked at the four recruits. "This attack on my home shows you the urgency of your mission. Follow Mothball's orders. She has weapons called Sound Slicers if you run into trouble. Please do me a favor and don't point them *at* each other. I'd rather you *not* return to me with your brains turned into runny oatmeal."

Sound Slicers? Tick wondered. He really wanted to voice a question, but the man in charge barely paused to breathe.

Master George held up a warning finger. "It is *imperative* you succeed in bringing back the Barrier Wand of Mistress Jane. We must seal her in the Thirteenth Reality forever. Or at least until we can properly prepare to fight against her evil magic hordes. If everything goes as planned, it should be quite, er, easy."

Tick didn't like the hesitancy in Master George's voice. He already felt like a rookie paratrooper about to be pushed out of the plane for the first time over a major battlefield, under heavy fire.

"Atticus, you enjoy chess, yes?" Master George said in a tight voice.

Tick couldn't think of a question that seemed more out of place. "Yeah."

"Good. Come here."

Tick moved closer to Master George, who put the Barrier Wand directly in front of his face. "It's been my experience that chess lovers are quite good at memorization. Am I correct?"

"Uh . . ."

"Excellent! Now look at each of the controls on the Barrier Wand and memorize their position. Exactly, now—there's no room for error, none at all."

"But—"

"Quickly!"

Tick swallowed the lump in his throat and did as he was told, scanning his eyes up and down the length of the golden Wand.

"Hurry, we only have a minute at most!" Master George said.

Pushing his panic away, Tick tried to freeze-frame the image of each dial, switch, and knob in his mind, storing it, *burning* it in his memory. He was still focusing on the bottom dial when Master George took it away and began switching everything again.

Master George spoke as he worked. "Mothball isn't . . . agreeable with Barrier Wands, so it'll be up to you, Atticus, to bring all of you back in case something happens to me."

Tick felt like someone had just poured acid down his throat.

"Mark your watches," Master George continued. "If I don't wink you back here in thirty hours—*precisely* thirty hours—that means that Rutger and I are in serious trouble. If that happens, Atticus, you will have to use Mistress Jane's Barrier Wand—which looks exactly like this one—in order to escape the Thirteenth Reality. Adjust it as I showed you, then hit this button on top." He pointed at a perfect circle cut into the top of the cylinder. "It will wink you to one of our satellite locations where you will be safe from harm. Understand?"

Tick nodded, scratching his neck through his scarf, nervous and afraid like never before. Another explosion rocked the building, throwing everyone off balance; a brick fell from the mantle of the fireplace, a poof of dust billowing out. Master George almost dropped the Barrier Wand but caught it just in time.

Paul cleared his throat. "And how're we supposed to steal a Barrier Wand from the most evil woman in history, as you put it?"

"We have a spy named Annika in place. All you have to do is meet her and she will help you retrieve it."

"Is that all?" Sofia said.

"Listen to me," Master George said, all semblance

of his normal, cheery, quirky self gone. "You have all shown tremendous resolve and courage in making it to me, and I am proud as buttons to know you. But you must do this one last thing before officially becoming Realitants. Show me you can do this, and a life of adventure and intrigue awaits you, I promise. Do we have an understanding?"

The building rumbled again as Tick made eye contact with Sofia, then Paul. They looked as scared as he felt, which for some sick reason made him feel better.

"Let's do it," Paul said.

"Yeah," Sofia agreed. "Psycho Jane'll be sorry once I get my hands on her."

They both looked at Tick, waiting for his answer. "You know I'm in," he said.

"Splendid," Master George said. "Sato?"

Everyone looked over at the disgruntled boy on the couch. He stood up, trying to bring the scowl back to his face but failing; he was just as scared as everyone else. "I'm only going because I don't trust Master George and I want to make sure you three don't mess up." He walked over and joined the small group standing around the Barrier Wand.

"Sato," Master George said, in an unusually kind voice for someone who had just been insulted. "I know more about you than you understand, and I feel no anger. When you succeed in this mission, I hope to gain your trust, and may I daresay, to become your friend."

Sato said nothing in reply, looking at the floor.

A horrible sound of crunching metal came from the hallway where Tick had first entered the building, followed by another rocking explosion.

"Best be gettin' a move on, don't ya think?" Mothball said.

"Quite right you are, my dear friend!" Master George said, holding the Barrier Wand out in front of him, his arm rigid, so the golden rod stood upright in the middle of the group. "All of you, hands on the Wand! It'll be much easier if you're touching it!"

Mothball was first, wrapping her huge hand around the very top of the cylinder. One by one, the others followed her example, clasping the Wand in quick succession—Paul, Sofia, Tick. All eyes went to Sato, who turned and spat on the ground. Then, with all the enthusiasm of putting his hand into a cage full of rattlesnakes, he grabbed the lower edge of the Wand.

"I'm very sorry indeed we didn't have more time to talk," Master George said, his tone solemn. "I expected a few more hours at least, but we must move on, mustn't we? Remember the plan, and remember your courage. May the Realities smile upon you, and may we see each other again very soon."

Without waiting for a response, Master George pushed the golden button.

CHAPTER 45

THE THIRTEENTH REALITY

Mistress Jane sat on her throne, eyes closed, deep in thought as she waited for her next visitor. *What a life mine has become.* So many people hated and despised her, wished she were dead. But they simply did not understand. All of her cruelty and harsh rule had a purpose, and someday the Realities would know of her goodness.

All she wanted was to make life better.

What a poor existence the wretches of Reality Prime eked out from day to day. It was a marvel they continued on despite the drab bleakness of their lives—no power, no joy, no *color*. Jane would change all of that. The new and improved version of Chi'karda made every second a wonderful moment, and it must be shared. It must be *spread.* The Realitants had always talked about finding a utopian Reality someday, a paradise on Earth; Jane could make it happen.

She was so close to implementing her plan. One by one, she would fragment and destroy the branching Realities until only Prime and the Thirteenth remained. Then, with an army such as never before witnessed in all of history, she would take over Reality Prime, consuming it with the mutated Chi'karda. Only then could the universe be rebuilt, one world at a time, a better place for all.

In a million years, her name would still be remembered with love and worship.

She needed help, of course. She'd sent a letter to a very important person, setting up a meeting on May thirteenth—a meeting that represented the final and most important part of her plan. *Only one more week,* she thought. If Reginald Chu agreed to her terms at that meeting, nothing could stop her. Nothing. Especially not the pathetic and laughable Master George and his dwindling Realitants. Just hours earlier, she'd finally initiated the attack on his headquarters, an act for which she'd shown much patience, having wanted to do it for years.

One more week until the meeting with Chu. The final piece of the puzzle.

Jane opened her eyes. It was time to speak with Gunn.

Frazier felt sweat seeping into his eyebrows from his forehead, as if the skin itself were melting.

He stood before the huge wooden door with its iron bindings and handle, barely able to breathe as he waited for the horrible thing to open. He had failed, miserably, and there was no telling how Mistress Jane might react. Sometimes she was very merciful to her failures—allowing them to die with a quick snap of her odd abilities in this place. At other times, she displayed much less kindness. Jane had immense amounts of control over the mutated Chi'karda that existed in the Thirteenth, and she loved to . . . experiment.

A muted thump sounded from the other side of the door, followed by the odd sound of something *dissolving*, like the scratchy rush of poured sand or the amplified roar of a million termites devouring a house. A hole appeared in the middle of the door, expanding outward like a ripple in a pond, devouring the wood and iron of the door as it grew until the entrance to Jane's throne room was completely open.

Why can't she just open *the door,* Frazier thought to himself. *Always has to show off her twisted power.*

Frazier steeled himself, promising himself he would remain dignified as he met his fate. He knew he had only one chance to redeem his folly and perhaps to save his life. Smoothing his filthy shirt, he stepped forward into the gaudy and ridiculous throne room of Mistress Jane.

From top to bottom, side to side, the room was a complete sea of yellow.

Tapestries of yellow people on yellow horses in fields of yellow daisies. Yellow padded chairs on yellow rugs on top of yellow carpets. The walls, the couches, the paintings, the pillows, the servants' clothing, the lamps, the books—even the wood and bricks of the fireplace had been painted yellow. It made Frazier sick to his stomach, and reminded him once again that the woman he'd chosen to follow was completely insane.

But Frazier knew one day Jane would snap, and someone would need to replace her. *That's where I come in,* he thought. *If I can only survive this day.*

A buzzing sound from above made him look up to see two large insects flying down toward him.

Snooper bugs, he thought. *Could she be any more paranoid?*

The enormous winged creatures flew around him in a tight circle, their cellophane wings flapping in a blur, their elongated beaks snipping at his clothes and poking at his skin. Frazier winced, but kept still and silent, knowing the vicious things could get quite nasty if you didn't submit completely. Finally, after inflicting dozens of tiny wounds all over his body, the two Snoopers flew back to their nests. They didn't need to communicate anything further to Jane—if Frazier had been holding any poisons or weapons, he'd be dead.

"Come forward," a gruff voice said from the side. Frazier looked over to see a grotesquely fat man who looked like a hideous cross between a dwarf and a troll, hovering ten feet in the air, his plump legs dangling. His head, face, and chest were covered in dark, greasy hair, and he wore nothing but a wide skirt around his middle, proudly displaying his disgustingly bloated skin. "The Mistress will see you now." He held out a flabby arm, gesturing deep into the throne room. "Hurry. She is a busy woman."

Frazier shuddered and followed the guard's instructions, staring straight ahead. He didn't stop walking until he reached the Kneeling Pillow of Mistress Jane, where he did as countless others had done before him, dropping to his knees and kissing the ground before him. Then, daring to show some boldness, he leaned back on his legs and looked up at the preposterous throne.

It was black.

Mistress Jane had never explained to anyone why her throne was made from completely nondescript, heavy, black iron, nor had anyone ever dared ask. But Frazier thought it must be a symbol that her seat of power was so important, she wanted it to stand out among the world of yellow.

She sat on her black throne, dressed from head to toe

in the color she so dearly loved. She wore a hat embroidered with lace and daffodils that stretched a foot above her bald head. Her sparkling gown fit her body tightly, covering every inch from the middle of her neck to her shiny yellow heels. Horn-rimmed glasses sat atop her nose, her emerald eyes peering through like focused lasers.

Everything about this woman is just . . . weird, Frazier thought as he waited for her to say something.

"I don't know *why* we rescued you," Mistress Jane said, her voice taut with barely veiled anger. "We could just as easily have destroyed the complex of that *buffoon* Master George while you still sat inside, bawling your eyes out."

"Yes, Mistress Jane," Frazier replied. He knew better than to say anything else—yet.

"We finally had a hope of knowing George's plan once and for all—and you threw it down the drain in exchange for a little fun with your Chu Industries toy and a car. You better hope the attack on George takes care of any loose ends. SPEAK!" She belted this last word, causing several nearby servants to gasp.

Frazier stumbled on his words. "Mistress Jane . . . I n-never intended to k-kill them. I only meant to scare them enough to t-talk. I failed, and I'm sorry."

Jane stood up, her reddening face all the fiercer against the yellow background of her hat and dress. "They did not *die*, you blubbering sack of drool!"

Frazier couldn't hide his shock at hearing this. *How in the world did they escape before the car . . .*

He knew that now was not the time to wonder, now was the time for apologies and groveling. "I am very sorry, Mistress Jane."

"Listen to me well, Frazier Gunn," Jane said as she sat back down on her throne. "And let my servants put this on record. I give you one spoken sentence—one sentence only—to convince me why I should not send you to your death at the hands of the scallywag beasts. And not the nice ones that only take a week to digest their food."

Frazier closed his eyes, throwing all of his mental powers into quashing the rising panic and constructing a single sentence that could save his life. He had nothing. Nothing! But then a single word popped into his head, giving him an idea. It was desperate, but his only shot. Quickly, in his mind, he visualized each word of a sentence one by one, going over them several times. Finally, he opened his eyes and spoke.

"Master George has a spy in your presence, and I know who it is."

Jane's eyes screwed up into tight wrinkles, her brow creased. She folded her arms, studying Frazier for a long moment. "Nitwit!" she suddenly screamed, causing even more servants to gasp.

Frazier jumped, his heart sinking to the floor. "But—"

Before he could utter another word, a young girl dressed entirely in yellow zoomed through the air from the back of the room, stopping to hover directly in front of Frazier, facing Jane. No one had figured out how Jane used the mutated Chi'karda to enable flight, but seeing people flying always gave Frazier the creeps. It seemed so . . . unnatural.

"Yes, Mistress?" a high-pitched voice asked.

"Fetch me a banana sandwich." Jane leaned to the side, peering down at Frazier. "We have much to discuss, and I'm hungry. And make it quick!" She clapped her hands, a booming echo that shook the walls.

As the little servant flew off to obey Jane's orders, Frazier tried to regain his breath after that frantic moment when he'd thought for sure he'd be killed, all the while in disbelief that Jane could stoop so low as to rename a child *Nitwit*. Of course, the last one had been named Nincompoop, but had been disposed of once Jane got tired of yelling "Nincompoop!" every time she wanted something.

"Frazier!" Jane snapped.

"Y-y-yes, Mistress?" he stammered.

"Start talking."

Frazier told her about Annika.

It truly did happen in the blink of an eye, a quick tingle shooting down Tick's spine.

The instant Master George pushed the button on top of the Barrier Wand, the room of the Realitant headquarters vanished, replaced by thousands of massive trees covered in moss. Tick and the other recruits, along with Mothball, stood in a dark forest, hazy sunlight barely breaking through the thick canopy of branches to make small patches of gold on the earthy floor. The haunted sounds of exotic birds and insects filled the creepy woods, smells of roots and rotting leaves wafting through the air. Tick had the uneasy feeling that the forest wanted to eat him alive.

"Where are we?" Paul asked, though he must've known the answer.

"In the Thirteenth, we are. Deep in the Forest of Plague," Mothball whispered.

"Forest of *Plague?*" Sofia asked with a snort. "Lovely."

"A great battle was fought 'ere," Mothball said, slowly turning as she scanned the ancient trees, most of which were thick enough to make an entire house. Gnarled, twisted branches reached out as if trying to escape their masters. "Many moons ago, it was. Thousands died, their rottin' bodies creating a plague that was downright nasty. So I've 'eard, anyway. Must be true, seeing as there's quite a bit of Chi'karda here. Come on, follow me."

THE JOURNAL OF CURIOUS LETTERS

"Wait," Sato said, trying to sound stern but coming across as a grumpy jerk. "Tell us the plan before we take a step."

Tick rolled his eyes, but quickly so Sato couldn't see him do it. *Things are scary enough*, he thought. *Why does this guy have to make it worse?*

"The plan's quite simple, really," Mothball said, not acting bothered at all. "Right over yonder"—she pointed toward an ivy-covered copse of pine trees— "there's some right dandy Windbikes that we can take to meet Master George's spy, Annika. She's been settin' things up for months to get close to the Barrier Wand. We meet Annika, we get the Wand, we come back 'ere in thirty hours, and home we go."

"Sounds too easy," Sato said with a comical sneer.

"Sure it is, old chap, sure it is." Mothball turned and walked toward the pine trees. "Got a better idea, let me know. But best be right quick about it."

As Tick and the others followed their eight-foot-tall guide, Sato said from behind, "How do we know we can trust this spy? Maybe she works for Mistress Jane."

"Find out soon enough, we will," Mothball replied, not slowing at all.

"Quit your whining and come on," Sofia snapped.

Tick cringed, wishing his friend would ease up on the poor kid. Tick didn't like him either, but Sofia seemed way too harsh—who knew what Sato might do to retaliate.

Begrudgingly, Sato finally started walking. The sounds of footfalls crunching the thick undergrowth of the forest suddenly filled the air, echoing off the canopy of interwoven tree limbs.

Tick moved to catch up with Mothball, practically running to keep up with her pace. "I have a question."

"Go on and ask it, then." Mothball pushed an enormous branch out of the way that everyone else simply walked *under*.

"The alternate versions of ourselves in other worlds— does that mean there is one of me in every Reality?"

"That's usually the case, it is. We call 'em Alterants. Strange how all that works—even though the Realities can grow in vastly different ways from each other, there seems to be a definite pattern when it comes to the *people*."

"What do you mean?" Tick asked, stooping to avoid a huge chunk of moss that drooped over a thick limb like a giant beard.

"Even though a Reality may have different governments and cultures and climates and all that from another Reality, the general pedigree of people remains quite similar—downright spooky, it is." A huge bird cawed from overhead, followed by the squeal of a small animal.

"So in your Reality—the . . ."

"The Fifth, it is."

"Yeah, the Fifth. There's a really tall version of me there? My Alterant? And he's alive right now, with parents named Edgar and Lorena?"

"Chances are ya be right. Course, I've never met 'em, and never tried. Dangerous stuff, messin' with Alterants."

Sofia and Paul had been following closely and listening to every word while Sato hung back, only a couple of steps behind them. Though he acted indifferent to the conversation, Tick had a feeling Sato was intently paying attention.

"Why is it dangerous to mess with Alterants?" Sofia asked.

"Since I had dealings with Tick in Reality Prime," Mothball said, pausing a second to reassess her bearings. She changed directions slightly and headed down a shallow ravine scattered with boulders among the trees. "I didn't want to meet his Alterant in any of the other Realities. Not only could it make me go mad, it could lead to the little sir meetin' his taller self in my Reality. Disaster, that."

"Why?" Paul asked.

"If two Alterants meet and truly recognize each other for what and who they are, well, then only one of the poor blokes can survive. Still trying to figure out the why and how, we are, but one of them ceases to exist. Sometimes that causes a nasty chain reaction that can rattle the Realities to their bones. Bet yer best buttons some of the worst earthquakes and such you've had were because of Alterants seein' each other. Master George and the Realitants have worked their buns off to avoid such meetings, but Mistress Jane likes to bring Alterants together. She thinks it's funny. Mad, she is. Crazy as a brain-dead Bugaboo soldier."

That was the second time Tick had heard Mothball refer to Bugaboo soldiers, but he was too busy thinking about Alterants to ask any more questions.

"Whoa, man," Paul said. "This is some downright freaky stuff. You're telling me there's all these Pauls running around the universe? I better be a big-time surfer in one of them. And a world-class pianist in another."

"Face it," Sofia said with a smirk. "You're a no-talent bum in all of them, just like you are here. Or, there. Or, whatever."

Paul stuck out his tongue. "Sis, you're hilarious."

"Call me 'sis' again," Sofia challenged, raising her fist.

"Sis."

Sofia pulled back and punched Paul solidly on his upper arm with a loud thump.

"Ow!" he yelled, rubbing the spot. "That's no fair. I can't punch a *girl* back."

Tick laughed, and Mothball surprised everyone when she did, too.

"Glad my pain can give everyone a nice chuckle," Paul said, still wincing. "Tick, a word of advice. Don't mess with Italians."

"I learned that just from her e-mails. Whatever you do, don't rip on her spaghetti."

"Tick," Sofia said. "I like you. You're smart . . . for an American."

Sato completely ignored all of them, never breaking his stoic expression.

Before anyone could throw out another sarcastic remark, Mothball stopped next to a big pile of fallen branches and twigs. She turned toward the messy heap and took a deep breath. "'Ere we are." She bent over and yanked on a large branch, pulling it off the stack. "A little 'elp would be nice."

Tick grabbed a branch and everyone joined in, even Sato, who was mumbling something Tick couldn't understand.

Tick saw a glimmer of metal when he pulled off a prickly branch, his curiosity increasing his pace. Soon, they'd cleared the entire pile, and all of them stared at what they'd uncovered.

Three sleek and shiny motorcycles were lined up in a row, silver with sparkly metallic red paint. They were the coolest things Tick had ever seen, but there was one thing about them that seemed a little odd.

None of them had wheels.

CHAPTER 46

CHI'KARDA DRIVE

They're called Windbikes," Mothball said, gesturing with a wide sweep of her arm. "Quite fun, they are." Everything about the strange vehicles looked exactly like a normal bullet bike you'd see zooming down the freeway: a small windshield, silvery handlebars, shiny body with a big black leather seat. But the machine ended in a flat bottom instead of two round wheels.

"I hate to break it to you," Paul said, "but somebody, uh, stole the *tires.*"

Mothball laughed, a booming roar that bounced off the overhanging branches. "You're a funny little man, you are, Paul."

"Are you telling us these things . . . fly?" Sofia asked.

"Well, I'd hope so, what with them not having wheels and all. Come on," she said while pulling the bike on the end away from the rest, pushing it across the ground. "There's three. One for me, and two for you kiddies to share. Methinks you'll be better off if ya go in pairs."

"Not me," Sato said. "I go alone."

"You'll go in a pair," Mothball said. "Or you'll sit 'ere and hug this tree all day." She stared down at Sato, daring him to argue. He said nothing in reply.

It was the first time Tick had seen Mothball use her size to intimidate someone. *I have a feeling this lady is a lot tougher than she acts.*

"Sweet biscuits!" Paul said as he grabbed hold of the next Windbike and dragged it a few feet away. "You're serious? This thing really *flies?* In the air?"

"Where else would it fly, Einstein?" Sofia said. "Underground?"

"You got me there, Miss Italy," Paul said, seeming to have grown accustomed to Sofia's smart mouth. "How does it work?"

Mothball sat down on her bike, her body taking up the entire seat that was meant for two. "You push this 'ere button, which turns it on, like so." She pressed a red button on the small dashboard under the handlebars. The Windbike came to life, humming like a big computer and not like a normal motorcycle at all. "Doesn't use gasoline. Takes hydrogen right out of the moisture in the air, it does, burns it right nicely. Come on, get on, now!"

"Who's going with who?" Tick asked.

"I'll go with you or Paul," Sofia said. "But not *him*." She nodded toward Sato, who scowled back at her.

"I don't want to go with you, either."

"Alrighty then," Paul said, clapping his hands. "Looks like it's me and Sofia on this one, Tick and Sato on that one." He pointed to the next bike in line.

Tick wanted to argue, but he didn't really want Sato any angrier than he already was. He looked to Sofia for help, but she only shrugged, not bothering to hide the smirk on her face. "Uh, great, okay."

Paul moved toward his bike and sat down right behind the handlebars, but Sofia would have none of it.

"I'm driving, tough guy," she said, pushing him backward as she squirmed her way in front of him.

Paul held his hands up in surrender as he scooted to the rear of the big seat. "You win, Miss Italy, you win." He looked over at Tick and mouthed the words, *"Help me."*

Sato pulled the last Windbike upright and pushed the button to turn it on as he swung his leg over and sat down in the driver's position. "Get on," he said, not bothering to look at Tick.

Tick felt like he'd rather pound his head against

the closest tree than get on the back of the humming machine. He hated how the mean kid from Japan was ruining everything.

Mothball must have noticed Tick's hesitation. "Come, now. Time's a wastin', it is."

"Yeah, sorry." Tick sighed as he sat behind Sato. The bottom edge of the Windbike had a railing with sticky pads for his feet. "Is this another invention from the Fourth Reality? Wait, let me guess—Chu Industries?"

"Nailed that one, you did," Mothball answered. "Chu rules a monopoly in the Fourth, he does—practically owns everything. Smuggled these bikes in a few months ago, we did, figuring they'd do right nicely for our little mission."

"What do we do now?" Sofia asked.

"Watch me very closely," Mothball said. She gripped the handlebars, then gently *lifted,* surprising everyone when the metal connecting her handgrips to the bike bent upward. As she did so, her Windbike rose several feet into the air with a slight surge in its humming sound; the top of her head almost bumped into a low-hanging branch.

"Cool!" Paul shouted.

Tick couldn't believe what he was seeing.

"Your hands control everything," Mothball said from above. "Push forward, go forward. The farther you push, the faster you go. Pull back and you slow down or stop, depending how hard ya do it. And ya go up or down by lifting and dropping the handgrips. Easy as breathin', it is."

Tick yelped and grabbed Sato's shirt as their bike suddenly leaped into the air and backward, then lurched forward and came to a sudden stop. A second later it shot forward again and flew around the closest tree, coming to a halt right above Sofia and Paul.

"It works," Sato said in a deadpan voice.

At the same time, all of them laughed. Even Sato broke into a smile for the first time since they'd met, looking back at Tick just as it turned back into a frown.

Tick had the strange feeling that maybe he was glad Sato had taken the pilot's seat after all, since he seemed to already have the hang of it. *I probably would've slammed us into the ground already, breaking all of our legs.*

Sofia tried it next, shooting straight upward until Paul's head slammed into the branch overhead.

"Ow, watch it!" he screamed. "I'm *tall*, remember!"

"Sorry," Sofia said through a snicker. Tick could see her push down and forward on the handlebars as the Windbike came down and flew around the same tree he and Sato had just circled. She came to a stop by pulling back with her hands, hovering right next to Tick.

"Told you it was easy, I did," Mothball said. She

revved her humming motorcycle. "Follow me!"

Her Windbike shot forward into the forest before she'd finished her sentence.

⁓

"You're sure of the meeting time and place?" Mistress Jane asked from her perch on the throne, glancing at her brightly yellow painted fingernails one by one.

"Absolutely," Frazier replied, trying his best to remain calm and professional, even though he knew how unpredictable his boss could be. He'd been put in charge of counter-spying on Annika since he'd returned and he had discovered some very interesting letters in the back of her closet. His relief at being right about her had far outweighed any fear he felt about damage she may have done. His hide had been saved and that was all that mattered.

"Tomorrow morning," he said, looking at the floor. "Dawn. Where the river meets the Forest of Plague. Annika will take the Barrier Wand from your throne room while you sleep, then deliver it to the Realitants."

"Why doesn't she just wink away with it herself? Why all the *drama?*" Jane said the last word with a low and sarcastic drawl.

Frazier swallowed despite his dry mouth. "She's under orders to keep her cover, stay infiltrated. Keep spying on you."

"Perhaps we should hide the Wand, end the plan this very minute." Jane lifted her hand and a small plate with a cup of steaming hot tea floated up from a nearby table and rested on her palm. She took a long and slurping drink.

"We could, Mistress, but then we might lose our chance to capture any Realitants who may have escaped George's Command Center before your attack. If Annika is not there with the Barrier Wand, they might suspect something and flee before we arrive."

"Frazier Gunn," Jane said with a sneer as she leaned forward in her throne, dropping the plate and cup onto the floor with a wet crash. She took off her lemon-decorated hat to reveal the shiny bald scalp underneath. Frazier shivered, knowing she did this only when she wanted to threaten someone. "This is your chance to redeem your pathetic failure of not bringing me those kids the *first* time I asked you to. If you fail me again . . ."

"You have nothing to worry about, Mistress. I'll have eyes on the Barrier Wand at all times and the army of fangen are ready to attack. Once the Realitants meet up with Annika, we'll charge in and take them all. They'll have nowhere to go."

"Are you sure the fangen are reliable? Last time I checked, they were still developing, still blind as bats."

Heat pulsed through Frazier's veins. "They're not at full strength, that's true. But they'll be plenty tough to take care of a few Realitants, I promise."

Jane paused a moment, staring him down as she considered his plan. "Fine, Frazier. But I want you personally to check and double check that the Chi'karda Drive in the Wand is disengaged before tonight. In fact, take the thing out altogether and give it to me so I can sleep with it under my pillow. Without it, they won't be able to wink away."

"And Master George's Wand? What if he tries to wink them back?"

Mistress Jane laughed as she placed the lemony hat back on her shiny head. "Oh, don't worry about him. He'll be far too *occupied* to do any rescuing." Her face flashed to red as she screamed, "Nitwit! Clean up this mess!"

By the time Mothball finally stopped next to an oak tree the size of a small building, Tick was desperate to throw up. After all the dodging and weaving through the maze of trees in the forest, his insides felt as if someone had shaken them like a maraca. When Sato pulled to a stop and lowered the Windbike to the mossy floor, Tick jumped off and ran over to a clump of bushes, where he spewed out every last morsel remaining in his stomach.

Paul made a wisecrack, but by the looks of his green

face, he didn't feel much better. Sofia and Sato seemed fine—as did Mothball—and Tick wondered if it was because they'd been driving.

Mothball removed her backpack and started pulling out all kinds of stuff. A tarp, some blankets, a little stove, packets of food.

"I thought we were in a hurry to meet our spy lady?" Paul asked, still walking off his nausea.

"What's that?" Mothball asked, concentrating on setting up the stove. "Oh, no, that be tomorrow morning when we meet Annika."

"Then why all the rush?" Sofia asked.

"Wanted to get far away from the deadies, I did." Mothball shivered. "The battleground where all those people died is downright spooky if ya ask me. Thought it best to be away a bit before we set up camp."

"So what do we do all night?" Paul asked as he leaned over Mothball's shoulder, not bothering to hide his interest in whatever she planned on cooking.

"Eat up, we will. Rutger prepared some right tasty dinners. Rest a bit, get some sleep. We'll be meetin' Annika just as the sun comes up, down by where the river that flows through Mistress Jane's fortress comes out and hits the Forest of Plague."

"How do we know for sure she'll be there?" Sato asked, still sitting on his Windbike. "Maybe she's turned on you."

"She'll be there, Mister Sato, no worries." Mothball ripped open a silvery pack of goop and poured it into a pot on her small stove. "One of our finest, Annika is."

"What if she's been captured?" Sato persisted.

"Then ya better be prayin' Master George survived his little battle and brings us back."

Tick sat down on a fallen log, unhappy that they had hurried to get here only to sit and wait for tomorrow. It was going to be a long night.

~~~

"Here you are, Mistress."

Frazier handed over the cylindrical pack of wires, nanochips, and instruments that made up the Chi'karda Drive, the heart and soul of her Barrier Wand.

Jane took the odd-looking package through her open bedroom door, examining it as though she suspected it wasn't the real thing. "You put the Wand back where it always rests for the night?"

"Yes, I did. The trap is set."

"I can't wait to find out why Annika has betrayed me," Jane said with a nasty smile. "How fun it will be to remind her why it's best to be on *my* side of things."

"Loads," Frazier muttered, almost forgetting himself. "The fangen are ready, Mistress, and are already moving into their hiding positions."

"That should be an interesting sight to watch—

them sniffing along, bumping into things." Jane pointed a finger through the crack of the door. "Remember, we need the Realitants alive. This is the perfect opportunity for me to learn what that weasel George is planning."

"Yes, Mistress Jane," Frazier said. "The fangen will be very . . . eager, but I'll do my best to restrain them."

The night was dark and cool, and Tick slept surprisingly well until Mothball shook him awake a couple of hours before dawn. He jumped at first, but his senses came back to him quickly.

"Time to be movin', it is," she whispered, then moved on to the next person.

They'd all slept on a wide blue tarp, each one of them given a single blanket to make it through the night. Tick had never felt *too* cold, and the soft undergrowth of the forest floor made for a nice mattress. All in all, he felt well rested once he got up and his blood started flowing.

After a quick breakfast of granola bars and apples, a unified hush settled on everyone as they helped Mothball pack up her things and stuff them into the backpack. The forest was mostly quiet, the occasional buzz of an insect or howl of an animal in the distance the only sounds.

Tick didn't know if he'd ever felt butterflies so intense as he did at that moment, waiting to hop back on his Windbike and fly off to meet Annika the spy. From what he'd heard about Mistress Jane, he doubted she would be very merciful if they blew the mission and got captured. What if Sato was right? What if this was all a trap? What if something went wrong? Tick tried not to think about his fears, putting his trust in Mothball and Master George.

"Everyone, gather 'round," Mothball said once she'd swung the backpack onto her shoulders. They moved together into a tight circle, intently awaiting instructions. "Just yonder there's a small break in the trees. Once there, we're going to fly up and over the roof of the forest to make it easy goin'. Just follow me, and we'll make our way to the meetin' point by the river. Once Annika comes with the Barrier Wand, we'll scuttle away right quick and head back for the old battleground in the forest. Got it?"

"Yeah," whispered Paul. "Sounds pretty easy to me."

"What do we do if something goes wrong?" Sato asked, seeming to show a little more interest in the group. "What is—how do you say?—our Plan B?"

"Yeah, what if this Annika lady doesn't get the Wand to us?" Paul asked.

Mothball paused. "Then we fly like the dickens back to the battleground to regroup."

"Why do I *not* feel assured this has all been thought out?" Sofia asked.

"Annika's been preppin' for months for this, she 'as," Mothball replied. "But if we don't get the ruddy Wand, won't matter much in the end. If we're to have any 'ope of defeatin' the Mistress, we need to trap her 'ere for a long time."

"Then let's do it," Paul said, holding his hand out, palm to the ground.

Tick got the idea and did the same, putting his hand on top of Paul's. Sofia followed suit, then Mothball. Everyone looked at Sato, whose face was hidden in the darkness. After a long pause, he finally gave in, placing his hand on top of the pile.

"Promise me," he said looking around the circle. "Promise me you people won't betray me."

His words surprised Tick, and by the shocked silence from his friends, he figured they were just as taken back.

"Promise me!" Sato yelled.

"Just who do you think——" Sofia began.

"No," Mothball said, cutting her off. "Sato 'ere had a bit of trouble in his past. Right deserving of his doubts, he is. Sato, I promise I won't be the one doin' any betraying. You can bet yer best buttons on that one."

"Me, neither," Paul quickly added. "Sato, we're in this together, man."

"Yeah," Tick agreed. "We're not going to betray you."

"And you?" Sato said to Sofia.

"I think you need an attitude—"

"Sofia!" Tick snapped, surprising himself.

She paused for a long time. "All right, all right. Sato, I promise I won't betray you, even though that sounds really lame. We're all a team, here. *Okay?*" She said the last word sarcastically, as if to preserve her dignity. "Can we quit holding hands now?"

"On three," Paul said, ignoring her. "On three, yell . . . *Go Realitants.*"

"Oh, come on," Sofia complained.

"Just do it," Paul replied. "Pump us up for some prime-time action and adventure. Ready?" He bobbed his hand up and down as he counted. "One . . . two . . . three . . . GO REALITANTS!" He threw everyone's hands up in the air as he shouted the last part with enthusiasm.

Tick and Mothball half-heartedly said the words with him, but Sato and Sofia didn't make a peep.

"Man, you guys are pathetic," Paul muttered.

"Let's just get on with it, Cheeseball," Sofia said. "Let's go get us a Barrier Wand."

And with that, they got on their bikes and flew toward the tops of the trees.

CHAPTER 47

ANNIKA'S TOSS

The dark sky had the slightest hint of purple as the Realitants shot out of the forest and skimmed along the canopy of trees, following Mothball in the lead. Tick knew he should be terrified, but he already felt completely confident in the workings of the Windbikes; they seemed invincible and effortless. The dark and puffy roof of the forest below them looked like a churning sea of storm clouds, making him feel higher in the sky than a few hundred feet. It was a little awkward holding on to Sato at first, but he enjoyed the rush of speed and the whipping wind.

For the first time in his life, he knew what it felt like to be Superman.

They traveled for a half hour before Mothball held up her hand to signal the others to slow down. The black purple of the sky had slowly brightened into a mixture of oranges and reds, streaks of fiery clouds scratched across it. Tick could see that the main forest ended a mile or so ahead, and almost swallowed his tongue when he saw what towered above the land beyond.

It was a massive fortress of stone and rock, still dark against the scant light of dawn. Dozens of towers and bridges dotted its skyline. It had to be the single largest structure Tick had ever seen—bigger by *far* than even the Seahawks' football stadium. It appeared that not only had Mistress Jane discovered a land full of something like magic, she'd set herself up in a castle fit for a king from any fantasy book in the library. Tick was in awe and had the sudden urge to explore the place.

The three Windbikes hovered next to each other, everyone in stunned silence as they gawked at the castle of Mistress Jane.

"Calls it the Lemon Fortress, she does," Mothball said. "Why that woman loves the color yellow so much is beyond me. Looney, she is."

"Are we sure they can't see us?" Paul asked.

"Not sure at'all. Come on, down we go. Got to be about our business." She pushed on her handlebars and flew toward the edge of the forest, the other two Windbikes right behind her.

They passed over the green cliff of the tightly packed trees and descended toward the ground, where a lush lawn of grass and wildflowers was sliced by the sinewy curve of a huge, sparkling blue river that spilled out from underneath the castle before finally disappearing into the forest. Not a person was in sight, and in a matter of seconds, the group had settled on the ground next to the deep, slowly moving waters, close enough to the trees to smell bark and pine.

"Where is Annika?" Sofia asked, not bothering to hide the frustration in her voice.

"Be along directly, she will," Mothball replied, but her face showed signs of worry as she stared at the Lemon Fortress with a creased brow.

From where they waited, they could see a cobblestone path running along the river and up to a large double-doored entrance of the castle, just a few hundred feet away. Next to it, the river seemed to magically appear from nowhere, bubbling up from under the cold blocks of the castle's granite. At the moment, not a thing stirred anywhere except for the trickling river and the early-rising birds of the forest.

Tick was about to say something when Mothball shushed him, holding up a hand as she perked her ears, looking around for signs of mischief. At first, Tick couldn't hear anything, but then the faintest sound of giggling and high-pitched chatter came from everywhere at once, bouncing along the lawn in front of them and from the trees behind them.

"What *is* that?" Paul whispered.

The creepy cacophony of hoots and howls and wicked laughter grew louder.

"That can't be good," Sofia muttered, her eyes wide in her frightened face. "Mothball, what's going on?"

"Methinks we've been found out, I do," she answered, standing to get a better look at the Lemon Fortress. "Sounds like the fangen to me, and they be comin' fast. We may have to fight a bit after all. Don't worry, the lugs are still blind and clumsy so all ya'll need to do is move a lot and shoot 'em with these little gems."

She pulled out several dark-green cylinders from a side pocket on her backpack and passed one to each of the kids. They were thin and several inches long, one end tapering to a point. Tick took his and examined the shiny surface, noticing a small button toward the thicker end.

"What's this?" he asked.

"That there's the Sound Slicer," Mothball answered. "Point the narrowed bit at the beasties when they get close and push the button. Keep 'em off ya, it will."

"What does it—" Sofia began.

Before she could finish her question, the sound of wood scraping against stone echoed through the air.

Everyone turned in unison to see the wide double doors of the castle opening outward like the gaping jaws of a monster. The seam in the middle had barely grown a foot wide before a woman with long black hair shot out of it, dressed in a bright green dress, running with strained and frantic effort. In her right hand, she held a long golden rod.

The Barrier Wand.

"It's Annika!" Mothball roared as she jumped back onto her Windbike. "Quick! Fly to her—fly to her!"

She shot into the air and down the path of the river, toward the running woman, who kept looking behind her, terrified. She shouted something as she ran, but they were too far away to hear. As Tick scrambled onto the Windbike behind Sato, he saw tall, gangly figures pouring through the castle doors, more and more as the exit opened wider. He couldn't tell what the creatures were, but they seemed . . . *wrong* somehow. They were basically human in shape, but all comparisons ended there.

Sato shot through the air and pulled up beside Mothball as they drew closer to Annika. "What are those things?" he yelled.

The creatures' skin was a putrid hue of yellow, like they'd been infected with a horrible disease. Clumpy patches of hair sprang from their bodies in random places and they wore only scant, filthy clothing that looked like tattered sheets that barely covered their thick torsos. Their eyes were mere slits, burning red pupils peeping out like a glimpse of hot lava. And their mouths . . .

They were huge, full of pointy spikes of enormous teeth.

"Them's the fangen," Mothball shouted. "Nasty beasties, they are. But we can fight 'em off with a bit of effort."

Even as she spoke, the hackles and cries from the fangen grew louder. Tick looked around in horror as he saw more of the sickly creatures appearing from everywhere, out of ditches, over the crests of the surrounding hills, out of the forest. They came from all directions, some bounding along on all four of their skinny arms and legs, others running upright; still others had *things* sprouting off their backs, membranous extensions resembling dirty sails, tautly flapping in the wind. With horror, Tick realized they were wings.

"By the way," Mothball yelled, readying herself to dive for Annika. "Fangen can fly."

High above the grounds, safe in her room, Mistress Jane sat next to the open air of her window, listening with glee to the horrific sounds of her attacking army. Amazing what the power of this twisted and evil

Reality could create. This was her first practical use of the fangen. How wonderful.

But with so many against so few, it hardly seemed fair.

She looked down in her lap, where she cradled the Chi'karda Drive like a newborn baby. Without it, the pathetic band of Realitants could never use her Barrier Wand to escape. And she had already received word that Master George's Wand had been damaged beyond repair in the battle at the Bermuda Triangle. Good news, all around.

She did feel a little saddened by Annika's betrayal. Jane had trusted her with so many trivial and demeaning duties. What a pity she'd have to be done away with.

Mistress Jane screamed for something to eat. She had a show to enjoy before she sat down to strategize for her meeting with Reginald Chu in a few days.

Her plan to make the universe a better place had officially begun.

Sofia had fallen far behind the other two Windbikes, too shocked by the sight of the onrushing creatures to push ahead any faster. She spun in a slow circle as she took it all in. The fangen were everywhere. The sight of the tall, awkward creatures, with their bony arms and legs attached to a thick, solid torso and their disgusting skin and patches of greasy hair, made her sick.

"Man, what are those things!" Paul shouted from behind her.

"Your long-lost cousins!" Sofia yelled back, knowing there couldn't possibly be a worst time to make a joke, but unable to stop herself.

"Hilarious—now hurry and catch up with Mothball!"

Sofia was about to push forward on the handlebars when something appeared right in front of them, shooting up from the ground.

One of the creatures, its enormous mouth baring fangs the size of small knives, hovered in midair, blocking their path. It looked hungry.

Sofia saw the wings for the first time, furled out behind the fangen like a horrific version of giant palm leaves.

From behind her, Paul suddenly screamed.

The fangen moved twice as fast as Annika could run, and they were almost on top of her as Mothball dove toward the ground like a hawk on a field mouse. Her heart hurt at seeing the terror on her old friend's face as she ran, the fierceness in Annika's eyes enough to turn water to stone. Mothball leaned on the handlebars, willing the Windbike to move faster. She wasn't close enough to use a Sound Slicer, and even if she were, she couldn't use it; the thing would turn Annika's brain to jelly.

A fangen jumped on Annika's back, throwing her to the ground. Annika rolled, gripping the Barrier Wand with both hands and swinging wildly. She hit the creature in the face, a strange bark coming out of its mouth as it reared back in pain. Annika scrambled to her feet and kept running, the horde of fangen right on her tail. The clumsy things constantly stumbled over each other, but never lost ground due to sheer numbers.

Mothball was almost to Annika, screaming at her to keep running. Though Mothball was bigger than the usual rider of a Windbike—leaving no room for another passenger—she felt sure she could somehow lift Annika up and away from the monsters. Of course, the disgusting things could just leap into the air with their warped Chi'karda-melded wings, but she'd deal with one thing at a time.

About forty feet away, Mothball realized she was too late. Several fangen had caught up with Annika, flanking her to make sure she couldn't fight her way out again. Her eyes met Mothball's, and they seemed so full of fear that Mothball worried Annika might drop dead of it.

Determined to fight her way into the melee and

save Annika and the Wand or die trying, Mothball surged forward.

She was almost there when Annika threw the Barrier Wand into the air as hard as she could, the shiny rod glistening in the morning sun as it wind-milled end over end toward Mothball. An instant later, Annika disappeared under a mass of writhing yellow skin and claws.

Mothball reached out and caught the Wand with her right hand, screaming with fury at the beasts below her, knowing it was too late to save her friend.

Tick and Sato watched the entire ordeal play out from dozens of feet behind Mothball, flying in to help. Tick didn't know if he should cheer or cry when their tall friend caught the Barrier Wand in her hand.

He had time to do neither.

A pack of three flying fangen attacked their Windbike in a swarm of sharp claws and spiky fangs and flapping wings.

Paul screamed when the claws raked down his back, trying not to picture in his mind what it had done to his skin. On instinct, he gripped Sofia harder for support and kicked behind him with his right leg.

He felt a solid thump as his foot connected, followed by a hair-raising shriek that faded as the creature fell to the ground.

Sofia gunned the Windbike forward; it smashed into a flying fangen and sent it reeling to the side, hissing in frustration. Paul felt himself slipping backward and had to pull himself back onto the seat, all the while looking below them at the unbelievable sight. Everywhere he looked, more and more of the nightmarish creatures appeared, snapping at the air with their vicious fangs.

"Use the thing Mothball gave us!" Sofia yelled from up front, pulling it out of her pocket as she spoke.

"Sound Slicer," Paul whispered to himself as he grabbed his own.

Together, they aimed the little cylinders at the nearest pack of fangen and pushed the buttons. A low sound vibrated through the air, barely discernible but heavy, rattling Paul's bones as if he'd been standing next to tolling cathedral bells. Below them, the fangen suddenly plummeted toward the ground like they'd been hit with an invisible tidal wave.

"Whoa," Paul said.

In tandem, he and Sofia swept the area below them, firing the Sound Slicer at anything in sight. Hordes of fangen fell from the sky.

"Find Mothball!" Paul yelled in Sofia's ear.

Tick had never really been in a fight his entire life. He'd always walked away from them or taken the punishment or *avoided* them. But now he had no choice. With one hand clutching Sato's shirt, he punched and kicked with his other three limbs, thrashing wildly as he frantically tried to avoid the fangs and claws of the fangen.

Sato swerved back and forth with the Windbike, alternately accelerating and slamming on the brakes, popping up and down, trying his best to get away from their attackers. But for every one that fell away, two more seemed to show up.

Tick felt his elbow connect with something solid, heard an eerie yelp. His feet kicked away a fangen on each side of the bike at the same time. He punched another one square between the small slits of its eyes. More of the beasts swarmed in. Tick reached into his pocket and pulled out the cylinder he'd received from Mothball, only to have it knocked out of his hands, falling to the ground below.

He felt something sharp on his shoulder blade, turning around to see that one of the fangen had grabbed his scarf, pulling itself closer with jaws wide open. Tick had to let go of Sato with his other hand as he swung his elbow up and around as hard as he could, slamming it into the beast's neck. It screamed and fell away.

At that very moment, Tick's stomach shot up into his throat as the Windbike suddenly plummeted toward the ground. He just barely grabbed the edges of the seat, turning toward the front of the bike.

His heart skittered when he saw that Sato had *disappeared*.

He looked up just in time to see two fangen flying away, Sato firmly in the grasp of their claws.

CHAPTER 48

DOUBLE DOORS

Frazier Gunn watched the action from his perch high atop the walls of the Lemon Fortress. Seeing the swarms of fangen descend on the few Realitants—especially the big one who'd kidnapped him in the Alaskan cemetery—gave him a grim sense of satisfaction.

His place in Mistress Jane's hierarchy would surely skyrocket after this victory.

He saw the tall woman, grasping the useless Barrier Wand, dodging and weaving through hundreds of fangen as she tried to escape. He worried slightly she might break it—even though it couldn't be used without the Chi'karda Drive, the shell itself was a complex instrument in its own right that would take months to replace—but the army of creatures had direct orders to retrieve it safe and sound. Everything would be fine.

Surprised by a sudden yawn, Frazier decided he'd had enough; the fangen were already boring him. He turned around and went back into the castle proper, hoping Mistress Jane might call on him for congratulations very soon.

Tick knew Sato's fate was sealed if Tick couldn't gain control of the Windbike before it crashed into the ground below. The bike twisted and pitched back and forth as it fell, throwing his senses into complete chaos. He steeled himself, forcing his eyes and hands to focus on the leather seat, pulling himself toward the handlebars. Though he didn't dare look, he could *feel* the lawn and river rushing up to smash him to bits. He only had seconds to live unless he . . .

With one last grunt, he yanked himself upright and squeezed his legs on both sides of the bike's body. He quickly grabbed the handlebars and bent them toward the sky. With a lurch that almost made his stomach implode, the Windbike slowed to a halt then shot straight back up into the air. As dozens of fangen repositioned themselves to attack him again, Tick looked in the direction Sato had been taken. He could just see his flailing body, resisting the two creatures that'd whisked him away.

They were on a direct course for the top of the castle.

In the next instant, a million thoughts seemed to flow through Tick's mind, processing and reprocessing.

A few months ago, he'd made a very difficult decision. Even though his life had become frightening—just as Master George had promised it would—and even though he could've made it all go away with a simple toss of the first letter into the fire, he hadn't done it. Some courage he didn't know he'd had, some sense of duty and right he didn't know was so powerful, had swelled inside his heart and given him the conviction to make an extremely hard choice. He remembered thinking of his little sister Kayla, and what he might do if her life were at stake.

And now, truly for the first time in his existence, Tick had a chance to risk his own life to save another.

The question posed by Master George so long ago popped back into his mind.

Will you have the courage to choose the difficult path?

Tick screamed Sato's name and slammed the handlebars up and forward, bulleting the Windbike in a straight path toward the fangen. Toward Sato.

⁓

Sofia continued to fly the Windbike as crazy as she dared, swerving and diving and skyrocketing upward in an attempt to evade the countless creatures coming after them. Her head hurt from the effort; her stomach begged her to stop.

Behind her, Paul continued to shoot as many fangen as he could with his Sound Slicer, defending her as she drove. He'd slipped and almost fallen several times, but she had no choice but to keep flying forward.

She caught a glimpse of Tick streaking past her on his Windbike.

Alone.

Where was—

Before she could finish her thought, one of the flying creatures slammed into them from the side, driving its head into the engine of the bike. Sofia lurched, barely hanging on as the body of the beast flipped under them and fell to the ground.

She felt Paul squirming behind her to right himself on the seat. "What was that thing *doing?*" he asked.

Unfortunately, they got their answer a second later.

With a loud sputter of electronic coughs, then a low whine that sounded like a baby elephant caught in a trap, the Windbike quit working. Completely.

This time, Sofia and Paul screamed in unison as they dropped toward the ground far below.

Tick had halved the distance to Sato and his captors in a matter of seconds. Even though they could fly, the fangen were no match for the Windbikes when it came to speed.

Tick leaned forward, keeping his eyes focused on his target.

He tried not to think of what would happen if they suddenly decided to drop Sato.

⌒

Mothball used the Barrier Wand like a staff, swinging it in wide arcs as she darted about on her Windbike, knocking the heads of the fangen, sometimes two or three at a time. She realized they'd be in a whole heap of mess if she broke the ruddy Wand, but Master George had always said the things were sturdy enough to withstand most punishment.

She'd just landed a particularly nice hit on a creature when she caught a flicker of dark movement to her right. She looked to see Paul and Sofia—and their bike—plummeting toward the ground.

She zoomed in that direction without an instant's hesitation.

⌒

Sofia's Windbike sputtered sporadically, humming to life with a jolt for the briefest of moments before dying again. Paul hugged Sofia tightly from behind, probably hoping she'd never bring it up again should they somehow survive.

But Sofia knew they'd be dead in seconds, and wondered what life as a Realitant might've been like. She thought she might have liked it.

Mothball didn't have time to think or ponder several options. Only one made sense, and she went for it, quickly stuffing the Barrier Wand through a belt loop with one hand while she steered with the other.

In a nosedive that made her eyes water, she rushed toward Sofia and Paul, who clung to their useless Windbike as it plummeted in a downward spiral. Their present course would smash them against a group of boulders clustered close to the river. Mothball intended to *change* that course.

At the last second before she caught up with the falling bike, Mothball swerved hard to the right then arrowed back in straight at Sofia and Paul, keeping pace with their rate of descent, knowing she only had one shot. As soon as she made contact, Mothball gunned her own Windbike, *pushing* the other one at an angle as it fell.

Toward the river.

What had been certain death was now a chance.

If the ruddy water was *deep* enough.

Tick flew up and over the stone parapet bordering the massive crown of the castle, then skimmed along the loose gravel covering the roof. The two fangen had touched down, folding their wings behind them; Sato was clutched between them, his head hanging low.

When they spotted Tick, the two fangen howled out a piercing cry, seeming to dare Tick to attempt a rescue. From both sides of the castle walls, more of the creatures charged in, hungry to join the fight.

Tick never slowed down.

"Sato!" he screamed. "Duck!"

The boy showed no signs he'd heard or even planned to do as he was told, but Tick knew he had no other choice. He leaned forward, trying to envision in his mind what he was about to do.

"Sato!" he screamed again, only thirty feet away. "Duck—NOW!"

To Tick's relief, Sato buckled his legs and fell toward the roof, catching his captors by surprise. Though they didn't let go, both fangen looked down at Sato, their attention diverted for an instant, their heads high enough to serve as a perfect target.

Tick yanked back and to the left on the handle-bars, leaning hard to the left as the Windbike spun, slowing as the back end swerved around and slammed into the upper bodies of the two fangen. Tick felt a jolt of pain as one of the creatures bit at his right leg before it toppled over. Both of the horrible creatures let go of Sato, stunned by the sudden impact.

Tick steadied the Windbike and lowered it all the way to the loose rocks of the roof. "Get on!" he yelled. Dozens of fangen were charging right for them.

Sato was bruised and battered, his face still pale with the terror of being captured, but he crawled to the bike and pulled himself onto the seat, Tick helping him the last few inches.

Out of the corners of his eyes, Tick saw a blur of yellowed skin and vicious claws. He felt an icy touch on his elbow. Before anything could take hold, Tick shot the Windbike up and away from the sea of disgusting monsters.

A storm of fangen took flight in pursuit.

⁓

Paul had absolutely no idea what happened.

His mind had been fading, shutting down into a blissful state of unconsciousness so he didn't have to feel the excruciating instant of pain when his body smacked into the ground. But everything changed in a sudden rush of intense cold and wetness.

Water engulfed him, filling his lungs as he instinctively sucked in air at the shock of impact. As he felt his feet slam into the river bottom—hard enough to almost break his legs—he sputtered and coughed, his instincts trying to prevent him from taking another breath and killing himself. The next instant, he felt a massive arm grab him around the chest and pull him through the water.

But not up—not toward air.

The arm pulled him to the *side*, skimming his body along the sandy river bottom.

Paul had one moment to wonder if he was dead before everything grew very dark.

~~~~~

Tick shot into the open air away from the castle, his blood freezing at the sight of countless fangen everywhere. The air was full of them, defying gravity as they flew with their pale, weak-looking wings. More crawled and ran across the grounds, an endless army of ants. Not knowing where to go or what to do, Tick frantically searched the sky and the ground for any glimpse of his friends.

A flash of red far below caught his eye. One of the Windbikes, in the *river*.

And no sign of anyone near it.

His heart sinking faster than he could ever fly, Tick slammed on the handlebars and catapulted toward the ground.

After swimming under the thick stone arch from which the slow-moving river exited the Lemon Fortress, Mothball kicked with all of her might toward the surface, dragging both Sofia and Paul in her arms. Desperate for air, she could only imagine how her two little friends were doing, if they still lived.

Her head broke through the surface with a loud splash; she sucked in the most refreshing breath of her life. Even as she did so, she pulled up with her arms, bringing Paul's and Sofia's faces above the water line.

Mothball's heart almost leaped out of her chest when both of the kids coughed and sputtered for air. With an inexplicable laugh, she dragged them to the side of the river where she helped them climb out and onto a wide stone walkway. Paul fell over, spitting and sucking, spitting and sucking. Sofia seemed better, taking in slow, deep breaths as she looked around, her eyes wide.

They stood next to the river in a long, dark tunnel that delved in one direction for what seemed like eternity, no end in sight. On the other side, the river disappeared under a thick stone wall, flowing outside the castle wall. Next to that stood the huge wooden doors they'd seen from the outside. They were still halfway open and letting in enough light to prevent them from being in complete darkness.

"This is where those creatures came from," Sofia whispered.

"Best be glad they're out there, now," Mothball muttered. She pulled the Barrier Wand out of the huge belt loop where she'd stuck it for safekeeping.

Paul had recovered enough to stand up, his chest still heaving as he fought to catch his breath. "What happened to Tick and Sato?"

As if in answer, they heard Tick shout from outside the doors. "Mothball!"

His Windbike had flown down from somewhere above; he hovered just outside, Sato on the back.

"Wait a minute," Paul said. "I thought Sato was driving the bike."

"Quick!" Mothball yelled, ignoring Paul. "Get in 'ere!"

She saw Tick obey immediately, shooting the Windbike through the narrow space between the half-open doors. Even as he did, Mothball grabbed the long ropes hanging on the inside of the huge slabs of wood that served as handles to pull them closed.

"Help me!" she yelled.

As the others moved to her side and pulled with her, Mothball looked outside. Just before the doors slammed shut with a loud boom, she saw the hideous sight of countless fangen charging directly for them.

CHAPTER 49

THE GOLDEN BUTTON

Mothball pulled an enormous plank of wood down into the slot that locked the double doors. "Won't hold 'em for long, bet yer best buttons." She looked at Tick, who'd parked the Windbike and now hugged his friends like they'd just won the Cricket tourney. "Save the celebratin' if you don't mind. Here." She held up the Barrier Wand, gesturing for him to take it.

"What?" Tick stammered. "Here? Now?"

"'Less you'd be wantin' to invite the fangen in first."

Tick frowned. "But I thought we had to get back to the battleground."

Something heavy slammed into the doors from the other side, followed by a thunder of heavy thumps and nerve-grinding scratches. The fangen wanted *in*.

"Only if we'd be wantin' Master George to grab us in a few hours," Mothball said. "No time for that now. It's up to you."

Without waiting for a response, she tossed the Wand in Tick's direction.

Tick caught the long golden rod with both hands, scared to death he'd drop it and break it. He hefted it in his hands, surprised at how light it felt.

"So . . . I just have to adjust the controls and poof— we're safe?" he asked Mothball.

"Be quick about it—and make no mistakes on the dials or we may end up in the wrong end of a beluga whale, we will. Once you're set, we all need to be touchin' it, then ya simply push the button."

A crashing thunk made them all jump. Tick saw the head of a huge axe embedded in the wood of the right door. With an ear-piercing squeal, the huge sliver of metal was yanked back out. A second later it landed again, throwing a shower of splinters all over the stone walkway. It disappeared and a red eye peeked through the rough slit, followed by a gurgly scream.

"Uh, Tick," Sofia said. "Maybe we should, I don't know, *hurry*?" She threw every ounce of sarcasm she could muster into the last word.

"Yeah, man," Paul agreed. "Giddyup."

"They're almost through . . ." Sato said, his voice taut.

"Okay," Tick whispered as he knelt down on the stone, holding the Barrier Wand in front of him delicately, like he held in his hands the most priceless artifact of the ancient Egyptians. "Here goes nothing."

More booms and cracks sounded from the doors. More cackles and deranged giggling. The left door started to buckle, like the fangen had just hit it with a huge battering ram.

"Take your time, Tick," Sofia muttered.

Tick ignored her, closing his eyes and bringing up the image of what Master George had shown him back at the Bermuda Triangle complex. He raised his mind's eye to look at the Doohickey, the uppermost control.

"Okay," he said, opening his eyes to focus on the real thing. While holding the rod with his left hand, he reached forward and turned the Doohickey three clicks to the right. He paused again, knowing it was better to get it right the first time instead of rushing and having to start all over again. He envisioned the Whatchamacallit, then the Thingamajig, slowly making the appropriate adjustments. He moved his attention to the next control down.

An ear-splitting crack made him yelp, looking up to see a huge seam had split the right door into almost two complete sections. Several yellowy arms squirmed through the opening, grasping and clawing to pull the pieces apart.

Tick, spurred into a fear-induced sense of focus, went back to work on the Barrier Wand.

———◦———

"The water ruined the ruddy Sound Slicers, no doubt," Mothball said as she ran forward to the doors, picking up a huge splinter of wood that had fallen inward onto the stone floor. She immediately got to work, whacking and stabbing any sign of the diseased yellow skin that squeezed through the large crack. With every shriek and scream of anger, she doubled her efforts.

Paul joined her, finding a smaller but sharper stick. Without a word to each other, they worked in tandem— Paul fighting the lower portion, Mothball the upper.

They only had to buy Tick a little more time.

———◦———

Sofia felt rooted to the ground, screaming inside with helplessness. Sato stood beside her, frantically looking around as if trying to find something to fight.

"What happened out there?" Sofia asked him.

Sato looked at her, his eyes drained of the hatred and mistrust he'd shown back at Master George's place. "He saved my life." Sato pointed at Tick.

"He did?"

Sato nodded.

"That's—" Sofia shrieked as something grabbed her ankle. She looked down to see a slick yellowed hand gripped around her, attached to one of the fangen, crawling out of the river. Behind it she saw another's head pop out of the water.

Before she could react, Sato kicked down with his foot, breaking the miserable thing's hand with a hideous crunch. It squealed and splashed back into the water, just as Sato got down on his knees and shot the other one with a muted *thump* from his Sound Slicer. The creature disappeared into the black water.

Sofia reached down and helped Sato back to his feet, then dragged him away from the river, seeing no signs of other creatures—for the moment.

The breaches in the doors were cracking wider, almost big enough for one of the monsters to squeeze through. A sickly arm reached inside, a glimmering silvery globe clutched in its hand. Sofia was about to shout a warning when Mothball whacked the thing's arm with her huge stick.

The tall woman turned around, her face on fire with rage, yelling at the others. "Run away from the door! All of you!"

Paul didn't argue, turning immediately to run down the dark tunnel. He grabbed Tick's arm as he passed, half dragging him along since Tick was still focused intently on the Barrier Wand.

"Come on!" Paul yelled. "We need to get out of their reach or they're going to fry us for dinner. Just a little farther in!"

Tick finally snapped his concentration and broke into a full run behind Paul. "I've almost got it," he said, panting. "Just one more dial."

The last word had barely crossed his lips when a horrible explosion of cracking wood boomed and echoed down the dark stone tunnel. The silver ball had been some kind of bomb.

The breach was complete.

❧

Tick tried to ignore the noise of screaming and howling fangen pouring through the shattered doors behind them. Knowing he had no time left, he quit running and knelt down again, bringing the Barrier Wand up to his eye level. "Everyone come here!" he shouted. "Grab the Wand!"

He focused on the bottom dial—the Whattzit. He turned it to the correct position, then glanced over the other six controls, verifying each of them one last time. The other Realitants had gathered around him, leaning over to grasp the Wand in different locations, being careful not to cover up or bump the dials and switches.

The nightmarish sounds of the onrushing fangen grew louder. Sato used his free hand to shoot with his Sound Slicer, keeping some of them at bay, but Tick knew it was only a matter of time.

"Everyone ready?" Tick shouted over the cackles and war cries of the fangen and the teeth-jolting thumps of Sato's lone weapon.

"Do it!" Mothball answered for everyone. "Be quick about it!"

Unable to prevent a smile from spreading across his face, Tick pushed the golden button on top of the Barrier Wand.

Nothing happened.

The haunting chorus of horrible sounds continued. Tick and the others were still trapped inside the Lemon Fortress.

Tick pushed the button again, then again, triggering his finger up and down several times.

Nothing.

"What's *wrong*, Tick?" Sofia yelled.

"Dude, hurry up!" Paul added.

Tick ignored them, studying the controls to see if he'd made a mistake. One by one, he quickly scanned them, matching their positions with the image burned inside his mind. Everything was right.

He pushed the button again, with the same result.

No, no, no, he thought. *Not after all we just went through. You will work. You will work!*

"Tick!" Sofia yelled, swatting him on the shoulders in panic.

Tick could hear the creatures coming, could feel them.

Focusing, funneling the surroundings out of his mind and heart, Tick gripped the Barrier Wand, staring at it like he could melt it with his eyes. *They'd come so far . . .*

He felt that strange reservoir of heat deep in his stomach bubbling to life. He'd tapped into it twice before and now he reached for it eagerly, letting the warmth flood through his entire body, filling him with certainty.

Tick shouted into the air, louder than he'd ever shouted anything in his whole life.

"YOU WILL *WORK* YOU STUPID PIECE OF HUNK-A-JUNK!"

He closed his eyes and pushed the button one last time.

Tick instantly felt a tingle shoot down his back and the world around him fell into dead silence.

CHAPTER 50

THE CALM
AFTER THE STORM

What do you mean, it *worked?*"

Mistress Jane glared at Frazier Gunn, who knelt before her chair by the window, like a criminal begging for his life. Surprisingly, Jane felt more intrigued than angry about this new development. Maybe she would let Gunn live after all.

"I don't know how it happened, Mistress," Gunn grumbled, sweat covering his face. "The Realitants disappeared and took the Barrier Wand with them."

Jane reached over and lifted the Chi'karda Drive from where she'd placed it on the stone ledge of the windowsill. "*How,* exactly, could they do that when I'm holding the heart of the Wand in my hands?"

"George must've winked them out somehow." Gunn kept his eyes fixed on the floor.

"Impossible," Jane said immediately. "I have first-hand reports that George's Wand broke in half. Plus, *you're* the one who said their plan was to go back to the ancient Plague battlefield and get winked hours from now."

"Then how did—"

"SILENCE!" Jane had endured this stupid man for quite long enough. "Leave me. I don't want to see you for a very long time." She dismissed him with a wave of her hand.

"Yes, Mistress."

Jane watched him get to his feet and shuffle away, murmuring incessantly his thanks for her gracious decision to let him live. He was lucky—losing the Wand was a major loss; its parts and mechanisms were equally as important as the Chi'karda Drive itself—but she had much more important things flying through the recesses of her brilliant mind.

How had they done it? How had they manipulated the Chi'karda powerfully enough without the Drive? And in the heart of her personal fortress at that? Did it have something to do with the twisted version of the mysterious force that existed in the Thirteenth Reality? Jane tapped a sharp fingernail against her lips, thinking.

Did one of those bratty kids have some kind of special power over the Chi'karda? Many questions indeed.

The implications were vast, the possibilities endless.

Despite the setback, Mistress Jane smiled.

To any outside observer, it would have seemed as though Tick and his friends had just won the Super Bowl, the World Series, and the NBA Championship in one fell swoop. Having been through so much, and after having hundreds of creepy yellow fangen within inches of tearing them to pieces, winking away to complete safety seemed reason enough to jump up and down, screaming and hugging and cheering and then to start all over again.

"What took you so long!" Paul yelled, whacking Tick on the back with a huge smile on his face.

"I was trying to decide if I wanted to take you or leave you behind," Tick replied, grinning.

They celebrated inside a room very similar to the one they'd left in the Bermuda Triangle, though a much smaller version—a couple of couches, a chair, a cold brick fireplace. A single window was placed directly across from the fireplace, and it looked out upon a dry palette of colors—oranges, reds, browns.

Tick brought his giddiness back to reason and

walked over to get a better look at the view. Beyond their room was a huge drop-off that led to a brown strip of river far below. Sheer walls of striated rock rose up from the valley on all sides, stretching in all directions as far as Tick could see. *This* was the satellite location Master George had said he'd send them to?

It was a canyon. No, it was *the* canyon.

"Are we inside the Grand Canyon?" he asked to no one in particular.

"That we are," Mothball answered. "This big crack's brimming over with Chi'karda, it is."

"Then where are Master George and Rutger?" Sofia asked.

A fallen mood filled the room like a sluggish oil spill, and no one said a word.

~⁓~

Master George worked furiously on his Barrier Wand, welding and wiring and hammering. He and Rutger had managed to repel the attack from Mistress Jane with an odd assortment of weapons, but not before the creatures had smashed his Wand in half with an axe. At least they'd missed severing the Chi'karda Drive.

Knowing his deadline to pull the Realitants out of the Thirteenth Reality was only a couple of hours away, he wiped the sweat off his brow and doubled his efforts.

"Master George!" Rutger yelled from the other room, followed by the quick series of heavy thumps that always marked the little man running on his short legs.

"What *is* it, Rutger?" Master George asked, annoyed. "Can't you see I'm under considerable duress?"

His friend stopped in the doorway, panting like he'd just run three miles. "Master George!"

"Speak, man, and be quick about it!"

"The nanolocators . . . Mothball, Tick . . . everyone— they winked to our station at the Canyon!"

His old friend's news made Master George regret the harshness of his words. "That's wonderful, Rutger! Wonderful, indeed!" He went back to work on the Wand, very encouraged indeed.

⌒⌒

Three hours after Tick and the others arrived at the Grand Canyon—three long and boring but happy hours—Master George and Rutger suddenly appeared by the fireplace without any warning, disheveled and dirty, but faces beaming.

Tick didn't know how to react; he felt shocked, relieved, elated, confused. He jumped up from the couch, his emotions swirling from all the highs and lows he'd felt since he'd awakened that morning. Mistress Jane's Barrier Wand lay on the couch next to him and he picked it up, excited to show Master George, who was already talking a mile a minute.

"I can hardly believe my eyes, old chaps! You did it, you really did it, indeed! I couldn't be more delighted if Muffintops bore twelve kittens this very instant. Why, I—" He stopped, catching sight of the now-filthy and battered Wand in Tick's hands. "Master Atticus, I simply *knew* you were up to the task. Congratulations to all of you." He focused on the Wand, holding his hands out timidly. "May I, er, see it?"

Tick handed over the golden cylinder, glad to be rid of it.

As soon as Master George took it in his hands, he frowned, his brow crinkling in confusion. "Why, it's so . . . *light*. Has Mistress Jane altered the construction somehow?" He turned the Wand over and unscrewed the bottom until it popped off. He then held the now-open cylinder up to his eye like a telescope, closing his other eye as he examined its insides.

Master George dropped the Wand to his side, a look of complete bewilderment on his face.

"What's the matter?" Mothball asked. "Look like a mum what's lost her kiddies, ya do."

Master George looked at Tick, dark thunderclouds gathering in his eyes.

"What?" Tick asked, taking a step back.

"Have you taken any pieces out of this Wand?"

Master George asked, his tone accusatory.

"Huh?" Tick looked over at Sofia, then Paul. Both of them shrugged their shoulders. "No. I didn't even know you could open it up."

Master George looked like he didn't believe him. "Young man, you are telling me you used *this* Barrier Wand to wink yourself and these good people to this place?"

"Um . . . yes, sir," Tick stammered, worried he was in serious trouble.

Master George harrumphed and paced around the room, mumbling to himself, throwing his arms up in frustration as if he were in a great argument. He looked like a gorilla on a rampage.

"What in the name of Reality Prime's wrong with ya, Master George?" Mothball asked.

Master George stopped, turning sharply to face the group. "My dear fellow Realitants—because you are all most certainly full-fledged members now—you have all witnessed something that could very well change the Realities forever. Tick, my good man, have you ever had anything remarkable happen before in your life? Something quite . . . miraculous, if you will?"

"Why? What do you mean?" Tick thought of the incident with the letter from Master George that Kayla had burned, and its magical return as though it had never happened. But he didn't want to say anything about it, feeling suddenly very embarrassed and confused.

"I don't *know* what I mean, actually," Master George said. "But you've just done something that defies logic."

"What are you talking about?" Paul asked. "What did Tick do?"

Master George held up the Barrier Wand for everyone to look at. "This Wand is *missing* its Chi'karda Drive." He paused, waiting for a response, as if he'd just revealed a mystery recipe stolen from the Keebler elves, but only Mothball and Rutger reacted, exchanging a startled glance with each other before turning to stare at Tick.

"Good people, this thing is completely useless without the Drive. It cannot *work* without the Drive. Better off using a turnip to wink between Realities."

Tick was stunned, his mind on the cusp of realizing what had happened, but resisting its huge implications.

"Then how did Tick make it work?" Sofia asked.

"I have no idea! All I know is that the only way he could've winked here is by a deliberate control of Chi'karda the likes of which I've never seen in my life."

Master George walked over to Tick, put a hand on his shoulder.

"You, sir, are a walking enigma. This changes everything."

CHAPTER 51

HOMECOMING

The next day and a half were a complete blur for Tick. Mothball broke the news of Annika's death to Master George and Rutger, neither of whom bothered trying to hide their emotions, weeping like children on each others' shoulders. Not much was said after that, except that Annika's courage in sacrificing her life to steal the Barrier Wand would never be forgotten. Tick hadn't known her at all, but he still felt sad she was gone.

As for how Tick had winked them away to safety, no one understood what had happened, least of all Master George. He kept saying that the amount of conviction Tick had channeled, the sheer *energy* of his desire to wink himself and the others back to Reality

Prime should've killed him. It must've been such an unusual display of Chi'karda that the instruments back in the Triangle didn't know how to measure it or surely Rutger would've noticed an anomaly.

Eventually, everyone grew tired of so many questions without answers, and looked ahead to what came next.

Going home.

Master George said that even though Mistress Jane had kept her Chi'karda Drive, it was useless without the Wand casing. It would take her several months to build a new Barrier Wand capable of using its power. For now, she—and her newfound dark and twisted magic— were trapped within the Thirteenth Reality. The new Realitants' successful mission had bought them considerable time, time which Master George needed to repair his headquarters, plan for the future, and think about the potential meaning of Tick's unexplained ability.

As young as the Realitants were, with worried families, Master George thought it best that they return to their homes, explain their futures, and continue their studies—all until such time came that Master George needed them again.

And need them he would, he assured them over and over.

And so late that night, Tick, Sofia, Sato, and Paul stood in a circle by the roaring fire—Master George *loved* fires, even in the middle of the desert in summer—

with Master George and his two assistants, Mothball and Rutger. Everyone was silent, the reality of saying good-bye a heavy weight on their hearts.

As for Tick, he felt like his *soul* hurt. Though he'd only known these people a short time, the experiences they'd been through had solidified them as the very best friends he'd ever had. He felt excited to see his family, but dreaded the thought of going to bed tonight, alone in his room, not knowing how long it might be before he'd see any of the Realitants again. It took every ounce of will in his bones to keep from crying.

"Sato, my young friend," Master George said, finally breaking the somber silence. "I'd like to invite you to stay with us, to help us at the Triangle. These others have families to return to, but, er, well—I think you'd likely agree that joining us at headquarters may be in your best interest. Your, er, guardians will barely notice you're gone, I expect."

Tick looked at Sato, shocked. The quiet boy from Japan hadn't said much since their return from the Thirteenth Reality.

Sato looked up, trying to hide the relief on his face, but failing. "I will stay." He looked at Tick, then the others, as if he wanted desperately to say something. Instead, he folded his arms and looked away.

Tick's whole perception of Sato changed in that instant. *What mysteries are hidden inside that brain of his?*

"We'll be simply delighted to have your help," Master George said. "Now, then, it's almost time to wink everyone back to their homes. But first, I have something to give all of you." He reached into the folds of his suit and pulled out a handful of thin gold-link chains, a heavy pendant swinging from each one. "These will forever mark you as official and bonafide Realitants."

Tick stared at the shiny gold ornament as Master George placed the chain over his head like he'd just won an Olympic medal. Tick studied the object hanging on his chain, bringing it close to his eyes for a better look. It was a miniature replica of a Barrier Wand, dials and all, solid and heavy.

"Be sure and wear them under your shirts," Master George said as he stepped back in front of the group. "No need to go around advertising you're a member of the most important society in the world. Plenty of enemies about."

As Tick tucked the Wand pendant under his scarf and shirt, feeling the cold hardness warm up against his skin, Rutger began passing out small pieces of thick paper to each of the kids. "These are your official membership cards, so don't lose them."

Tick accepted his, a stiff brown card that simply said, "Atticus Higginbottom, Realitant Second Class."

"Whoa," Paul said. "No one will mess with us now.

I'll just whip this puppy out and they'll run like scared dogs."

"Very funny, young man," Rutger said, folding his chubby arms. "You just be sure and hold on to your Wand pendant and that card—you've earned them both."

"Yes, indeed," Master George said. "And now, we must really let you be on your way. Atticus, your name begins with an A, so let's send you off first."

Tick's stomach leaped into his throat. "Um, okay." He stepped forward.

"Wait a second," Paul said. "We need a send-off to pump us up." He held his hand out to the middle of the circle.

Tick joined him, then Sato, then Rutger, and Mothball. Master George chuckled and put his hand out, too. Rolling her eyes, Sofia finally did as well.

"Go Realitants!" Paul yelled. He groaned at everyone else's half-hearted attempt. "You guys need more team spirit."

"Please tell me we don't have to do that every time," Sofia muttered.

"Yeah," Tick agreed. "I think I'm with Sofia on that."

Paul looked devastated. "She's corrupted you."

Tick shrugged. "It *is* kind of corny." He paused, grinning. "Dude."

Master George cleared his throat. "Time to be off. Atticus, step up here, please."

Tick did so, adjusting the tattered and soppy scarf that clung to his neck like a frightened ferret. Mothball began the good-byes.

"Best of luck, little sir," she said, leaning down to give him a quick hug. "Get a little older and I'll be bringin' ya a nice tall girlfriend from the Fifth, I will. Better than a short fat one from the Eleventh, don't ya think?" She winked and stepped back.

"See ya, big guy," Rutger said, reaching up to pat Tick on the elbow. "Sorry about all the rock-throwing."

Tick laughed. "No problem."

"Later, dude," Paul said next. "See ya on the e-mail."

"Definitely."

Tick turned to Sato, who reached out and shook Tick's hand.

"Thank you," Sato said. "Next time I will save *your* life."

"There's a good plan," Tick replied with a smile. He turned to face Sofia.

She looked at him, her eyes revealing that she was trying to think of a smart-aleck remark. She finally gave up and pulled Tick into a hug, squeezing tightly. "E-mail me," she said. *"Tonight."*

Tick awkwardly patted her on the back. "Remember our bet—you have to come visit me in America. And I want some more free spaghetti sauce, too."

"Count on it." She pulled away, not bothering to hide her tears.

Tick turned to face Master George again, relieved the good-byes were over.

"Master Atticus, my dear friend," the old man said, his ruddy face beaming with a smile. "Your family will be so proud of you, as well they should. Quite a puzzlement you've given us to figure out, I must say. Busy, busy we'll be."

Tick nodded, not knowing what to say.

"Very good, then." Master George held up the Barrier Wand, having already set the controls. "Put your hand on the Wand. There we are."

"Bye everybody," Tick said, closing his eyes, hurting inside.

Master George had one final thing to say, though, whispering in Tick's ear. "Atticus, never forget the inherent power of the Chi'karda. Never forget the power of your choices, for good or for ill. And most importantly, never forget your courage."

Before Tick could reply, he heard a click.

He felt the now-familiar tingle.

Then came the sounds of birds and wind.

⁓

Edgar Higginbottom sat on his favorite chair next to the window, staring at the floor, wringing his hands together as he wondered for the millionth time what had happened to Tick. *He's lucky*, Edgar kept telling himself. *All those times as a kid—something's protecting him. He'll be fine.*

But it had been almost four full days since the boy vanished, and the worry ate at Edgar's heart like a hideous disease. Lorena was no better; they could barely look at each other without bursting into tears. Even Lisa was worried.

And yet Edgar knew it had been the right thing to do. Somehow, some way, he *knew*. Atticus Higginbottom was out saving the world, and when he was done, he'd come back home, ready for a new game of Football 3000. But when—

Edgar heard someone shouting outside. A kid's voice. *Tick's* voice.

He looked up, his heart swelling to dangerous sizes when he saw Tick running down the street toward the house. For a second, Edgar couldn't move, couldn't breathe, practically choking as he tried to yell for his wife. *It was him. It was* really *him!*

"Lorena!" Edgar finally managed to scream, squirming to get his big body out of the chair. "Lorena! Tick's back! I *told* you he'd be back!" He found himself laughing, then crying, then laughing again as he ran for the front door.

Lorena thumped down the stairs, faster than he'd ever seen her move in his life. Kayla and Lisa bolted out of the kitchen, eyes wide in surprise.

"He's really here?" Lorena asked, her hand on her heart as if she didn't dare hope Edgar had been telling the truth.

"He's back, he's back!" Edgar yelled with delight as he ripped open the door and ran outside.

Tick ran into his dad's arms, then, almost knocking Edgar down. They hugged each other, then parted to bring Lorena and the girls into the group. In one big tangle of arms, the Higginbottom family hugged and laughed and jumped and generally made complete fools of themselves. The world had suddenly become a very bright and cheerful place to be.

Finally, Tick pulled away, looking at each of his family members in turn.

"I've had a crazy couple of days."

Later that night, well after dark, Tick stood in the front yard under a sky thick with black clouds, not a star or moon in sight, thinking.

He thought about everything that had happened to him, but his thoughts kept returning to the bizarre incidents of the letter reappearing in his *Journal of Curious Letters* after Kayla had burned it, and how he'd made the Barrier Wand work even though Mistress Jane had broken it. Somehow, the two events were linked, but Tick couldn't begin to understand why or how. Did he have some kind of weird, freaky power? Or did Mistress Jane do something to the Realities, altering how the Chi'karda functioned?

Master George'll figure it out, Tick thought, trying to ignore how much it scared him.

He turned to walk back inside when the ground around him brightened, the slightest hint of a shadow at his feet. To the east, the full moon appeared, shining through a brief break in the clouds.

As if it were a sign, Atticus Higginbottom, Realitant Second Class, pulled out the Barrier Wand pendant from beneath his shirt and squeezed it in his fist.

EPILOGUE

THE THWARTED MEETING

Reginald Chu, the second best inventor and greatest businessman of all time, looked at his skin-watch again. He sat atop a park bench made from the new Plasticair material his company had created, growing more furious with every passing second. The person who'd asked to meet him here was *late*.

And no one was ever late for the founder, owner, and CEO of Chu Industries.

He reached into his pocket and pulled out the odd note that had been mailed to him several weeks ago, without any kind of return address or postmark. He unfolded the wrinkly paper and read through the handwritten message once again.

Dear Mister Chu,

You don't know me, but we must meet very soon. I know you are aware of the Realities, but that you have never had much interest in them because the Fourth is so much more advanced than the others. But I have a proposition for you that I am certain you will accept. I know of your love for power.

As a measure of my sincerity, I will come to your Reality. Meet me in Industry Park by the Lone Oak at noon on the thirteenth of May.

Your future partner,
Mistress Jane

Reginald crumpled the note up into a ball, squeezing it in his fist. The audacity of this woman. Commanding him to meet her like he was some errand-running schoolboy—and then having the nerve to not even show up? Who called themselves *Mistress* anyway?

He looked at his skinwatch one last time, then stood up. The lady was obviously not coming.

As he walked back toward his building, Reginald

threw the mysterious note into a roving Recycabot, angry about the time he'd wasted. There was much to be done, things he'd mapped out and set in motion long before he'd received a letter from today's no-show, Mistress Jane.

Reginald was a very busy man.

THE HUNT FOR
DARK INFINITY

This book is dedicated to my siblings:

Michael, Lisa, David, Paul, and Sarah.

Thanks for making life fun and adventurous.

I just wish you had shared more of the Dashner

good-looking genes. I love you guys.

PROLOGUE

THE ILLNESS

The boy stared at his world gone mad.

The wintry, white face of the mountain housing the End of the Road Insane Asylum towered behind him, its forever-frozen peak lost in the gray clouds blanketing the sky. Before him, the boy saw the last person of his village succumb to the claws of insanity.

The man was filthy, barely clothed, scraped from head to toe. He thrashed about in the muddy grass of what used to be the village commons, clutching at things above him that were not there. The man's eyes flared, wide and white, as if he saw ghosts swarming in for the haunt. He screamed now and then, a raw rasp that revealed the condition of his ruined throat. Then, spurred by something unseen, the man got up and sprinted away, stumbling and getting back up again, running wildly, arms flailing.

The boy finally tore his eyes away, tears streaming as he looked back toward the icy mountain. A lot of the crazies were already there, filling the asylum to capacity—prospective inmates had been turned away for a week now, left to wander the streets and fight others who were as mad as they were.

The boy had not eaten in two days. He'd not slept in three, at least not peacefully. He'd stopped grieving for his parents and brother and started worrying about how to survive, how to live. He tried not to think—

You are mine, now.

The boy jumped, looking around for the source of the voice. Someone had spoken to him, as clear a sound as he'd ever heard. But no one was there.

There's no need to be alarmed. The Darkin Project will be fully functional soon. Until then, survive. This is an automatic recording. Good-bye for now.

The boy spun in a tight circle, searching his surroundings. He saw only the burnt ruins of his village—weeds, dust, trash. A rat skittered across the ruined road. Someone was screaming, but it was very far away.

The boy was alone.

The voice was in his head.

It had begun.

PART 1

✴

THE
UNWANTED
WINK

CHAPTER 1

THE TWO FACES OF REGINALD CHU

Mr. Chu hated his first name. It was evil.

Crazy, perhaps, for an adult to think such a thing—especially a science teacher—but as he walked down the dark, deserted street, he felt the truth of it like a forty-pound weight in his gut. He'd felt it since childhood—an odd uneasiness every time someone called his name. A black pit in his belly, like rotting food that wouldn't digest.

"Mr. Chu!"

The sharp ring of the woman's voice slicing through the air startled him out of his thoughts. His breath froze somewhere inside his lungs, sticking to the surface, making him cough until he could breathe again.

He looked up, relieved to see it was only Mrs. Tennison poking her frilly head out a high window, no doubt spying on her neighbors. Her hair was pulled into dozens of tight curlers, her face covered in a disgusting paste that looked like green frosting.

Mr. Chu drew another deep, calming breath, embarrassed he'd been jolted so easily. "Hi, Mrs. Tennison," he called up to her. "Nice night, huh?"

"Yeah," she said in an unsure voice, as if suspecting him of trouble. "Why, uh, why are you out so late? And so far away from your house? Maybe you'd like to, uh, come up for a cup of tea?" She did something with her face that Mr. Chu suspected was supposed to be a tempting smile, but looked more like a demented clown with bad gas.

Mr. Chu shuddered. He'd rather share a cup of oil sludge with Jack the Ripper than spend one minute in Mrs. Tennison's home, listening to her incessant jabbering about town gossip. "Oh, better not—just walking off some stress," he finally said. "Enjoying the night air." He turned to walk away, glad to have his back to her.

"Well, be careful!" she yelled after him. "Been reports of thugs in the town square, mobbin' and stealin' and such."

"Don't worry," he replied without looking back. "I'll keep an eye out."

He quickened his step, turned a corner, and relaxed

into a nice and easy gait. His thoughts settled back to the strange fear he had of his own first name. The name he avoided whenever possible. The reason he always introduced himself as "Mr. Chu" to everyone he met.

Having taught science at Jackson Middle School in Deer Park, Washington, for more than twenty years, he'd hardly ever been called anything *but* Mr. Chu. Single and childless, his parents long dead, and separated from his brothers and sisters by thousands of miles, he had no one to call him anything more intimate than those two lonely, icy words. Even the other teachers mostly hailed him by his formal title, as if they dared not befriend him. As if they were afraid of him.

But it was better than the alternative. Better than hearing the word he despised.

Reginald.

Wiping sweat from his brow, he thought back to an incident several months earlier when a fellow teacher had uttered aloud the rarely heard *Reginald* when poking her head into his classroom for a question. A student had stayed after school that day, and the look that had swept over the boy's face upon hearing Mr. Chu's first name had been a haunted, disturbed expression, as if the kid thought Mr. Chu stole children from their beds and sold them to slave traders.

The look had hurt Mr. Chu. Deeply. That cowering wince of fear had solidified what he had considered until then to be an irrational whim—the childish, lingering superstition that his name was indeed evil. The knowledge had always been there, hidden within him like a dormant seed, waiting only for a spark of life.

The student had been Atticus "Tick" Higginbottom, his favorite in two decades of teaching. The boy had unbelievable smarts, a keen understanding of the workings of the world, a maturity far beyond his almost fourteen years. Mr. Chu felt an uncanny connection to Tick—an excitement to tutor him and guide him to bigger and better things in the fascinating fields of science. But the look on that fateful day had crushed Mr. Chu's heart, tipping him over a precipice onto a steep and slippery slope of depression and self-loathing.

It made no sense for a man grounded in the hard science of his profession to be so profoundly affected by such a simple event. It was an elusive thing, hard to reconcile with the immovable theorems and hypotheses that orbited his mind like rigid satellites. A name, a word, a look, an expression. Simple things, yet somehow life-changing.

Now, as he walked home in the darkness of night, the new school year only a few days away, the air around him mirrored his deepest feelings and unsettling thoughts. Instead of cooling off, it seemed to get hotter. The suffocating heat stilted his breathing despite the sun having gone to bed hours earlier. Since

Mrs. Tennison's intrusion, neither people nor breeze had stirred in the late hour. The muted thumps of his tennis shoes were the only sound accompanying him on this now habitual midnight walk, when sleep eluded him. He turned onto the small lane leading to the town cemetery—a shortcut to his home—a creepy but somehow exhilarating path.

It had been a long summer—weeks of huddling under the burning lamp in his study, scouring the pages of every science magazine and journal to which he could possibly subscribe. He'd channeled his growing self-pity into an unprecedented thirst for knowledge, his brain soaking it up like a monstrous, alien sponge. Oh, how he'd enjoyed every single minute of his obsessive study binge. It kept him sane, helped him—

Mr. Chu faltered, almost stumbled, when he realized a man stood just outside the stone archway of the cemetery, arms folded across his chest, silhouetted against the pale light of a streetlamp in the distance. He seemed to have appeared from nowhere, as Mr. Chu had detected no movement prior to noticing the stranger. Like a black cardboard cutout, the figure didn't move, staring with unseen eyes, sending a wave of prickly goose bumps down Mr. Chu's arms.

He recovered his wits and continued walking, refusing to show fear. Why was he so jumpy tonight? He had no reason to think this man was a thug, despite

Mrs. Tennison's absurd warning. Even if the still figure, standing there like a statue, was a bad guy, it would do no good to act afraid. All the same, Mr. Chu slyly changed his course to cross the lane, knowing the small, wooded area between here and the town square would provide cover if he needed to run and hide.

Quit being ridiculous, he chided himself. However, he kept the mysterious shadow of a man in the corner of his vision.

Mr. Chu had just reached the gravel-strewn side of the road when his late-night visitor spoke—a slippery, soft-spoken whisper that nevertheless carried like clanging cowbells through the deep silence of the night.

"Where do you think *you're* going?"

Bitter mockery filled the voice, and Mr. Chu stopped walking, falling through the thin ice of apprehension straight into an abyss of outright terror, something he had never truly felt before. It turned his stomach, squeezed it, sending sour, rotten juices through his body; he wanted to bend over and throw up.

Another man stepped out of the woods to his right. At the same moment, a finger tapped him from behind on his right shoulder. Shrieking, Mr. Chu spun around, his fear igniting into panic.

This time, he saw a face—a shadowed mug of hard angles, rigid with anger. Mr. Chu saw a flicker of movement, then a flash of blue light. An explosion of heat and electricity came from everywhere at once, knocking him to the ground in a twitching heap. He cried out as pain lanced through his body, tendrils of lightning coursing along his skin. With a whimper, he looked up and saw the person holding out a long device that still crackled with static electricity.

"Wow, you look just like him," the nameless face said.

⌒

Reginald Chu, founder and CEO of Chu Industries, stood within his massive laboratory, studying the latest test results from the ten-story-tall Darkin Project as he awaited word on the abduction of his Alterant from Reality Prime. It amused him to know the science teacher would be brought to the same building in which he himself stood—a dangerous prospect at best, certain death at worst. Mixing with alternate versions of yourself from other Realities was like playing dentist with a cobra.

Which is why his employees had been given strict instructions to never bring the *other* Reginald Chu within five hundred feet of the *real* Reginald Chu (the one who mattered most in the universe anyway). They'd lock the look-alike away in a maximum-security cell deep in the lower chambers of the artificial mountain of glass that was Chu Industries until they needed the captive to serve his dual purpose in being kidnapped.

Dual purpose. Reginald took a deep breath, loving the smells of electronics and burnt oil that assaulted his senses. He reflected on the plan he'd set into place once the information had poured in from his network of spies in the other Realities. They brought news of intriguing developments with massive potential consequences—especially the bit about the boy named Atticus Higginbottom.

If Reginald was not the most supreme example of rational intelligence ever embodied in a human being—and he most certainly *was*—he would have doubted the truth of what he'd heard and had verified by countless sources. It seemed impossible on the face of it—something from a storybook told to dirty urchins in an orphanage before they went to bed. Tales of magic and power, of an unspeakable ability in the manipulation of the most central force in the universe: Chi'karda. A human Barrier Wand, perhaps.

But Reginald knew the mystery could be explained, all within the complex but perfectly understood realm of science. Still, the idea thrilled him. The boy had no idea what was at stake—he had something Reginald Chu wanted, and nothing in the world could be more dangerous than that.

Reginald walked over to the airlift that would ascend along the surface of the tall project device. He allowed his retina to be scanned, then stepped onto the small metal square of the hovervator. He pressed the button for the uppermost level. As the low whine of the lift kicked in, pushing him toward the false sky of the ridiculously large chamber, he heard the slightest beep from the nanophone nestled deep within the skin of his ear.

"Yes?" he said in a sharp clip, annoyed at being disturbed even though he'd *told* them to do so as soon as they returned. The microscopic particles of the device he'd invented took care of all communication needs with no effort on his part.

"We have him," the soft voice of Benson replied, echoing in Reginald's mind as though from a long-dead spirit. Benson had been the lead on the mission to Reality Prime.

"Good. Is he harmed? Did you raid his house, gather his . . . *things?*" The airlift came to a stop with a soft bump; Reginald stepped onto the metal-grid catwalk encircling his grandest scientific experiment to date. From here, all he could see was the shiny golden surface of the enormous cylinder, dozens of feet wide, reflecting back a distorted image of his face that made him look monstrous.

"Everything went exactly as planned," Benson said. "No blips."

Reginald stabbed a finger in the air even though he

knew Benson couldn't see him. "Don't you dare bring that sorry excuse for a Chu near me—not even close. There's no guarantee who'd flip into the Nonex. I want him locked away—"

"Done," Benson barked.

Reginald frowned at his underling's tone and interruption. He took note to watch Benson closely in case his lapse in judgment developed into something more akin to insubordination or treachery.

"Bring his belongings to me and ready him for the Darkin injection."

"Yes, sir. Right away, sir." Reginald's nanophone registered a faint quiver in Benson's voice.

Ah-ha, Reginald thought. Benson had realized his mistake and was trying to make up for it with exaggerated respect. *Stupid man.*

"As soon as we inject him," Reginald said, "we can begin phase two. You've checked and rechecked that the others are still together?"

"Yes, sir. All three of them, together for another two days. School starts after the weekend."

"You're *sure?*" Reginald didn't want to waste any more time away from his project than he must.

"Seen them with my own eyes," Benson said, the slightest hint of condescension in his voice. "They'll have no reason to suspect anything. Your plan is flawless."

Reginald laughed, a curt chortle that ended abruptly.

"You always know what to say, Benson. A diplomat of diplomats—though one not afraid to squeeze a man's throat until he sputters his last cough. A perfect combination."

"Thank you, sir."

"Call me when you're ready." Reginald blinked hard, the preprogrammed signal to end his call with the synthesized sound of an old-fashioned phone slamming into its cradle.

Clasping his hands behind his back, Reginald continued pacing around the wide arc of the Darkin Project, his carnival-mirror reflection bobbing up and down in the polished, cold metal. He loved doing this, loved the feeling he got when the words that lay imprinted in large, black letters appeared on the other side. He slowed for dramatic effect, running his left hand lightly across the indentation of the first letter. A few more steps and he stopped, turning slowly toward the cylinder to look at the two words for the thousandth time—the thrill of it never ceased to amaze him.

Two words, spanning the length of his outstretched arms. Two words, black on gold. Two words that would change the Realities forever.

Dark Infinity.

CHAPTER 2

SPAGHETTI

"Dude, that stuff smells like feet."

Tick Higginbottom stifled a laugh, knowing his friend Paul's brave statement would bring down the wrath of Sofia Pacini, who was hard at work kneading a big ball of dough in the Higginbottoms' kitchen. Tick loved watching the two of them go at each other. He adjusted the red-and-black scarf around his neck, loosening it to let more air in, and settled back to enjoy the show.

"What?" Sofia said, using her pinky to push a strand of black hair behind her ear—the rest of her fingers were covered with flour and yellow goop. "*What* smells like feet?"

Paul pointed at the kitchen counter, where a mass of raw pasta dough rested like a bulbous alien growth. "*That*—the famous Pacini spaghetti recipe. If I wasn't helping you make it, I'd swear my Uncle Bobby had just walked in with his shoes off." He looked over at Tick and squinted his eyes in disgust, waving his hand in front of his nose. "That guy's feet sweat like you wouldn't believe—they smell like boiled cabbage."

Sofia turned toward Paul and grabbed his shirt with both hands, obviously not concerned about how dirty they were. "One more word, Rogers. One more, and I'll shove this dough down your throat. You'd probably choke and save Master George the trouble of firing your skinny Realitant hide. Plus, it's the feta cheese that stinks, not the dough."

"Whatever it is, I'll eat it," Paul said. "Just hurry—I'm starving."

Sofia let go and turned back to her work. "You Americans—all you want is fast food. We still have to make the sauce while the pasta dries."

"Tick," Paul groaned, "can't we just make some hot dogs?"

"Grab some chips out of the pantry," Tick said, pointing. "I'm waiting for the world-famous Pacini spaghetti."

More than six months ago, Sofia had won a bet

to visit Tick. Since her family had more money than most movie stars, she not only paid for her trip from Italy, but she also paid for Paul to come from Florida at the same time. Tick had looked forward to the visit all summer, thinking every day about his friends and their crazy experience in the Thirteenth Reality where they'd all been lucky to escape alive. Although this was only the second time the three of them had been together, they were already friends for life, not to mention members of a very important group—the Realitants.

"All right," Sofia said. "Time to get busy. Help me spin out the strands." She grabbed a small wad of dough and showed them how to shape it into a long, slender rope. Like soldiers following orders, Tick and Paul got to work while Sofia started on the sauce, chopping ingredients and pouring one thing after another into a huge metal pot.

"So is Master George going to call us or what?" Paul said. After stealing Mistress Jane's Barrier Wand, they'd been assured from their leader that it wouldn't be long before the Realitants would gather again.

"It's been almost three stinkin' months," Tick replied. "I check the mailbox every day."

Sofia snorted and shook her head. "He can track people all over the world using nanolocators, but he still sends messages in crumpled old envelopes." She measured a teaspoon of something orange and dropped it in the pot. "You'd think the old man could figure out how to use e-mail."

"Chill, Miss Italy," Paul said, holding up a long strand of dough and swinging it back and forth, grinning like it was the grandest form of entertainment in the world. "It's so he can't be tracked down by all the bad guys. Don't you ever watch TV?"

Tick spoke up before Sofia could reply—he was hungry and didn't want any more delays from his friends' bickering. "I just hope he's figured out how we winked out of the Thirteenth with a broken Barrier Wand."

"How?" Paul asked. "I'll tell you how. You're a regular Houdini—all you need is a cape and one of those funky black hats."

"And a wand," Sofia said as she began stirring her cauldron of blood-red sauce.

"He *had* a wand," Paul said. "It was just broken."

Tick's spirits dampened a bit, his heart heavy at remembering the terror of that moment when the Barrier Wand hadn't worked, when he'd pushed the button over and over again as hordes of screaming, sharp-toothed fangen rushed at them. Any reminder that such monsters existed in the world—or worlds— was enough to make a spaghetti feast not quite as appealing.

"He made it work somehow," Sofia said, nodding at Tick as she stirred. "Magic Boy himself."

Tick did his best to smile, but it didn't last.

⟍⟋

Two hours later, the homemade meal passed Sofia's inspection—barely. She kept insisting the sauce needed to simmer the rest of the day to taste perfect, but finally gave in to the impatient hunger groans of Paul and Tick. *It was worth every minute,* Tick thought as he shoveled in the food, not caring that he'd already spilled sauce on his scarf once and his shirt twice. He felt much better about things now that he wasn't starving.

"I'm not gonna lie to ya," Paul said through a huge bite, a vampire-like drip of red sauce streaked on his chin. "This is the best thing I've eaten in my entire life."

Sofia sat back in her chair, pressing a hand to her heart. "Did you, Paul Rogers from Florida—King Smarty Pants himself—just say something nice to me?"

"Yes, ma'am, I did. And I meant every word of it. Dee-lish."

"It's really good," Tick chimed in. "I'll never doubt you again about your family's claim to fame."

Several moments passed, everyone too busy eating to talk. Sofia slurped her spaghetti, sounding like a renegade octopus trying to climb a slippery metal pole. Tick almost made a joke, but didn't want to waste any breath when there were still noodles on his plate.

Paul wiped a big swath of sauce from his plate with a piece of garlic bread and shoved the whole thing in his mouth. "Man," he mumbled as he chewed, "I can't wait to visit more Realities so I can check out the ladies."

Tick almost choked on a laugh. "Yeah, right. You'd be lucky to get a date with Rutger's little sister." Tick's friend Rutger was an incredibly short and fat man from the Eleventh Reality. And full of pranks.

Paul shrugged. "As long as she's not quite so . . . bowling-ballish, I'm cool with that. Paul ain't picky."

"Good thing, too," Sofia said. "No girl I know would give you a second glance."

"Oh, yeah? And why's that?"

Sofia put down her fork and looked him square in the eyes, her face set in matter-of-fact stone. "Your ears are crooked."

"Excuse me?"

"Your. Ears. Are. Crooked." Sofia emphasized each word as if Paul spoke a foreign language, then folded her arms and raised her eyebrows.

"My ears are crooked," Paul repeated, deadpan.

"Yes."

"My ears are *not* crooked."

"Yes, they are."

"No, they're not."

"Crooked."

Paul reached up and felt both of his ears, rubbing them between his thumbs and forefingers. "What does that even mean? How could they be crooked?"

Sofia pointed at Paul's face. "Your left ear is almost half an inch lower than your right one. It looks ridiculous."

"No way." Paul looked to Tick for help. "No way."

Tick leaned forward, studying Paul's face. "Sorry, big guy. Crooked as bad lumber."

"Where's a mirror?" Paul half-yelled, standing up and running for the bathroom. A few seconds later, his shriek echoed down the hall: "Tick! My ears are crooked!"

Tick and Sofia looked at each other and burst out laughing.

A dejected Paul came slouching down the hall; he pulled back his chair and collapsed onto the table. Then he held up a finger, like he had a brilliant idea. "Fine, but I have beautiful toenails—here, let me show you—"

"*No!*" Sofia and Tick shouted together.

Thankfully, the low rumble of the garage door opening saved the day. Tick's family was home.

⌒

"Well, if it's not my three favorite heroes in the world," Tick's dad said as he stumbled through the door, both arms full of packages and bags—new school clothes, by the looks of it. "How'd the spaghetti experiment go? Smells great." Tick knew what his dad was really thinking: *Give me some. Now!* The guy loved to eat, and his big belly showed it.

"The way these boys ate," Sofia said, "I'd say it went pretty well."

Paul moaned with pleasure, rubbing his belly. "Yes, sir, Mr. Higginbottom. The chef is a tyrant, but she can cook like you wouldn't believe."

"Best I've ever had," Tick agreed, just as his mom entered from the garage. "Oh, sorry, Mom. Yours is good too."

"It's okay, Atticus," Mom said as she set a couple of bags down on the counter. "I'd hope a young woman from a family well-known for their spaghetti would be able to beat mine any day."

Dad shook his head. "I don't know. You sure do know how to add spices to that Ragu sauce."

"Very funny," Mom replied.

Newly driving Lisa and newly turned five-year-old Kayla came through next, both holding bags of their own.

"Whoa, Mom," Tick said. "How much stuff did you buy?"

"Enough to keep three kids clothed for a year." She pointed a finger at Tick. "No growing until next summer. That's an order."

"Did you kill anyone driving to the mall, sis?" Tick asked.

Lisa gave him a mock evil stare. "Just one old lady—and I hit her on purpose."

"Wow," Paul said. "Sounds like—"

A sudden *crack* from upstairs interrupted him; a booming sound of splitting, shattering wood shook the entire house. A plate fell from the counter and broke on the floor. Kayla shrieked and ran to her mom.

"What the—?" Dad said, already on the move out of the kitchen and down the hall, everyone following behind him. As his dad bounded up the stairs as quickly as he could move his big body, Tick anxiously looked around him to see what had caused the commotion.

Through a swirling cloud of dust and debris, Tick could see a large, silvery metal tube with a sharp, tapered end jutting from the wall outside Tick's room, splinters of ripped wood holding it in place. It looked as if it had been shot from a cannon, a dud bomb lodged in the drywall.

"What on *earth?*" Mom said in a shaky voice, putting a hand on her husband's arm.

Dad had no answer; Tick hurried past him to his bedroom door and opened it, expecting to see a disaster area—broken windows, a gaping hole in the side of the house, something. But his breath caught in his throat when he saw no damage at all—not a crack or tear in the ceiling, the windows, or the walls. His room was in perfect shape. The only thing out of place was the other end of the metal tube, which stuck out of the wall to his left. It also had a tapered end.

Tick poked his head back into the hallway, examined the ceiling. No damage there, either. Everyone looked as perplexed as he felt.

Dad leaned forward and studied the strange object. "Where'd that thing come from? And how in the *world* did it get stuck in our wall?"

CHAPTER 3

SOMETHING ODD IS HAPPENING

Tick stepped forward; everyone else seemed frozen to the floor in amazement by the sudden and violent appearance of the strange metal tube. Dad stood there and shook his head, muttering under his breath.

Tick reached up, his hand slowing as he approached the sharp end of the cylinder sticking out into the hall.

His mom yelped. "Careful! Maybe we shouldn't touch it."

"It's fine, Mom," Tick replied. "There's gotta be some reason it was sent here."

"Yeah," Paul said, "like, maybe to kill the state of Washington once you trigger its thermonuclear reactor inside."

Ignoring Paul, Tick tested the side of the object with a quick tap to see if the metal was hot. Feeling only hard coolness, he wrapped his hand around the tube and yanked as hard as he could. With a high-pitched groaning squeal, it gave way and slipped out of the splintered hole. Finding it to be quite light, Tick bounced the three-foot-long cylinder in both hands as he turned to show it to everyone else.

"But what is it?" Sofia asked.

"Here, son," Dad said, sticking his chest out as if to show he was the brave one who should examine the cylinder. "Let me check it out in case it explodes or something."

"You're so brave, sweetie," Mom said, rubbing her husband's shoulder with affection.

"Yeah," he mumbled back. "A regular Iron Man."

Tick handed the tube to his dad, who took it, turning it this way and that in front of his face, examining it with squinted eyes. He peered down its length as if he were aiming a sniper's rifle.

"Having inspected this object fully," Dad finally said, "I hereby declare it to be nothing but a solid metal rod."

Tick cleared his throat, having just noticed something as his dad tilted the tube just right. "Well, um, there *is* a seam circling the middle."

"Huh?" Dad lifted the thing until it was an inch

from his eyeballs, then squinted again. "Oh. Yeah. You're right." With both hands, he gripped the ends of the rod, right before they tapered to sharp points, and pulled in opposite directions.

With a metallic scrape, the object split into two pieces. As soon as it did, a smaller tube fell to the floor, a flash of white that bounced once, rolled, then came to a stop by Sofia's feet.

Sofia snapped it up and quickly unrolled the piece of paper. Her eyes quickly scanned the contents, then she looked up with a wide grin on her face.

"It's a message. From Master George."

⁓

They went back downstairs, the group huddled around Sofia as she sat in a chair at the kitchen table. Tick wiggled his way to be closest to her, looking down at the typed message as Sofia read it aloud.

Dear Fellow Realitants,

I hope this day finds you all warm and happy. If so, enjoy it. Dark times are upon us, and I fear we must gather as soon as possible.

Something odd is happening within the Realities. Something unnatural, indeed. Sinister forces are about, and

I have my suspicions as to the source.
And no, it is not Mistress Jane. I
shan't write about it any further; you
will be briefed during our meeting.

On the twenty-second of August,
please report to the nearest cemetery
at your earliest convenience,
whereupon I will wink you to
headquarters straightaway, based
upon your nanolocator reading.

Now I really must be going, as
poor Rutger appears to have hung his
malodorous socks in front of the
cooler vent, creating quite a smell, I
assure you. Wish me luck in finding a
can of powerful air freshener.

Most sincerely,
Master George

P.S. Muffintops sends her warmest
regards.

P.P.S. Please attach the Spinner
to a blank wall and observe
carefully to learn about entropy
and fragmentation.

"Spinner?" Paul asked. "What's he talking about?"

"The twenty-second? That's only two days away," Tick's mom whispered, her voice not hiding the sudden dismay at the possibility of her son running off again.

Tick's initial excitement at hearing from Master George quickly faded into a sickly pang in his gut. He had dreaded this moment in many ways, knowing he'd be summoned again, leaving his poor mom to worry about him. Even though she'd been convinced of the truth about the Realities, Tick knew that when the day actually came for him to leave again, she'd throw a fit.

Like any good mother.

"Mom . . ." Tick said, but no other words filled his mouth.

His dad reached over and squeezed Tick's shoulder, then shook his head ever so slightly when they made eye contact.

"Honey," Dad said, "let's go for a drive and talk a bit. Lisa, Kayla, you come with us—we'll get some ice cream."

"But I want to hear—" Lisa protested, but Dad cut her off.

"Just come on. In the car. Let's go."

Tick didn't completely understand what his dad was doing. He had insisted all summer that he believed in Tick and in his responsibilities as a Realitant, and that he would do whatever it took to support him and make sure nothing got in his way. But now, in the moment, Tick couldn't believe his dad was going to leave them to discuss the message and its meaning alone.

He was treating Tick like an adult, and Tick wasn't sure he liked that as much as he thought he would.

As his parents left for the garage, half-dragging Kayla and Lisa, Mom staring at the floor with dead eyes, Tick tried to push aside the swirling, conflicting emotions he felt about involving his family with the Realitant stuff. He wished he could somehow separate them into two different worlds, independent and unaware of the other. But he couldn't. And he was a Realitant Second Class with people depending on him. He pulled out a chair and sat next to Sofia; Paul did the same.

"So, what do you think?" Paul asked.

Sofia threw her arms up. "What's there to think? Instead of flying back to our homes, we're going to the cemetery with Tick."

"But my ticket is for tomorrow night," Paul said. "Just because your parents don't give a—"

He stopped, looking quickly at the floor. Tick groaned on the inside. The more they got to know Sofia, the more they realized her parents didn't seem to care too much about what she did. This time they'd even let her come without her fancy butler, Frupey. But the verdict was still out as to *why* they didn't care; Sofia refused to talk about it.

"Go home if you want," she said with a sneer. "They have dead people in Florida, too, don't they? Find a cemetery there."

"Ah, man," Paul said as he dropped his head into his hands with a groan. "You have no idea how hard it was to explain this stuff to my family. I don't know if I can go through that again."

"Fine. Then quit."

"Oh, give me a break. I didn't say squat about quitting."

"It's gonna be hard for all of us," Tick interjected. "We just need to make them understand."

"Easy for you to say," Paul said. "I swear your dad is the single coolest person that's ever breathed."

"Maybe. But none of us can quit. Ever."

Paul leaned back in his chair, crossing his arms in anger. "Dude, quit preachin'. Paul Rogers is not gonna quit. I was just saying, man, it's gonna be killer telling my old lady I'm running off again."

The full load of spaghetti in Tick's stomach was starting to churn. "Our parents just have to trust us. That's all there is to it."

"Yeah," Paul agreed in a murmur.

"Okay, you know what?" Sofia said, her voice laced with annoyance. "You guys are getting on my nerves. We just got a letter from Master George—which we've been waiting for all summer—and you both are sitting here moping like you just found out you have two hours to live." She stood up and started walking toward the stairs. "Let's go look at the tube again to see if we can figure out what M.G. meant by *Spinner*."

When neither Tick nor Paul moved a muscle, Sofia turned and cleared her throat loudly. "Come on." She paused. "I promise I'll be nice." Another pause. "Please."

Paul looked at Tick, as surprised as if he'd just seen an extra arm bloom from Sofia's shoulder. Tick shrugged.

"Now!" Sofia yelled.

Paul and Tick jumped from the table, stumbling over each other as they followed her up the stairs.

Sofia picked up the broken metal tube and started shaking the two pieces toward the floor of the hallway. A small object fell out of one end and clinked when it hit the carpet. Paul reached it first, holding the odd thing up for everyone to see.

"What *is* it?" he whispered as he studied it.

Tick took it from him to get a better look. It was a two-inch wide, red plastic suction cup. Attached to the back of the cup was a thin, silvery metal rod bent at a ninety-degree angle. The L-shaped rod was about the size of Tick's index finger. Tick clasped the cup in one hand, then flicked the tip of the rod with his finger. The small rod spun so fast the metal became a circular blur of silver.

Sofia flicked the rod again, watching it twirl. "Spinner. Master George is *so* brilliant when he names things."

"I wonder if it's from Chu Industries," Tick said. "Does it say that anywhere?"

Sofia stopped the spinning rod and looked closer. "I don't see anything."

"What do you think it does?" Paul asked.

Tick pointed back down the stairs. "Master George said to attach it to a blank wall—let's try the one in the dining room."

"Let's go," Sofia said, already on the move.

CHAPTER 4

THE WRETCHED BOY

The Spinner's suction cup stuck to the middle of the wall with a simple push; the bent end of the "L" pointed toward the floor and swayed back and forth until it finally came to a rest.

"What now?" Tick asked.

"Spin it," Paul said.

Sofia leaned forward and flicked the rod to make it spin, then stepped back. Without a word, the three of them quickly moved all the way to the other side of the room, pressing against the wall to watch. You couldn't be too careful when it came to gadgets sent from Master George.

Strangely, the spinning metal rod didn't slow at all,

instead going so fast it appeared as a perfect circle of shimmering silver. A slight hum filled the room, like the soft sound of a ceiling fan. After several seconds, Tick's eyes started to water as they tried to focus on something. Anything. Then the Spinner changed.

A red light flared from the tip of the metal rod, instantly creating a much larger circle that took up most of the wall, a hazy, flat disk of redness. Sofia gasped; Paul let out his usual, "Dude." Tick could only stare.

"How's it making a perfect circle?" Paul asked.

Sofia answered. "It must be shooting out some kind of scaled laser."

"Ooh, like a light saber," Paul said.

"But—" Tick stopped.

The red color faded from the projected, spinning disk, replaced by a large image of Master George, dressed in his dark suit, standing in front of a fireplace, staring out at them; he caressed Muffintops the cat in his arms. The picture quality was perfect—as good as any theater—it was just . . . *round*.

"My fondest greetings to the three of you," Master George said. The sound of his voice seemed to come from everywhere at once, though slightly warbled. Tick couldn't help but wonder what kind of speaker could have such power and still be so small—they certainly hadn't noticed anything when they studied the Spinner a few minutes earlier.

Master George held out a hand. "Don't attempt to reply—I assure you it will be a waste of your breath. This is only a recording, you see. Quite nice, don't you think? The Spinner comes in handy when you get a bit depressed and want to watch an old black-and-white. It's one of my favorite things. Although, it's a bit difficult to use when you're in a forest—particularly when you're being chased by wolves . . ."

Tick exchanged a look with Sofia, both of them trying to hold in a laugh.

"Oh, dear, I've already gone off on a tangent," Master George said, clearing his throat and growing very serious. "My apologies. There is a *point*, you see, to my sending you this Spinner. I must show you footage of something very frightening—something you must see and prepare yourselves to study with the greatest vigor. I want you to remember two words—*entropy* and *fragmentation*. These two things serve as our greatest challenge when studying the Realities; they are also the source of much heartache."

Master George paused, looking past the camera or whatever was recording him. "Rutger, please put *down* that pastry—get ready to cut to the footage you filmed in the fragmenting Reality." Master George focused back on Tick and the others. "No wonder I constantly find sticky goo on my camera. Now, I want you to watch closely. We have no sound, as Rutger had to get in and out very quickly and almost ruined the film entirely. I will narrate as you observe."

The image on the circular screen changed. All three of them sucked in a quick breath when they saw *Tick* huddled next to a tree, shivering, his terrified eyes darting back and forth, looking all around him.

Tick swallowed. He was filthy in the film, his clothes ripped to shreds. Wind tore at his shaggy hair, and his bare feet were covered with grime. Of course, it couldn't be him—it had to be someone who just *looked* like him. It had to be . . .

Master George's narration cut off his thoughts. "Master Atticus, this trembling wretch is one of your Alterants—created last year when you made the choice to follow the Twelve Clues and solve my mystery. A branching reality was created in which you *didn't* make that brave choice, and here you see the result."

Tick felt like everything around him disappeared, his eyes riveted to the image of himself on the screen, his heart aching for the boy there. *How can that be me?* he thought. *Is it me? It can't be me.* Confusion swirled in his mind like poisonous gas.

"This is a terrible thing," Master George continued. "One of our goals as Realitants is to prevent this type of fragmenting event from happening. In a very twisted way, this boy *is* you, Atticus. He has your mind and heart, your goodness and courage. And he doesn't deserve the fate that's come upon him. Watch closely."

The trees around the Alterant Tick started to shake; the brisk wind picked up even more, tearing at Tick's pitiful, filthy clothes. There was no sound, but Tick saw the boy scream, hugging his arms around himself tighter. Above his head, the wood of the tree *vibrated,* then broke apart into a million tiny pieces, swept away by the wild wind. The other Tick screamed again, scooting away until he hit another tree. An instant later that one liquefied into a horrific brown goo, splashing all over the Alterant. Another scream, as if the tree burned him.

The real Tick watched in horror at what happened next.

The boy on the screen started to *dissolve.*

CHAPTER 5

THE ENTROPY
OF FRAGMENTATION

The image flashed to black. Master George reappeared, his ruddy face creased and frowning. "I'm very sorry you had to see that."

Tick felt his back pressed against the wall, felt the slime of sweat on his palms. The movie had stopped before getting too bad, but he'd seen enough. The boy's skin and hair and clothes—all dissipating into a million pieces, breaking apart, dissolving, whipped away by the wind.

That was me, he thought. *That was* me.

"Now listen closely," Master George said. "You may already have heard the term *entropy* in your studies. It describes the natural . . . urge of the universe to destroy itself, to cease to exist, to *deconstruct*. All things—no matter what, no matter how strong—will eventually erode into nothingness, into chaos. It is an unchange-able law. All things fade away. This is called entropy."

Master George looked down at Muffintops, petting her as she purred. "The process of entropy can take a few years or billions of years. Think about your bodies. When you die, your flesh and bone will slowly turn to dust. A towering mountain can stand for millions of years before it slowly but surely breaks down. Nothing can stop the inevitable—entropy wins. Always."

"What does this have to do with—" Paul began to ask, obviously forgetting they were watching a record-ing. Master George kept talking.

"Here is the disturbing part. The Thirteen Realities we know about are solid and permanent. But *fragmented* Realities are not—we've told you before how unstable they are, and how they eventually fade away or destroy them-selves. Now you know the reason—an extreme heighten-ing and acceleration of entropy. And I mean *extreme*. It almost becomes a living entity, devouring everything in its path, as you just witnessed. Once fragmented, a Reality doesn't last long—and its final moments are pure terror for the poor chaps living there. It is an awful thing."

Master George took a deep breath. "We don't under-stand all of it. There's much to learn, much to discuss. It's time the three of you started your Realitant studies, and this is the first lesson of many. And most importantly, I wanted you to see firsthand the severe consequences of your choices. If you'd lacked the courage to pass my tests, perhaps . . . well, it is a very deep and complicated situation. But we must stop the fragmenting. Even though we will never feel the pain and terror of those temporary Alterants, it's very real to them, if only briefly. Makes it hard for me to sleep at night."

Muffintops jumped out of his arms and disappeared off screen. "Very well, thank you for watching. There are many other mysteries to discuss—like the odd properties of *soulikens* and the Barrier Haunce. All in good time. We'll look forward to the gathering of Realitants. Until then, remember your courage, my good friends. Good-bye for now."

Master George smiled at the camera for a few seconds, saying nothing. His eyes flickered to the side, as if he looked uncomfortable. Finally, he mumbled something out of the side of his mouth. "Turn the camera *off*, Rutger."

The screen went black, then red, then silver. The hum of the Spinner died out as the metal rod slowly came to a standstill. All the while, no one said anything.

"What was *that?*" Sofia finally asked.

Tick ignored her, pushing past and walking out of the dining room. The spaghetti churned inside his stomach, and he didn't know how much longer he could last before throwing up. A throbbing ache raged behind his eyeballs.

"Tick?" Paul asked from behind.

"I don't wanna talk about it," was all Tick could get out.

He barely said a word the rest of the evening, ignoring his friends and family equally. The image of that boy on the screen—of *himself*—screaming and then dissolving . . .

How could he ever get that out of his head?

He went to bed early that night while everyone else watched a movie downstairs.

~~~

The next morning, Tick, Paul, and Sofia decided to get out of the house and talk over things—maybe do some research at the library. Tick felt a little better on waking up; every time the disturbing image of his fragmenting Alterant popped in his head, he tried to picture Muffintops. After another excellent Lorena Higginbottom breakfast of eggs and fried potatoes, the three of them headed out.

They stayed mostly silent until they reached the long road that led from Tick's neighborhood to the town square of Deer Park. The rising sun kept the east side of the street in shade, the towering evergreens and oak trees of the forest providing relief from the late summer heat.

The humidity had dipped considerably in the last couple of days, giving the air a hot but pleasant feel. Birds and crickets sang their songs in the woods; somewhere in the distance a lawn mower cranked up.

"Man, feels good out here," Paul said, bending over to pick up a rock. He threw it deep into the woods; it cracked against a tree.

"You guys need to come to Italy sometime," Sofia said. "In the summer, we can go up to the Alps and cool off. Best place in the world."

"No argument here," Paul replied. "Florida downright stinks this time of year. You go outside for two seconds and presto—sweaty armpits."

"Lovely," Sofia said.

Tick only half-listened to the conversation, staring into the woods as they walked. They neared the spot where so much had happened a few months ago—meeting Mothball, the sign from Rutger about the midnight meeting on the porch, getting clues from the two of them, screaming in desperation after Kayla had burned his original letter from Master George. It all seemed like a dream now.

"—to Tick, Earth to Tick." Paul had stopped, snapping his fingers in the air.

"Oh, sorry," Tick said. "Just daydreaming."

Sofia sighed. "Better than listening to Paul drone on, trust me."

"Miss Italy, be nice to me. I might have to save you on our next mission."

"I better update my will."

"Hilarious."

"I know."

The Muffintops distraction trick wasn't working so well for Tick as they walked. *That kid. That poor kid.* The whole concept of Alterants was confusing—especially when you threw in the whole thing about fragmented Realities. What was the difference between the Tick they'd seen in Rutger's film, Tick himself, and the Ticks that existed in the stabilized Thirteen Realities? It made his head hurt thinking about it.

"What do you guys think of all that entropy stuff?" he asked, kicking at a pebble on the road and watching it skitter across the pavement.

"I remember studying it in science," Sofia said. "Seems crazy that it could be accelerated like that and just . . . eat away at the world."

"It's freaky, dude," Paul said. "I mean, if I decide to turn left instead of right up here, am I gonna create a nasty Reality where I get eaten alive by monster air? That ain't right."

"It's weird that—"

Sofia never finished her sentence, cut off by a loud yelp in the woods to their right, followed by the sudden, rushing sound of crunching leaves and breaking twigs. Someone, or some *thing,* was running toward them through the trees.

Tick and the others froze, staring toward the sounds, which grew louder as the whatever-it-was came closer. *Crick-crash, crick-crash.* Another yelp, this time more of a short scream, echoed off the towering trunks and leafy canopy.

"What *is* that?" Paul asked.

"Maybe we shouldn't stick around to find out," Tick offered. Every nerve in his body had just lit up with warning flames.

Before anyone could respond, a man burst through a wall of thick foliage fronting two large trees, hurtling himself forward until he lost his balance and fell onto the steep slope that led up to the road. As soon as the skinny, dark-haired man hit the ground, he scrambled to his hands and feet and started clawing his way toward them. With growing dread, Tick stared at the stranger's tattered clothes and bloody splotches on his shirt.

Just a few feet away, the man finally reached the road and stood up, lifting his head enough to be seen clearly for the first time. Disheveled, dirty hair framed an olive-skinned face covered with terrible scratches and terror alive in his eyes.

Tick sucked in a huge gulp of air, half-relieved and half-shocked.

It was Mr. Chu, his science teacher.

CHAPTER 6

INTENSE PAIN

Mr. Chu!" Tick yelled, running forward to help his favorite teacher, who looked ready to collapse. Sofia moved to assist, both of them grabbing an arm of Mr. Chu and lowering him to the shoulder of the road. The poor man crumpled into a ball, great heaves of breath making his chest rise and fall as his eyes darted between Tick, Sofia, and Paul. A leather satchel was slung over Mr. Chu's shoulders with a thin strap, its bulky, sharp-angled contents clanking when it hit the ground.

"What happened?" Tick asked, fighting the panic he felt. *What if he's dying? Did someone out there attack him?* He couldn't help but look up at the trees, which suddenly seemed dark and ominous.

"Atticus . . ." Mr. Chu said with a dry rasp.

Tick knelt on one knee, lowering his head until he was close to Mr. Chu's face. "What happened to you, Mr. Chu?"

"Atticus . . . I barely escaped . . ." A racking cough exploded from his lungs, shaking his entire body.

"Escaped?" Tick repeated. "From what?"

Sofia and Paul knelt right behind the teacher, both of them looking at Tick with wide, confused eyes. So far, a car had yet to pass by the woods, and Tick hoped one did soon so they could ask for help.

"From . . ." Mr. Chu whispered, starting to gain control of his breath. "From . . . a very bad man. Looks like me. *Is* me."

Tick exchanged a puzzled look with his friends. He'd never seen his teacher like this, or heard him say such crazy things. He'd never seen *anyone* act like this. An idea hit him. "Do either one of you have a cell phone?"

Mr. Chu's hand shot out and grabbed Tick's shirt, pulling him closer with surprising force. "No!" he yelled, a sharpness narrowing his eyes with a clarity that hadn't been there moments earlier. "Help me back into the woods—we need to hide."

"Mr. Chu, I don't—"

"Just help me!"

With a grunt and another dry, loud cough, Mr. Chu pushed himself back into a sitting position, then held up his hands. Tick and Paul lifted the miserable man to his feet and wrapped his arms around their shoulders. Then, half-carrying, half-dragging Mr. Chu, the three of them stumbled down the small slope and entered the woods, Sofia right behind.

They made their way past a few smaller trees and then rounded a massive, towering oak, finally finding a secluded patch of ivy-strewn forest floor with enough room for all of them to sit. Specks of sunlight littered the ground, the call of birds in the air far too cheerful for the situation. The smells of pine and earth and wood were strong—scents that Tick loved but for some reason made him uneasy at the moment.

They settled into a circle, facing each other. Mr. Chu appeared to be gaining his strength back with every passing minute, though his hands shook with apparent fear; a small drip of drool crawled down his chin. No one said a word, a silent understanding hanging in the air that Mr. Chu would tell them what was going on when he was good and ready.

"It was terrible," he finally whispered, barely audible.

"*What* was?" Sofia asked. Tick cringed; it seemed like a really bad time for her usual impatience.

Mr. Chu continued to stare at the ground in front of him. "These men . . . with some kind of electricity weapon, kidnapped me and took me to a place that was like the barracks of a battleship—metallic and cold.

They . . . did things to me. . . . Unspeakable things." He quit talking.

"Who were they?" Tick asked. His mind couldn't settle on any possible reason someone might want to take Mr. Chu, who was one of the nicest people Tick knew.

"It was . . . *him.*" Mr. Chu squeezed his eyes closed as if in pain.

"Him?" Paul asked. "Who's *him?*"

"The other me. The bad me."

Tick felt his breath catch in his throat. An Alterant Mr. Chu?

Tick looked at Sofia; she mouthed the word *psycho.* A storm of anger surged inside Tick. His face flushed hot, and for the first time since he'd known her, he wanted to scream in fury at Sofia. This was one of his favorite people she was talking about. He was just about to say something nasty when Mr. Chu unexpectedly shot up from the ground to his feet.

"Did you hear that?" he whispered, twisting and turning, searching the surrounding forest.

Tick stood, as did Paul and Sofia, the three of them looking for any sign of what had alarmed the teacher.

"Did you hear that?" Mr. Chu repeated.

"No," Tick answered. "What was it?"

"Something's out there. What was I thinking? What was I *thinking!*" Yelling the last word, Mr. Chu knelt down beside his leather satchel and opened it up, rummaging inside before pulling out three strange objects. "They followed me here. How could I be such an idiot?"

As Mr. Chu got back to his feet, Tick finally heard it. Coming from deeper in the woods, it sounded like hundreds of spinning circular saws, sharp and shrill, accompanied by the horrible crunching and breaking of trees, as if King Kong himself were trampling through the forest with the world's largest electric razor buzzing at full speed.

"What the heck is that?" Paul asked, a look of alarm spreading across his face that Tick thought must surely mirror his own.

Sofia took a few steps toward the sound, rising onto her tiptoes and tilting her head as if that would help her hear better. "That doesn't sound good," she finally said.

Paul rolled his eyes and stomped his foot, clearly impatient to be away from this place. Tick felt a thick veil of creepiness hanging over him.

"They let me go; they let me go," Mr. Chu murmured, handling the objects he'd pulled from his bag. Tick got a good look at them for the first time, but had no clue what they were. All he could see were a bunch of cloth straps and pieces of dull metal.

"They let me go. . . . They knew I'd come to you. I'm such an idiot! Atticus, I'm so sorry."

Something was wrong about the whole situation, and Tick knew it wasn't just the rush of ominous sounds that were growing louder by the second, filling the air with horrible screeches of metal and the splintering crack of wood. Nor was it just the overall strangeness of Mr. Chu's sudden appearance. Something was *wrong*, out of place—but Tick couldn't pinpoint it exactly.

"Shouldn't we get out of here?" Paul said.

"Won't do any good," Mr. Chu replied, stepping close to Tick. He stretched out one of the things in his hands, two strips of cloth attached to a circular ring of metal in the middle. "Until we get these on you, they'll follow you wherever you go, until you're dead."

Mr. Chu grabbed Tick's right arm and started wrapping the cloth strips around his bicep. Tick was so stunned by the odd situation that he didn't move or resist. In a matter of seconds, Mr. Chu had snapped the metal ring around Tick's elbow, and wrapped the attached strips of cloth, like sticky gauze, in candy-cane fashion down the length of his entire arm.

"What . . . what are you doing? What is this thing?" A sick, uneasy feeling spread through Tick and he started to sweat.

"Yeah, what is that?" Sofia asked.

"You all have to put them on," Mr. Chu answered.

But when he stepped toward Sofia, she swiped his arms away and held up her fists. "You aren't touching me, you crazy old man."

The sounds—the spinning saws, the crunching

and crashing of trees, a mechanical roar that sounded like something out of an old sci-fi movie—it was all coming very close, very fast. Though Tick couldn't see anything yet, he could *feel* whatever was approaching, as if it were pushing the very air away as it rushed through the woods.

Mr. Chu tried again to wrap his gadget around Sofia's arm, but she swatted him away, then actually swung a fist at his face, barely missing. "I said, stay away!" she screamed at him.

Mr. Chu turned toward Tick, his face intense. "Atticus, I've known you and your family for a long time. I taught your sister, I taught you. We're friends, are we not?"

"Yeah." Tick looked at Sofia, then Paul. His head swam in confusion. How could this be happening? Why did he feel so . . . *wrong?* Was this a dream?

"They'll be here in seconds. If we put these devices on our arms, they won't see us. Do you hear me?"

Tick didn't say anything.

"Just wink us away again!" Paul said. "You can do it, Tick. Concentrate and wink us away. Forget this dude."

"Give me a break," Tick said. "I have no clue how I did that."

"Just try," Sofia said in a calm voice, as if she were trying to talk someone out of jumping off a skyscraper.

Tick barely heard her over the mechanical chorus of horrible sounds.

"Atticus!" Mr. Chu yelled. "We have only seconds left! They . . . are going . . . to eat us . . . alive!" He pointed toward the sounds with every pause, his voice filled with fire.

"Just do it!" Tick finally said. "Sofia, just let him do it!"

"Tick, you expect me to trust this nut—"

"Just do it!"

Completely surprising Tick, she obeyed with a huff, sticking her arm out to Mr. Chu. He quickly wrapped the second device on her arm, just as he'd done with Tick. Nearby, a thunderous, ear-splitting crack of wood was followed by the sound of a tree crashing to the forest floor. The mechanical sounds whirred and buzzed, roaring like monstrous robots.

Mr. Chu worked feverishly, wrapping the third and final . . . whatever it was . . . on Paul's right arm, who protested the entire time that this was crazy and stupid and that they should *run*.

"What about you?" Tick asked Mr. Chu.

His teacher pulled out a small, rectangular object from his pocket that looked like a TV remote control. He looked down at it as his finger searched for one of the many buttons scattered in rows across its front side. Then he looked up at Tick.

"Don't worry about me," he said. He held up the small remote device and pushed the button.

In that instant, a pain like nothing Tick had ever experienced or thought possible lanced through his body from head to toe, and the world spun away, leaving him in darkness and agony.

CHAPTER 7

MASTER GEORGE'S
INTERVIEW ROOM

S ato was bored out of his mind.

The Big Meeting wasn't for another couple of days, but Realitants had been arriving at the Grand Canyon Center from all over the world—well, *worlds*—since last week. And George made Sato sit with every last one of them, sometimes for hours, asking them questions, gathering information on their assigned areas, looking for clues on the strange happenings in the Realities. As if the long, tedious interviews weren't enough, Sato then had to compile everything into very specifically outlined reports for George's later analysis.

As Mothball would've said, it was driving Sato batty.

A lot had changed in the last few months—since the day in the Thirteenth Reality when everything he'd thought and felt for years had been turned upside down. The pain of losing his parents hadn't faded—it never would—but the anger and drive for vengeance he'd fostered and groomed for so long had been . . . altered, forged into an entirely different sword. In many ways, Sato thought that was a bad thing, not a good thing. He felt more lost than ever, floating in a pool of confusion and misdirection. The sword wasn't as sharp as it used to be.

Tick had done this to him. Tick had changed everything, forever.

And Sato didn't know how he felt about that.

A knock at the door snapped him to attention; he realized he'd been staring at a small smudge on the wall to the right of his desk. At the moment, Sato felt for all the world like he and the dirty spot shared a lot in common.

Though he already knew the answer, Sato asked anyway. "Who is it?"

"It's me—who else?" replied the muffled voice of Rutger. "Do you really have to keep the door closed? My poor knuckles are getting bruised from knocking every time."

Yeah, right, Sato thought. *You've got enough cushion on those hands to protect you from a sledgehammer.* "Hold on."

THE HUNT FOR DARK INFINITY

Sato quickly gathered his latest notes and reports and filed them away in his desk drawers. Though he'd acted the part of a trusting friend to Rutger for weeks, he still had his doubts about the short, fat man. *Anyone can be a spy.*

He stood up and walked over to the wooden door, slightly warped from a small leak that had crept through the tons of solid rock above them. He unlocked the door and yanked it open, jerking it harder than necessary.

Sato looked forward with a glazed expression, then left and right, as if searching for someone. Finally, he slowly lowered his gaze until he met Rutger's eyes. "Oh, it's you. Down there."

"Very funny, very funny." Rutger's short, round body barely fit in the hallway. He took in a deep breath, inflating himself even larger than he'd been a second earlier. "At least it was funny the *first* hundred times. Come on. Our next visitor has arrived."

Grumbling inside—no, *screaming* inside—Sato stepped into the hall, turned and closed the door, and then locked it. Without a word to Rutger, he walked toward the welcoming room at a brisk pace, knowing the poor little man could never keep up on his tiny legs.

When Rutger yelled, "Wait up!" from behind, the briefest hint of a smile flashed across Sato's face before he swiped it away with his trademark scowl.

"Ah, Master Sato!" George said, his usual jovial self, when Sato entered the room. Even though it was August, large flames licked and spit at the air inside the stone fireplace, warming the room to an uncomfortable level. A couple of nice leather couches hugged the walls; an armchair was set at the perfect angle for someone to sit by the fire and read a book. But at the moment, the only other two people in the room were standing next to the small window that overlooked the canyon river far below.

George stood to the right of the window, dressed in his Tuesday Suit, which only varied from his Monday Suit in that it was a very dark blue instead of a very dark black. One of his hands was outstretched toward Sato, the other toward the stranger standing to the left of the window. "Sato, I would like you to meet a very dear friend of mine, Quinton Hallenhaffer."

The man bowed his head in greeting, and Sato couldn't believe the guy could take himself seriously. He wore a twisty turban on his head made up of no less than ten different colors, all of them bright and swirling in a whirlpool pattern so that it looked like Mr. Hallenhaffer had ribbons for hair and had been caught in a tornado. The rest of his clothes were no different— a loose robe with dozens of colors splashed about with no definite pattern, purple gloves, and red shoes that appeared to be made out of wood.

Sato gave a curt nod. "I'm ready for the debriefing."

George's face flushed redder than usual. "Er, yes, Sato—though I think we could show our guest a little more, er, courtesy . . ."

"Oh, it's all right, George," Quinton said, waving at the air as if to swat away gnats. He had a trilling, lilting voice, like he couldn't decide whether to sing or talk. "The boy obviously means business, which is what we need in the new Realitants, don't you think?"

"Yes, indeed," George replied, giving the slightest frown of disapproval. "If Sato is anything, he is straight to the point." George clapped his hands once. "Very well, then. I'll leave you two alone. Quinton, please fill Sato in on any information you may have gathered since we last met. I have other things to attend to."

After George left the room, Sato sat down on one of the couches, gesturing for Mr. Hallenhaffer to sit across from him on the other couch. Once settled, Sato asked the question he'd been asking first ever since the fourth such interview, when a common theme had become evident.

"Are people going insane in your Reality? Lots of people?"

Rutger was spouting off at the mouth before Mothball could say one word upon entering the kitchen. "I tell you, that boy is an insolent, inconsiderate, rude—"

"Calm yerself, little man," Mothball muttered, grabbing the milk bottle from the fridge. "'Eard enough of yer gripin' for one day, I 'ave. We all know he's a bit rude, no need yappin' off about it one second more."

"A *bit* rude?" Rutger sat at the large table, munching on something that looked suspiciously like Mothball's cheesecake leftovers from the night before. "A *bit*? That's like saying you're a bit tall."

"Well, I am, now, ain't I?" Mothball pulled out a chair and sat beside her oldest friend, pulling the plate away from him. "Pardon me, but I don't quite remember givin' ya the go ahead on eatin' me hard-earned sweets."

"Sorry," Rutger said, head bowed in shame. "You know I get . . . kinda hungry sometimes."

"Ya reckon so, do ya?" Mothball let out a laugh. "That there's like saying Sato is a bit rude."

"Touché," Rutger muttered.

A long pause followed. Mothball had enjoyed seeing her fellow Realitants come to the Center over the last few days—many of them she hadn't seen in years—though the reunions were somewhat bittersweet. The reason for the gathering was not a good thing. People going bonkers everywhere, Chi'karda getting loopy here and there. Something very strange was happening.

"Can't wait to see Tick and the others again," Rutger said.

Mothball couldn't stop a huge smile from spreading across her face at the mention of the boy, Atticus. "I hear ya, there. Goin' to give 'im a big 'ug, I will. Paul and Sofia, too."

"I just wish it were under better circumstances." Rutger sat back in his chair, hands resting on his round belly. "All this time we spent worrying about Mistress Jane and the Thirteenth, and then this comes along. Nasty stuff."

Mothball thought back to several weeks earlier, when the first sign of the craziness showed up in the form of a madwoman running through the streets of downtown New York City in the Twelfth. The resident Realitant had witnessed it firsthand, and thought nothing of it until the woman started screaming, "I can't get it out of my head! I can't get it out of my head!" and then *disappeared,* winking away to some unknown destination. Thinking on it gave Mothball the creeps.

"'Tis gettin' worse," she said. "From what I 'ear, there's a fragmented Reality that's gone good and batty through and through, every last one of 'em. A literal madhouse."

Rutger huffed. "I heard there's a town in the Sixth

where every last person is acting like a cat, crawling around, purring, fighting over milk. Can you imagine how *disturbing* that must be?"

Just then, Master George entered the kitchen, his golden Barrier Wand—its dials and switches set to who-knew-what—clasped in his right hand like a walking cane, and Muffintops right at his ankles. Mothball had the odd thought that she hoped the little tabby cat hadn't heard the bit about the people-kitties in the Sixth. Could be quite traumatizing for the poor thing.

"Having a bit of a snack, are we?" Master George said as he joined them at the table. "I must admit, I'm quite hungry myself." He looked around the kitchen as if some food might magically appear in front of him.

"Did you get the letter delivered to Tick okay?" Rutger asked.

Master George blushed, fidgeting with the Wand. "Why, er, yes, yes, it arrived just fine, I believe. Though I might have miscalculated a bit on the exact delivery location."

"Miscalculated?" Mothball repeated.

"Why, er, well . . . I may have sent it a little . . . to the . . . *left,* if you will."

"The left?" Rutger asked.

Master George slammed his hand on the table. "Fine! I put the blasted thing right in the middle of their wall! And yes, I'm quite embarrassed."

"Ya could've sliced someone's ruddy head off," Mothball said.

"I'm quite aware of that, thank you very much." Master George looked angry, but it quickly flashed into a smile and a snicker. "I imagine it gave them a jolly good fright, don't you?"

"I bet you did it on purpose," Rutger said. "I know I would have."

"But they got it?" Mothball asked.

"Yes, yes, they got it. I hope they'll forgive me the debt of mending their wall, however." Master George cleared his throat, then his face grew serious again. "I'm afraid we have tough times ahead, my friends. This . . . problem is growing, and we haven't the slightest clue as to its source. If I could, I would begin our meeting this very instant. But, alas, not everyone will be here until the appointed time."

"What do you have planned for Tick and his friends?" Rutger asked.

Master George put the Barrier Wand on the table and absently rolled it back and forth. "Well, the most essential matter is to figure out Master Tick's odd ability to manipulate the Chi'karda. Perhaps we can use it to our advantage in this dreadful mess."

"Figured out where yer gonna send 'em yet?" Mothball asked.

"Oh, yes, indeed I have."

Mothball and Rutger waited, expecting their boss to tell them the plan. But he stayed silent, staring at an empty spot on the other side of the kitchen.

"And . . ." Rutger prodded.

Master George finally looked up, focused on Rutger, then Mothball. "My dear friends, I'm afraid my plans for them are quite . . . hazardous."

"Hazardous?" Mothball repeated.

Master George nodded. "I daresay I hardly expect all three of them to survive."

CHAPTER 8

GUILTY

Tick's eyes flickered, then opened.

Though shaded by trees, the faint forest light looked like atomic explosions, blistering his eyeballs with pain, making him squeeze his eyelids shut once more. He groaned, every inch of his body feeling like someone had mistaken him for a human piñata. He hurt. He hurt *bad*.

To his right, he heard movement—the rustling of leaves, moaning. Tick brought his hands up to his face, wincing as the movement sent shock waves of pain coursing through his body again. He froze until it died down, then rubbed his eyes. He finally opened them again, and the light didn't seem nearly as bad.

Carefully, delicately, he pushed himself into a sitting position.

Darkness had crept into the forest, more and more insects revealing their presence in a growing chorus of mating calls. Paul sat with his arms folded, leaning against a nearby tree, his face set in a grimace. Sofia was curled up in a ball several feet to Paul's right, still moaning, leaves sticking to her clothes as if she'd been rolling around in them since morning. The strange devices Mr. Chu had attached to them were gone.

Surprisingly, Tick felt the pain sliding away, feeling better by the second. Pushing against the ground, he got his feet under him and stood up. Though sore, he no longer felt the pinpricks and bruises he'd suffered from just moments earlier. It was as if someone had injected him with two shots of morphine.

"Dude, what *happened?*" Paul said through a groan, stretching his arms out before him.

Tick stepped over to Sofia, who seemed to be regaining her strength as well. She rolled onto her back, blinked up at Tick, then held up an arm; Tick helped her to her feet.

"Is that guy still your favorite teacher?" she asked, brushing leaves off her clothes. "He's a real joy to be around, that's for sure."

"I . . . I don't know what—" Tick stopped in mid-sentence, staring at something over Sofia's shoulder.

He squinted to see through the dim twilight, then squeezed his eyes shut and opened them again. "What the heck is *that?*"

"What?" Sofia and Paul asked in unison, turning to look in the same direction as Tick.

Without answering, Tick walked toward the oddity that loomed over them just a few dozen feet away.

"Whoa," he heard Paul say from behind him.

Deeper into the forest, several trees had *melted* into a twisting, gnarled, monstrous-looking mass of wood that was as tall and thick as a house. Several other trees had been lifted out of the ground, their roots sticking out like naked fingers, clods of dirt swaying back and forth. Tick could only stare, disbelieving his own eyes. It looked like some giant magician had grabbed dozens of trees, transformed them into liquid wood, and then smashed them together, twisting and squeezing all of it into a deformed, hideous shape.

Sofia gasped, then pointed to a section of the wood-blob near the ground. "Is that what I think it is? Oh!" She covered her face with her hands and turned around, her body visibly shuddering.

"What?" Paul asked, stepping closer to take a look. Tick joined him, and immediately saw the source of her disgust.

Somehow *twisted* into the wood was the body of a deer. Three legs poked out of the main trunk; its face was half-sunk into the wood, the one visible eye some-how displaying the fear it must have felt at the last sec-ond before death.

"That's downright creepy," Paul whispered.

⸻

By the time they reached Tick's house, almost all of the intense pain they'd felt had disappeared, leaving only a weary soreness. Tick, like Paul and Sofia, had hardly said a word on the walk back, trying to figure out which had been more disturbing—the agonizing pain or the deformed super-tree with the dead deer sticking out of it.

"Could this day have been any weirder?" Paul asked as they walked up the porch steps to Tick's house.

"Maybe if we'd grown bunny ears," Sofia replied.

Paul let out a bitter laugh.

They walked in to the wonderful smells of dinner, all of them pausing to take a deep breath. Tick was starving. He couldn't tell what his mom had cooked, but he had a feeling she'd felt the need to prove to Sofia that *she* could cook, too.

"So are we gonna tell your parents what just hap-pened?" Paul whispered.

Tick thought a minute. "Maybe later. My poor mom's worried enough as it is. No harm, no foul, right?"

"Yeah," Sofia agreed. "Let's just stay in the house and stare at each other until it's time to go meet Master George."

"Sounds good," Tick said. "Hopefully we can stay out of trouble for one more day."

They walked into the kitchen.

～～～

Mistress Jane felt discouraged.

She sat next to the large stone window of her apartment in the Lemon Fortress, closing her eyes every time the soft, warm breeze filled with the sweet smell of wildflowers blew up from the meadows below. The day was beautiful, the slightest hint in the air that autumn lay just around the corner. Everything was perfect.

And yet, a stinging sadness tempered all of it.

It had been four months since her Barrier Wand had been stolen, trapping her inside the Thirteenth Reality. At the time, she'd been so intrigued by the Realitants' ability to wink away with a broken Wand, and its potential implications for her, that she'd gotten straight to work—studying, experimenting, *building*. There was a lot about the mysterious power of Chi'karda she'd not yet discovered, and the little group's seemingly miraculous disappearance had led her to change her thinking. She had already made some exciting discoveries.

However, at the moment, she was very frustrated.

For one thing, her efforts to build a new Barrier Wand had hit a major snag. Frazier Gunn, the leader on the project, couldn't find one of the key elements for the wire that would transmit the Chi'karda from its Drive packet to the body of the Wand. The needed material was a complicated alloy of several rare metals, and one of them was proving impossible to find within the Thirteenth. Frazier had grown noticeably irritable, obviously realizing the potential consequences if he failed in this project. His room for error with Jane had grown very thin.

But all of this was secondary to what troubled her most.

She was starting to feel *guilty*.

She couldn't remember when it started, or when it had grown to such a staggering weight on her heart. But now, every minute of the day, all she could think about was how evil she had become. When had it come to this? *How* had it come to this? In the beginning, all she'd ever wanted was to make the world a better place, to improve life for all her fellow human beings. It was to fulfill those lofty and noble goals that she'd joined the Realitants years ago, devoting her life to studying the Realities. Though she'd never voiced her intentions, she'd planned from the first day to seek out those things in other Realities that would lead to her ultimate goal.

A Utopia. A perfect world. A haven for all people, where pain and sorrow would cease to exist. Where everyone could be happy.

That was all she'd wanted. That was all she *still* wanted.

And yet, here she was, a fierce and cruel ruler of an entire world, using its mutated powers to create horrific armies of creatures, to repress those who opposed her, to destroy those who dared to fight back. She was a despicable, disgusting person. A terribly *unhappy* person.

But she couldn't change. Not now. She knew that as clearly as she'd recognized what she had become. It was too late for change. Her plans were in full motion, and if it took her full cruelty and reprehensible reputation to win the battle, then so be it.

She realized what that meant. She was willing to sacrifice her own dignity, her own reputation, her own . . . soul. In the end, though, the worlds would thank her. In the end, everyone would be better off. In the end, life would be perfect.

She looked to her right just in time to see her latest servant-girl, Doofus, stumble through the door and drop a tray, dishes clattering all over the floor.

The timing couldn't have been worse. Jane's *mood* couldn't have been worse.

She threw her hand forward, unleashing a burst of the mutated Chi'karda. Doofus shot into the air and slammed high against the stone wall, pinned near the ceiling by the invisible force. Choking sounds filled the room as the poor girl kicked at the air, her heels thumping the wall.

"How dare you enter without knocking, you pathetic slob." Jane's voice remained calm and cool, belying the rage and guilt she felt within. With a quick wave of her hand, she made Doofus spring away from the wall and fly across the room. Screams burst from the girl's throat as the chokehold was released. They quickly faded when the servant shot through the open window and plummeted toward her death far below.

"I'm tired of coming up with names for these people," Jane grumbled to herself.

She stood up, took one last look at the beauty of her fortress grounds, then went back to work. There was much to be done.

CHAPTER 9

A MAJOR RULE VIOLATION

On the morning of August 22, Tick and his friends barely said a word during breakfast with his family, scared to death that somehow they'd slip up and say something about the incident in the forest. They were having enough trouble already with his mom—she kept insisting Dad should go with them, that they should demand Master George allow Edgar to be a Realitant or they would all quit.

Tick hated seeing how much his mom worried. She'd never looked so distressed and unhappy. Seeing his mom sobbing uncontrollably was just about enough to rip Tick's heart into two pieces. But he knew they had no choice, and he also knew his dad would figure out a way to console her after they were gone.

Luckily, Dad was firmly on their side, though he, too, often failed to hide the worries and concerns inflicted on his own heart.

After stuffing food and clothes into their backpacks, and after a terribly tearful good-bye with Tick's family, the three Realitants set off for the cemetery near the town square of Deer Park. Tick thought it was a little surreal, like his parents had packed him off to summer camp instead of to another reality.

"Man, your mom *really* loves you, dude," Paul said, adjusting his backpack.

"Yeah, I guess," Tick replied.

"You *guess?*" Sofia said. "My parents are just glad to get me out of the house. 'Yes, sweetie, run along to your adventures. Don't forget to brush your teeth!'"

Paul kicked a loose rock on the road. "You know my strategy—ask for forgiveness when I get back."

Tick didn't respond, unable to get the look on his mom's face out of his head.

They walked in silence the rest of the way to the cemetery.

"So good to see you!" George said for the hundredth time that morning. He reached out to shake the hand of William Schmidt, an old man from the Third Reality who Sato thought looked like someone three steps from death's door. Sato stifled a yawn, wondering why George always made him do stuff like this with him.

They stood at the entrance to the large assembly hall, a wide auditorium cut into the stone with a stage in the front and a tinted window at the back overlooking the Grand Canyon. Sato knew they'd somehow camouflaged the windows in the complex, but it still seemed like a foolish thing. He could only imagine the news explosion that would happen if they were discovered.

The Big Meeting wasn't scheduled to begin for another ninety minutes, but the Realitants had been pouring in for hours, wanting to meet and greet and speculate. Sato had never met such strange and diverse people in all his life, and couldn't help but feel amazed at the sheer effort of maintaining such an organization.

A slender woman with flaming red hair entered the assembly hall next, enough makeup on her face to hide a dozen boils. She smiled as George shook her hand, then focused on Sato, nodding her head.

"Is this one of the new recruits?" she asked, her high voice filled with a creepy sweetness.

"Why, yes, yes, he is," George replied, his voice loud and prideful. "Young Sato here has proven himself quite valuable in the last few months. A real worker, eh, Sato?"

Sato shook the lady's hand. "Nice to meet you." He

wanted to add, *Would you mind killing me, please? I'm bored.*

"My name is Priscilla Persephone," the redhead replied in her slightly disturbing, shrill voice. "I've heard great things about your mission to obtain Mistress Jane's Barrier Wand. Good to know Master George can trust such . . . important duties to someone so young, instead of depending on veterans like myself."

Priscilla gave George a hard stare, then walked off to grab a glass of orange juice and a pastry.

George mumbled something under his breath; it sounded like he'd used the words *ugly hag* and *yapping dog.*

"What did you say?" Sato asked.

George waved at the air. "Oh, nothing, Master Sato, nothing at all."

The next person George greeted was a younger, much prettier woman named Nancy Zeppelin. Her golden hair and brilliant blue eyes made her look like she'd just stepped off a Paris fashion runway. Sato didn't realize he was staring until George nudged him with an elbow.

"Oh, um, my name is Sato," he said, feeling his face grow warm.

"Nice to meet you. Congratulations on joining the—"

Before she could finish, Rutger rushed into the auditorium, yelling George's name, waddling like a fat duck trying to catch its ducklings before they crossed a busy road.

"Goodness gracious me," George said, trying to calm the short man. "What is it, Rutger?"

Rutger spoke in short bursts, sucking in gasps of air between words. "Tick . . . and the others . . . their nanolocators . . . everything seems normal . . . at the cemetery . . . but it won't work . . ."

George reached down and grasped Rutger by the shoulders. "Take a deep breath, man, then explain yourself."

Rutger did as he was told, closing his eyes briefly before opening them again. But when he spoke, it came out just like before. "I don't understand . . . all their readings . . . normal . . . no malfunctions, no blips . . . but the Wand won't wink them in. They're standing there . . . waiting! It won't work!"

George tapped his lips, looking down at Sato then at the mingling Realitants gathered in the assembly hall. His eyes seemed afire with concern. "Oh, dear."

"What's going on?" Sato asked.

"Unfortunately, I think I know *exactly* what's going on." George started walking toward the stage, his steps brisk.

Sato looked down at Rutger. "Do you?"

Rutger shook his head, his face so lined and creased that Sato worried he'd drop dead of a heart attack. He was about to say something when George's voice boomed across the room, echoing off the walls. Sato turned to see George standing at a microphone on the stage.

"My fellow Realitants," he announced. "This meeting must start immediately. Please, find anyone lingering in the halls, bring them here, and take your seats."

"What's wrong?" someone yelled from the audience.

George paused before answering. "We've had a violation of Rule Number 462."

Tick fidgeted, rocking back and forth on his feet, wiping his sweaty hands on his pants. Sofia stood to his left, Paul to his right. The sun made its way toward the top of the sky, beating down on the cemetery with a ruthless heat. Tick hoped Master George would wink them away to a nice, cool place; he couldn't wait to tell him about the bizarre incident in the woods with Mr. Chu. They'd seen no sign of him since, and several calls to the school had only hit the answering machine.

"Come on, already," Paul muttered, looking up at the cloudless blue sky as if he expected Master George to float down in a balloon and pick them up. He cupped his hands around his mouth and shouted to the air, "Yo! We're ready! Wink us, man!"

"Maybe he will once you quit acting like an idiot," Sofia said.

"At least I'm *acting*," Paul replied.

Sofia pulled back to punch him for his troubles when the screeching sound of a car slamming on its brakes in front of the cemetery entrance made them look in that direction. Tick's heart skipped a beat when he realized it was his mom. She was already out the door and past the stone archway, running at full speed.

"Mom!" Tick yelled. "What are you doing?"

"Atticus, don't leave yet!" she said, looking ridiculous as her arms pumped back and forth. Tick realized that he'd never, not once, seen his mother run before.

"What's wrong?" he asked, lowering his voice now that she'd almost reached them, only twenty feet away.

"I have to tell you something—I have to tell you before you go." She slowed, then stopped, sucking in air. "It's very important."

Tick was so relieved she wasn't going to prevent him from leaving, he failed to realize how odd it was that she'd raced here to tell him . . . what?

"You okay?" he asked. "What is it?"

Having regained her breath, she began talking. "I should've told you this years ago—at the least, I should've told you four months ago. I—"

But Tick didn't hear the rest of her sentence. Instead, in that instant, he and his friends were winked away to a very strange place.

CHAPTER 10

A VERY STRANGE PLACE

Tick got his wish in one regard—the place was cold. Beyond that, he couldn't find one positive thing about it.

They stood on a cracked stone road, small pools of stagnant water filling the gaps. The smoggy air reeked of things burnt—oil, rubber, tar. Metal structures lined the long street on both sides, towering over them, black and dirty. Tick first thought they were buildings of some kind, but that notion quickly evaporated. They were more like sculptures, the dark and twisted vision of some maniac artist.

"Man," Paul whispered, "it's like Gotham City."

In some spots, wide, arching pieces rose fifty feet

in the air, ending in a jagged, ripped edge as if some enormous monster had ripped the top off with its teeth. In other places, huge, towering cylinders—some taller than New York City skyscrapers—ascended to the sky until they disappeared into the menacing, storm-heavy clouds. Squat, deformed lumps sat in the nooks and crannies, like weathered statues of ancient Greek gods. Hideous carvings of animals, worse than the ugliest gargoyle Tick had ever seen balancing on the outer walls of a cathedral, lay strewn about like stray dogs, frozen in place by a rainstorm of molten metal. Random triangles and pentagons hung oddly from various structures, seeming to defy the laws of physics.

All of it, everything in sight, was made out of a dark gray metal that dully reflected the scant light filtering through the clouds above. And there was no variation—the bizarre structures and sculptures lay everywhere, in every direction, as far as Tick could see.

One word seemed to describe the place better than anything else: dreary.

"Where are we?" Sofia asked, slowly turning in a circle, just as Tick and Paul were.

Good question, Tick thought. He didn't know if he was looking forward to any locals showing up to answer it.

"What kind of people would *live* here?" he asked,

trying to shake the worry of his mom and her undelivered message.

"People who like to gouge their eyes out, obviously," Paul said. "This has to be the ugliest place I've ever seen."

"They ever heard of flowers?" Sofia said. "Maybe a splash of color here and there?"

"Do you think we're in one of the Thirteen Realities?" Tick asked. "One we haven't heard of yet?"

"Where else could we be?" Paul answered. "Does this look like something in Reality Prime to you?"

"I don't know—maybe these are ruins or something."

Paul coughed. "Uh . . . don't think so, big guy. Pretty sure we would've heard about a place this weird."

"What could've led to something like this?" Sofia asked, sliding her hand along the flat side of a large, boxy structure, big spheres bubbling out the side of it like pimples. "How could they be so different from us?"

Tick stepped toward one of the cylindrical towers, following Sofia's lead and touching the black metal. It was as cold and hard as it looked.

A faint buzzing sound filled the air. At first, Tick panicked because it reminded him of the Gnat Rat and its mechanical hornets that had attacked him in his bedroom the previous fall. But an instant after the droning began, a burst of light to the left caught his attention.

Near a large circle of metal, jutting up from the ground like a half-buried flying saucer, sparks of brilliant white light popped and flashed, igniting into existence only to disappear a second later, like the brief flames shooting off a welder. The sparks seemed random at first, exploding all over the place, high and low in the air, across an area dozens of feet wide, reflecting off the metal circle in dull smears of color. But then the strangest thing happened.

The sparks began to form words.

Tick thought his mind was playing tricks, the constant flashing of lights wreaking havoc on his vision. But soon it became obvious as large letters of bright, streaky light appeared, hanging in the air, flashing and dancing but remaining solid enough to read. In a matter of seconds, a wall of words flickered before them, as big as a movie screen.

Tick swallowed his awe and confusion, reading the words as quickly as possible, scared they might disappear at any second:

Inside the words of the words inside,
There lies a secret to unhide.
A place there is where you must go,
To meet the Seven, friend or foe.

Of course, an order there must be,
To hill and rock and stone and tree.
Of worlds above and worlds below,
Of worlds with water, fire, snow.
Of worlds that live in fear and doubt,
Of worlds within and worlds without.
The Path begins where dark is clear,
Where short is tall and far is near.
All this you must ignore and hate,
For you to find the wanted fate.
There lies a secret to unhide,
Inside the words of the words inside.

Tick read it three times, his eyes wide. He had no clue what the words meant, but they mesmerized him, held him captivated. He felt just like when he'd first read the original invitation from Master George.

Master George!

"You've gotta be kidding me," Tick said, surprised at how loud his voice sounded, echoing off the world of metal around them. He looked over at his friends.

"What?" Paul asked without returning the glance. He still stared at the poem, which shimmered as brightly as ever, his lips forming the strange words silently. Sofia was doing the same thing a couple feet from him.

Tick returned to the poem, quickly rereading it. "I can't believe Master George is messing around with riddles and clues again. I thought we'd proved our-selves already."

"How do you know it's from Master George?" Paul asked.

"Hmmm," Sofia said. "Maybe because he told us to go to the cemetery then winked us here? I know it's a little complicated for—"

A loud, electric *crack* cut her off, followed by a series of hissing sizzles. The letters of the poem quickly sparkled and flashed before disappearing altogether, the wispy, streaming trails of smoke the only sign they'd ever been there. Without any wind, the smoke lingered, slowly coalescing and melding into one hazy glob.

Just when everything seemed utterly silent, another loud crack of electricity made Tick jump, one last explo-sion of light igniting on the ground a few feet in front of Sofia. It was gone as quickly as it had come, and in its place stood a small metal box, a tiny latch on the front.

Paul got there first, dropping to his knees and reaching out for the box.

"Wait!" Sofia said.

Paul's hands froze in midair; he looked over his shoulder. "Why? This is obviously from Master George, right? You just said I was an idiot for doubting it."

"Well . . . yeah, I guess. Just . . . I don't know, be careful."

"Open it," Tick urged. "We're lucky he didn't wink it into one of our skulls."

Paul reached out again and flipped up the latch, then carefully lifted the lid open. He leaned forward and looked down into the small space of the container; Tick and Sofia stood behind him, looking over his shoulder.

Inside, there lay only a small piece of paper. Stiff, white paper—cardstock.

"Definitely M.G.'s MO," Paul said as he picked up the message. He held it up in the scant light for everyone to see.

In the same typed writing of the Twelve Clues from their first adventure with Master George, the paper contained the exact poem, word for word, they'd just seen floating in the air like the world's most sophisticated fireworks. Paul flipped the paper over and read another mysterious clue:

```
Miss Graham is the key. Repeat: you
must find Anna.
```

"Man, he's getting all fancy on us," Paul said, standing up. "Why use all the Christmas lights if he was gonna send us this anyway?"

"Guess he wanted to show off," Sofia said, taking the message from Paul. She sat down on the stone-paved road and read through the poem again.

Tick folded his arms and shivered, looking up at the sky. There was no sign of the sun, but it seemed to have grown a little darker since they'd arrived. The temperature had dropped too, and for the first time in months, he felt justified wearing his scarf. He wrapped it a little tighter, then walked over to sit on a small metal cube next to the road.

"Hurry up and figure it out, Sofia," he said before letting out a huge yawn. "I don't really wanna hang out here much longer."

"You could help, ya know," she mumbled, still studying the paper.

Actually Tick was doing just that, reviewing the poem in his mind's eye; without meaning to, he'd memorized it. But he didn't know what to look for or try to solve. The riddle seemed to have only one purpose—to confuse its reader.

Paul yawned and stretched. "Man, I can't just sit here. Let's get moving."

"Where to?" Tick asked, looking down one length of the endless road, then the other. The heavy clouds had sunk to the ground, as if seeking warmth and companionship. The only things Tick could see were the countless heaps and angles of dark metal, covered in a mist that grew thicker by the minute. Tick shivered again.

"I don't know, dude," Paul said. "That way." He

pointed to his left, then changed his mind, pointing the other direction. "Nah, that way."

Sofia stood, shaking her head; she seemed as frustrated as Tick about the riddle. "Sounds good to me. Let's go." Without waiting for a response, she started walking down the cracked and pitted road.

Thirty minutes later, nothing had changed except for the air around them, which continued to grow thicker with wet, heavy mist. The world of metal was almost lost in darkness. Obscure, creepy shapes appeared and disappeared, all sharp angles and looming curves. The burnt smells intensified, as if the kids were approaching a huge factory or garbage dump.

Tick officially hated the place, his panic growing at the thought that maybe they'd be stuck here, that they'd have to *sleep* here. If the stupid riddle was their only way out . . .

He kept running through it in his mind, trying to recall the methods he'd used to solve the original Twelve Clues. Those had seemed so easy in comparison, almost childish. Magic words, thumping the ground with your foot, figuring out a day and a time. Compared to that, this new one seemed like advanced calculus.

For some reason, the lines "All this you must ignore

and hate, for you to find the wanted fate" kept returning to his mind. Something told him that was the key
to figuring everything out.

They approached a wide, thick span of metal arching across the road—rusty, linked chains of varying
lengths hanging down every couple of feet. The chains
swayed slightly despite the lack of wind. That gave Tick
the creeps more than anything else, and he quickened
his pace until the odd structure was way behind them.

"Spooked?" Paul asked. His voice was muffled,
swallowed up in the mist.

"Yeah," Tick answered. "You're not?"

"Maybe."

"Oh, please," Sofia said. "If it weren't for me being
here, you two would be running around bawling your
eyes out. Just keep moving."

"Miss Italy, you're probably right, but do you have
to be so annoying?"

They walked for another couple of hours, but nothing changed. The path only led to more of the same—
mounds of dark metal and looming, odd shapes. Tick
finally couldn't take it anymore; his feet hurt and his
stomach rumbled with hunger.

"We need to eat," he said. "And sleep."

"Amen," Paul agreed.

Sofia didn't say anything, but she almost collapsed
to the ground, sighing as she leaned back against a

black wall and pulled out a granola bar and a bottle of water from her backpack. Tick sat across the road from her, diving into his own food.

"How can I possibly sleep here?" Paul asked as he bit into an energy bar. "I don't have my feather pillow."

Tick half-laughed, but he already felt his eyes drooping, despite sitting up. Feeling like he'd been drugged, he leaned over and lay on his side, pulling his backpack under his head for a pillow. He fell asleep instantly.

Two days passed, though the only way Tick knew for sure was by looking at his watch and noticing the subtle changes in the darkness of the sky. Tick's anxiety and panic faded into a dull indifference as they trudged along the endless path, finding nothing. For all he knew, they were walking in circles because everything looked so similar.

They grew quiet as they walked, discouragement acting as a gag in their throats.

On the morning of their third day in the miserable place, Tick finished off his measly breakfast of a candy bar, half a bottle of water, and a stale piece of bread— he was almost out of food. As he stood and put on his backpack, Paul gave him an ugly look.

"Dude, where are you going?" he said through a yawn. "I'm barely awake—what's the rush?"

"There has to be something we're missing," Tick replied. "I think we need to get off this stupid road and climb up one of these structures. Try to get inside one of them."

"Tick's right," Sofia said, getting to her feet as well. "This road isn't leading us anywhere except in a big circle—everything looks familiar."

"It *all* looks the same to me." Paul stretched, then stood up. "Fine, whatever. It's not like I wanna retire and live on this road someday. Maybe we could try to climb—"

A loud, crashing sound to their right cut him off. All three of them froze, waiting, listening.

A metallic *clang* rang out from behind a jutting rectangle of metal, followed by a scrape, then the grunt of a man. Tick heard the shuffling of feet, then a cough. Although he knew someone was approaching the road, about to appear at any second, he couldn't move. After almost three days of complete boredom, hearing the presence of another human being was like finding an alien in his backyard.

A man of medium height and enormous build stepped around the corner of the metal obstacle, limping slightly. He had tangled, red hair and a scruffy beard; he wore a plaid red flannel shirt, dirty denim overalls, and heavy work boots. Tick was half-surprised the guy didn't have a huge axe slung over his shoulder.

When the man noticed Tick and the others, he stopped and stared at them with wide eyes. After a long, awkward pause, he spoke, his voice as scratchy as his beard.

"Well, butter my grits," he said with a heavy Southern accent. "What you chirrun doin' up in here?"

Tick didn't say anything, not sure why he felt so odd. Maybe it was the absurdity of seeing a lumberjack in a world made of metal. Sofia saved the situation.

"We're, uh, kind of lost," she said.

"Lost?" the man repeated, leaning back and putting his large hands in the pockets of his overalls. "How you reckon on gettin' lost up here on da roofens?"

Tick blinked, unsure if the guy was still speaking English.

"Um, pardon me?" Paul said, clearing his throat. "Didn't quite catch what you just said."

The man squinted, looking at each of them in turn, as if doing some deep thinking and analysis. Finally he said, "Ya'll look as twittered as a hound dawg at a tea party. Whatcha lookin' fer?"

Tick felt it was his turn. "Sir, we're, uh, like my friend said—we're lost. We're not familiar with this . . . place. Where are we? Where are all the houses and buildings and people?"

The man folded his arms, a smile spreading across his face; he had a huge gap between his two front teeth.

"Boy, you must be dumber 'an roadkill in math class. You hear what I'm sayin'?"

Tick shook his head, trying to look as confused as possible—which wasn't hard.

The man stepped forward. "Boy, you is standin' on the Roofens." He pointed down to the ground with exaggerated enthusiasm. "All the people is down *there*."

CHAPTER 11

BELOW THE ROOFENS

Tick looked at his feet, almost expecting to see little fairies running around to avoid being squished. But of course all he saw were his shoes and a thin crack on the stone road.

"Down there?" he asked.

The man made a noise somewhere deep in his throat, a cross between a cough and the clearing of phlegm. "I reckon that's what I said, ain't it? Who in the guppy-guts are you people?"

Tick fumbled for words, glad Sofia spoke up first. "We're just up here exploring, that's all. Of course we know what the Roofens are and that we're *standing* on them." She gave Tick an annoyed look. "That we're *on top* of the buildings."

"Ain't usin' dem brains a'yorn too much up here, wanderin' 'round like three hillbillies lookin' for moonshine. No, ma'am, ain't too smart." The man leaned over and spat something dark and disgusting on the road.

"My name's Sofia, and this is my friend, Tick." She gestured with her thumb. "And this is Paul. To tell you the truth, we *are* really lost, and kind of hungry and cold."

"Mmm-hmm," the man said with a grunt, eyeing Sofia up and down as if checking for ticks. "Come along, then. Ol' Sally'll take right good care of ya."

Paul spoke for the first time since the appearance of the strange man. "Is Sally your wife?"

The man laughed, a guffaw that hit the mist with a dull thump. "My wife? Boy, I ain't got me no wife. You're lookin' at him."

Tick was confused. "What do you mean?"

"Boy, what you mean, what I mean?"

"He *means,* what do you *mean?*" Sofia said, her voice returning to its normal arrogance.

The lumberjack threw his arms up in the air. "Feel like I'm talkin' to kai-yotes who done got their ears chopped off. I'm tellin' ya that yer *lookin'* at Sally, and you best not say a word about it."

"*Your* name is Sally?" Tick asked.

"Sally T. Jones, at yer service." He bowed, sweeping his arms wide, then righting himself. His face had reddened from the blood rushing to his head; it matched his beard. "Named after my grandpappy, who was named after his grandpappy. See, Sally's short for Sallivent, a name older than expired dirt, ya hear?"

"We hear," Sofia said. "You have a woman's name."

Tick elbowed his friend. "Be nice," he whispered.

"I like it," Paul said. "Beats the heck out of being named Princess or Barbie, right?"

Sally gave Paul a confused look. "I'll eat my own dandruff if you ain't the strangest group of chirrun I ever done seen."

"What's a chirrun?" Tick asked.

Sally squinted in disbelief. "*Chirrun.* Ya know—you's a kid, a child. More than one of ya—*chirrun.*"

"I think he means *children,*" Sofia said.

Sally took a step to the side, then motioned around the back of the metal block. "You kids wanna come back with me? Get ya sumthin' to fill dem tummies?"

"Where'd you come from?" Paul asked, leaning to get a look around the metal wall. "Is there seriously a whole city under us? Under these roofs?"

"Like I said, boy, we standin' on the Roofens. Probably done shaved purtin' near six months off your life stayin' out chere for so long. Dis dirty air'll eat yer innards quicker than a beaver on balsa wood."

"What's wrong with the air?" Tick asked.

Sally did his funny squint again. "I reckon you folks ain't lyin' when you says yer lost. These parts 'bout as polluted as my granny's toenails. Why do you think they built dem cities under all this here metal?"

"Why'd you come up here, then?" Sofia asked.

Sally paused, his eyes darting back and forth. "I, uh, well, ya see, the thing is . . ." He scratched his beard. "See, I done heard yer little twitter feet up on my ceilin' there, so I come up to do some investigatin'. Yep, that's what I reckon, far as I recall."

Tick exchanged a baffled look with Sofia and Paul. It didn't take a genius to realize they'd already caught Sally in his first lie.

"Well," Tick said, "we need a minute to talk about what we're gonna do."

"Go on, then," Sally said. "I ain't got a mind to bother dem there bid'ness and matter, such as it were."

"Huh?" Paul asked.

Tick quickly grabbed his friend by the shoulders and turned him away from Sally, pulling him into a huddle with Sofia.

"So what do we do?" Tick whispered.

"That guy's something else, ain't he?" Paul asked. "I can barely understand a word he says."

"I'm already getting used to it," Sofia said. "If you ignore every third word or so, it makes perfect sense."

"But what do we *do?*" Tick insisted.

"What else?" Paul said. "Go with this dude and get something to eat."

"How do we know he's safe?" Tick asked.

"Dude, get off the sissy train. There are three of us and one of him."

"He seems perfectly harmless," Sofia said. "I vote we go with him. We can't walk around up here for the rest of our lives."

"Plus," Paul said, "he said this air's really polluted. I'm not real cool on the whole lung-cancer thing. Let's do it."

Sofia nodded. "I'm dying to see what's down there."

Tick thought for a second. He felt uneasy, but he knew it was because their lives had gone flat-out crazy the last couple of days. Sally was definitely holding something back, and that made Tick nervous, but Paul was right—they had him outnumbered.

"All right," he whispered, then turned to Sally. "Sir, we really appreciate the offer to go to your house. We're really hungry, and, uh, lost."

Sally smiled and rubbed his belly. "I ain't said nothing about goin' to my house. But I know a restaurant's got some good eatin'. Come on, den." He waved his arm in a beckoning gesture as he turned and walked back the way he'd come.

Tick, Sofia, and Paul paused. But then they followed.

—

Sally led them through a small trapdoor and down a very long and steep set of wooden stairs, which looked out of place amidst all the surrounding metal. The way was dark and hot, humid and reeking of something rotten. Tick felt more nervous by the second, worried they were walking into a trap, but he didn't know what else to do. Where could they go? Who could they trust?

For now, Sally was their only friend in the world. *This* world, anyway.

They reached the bottom of the stairs and proceeded down a long hallway, their surroundings remaining unchanged. A faint light from ahead revealed black water seeping down the wooden walls. A rat scurried by Tick's foot; he barely stopped himself from crying out like the startled maid in an old cartoon.

Sally finally stopped next to a warped door of splintered wood, an iron handle barely hanging on. "Prepare dem hearts a'yorn," he said. "This place ain't like none such you ever saw." He pushed the door, and everyone watched as it swung outward, creaking loudly.

"Follow Uncle Sally and you chirrun might live

another day or two." He stepped through the doorway.

Sofia went first, then Paul, then Tick. For the next several minutes, Tick felt as if his brain might explode from taking in the completely alien place.

Stretching before them, below them, above them, was an endless world of chaos. Long rows of roughly cobbled pathways ran in every direction, with no pattern or regularity. Shops and inns and pubs crowded close on all sides. Hundreds of people bustled about. Dirty, ripped awnings hung over the places of business, wooden signs dangling from chains. On these signs were printed the only means of distinguishing one building from another—their names carved and painted onto the wood. Places called such things as The Axeman's Guild and The Darkhorse Inn and The Sordid Swine.

Some of the pathways were actually bridges, and Tick could see the levels below, overlapping and seemingly built on top of each other. The same was true above them, balconies and bridges spanning every direction, up and up and up until Tick saw the black roof that covered everything. The ceiling was filled with small rectangles of fluorescent lights, half of which were flickering or burned out altogether.

It was the universe's worst mall.

Paul leaned over and whispered to Tick, "Dude, check these people out."

Tick focused on the occupants of the enormous indoor town. Most of them slumped along, barely speaking to each other, many with hunched shoulders or an odd limp. Black seemed to be the color of choice for their clothes, everyone wearing drab and dirty garments with rips and tears aplenty. The people's faces were dirty too, with disheveled, greasy hair. The only spots of color were an occasional red scarf or green shawl or yellow vest, worn by those who seemed to walk with a little more confidence than the others.

And the smell—it was like a port-a-potty dumping ground, a foul, putrid stench that made Tick gag reflexively every few seconds until he grew somewhat used to it.

"Sally," Sofia coughed, "I think we were better off on the Roofens."

"Quit yer poutin' and come on," Sally replied, shuffling off to the right.

Tick and the others followed, dodging through the lazy crowd of sullen, black-clad residents, who seemed to be marching toward their destinations with no purpose whatsoever. Tick didn't see one person smiling. For that matter, none of them showed emotion at all— not a sneer, not a grimace, not a frown to be found.

"We've gotta get out of here," Tick whispered, scared to offend anyone around him but feeling a surge of panic well up inside him. He didn't know how much longer he could last in this horrible place. "We need to solve that riddle, quick."

"No kidding," Paul said. "I've just about had my fill of Happy Town."

"It's not just that," Tick said, still speaking quietly. "Something's not right here—it's not safe."

Sally moved them to the side of their current path, next to a small iron table outside a restaurant called The Stinky Stew.

"Have'n yerselves a seat on dem cheers." He pointed to the four crooked wooden chairs surrounding the table. "I'll be back with some eats."

As their guide entered the restaurant, a rusty bell ringing with the movement of the door, Tick and the others pulled out the chairs and sat down. Tick eyeballed the people walking by, looking for potential trouble. Seeing nothing but the unchanging mass of zombie-like shoppers, he said to Sofia, "Get the riddle out."

Sofia did, putting the paper on the table in front of her. Tick and Paul scooted their chairs across the uneven stones of the floor until they could see the words of the long poem.

Inside the words of the words inside,
There lies a secret to unhide.
A place there is where you must go,
To meet the Seven, friend or foe . . .

Tick read through the whole thing, then sat back in his chair, racking his brain. The poem seemed to offer no direction, nothing specific to grasp on to. At least the Twelve Clues had made it pretty clear that he was to figure out a date, a time, the magic words. This was a bunch of poetic nonsense.

Sofia flipped the page over where the second note was printed. "Who are Anna and Miss Graham?"

Paul leaned onto his elbows, resting them on the table. "Do you think it's the same person?"

"Maybe," Sofia replied. "We should start asking around here—see if anyone's heard of her."

"That's the only thing I can think of," Paul said. He stood up, almost knocking his chair backward.

"What are you doing?" Tick asked.

"Asking around, dude." He reached out and tapped the arm of the first stranger to walk by, an older woman in a filthy black dress, her gray hair sprawled across her shoulders in greasy strings. "Excuse me, ma'am, do you know who Anna Graham is?"

The old lady recoiled, barely casting a glance at Paul before quickening her step to get away. He didn't give up, tapping the next person, then the next, then the next, each time repeating his question. And the response was the same each time—a flinch, as if the name frightened them.

"Dudes, we don't have leprosy, ya know?" Paul

called out. Cupping his hands together, he shouted in an even louder voice, "Does anyone here know Miss Anna Graham?" The sounds of shuffling feet were all he got in return.

Sitting down with a huff, Paul shook his head. "This is ridiculous. What's wrong with these people?"

Tick's thoughts had wandered slightly. Something about Anna's name bothered him, tickled something in the back of his mind. *Miss Graham. Anna. Anna Graham.*

"This phrase has to be the key," Sofia said suddenly, pointing at the lines near the end of the poem: "All this you must ignore and hate, for you to find the wanted fate."

"Yeah, I thought the same thing," Tick said.

"Maybe it means—" Sofia began, but stopped when Sally came bustling outside, clanging the door against the wall with his elbows as he balanced several plates and bowls heaped with steaming food.

"As promised," he said, setting the meal on the table. He almost dropped one plate onto the ground, but Paul caught it and pushed it to safety. "Grab yer grub and eat. I'm as hungry as a one-legged possum caught in a dang ol' bear trap."

Sally sat down in the remaining chair and picked up his food with his hands; there wasn't a utensil in sight. Tick couldn't believe how delicious everything looked—chicken legs thick with meat, slabs of beef, celery and carrots, chunks of bread, sausages. It was so unexpectedly appetizing; he'd half-expected Sally to bring out a trash can full of fly-infested garbage.

Paul was the first to join in, then Sofia, both of them grabbing a roasted drumstick and chowing down.

"This ain't bad," Paul said with a full mouth, throwing his manners out the window. "Tastes a little stale and smoky, but it's pretty good."

Tick reached over and grabbed his own piece of chicken and a roll. Paul was right—it tasted a little old, even a little dirty, but it was like Thanksgiving dinner all the same—and Tick was starving. No one said a word as they munched and chewed and chomped their way through every last morsel of food.

Tick had just sat back, rubbing his belly in satisfaction, when a young boy in a dark suit stepped up to their table and cleared his throat. His dirty blond hair framed a face smeared with grime, and his eyes were wide, as if he was scared to death.

"Whatcha want?" Sally asked, wiping his mouth on his sleeve. "What's yer bid'ness, son?"

The boy swallowed, rocking back and forth on his feet, glancing over his shoulder now and again. But he said nothing.

"Got some dadgum cotton in dem ears, son?" Sally asked. "I say, what's yer bid'ness?"

The boy's arm slowly raised, his index finger extended. One by one, he pointed at the four people sitting at the table. Then he spoke in a weak, high-pitched voice full of fear.

"The Master . . . told me to . . . he said . . . he said you'll all be dead in five minutes."

CHAPTER 12

LONG, SPINDLY LEGS

All four of them stood up in the same instant; this time, Paul's chair did fall over with a rattling clang.

"What kinda nonsense you talkin'?" Sally asked.

The boy looked up at him, his face growing impossibly paler; then he turned and ran, disappearing in the dense crowd of mulling citizens.

"What was *that?*" Paul said.

"The riddle," Tick said, leaning over and twisting the paper from Master George toward him. "We have to solve the riddle. Now."

"Yeah, that'll be extra easy knowing we're about to die," Paul said.

"Quit whining and think," Sofia said, joining Tick to study the poem.

Tick tried to focus, reading the words through and then closing his eyes, letting them float through his mind, sorting them out. He thought of the lady's name, Miss Anna Graham . . .

Sofia spoke up, breaking his concentration. "The part about ignoring everything else—it must mean the two lines after it are all that matters—the last two lines. The rest of it seems like nonsense anyway . . . but . . . 'There lies a secret to unhide . . . '"

"'*Inside the words of the words inside,*'" Tick finished for her.

"What is *that?*" Paul said, his neck bent back as he looked up at the ceiling.

Tick ignored him, staring at the last two lines of the poem as if doing so would make them rearrange themselves. Rearrange . . .

Paul slapped Tick on the shoulder, then Sofia, who was also ignoring him. "Guys, cut the poetry lesson for a second and *look.*" He pointed upward.

Far above, odd shapes crawled across the black roof, defying gravity and blotting out the sputtering lights as they moved around. Impossible to make out clearly, the . . . *things* were squat and round with several long, angled limbs that moved up and down rapidly, bending and unbending as they scuttled about. They looked like big spiders, but *false* somehow—artificial. As if their legs were made out of ... .

"Bless my mama's hanky—what *are* those buggins?" Sally asked.

One of the creatures jumped from the roof and landed on the closest balcony with a metallic clank. As it flew through the air, its awkward limbs flailing, Tick noticed a flash of steel. Another creature followed its companion, then another, then another. By the time the leader had jumped down to the next balcony, the dozen or so others had reached the first one. Balcony to balcony, down they came.

Straight for Tick's group.

"This is gonna be trouble," Paul said.

A sharp pain built behind Tick's eyes, his mind spinning in all kinds of directions. He knew these mechanical spiders must be like the Gnat Rat or the Tingle Wraith, things sent by Master George to test them. At least he *hoped* they were from Master George.

"'Inside the words of the words inside,'" Sofia said in a burst, her eyes widening in revelation. "'Inside the *words* of the words inside!'"

The spider-things were two levels away, close enough for Tick to make out their features. The long, spindly legs were jointed metal, supporting a round ball of steel with all kinds of devices jutting from its body—spinning blades and sharp knives. The clanking and clicking and whirring of the horrible creatures made Tick's insides boil.

Sofia grabbed Tick's arm. "*The words inside.* Those three words are the main part of the riddle!"

The answer hit Tick like a catapulted stone. Anna Graham. Rearranging. Tick had always loved the puzzles in the Sunday paper, everything from Sudoku to number pyramids, but one game had always been a favorite . . .

Anna Graham.

"Anagram!" he yelled, probably looking insane to his friends because of the huge smile that spread across his face. The clanking sounds of the oncoming metal-spiders grew louder.

"Yeah, but who is she?" Paul asked. "How do we find her?"

"No, no," Tick said. "Not a name—a thing. An anagram."

"What the heck is an anagram?" Paul asked, stealing a glance at the creatures, now only seconds away from reaching them.

Sofia answered. "It's when the letters of a word or phrase are rearranged to spell something else."

"Yeah," Tick said. "Whatever we're looking for must be an anagram of '*the words inside.*'"

"Yes!" Sofia yelled.

But their joy was short-lived. The first spider landed on their table with a horrible crash.

~⁓

The boy named Henry ran, bumping into people, bouncing off them, falling to the ground, getting back up—running, always running. He'd hardly said one word to a stranger his whole life, living in fear of the metaspides and their all-seeing eye. They were always there, waiting, watching.

But he'd done his job. He'd said the words, delivered the message. In doing so, he'd made enough money to buy medicine for his mom for another six months. He knew the docs were overcharging him, but he had no choice. He didn't want his mom to die.

The creepy man who'd offered him the job stood in the same spot, lurking inside an alcove between two pubs. The man had paid him half the money beforehand, promising the other half when the deed was done. Henry walked up to him and held out his shaking hand. When they made eye contact, he couldn't help but take a step backward.

The man looked at the boy with fierce eyes, his brow tensed in anger, his dark hair hanging in his face. A long pause followed, filled with the sounds of the metaspides launching an attack behind him.

"You did it, then?" the man said. "You think you deserve some money, do you?"

"Y-y-yes, sir," Henry replied.

"So you do, boy. You deserve every penny. I'm a businessman, you know, and I've never faltered on a deal in my life." He reached out and tousled Henry's hair. "It's why I am who I am. Where do you think the metaspides came from, anyway?"

Henry shrugged, wishing with all his heart he could get away from this strange, scary man.

The tall stranger reached into his pocket and pulled out several bills, which he placed in Henry's hand. "Take this, boy, and use it wisely."

"Yes, sir," Henry said, turning to run.

The man grabbed his shoulder, gripping tightly. "Grow up smart, boy. Grow up smart, and one day you may work for me." The man leaned in and whispered into Henry's ear. "For Reginald Chu, the greatest mind in all the Realities."

Henry squirmed out of the man's clutches and ran. He ran and ran until he collapsed into his sick mother's arms.

~⁓~

For an instant, Paul couldn't make himself move. He stared down in horror at Tick, who was lying on the ground, the weird metal spider thing on top of him. Its eight segmented legs of steel pinned each of Tick's limbs while a pair of slicing blades popped out of its silver belly and headed for his friend's head. Somehow, in the midst of all this, Paul noticed words printed on the back of the spider's round body:

METASPIDE
Manufactured by Chu Industries

Just like the Gnat Rat.

He snapped himself out of his daze and grabbed the closest chair. Picking it up by the back, he swung it as hard as he could and smashed it into the creature, sending it flying off Tick and clanking along the paved stones of the pathway. Tick scrambled to his feet and joined Paul; Sofia and Sally were right next to them, staring at the thing Paul had just whacked.

The metaspide righted itself, turning to look at the group, though it had no eyes as far as Paul could tell. The thing's buddies had dropped down to the same level of the indoor mall and joined their leader in a pack, as if readying for a charge. Most of the darkly dressed people had fled the scene, somehow finding the spirit to move quickly when vicious robot spiders came calling. A few stragglers pressed their backs against the walls of the buildings, looking on in terror. The place had become eerily silent.

"I just can't buy that Master George is doing this," Sofia said.

"You chirrun ain't tellin' me the whole truth!" Sally said.

Paul tried to calm his heavy breathing. He knew the only way to get out of this was to solve that stupid riddle. An anagram of "the words inside." He quickly started visualizing options in his head, other words those letters could spell: *sword . . . died . . . snow . . . wine . . . news . . . odd . . .*

It was easy to come up with individual words, but using every last letter—and only those letters—was really hard without pen and paper.

"What are they waiting for?" Sofia said.

The metaspides stood in a line, at least a dozen of them, their bodies turning and nodding, clicking and clacking, buzzing endlessly. They seemed to be communicating, deciding what to do next. It didn't make Paul feel very good thinking that those things were smart enough to call plays, like in football.

"I don't know," Tick said. "Sally, where can we go? Where do you live?"

Sally grunted. "Ain't be leadin' them buggers to my place, no how."

"Is there a place to hide?" Sofia asked.

"Mayhaps if we go into one of dem there stores or such." Sally pointed to nowhere in particular.

This triggered a thought in Paul's head. Maybe they were supposed to figure out the *name* of a place, and go there. Maybe they'd be winked away if they made it.

"Look at all the signs," he said. "I bet one of them is an anagram of 'the words inside.'"

Tick's eyes lit up in agreement. "You're right! Every little place here has a sign out front. That has to be it!"

An abrupt whirring sound made them all return their attention to the metaspides. The creatures had started to move, slowly spreading out in an obvious attempt to surround Paul and his friends.

"We need to split up," Paul said. "Run around, level to level, look at every sign. It'll be easy to find the right one. Just keep saying 'the words inside' over and over in your head."

"What do we do if we find it?" Tick asked.

"Scream like bloody murder. We'll come to you."

The metaspides had formed a semicircle, still moving slowly, closing their trap. Every few seconds, on each creature, a spinning saw would pop out, or twin blades would scissor shut with a snap. They were like gang members taunting their opponent.

"Are you in?" Paul asked Sally.

"Ain't got much choice, I reckon. Fine friends you chirrun turned out to be."

Sofia spoke, her voice steady. "We need to go. *Now.*"

Paul quickly pointed out directions of who should go where. "Okay . . . ready . . . *Go!*"

Paul shot down a pathway to the left, having to run in between two of the robots. They snapped at him, but he slipped through easily. Sprinting, he made it thirty or forty feet before something became very obvious. He turned, baffled.

None of the metaspides were behind him.

They'd all gone after Tick. Every single one of them.

CHAPTER 13

FLYING METAL

Tick looked over his shoulder when he got to the end of the bridge, shocked to see all of the creatures following him. He caught a quick glance of Paul standing in the distance, staring.

"I'll keep them busy—you just find the place!" Tick yelled. "Find it!"

He turned and set off running again, winding his way down another cobbled path and then down an alleyway, then back onto a wider, main road. The clicking sounds of his pursuers' metallic feet sounded like a typist overdosed on caffeine. Tick looked up at the signs of the various establishments as he passed by.

Tanaka's Feet Barn . . . The Hapless Butcher . . . Ted's

Cups and Bowls . . . The Shack Shop . . . Mister Johnny's Store . . .

None of them came close to matching an anagram for "the words inside."

He came to an intersection and hesitated too long deciding which way to go. One of the spider robots caught up with him and jumped on his back, some kind of clamping device shooting out and gripping his neck. Tick shouted out in pain and fell down. He twisted to see his attacker, but could barely move. Two more spiders grabbed his arms, another two grabbed his legs, pinching him viciously.

Tick squirmed and kicked. The rising panic thumped his heart, blurred his vision. He heard metallic snaps and whirring, like the sounds of a futuristic torture device. Something sharp sliced across the length of his back; something pointy stabbed into his left calf. Tick could do nothing but scream as the heat of rage filled him.

A new sound filled the air—something like sizzling bacon or bubbling acid, but a hundred times louder. This was followed by a booming *warp,* the sound of crumpling, twisting metal. Something knocked the spiders off Tick with a ringing clank. Their sharp legs ripped new wounds where they'd been clutching him. Pain lanced through him and all over his body. Groaning in agony, he flipped onto his back.

Above him, the indoor world had gone berserk.

Sofia found it near the very spot from which they'd entered the underground complex.

The Sordid Swine.

The rickety sign swung crookedly on a single chain above the entrance to a squat, brick building. Sofia thought it looked like a seedy gambling hall. Etched into the wood, the three words grabbed her attention; her eyes locked in.

It wasn't obvious on first glance, but the phrase had no letters that immediately ruled it out. In a matter of seconds, she'd worked through it. The Sordid Swine was definitely an anagram for "the words inside," letter for letter, rearranged.

She turned to face the way she'd come, ready to yell out that she'd found it, but faltered. In the distance, in the direction Tick had run, she saw something impossible. After all, they were *indoors*.

But there, a couple hundred yards away, countless pieces of debris swirled and flew through the air.

It looked like a tornado.

Paul heard it before he saw it. Crumpling metal, banging, clanking, a roaring wind—it all sounded like the world was coming to an end. He rounded a corner shop and saw a spinning mass of debris up ahead, mostly made up of chunks of metal and wood, some large and some small. As he watched, a long, steel beam hit the rail of an upper balcony then windmilled, smashing through a barber shop window.

"Paul!"

He turned to see Sofia just a couple of paths over, running toward him.

"Tick's over there!" he yelled. Without waiting, he took off, crossing a cobbled path, heading for the same bridge he'd seen Tick cross a short time ago.

"Wait!" she called out, but he ignored her. He knew Tick might be caught in the middle of the weird tornado—of course, he didn't know how he could help if that were the case, but he ran on anyway, making it half-way across the bridge before he stumbled to a stop.

Tick lay on the ground up ahead, bruised and bloody, staring up into the twister that spun right above him, railings and pipes and poles and sheets of metal flying through the air in a circle. He looked to be in the exact center of the steel storm, the buildings and walls around him ripped to shreds as they provided fuel for the impossible tornado. Nearby, several crumpled metaspides twitched and sparked; one of them had most of its body torn off and another had partially melted, two limbs and a chunk of its torso reduced to a pile of silvery goop.

"What the heck?" Paul said, just as Sofia caught

up with him, almost knocking him forward.

"We've gotta grab him!" she said.

"I know, but how?" He turned toward her. "You got some body armor I don't know about?"

"Look!" she said, pointing at Tick.

Their friend was crawling toward them.

Tick didn't understand how this could be happening. Above him, solid metal objects ripped in half, dissolved, and reformed. Everything around him had gone nuts, breaking apart and spinning in the air above him, only to melt together into new shapes. The clank of stuff crashing into each other mixed with the roaring wind, sounding like freight trains were playing bumper cars.

And he'd had enough.

He crawled toward Paul and Sofia, thankful that the raging twister was several feet above him. Worried it might drop at any moment, or that one of the hundreds of pieces of debris would fly at him and skewer him, he scrambled on his hands and knees as fast as possible. When he reached what seemed to be the edge of the twister, he pushed himself to his feet and sprinted across the bridge to his friends.

"What's going on?" Paul asked, staring over Tick's shoulder at the chaos.

Tick turned to see it from this angle. The twisting

body of debris contracted into a thin column, spinning faster the tighter it got. The destruction sounded like a loud swarm of bees, the small bits forming a tall, black cloud. Seconds later, the mass fell toward the ground, where it landed in a lump, a twisted structure of metal, a hideous pile with several crooked steel beams sticking out. Then everything grew quiet.

"How did that just happen?" Sofia said in a dead voice.

"Yeah," Tick agreed. "Could this place get any freakier?" He immediately regretted the question, superstition telling him the answer was *yes*—just because he'd asked.

"I found the place," Sofia said, turning from the pile of metal junk. "A perfect anagram. It's called—"

A loud clank cut her off, followed by the horrible screech of scraping metal. On the other side of the pile, a large door slid upward, revealing a wall of darkness behind it. A shape appeared, stepping into the light. It was huge and silver and spherical, eight massive legs of jointed steel protruding from its body.

The word *Metaspide* was spelled across it in large, black letters.

The clicking, clacking, buzzing monster was twenty times the size of its little brothers. With clumsy, yet strangely graceful movements, it started walking toward them.

"Come on," Sofia said, grabbing both Tick's and Paul's arms and dragging them after her.

Tick cried out and pulled his arm away, wincing from the cuts on his body as he sprinted after Paul and Sofia. They reached an intersection; Sofia hesitated, trying to remember which way to go.

"This way," she said, pointing to the left.

Before they took a step, another booming *clank!* rang out behind them, the loudest so far, like the sound of a horrible car wreck. Tick couldn't help himself—he turned to look. The huge, clunky spider had jumped across the large gap, clearing the bridge in one leap. It crashed and rolled, smashing into a whole row of shops, obliterating them entirely. A second later, it sprang back onto its thin legs and started after them.

"Run!" Paul yelled.

Sofia took off on the path, followed by Paul, then Tick. The crashing and banging and clanking of the pursuing metallic monster filled the air like a lightning storm. The ground shook with the booming footsteps of the giant spider, joined by the sounds of breaking glass and splintering wood. Tick knew that if it kept gaining speed and strength, they'd be smashed to bits in less than a minute.

"How far is it?" he yelled to Sofia as they turned a corner and ran up a narrow set of stone stairs. They reached a wide alleyway and kept running. The smash of shattered buildings thundered from behind as the monster forced its way after them, destroying everything in its path.

"We're almost there!" Sofia answered.

They rounded the next corner to see Sally running straight toward them, covered in dirt, his face lit up with fear. "Dadgum world's endin'!" he screamed. Then his eyes rose up to look over them, his mouth falling open. "How'd it get so big!"

Sofia grabbed Sally by the arm as she ran past. "Just come on!"

He stumbled until he got his feet set and joined the escape.

Tick saw it before Sofia pointed. A crooked sign indicating The Sordid Swine, swinging on a single pathetic chain. The clanging sounds of pursuit were getting closer and closer.

Paul passed Sofia, ripping the wooden door of the shop open. All four of them stumbled across the threshold and into The Sordid Swine without so much as a peek behind them, afraid that looking would somehow allow the metal monster to gain ground. Sally was last, slamming the door shut, leaving them in almost complete darkness. A shaft of pale light from a small window gave the musty room a haunted glow. The place was empty except for a crooked wooden chair in the corner.

"What now?" Sofia whispered.

Before anyone could answer, something smashed into the wall from the other side, shaking the room and sending a cascade of debris rattling down the brick walls. The group instinctively ran across the room to get as far away from the door as possible, pressing their backs against the brick wall. The giant metaspide slammed into the wall again, then again; a hinge broke, rattling to the floor. Light seeped through the broken door.

"What are we supposed to do now!" Sofia yelled.

Another crash rattled the door—half of it broke apart and tumbled to the ground. The spider was too big to fit through the hole, but a nasty-looking piece of steel came shooting in, sharp as a blade on one edge, swiping around like a cat trying to get a mouse out of its hole. It was nowhere close to them.

Yet.

"Tick," Paul said, "sure'd be nice for you to use those nifty superhuman winking powers right about now."

"Would you shut up—I don't know how I did that!" Tick yelled back, sick of everyone expecting him to be the stinkin' Wizard of Oz. He wished he hadn't said it as soon as it came out.

"Whoa," Paul said, looking hurt. "Sorry, dude."

"Guess we were wrong about the anagram thing," Sofia said.

"No, we weren't," Tick said, pushing aside his regret

at yelling at Paul. "There has to be something. *Think*."

The huge metaspide slammed into the door again, making the hole bigger. Several bricks clattered across the ground. Its blade-arm swiped a little closer, only a few feet away.

"You chirrun better get me on out dis here mess," Sally said. "Ain't too particular 'bout how ya'll do it, neither." He grimaced as the metal arm swung close enough to stir his hair as it passed.

"The only thing in here is that stupid chair," Paul said. The rickety thing sat in the corner, looking like a sad punishment place for a naughty child.

"Well," Tick said, "then maybe we're supposed to do something with it." He felt defensive, like his inability to recreate the winking trick he'd pulled off in the Thirteenth Reality made him responsible for figuring out another solution.

"What can we do with a *chair?*" Paul retorted.

"I don't know!" Tick snapped back. The room shook again with another ram from the spider; an alarming chunk of the entrance crumbled to the ground, the hole getting wider. A second metal arm squeezed through, two rough blades attached at the end, snapping together like alligator jaws.

"Boys!" Sofia said. Tick was shocked to see her smiling. "You're so busy thinking, you forgot to use your brains."

With a smirk, she darted over to the corner, ignoring the steel blade of death that sliced through the air a few inches from her shoulder. Then she sat down on the chair.

The second her bottom touched the warped wood of the seat, she disappeared.

CHAPTER 14

THE COUNCIL ON
THINGS THAT MATTER

Tick felt like an idiot. Sofia was right; sometimes
they thought *too* much.

He grabbed Paul by the shoulders and pushed him
toward the chair, following right behind. "Hurry!" A
blade whipped past his left shoulder, slicing his shirt.

Paul reached back and shoved Tick against the
bricks. "Careful, dude. Inch along the wall."

Sally stood next to the chair, looking confused as
he glanced back and forth between the chair and Tick.
Paul and Tick scooted along the wall until they reached
the corner.

"Sit down, Sally!" Paul yelled. "Don't worry, it'll
take you somewhere safe."

Sally didn't reply but leaned toward Tick's ear until Tick could feel Sally's beard scratching his cheek.

"What are you doing?" Tick asked, feeling uncomfortable. "You need to tell me something?"

"Just lookin' at yer dadgum ear, boy."

Before Tick could stop him, Sally reached up and rammed his pinky finger into Tick's ear canal. Tick stumbled backward into Paul's arms, a sharp pain exploding inside his head like an eardrum had just ruptured. The pain went away as soon as it had come, and Paul helped him back to his feet.

"What'd you do that for?" Tick yelled at Sally, glaring at the man who'd seemed completely harmless until that very moment.

"Weep to yer mama, boy, not me."

Sally sat down on the chair, not bothering to hide the grin on his face. He shrugged his shoulders as if to say, *Sorry, can't help myself,* and disappeared.

"What in the world was that all about?" Paul asked.

"No idea," Tick replied. "But we've gotta get out of here."

"You first," Paul said.

Tick wanted to argue, act brave, be the last one out. Then he realized that'd be the stupidest thing in the world and hurried to sit on the chair. Every second they wasted meant the spider was that much closer.

He had just enough time to see the entire front of

the building collapse in a swirl of dust and flashes of metal before everything around him turned bright.

⁓

Sofia stood on a slippery slope of rust-colored sand, squinting in the brilliant sunlight at the small, iron chair that stood rigid on top of the dune as if held in place by magic. She'd stood up and gotten away from it the second she'd winked there, not wanting someone else to come through and squish her.

Tick showed up a minute later, an instantaneous appearance that shocked her even though she'd been expecting it. There was no effect—no smoke, no sound. One moment the chair was empty. The next, it wasn't. Tick's face looked like he'd just bungee-jumped off the world's tallest bridge.

"What took you so long? Hurry. Get up," Sofia said, slipping in the sand as she stepped forward to help him, sliding down the steep dune. The hot sand seemed to find its way through every teeny hole of her clothes and scratch at her skin.

Tick didn't answer, but stood up and was making his way down the loose sand to Sofia when Paul appeared, a small cut on his right cheek.

"Dang thing got me," he said, wiping the blood away with his fingers. "Couple more seconds and I'd be . . ."

He trailed off, looking around him with huge eyes.

With her friends safe, Sofia finally had a chance to take a good look at their surroundings as well.

They stood in the middle of an enormous desert, an endless sea of dunes stretching for miles in every direction. The white-hot sun blazed down so the distant horizons shimmered in a wavering haze. The only thing breaking the monotony of sand was a large, shiny pipeline about a half-mile away. The tube of opaque glass sat above ground, at least twenty feet in diameter, and ran from one direction to the other for as far as Sofia could see.

"Where are we?" Paul asked. "And what *is* that?" He motioned to the giant pipe.

"Looks like a huge straw," Tick said. "Maybe a giant sand monster dropped it."

Sofia ignored them and started walking toward the glass structure. Her heart hammered in her chest, a rise of panic as she thought about their situation. They'd just barely escaped a horrible metallic spider and now they were stuck in the middle of a scorching desert. Anger at Master George rose in her as well. *How can he waste our time with this? What if we'd been killed?* But deep inside, she didn't think it was him. Something had gone wrong.

"Wait!" Paul called from behind her. "Where's Sally?"

Sofia stopped; she'd completely forgotten about the

odd man. She turned and said, "Maybe he didn't want to follow us."

Paul was standing on the dune next to the chair, looking around. "No way—he winked away before we did."

"Yeah," Tick said, also searching. "He went right after you."

Sofia felt a disorienting chill in her gut. "Well . . . he never showed up here. I've been watching the chair since I winked in."

Paul stumbled through the soft sand to stand next to Sofia; Tick joined them as well. Both of the boys had baffled looks on their faces, still glancing at the chair now and then as if expecting Sally to show up.

"You're *sure* he didn't wink in?" Paul asked.

Sofia rolled her eyes. "Yes, I'm sure. Where would he possibly hide?"

"Dude," Paul whispered, and that one word summed up how they all felt.

"What could've happened to him?" Tick asked. "Why would *we* wink here and not him? And what was up with him poking me in the ear?" He rubbed at the side of his head.

"What?" Sofia asked.

"Right before he winked away," Tick explained, "he acted all weird and slammed his finger into my ear. It hurt, too. Then he sat down and disappeared."

"He slammed his finger into your *ear?*" Sofia repeated. "While a giant spider monster was trying to kill you?" It was such a bizarre thing, she couldn't believe she'd heard him correctly.

Tick shrugged. "Don't ask me—maybe he went crazy from the panic."

"What if he's in trouble?" Paul asked. "I like him— we need to help him. Even if he did try to stab you in the brain."

Sofia felt the same sadness at Sally's disappearance. He'd been so humble and sincere; there was just something likable about him. But she also knew that standing there waiting on a nice sunburn wouldn't help anybody.

"Not much we can do," she said. "Someone must've sent us here for a reason. Let's go check out that glass thing." She pointed at the tube that looked like a giant crystal worm stretching into the distant horizon.

"What if Sally shows up and we're not here?" Paul said.

"He's an adult," Tick said. "He can take care of himself or come find us. I agree with Sofia—we should see what that thing is."

Sofia started walking again. "Come on, then."

Paul and Tick joined her, all of them marching as best they could up and down the slippery, hot dunes.

Master George sat at the head of a long, wooden table, looking around at the few people he'd asked to join him in this special Council on Things That Matter. His last guest had yet to appear, and Master George hoped he would arrive soon. It had been a near thing, winking him away as fast as he had. A large fire roared in the hearth at his back, but it wasn't enough to rid him of the chill that iced his heart. Things were going badly. Very badly. He reached down and petted Muffintops, who purred and rubbed her back against his leg.

Most of the other Realitants had left the Grand Canyon complex already, carrying out various orders and missions agreed upon by the larger meeting earlier. That was good. Things would be said here that not everyone should hear.

Mothball sat to his left and Rutger to his right, balanced precariously on his booster seat. To Rutger's right was Sato, looking as bored as ever, ready to take notes. Then came Nancy Zeppelin, wrapping and rewrapping a long string of her golden hair around a finger; William Schmidt, his ancient face pulled down into a frown that made him look like the Grim Reaper; Katrina Kay, her buzz-cut hair framing a pretty face with eager eyes; Priscilla Persephone, invited only because Master George knew he had offended her enough already (oh, how he hated that snooty smirk on her face; and her *hair*—it was orange, for heaven's sake). Finally, next to Mothball on his left, sat Jimmy "The Voice" Porter. His nickname was sadly ironic now because the poor man's tongue had been ripped out by a slinkbeast in the Mountains of Sorrow in the Twelfth Reality.

"Very well," Master George said. "I think it's time we begin."

"Yes, *let's,*" Priscilla said in her annoying, lilting voice. "We've only been waiting on you. Wasting valuable time, no doubt."

Rutger shifted forward in his seat, a slight rolling motion that brought his arms and hands to rest on the table. "Priscilla, why don't you open up a can of shut the—"

George quickly interrupted his loyal friend. "Yes, Priscilla, I appreciate your patience." He wanted to add that perhaps she'd like to take on a mission to the icy wastelands of the Third Reality, but refrained. "We have much to talk about, indeed."

"Wasting time," Rutger mumbled under his breath. "I'll show you . . ." The rest was too low to hear, but Master George thought he caught the words *rat fink.*

"First things first," Mothball said. "Methinks we best be talkin' 'bout Master Tick and his friends."

Master George agreed. "Yes, yes, quite right, Mothball. Based on the evidence, I have no doubt that someone has violated Rule Number 462 and taken hostage the nanolocators implanted in our dear young friends from Reality Prime. We can track their general location, but nothing more—and even that signal is weak. We have tried repeatedly to wink them here, but they have remained out of our reach. This act violates no less than three Articles of Principles established by the First Realitant Symposium of 1972. It is outrageous, despicable, irresponsible, reprehensible—"

"We get the point," Rutger said.

Master George slammed his hand on the table. "Yes! I hope you do, Master Rutger, because this is very serious indeed. Not only can we not wink in our most important recruits in years, but we have a renegade out there capable of such things as hijacking a nanolocator! The technology for such an act—"

"It has to be him," Nancy Zeppelin interrupted quietly. "Has to be."

A long moment of silence passed, broken only by the crackling fire. Master George closed his eyes. No one in the room doubted who the culprit could be. But if Reginald Chu had finally decided to use his significant technological powers to branch out and cause trouble in other Realities, then they were all in for a great deal of trouble. Until today, they'd all hoped, perhaps foolishly, that Chu would be happy ruling his own world with an iron fist.

"Yes, Nancy," Master George finally said, opening

his eyes and sighing. "We should all be quite nervous that Reginald Chu would stoop to such a thing. He obviously has plans for our new friends."

William Schmidt cleared his throat, a wet, gurgling hack that made Master George wince. Then the old man spoke in his ghost-soft voice. "Chu's spies must have learned of Higginbottom's mysterious winking ability. Chu would do anything to have him under his control."

"For all we know," Katrina said, "Tick is strapped on a laboratory bed as we speak, his brain being examined for anomalies."

Master George held up a hand, wanting the terrible talk to stop. "We must keep our minds on solutions, my dear associates. Solutions. And we mustn't give up hope. Master Atticus is a special boy, as are his friends, and their recovery is our number-one priority."

"What about all the people going crazy everywhere?" Priscilla asked. "That should alarm us a little bit more than a few missing brats."

Mothball stood up—Master George reached out too late to stop her. She towered over everyone, her suddenly angry glare focused on Priscilla. "One more nasty word about them three children, and I'll lop off yer 'ead, I will. That's a promise."

"Yeah," Rutger chimed in. "And I'll bite your kneecaps."

"Please, let's all remain calm," Master George said. "Mothball, please be seated. I appreciate your concern for Atticus and his friends. Priscilla hasn't met them, of course, so let's give her time to appreciate their importance."

Mothball sat, not taking her eyes off Priscilla, whose suddenly pale face made her look like she might never speak again.

"Now, er, we do need to talk of this matter," Master George continued. "Sato here has put together a summary of his interviews, and the reports of people going insane are numerous, indeed. Something is very wrong, and it's spreading throughout the Realities at an alarming rate. Almost like a—"

"Disease," Nancy Zeppelin said. "Like a disease."

Master George paused, studying the beautiful woman as he thought about what she said. She didn't look back, staring at the table in front of her with a blank expression.

"Yes," he finally said. "Yes, quite like a disease, actually. The pattern shows it spreading from a fragmented Reality—all cases link back to it eventually, with no exception. It is *exactly* like a disease or a virus."

"Need a sample, then. One of the crazies," Mothball said.

Before Master George could reply, an urgent knock rapped at the closed door from the hallway. Finally.

Perhaps now they would have some answers. He stood up. "Mothball—"

The door opened before she could do anything. A wave of relief washed through Master George as he saw one of his oldest friends enter the room, though he looked like he'd just taken a bath in a pile of dirt—his overalls were *filthy*.

"Master Sally," George said, smiling.

Sally grinned through his thick, red beard. "It was harder 'an findin' a tick on a grizzly bear, but I did it."

"Did what?" Rutger asked, shocked.

"I found dem kids a'yorn."

PART 2

❋

THE BEAST
IN THE
GLASS

CHAPTER 15

NICE MISTRESS JANE

Frazier Gunn was worried about his boss.

As he walked up the winding stone staircase of Mistress Jane's tower, enjoying the smell of burning pitch from the torches ensconced on the hard granite walls, he wondered which version of her would answer the door. The flickering, spitting flames cast haunted shadows that seemed alive, hiding and reappearing like dark wraiths. A team of seven servants maintained the torches throughout the Lemon Fortress, even though Jane probably could have lit the place using only her growing abilities in the mutated Chi'karda.

But she had her own way of doing things, and that was that.

Frazier felt a trickle of sweat slide down his right temple as he passed the halfway point. He'd been sick the last few days, unable to keep any food down, and he felt the effect of his illness now. He almost paused to rest, but his pride wouldn't let him. He kept moving up the staircase, step by step.

His thoughts slid back to Jane's recent mood swings—episodes of inexplicable kindness mixed in with the usual displays of anger and violence. He'd witnessed with his own eyes several of the bizarre occurrences. Just the other day, he'd almost swallowed his own tongue when he saw his boss help her servant Brainless clean up a broken dish Jane had slammed against the wall. The child's face had paled during the incident, sure it was a trap, but when they finished, Jane apologized for losing her temper, dismissed her with a wave, and went back to work.

Frazier would've been less surprised to see a duck-billed platypus knock on his door and ask for tea.

Rumors of other surprising acts had spread through the castle like flames through a heat-wilted cornfield. Stories of kind words, apologies, thank-yous, compliments. Tales of Jane using her special powers to help servants lift heavy objects. It was crazy. Frazier had known this evil woman for years, and he couldn't reconcile in his brain how it could be the same person. And yet, interspersed among these un-Jane-like anomalies, there were many moments where she exploded in rage, sometimes worse than ever before.

The whole thing was fishy, and in an odd way, Frazier longed for the days when Jane acted the tyrant every minute of every day. At least then he'd known what to expect.

He finally reached the top step, pausing to take three long breaths to calm his heart. He wiped the sweat from his face, not wanting Jane to see him so weak. After a very long minute, he finally crossed the stone landing and knocked on her wooden door.

It disappeared in a swipe from left to right, as if it had slid into the stone. It was only a trick, however, a manipulation of Chi'karda. Jane loved using her power for such trivial things, always opening her doors in creative and unexpected ways. One time she'd simply made it explode outward in a spray of dagger-like splinters, permanently scarring the poor sap delivering her mail.

Jane stood there, dressed in a simple yellow gown, her feet and hands bare. Her emerald eyes shone, almost glowing like green embers. Something was off, though. For a second, Frazier couldn't figure out why she looked so odd, but then it hit him.

Jane had a layer of stubble growing across her head, tiny black sprouts of hair. Never—not once since he'd first met her so long ago—had Frazier ever seen so much as one hair on her head. She'd always insisted on baldness for some mysterious reason. Frazier balked and looked toward the floor, almost as if he'd caught her unawares coming out of the bath.

"Good morning, Mistress," he said, keeping his eyes down. "I've come to report the latest on the Barrier Wand, and to, uh, report some interesting news."

"Frazier, dear Frazier," Jane said, her voice soft. "Please, come in."

He looked up to see she had moved aside, gesturing toward her large, yellow velvet couch, beside which a fresh fire burned in the comforting hearth, its bricks freshly painted her favorite color. Clearing his throat, using every ounce of his will to avoid a single glance at her head, Frazier stepped past her and took a seat, sinking into the wonderfully comfortable cushions.

Mistress Jane sat next to him on his right, crossing her legs so that she faced him only a foot away. The fire reflected in her bright eyes, seeming to ignite them into some odd, molten metal. Frazier didn't like this. No, he didn't like this one bit.

"Frazier," Jane said, reaching out to caress his arm, just once, before clasping her hands in her lap. "I know people are talking about me—about my . . . change."

Frazier cleared his throat, faked a cough, hoping to buy time. He didn't know how to respond to this. "Um, yes, Mistress, the servants have said some very . . . um, nice things about you. They are, of course, very grateful when you, uh, show them kindness." He stopped; every word that came out of his mouth sounded worse than the one before it.

"Kindness?" she said with a disgusted tone, as if the word were a highly contagious disease. "That's the best they can come up with? *That's* how they honor my attempts to elevate my leadership skills?"

"Well," he said, doing his best to speak clearly without stuttering. "No, I meant, well, I just meant they're noticing your efforts, saying many *different* words—all very glowing words, actually. Your esteem has skyrocketed in their eyes. In, uh, mine, too."

Jane folded her arms, glaring directly into Frazier's eyes. "Do you think I'm stupid, Frazier?"

She's going to kill me, he thought. *Right now, after all these years, she's going to kill me because she's finally gone completely and totally insane.*

"Stupid?" he repeated. "Of course I don't think you're stupid."

Jane leaned over and whispered in his ear. "Then don't *speak* to me like I'm stupid."

She sat back, looking at the fire, her face expressionless. After several seconds, Frazier followed her gaze and caught his breath.

Several burning logs had floated up into the air and out of the main hearth, hovering above a rug made from the skin of a scallywag beast. Sparks and hot cinders fell from the logs, igniting several long hairs of the soft fur, which flared and died out quickly. A mess of white ash flew up from the fireplace, swirling around the flames in midair in fancy patterns, spelling words and making faces. Frazier felt a familiar icy fear in his gut, thinking of such power in the hands of a woman as unstable as Mistress Jane.

With a hiss and crackle, the whole show collapsed back into the fireplace; in seconds, it looked like the fire hadn't been disturbed at all.

"Now," Jane said, folding her arms and returning her focus to Frazier. "I know people are worried that my attempts to change are insincere. If anything, they seem *more* frightened of me than ever. Correct?"

Frazier nodded, not daring to say a word.

"This doesn't bother me. Not in the least. I've been . . . *unwise* in some of my leadership methods. Perhaps even cruel. I know it will take time—a long time—to change." Jane shifted in her seat, looking toward the window on the other side of the room, muted light from the cloudy day spilling through onto her bed. "All I ever wanted was to make things better, Frazier. That's all I still want. If I need to adapt how I rule things, then so be it."

She turned her neck, looking once again at Frazier, her eyes narrowed. "But we *will* take over the Realities. We *will* spread the goodness and power of the Chi'karda from the Thirteenth Reality to the others. And in the end, we will make the universe a better place for all. This, I promise you."

Frazier nodded again, throwing all the sincerity he could into his expression. Jane's words, filled with passion, had moved him greatly. He remembered why he had followed this woman for so many years, despite the constant danger. He remembered . . . and felt ashamed of the many times he'd hoped to topple her and take over.

"Mistress Jane," he said. "I . . . I . . . I don't know what to—"

"Say nothing," she snapped, a sudden thunderclap shaking the room. It was a trick she performed often. "You've earned yourself back into my full graces. You're my most loyal servant. You will be beside me, always. Nothing else needs to be said."

A long pause followed, thoughts churning inside Frazier's mind. *How do I act now? What do I say?* His fear of Jane hadn't diminished in the least—if anything, it had grown stronger.

Thankfully, Jane got back to business. "You said you had an update on the Barrier Wand and some interesting news. Well, get on with—" She paused, forcing a smile. "Please, report."

Frazier leaned forward, grunting as he pulled himself out of the soft cushions, and put his elbows on his knees. "They've found a place in a small mountain range about five hundred miles away—they've spotted signs of ore. It looks encouraging. The Diggers are hunting as we speak. As soon as they find a deposit, I'll let you know."

"Once they do," Jane said, "we should need only two or three more weeks."

"That's right. The metal is the last thing we need to reconstruct the Wand."

Something floated up from a shelf near the bed, flying through the air and landing with a thump in Jane's outreached palm. She held it out for Frazier to see—a complex bundle of wires, pipework, gears, and nanochips—the Chi'karda Drive she'd removed from her previous Barrier Wand. The one Atticus Higginbottom had stolen.

"What's the other news?" Jane asked.

Frazier shifted uncomfortably. His news was very strange, and he worried about her reaction. "Well, some of our hunters discovered an interesting . . . thing." He paused, unsure how to proceed.

"A *thing?*" Jane repeated. "Your descriptive skills are less than apt, Frazier."

"Sorry." He rubbed his hands together. "I guess I'll just say it how it is."

"Brilliant idea."

Frazier tried to laugh, but it came out as a snort.

"Way out in the Forest of Plague, near the spot of the old battleground, they found a place where hundreds of trees have been cut down. Each stump is perfectly flat, as if the trees had been cut with a laser or something."

Jane tilted her head, obviously intrigued. "Interesting. I can't think of anyone . . ."

When she trailed off, looking at the fire, Frazier continued. "Right, no one in our Reality has that kind of technology. But, um, that's not the weird part. Not even close."

That caught Jane's attention; her eyebrows rose.

"The trees . . ." Frazier said.

"Did someone take them? Did they burn them? That area has enormous trees—some taller than the fortress."

Frazier shook his head. "I know, which makes the next part really bizarre. I couldn't tell what had happened until I flew on the back of a fangen and looked down from above."

"What do you mean?" Jane asked.

"Somehow, whoever cut those trees down . . . *arranged* them on the ground so they spelled out words."

"Spelled out words?" Jane repeated. "With *trees?*"

"Yes. They formed letters out of the tree trunks. Really big trees that made really big words." He laughed at himself but stopped abruptly.

"What did they say?" Jane asked, not smiling.

Frazier braced himself, knowing he had no choice but to repeat the mysterious message word for word.

"It said, 'Mistress Jane, you are a coward. Come and find me.'"

CHAPTER 16

TUNNEL OF GLASS

Tick slid his hand along the warm, hard glass of the big tube as he walked beside it in disbelief at the sheer height of the structure. It rose at least twenty feet above him, maybe more, and appeared to be a perfect cylinder. The bottom third was buried underneath the shifting sands of the desert. The glass was clear, but so thick he couldn't tell what lay inside the big pipe; he could only see distorted images of varying color.

"Okay," Paul said. "I've seen some strange stuff since hanging out with you two, but this might beat all." He stepped back and spread his arms wide, looking up at the curved glass. "What could this thing possibly be?"

Sofia squatted on the ground, digging through the sand to see if the structure changed at all underneath. "Looks like it just keeps curving in a perfect circle. Maybe if we dug all the way to the bottom we'd figure something out."

"Do I look like a shovel to you?" Paul asked.

"Well . . . actually, you kind of do," Sofia said. "You look like a shovel with crooked ears."

Tick ignored them, walking along with his hand pressed against the glass, hoping for some change or sign of what they were supposed to do next. Sweat soaked his clothes, the sun beating down on them as if trying to cook them for dinner. He could feel his skin beginning to burn—especially his neck. In all the chaos with the giant spider robot monster, he'd lost his scarf.

What is *this thing?* he thought as he studied the glass structure. Master George—if it really had been him—must have sent them here for a reason, and a clue or riddle must be hidden somewhere. He kept walking.

"Yo, where you going?" Paul called out.

Tick turned to look, surprised at how far he'd walked—at least a hundred feet. "I don't know!" he yelled. "Trying to find a clue!"

He stopped, squinting to examine the endless tube as it stretched into the horizon, diminishing in a shimmering haze of heat in the distance. Nothing appeared to break the consistency of the smooth glass—no ladders, no doors, no connected buildings. He finally gave up and walked back to his friends, both of whom were digging in the sand.

"See anything?" he asked.

"No," Sofia answered. She sat back on her heels, letting out a big sigh. "Seems like a perfect cylinder. A really big one."

Before he could reply, a deep humming sound filled the air, a short burst lasting only a few seconds, but so loud it made the glass vibrate. *Or maybe it was the other way around,* Tick thought. Maybe the glass had shaken and *made* the sound.

Sofia and Paul jumped to their feet and moved next to Tick.

"Please tell me you guys heard that," Paul said.

"Yeah," Tick said, almost in a whisper. He thought he might've seen something from the corner of his eye— a slight movement in the glass to their left. "Something happened when it made that sound—I didn't really get a good look." He pointed to where he thought he'd seen the anomaly and walked closer; the others joined him.

"What do you mean?" Sofia asked.

"I don't know. I thought I saw something move across the glass, a shadow inside or water pouring down it."

Paul reached out and ran his hand along the curved wall. "Serious?"

"Yeah, positive."

"Let's wait to see if it happens again," Sofia said.

Tick folded his arms, staring at the tube. No one said a word, silently hoping for a clue as to what they should do next.

A minute went by. Then another. Then several. A half-hour passed and nothing happened. Tick felt so uncomfortable from the sweat drenching his clothes and the sticky salt on his face and the burning in his skin and the sand in his shoes—

VRRMMMMM!

The sound boomed out again for five or six seconds, and this time, they all saw it. Right where Paul had touched earlier, a section of glass slid down, as if it were simply melting open, creating a rectangular hole the size of a typical door. Inside, filling the entire cylinder, something huge and dark zoomed past like a train, going at an incredible speed. Tick couldn't see any details, scarcely believing that whatever it was could move at such a velocity.

The train thing was gone as soon as it had come, and the glass melted upward, closing the door and reforming until not a single blemish or mark revealed it had ever been there.

"Whoa," Paul said.

"This must be a tunnel for some kind of bullet train," Sofia said. She gingerly reached out to where the doorway had appeared, then tapped the glass with her fingertip and pulled away. "It's not any hotter than the rest of the tube."

"We're obviously supposed to go inside," Tick said.

"And get smashed by that thing?" Paul said. "Wasn't much room for a nice stroll in there if that train comes flying by again."

Sofia turned toward the two of them so they stood in a small circle, facing each other. "Tick's right. It can't be a coincidence that we showed up here next to this big tunnel, right where a door opens up. We have to go inside."

Paul shook his head. "Well, I'm not too keen on the idea of getting run over by a monster train. That door seems to open only every half-hour or so and it only stayed open a few seconds. Jumping in there sounds like the worst idea I've ever heard."

"There has to be a path and a railing, right?" Tick said. "Even if it's small. Any subway in the world has a walkway, doesn't it? For people to make repairs and stuff?"

Paul shrugged. "Maybe, but it sure seemed to me like that thing was right next to the glass."

"Yeah, it was," Sofia agreed. "But what else are we going to do? Sit out here in the sun and bake to death? There's no sign of anything for miles and miles except that stupid chair—I guess we could try sitting on it again, but—"

"We have to go in *there*," Tick interrupted, nodding toward the tube, knowing he was right.

Paul held out his hands in surrender. "All right, all right, all right. Look, here's what we'll do. We sit here and wait for the door to open again. When it does, we'll peek in and see what we see—all while making sure we don't let anything slice our heads off or smash our faces in. Ya know, just for kicks. Like I've said before, we wouldn't want to mess up this pretty face of mine or you *know* the ladies would be devastated."

Sofia groaned.

"That works for me," Tick said. "If this door opens every half-hour or whatever, we don't need to rush it. Next time, let's just lean in real quick and take a look around. Hopefully there'll be a walkway with a railing. If not, we'll decide what to do from there."

"Deal," Paul said.

"Who's going to poke their head in?" Sofia asked.

"All of us—it looks big enough," Tick said. "Sofia, you look left. Paul, you look straight ahead. I'll look to the right—and make sure you look *down,* too. Get in line and let's get ready. Who knows when it'll open next."

They lined up in the order Tick had indicated and stood just inches from the invisible door in the shiny curved glass. The seconds dragged into minutes as Tick stared at his distorted reflection, trying to stay focused so he could lean forward the instant things changed. The sun had moved further west, but it still shone down with ruthless heat.

"What if the door closes before we pull out?" Paul said after what seemed like an hour of waiting.

Tick rolled his shoulders, surprised at how stiff his muscles were, tensed as he kept himself prepared to move. His injuries from the metaspides still stung as well. "Just count to three inside your head then pull back. It stayed open at least—"

The humming sound cut him off.

Tick tried not to blink as he stared at the unbelievable sight of the doorway opening. Like liquid silver, the glass melted and disappeared into itself, dropping in a straight line until a perfect rectangle once again revealed the inside of the tube.

"Now!" Tick said, but the other two were already leaning forward with him.

Everything felt different—the *vrrmmmmm* sound wasn't as loud and nothing shook. Even as Tick's head passed through the opening, he could see that no train or anything else was close by. Mentally counting to three, he stared across the tube and took it all in, hoping his friends were doing the same.

He saw no sign of rails or anything else to indicate train tracks. There wasn't even a sunken floor running along the bottom. The inside of the structure looked much like the outside, a long tunnel of smooth glass

almost completely unblemished by objects. It was much darker inside, the sunlight filtering into dark shades of blue and purple as it passed through. Here and there, small, odd-shaped formations of glass jutted into the tunnel. Tick had no idea what they were for.

Tick felt someone tugging on his shirt. He snapped back to his senses and jerked himself out of the tube. A second later, the humming sound returned as the glass magically formed upward, a gravity-defying sheet of molten crystal, and sealed off the doorway.

"Dang, Tick!" Paul said. "Weren't you the one who said count to *three?*"

"Sorry—I just . . . I guess I lost track of time."

"How do you lose track of three seconds?" Sofia said.

"Yeah, man—one more second and you'd have been running around here without a head."

Tick ignored them, still fascinated by the inside of the tunnel. "So what did you guys see?"

"Glass," Paul said. "A bunch of glass."

"Me, too," Sofia agreed.

Tick frowned, having hoped they would have seen something different. "No sign of a walkway or anything?"

Paul shook his head. "Just smooth glass with little things sticking out here and there—no idea what those were."

Sofia nodded. "Below us the glass just curved toward

the bottom in the middle then started back up again. It's just a big glass tunnel. That's it."

Tick folded his arms and leaned back against the tube—a few feet away from the doorway, just in case. "What was that thing we saw zing past last time?" He wondered if maybe they'd gone to a Reality with extremely advanced technology, some form of travel they couldn't even comprehend.

Sofia seemed to be on the same wavelength. "Maybe it's some kind of futuristic invention—a train that slides through the tube at lightning speeds. Maybe this is a special kind of glass mixed with a metal we don't know about and super-magnetized. Maybe."

"Man, that sounded smart," Paul said as he joined Tick, leaning against the tube.

Sofia put her hands on her hips and stared at them, as if picking out a criminal from a police lineup. "Okay, so what do we do?"

A long pause answered her. Tick finally broke the silence. "We go in."

"Now, wait a minute—" Paul began.

"He's right, Paul," Sofia said. "What else can we do? We go in and let the door close behind us. Someone is testing our bravery. If we're willing to just stand out here and roast to death, what good are we as Realitants?"

"What good are we if we get smashed by a big old train?" Paul retorted.

"Courage," Sofia said. "Master George expects us to be brave."

"He also expects us to be smart."

"How about this?" Tick interjected. He stepped away from the tube. "We'll wait until the door opens *and* we don't feel the big vibration of the train-thing. The door opens every half hour, but maybe the train only comes by at certain intervals. We've been here for at least three hours and we've only felt the vibration of the train twice."

"I'm in," Sofia said quickly.

They both looked at Paul, who took a long moment to think. "Fine—but only if there's no doubt the train isn't coming."

"Sweet," Tick said. "Line up again."

They did, and time seemed to move slower than ever. When the door opened next, it was accompanied by the violent vibration of the traveling machine. Tick caught a blurry glimpse of the dark shape as it zipped past.

"See," Sofia said. "It's totally obvious when the train is coming. We can probably go in next time. If we don't see or find anything in thirty minutes, we'll just come back out."

Again, the waiting game. Tick felt like the heat and the boredom were slowly driving his mind crazy; his stomach ached for food. He thought of his family, picturing each one in turn. Kayla, finally reading and loving every minute of it. Lisa, getting better at the piano and yapping on the phone constantly. His mom, the best cook he'd ever known—though old Aunt Mabel in Alaska was a close second. Finally, he pictured his dad: big belly, funny hair, gigantic smashed nose and all. Thinking of them made him feel a little better, but his heart panged with sadness as well.

What if this time, he didn't make it back to them?

His attention came back to the hot desert and big tube when he heard the humming sound again, this time much quieter with no vibrations. The glass doorway melted open, and no one said a word. Together, the three of them jumped through the hole and into the tunnel.

As they slid to the curved bottom of the huge cylinder, Tick heard the swishing sound of the door closing shut behind them.

CHAPTER 17

STREAMS OF FIRE

Tick was surprised at how the glass felt on the inside—cool, but hard as steel. The light came from everywhere and nowhere at once, a muted glow that made Paul's and Sofia's skin look purple. Glimmering shapes skittered along the interior surface of the tunnel, like reflections from a swimming pool. As Tick stood, he thought he might slip on the shiny surface, but the material had plenty of friction—it was almost sticky.

"What's that smell?" Paul said, taking a big sniff with a wrinkled nose.

Tick took a deep breath. "Ooh, that does stink." The air smelled like the chemicals in a portable toilet.

Tick walked as far as he could up the curved side

of the tunnel, almost making it to the part where it was completely vertical. He saw a round bubble of glass, about three inches tall, bulging out from the wall. Scared to touch it, he leaned forward and took a closer look. A freaky distortion of his own image stared back at him, but nothing else.

"You're gonna break your neck," Sofia said. "Come back down, and let's figure out what we need to do."

Tick scooted down on his rear end, then stood back up. "Maybe we should just start walking."

"Which way?" Sofia asked.

"Whoa, whoa, whoa," Paul said. "It was a borderline eight on the dumb-guy scale to come in here in the first place. If we start trottin' off away from this door, we'd be complete idiots. Did you forget about that really big train that goes really fast?"

"Maybe we could stand to the side and jump onto it when it flies by," Tick suggested.

Paul and Sofia both looked at him with blank faces. Then Paul said, "Dude, you just hit number one on the Top Ten List of Dumbest Ideas Ever Spoken Aloud."

Tick shrugged. "Maybe. Got any better ideas?"

"Yeah, let's stand here and hope Santa Claus shows up to tell us what to do."

"Oh, would you two—" Sofia began.

"Shhh!" Tick said. He thought he'd heard something.

"What?"

"Just be quiet for a sec." He stilled his body, perked his ears. There it was. A very quiet beeping sound, like a car alarm honking from miles away. "Do you hear that?"

"No," Paul answered.

"Yeah, I hear it," Sofia said. "Sounds like it's far away but I can't tell from which direction." She looked down one end of the tunnel, then turned to the other. "That way?"

Tick shook his head, still straining his ears. "No, it sounds like it's coming from outside the tunnel. Or below us, maybe."

"Do you people have Superman hearing or something?" Paul said, throwing his arms up in frustration. "I don't hear a dang—hey, what's that?" He pointed toward the ceiling.

Tick followed the line of direction, at first not seeing what Paul was pointing toward. Then he spotted it—a blinking red light.

"That looks like a button," Sofia said.

Tick squinted to get a better look and agreed. "It's definitely a button. With some words next to it, on a sticker." The ceiling was about twenty feet above them, just far enough that Tick couldn't make out the words.

"If you can read that, you *are* Superman," Paul said.

"I can't. But I bet we're supposed to push that button."

"You think?" Paul frowned. "Master George built this entire gigantic tube thing just to test us to see if we could push a button?"

"I don't know," Tick muttered, feeling confused and discouraged.

After a long pause, all of them staring up at the flashing button, Sofia spoke up. "Maybe if we stood on each other's shoulders, we could reach it."

"On each *other's* shoulders?" Paul asked. "What does that mean?"

"Well . . . you're probably the strongest, though that isn't saying much." She looked Tick up and down, weighing him with her eyes. "I'll get on Tick's shoulders, then you lift both of us up."

Paul flexed his arms, showing off his not-so-impressive biceps. "I might have some guns, Miss Italy, but that sounds ridiculous."

"Let's just try it," Tick urged. "Show us you're a man."

Paul laughed. "You two are crazy. But whatever, I'm game."

Tick got down on his knees and let Sofia crawl onto his shoulders, wrapping her legs around his neck so that her feet dangled over his chest. As Paul helped him stand up, Tick thought the blood vessels in his brain might burst from the effort. He couldn't help but groan out loud as he struggled to balance with Sofia on top of him. He opened his mouth to say something, but Paul held a finger to his lips.

"Don't say anything," he said. "Nothing. No matter what you say, you'd be calling her fat. So just zip it."

"You're not so dumb, after all," Sofia said from above.

Tick braced his feet and finally steadied himself. "How in the world are you going to lift both of us?"

"I surf, man. My legs could lift an elephant." He looked up at Sofia. "Not that I'm saying you weigh as much as an—"

"Just get on with it," Sofia said, kicking out at Paul.

Paul smiled at Tick, then walked behind him. "All right, dude. Let's do this thing."

Tick shuffled his feet apart and soon felt Paul grabbing him by the thighs and lifting with his shoulders. To his complete amazement, he rose slowly into the air.

Paul screamed out words as he struggled to stand. "Good . . . gracious . . . mercy . . . mama . . . you people . . . are *FAT!*"

The three of them swayed slightly as Paul fought to keep his balance and strength. Tick's stomach turned; he couldn't believe what was happening. *I've been zapped into a Saturday morning cartoon.*

"I can't reach it!" Sofia yelled from above. "I'd have to *stand* on Tick's shoulders!"

"Then *do it!*" Paul screamed from below. "Hurry!"

Sofia lifted her right foot and wedged it between Tick's neck and shoulder, grabbing his head with both hands and pulling his hair.

"Ow!" he yelled.

Sofia ignored him and tried pushing down and lifting her other leg up to his left shoulder. That's when everything came apart and they fell on the ground in a chaotic heap of arms and legs.

After they'd finally squirmed away from the pile and stood again, the three of them stared at each other, panting with red faces.

"You're right," Tick said between breaths. "That was ridiculous."

"I don't think my body will ever heal," Paul said through a wince.

Sofia stared up at the button with a grin. "Well, at least I got a closer look at the words on that sticker."

"Really?" Tick asked, his hope rising. "What did it say?"

Sofia let out a discouraged sigh. "Two words: *Push me.*"

Sato lay on his back, staring at the ceiling. He'd focused so long on a bear-shaped shadow caused by the pale moonlight seeping through his window that it seemed to be moving, growing smaller and larger as if breathing. He knew it was only a trick of his eyes, but it still gave him the creeps.

He'd dreaded going to sleep lately because of an old dream that had come back to haunt him. He had no idea why it had returned in recent days, causing him to jerk awake every night, a sheen of sweat covering his whole body. Actually, it wasn't a dream at all—it was a memory.

The memory of his parents' murder.

What a day that had been, almost eight years ago. A terrible, frightening, horrible, horrible day. Master George had been there. Mistress Jane had been there, too. Others as well, but for some reason he couldn't remember their faces. But he'd never forget the way the old man had looked that day, or his closest ally— the woman dressed in yellow. He'd never forget. Sato would never, ever forget.

He closed his eyes, knowing the dream would come but giving in to exhaustion, hoping the memory might strengthen his hopes for revenge. Revenge on Mistress Jane.

Revenge . . .

"Yama Kun, come meet our guests!" his mother called

from downstairs. She'd always called him that. It meant Little Mountain.

Six-year-old Sato stepped out of his room and slowly walked down the stairs, not wanting to meet a bunch of strangers. While preparing for the big dinner, his father had called them "Realitants" as if any person in the world should know what that meant.

Realitants. A strange word, especially for a six-year-old. But after witnessing what Sato saw that night, the word burned a place in his mind, never to be lost. Realitants. In years to come, he'd end up thinking the word every day, sometimes repeating it aloud as he looked in the mirror. Realitants. The word came to mean evil and death to him, and he made a pact to one day rid the world of them.

He'd known so little back then.

He entered the front room, where several people sat on the leather couches and fancy armchairs, sipping ocha tea and speaking with each other as if discussing the weather or the latest sumo tournament. Most of them were unrecognizable, their faces a blur. The only ones he saw clearly were the slightly chubby man in the suit—Master George—and the beautiful but chilling bald woman, Mistress Jane. They sat together on the couch, mumbling something he couldn't quite hear.

It was the image of those two sitting side by side on the couch that stayed in his memory more than anything else. It was that image that many years later would make him distrust Master George with a passion. At least for a time.

Without warning, the room grew silent, and everyone turned to look at Sato.

"I'd like you all to meet my son," his father said, gripping Sato's shoulders from behind and squeezing. His mother joined them, pulling Sato's hand into hers.

The dream froze for a moment, as if paused on television. It always did at this exact point, and Sato knew why. Although he was nervous at meeting strangers, uncomfortable in his nice clothes, perhaps even hungry at the time, it would be the last time Sato ever felt the comforting touch of his parents. The last time he ever felt safe and protected.

That moment with his parents would be the last time Sato ever felt happy.

The dream continued playing out.

Mistress Jane stood, then Master George and the rest. Each of them stepped forward around the great, round coffee table and shook Sato's little hand. George knelt on the ground, a big smile creasing his face.

"Goodness gracious me," the old man said. "I can see it in the boy's eyes. The passion, the hunger, the intelligence. A splendid Realitant he'll make, Master Sato"—he looked up at Sato's father—"a splendid Realitant, indeed. We'll begin the testing shortly."

Mistress Jane was next, also kneeling before Yama Kun. Though her smile shone and her face was pretty, even then, Sato felt that something was wrong with her.

"Yes," she said. Sato almost expected her to cackle like an evil old witch. "A smart child by the looks of it." She leaned forward to whisper in Sato's ear, so quiet only he could hear her. "But whose side will you fight for? Everything is about to change, little boy."

Mistress Jane stood. "This is as good a time as any," she announced, turning slowly as she spoke so everyone could see her face. "My team has discovered a new Reality—a stable one. It's solid enough to officially call it a branch."

"Really?" George shouted. "That's delightful, simply delightful!"

Jane looked down at Sato, who returned her glare. She rolled her eyes and stuck out her tongue, as if disgusted by George's enthusiasm.

"The Thirteenth Reality," she continued, not taking her eyes off Sato, "has . . . unusual qualities. We've explored it extensively, realized its potential."

"Why didn't you tell us before?" Sato's father asked, his voice laced with anger. "If you've been exploring it this long—"

"The Chi'karda there," Jane said, ignoring the interruption, "is different. More powerful. More potent. It's mutated into something quite extraordinary. We may finally have the secret to finding our Utopian Reality. If

this place isn't it, the power in the Thirteenth will help us make it ourselves."

No one spoke for a long time; a few people exchanged nervous glances.

"Why all the sad faces?" Jane asked. "Haven't you trusted me all these years? Don't you still trust me?"

"Not if you break the rules," Sato's mother said. "How can we trust you if you break the rules and hide things from us?"

"This calls for an immediate Discretionary Council," Sato's father said. "George, you know it does. I demand you call in the Haunce, this instant."

George stood. "Now, Master Sato, let's not be hasty—"

That was the line. Those seven words would stick in young Sato's mind, making it even harder for him to trust the man in the future, when his own recruiting call came. That was the line, because after George said it, not another word was spoken by him before Sato's parents were dead.

"I don't have time for this," Jane said. "I thought this might be the reaction, so I brought along something to show you all how important this discovery is. For all of us. For the Realities. For humanity."

"Stop," Sato's father said. "Stop this instant. I demand it."

"You . . . demand it?" she replied, her lip curled ever so slightly. "You demand it?"

"Yes," Sato's mother answered for her husband. "You're scaring us. This doesn't feel right."

Mistress Jane smiled then, an image Sato would never forget. The smile held no humor, no joy, no kindness. It was an evil smile.

The next moment, the windows erupted, blowing inward with a shower of tinkling glass shards. Shouts of pain surrounded him as streams of fire poured in from outside, streaking spurts of lava that whisked around the room like flying eels of flame.

The dream always grew dim at that moment, the memory fading into horror. He remembered his father's comforting grip on his shoulders disappearing, his mother's hand letting go of his own. He remembered intense heat. He remembered people running around, their clothes on fire. He remembered Jane vanishing into thin air. He remembered crying, turning to find his parents, wanting to run away.

But then, like always, he saw one last thing in the dream before it ended. One last image that would haunt him forever. His mother and father, lying on the ground, side by side.

Screaming. Burning.

Dying.

Sato woke up.

CHAPTER 18

A VERY SCARY PROPOSITION

O kay, it's my turn," Sofia said as she took off her right tennis shoe. "You guys couldn't poke yourselves in your own eyeball."

Tick wanted to argue, but didn't have much evidence to the contrary. He and Paul had been trying to hit the button with a shoe for at least ten minutes, their only reward being smacked in the head a couple of times as the shoes fell back down.

"'Poke yourselves in your own eyeball?'" Paul said. "Never heard that one before."

Sofia ignored him, planting her feet and staring up at the button with intense concentration, swinging the shoe up and down with both hands as she readied herself. Finally, she swung hard upward and let the shoe fly. It missed by three feet.

Paul snickered. "Ooh, so close. Hate to break it to you, but you throw like a girl."

Uh-oh, Tick thought.

Sofia bent down to pick up her shoe, then bounced it up and down in her right hand like a baseball. "What did you say?"

Paul folded his arms. "I said, you throw like a girl."

"Huh," Sofia grunted, staring down at her shoe. Then she reared back and threw it straight for Paul's face, smacking him square on the nose.

He grabbed his face with both hands, jumping up and down. "That hurt, man!" he shouted. But a second later, he started laughing. "Ah, Tick, it was worth it to see Miss Italy mad. Her face looks like her daddy's spaghetti sauce."

This time Sofia punched Paul in the arm with a loud thump. "You want some more?" she asked.

Paul rubbed the spot. "Dang, woman, I give up. How'd you get so mean, anyway?"

Tick was loving every minute of the exchange, but he knew they had to push that button. He felt something—a pressure in his chest—that told him they'd better get serious quick.

"You lovebirds cut it out," he said. "Start throwing."

They tried for another five minutes, dodging each

other's shoes and scrambling around to pick up their own. Sofia finally hit the bull's-eye.

When her shoe connected, a quiet click echoed off the round glass of the tunnel and the blinking light stopped, turning off completely. All three of them stared, waiting for something amazing to happen. Nothing did. Tick rubbed his sunburned neck, sore from craning it upward for so long.

"Great," he said. "Just great."

Sofia huffed and looked down; Tick noticed her body tense, her eyes widen. She stared at the floor, trans-fixed, as if hypnotized. Tick quickly followed her gaze. He couldn't stop the gasp before it escaped his mouth.

On the very bottom of the tunnel, at their feet, a perfect red square had formed on the glass, about five feet on each side, as if a neon light were glowing right beneath them. In the middle of that square, several lines of words appeared like text on a computer screen, black on white.

"Guess we *were* supposed to push the button," Paul said.

Tick fell to his knees and scooted around until the words were right side up. It was another poem—a pretty long one. He started reading.

You pushed the button; it called the beast.
It moves real fast; it likes to feast.

You can stop it once, but cannot twice,
It's the only way to save your life.
How to do it, you may ask;
This will not be an easy task.
Your mind will beg of you to quit,
But if you do, your mind will split.
On this very spot you'll stand;
You will die if I see you've ran.
I'm testing strength and will and trust.
Move one inch, and die you must.
Do not step outside the square.
No matter what—don't you dare.
When this is over, you will see
A grand reward for trusting me.

"Dude," Paul breathed. "There's no way Master George is behind all this."

Sofia sat down next to the poem. "For the first time in my life, I think I agree with you. He said in the letter we were going to a gathering, not doing more tests."

Tick read through the poem again, feeling very uneasy. Paul and Sofia were right—this was getting weird. Even though Master George had sent the Gnat Rat and the Tingle Wraith after them during their initial recruiting test, this seemed too sinister for the jolly old man. It felt dark and threatening.

"This isn't even a riddle," Tick said, standing up.

"What do you mean?" Sofia asked.

Tick pointed down the long tunnel in the direction from which he thought the train thing had come the first time they'd seen it blur past. "There's nothing to solve. We have to stand inside this square no matter what happens. No matter what . . . *comes*."

He couldn't get over the sick feeling in his gut. Something felt wrong, like he'd left a fat wallet full of money on a city park bench. Or probably how his mom would feel if she realized she'd left the oven on, right after taking off in the airplane to go visit Grandma. The world seemed twisted, off balance.

After a long pause, Sofia spoke up in a confident voice. "It doesn't matter."

"What doesn't matter?" Tick and Paul said at the same time.

Sofia shrugged. "If it's Master George—which I doubt—we need to do what the poem says. If it's not him, we *still* need to do what it says. We'll be really tempted to leave the square, but we can't. Then, at the last second, whoever it is will wink us away. Poof, nice and easy—just like the chair thing."

"How do we know for sure we'll get winked?" Tick asked, even though the answer had just clicked in his head.

"If somebody else is doing this," Sofia said, "they could obviously just kill us if they wanted to. Why would they go through this whole ordeal to get rid of us? If anything, now we have even more pressure to pass these tests." She shook her fists and screamed in frustration. "This is so stupid! Stupid, stupid, stupid!"

"Way to sum it up intelligently," Paul muttered. When she gave him a cold stare, he threw his hands up. "Hey, I agree with you!"

"Wait," Tick said, shushing them, holding a hand out. He felt a slight tremor beneath his feet, a small vibration with no sound.

"It's coming, dude," Paul said. "It's coming!"

The shaking grew stronger, almost visible now; Paul and Sofia seemed to jiggle up and down. Tick had never been in an earthquake, but he knew this must be what it felt like.

"What do we do, man, what do we do?" Paul was looking left and right as if trying to decide which direction to run.

Sofia reached out and grabbed Paul by the shirt, jerking him toward her until their faces were only inches apart. "We stand in this square, Rogers, you hear me? We stand in this square!"

At once, they all looked down at their feet. Tick had to shuffle a foot closer to the others to be inside the red-lined boundary.

"She's right," he said as Sofia let go of Paul. "No matter what, we have to stay in the square."

The tunnel trembled violently; Tick had to spread his feet a little and hold out his arms to maintain his balance. A sound grew in the distance, a low rumble of thunder. Whatever it was—the poem had called it a beast—was coming from the direction Tick had thought it would. He narrowed his eyes and stared that way, though nothing had appeared yet in the distance.

"This is crazy, man," Paul said. "Are you guys *sure* about this?"

"Yes," Tick said, not breaking his concentration. He thought he could see something dark, far down the tunnel.

"My brain wants me to run," Paul insisted.

This time, Tick did turn, pointing at the poem still printed on the ground. "The message said we'd think that. Don't move." He looked back down the tunnel. There was definitely something dark way down there, growing larger, bit by bit.

"I'm watching you, Rogers," Sofia said, almost shouting as the rumbling and shaking increased. "We're going to wink away. No one's going to kill us!"

"Fine! Quit treating me like a baby."

Tick strained his eyes as the dark shape grew bigger. Something about its movement made him think it was *twisting*—corkscrewing through the tunnel like a roller coaster.

"What *is* that thing?" he said, though the roar had

grown so loud he knew no one could hear him. He braced himself, knowing it would be easier if he didn't look, didn't see it coming. But his curiosity was too strong.

Then the air around them suddenly brightened, flashing a blinding white.

"Look!" Paul shouted from behind him.

Tick turned to see sand dunes and sunlight through a gaping hole in the side of the tunnel.

The door had opened.

CHAPTER 19

THE TRAIN THING

A shot of elation and relief surged through Tick's nerves, like he'd been rescued from a burning building. There it was, their escape! He even took a step toward it before reason pulled his thoughts back to reality. Sofia grabbed his arm.

"No!" she screamed.

"I know!" he answered, looking down at his feet. His toes were within inches of the red line. The world around them shook and roared, as if they were in a small building pummeled by a tornado. The wind had picked up, rustling their hair and clothes.

Paul stared at the open door, his eyes glazed over.

"Don't even think about it!" Sofia shouted at him.

"No matter what, remember? If we run, we die!"

Paul snapped out of his daze, looked at Tick. "Dude, it's right there!"

"Whoever it is, they're just tempting us!" Tick yelled.

He moved as close to Paul as he could, then pulled Sofia in. "Link arms!" He could barely hear his own voice.

Sofia obeyed immediately, but Paul hesitated, the wind ripping at his shirt.

"Do it!" Tick yelled.

Paul's face sank into a frown as he wrapped his arm around Sofia's elbow, then his other around Tick's. All this time, the door remained open, staying open far longer than it ever had before. *This was all planned out,* Tick thought. *But by who?*

From the way they stood, only Sofia faced the onrushing nightmare, her face set in cold fear, eyes wide, mouth in a tight line. The air swirled around them, making them sway dangerously close to the line. Tick thought Sofia's hair might simply fly off at any second. And the noise. The *noise.* Like screaming brakes and revved jet engines and pounding hammers and hissing steam—a chorus of terrible sounds that pierced Tick's ears with sharp pain.

Finally, as if giving in to some inevitable fate, he twisted his neck to look behind him.

The thing was very close now, dark and hideous,

spinning upside down and right side up again, cork-screwing as it sped toward them, faster and faster. Tick squinted, thinking the panic must have scrambled his brain—what he was looking at didn't make any sense.

The poem had been more accurate than he'd thought. The train was not a train at all. It wasn't a car, truck, or plane. It wasn't even a spaceship. The thing thundering toward them at unbelievable speeds was an *animal*. The biggest, strangest, ugliest beast Tick had ever seen.

"What . . ." he said, trailing off, knowing his friends couldn't hear him. Nothing made sense any-more. Nothing.

As the beast got closer, Tick felt the fear in him swell, burning like fire, surging through his veins, hurt-ing him. The animal had at least a dozen sets of thick, muscled legs, almost a blur as they churned back and forth to move the creature in its twisting pattern. Its huge head spun but, impossibly, didn't turn as quickly as the rest of its body, as if the legs were on springs or gears. Dark, scaly skin covered a hideous head, spikes and stunted bones sticking out in random places, enor-mous teeth jutting from its mouth.

As it approached within a half mile, then a quarter mile, Tick felt more scared than ever before, despite the things he'd been through. His mind couldn't come up with any possible explanation why a gigantic glass tube would exist in the middle of the desert, made for a terrible beast to run through at ridiculous speeds. Confusion and fear mingled together inside his brain, squeezing his thoughts until his head pounded with a drumming pain.

Wink us away, he thought. *Time's almost up, wink us away. Wink us away. WINK US AWAY!* The wind, the noise—the horrible noise. *What is making that stupid noise?* He thought he heard a scream, maybe two. Maybe it was him.

When the beast was only fifty feet away, growling and snapping its jaws and twisting and pumping its powerful legs, bulleting toward them, everything went crazy.

For the slightest of moments, a hush swallowed the area, the noise ending in an abrupt clap of empty silence. Then a booming, deep toll, like millions of huge bells and French horns playing at once, rang out, drowning out all other sound. Tick let go of Paul and Sofia and clapped his hands over his ears. The volume became unbearable; the ache in his head became a splitting pain behind his eyes.

The entire tunnel rocked upward and crashed back to the ground, sending a web of cracks shooting in all directions, spreading like a branching tree with the sound of ice breaking over a frozen lake. Tick crashed to the ground, his knees buckling from the impact; Paul fell on top of him, then Sofia.

Somehow Tick got out the words, "Stay in the box!"

In both directions, the tunnel started *warping*— impossible waves rippling in the glass up and down its length. The massive beast had stopped a few feet away, its many legs coming to a rest on the bottom of the tube. Its head swiveled around at the chaos as if it were as frightened as the humans. The deep, vibrating horn-like sound continued to boom through the air.

Tick and the others scrambled to the center of the square and clasped arms around each other, huddled on top of the still-glowing words of the poem. Everything shook, much worse than before. The glass rippled and cracked; the tunnel bounced in places like a writhing worm. The beast let out a roar, its huge mouth opening to show dozens of teeth; saliva flew everywhere. Still, the sound of it was nothing compared to the clanging, ear-piercing toll of the mysterious bells.

"What's happening?" Sofia shouted. Tick barely heard her and had no answer.

The creature moved toward them, anger ignited in its black eyes that looked through a hooded brow of horns and scales. Almost on top of them, it roared again, this time louder. The air reeked of something foul and rotten.

"Stay in the box!" Tick shouted again. *Wink us away. Wink us away. WINK US AWAY!*

The beast lunged at them, its legs catapulting it into the air. Its outermost horn came within inches of Tick's face when something suddenly slammed the whole creature away from them and against the wall of the tunnel to their right, where the door still stood open—though it was way too small for the beast. The glass exploded outward, the huge animal crashing through and into a steep desert dune.

As it landed, sending up a massive spray of sand, large sections of the tunnel began melting into liquid, forming huge flying globs that looked like molten silver as they moved through the air. More and more of them appeared, completely destroying the tunnel except for the small spot on which Tick and the others stood. All at once, the melted glass hurtled toward the monster, engulfing the beast completely. The liquid hardened back into glass, tinkling and crackling.

As quickly as it had started, everything stopped. Tick sat next to Paul and Sofia, all of them squeezing each other, gasping to catch their breath. Only a few dozen feet away stood a horrific sculpture of glass, twisted and bent, parts of the poor animal's body sticking out here and there. One large horn jutted from the front, pointing at them as if it had all been their fault.

No one said a word. They had stayed in the square. They had done what they were supposed to, despite everything.

A few seconds later, someone winked them away to another Reality.

CHAPTER 20

AN INVITATION

Mistress Jane walked through the darkening woods, enjoying the smells of the forest and fresh air more than she thought she would. She'd rarely ventured out of the Lemon Fortress since losing her Barrier Wand to the Realitants, too busy working and planning. Too busy thinking.

A bird cawed in the distance, a shriek that sounded like someone being tortured. She faltered a moment, then stepped over a log and continued walking. *There you go again,* she thought. *You can take anything and see the worst in it.* Why couldn't she just hear the sound of a bird and appreciate the beauty in it—the joy of nature? When had she become so dark and morbid? How had it gotten this bad?

She closed her eyes and took a deep breath, loving the strong scent of pine. Such simple things used to please her, make her happy. Until her mission to find the Utopian Reality consumed her and turned her into what she'd become. Someone feared and hated. When it came down to it, Jane didn't like herself very much. Not one bit.

She reached a sudden break in the trees, the place Frazier had described to her. He'd wanted to come with her, insisted on it with more bravery than usual. Jane had finally ordered him to clean the kitchens for being obstinate. If anyone could take care of themselves in the Thirteenth Reality, it was Mistress Jane.

The sun had fallen behind the line of trees on the other side of the huge clearing, a random twinkle shining through the leaves as she kept walking. She'd believed Frazier's report, but she still felt a thrill of shock at seeing it for herself.

The gap in the forest was at least a quarter mile in diameter, almost perfectly circular. She saw no signs or tracks of heavy machinery that had mowed down hundreds of trees overnight. She saw only a few footprints, and they looked to be those of the hunters and Frazier's investigating party.

Who did this? And how?

As she neared the center of the clearing, she tried to come up with possibilities. It certainly wasn't a natural phenomenon—especially considering the felled tree trunks spelled out words in massive letters. From this low vantage point, she couldn't make out the words, of course, only a general sense of the individual letters—even though they were almost too big to recognize. But she had no doubt as to what it said, trusting Frazier implicitly.

Mistress Jane, you are a coward. Come and find me.

She continued on, knowing exactly where she wanted to end up. The message had a hidden meaning, a literal clue. *Come and find* me. That's exactly what she was doing, counting on her budding powers to help her if she ran into any trouble.

She made it to the other side of the clearing, her arms and legs weary from crossing over—and sometimes *climbing* over—the many logs. She could have levitated herself, flown to her destination without another thought, but she was enjoying the nostalgic effort of physical exertion. Finally, in the center of where she estimated the word "me" was spelled out, she stopped.

"Here I am," she said, not stooping so low as to shout; she had her dignity to preserve. "We're near enough to the old battleground and its thick Chi'karda. Wink in and be done with it."

A few minutes passed in silence. Jane grew restless far

quicker than she expected, and stilled herself to be sure her emotions didn't show. She would not utter another word or move another muscle, no matter how long the mystery person made her wait.

Ten more minutes went by, the cloudless sky growing ever darker, a deep blue slowly bleeding to purple. Then, with no fanfare or smoke, a man appeared ten feet in front of her. Dressed in a pinstripe suit, he had dark hair and olive skin. He was tall and almost handsome, but not quite. His arms were clasped behind his back, perhaps holding something, hiding it from her. Though she'd never met him, she knew his name immediately. After all, just a few months ago she'd tried unsuccessfully to arrange a meeting with him.

Reginald Chu, perhaps the most dangerous man in the Realities.

But surely he couldn't possibly know her powers in the Chi'karda were growing enough to match his technological gadgetry. *Why is he here?*

"Hello, *Mistress* Jane," Chu said, mocking her title. "We finally meet, several months later than you had hoped."

"You got my note, then?" she asked.

"I did." He paused, not moving, staring at her. "I waited for you in the park, but you never showed up. You wasted time that was not yours to waste."

It took every ounce of willpower for Jane to remain

calm, to not lash out and whip this man with one of the fallen logs. She could do it, and the man spoke to her as if she were inferior. *No,* she told herself. *He's here for a reason.*

"My apologies, Mister—"

"Call me Reginald," he snapped. "Never call me Mr. Chu. Never."

Jane bowed her head ever so slightly. "My apologies . . . Reginald. I had a proposition for you, a good one, but the Realitants stole my Wand, trapping me here. I'll soon have another one built."

Chu moved his arms from behind his back to reveal what he'd been hiding—a brand new Barrier Wand, its golden surface sparkling despite the diminishing light, seven dials and switches running along its length.

He hefted the three-foot-long device in his left hand, holding it out to her as a gift. Then he dropped one end of it toward the ground and leaned on it like a cane. "I've had spies here since the week you stood me up. I know a lot about you. I also know about this Reality and its twisted version of Chi'karda."

It took considerable effort for Jane not to look at the Wand, staring Chu in the face instead. "I'm glad you know how to do your research."

"That's not all I found. You're missing one of the metals. It'll be months before you can extract enough from the ore you've discovered." He nodded toward the

Wand at his feet. "So I've brought you a new Wand to save you the trouble."

Jane folded her arms. "At what price?"

Chu broke into a smile, something Jane would never have expected to see on such a man. "I can see you're as wise as I hoped. Nothing, of course, is free. Especially in my Reality."

"Tales of your business skills are widespread, I assure you." She wanted to add, *And your ruthlessness and greed are likewise well-known.*

"That's good to know."

She expected him to say more, but he grew silent, keeping his gaze locked with hers. *Oh, I do not like this man.* "Your price?" she asked again.

"I've developed something that will completely change the Realities. It's a new invention—"

"What is it?" Jane asked, trying to assert some authority, show her impatience.

Chu paused, his face pulling tight, his eyes narrowing. "Listen to me, *Mistress.* Never interrupt me. You will stand there and listen to my proposition and you will not utter a word until I am finished. Do you understand? Indicate with a nod of your head."

Jane felt her face fill with blood, heat up, and burn. A small sound escaped from somewhere in the back of her throat, a mortifying squeak. At that moment, she swore to herself that when this man died, he would be looking at her smiling face. The only thing staying her hand from unleashing her powers was curiosity. Intense curiosity.

She nodded.

"Good." He pulled up the Barrier Wand and held it in front of him, parallel to the ground. "My project is called Dark Infinity, a tool that artificially creates massive amounts of Chi'karda—far stronger than anything you've encountered here. It's more powerful than all of my previous accomplishments combined. However, there is still one missing piece."

Jane almost asked him what, but stopped just in time. Her curiosity burned like an itch.

"It's so strong that I can't control it alone," he continued. "I need another person, someone of proven strength, someone extraordinary. I've studied and searched every Reality, every region. I have narrowed it down to only two people. I don't fully understand yet what sets these two apart, but I do know that one of them will do. And I only need . . . one."

He paused, and Jane was dying to speak. She didn't know what she had expected, but it was certainly nothing like this.

Chu continued. "One of the two is you. Your powers here do not exist solely because of the mutated Chi'karda in this place. Otherwise, everyone would be able to do what you do. There is something extraordinary about you, and I do not say that lightly."

Who is the other? she screamed inside her head, completely ignoring the compliment.

"You might be wondering about your competition," Chu said, smiling. "And here is the proposition. It's very simple. I'm currently sending the other person through a series of tests. If he passes them and ends up where he's supposed to, he will win the honor of standing by my side as we rule the Realities. Meaning, of course, you lose and will be disposed of." He paused. "You may speak now."

"I . . . I'm not sure I completely understand," Jane mumbled, hating herself for appearing so weak. Chu had said she could be "disposed of" like a sickly fly. *How dare he?* And yet, she felt uneasy. "How do I win?"

Chu walked forward, holding out the Barrier Wand and gesturing for her to take it. She grasped the golden rod with its dials and switches eagerly, like a child grabbing for candy. It was cold and hard in her hands.

"Like I said," Chu continued, "it's very easy. If the boy makes it to me, you lose. If he doesn't, you win. Only one of you will survive in the end—only one of you will be worthy to serve with me in controlling Dark Infinity. That's it."

"That's it?" she repeated, her courage returning. "Nothing else?"

Chu nodded. "You've been given your test, and I assure you, it's not a simple task. You must kill Atticus Higginbottom."

CHAPTER 21

AN ELEVATOR IN STONE

"C ome on," Mothball said, stopping for the tenth time to allow Rutger to catch up. "You're slower than a sloth with no legs, you are."

Truth be told, Mothball appreciated resting for a spell. It was blazing hot in the Arizona desert, and she was hauling a big load of logs she'd gathered from the riverside. Carried down by the Colorado River, stray wood often lodged in one particular bend, and Master George had to have his fires, didn't he?

Rutger, sucking in every breath, his face the color of boiled cherries, stopped and craned his neck to look up at her. He was like a big ball rolling backward, pivoting on little legs. The man looked absolutely exhausted.

"Can't . . . really run when I'm . . . carrying all of this . . . wood . . . now can I?" he managed to get out between breathing spells.

Mothball glanced at Rutger's short arms, holding all of two sticks—one of them barely more than a twig. "Yeah, I'm quite shocked you haven't called someone on the telly to announce you've broken the world's record for stick-luggin'."

"It probably is a record for someone from the Eleventh." Rutger nodded toward the door hidden in the canyon crevice, about forty yards away. The two of them stood at the bottom of the Grand Canyon, its majestic red walls of stone towering over them, reaching so far to the sky they couldn't see their tops. Having finished gathering firewood, they were making their way back to the elevator shaft entrance.

"I reckon Sofia would call you a *flimp* right about now," Mothball said as she resumed walking toward the hidden crevice.

"It's *wimp,* you tall sack of bones, and if she did call me that, she'd pay the price."

"Oh, really?" Mothball called over her shoulder. "And wha' exactly would you do? Sit on her toesies? Bite her shins, perhaps?"

"I'd do whatever it took to teach the young lady some proper manners, that's what."

Mothball made it to the small crack of a cave that

led to the elevator and dropped her stack of logs onto the ground. She reached her arms to the sky in a long, satisfying stretch. When Rutger finally waddled over and dropped his pathetic two sticks onto the pile, he put his hands on his waist and took deep gulps of air, as if he'd just completed a marathon.

"Congratulations," Mothball said. "You're the first tiny fat man to haul two twigs across a weed-scattered spit of sand. Right proud of yourself, I reckon?"

Rutger looked up at her and grinned. "Push the button, or it'll be *your* shins that get bitten."

Mothball's booming laugh escaped before she could stop it. She looked around to make sure no stray hikers were around to hear it. "Quit makin' me laugh, ya little ball of bread dough. Get us in trouble, ya will."

She stepped through the thin crevice and pushed a button that looked like the nub of a rock. She heard the rumble of machinery and pulleys from deep within the mountain, then the low whine of the descending elevator. She groaned, having expected the doors to pop right open since they'd just exited an hour ago and no one else should've used it.

"Blimey, who called up the ruddy thing?" she said as she stepped out of the cave and back into the sunlight. "Probably that rascal Sally, playin' one of 'is jokes."

"Oh, calm yourself," Rutger said, his face finally returning to its normal color. Sweat poured down his face, however, and his hair was matted and wet. "It only takes a couple of minutes. Master George has Sally too busy to mess with jokes anyway."

"I'll bet ya tonight's dessert that when the door pops open, Sally'll be there with a trick up his sleeve."

Rutger looked up at her, his face creased in concern. "D-d-dessert?" he asked, as if she'd just suggested wagering the man's life savings. "Let's not get foolish, Mothball."

"Then you'll take it?" she asked, folding her arms and peering down her nose at him.

Rutger hesitated, fidgeting as he rocked back and forth on his tiny feet. "Um, no, I think you might be right on this one." He cleared his throat. "Probably, um, going to throw a bucket of water on us. That silly lumberjack."

Mothball shook her head, pretending to be disgusted. "You'd throw your own mum in the sewer for a dessert, you would. You can 'ave mine—s'long as you give me some of your bread and jam. Quite tasty stuff, that is."

Rutger rubbed his chin, deep in thought. After a few seconds, he said, "No, I like the bread and jam, too. Let's just stick with our own portions. Deal?"

Mothball reached down and patted him on the head. "You're a good man, you are. A bit short for my likin', but a good man indeed."

"Oh, stop—look, it's here."

A few feet inside the crevice, a rock wall slid to the side, revealing the lighted cube of the elevator, its walls made of fake wood panels. Master George stood inside, dressed in his usual dark suit, arms clasped behind his back.

Mothball's surprise quickly turned to concern. "What's wrong?" she asked.

"Oh, nothing, nothing," he said, breaking into a smile that was obviously forced. "Just wanted to come down and get a bit of fresh air."

He stepped out of the elevator and squeezed past the narrow walls of the cave and into the open canyon. He took a deep breath, then let it out in a satisfied sigh.

"Simply beautiful, don't you think?" he asked, turning back to look at them. "I really should come out here more often. Good for the heart, I'm quite sure."

Mothball rolled her eyes at Rutger. "Out with it, Master George. Somethin's botherin' ya."

Master George tried to look startled, an expression that for some reason reminded Mothball of a frightened chicken. Then his face wilted into a frown, and he huffed.

"Goodness gracious me," he said. "I can't get anything past you two."

"That's a good thing," Rutger said. "What's going on?"

Master George put his hands behind his back again and paced in a wide circle for a full minute. Mothball knew better than to interrupt him. He finally stopped and looked at both of them in turn.

"I've just read through Sato's final report of his interviews, and it concerns me greatly. He's made conclusions with which I can't disagree, and given me a proposal, in private, that frightens me to no end."

"You have our full attention," Rutger said. Mothball nodded.

Master George continued. "I've known all along that Reginald Chu was behind the strange things happening throughout some of the Realities. There've been whispers that he has a new invention, something terrible—something abominable. And I no longer have any doubt it's directly related to the people who are going insane. I'm quite sure of it."

"What is this invention?" Rutger asked.

Master George paused. "Let's go back up to the complex. I'd like Sato and Sally to join our discussion. We've much to talk about."

Mothball, troubled, bent over to pick up her large pile of logs, wet from soaking in the river; she grimaced at how filthy they were after lying in the dirt.

"Could you take mine, too?" Rutger pleaded. "It's hard enough for me to fit through this ridiculous cave as it is."

"Don't know if I can handle your twigs," Mothball muttered. "Might tip me over."

Rutger happily picked them up, then threw them on top of the stack bundled in her arms. One end smacked her in the nose.

"Blimey, that hurt! Go on with ya, get in the ruddy lift."

Master George had already entered the well-hidden elevator, waiting with arms folded and slightly shaking his head, as if observing the antics of misbehaving children. "Please, would you two *hurry?*"

Rutger sucked in a huge breath, trying to shrink his tummy, then ran forward into the dark slice of air between the two vertical walls of the cave. He made it two feet before he came to an abrupt halt; his legs dangled below him, his body lodged in place.

"Help!" he cried out, like a monster was coming to eat him.

Mothball snorted as she held in a laugh. With glee, she balanced herself, lifted one leg, cocked it, then kicked Rutger in the rear end as hard as she could. As he tumbled forward into the elevator, he managed to say, "Thank you!"

Mothball stepped onto the lift and pushed the *up* button.

Buzz.

Sato looked up from his bed where he'd been reading through his reports again. The intercom had rung for him. He put his papers aside, swung his legs off the bed and onto the floor, then reached over to hit the button on the wall.

"Yes?" he shouted.

"Ow, do you have to answer so loud?" It was Rutger, his voice a hollow echo of itself.

"Sorry. What do you want?"

"We're meeting in the conference room in ten minutes. I'll be providing refreshments, so snap-snap!"

Click.

Sato put his elbows on his knees and rubbed his face with both hands. The nightmare of his parents' death had seemed more vivid lately, the horrific images floating in his thoughts for hours after waking up. They hung in his mind like dirty, tattered drapes blocking out the sunlight. He shook his head and bent over to put his shoes on.

"Another meeting," he mumbled. "Joy."

A few minutes later, he slid into a cushy chair around the conference table, reaching out to grab a Chocolate Chip-Peanut Butter-Butterscotch-Pecan-Walnut-Macadamia-Coconut-Delight, one of Rutger's specialties. The little man always said the name in full, despite its length. No one in the complex cared what they were called because they tasted delicious.

Everyone else was already seated: Mothball and Rutger to his right, Master George across from him, Sally to his left. They were the only Realitants at the Grand Canyon Center at the moment—the others had gone off with various duties and assignments.

"Sorry to bother you, Sato," George said. "I know you wanted some time for a bit of relaxing after we spoke earlier, but I felt this gathering couldn't wait."

"No problem," Sato muttered. He'd tried so hard to improve his mood lately, but the recent spout of dreams had quashed his efforts. The world seemed bleak and grim—the only thing that gave him reprieve was trying to figure out the mystery of the crazy people.

George rested his clasped hands on the table in front of him. "First, let's summarize where we are at the moment. Thanks to our good man Sally, here"—he gave a nod to the lumberjack, who seemed lost in thought, his thumb picking suspiciously at his nose—"for putting the Earwig Transponder inside Tick so we could track him better and scramble Chu's eavesdropping capabilities. For as long as I shall live, I shan't forgive that man for his violation of Rule Number 462 on those poor kids. Hijacking a nanolocator . . . it's evil, I tell you!"

George's hands squeezed together as his face reddened. "But the milk's in the kitty litter, as my mum was fond of saying—no use weeping and wailing. With the transponder in Tick's ear, we'll have much more information." He cleared his throat. "For example, we know they've just had a bizarre incident in the Tenth Reality, but we're not quite sure what happened."

Rutger slammed his hand on the table. "Don't tell me that wretch stuck them in the Grinder Beast's training tunnels?"

Sato leaned forward at this question—the words *Grinder Beast* would perk anyone's attention.

George nodded. "Indeed. I must say, I was rather tempted to go rescue them, but I didn't want to ruin our chances at getting on the inside of Chu's plans. I believe we all agree that Chu would not put them in total danger—not yet, anyway. It appears he's running them through some sort of test, and I can't imagine he'd waste their potential by letting one of the Grinders kill them so easily. They serve us best as spies—albeit unknowing spies—at the moment."

"That's a big risk on your part, it is," Mothball said, the most accusatory thing Sato had ever heard her say to George. The tall woman loved those kids like her own children. Sato felt a little jealous; she didn't seem to care so much for him.

"That's neither here nor there," George responded. "I was right to wait. They've been winked to the Sixth by Chu, where they seem to be safe and sound for the time being."

"What was that you said about a bizarre incident?" Sato asked.

"I can't say for sure. There was a surge in Chi'karda in that area, some kind of great disturbance that caused a Ripple Quake in one of the fragmented Realities. If I had to guess, I'd say Chu destroyed one of the training tunnels in order to wink them out. That glass is particularly resistant to Barrier Wands."

"But how would he do that?" Rutger asked.

"Well . . . that brings us to our next item of discussion." George looked over at Sato. "Based on the information Sato has gathered, combined with the evidence of our spies and the disturbances we've seen this past summer, I believe Chu has built some sort of superweapon that contains more simulated Chi'karda power than anything ever built previously. I believe it's responsible for some of the odd things happening to Tick and the others, as well as for spreading the plague of insanity."

Everyone turned to look at Sato, as if he would follow this up with a brilliant statement supporting George's theory.

"Everything points to that," he said, unable to think of anything else. George had said it better than he ever could.

"We can dig more into the details later in the meeting," George continued, "but I want to put something on the table now before we say another word. It's rare that I must give an assignment as terribly important as the one I'm about to ask of Sato."

Sato's mind had been drifting, and he wasn't sure he'd heard correctly. "What was that? An assignment?"

"Yes, a mission of sorts."

Sato swallowed. He felt as if the temperature in the room had risen twenty degrees. "You want *me* to . . ." He had mentioned the possibility of sending someone to gather samples, but he'd never guessed the old man would choose *him*.

"I can think of no better Realitant for this than you, Sato. You have stealth and wit about you. Plus, no one will suspect someone so young, and if you do get in a bind, I trust your ability to get out of it."

"Wait, wait, wait," Rutger said, squirming on his booster seat. "What mission are you talking about?"

George paused before answering. "Sato and I are positive the explanation for people going crazy is some type of plague—literally. And we're quite sure it's linked to Chu's superweapon. I want to send Sato into the area most infected with this plague and obtain a blood sample from one of the victims. Until we understand the disease, we won't know how to fight it."

Sato barely heard George's words, as if they were coming down a long, dark tunnel. George wanted to send *him*. What if . . . what if he *caught* the plague?

He was perfectly willing to face danger in his quest to avenge his parents' death, but the prospect of a nasty disease that made you crazy sickened him. Frightened him.

"Are you up to it?" Mothball asked, reaching over and patting Sato's arm.

"Huh? What?" he said.

"Are you up to it, I said."

Sato looked around at the others in the room. Several beads of sweat finally let go and slid down his temples. He hadn't expected *this*.

"I . . . uh . . ." In that moment, the image of his parents burning popped into his head, and his squishy fear hardened into concrete resolve.

"I'll do it," he said, trying his best to keep his voice firm. "I'll be fine."

Sally stood up, folding his arms across his broad chest. "I reckon I'll go wid the young fella."

George shook his head. "No, Sally. I have an entirely different mission for you."

CHAPTER 22

LOTS OF LEFT TURNS

They'd been walking for hours.

This new Reality seemed the most normal of any Tick had visited so far. Aside from a few oddities, it wasn't much different from his hometown in Reality Prime. One of those differences was the style of the buildings and the clothes of the citizens. It was slight, but everything here seemed a little more elaborate, a little fancier. Many businesses had huge fountains in front, with complex displays of shooting water; the moldings on the houses had carved pictures of animals and trees. The men wore fancy dark suits and greased back their hair, and the women wore dresses with white gloves pulled clear past their elbows. Also, an eerie, operatic soprano voice sang from speakers throughout the town.

Another odd thing: the place appeared to only have left turns—at least off the road on which they currently walked.

"Dude, what's up with this?" Paul said, pointing to his right, where a thick forest of tall trees loomed like an ominous wall. "Look at all that land out there. Why aren't they building on it?"

"Who cares?" Sofia said, annoyance creeping back into her voice. "Maybe they're a bunch of idiots."

Tick understood her mood. Even though the weather was pleasant here—partly cloudy sky, soft breeze, warm but not hot—he felt like they were going nowhere fast. Not to mention the sick feeling he still had from almost being trampled by a raging monster inside a gigantic glass straw.

Paul yawned. "Just seems a little weird that there's this huge town to our left, but nothing at all to our right. We should open a real estate office."

Sofia ignored him. "Well, our plan to stay on this road isn't working. I say we go into the city."

"Me too," Tick agreed. "Everything is starting to look the same—I swear I saw that exact building a couple of hours ago." He pointed to a tall office complex made of dark granite with shiny, black windows that sparkled as if inlaid with gold.

"Whoa," Paul said, stopping.

"What?" Tick and Sofia asked at the same time.

"That building doesn't just look familiar—it *is* the same one we saw earlier. I'm positive. Man, this road is a ginormous circle that goes *around* the city. No wonder we're not getting anywhere."

"That explains all the left turns," Tick added.

"I thought we were all supposed to be smart," Sofia said. "It took us *how* long to figure this out?"

"Come on," Paul said. "Let's go into the town and find a sweet old lady who's willing to feed some starving kids."

Right on cue, Tick's stomach rumbled with hunger. "Hope our money works here."

"I doubt it, but we can try," Paul said.

At the next road, they turned left, the wall of trees now at their backs.

～

Reginald looked down at the weasely little hotel owner of Circle City, rocking between his two feet, fidgeting with the buttons on his fancy red vest. Chu was astonished that someone could show so much weakness in front of another grown man. His name was Phillip, and he couldn't be more than five feet tall, fat, with streaks of black hair pasted in greasy lines across his obviously bald head.

Ah, yes. The comb-over. Delightful. Reginald swore

that if he ever went bald, he'd simply invent a way to make his hair grow back. *Hmm,* he thought. *I can't believe I haven't done that yet . . .*

"What do I get out of all this?" Phillip said, his voice sounding to Reginald like a talking rat high on helium. "And how do I find the kids?"

"They're in the city. Three young teenagers—a Caucasian with brown hair, a girl with black hair, and a dark-skinned boy who's a full foot taller than you and ten times as handsome. They'll be wandering around, obviously lost, smelling like a bag of three-week-old tuna—the brats haven't showered in days."

Frankly, Reginald was annoyed that Atticus still had the other two kids with him. He'd hoped they'd have been killed by now, but they seemed as determined as their powerful friend. No matter. That was the beauty of the test—there were no rules, not really. If Atticus made it to the end, he made it to the end. Even if he had the help of friends and the Realitants.

Realitants. What a waste of human DNA.

"All right," Phillip said. "I'll send out my boys to find them, bring them here, offer them rooms, as you said."

"And feed them. They'll be here at least a week, probably longer. I want the boy—I mean, I want *all* of them—well-rested and strong for what lies ahead. I will pay you double your rates, plus a bonus."

"What kind of bonus?" The hotel owner tried his very best to display an expression of professional hard-ball on his face, but it looked more like a fat squirrel eyeing an acorn.

Reginald stifled a laugh. "The value of one week's worth of rent for all your rooms."

Phillip choked, his eyes wide with the prospect of such a sum for doing almost nothing. "I'll have to think about—"

"Shut up and take the deal," Reginald said.

Phillip nodded, his face flushed red. "Okay, it's a deal. I'll have them here, safe and sound, by tonight."

"Good." Reginald reached into his pocket and pulled out two sealed envelopes, then handed them over. "The thick one is half your money, including the bonus, plus money for the kids to spend. You'll get the rest of your portion when they . . . disappear."

"And this other one?" The hotel owner held up the thin envelope.

"I want you to deliver that to them at precisely six o'clock. If you can't get them to the hotel before then, wait until morning to deliver it. I don't care if it's AM or PM, just give it to them at *six* o'clock."

Phillip's eyes squinched up in confusion.

"Don't ask any more questions," Reginald said. "Just do as I say and enjoy the money."

After giving Phillip a few more instructions, Reginald turned and walked away, enjoying himself and his clever ways even more than usual.

⁓

"All right," Paul said as they passed a small group of kids playing a version of soccer with a square ball. "I've known for a while that *you* guys stink, but now I can smell *myself.* I don't care if it's in one of those fancy fountains—I need to get clean."

Tick lifted up his arm and smelled his armpit. "We do stink. Dude."

"I don't," Sofia said. "But I'm starving."

"I'm glad you think you smell so nice," Paul said, stopping to study Sofia up and down. "What's your secret?"

Sofia halted as well, folding her arms and returning the stare. "I don't sweat."

"You don't sweat?" Paul looked over at Tick. "She doesn't sweat, Tick. Now I've heard everything." He continued walking toward the center of town, shaking his head.

Nothing much had changed since they'd left the border road and headed deeper into the city. The buildings had gotten a little bigger with fewer pillars and less frilly decoration; apartments and condos had replaced the extravagant neighborhood homes. The sun had sunk lower in the sky, the darkened glow of twilight fast approaching. None of the people they passed paid them much mind, despite their dirty clothes and haggard appearance. Everyone seemed extremely busy—all made up and pressed clean.

"Look up there," Sofia said, pointing straight ahead.

Less than a quarter-mile ahead of them, twelve roads came together like spokes of a wheel, intersecting in a huge open-air mall where hundreds of people milled about. Tick realized something, and he couldn't believe he hadn't noticed it before.

"Where are all the cars?" he asked.

Sofia and Paul stopped, as if stunned by the simple question.

Paul snapped his fingers. "I knew something was missing. We haven't seen a single car."

"That doesn't make sense," Sofia said. "There's nothing primitive about this place. If anything, it seems a little more advanced than our reality."

"Ah, dude," Paul said. "What if they beam around like in *Star Trek?*"

Sofia snorted. "I'll be sure to ask Dark Gator if I see him."

Paul burst out laughing; Tick held his laugh in, pressing his mouth closed.

"What?" Sofia said.

"What did you call him?" Paul asked.

"Dark Gator."

"Man, oh, man, you are too good to be true, Miss Italy, too good to be true." Still chuckling, he walked toward all the people. "I think I see a restaurant up there. Let's check it out."

Sofia looked at Tick, her eyebrows raised.

"It's Darth *Vader*," he whispered. "And he's from *Star Wars*, not *Star Trek*."

"Well, they both sound stupid," she concluded, then followed Paul.

The mall was a collection of all sorts of shops and eateries, surround by a broad expanse of inlaid bricks. The three of them stopped to see which restaurant looked most appetizing—assuming, of course, they accepted Reality Prime money. Tick's hopes were rising, because this place had some of the same fast-food chains as back home—their logos were just slightly different.

"Ooh, look—" Tick started to say, but a man stopped him by pulling on his elbow. Tick looked behind him to see a short, fidgety man with the worst comb-over Tick had ever seen.

"Excuse me," the man said, his face breaking into a smile that would have looked more natural on a rattlesnake. "Is your name, er, Atticus Higginbottom?"

Tick didn't know what he'd expected the man to say, but his mouth dropped open and his heart started thumping.

"Um," he said, looking over at his friends to see if

they'd heard. By the stunned looks on their faces, he figured they had. He turned back to the man. "Yeah, I'm Tick, I mean, Atticus."

"That's great, real great," the man said, more relieved than happy. "Someone named, um, Mothball asked me to find you and offer you rooms in my hotel, The Stroke of Midnight Inn. My name is Phillip, and I'm happy to accommodate you."

Then he bowed. He actually *bowed*.

Tick felt immediately suspicious, and it only took a second for him to see his friends felt the same.

"Mothball sent you?" Sofia asked.

"Why didn't she come herself?" Paul added.

Phillip pulled his head back, looking like a startled—albeit pudgy—chicken. "I don't know—why would I make something like that up?"

"What does she look like?" Tick asked.

The man didn't hesitate. "She's very tall—the tallest person I've ever laid eyes on. Black hair, thin, not very . . . well, what I mean to say is . . . well, she's a bit homely, to be honest."

"A-plus on that quiz," Paul muttered, and Tick felt himself relax a little.

"She said you'd be staying here for a week or so," Phillip continued. "She paid me in advance and asked me to provide you three meals a day, plus whatever else you might need."

The prospect of a nice hotel room, a hot shower, and all the food he could eat sounded to Tick like the single best idea in the history of best ideas.

"Good enough for me," Paul said. "Where do we go?"

"Wait a minute," Sofia said, holding out her hand. "There has to be something else. There's no message, no reason, nothing? I don't like this."

"Actually," Phillip said, "she did leave you an envelope. It's sealed, so of course I don't know its contents. Oddly enough, she asked me to give it to you at exactly six o'clock." He looked at his watch. "Um, tomorrow morning."

Tick looked at his own watch—it was just past six-thirty. "Sounds pretty legit to me. I actually feel a ton better—like maybe Master George is behind all of this after all."

"Yeah," Paul agreed. "Let's go eat."

Sofia didn't answer at first, her eyes distant as she thought it over. "Where's the hotel?" she finally asked.

"Right this way," Phillip said, stepping aside and sweeping his arm wide. "If you'll follow me, it's on the edge of town. In fact, I've reserved rooms for you with a great view."

As Phillip led the group north along the road, Paul asked, "A view of what?"

"The forest, of course," Phillip said without missing a

step. "If you look out your window after dark, you might see the glowing monkeys."

Tick waited for the man to laugh, but the only one who did was Paul. Tick almost asked if he'd been serious, but with everyone else silent, he felt stupid for even thinking it. Of course the guy was kidding. Wasn't he?

CHAPTER 23

THE TIME RIDDLE

The hotel was like something out of Hollywood. Big pillars, stamped gold everywhere, doormen in green velvet coats running around, treating their guests like royalty. A huge sign hung above the entrance with *The Stroke of Midnight Inn* written in fancy script. Inside, everything sparkled and shone, and not a person in sight had a grimace or the slightest hint of a frown. Plush red carpet blanketed the floors and grand staircase, over which an enormous chandelier hung with hundreds of crystalline lights.

I've died and gone to heaven, Tick thought.

He knew Paul must feel the same, but Sofia would

surely find something to complain about, having come from such a rich family.

Phillip led them to the fourth floor—walking up the stairs, the poor man sucked in huge gasps of breath with every step—and down a long hallway to their rooms. When Paul asked him why they hadn't used the elevator, Phillip responded with a baffled look, as if he'd never heard of such a thing.

Phillip opened up a room with an old-fashioned key. Tick was surprised since he'd only ever seen the magnetic-stripe key card at hotels. The room was filled with normal hotel things: a king-sized bed, a small refrigerator, a couch, a desk, and a bathroom. The only difference was that the items were ten times nicer than the stuff in hotels Tick had been in when his family traveled.

"There are three rooms in all," Phillip announced, passing out keys accordingly. "There's a menu on the desk for you to order food from the restaurant. Please be reasonable, but make sure you feed yourself nicely. Is there anything—"

"Where's the TV?" Paul asked.

Phillip gave him that same bewildered look, his brow crunched up into dozens of wrinkles. "A TV? What's that?"

"Television. You know—movies, shows, commercials, *television?*"

"Sorry, I don't know what you're talking about."

Tick looked at the light on the wall, which Phillip had turned on when they'd entered the room. They obviously had electricity here, but seemed to be missing a lot of other things common to Reality Prime.

As if reading his mind, Sofia asked, "Where are all the cars?"

Phillip put his hands in his pockets, his confused look morphing into suspicion. "Cars have been banned for at least twenty years."

"Banned?" Tick asked. "Why?"

"And how do you get around?" Paul asked before Phillip could respond.

The hotel man shook his head, looking at his three guests in turn. "When that . . . when Mothball made me this deal, I didn't realize she'd be sending such odd people. Where are you kids from?"

"Florida," Paul answered. "Well, originally from California—"

Sofia cut him off. "It doesn't matter. But we're curious about the cars. Where we come from, they still use them."

"The darn things were polluting us to death," Phillip said, still appearing uneasy as he rocked back and forth on his feet. "So they banned them, made towns where everything was in walking distance. If you want to visit another town, you take the Underground Railroad—

named after the lady who escaped the slave drivers a long time ago—the one who became president, Harrietta Tubben."

Tick and Sofia exchanged baffled looks.

"So you've got trains, underground?" Paul asked.

"Fastest ones in the world," Phillip answered, eyeing the door. "If there's nothing else . . ."

"Thanks for letting us stay here," Tick said, liking the idea of seeing Phillip leave and finally ordering some food. "Don't forget to bring us that message from Mothball."

"I won't, I won't," the man assured them, already backing out the door into the hallway. "Order a nice dinner and get some rest."

Tick closed the door before the last word made it all the way out of Phillip's mouth.

"Well," Sofia said, "this place is just like home compared to the last Reality—desert, glass tunnel, raging beast."

"All I care about right now is food," Paul said. He'd already picked up the phone to call room service.

⁓

Later that night, his stomach stuffed with roasted duck and asparagus (they didn't have pizza or hamburgers in this place), fully showered and clean, Tick lay in his bed and stared at the ceiling. Every ounce of his body begged for sleep, his mind deadened with exhaustion. And yet, he remained awake.

Man, I have a weird life.

He'd lost track of how long they'd been gone—it seemed like a month, but he knew it was only a few days, maybe a week at most. He knew his mom and dad were back home, worry eating at them like ferrets trapped in their gut, trying to stay chipper for Lisa and Kayla. Tick wished he could send them a message, talk to them somehow. Just to let them know he was okay.

A hard knock at his door made him jump. Crumpling up the sheets in his bed, he wiggled into a sitting position, his back pressed against the wall. He stared at the small space under the door, where two small shadows marked someone's feet.

"Who is it?" he called out, embarrassed at how shaky his voice sounded to his own ears.

"It's me, sleepyhead," Paul replied, the words muffled through the wood.

Tick sighed with relief as he threw the covers aside. He hurried over and opened the door. Sofia was behind Paul, her eyes puffy with sleep. Each of them wore fancy-looking flannel pajamas provided by the hotel, and Sofia's looked about three sizes too big.

"What's going on?" Tick asked.

"Dude, have you looked out the window?" Paul stepped into the room, pushing past Tick.

"Um, no." Tick stepped aside to let Sofia in, then closed the door. He flicked on the light, but Paul quickly waved his hand at him.

"No, dude, turn it off!"

Tick did as he was told, grumbling a little. All he wanted right now was to be left alone and sleep for days. He felt so tired and his body hurt like he had the flu. The only light in the room was a mysterious panel on the wall that shone a dull yellow. Something about it gave Tick the creeps.

Paul leaned next to the window, carefully pulling aside the curtains to peek through the corner, as if spying on someone in the parking lot. Tick faltered as he joined Paul—this place didn't *have* a parking lot.

"What are you looking at?" Tick asked.

Sofia knelt at the other end of the window, lifting that corner of the curtains to peer out. The two of them looked ridiculous.

"Santy Claus," Paul whispered. "What do you *think* we're looking at?"

"I don't know—that's why I asked."

Sofia turned toward Tick, the disgusted look on her face barely discernible in the faint light. "The glowing monkeys."

"Oh, yeah!" Tick couldn't believe he'd not even looked—a sign that his brain had gone to sleep even though his body had refused. He squatted on the floor between his friends and slowly lifted the bottom of the curtain to take a peek.

Outside, the dark forest stood like a fortress wall, massive trees silhouetted by the pale moonlight seeping through the thick clouds above. The city behind the hotel had a surprising lack of nighttime lights, making Tick feel like they were in a cabin deep in the wilderness. And there in the woods, radiant and eerie and constantly in motion, dozens of creepy glowing shapes moved about the trees.

"Those don't look like monkeys," Tick whispered. When he'd heard the word *glowing*, he'd imagined his old skeleton Halloween decoration back home, which appeared as a whitish-yellowish blur in the darkness. But this light was much different. This light was bright and stark and reddish, and the creatures looked a lot bigger than monkeys. "They look more like . . . radioactive bears."

"Yeah," Paul whispered back. "Demon bears."

"Why are you guys whispering?" Sofia said, so loud that both Tick and Paul quickly shushed her. "What? You think those things will come and eat us? I'm pretty sure the hotel would've gone out of business if their customers were routinely eaten by monkeys whenever they spoke louder than a whisper."

"I don't know," Paul said, still in a low voice. "Just seems like you should whisper when spying on monstrous, glowing creatures. So be quiet."

"Pansy," Sofia muttered, returning to the window.

Paul reached over and elbowed Tick. "Did you teach her that word?"

"No."

"She's getting way too American—makes me uncomfortable."

Sofia tsked. "I love it when you guys talk about me as if I can't hear you."

"What do you think those things are?" Tick asked, trying to steer the conversation in a different direction before Paul ended up getting punched again.

"I bet it has something to do with the ban on cars," Sofia said. "Something really weird happened here. Maybe it affected the animals. Maybe they *are* radioactive."

"Remind me not to go on a walk out there tomorrow after breakfast," Paul said.

Tick let the curtain fall into place and leaned back against the bed. "That's enough monkey-watching for me. Phillip's bringing us that message from Mothball in just a few hours. We need some sleep."

"How can you sleep with psycho-radioactive-gorilla-bears playing outside your window?" Paul asked, his nose seemingly glued to the glass.

"I think I'll manage. Get out."

Surprisingly, Sofia grumbled more than Paul did as Tick kicked them out of his room.

~

The next morning, Phillip didn't pound the door nearly as hard as Paul had done just a few hours earlier. At first, the light tapping came in the form of a woodpecker in Tick's dream, one where he sat in the backyard laughing while his dad jumped about trying to put out flames on the barbecue. It happened every time the man made hamburgers, which is why Tick always made sure he had a front-row seat.

A woodpecker had never been there, however, and even in his dream, Tick knew something was wrong. When it kept knocking and pecking and tapping, he somehow pulled himself out of sleep. With groggy eyes and cottonmouth, he got out of bed and stumbled to the door, sad that the dream had been interrupted.

Phillip wore the exact same clothes as he had yesterday, still rocking back and forth on his feet. He handed over a yellow envelope—one that looked very familiar to Tick, who snatched it without meaning to.

"Sorry," he said. "Just eager to read it."

"Are you finding your stay pleasant?" Phillip asked, no emotion or sincerity in his voice whatsoever.

"Yes, we really appreciate it," Tick said, unable to

take his eyes off the envelope, which bore no marking or writing. When he finally looked up, Phillip had already begun walking down the hall toward the stairs.

Thoughts of the odd man quickly evaporated as Tick hurried to knock on Paul's door. It took three tries, but Paul finally answered, rubbing his eyes.

"Come on," Tick urged, heading next door to Sofia's room.

He'd just held up his hand to knock when the door flew open, Sofia waiting there—fully dressed in her newly provided clothes and looking surprisingly pretty. "Did you get the note?"

Tick held up the envelope.

"Then get in here and let's open it," she said, stepping aside and almost comically jerking her head toward the inside.

Tick entered and sat in the desk chair, with Paul looking over his right shoulder, Sofia his left. With slightly trembling hands, Tick opened the envelope and pulled out a piece of white cardstock paper. With the others following along, he read the typed words out loud:

This place is nice, but not quite
  heaven.
You must start on the hour of seven
Add six hours then take away three,
Then add ten more and do it with glee.

Let one week of time go by,
Sit and rest and eat and sigh.
Then twenty-two hours less three
 plus two,
At that time decide what to do.
It does not matter; I do not care.
Just make sure your feet find air.

"It's easy," Sofia said.

"Yeah, too easy," Paul agreed. "Which means we're in deep trouble."

Tick shook his head. "It'll be easy to figure out the time, but there's nothing that tells us what to do *at* that time."

"Yowza," Paul said, then whistled. "You're dead on. What are we supposed to do at five in the afternoon one week from tomorrow?"

Tick jerked his head around to look up at Paul. "You already figured it out?"

"I told you it was easy." He slapped Tick on the shoulder. "Don't worry, little dude, not everyone can be as brilliant as the Paulmeister."

Sofia snorted. "I figured it out, too, Einstein."

Tick quickly ran through the riddle in his head. Sure enough—5:00 PM, one week from tomorrow.

"A whole week?" he said. "What are we supposed to do until then?"

"I'll tell you what we do," Paul said, flopping onto the small couch and sticking his feet up on the armrest. "What my grandpa calls a little R and R."

Sofia walked over and slapped Paul's feet to the floor, almost knocking his whole body off the couch.

"If you ever did that in my house, my butler would chop off one of your toes." She sat next to him, ignoring his stuck-out tongue. "It does sound good to relax for a while, but we'd better start thinking hard about what's hidden in that message."

"Yeah," Tick said. "What happens if five o'clock rolls around and we don't do what we're supposed to?"

His only answer was a very long silence.

CHAPTER 24

AN INSANE MISSION

Sato adjusted the straps on his backpack, pulling them tight so they wouldn't rub blisters on his skin. It was heavy, Mothball and Rutger having gone overboard as usual to make sure he had everything he needed.

"What did you put in here?" he asked. They stood by the window overlooking the Grand Canyon, the early streams of sunrise reflecting off the sheer stone walls with a reddish glow. "Some bricks in case I need to build a house?"

Mothball laughed. "Methinks you've a sense of humor after all, Sato." She reached down and tousled the hair on Rutger's head. "Almost as funny as this one, 'ere."

Rutger huffed. "He only seems funny because he's the world's biggest grouch. Anything slightly different pops out of his mouth, and everyone laughs like he's Bojinkles the Clown."

"Who?" Sato asked.

Rutger slapped his hands to his face. "Who? *Who?*" He stomped his right foot. "Don't tell me you haven't heard of Bojinkles! Oh, how he made me chuckle when I'd read him in the funny parcels as a kid . . ."

His voice wandered off as he stared at something through the window, seemingly lost in childhood memories. Sato and Mothball exchanged a look, both of them stifling a laugh.

Just then, George entered the room, his face flushed like he'd been running a race. He held a Barrier Wand in one hand, so sparkly and shiny it appeared brand-new.

"Ah!" he said. "Looks like Master Sato is all set and ready to go."

George stepped in front of Sato, inspecting him like he was a soldier going off to war. Sato still felt confused inside, his mind and heart full of swirling, haunted images and feelings. He'd grown to trust George and the others, had grown to accept his role as a Realitant. He'd especially solidified his resolve to avenge the murder of his parents.

And yet . . . for so many years, the man before him had represented all the terrible things in his life.

George had been there that day. Why hadn't he saved his parents?

"Ready as I'll ever be," Sato said, momentarily closing his eyes to squeeze away his ill thoughts.

"Splendid," George said, taking a step back so he could look at the three of them. "Our dear friend Sally is off, too. He, er, didn't want to say good-bye because of, er, well, you know—what we did to his hair to disguise him. The old chap's surprisingly vain about his looks after all."

"Well, I *do* know how he feels," Rutger said, smoothing his black hair.

George turned to Sato, his face serious, squinting as if he couldn't quite focus on Sato's face. "Are you *certain* about this?"

"I'm doing this for my parents."

George nodded absentmindedly. "Yes, yes, indeed. Your bravery would make them proud."

Sato fumed inside. He wanted to scream at the old man, blame him for their deaths. But he stayed silent, channeling his thoughts into the task at hand.

"The needle and vials are in the outer pocket of your pack," Rutger said. "They're bubble-wrapped for protection, but please be careful. You have only a couple of extras."

George grunted, but Sato wasn't sure what that meant. "We want you to get in and get out. You'll be winking to the original Reality, the . . . *host* Reality where all of this nonsense began. It's not one of the major branches, and it's fragmenting as we speak. Still not sure of the event that was so powerful as to make them completely unstable." He shook his head. "I need not remind you of the necessity of caution."

"In and out," Sato said, staring at the wall in front of him. An old picture of Muffintops hung there, a close-up from when she was a kitten, licking something that looked suspiciously like George's foot. "The first crazy person I meet. No problem."

Rutger cleared his throat. "It might not be *that* easy. Most people won't let you walk up and stick a needle in them."

"'Specially the crazies," Mothball added.

"Then I'll use the . . . thing you gave me." Sato jerked his head toward the top of his backpack.

"Only as a last resort," George said, holding up a finger. "A last resort."

Sato shrugged. "Last resort. What does it matter—they're all crazy."

"It matters because we're trying to *save* them, find a cure," George answered.

"But it's a fragmented Reality," Sato countered. "Again, what does it matter?"

George shook his head. "It's not our place to determine the value of their lives, Master Sato. They're people, just like you and me."

"Chances are one of 'em *is* you, actually," Mothball said with a quick snort of a laugh. When no one responded, she continued, "His Alterant. Get it?"

"Yes, Mothball, we got it," Rutger muttered as he shot a look at Sato as if to say, *just humor her.* "Good one, very funny."

As for Sato, his head spun; it was impossible to wrap his rational mind around the confusing facts of how the multiverse functioned. "I'm ready. Wink me away."

George held up the Barrier Wand in both hands. "You'll appear on the stone outcropping of a mountain; it's soaked in Chi'karda, for reasons we don't know. Return there when you've obtained the blood sample. Rutger will have his eyes glued to the command console and will wink you back the instant you're ready. Your nanolocator is in good working condition."

"Okay," Sato said, taking a deep breath as he reached out and clasped his hands around the bottom of the golden cylinder. *Just do it before I change my mind.*

"Best of lu—" Mothball started to say, but she was cut off with the click of the Wand ignition button.

Sato winked away.

⟳

"Mmm, this rabbit food ain't so bad," Paul mumbled through a bite of fancy salad—walnuts and pears scattered over dark green leaves.

They sat at a table in the hotel restaurant, the last gloomy glow of sunset painting the large windows a sleepy amber. They'd spent most of the day walking, making three complete trips around the main road that circled the town—aptly named Circle City. They saw nothing new—more buildings, more nicely-dressed people, more glittering fountains, more eerie opera music—as they discussed the riddle and the possible hidden meaning behind it between long bouts of silence.

"This Reality must not have an Italy," Sofia said. "Nothing on the menu even comes close to real food."

Tick nodded, too busy eating to say anything. He'd ordered something he couldn't pronounce but which looked and tasted like pork chops, and he was loving every bite. Sofia, stubborn as usual, hadn't even ordered yet, still staring at the menu like an impossible homework problem.

"Just get the chicken stuff," Paul said, wiping his mouth. "They eat chicken in Italy, don't they?"

"Well . . ." Sofia said, her eyes focusing on one item. "This one does have some kind of cheese on it."

"Really?" Paul said, leaning over to take a look at where her finger pointed. "Chicken and cheese. I'm getting that next time."

Tick quit listening to them, having noticed a strange man enter the restaurant, looking about as if he was lost. He was heavily built, head shaved bald, and dressed in a suit as fancy as any Tick had ever seen worn by Master George. The man's eyes finally fell on Tick and his friends, and he started walking directly for them, stumbling twice in his polished new shoes.

"Uh-oh," Tick whispered. When Paul and Sofia looked at him, he nodded toward the stranger.

"Who's that guy?" Paul asked.

Tick only shrugged.

When the man reached their table, he bowed awkwardly. "Good . . . day," he said very slowly, taking time to carefully pronounce each word. "I . . . welcome . . . you . . . to . . . our . . . city."

He bowed again, then turned to walk away. As he took his first step, he reached into his pocket, pulled out a slip of paper, and let it fall to the floor. It was such an obvious act that none of them called it to the man's attention. He kept moving, continuing in his halting gait until he'd left the restaurant, never once turning around to look back.

Paul practically jumped onto the floor to pick up the paper, then unfolded it on the table. Tick and Sofia scooted their chairs around to see the message:

> DO NOT READ THIS ALOUD!
> I'm a friend of Master George.
> Meet me in Tick's room at 9:00.

Don't say a word to me.
We must communicate in writing.
People are listening.

⟳

The first thing Sato felt was frigid air, gusting in short bursts of wind that bit through his clothes, pricking his skin like dagger points. Feeling as if he'd just plunged into an icy lake, he gasped for air as he swung off his backpack and searched for the thick down coat within. As he pulled it out and stuffed his arms inside the soft, warm lining, he gaped at the place George had decided to send him.

The highest reaches of an enormous mountain, blanketed in snow.

He stood near the edge of a rocky outcropping that overlooked an infinite expanse of clouds, thin peaks of smaller mountains thrusting through the cottony layer here and there, black stone frosted in white. Above him, the sky was deep and dark and blue, like an ocean hanging impossibly over him. Realizing how high up he was, Sato stumbled backward, falling into the soft snow. The world seemed to sway around him.

He scrambled up and turned his back to the cliff, brushing the snow off before the cold stuff melted and soaked through. To his left, a steep path led up the mountain, the barely visible steps of roughly cut stone glistening with ice. If that was the way he needed to go, it would be a treacherous journey. Other than a sparse bush and a few dead trees, he saw no sign of life anywhere—just endless rock and ice and snow.

Sato took a few steps to the right, hoping to see a more reasonable trail he could follow, but the jutting slice of rock ended in a sheer, knife-edge cliff, as if a recent earthquake had sent a huge chunk of the mountain falling to its splitting, crumpled death far below.

There was only one way to go.

Securing his pack, he started up the ancient stairway. He placed his feet very carefully, bracing them against the small vertical slab of stone marking the next step. Just when he thought he had the hang of it, his left foot slid backward, throwing his whole body forward; his chest slammed into a jutting edge of rock. Holding back a cry of pain, he chastised himself and took more care, leaning forward to grip the stairs above him with his hands, as if he were climbing a ladder.

The wind picked up, throwing spurts of snow into his face like cold, rough sand. The sun, though unhindered by clouds above him, failed to provide even a spark of warmth. He had to stop every few minutes to blow warm air into his cupped hands, rubbing them together to create friction. His ears and face grew numb. He looked up, hoping to see signs of life, a building, anything. Nothing.

He kept going, step by frigid step.

A half hour went by. Sato started to worry that George had made a serious mistake, sent him to an abandoned nowhere by accident.

"George," he spoke aloud, though the wind seemed to snap his words out of the air and whisk them away. "If you can hear me through the nanolocator—what's going on? I'm freezing to death!"

Half-hoping he'd be winked away, Sato kept moving up the stairs.

Forty or fifty steps later, he finally saw the end of the staircase—a place where the stone stopped and all was white, a wall of snow and ice reaching for the sky. His heart sank at the thought that he might've reached a dead end.

Legs burning, limbs aching, skin frozen, he reached the uppermost step, which led out onto a small landing that faced a solid wall of dark granite, crystalline icicles hanging from the brief canopy of rock that protected it. In the middle of the wall was an iron door, ridges of rusty bolts lined around its outer edges. On the door was a sign, faded letters barely legible in the awful weather conditions.

Sato took a few steps forward to read the sign, his eyes squinted. They widened when he realized what it said:

End of the Road Insane Asylum
Mountaintop Exit
To Be Used for the Execution
of Inmates Only

CHAPTER 25

COTTON EARS

No one said a word, their eyes glancing at the clock every few seconds. In eight minutes, it would be nine o'clock—when they expected the visitor.

Tick sat on the bed, his back resting on a stack of pillows he'd pushed against the wall. In his mind, he'd been picturing the stranger who'd dropped off the note, trying to decide if they'd ever met. There was something vaguely familiar about him, but all Tick could remember was how strange the man acted, sounding out each word and looking about nervously.

Three minutes to go.

"What do you think—" Paul whispered, but Sofia punched him on the arm, then made a slashing gesture at her neck. Paul winced as he rubbed his shoulder.

They'd been dying to talk about the note since dinner, but paranoia kept their mouths shut—except for the occasional slipup from Paul. The stranger's message said people were listening, and now Tick couldn't sneeze without wondering what the snoopers might think. If the note was even true in the first place.

A barely discernible click sounded as the big hand on the old-fashioned clock struck nine. All three of them turned their heads toward the room's door, as if expecting the stranger to walk in precisely on time. He didn't.

Several minutes went by with no sign of their visitor. Paul finally got out of his chair and paced the floor, shaking his head and mumbling something under his breath. He stopped at the desk and wrote a few words on the pad of paper provided by the hotel, then tore the piece off and showed it to Sofia. She shrugged, and then Paul brought it over to Tick.

Don't we seem suspicious sitting here and not saying anything?

Tick nodded, but didn't know what else they could do. If people were really spying on them, they'd certainly be alarmed at how silent their prey had become.

I wish the guy would just hurry up and get here, Tick thought.

Paul sat back down in his chair. A few more minutes passed. A shadow crossed over the small slit under the door, catching Tick's attention out of the corner of his eye. He shifted on the bed and put his feet on the floor, leaning forward, expecting to hear a knock.

Nothing.

Tick exchanged questioning looks with Paul and Sofia, then got up and walked over to the door. It didn't have a peephole, so Tick reached forward and slowly pushed down on the lever handle. A loud *click* filled the room like a clap of thunder; he squeezed his eyes shut, not even sure what he was afraid of.

After a few seconds of silence, he jerked the door open and looked into the hallway, ready to slam it shut again at any sign of trouble.

The stranger from the restaurant sat on the red-carpeted floor, his back against the opposite wall. He still wore the dark suit, his shoes so shiny that the hallway light reflected off them and into Tick's eyes. As soon as he saw Tick, he put his right index finger to his lips—a reminder they weren't supposed to talk.

Feeling uneasy, but unsure what else they could do, Tick stepped back and opened the door wide, gesturing with a sweep of his arm that the stranger should come in. The large man—bald head and all—got to his feet and entered the room, giving a quick nod to Paul and Sofia. Tick closed the door as quietly as he could.

The man sat on the bed, waving for the others to come and stand around him. As Tick and his friends obeyed, the stranger pulled out a photograph, a few pieces of paper, and a ballpoint pen. He'd already written one note and handed it to Tick along with the picture. In it, the man stood with Master George in front of the fireplace at the Grand Canyon Realitant complex, both of them with wide smiles; Muffintops perched on the mantle behind Master George's right shoulder.

The message was clear: they could trust the guy.

Paul and Sofia crowded closer as they read the note together:

> Your nanolocators done been hijacked.
> And this hotel is bugged like a bugger.
> It's not Master George winking
> you willy-nilly. Reginald Chu is behind
> everything.
> You MUST keep passing that
> sucker's tests.

At first, Tick felt like he was reading Spanish or French or Chinese—the words didn't click inside his brain. Such a monumental statement surely couldn't be said in a quickly scribbled note. He looked at the stranger, knowing his face showed the confusion he felt.

Master George's friend rolled his eyes and wrote another message, hastily scratching the paper with the pen. Then he held it up for them to read:

You've been under the control of
Reginald Chu all along. He's testing you.
Not Master George.
    It's Chu—it's all been Chu.

Something shuddered in Tick's chest; the room swayed. Losing his balance, he stumbled backward, falling into the chair where Paul had been sitting earlier.

Everything they'd just been through . . . the pain they'd felt in the forest, the riddles, the metaspides, the weird tunnel with its beast? All of it had been orchestrated by *Reginald Chu?* They'd suspected all along it wasn't Master George, but Chu? The man Rutger called the most evil in the universe?

"How—" Sofia said, then snapped her lips closed.

Tick felt like he was watching from a distance, the room still spinning. He kept picturing Mr. Chu, his science teacher, appearing in the woods, filthy and acting crazy. Had that really been him? Or had it been *Reginald* Chu from the Fourth Reality? Were they Alterants of each other? Was it possible they were the same person?

When Tick had been a small boy, he'd fallen off a ride at the water park, dozens of feet in the air. If he hadn't landed on the pile of large rafting tubes, he would have smacked into the cement and been one dead kid. It had taken him weeks to get over that "too close for comfort" feeling.

That was exactly how he felt now. To know they'd come so close to being killed by the metaspides and the tunnel monster scared him. What if they hadn't figured out the name of the pub where they escaped by sitting in that chair? What if they'd left the red square in the glass tube? How would things have turned out if they'd *known* someone so sinister was behind it all?

Tick leaned back in his chair, staring at the stranger on the bed as if the man could read his thoughts, expecting him to answer everything.

The man nodded, seeming to understand the shocking news he'd brought. He scribbled a few sentences on another piece of paper then handed it to Sofia. Tick and Paul leaned over to see:

> By the way, I thought you'd done recognized me. It's Sally—ain't my shaved head a beaut? Don't worry, I'll explain purtin' near everything. But you gotta trust me for a minute.

As soon as Tick read it, he knew it was true. The guy sitting on the bed was Sally, head and beard shaved, dressed in disguise. But the thing that made Tick's mouth drop open was the realization that *Sally* was a Realitant.

"You've gotta be kidding—" Paul whispered. He stopped when Sally shook his head curtly, holding a finger to his lips again.

Sally stood, holding his hands out, palms forward as if to say, *Hold on—give me a second.* Then he reached into the inner pocket of his suit coat and pulled out a small white box—the type in which you'd expect to find a necklace or bracelet, laid out all nice and pretty on a piece of velvet. He knelt down on the floor, placing the box gingerly on the bed, eyeing it like a ticking bomb he needed to disarm.

Paul elbowed Tick, then raised his eyebrows. Tick shrugged and quickly looked back.

Sally reached over and pulled off the top of the box, scooting as far back as he could.

Something shot out of the box and into the air— Tick lost track of it before he could tell what it was. An odd thump filled the air, like the sound of a distant thunderclap. Tick reached up and rubbed his ears; they felt like someone had stuffed cotton balls in them. He heard a faint buzz, like static on the radio.

Sally stood up, folded his arms, then grinned with satisfaction.

"Finally! Dadgum thing actually worked," he said. "George ain't never failed before—I reckon one of these

days I'll quit doubtin' the old feller. But I didn't wanna whip that sucker out 'til you knew who I was. We can talk now."

Tick didn't say a word—neither did his friends. The last few minutes had been so strange, so . . . *weird,* what were they *supposed* to say?

Sally laughed, a deep rumble that Tick swore shook the building. "You three look as twitterpated as a coon done found itself fallen in the outhouse bucket. Right diddly-widdly, I ain't never seen such a sight before. What ya'll a-feared of? I had to play dress-up so Chu wouldn't get all suspicious-like. Spies and such about, ya know."

Still, none of them responded. Tick blinked, then swallowed. Then he blinked again.

"Snap out of it!" Sally roared. "We ain't got no time to sit here throwin' peepeyes. I got to hurry and gets myself on outta here."

Sofia was the first one to speak. "It's just, well, we didn't . . . we didn't know you were a Realitant."

"Not to mention the news you just dropped in our laps," Paul added. "I think I'm gettin' too old for this stuff."

"Nonsense," Sally said, sitting on the bed and crossing his legs. As soon as he did, he winced and put both feet back on the floor. "Never did get how dem fancy lads like George sit that way. Yipes."

The static-laced buzzing sound still filled the air; Tick rubbed his ears again. "Why is it okay to talk now? What was in the box?"

Sally huffed. "Boy, you think I got da first nary a clue what dat dang thing was? Round dem Realitant parts, I'm known for my brawn and grits-cookin', not much on da brains. Ol' George said pop that sucker open—called it a dang ol' airborne nano whatchamerbucket—and we can talk. I done did it, and here I sit, talkin' my silly head off, and we ain't got nowhere fast."

Tick took a deep breath before he'd realized it—a sigh of relief. Maybe the world wasn't over after all.

"Sounds like you have a lot to tell us," Sofia said.

Sally nodded. "Reckon so. Good gravy on raw beef, I ain't got a clue where to git to start yappin' on."

Tick felt like he understood about one third of what came out of Sally's mouth, but he liked him all the same. "Just start from the beginning. How'd you find us in that weird place with the metal spiders? And what's going on with Reginald Chu?" Saying the name slammed a fist of reality back into Tick's gut, and his temporary good mood soured.

"All right, den." Sally shifted on the bed until his back was up against the wall. "Ya'll git yerselves comfy, and I'll tell ya every last bit I got in dis here noggin. Ain't much, mind ya, but listen up anyhow."

Sally started talking.

CHAPTER 26

NEEDLES

Sato didn't know what else to do—he pounded on the huge metal door of the icy alcove with his fist. A deep, hollow boom echoed down the rocky mountainside. Sato shook his hand, needles of pain vibrating through his cold skin after the impact.

No one answered at first, though Sato hadn't really expected them to. His theory that George might have made a mistake had taken root, entrenching itself deeper into his heart, sickening him. Freezing to death didn't sound like the best way to go.

But it wasn't long before something scraped on the other side of the door, followed by a loud clunk of metal against metal. Sato stepped back as the door slowly swung inward, the wind blowing wispy trails of snow into the dark interior of the mountain. He braced his feet, held his hands up in defense, not having any idea of what might lunge at him from the gloom.

"What's that?" a raspy voice called out. A pale face appeared, ghoulish with sunken cheeks, like a ghost peeking from beyond the grave. "What's that, I say?" The man's whitish eyes darted about. Sato was surprised the light from outside wasn't blinding him.

"I'm . . ." Then it hit Sato—he had absolutely no idea what to say. "I . . . my name is Sato, and I'm looking for someone."

"What's that?" the man repeated, stepping forward to reveal his whole body—rail-thin with tattered, filthy clothes hanging on by threads. His eyes still hadn't settled on Sato. "Lookin' for someone, are ya? What, you one of them Snarkies? Come to help, have you? No help for the Loons—too late for that, I can promise ya."

The initial shock of seeing an insane asylum on top of a mountain having finally worn off, Sato's hopes lifted. George had sent him to the perfect place to find people who'd gone crazy. Now, if he could just get inside, get a blood sample, and get out. But how would he know if his target patient was *normal* crazy or Reginald-Chu-plague-infected crazy?

Sato felt his courage building. "I'm looking for someone. I want to visit him. He's one of the people who got sick recently—went insane from the new plague that's been going around."

"What's that?" the man said, spittle flying from his mouth. "Plague? There's a plague about?"

"Haven't you had a lot of people brought in recently?" Sato asked, trying to fight off the shivers that racked his body.

"Don't know 'bout brought in." The man pointed to the treacherous stairs leading down the face of the mountain. "But an awful lot brought *out,* if ya catch my meanin'."

Sato turned to look at the stone steps, thinking about the man's words. The sign stated this door was for the execution of inmates—did that mean they threw them off the knife-edged cliff below? Sato felt his stomach twist.

He faced the man again. "May I *please* come in? I'm freezing to death out here."

"Right, in ya go," the poor excuse for a guard replied, stepping back and opening the door until it bumped against the stone wall inside. "Beats me how ya got here in the first place, but in ya go, nice and toasty. Lots of Loons in here—not much hope of findin' your mate, I can tell ya that. Name's Klink, by the way."

Sato stepped through the doorway, trying not to show his eagerness too much. "Nice to meet you, uh, Klink." Though *toasty* wasn't exactly the word Sato would use to describe the air inside, it sure beat the frigid bite of the outside.

Klink walked down the long, dark tunnel; Sato followed, listening, observing.

"Can't say as I've ever had a stranger knock on that door before," Klink said. "Only when the Cleaners come back after droppin' some Loons, that's all. Quite nice to have a visitor after all these years."

"They throw crazy people off that cliff down there?" Sato asked. "When they do something bad or what?"

"If they've done somethin' bad, or grown too old, or if they just need more room—whatever tickles them Cleaners' fancy. They ain't too particular when it comes to shovin' off the Loons, ya know."

They reached the end of the hallway where a small opening led through the stone to a sparsely decorated room: a floor rug, a chair, a filthy mattress. An old kerosene lamp flickered as it burned, somehow making the pathetic place look welcoming.

"Spend most of my days here," Klink said, looking around with his hands on his hips, proud of his homestead. "Beats the socks off where I used to live, that's for sure. If anyone ever offers ya to live in a cave full of flying rats, I recommend you say no thanks and move right along."

"I'll remember that," Sato half-mumbled.

"Want to sit a spell? Take a blink or two?"

Sato shook his head. "No, I feel much better now that we're inside. Could you take me to where they keep the inmates locked up? Maybe where they have the more recent ones?"

"Right, come on then," Klink said, moving along the hall again. They reached a metal grid door, which he slid open, a horrible screech piercing Sato's ears. On the other side, a boxy elevator awaited.

"This lift will take you all the way down to the Loons," Klink said as he gestured for Sato to enter. "Down ya go, then."

Sato, fighting his uneasiness, stepped inside and turned to face Klink just as the man slid the grid door shut. His pale eyes peeked through the slits.

"Best stay on your toes," Klink said.

"What do you mean?" Sato replied.

Klink reached through a large space in the door—mangled and jagged like it had been ripped out with teeth—and slammed a lever inside the lift toward the floor. The elevator lurched and slowly started going down, the squeaks and squeals of chains and pulleys filling the air.

"Didn't you know?" As Klink's body seemed to move upward, he called down to Sato just before he was out of sight. "Ent no one locked up 'round here!"

The trip down the dark elevator shaft was long and cold—especially in light of Klink's pronouncement that the crazies weren't locked up at all. Sato's stomach turned queasy from the jostling and bumping of the steel cage. He saw nothing outside the mesh of metal but black stone, heard nothing but the screech of the lift's mechanics. Impossibly, the seconds stretched into minutes, and he thought Klink surely must have sent him to the middle of the Earth.

Without any hint of slowing down, the elevator jolted to a stop, making Sato's knees buckle. He sprawled across the cold mesh floor, biting his tongue when his chin slammed into the hard surface. He quickly pushed himself back to his feet, rubbing his jaw as he stepped forward to look through the lift door.

Another dimly lit carved passageway led into the distance, no sign of anyone nearby. Having expected someone to greet him—crazy or not—he warily reached out to test the sliding door. It pushed aside easily, groaning as Sato slammed the metal mesh all the way open. The sound of the squeal echoed off the stone walls, and any doubt of his arrival was now wiped away. But still, no one came.

He stepped out of the lift, his eyes focused along the dark tunnel since that seemed to be the only place from which someone could appear. He took another step. Another.

And then he heard a scream.

It started low, an eerie moan that rose in pitch, escalating quickly on the creepy scale to a perfect ten. Sato stopped moving to listen, the hairs on his neck stiff as arrows. The sound was the wail of a lost child mixed with the terrified squeal of an animal in the butchering house. The effect of it bouncing off the walls made it seem like it was coming from every direction at once. Sato felt like getting back into the steel cage of the lift and going back up to safety.

The sound stopped, slicing silent as quickly as if someone had turned off a loud television. Shouts rang out, several voices yelling something incomprehensible—but Sato could clearly hear the anger and the *lunacy* in the voices. Sato's wariness turned into downright terror.

He closed his eyes, breathed, worked to calm himself. His heartbeat slowed; the blood in his veins stopped acting like it was trying to find a way to escape. After a full minute, he opened his eyes and took off his backpack. He rummaged around its contents until he found the packet containing the blood sample kit. There were three syringes in case one of them broke, each with a very long and nasty-looking needle covered with a plastic sheath to prevent unwanted pokes. He'd never been fond of shots, and the sight of the needles made him thankful he'd not be the one getting stuck.

Sato set the syringes on the stone floor, then looked

back at the elevator, checking to make sure he knew how it worked. Just inside the cage, the lever Klink had used jutted out of a dented box of rusty steel, slanted toward the ground.

Sato entered the elevator, gripped the lever with both hands, and lifted; he groaned and felt blood rush to his face until the lever finally gave way and snapped up. With a loud clunk the elevator started moving upward. Sato quickly slammed the switch back down. The steel cage jolted to the floor with a metallic boom.

Some escape route, he thought.

He stepped out of the elevator, slung the backpack onto his shoulders, then very carefully put two of the syringes in his left jeans pocket, making sure not to push down on them. The other he held in his right hand, gripped like a dagger, and removed the protective plastic covering. Having no idea what he was about to get into, he had to be ready for quick action. *Stab, extract, run,* he thought.

His only problem—other than perhaps being mauled to death by a bunch of crazy people—was knowing which of the asylum inmates were infected with Chu's mysterious disease and which were simply crazy. They probably wouldn't be too keen on chitchatting about it.

Blowing a breath through his lips, Sato walked forward.

CHAPTER 27

A SAMPLE OF BLOOD

ll righty den," Sally said after taking a long
swallow from his water glass. He set it down on the
nightstand, then turned his eyes toward Tick. "Your
turn."

Sally had made Paul and Sofia summarize in their
own words what he'd come to tell them. He said it was
to make sure the gist of it got "nailed up in dem there
noggins a'yorn." As the weight of Sally's information
settled on their shoulders, Tick at least felt some ease in
knowing more about what lay behind the craziness of
the last few days.

He put his right foot up on his left knee. "Well,
we were supposed to be winked to the Realitant Head-

quarters at the Grand Canyon for a meeting about the weird stuff Reginald Chu is up to. But before that could happen, Chu tricked us and put a device on our arms that hijacked our nanolocators."

"Which means what, now?" Sally asked, his eyebrows raised.

"That Reginald Chu controls us now. He can track us and wink us wherever he wants to. And there's not a thing anyone can do about it."

Sally shook his head in disgust. "Purtin' near one of da worst things I reckon a man can do. Matter-fact, breakin' Rule Number 462 bans you from dem there Realitants 'til the day you is deader than a squirrel on a tire's underbelly."

"Hey, let Tick finish," Sofia said. "We need to make sure we all understand everything you told us."

"Fair 'nuff," Sally said.

"Anyway," Tick continued, "you said it looks like Chu is testing us and some other people to see who's most worthy to help him in a secret project he's working on. And the project has something to do with a disease or plague that's making people go crazy in some of the Realities."

Tick paused, not really wanting to say the next part.

"Get on wid it," Sally prodded.

"Master George wants us to keep going. He wants

us to be the ones who make it. He wants us to win Chu's contest. It's the only way we can make sure the Realitants get there to stop it—whatever it is."

After a long pause, Paul said, "You're the man, Tick. Took Sofia about three hours to say what you just said."

"Well," Tick said, "that's pretty much it, isn't it? We have to keep going, even though it seems like Chu doesn't care if we make it or die trying. Not that much fun to think about, let alone talk about."

Sofia stood from her chair and walked to the window, where she parted the curtain just enough to peek out. "This is so creepy. It was bad enough knowing Master George tracked us last year. Now we've got some power-hungry mad scientist controlling our lives. There has to be a way to get rid of those nanolocators, right?"

"Then you'd be missing the point," Paul said. "Which is shocking considering how long you took to talk about it."

"I'm not missing the point," Sofia said as she turned back toward the group. "Even if we could get rid of them, we wouldn't because we need to keep pretending that we're trying to win."

"Not only that," Tick said. "We need Chu to think we don't know he's behind it all."

"Dang, you kids are plumb smart," Sally said. "When I's a youngun like you, I was happier than a crawdaddy at high tide if I could add up my own two feet."

"I think you're wrong, Tick," Paul said, ignoring Sally. "I don't think Chu gives one flip about what we know. He seems like a ruthless dude who doesn't care jack-squat about rules or whatever. All he cares about is who's standing at the end. It doesn't matter how we get there."

"Maybe," Tick said. "But it still seems smarter to play along as much as we can."

"Say we do make it," Sofia asked, sitting on the corner of the bed, addressing Sally. "What are we supposed to do once we get there?"

Sally nodded, pausing a long time before he answered. "Dat there's a dang ol' good question, miss. I reckon George is tryin' to figger dat one out as we sit here talkin'."

"What are *you* going to do?" Paul asked.

"I'll be gettin' on back to the homestead," Sally said, rubbing his hands together. "Ya'll keep mosin' along on dis here joyride, and I'll come find ya when we's got further word."

"How are you going to find us? How *did* you find us?" Tick asked.

"I'd reckoned you woulda done asked me dat. Took me forever to find ya the first time 'cuz the signal was weak. But don't you remember me shovin' my finger in ya ear?"

Tick couldn't have forgotten. "Yeah, what was that for?"

"I put one of dem fancy Earwig Transponder thing-amajigs in there. Now George can track ya better and stifle some of dem spyin' devices inside ya."

Tick reached up and rubbed his ear, then poked his index finger in as deep as it would go. "You put *what* in my ear?"

"Doncha fret, now," Sally said. "Ain't like it's gonna eat your dang ol' brain or nuttin'."

Tick was about to protest further when someone rapped on the door with a hard and urgent knock. Sofia and Paul jumped to their feet; Sally moved faster than Tick would have believed—running to the door and yanking it open in a matter of two seconds.

No one stood there, but a note had been stuck to the door with a piece of clear tape. Sally ripped it off, read through the words, then walked over and handed it to Tick.

"Read it," Sally said. "I'm goin' to look for the rat who left it." He left the room, marching like he was going off to war.

Tick shot a glance at Paul and Sofia, then read the note to them. "'You people must think I'm an idiot. But I know everything. Everything. The sooner you accept that, the better. The game is on. Win or die.'" Tick paused, swallowed. "'Sincerely, Reginald Chu.'"

No one said a word for the longest time. Finally, Sofia spoke: "Looks like you were right, Paul."

Win or die, Tick thought. *Win or die.*

⁓

The sounds grew louder—and more haunting— as Sato made his way down the long tunnel. A man screaming as if going through a horrible surgery without anesthetic. People arguing, their words impossible to make out. Someone crying. *Lots* of people crying. Mumbling, moaning, retching. Sato couldn't imagine anything worse than being in this place.

The roughly carved walls of the tunnel were dark and shiny, wet with rivulets and flat streams of water sluicing down its sides, disappearing into cracks on the floor. Odd lamps were set into the stone about every thirty feet, filthy glass surrounding a milky light that seemed a mix of old-fashioned wicks and electric sparks. Sato fully expected to see rats scurrying about, but thus far had seen no sign of life.

Just the sounds. The terrible, terrible sounds.

Up ahead, the tunnel made a turn to the right, a somewhat brighter light glowing from that direction. Huddled on the floor was a woman, her face draped in shadow, clutching her legs to her chest, shivering and mumbling the same phrase over and over. Sato couldn't quite make out the words.

His heart pounded as he walked toward the woman, sweat making the syringe clasped in his right hand slippery; he hid it behind his back. Was she infected? Could it be this easy? He stopped a few feet in front of her, thinking about each breath, trying to slow his heart down.

"Excuse me," he said, his voice breaking on the second word. He cleared his throat. "Excuse me, I'm looking for someone."

The woman looked up; Sato took a step backward. He didn't know what he'd expected to see—someone hideous, scarred, a wart-infested witch, maybe—but the lady sitting in front of him was very pretty. She had perfect skin, and blue eyes that shone like crystals in the pale light. Her dark hair sprawled across her shoulders. White teeth flashed behind her still-moving lips, uttering the indecipherable words repeatedly.

Despite her pleasant looks, she looked sad, tear streaks lining both cheeks.

"Can you help me?" Sato said, fingering the syringe hidden from her sight. He took a step closer.

The woman finally fell silent, pressing her lips together. Then she spoke, her voice soft but firm. "We're only crazy when he's not in our heads."

Sato reached for words to reply. The lady's eyes showed no lunacy, no fear, no confusion. She seemed perfectly sane.

"What do you mean?" he finally asked.

"My name is Renee," she replied, ignoring his question. "But right now he *is* in my head, and I will do whatever he says."

"I don't know what you mean," Sato said, taking a step back.

Renee stood up. Her beauty shined despite tattered, dirty garments. She was short and thin, but held herself with confidence—back straight, shoulders square, chin up.

"Why has George sent you here?" she asked.

Sato took another step backward, this time bumping into the stone wall across from the woman. "How . . . how do you know—"

"Stop acting the fool, young man. I know everything. I'm Reginald Chu, and I find it very interesting that you've come here, to this strange place, with a syringe in your hand. *Why?*"

Sato pulled his right hand from behind his back, looking down at it as if ashamed. He didn't know which felt worse right then—his head or his stomach. "I don't understand. What do you mean you're Reginald Chu?"

"I think I'm the one who doesn't understand," Renee replied. "George seems to know so much about my project, yet here you stand, without the slightest clue of the danger you are in. How can you trust such a leader?"

"Nothing you say makes sense."

"Everything I say makes sense." Renee crossed the short span of the tunnel, stopping directly in front of Sato. "Once I have my partner, once Dark Infinity is fully functional, you'll understand. The Realities are about to have a great change, my friend."

Sato swallowed, trying to build his courage. "You're crazy, lady. You think Reginald Chu is controlling you somehow. Don't you see how crazy that is? You need help."

"I told you," Renee said with a sneer. "We're not crazy until he leaves our heads."

"My boss—he thinks he can find a cure for you. If you'll just let me . . ." He held the syringe up, raising his eyebrows in question.

"A cure?" Renee backed off two steps, shaking her head. "A *cure*? Does that man think I'm a toady research assistant at some underfunded university? He thinks he's going to stop me with a *cure*? He'll sooner cure cancer, Parkinson's, diabetes, and regenerate amputated limbs before he'll stop Dark Infinity."

Confusion swarmed like a pack of bees inside Sato's head. The lady really and truly thought she was Reginald Chu. And it worried Sato that he was sliding toward that same belief as well. "What *is* Dark Infinity?"

Renee folded her arms. "As they say in your Reality, that's on a need-to-know basis and you don't need to know. A cure. Ha." She barked a laugh.

"If you're so confident, why not give me a blood sample? And then I'll leave."

Renee held out her hand to him. "Come with me," she said. "I want to give you a taste of what Dark Infinity will become. And then I want you to go back and report it to your buffoon of a leader. All the Realitant do-gooders can then have fun dreading the day I take over their lives."

Sato shook his head. "Give me a sample first. Then I'll go."

Renee stared at him for a long minute, her blue eyes seeming to glow. "You're brave for someone so young. Maybe you should have been included in my special trials. Of course, I need a lot more than bravery—too bad you're not more like your friend Atticus Higgin-bottom."

Sato almost fell to the ground at the mention of Tick. This lady had no way, absolutely no way of knowing anything about Tick or the strange ability he'd displayed in the Thirteenth Reality. "How do you know about him?"

"Come with me." She beckoned again with her hand.

"The sample first." Sato wiped sweat from his brow, thinking too late how much weakness the action prob-ably showed. "You said yourself there's no way George can find a cure."

"Yes, I did say that. But I'm not an idiot—I won't take chances. This isn't some lame movie from your Hollywood."

Sato steeled his nerves. "I'm not going anywhere until you give me a blood sample. You may think you have Reginald Chu inside your head, but I bet he won't be much help in a wrestling match between us."

Renee laughed, such a pleasant sound in the otherwise dreary place that it disturbed Sato.

"A compromise, then," she said. Or *Chu* said. "I'll give you your sample, but you let me carry the vial until we're done. I want—no, I *need* you to report back to George what you see here today."

"No way," Sato said. "I'm not giving you the vial."

Renee's face creased into a scowl so frightening that Sato would have melted into the stone at his back if he could have. "You tire me, boy. Do you really think I'm going to let you leave here alive with a sample of my blood? You'll be signing your own death warrant."

Sato felt his own blood chill. *George will get me out,* he thought. *George will get me out.*

"I'll take my chances," he said. "Give me your blood and I'll go with you."

Renee stuck her arm out. "Do it, then."

Sato stepped forward and grabbed her thin arm, leaning over to look at the soft skin in the bend of her elbow. A big vein pulsed, purple in the faint light.

"This might hurt," he said, not sure why he showed any compassion. "I've never done this before."

"Just do it. Nothing you do to me will be worse than when *he* leaves my head."

As Sato readied the syringe, the needle only an inch from the vein, he looked up at Renee's face. "Sometimes you talk like you're this Chu guy, and sometimes like yourself. You really are crazy."

"You wouldn't understand unless you were infected. Stick me."

Sato held his breath, then jammed the needle into Renee's vein. He quickly pulled back on the syringe pump, relieved to see dark red fluid fill the plastic vial. He finished, pulled out the needle, then replaced the plastic cover. He put the whole thing into his right pocket. He put a bandage on her arm to stop the bleeding.

"Done," he said, finally taking in a huge breath like he'd just surfaced after diving for oysters.

"That blood will never see the light of day; you understand that, right? The only way you will leave this mountain is by giving it up."

"Just show me what you wanted to show me." Half of him wanted to push her down and run for the elevator, but he knew he couldn't. George would desperately need any information he could gather in his quest to find a cure or antidote.

"This way." She walked toward a branch of the tunnel leading to the right, but paused after a couple of steps and turned toward Sato, her face devoid of expression. "What you're about to see, you'll never forget. Never. I promise you."

CHAPTER 28

TRAPPED

With each step down the wet and musty passage of stone, the noises around Sato grew in volume. The screams and wails and shouts and piercing cries for help made him feel as if invisible bugs were crawling across his skin, trying to find a place to burrow toward his heart. His stomach clenched into a tight wad of tissue. He braced himself for the sight ahead, wondering if he'd ever see George or Mothball or Rutger or his other friends again.

They reached a place where a dirty curtain was stretched across the entire width of the hallway, swaying slightly from a breeze behind it. The awful sounds became ear-piercing, no longer muffled by distance.

Sato was now only a few feet away from discovering whatever was wrong with these people.

"Prepare yourself," Renee said. Then she reached out and yanked the curtain to the side.

For the second time in the last hour, Sato's knees buckled. He fell to the ground, his shins slamming onto the hard stone as he stared at the chaos in front of him.

The passageway opened into a large chamber, tables and chairs scattered about the raggedy carpet, most of them broken or turned upside down. Hundreds of people—horrible, terrified, creepy-looking people— filled the room in a state of utter madness.

Their clothes were torn; bloody scrapes and gashes covered their bodies; big splotches of hair had been ripped from their heads. They attacked each other at random, moving from one to the other without warn- ing. They coughed and spit and snarled and bit any- thing in sight. They cried one second, laughed the next, then screamed as if their very throats would burst. They climbed the walls until they fell crashing to the floor. They jumped and huddled and kicked and flailed their arms.

It was, without any doubt, the most horrific thing Sato had ever witnessed, and he knew he would spend the rest of his life trying to purge it from his memory.

"What is this?" He had to force the words out, rage

clogging his throat. "What's wrong with them? How could you do this to them!"

Renee knelt on the floor next to him, not taking her eyes off the mayhem before them. "So you believe me now, do you? You believe that he's inside my head, controlling me, talking to you? That I am Reginald Chu at this moment?"

"I don't care who you are," Sato said. "I'll spend the rest of my life making you pay for it."

Renee tsk-tsked as she shook her head. "Hard to believe you're only a young man—you speak more like an adult than most men I know." She shifted until she was sitting comfortably with her legs crossed beneath her. "But this isn't what I *really* wanted to show you. Let me show you the future."

Sato finally tore his eyes from the sickening display and looked at Renee. "What?" he said, throwing all the hatred he could into the word.

Renee didn't return his stare, looking instead at the people around them. "They're like this because I underestimated the power of Dark Infinity. I can't control it on my own—I need help. I need a partner."

She pushed herself to her feet and walked forward, seemingly oblivious to the danger she entered. But then, as if spurred by the flip of a switch, every person in the vast room grew silent, freezing in place. After a few seconds, the people—every single one of them—calmly gained their composure and joined Renee in the middle of the chamber, lining up in perfectly straight rows. The formation filled the floor, as ordered and organized as any military group in the world. Not a sound could be heard as they all stood still, each one staring at Sato.

"He is in all of our heads, now," Renee called out, standing rigid as she spoke. "We will do his bidding, whatever he asks, until that time he must leave us, and then we will return to the horror that is life without him. The day comes when he will never leave us again."

Sato slowly got to his feet, nausea and despair threatening to consume him. In the understatement of his young life, he told himself he had seen enough.

"I'm sorry he's doing this to you," he half-whispered. "Fight it if you can. I promise we'll try to save you."

He didn't wait for a response. He turned and ran.

Behind him, he heard the piercing cry of Renee's voice, echoing up and through the air as if she'd used a bullhorn. "He has my blood in his right pocket! Don't let him leave with it!"

And then came the sound of hundreds of people running and screaming in a synchronized cry of pursuit.

◦⌐⌐◦

"Can you pull him out yet?" Master George asked for the twentieth time in the last ten minutes, pacing the floor of the command room.

"No," Rutger replied, his eyes riveted to the nano-locator monitor. "But his heart rate is spiking again—I didn't think it could possibly get higher, but now it's in the danger zone." In his hands, Rutger held the Barrier Wand, programmed to wink Sato back from the mountaintop.

"Oh dear, oh dear, oh dear," Master George whispered under his breath.

"Should've gone with 'im, I should," Mothball said from her chair in the corner. "Bugger, I should've ruddy gone with 'im."

Master George stopped, turning toward his tall friend. "Perhaps, my good Mothball, perhaps. However, we all agreed that this was the perfect opportunity for Sato to snap out of the haze of his past and find himself. If you were there to save him, he might never truly join us."

"He needs to make it back to the execution cliff," Rutger said. "Until then, there's nothing I can do."

"He'll make it," Master George said. "I know it. And when he returns, he'll truly be a Realitant, the shade of his parents' death no longer a crutch to bind him in shadow."

"Very poetic," Rutger muttered. "But the way his heart's racing, we'll need to give him a transplant as soon as he gets back."

"Just keep that Wand ready, Rutger. Keep it ready."

Sato gasped for breath as he ran through the dimly lit tunnel; it hadn't seemed so long the first time he'd walked through its winding path. The escalating screams behind him brought horrible images to his mind of what would happen if he were caught. Every muscle in his body begged him to stop, but he kept running, limping slightly from the pain in his shins, especially on his right leg.

Worried the blood-filled syringe in his right pocket might break, he reached in and pulled it out, gripping the plastic cylinder once again like a dagger in his hand. It almost slipped from the sweat on his palm— he shifted it to his left hand while he wiped his fingers dry, then switched back.

He kept running.

He turned a corner and saw the elevator up ahead, its steel cage open and ready for him. He could see the lever mechanism inside the sliding mesh door. He was almost safe.

The hollow echoes of his pursuers bounced through the tunnel like thunder crackling along open plains. Sato heard noises of feet stomping on stone, kicked rocks, heavy breathing, grunts. He heard Renee shout something; he couldn't make out the words, but the intensity of the screams jumped a notch.

Sato looked over his shoulder and saw the pack of crazies only thirty feet behind him and gaining ground. Renee led them, her eyes focused, her hoard of followers on her tail, waving their arms, shaking their fists. It was like the villagers chasing Frankenstein's monster—the only things missing were pitchforks and torches.

Sato faced forward again; so close, the elevator was only a few feet away. He reached up, slipped the backpack off his left shoulder, then his right, still running, still holding tight to the blood sample.

He windmilled his left arm and threw the backpack forward. It landed with a thud in the back corner of the elevator just as he crossed the threshold of the cage. He reached out with his free hand and slid the door shut with a squeal and a clank as it landed home. The latch to close it was small and weak—Sato knew it wouldn't last long. He closed it anyway then knelt on the floor and pushed up on the lever with his shoulder, screaming with the effort until the thing finally snapped into position.

With a lurch, the elevator started moving upward just as Renee and dozens of the screaming mob slammed into the cage, clawing at the steel, screaming and spitting. Hundreds of scabby fingers squirmed through the small openings, some of the crazies climbing onto the elevator, others violently pulling and pushing on the door. Sato scrambled to the far corner, staring at the sickening sight.

The elevator had only gone up a few feet when dozens more of his pursuers crawled beneath it and gripped the floor through the checkered holes, hanging on, pulling toward the ground. The cage slowed to a stop, the weight of the people too great. Sato knew if he could make it to the narrow shaft cut into the stone above, then the psychos clinging to the side would have no choice but to let go or be crushed to death. He jumped to his feet, kicking at the fingers below him, stomping repeatedly in a ridiculous dance, watching in triumph as those he smashed let go and fell to the floor.

The elevator stuttered and paused, screams coming from above as the topmost section entered the main elevator shaft and crushed several of the inmates who still clung to the side. The cage slowed again, and Sato closed his eyes before he could see the gruesome results. He heard the thumps of bodies on the stone below, and the elevator lurched upward again, regaining its normal speed.

Please, he thought. *Please be over, please let me go home.*

A wrenching click of steel made his eyes pop open just as the door to the cage slid open with a screech. Renee had somehow broken the latch, squeezing her body against the elevator until she could get it open.

She and Sato were alone, having left everyone else
below, their wails and cries already dying out with the
distance.

"Almost made it, didn't you?" Renee said, her chest
heaving with her deep breaths.

Sato reached down and pulled the plastic cover off
the blood-filled syringe, then held it out like a knife.
"Stay back," he said, bending his knees in a crouch.
"There's no way you can win a fight with me."

"You still don't get it, do you?" she replied. They
circled, each staying as far apart from the other as possible in the small cage. "He's in my head. I'll do whatever he asks."

"Why are you doing this?" Sato asked.

"I told you, he's in my—"

"Not you!" Sato screamed. "Reginald Chu! Why
are you doing this!"

"If you have to ask, then you'll never understand
why."

Renee lunged forward, surprising Sato despite his
stance. She crashed into him, slamming his back against
the side of the cage. On instinct, Sato stuck the needle
into her back. She cried out in pain then lashed out at
his face, scraping her nails across his right cheek. Sato
pulled out the needle and bent his knees, letting his
body fall to the floor, Renee landing on top of him.

They rolled and wrestled, Renee punching and

clawing like a panicked bear. Sato had the syringe under her, pointed it at her face, trying to threaten her because he didn't know what else to do. She grabbed his hand, thrusting the needle away, twisting his wrist so the syringe was heading toward his own skin. He couldn't believe her strength. He groaned with effort, but she kept winning, pushing the needle closer and closer to the soft skin of his lower neck.

He pushed her away with a final burst of exertion; she surprised him by pulling back instead of fighting it. Caught off guard, his grip on the syringe slipped and Renee yanked it free. She twisted backward and pressed the point of the needle against his leg.

"You . . . had . . . your . . . chance," she spit out, her face red with exertion and anger as she drove the needle *into* Sato's skin. He felt the prick, the achy slide of the sharp sliver of metal. Then Renee slammed downward on the plunger of the syringe.

Pain exploded through Sato's body as the needle dug in deeper, as the blood sample rushed into him. He cried out as the syringe emptied, its infected contents now swimming inside his tissue and veins. It felt like millions of tiny bugs squirmed underneath his skin.

"No!" he screamed, a surge of adrenaline giving him the strength to throw Renee off his body completely. *"NO!"*

He scrambled to his feet, unable to stop the tears

from flowing as pain racked his body. "What . . . what . . . have you done to me?"

"You'll be one of us now," Renee said, crouched in the corner with a smile on her face.

"No, I won't. Never."

The elevator slammed to a stop.

"What the devil's goin' on here?"

Sato looked over to see Klink, his eyes moving back and forth between Sato and Renee, surprise and concern on his face.

Sato didn't hesitate. He grabbed his backpack, ran from the lift cage, down the tunnel, and toward the steel door that led outside. He ran.

"Go, then!" Renee called out from behind him. "It won't matter—you'll be mine anyway. Run and take me to Master George. It'll be fun to have a spy—"

Sato didn't hear the rest. He was through the door, squinting his eyes against the blinding snow, scrambling down the stone stairway, slipping and falling and not caring.

Down the mountain he went.

⌒

"I've got him!" Rutger yelled.

He pushed the golden button on top of the Barrier Wand, and Sato appeared in front of them. The boy collapsed to the ground, a terrible mess of blood and dirt and torn clothing, sweat-ice crusted all over him.

"Goodness gracious me!" Master George yelled as he and Mothball reached forward to help Sato. They grabbed him by the arms and pulled him over to a leather chair, plopping his exhausted body onto the cushions.

"What happened?" Mothball asked.

Sato answered, his voice shaky and barely audible. "Lock . . . me . . . up. Chain me. Then . . . I'll explain."

"Lock you—" Rutger began.

"Just do it!" Sato snapped, his hand pressed to a wound on his leg. "Just do it before Chu can control me!"

"What happened?" Master George asked, leaning over to look at the boy. "Did you get the sample?"

"Yes," Sato said through a moan of pain. His eyes narrowed, like a wolf on the hunt. "It's . . . *inside* me."

"Oh, lad. Oh, you poor, poor lad." Master George paused. Then he straightened, his shoulders square. "Ready the holding cell, Rutger. And get me some rope."

PART 3

THE CIRCLE
OF TIME

CHAPTER 29

TICKETS TO
FOURTH CITY

I'm really getting sick of this place," Paul said.

Tick couldn't have agreed more as he scanned the walls and ceiling of the small restaurant where they had stopped to eat something that was a cross between pizza and toast. Five days had passed since Sally winked back to Master George, and they'd spent every waking hour investigating the town for signs of where they were supposed to be at five o'clock the next afternoon. Though they didn't know what they were looking for, they looked nonetheless.

And, just like this place—one of the last buildings they'd yet to explore—they'd found nothing. No signs, no clues, no Barrier Wands, no magic portals, no further riddles. A big fat zero.

And time was running out. Reginald Chu's riddle had been clear—5:00 PM, tomorrow. Maybe they'd finally been stumped.

"Maybe it's a good thing if we don't figure it out," Paul said. "Beats going off to have more adventures with a psycho mad genius of the universe."

"He said, 'win or die,'" Sofia said. "Dying sounds worse to me."

Tick picked up his last piece of dinner, but then put it back down, his appetite gone. "Sally said we need to be the ones to win it—so we can put a stop to whatever Chu's doing."

"Yeah, and I'm sure that'll be a piece of cake," Paul muttered. "Hey, Chu dude! We won, but please stop that knuckleheaded horseplay you're up to. Thanks kindly."

"You want to give up?" Sofia asked. "Then quit. I'm sure Master George will wink you away if you cry enough."

"No, Miss Italy, I don't want to quit. Someone has to protect you." Paul leaned back and rubbed his belly. "Man, that was pretty good."

"Come on," Sofia said as she got up from her chair. "It's our last night—we'd better get searching."

They searched until well past dark. They looked on every corner, behind every bush, under every sidewalk bench. They walked the underground pathways of the train stations again. Nothing. Absolutely nothing. Even the trains seemed to avoid them; they'd yet to actually see one despite several trips to the stations.

Tick thought about quitting more than once that night, but the urgency of the dwindling time spurred him on, despite his exhaustion. Finally, a roving police-man told them they needed to get off the streets, that curfew was far past. Sofia complained, but the officer made it clear they'd get one warning and one warning only.

And so they went back to the hotel, back to their beds.

Tick set his watch alarm for 6:00, but he had no idea what he'd do when he woke up. Imagining the glowing monkeys prowling the woods outside his window, he fell asleep.

His alarm had just sounded when he heard some-one knock at the door. It was Sofia, dragging a sleepy-eyed Paul behind her.

"We need to get out there," she said. "We only have eleven hours left."

"But what are we going to *do?*" Paul asked. "We've

looked everywhere. There's no point in looking any-more. We're just as well off staying here."

"Well, we have to do something!" Sofia insisted.

Tick groaned as he flopped back on his bed. "I'm with Paul on this one. All we've figured out is that something is supposed to happen at five o'clock. At this point, run-ning around the town makes no more sense than sitting here, holding hands and chanting to the time gods."

"Chanting to the time gods?" Paul asked. "Tick, you're losing it."

Sofia huffed as she took a seat. "Then *think*. What are we missing?"

No one answered, and they all remained silent for several minutes.

Paul snapped his fingers. "The last line of the riddle says, 'Make sure your feet find the air,' right? Well, maybe we're supposed to catch a train and go somewhere *else* by five o'clock. Someplace called 'air' or something like that."

"Hmm," Sofia said. "That's possible. The whole underground railroad system is kind of weird. There must be something about this place, a reason he sent us here—maybe it *is* the train!"

"I'll admit it's better than chanting to the time gods," Tick said. "Let's go."

The streets were surprisingly busy for so early in the morning; most of the people out and about were heading down the stairs that led to the underground railroad.

"These people must all work in another city," Tick said. "No wonder they have to leave when the sun comes up."

"Good thing we're not the only ones awake," Paul said. "I didn't want that cop barking at us again."

They followed the crowd to the ticket counters, old-fashioned brick windows where old men took money and gave out printed slips of paper. Holding some of the local currency given to them by Phillip, they waited their turn.

"Next!" a white-haired man called out, a scowl scrunching up his face like he was having a kidney removed.

Sofia stepped up first. "We'd like three tickets for . . . a train."

Somehow, the man's face screwed up even tighter. "Well, that's real nice to know you have that figured out, missy. How about telling me *where* you want to go?"

"Oh." Sofia looked back at Tick, who shrugged.

"How many trains are leaving soon?" Paul asked.

"What kind of a fool question is that?" the old man grunted. "As many as you'd like. As few as you want. Now are you going buy a ticket or not?"

Just when I thought it couldn't get any weirder, Tick thought.

"What are our options?" Sofia asked. "We're tourists, and just want to do some exploring."

"Oh, well isn't that just peachy?" the man replied, rolling his eyes under his bushy white brows. "Good thing you got me, kids. One of the grumpy ticket masters would've sent you walking already."

Tick could sense that something smart was about to fly out of Sofia's mouth, so he kicked her gently on the calf.

"Please just give us our options," she said instead.

"From this station, you can go to Martyrtown, Cook Reef, Falcon Bay, or Fourth City. Now choose and be done with it."

"Okay, please give me just one second, sir," Sofia said, so gushy polite that Tick was sure the man would kick them out for being smart alecks.

"Did you hear that?" Paul whispered. "He said Fourth City."

"That's the number of Chu's Reality!" Tick said.

"Bingo," Paul said.

"You really think that's it?" Sofia asked, staring at the floor as if deep in thought. She finally nodded to herself and turned toward the old man. "Three tickets to Fourth City, please."

"Well, congratulations on making a decision.

I hope you have a swell time. That'll be thirty-four yecterns."

"Oh," Paul said to the man as Sofia handed over the money. "Make sure we'll be there by five o'clock."

The ticket master printed out three tickets from a rickety metallic machine and handed them over the counter. "Boy, say one more snide remark and I'll have the police boot you out of here. Now go."

"Sir," Paul replied, sounding more sincere than Tick had ever heard him before. "I promise I'm not trying to be difficult—we just don't understand how the trains work here. And we need to be there by five o'clock."

The man frowned deeper than ever, then looked at each of them in turn. "You three are just about the strangest kids I've ever seen. You go over to the portal that matches the number on your ticket"—he pointed at a series of large white cubicles—"step inside, and it'll take you from there."

"But—" Paul started.

"Go!" The ticket master's face reddened as he pointed toward the booths.

Like three startled mice, they scuttled away. Tick hoped he never had to talk to the man again.

When they were sufficiently far enough away from the old buzzard, Sofia handed out the tickets.

Tick took his ticket. Printed in faded black letters

as if the ink were running out in the old guy's machine were the words, "Portal Number Seven. Fourth City. Round Trip."

"Well, let's go," Paul said. "Hopefully we'll get there in time to search around."

The portals—tall, rectangular cubicles, white and shiny—were lined up in order along the sunken line of what Tick had thought were train tracks. He peeked into the ten-foot-deep trench and saw a series of long, metal rods stretching into a dark tunnel at the end of the station.

"Come on," Paul said, holding open the door. It was made out of the same material as the rest of the small building and fitted to match its shape.

Sofia went in first, then Tick, then Paul, who closed the door behind him.

The inside was a perfect cylinder, completely covered in thick, rubbery padding that was a burnt-orange color. Along the bottom, a bench protruded from the walls—also covered in soft padding—making a circle for the passengers to sit and stare at each other.

"This is a train?" Tick asked no one in particular. An uneasy feeling crept into his bones.

"What do we—" Paul began, but was cut off by an electronic woman's voice coming from unseen speakers.

"Please present your tickets," it said, a soft monotonous tone that made Tick feel sleepy. He clasped his

ticket between his thumb and forefinger, holding it up into the air; the others did the same.

"Cleared. State your desired time of departure."

"As soon as possible," Sofia said in a loud voice.

"It's not deaf," Paul whispered, getting an elbow in the gut from Sofia in return.

"Checking departures. One moment, please." A pause, then: *"Six Forty-Four is acceptable. Please stand on the foot rest, backs against the wall."*

"Huh?" Paul asked.

"Just do it," Sofia said, climbing on to the bench.

"Three minutes to departure."

Tick stepped onto the padded bench, surprised at how firmly it held him. He rested his back against the soft wall; Paul and Sofia had done the same, the three of them spaced evenly apart, exchanging worried glances.

"This is weird," Paul said.

"That about sums it up," Tick agreed.

"It's obviously okay. All those other people are doing it," Sofia said. "We can't expect every Reality to be just like ours."

"One minute to departure."

"What do we do—just stand here?" Paul asked.

Sofia rolled her eyes. "You can do jumping jacks if you want."

"You're telling me you're not a little scared?"

"I am," Tick said.

"Maybe a little," Sofia said.

"Thirty seconds to departure."

No one said a word after that; Tick counted down inside his head.

"Ten seconds." A pause. *"Five. Four. Three. Two. One. Departure initiated."*

The room began to rotate clockwise, slowly at first, but then it picked up speed.

"Oh, no," Tick said. "I can't do this—I'll throw up all over you guys."

They spun faster and faster. Tick felt a pressure on his skin, squeezing his limbs and his torso, like an invisible force pushing him against the curved wall at his back. In a matter of seconds, he'd lost track of their rotation speed, his mind and stomach disoriented, his body sinking into the padding. His thoughts whirled as fast as his body, spinning clockwise in a tight circle.

Something clicked in Tick's mind.

He envisioned the city they'd just left, the layout, the circular road—and the solution to Chu's riddle crystallized in his head, as clear as anything he'd ever known. In that moment, he knew they shouldn't be on the train.

They had to stop. *They had to go back!*

He wanted to say something, but he couldn't. He felt like the world was crushing him. Grunting, he tried to push his arms up into the air. It felt like he had fifty-pound dumbbells in his hands. The second he relaxed, his arms slammed back onto the wall.

Then it got worse.

A horn sounded, coming from everywhere and nowhere at once, and then the room *shifted*. With the spinning and the pressure, it was hard to tell which direction the room was moving, but it seemed to have dropped into a black hole, catapulting forward at a speed that was too much for Tick's mind and body to handle.

He passed out.

CHAPTER 30

FOREST EXIT

"Tick."

He heard someone say his name, but it sounded hollow, like an echo coming down a long tunnel.

"Tick!"

There it was again. Louder this time. A sharp pain splintered across his mind, and that seemed to do the trick. Groaning, blinking through squinting eyes, he woke up.

"Dude, are you all right?"

Paul. It was Paul.

"Come on. Help him up."

Sofia.

Tick felt hands grip him by the arms and haul him

off the floor, setting him down on a soft bench. Every time he opened his eyes, all he could see were things spinning and rocking back and forth. His mind felt like a pack of termites had been set loose inside for lunch. And the nausea . . .

"I gotta throw up," he whispered.

"Not on me, you don't," Paul said. "Hurry, let's get him out of here."

They grabbed him by the arms again. He heard a door open, felt refreshing cool air wash over him as they helped him stumble outside the portal.

"There's a garbage can," he heard Sofia say; they changed directions.

"Hurry," Tick groaned, trying his best to get his feet under him. A cold line of metal pressed against his neck.

"Go for it," Paul muttered.

Tick let it all out, then slid to the ground and leaned back against the garbage can. "Ah, that feels much better." He opened his eyes fully and got his first good look at where they'd arrived.

The station looked much like the one they'd left earlier—maybe a little dirtier, less well-kept. Just as many people milled about, though, some leaving portals, some entering them.

"What happened?" he asked.

"You passed out," Sofia said. "I think I might have,

too, just for a few seconds. When we finally stopped, Paul and I slid down onto the bench, but you crashed straight to the floor."

"Yeah, man," Paul said. "You were out like a light."

"How long were we in that thing?" Tick asked.

Sofia looked at her watch. "Only a half hour or so."

"Worst half hour of my life," Paul said.

Tick rubbed his face with both hands, then stood up, wobbling for a second before he felt his legs strengthen and solidify beneath him. "We have to go back. Now."

"Go back?" Paul asked. "Are you crazy?"

"We need to look around," Sofia said. "Figure out what Chu wants us to do."

Tick shook his head, which sent another wave of nausea through his gut. "No, we got it wrong. We weren't supposed to come here. The trains have nothing to do with the riddle."

"How do you know?" Paul asked. "Fourth City—it's the closest we've gotten to anything that makes sense."

Tick started walking toward the ticket counter. Paul and Sofia followed, but they didn't look happy. "Our tickets are round trip—does that mean we just get back on Portal Number Seven?"

"Whoa, man," Paul said, grabbing Tick by the arm. "Tell us what you're thinking. If we're getting back in that death machine, we need to at least let our brains unscramble for a minute."

Tick nodded, anxious to leave but knowing Paul was right. He found a bench and they sat down, Tick in the middle.

"All right," he said. "Think about everything. The town Chu sent us to is a perfect circle. We counted *twelve* main roads that are basically spokes in the huge wheel of how the place is organized. Even the hotel he set us up in—it's called The Stroke of Midnight Inn. You gettin' it yet?"

"Holy toothpick on a hand grenade," Paul whispered.

"I don't think I've ever felt as stupid as I feel right now," Sofia said.

"It never had anything to do with an actual *time,*" Tick continued. "It was such an easy riddle because he wanted to throw us off track. We were so sure something had to happen at five o'clock today, we never considered that he might be describing a *place.*"

Paul finished for him. "If we look at the town from a bird's-eye view, it's a big clock. Our hotel is midnight—twelve o'clock. We need to go to the road that represents *five* o'clock."

"But we already looked there," Sofia said. "We scoured that whole town."

Tick stretched his arms, feeling better already. "Yeah, but we had so much area to cover, we didn't really have time to study anything in detail. I bet we find something where the five o'clock road hits the outer circle."

"Ah, man, what if we're too late?" Paul asked. "If you're right, maybe we didn't have to wait a week. Maybe we should've gone to the place a lot sooner."

Sofia stood up. "Maybe it's a double riddle."

"You're right," Tick said. "I bet we have to be at the five o'clock road *by* five o'clock today."

"Well, then," Paul said, "we have plenty of time. Let's go get something to eat."

"No way," Tick said. "You really think it's going to be that easy? Something will try to stop us, I guarantee it."

"Well, we have to *eat*," Paul insisted.

"Yeah, but we should get back to Circle City first," Sofia said. "The sooner the better."

All of them slowly turned their heads to look at the spinning nightmare train from which they'd just exited. Tick couldn't think of anything he'd rather *not* do than get back on that thing.

"We have to do it," Sofia said, as if reading Tick's thoughts.

"I know," Tick replied.

"Yeah, eating right now would be really stupid," Paul said. "I don't want Tick's bacon and eggs on my lap when we get there."

"Come on," Sofia said. "Let's figure out how to get back."

They had to wait only twenty minutes for Portal Number Seven to open up for the return trip to Circle City. Tick had never felt so nervous about a trip before; butterflies swarmed in his chest like it was mating season. He remembered his mom lecturing him at the amusement park: *"Now, Atticus, you* know *what the Spinning Dragon does to your poor tummy."*

"One minute to departure," the nice electronic lady said.

Tick squeezed his eyes shut, pressed his back against the soft padding. *Thirty-minute trip,* he told himself. *It's only thirty minutes.*

The warning for thirty seconds sounded, then ten, then the five-second countdown. When the room started spinning, Tick opened his eyes to look at Paul and Sofia, both of whom were trying to look very calm but failing miserably. This made Tick feel better, and he closed his eyes again.

The portal spun faster and faster, twisting like a tornado, throwing all of his senses into chaos as the invisible force once again pushed him into the padding, pressing against his body. He held his breath, anticipating the explosion of speed—reminding him of how he felt that split-second before the free-fall ride at the Seattle amusement park dropped fifteen stories to the ground far below. But this was far worse.

The horn sounded.

Tick tried to scream as the train exploded into instant acceleration, shocking his mind as it bulleted away from Fourth City. He didn't know if any noise escaped his throat. Nothing seemed to be working inside his brain, all of his nerves dead to the world, confused and compressed.

He felt himself sliding away again, moving toward the bliss of unconsciousness. *Do it,* he thought. *Pass out. Anything is better than this.* He faded in and out, feeling like every second lasted an hour. He had no idea how much time had passed when everything suddenly went wrong.

The train jerked, a quick and loud jolt as if they'd hit a cow on the tracks like the steamers in the old days. Then the room shook, rattling up and down, creaks and groans ripping through the air, as if the whole vehicle were about to fall apart. Tick would've thought it impossible, but everything had just gotten much, much worse. His stomach twisted into a knot of panicked nausea.

His eyes snapped open, but they didn't seem to work. Everything was a blur of color, images and streaks, flashing and tilting—*vibrating.* He couldn't even make out Paul or Sofia; everything was messed up.

What's happening? he thought. *Maybe it's okay. I passed out last time—maybe this is totally normal.*

But the train shook again, twisted, bounced and rattled. Pain seared through Tick's head like someone had driven a crowbar into the top of his skull and worked it open, wedging the long piece of steel against his brain.

A booming crash sounded through the room, a horrible crunch of metal. The train jolted, and the pressure forcing Tick against the wall abruptly vanished. He fell forward and crashed into Paul. They both fell to the floor, landing on top of a crumpled Sofia.

The next few seconds were complete insanity. The vehicle bounced and twisted and shook, throwing Tick and the others in every direction, slamming them against the curved walls, the floor, into each other. Tick tried to ball up, squeezing his knees against his chest and covering his head with his arms, but it proved impossible. Like a giant gorilla shaking a can of peanuts, the three of them were tossed and jostled about until Tick thought for sure their lives were over.

And then, with one final crash that slammed them all into one padded side of the curved structure, it ended.

Everything stopped, grew still, silent.

The only sounds were the moans coming from the battered humans inside.

"My arm!" Paul screamed out. "I think I broke my stinking arm!"

THE HUNT FOR DARK INFINITY

"What happened?" Sofia asked, her voice strained and tight.

Portal Number Seven lay on its side. Tick and the others were in a crumpled heap on top of each other, resting on one of the curved, padded sections that used to be vertical. With more groans and moans, they crawled away from each other. A hissing sound came from outside, followed by something that sounded like electric sparks.

Tick sat up, every inch of his body in pain. He looked over at Paul, who cradled his left arm with his right.

"You okay?" Tick said.

Paul looked up, a tear streaking out of his right eye. "Dude, it hurts, it really, really hurts."

"You think you broke it?" Sofia asked, rubbing one of her ankles.

"Yeah," Paul said, his face squeezed into a grimace of pain. "Ah, man, it kills!" Another tear slid down his cheek. Tick looked away, worried Paul would be embarrassed at being seen crying.

Sofia stood up, wobbling a second before she caught her balance. "We must have crashed or something. We've gotta get out of here, get Paul to a hospital."

Tick joined her and together they walked across the curved wall to the door, which was about four feet in the air, sideways. It was twisted slightly, and it took both of them ramming it with their shoulders before it finally popped open and slammed against the crumpled white wall of the portal.

Tick and Sofia made surprised grunts at the same time when they saw where they were.

"What's . . . out there?" Paul asked through clenched teeth.

Tick couldn't answer, his eyes glued to the wall of thick, enormous trees beyond the doorway.

"We're in a forest," Sofia said.

As if the pain had finally sent him over the edge, Paul started laughing.

CHAPTER 31

THE SICKNESS
OF SATO

Master George felt his heart breaking in two as he stared at Sato.

The poor lad thrashed in his bindings, twisting his arms and legs, arching his back as he strained against the ropes tied to his ankles and wrists. He lay on a bed in the holding cell, the sheets a jumbled mess from his spasms and fits of lunacy. Deep bruises marked where the ropes touched his skin, yet he didn't stop his fruitless efforts to escape.

He had the illness, the disease.

Sato had gone quite insane.

Master George gripped his hands together, wishing so badly he could have just a few seconds of conversation with the *real* Sato, who was locked somewhere inside the mind infected by Chu's mysterious plague. The bravery shown by the boy in entering that mountain insane asylum made Master George so proud it hurt. He also felt again the pains of losing Sato's parents all those years ago, a dreadful death that still made him feel hot, as if the heat from the flying fires of that fateful day had never quite left his skin.

"We're going to make everything right," Master George said aloud, even though he doubted Sato could hear, let alone understand, his words. "Rutger and I are working on the antidote every second of the day. And we're getting close, very close. Hang in there, lad, hang in there. Your suffering may be the very key that saves us all."

Sato stilled, then, letting out an enormous sigh as his body came to rest on the sweaty, crumpled sheets of the bed. Master George leaned forward, terrified he'd made a huge mistake in saying anything.

"He's back in my head," Sato whispered in a chant-like voice that sent chills up Master George's arms. "He wants to speak to you."

"Sato, are you there?" Master George asked. "Even with him in your head, are you there, listening to me?"

"He wants to speak to you," Sato repeated.

"I don't care about him, Sato. I want you to know that we're doing everything we can to save you, and that your mission was an enormous success. We *are* going to take care of you."

Sato slowly turned his head until his eyes—glazed over as if drugged—met with Master George's. "That's very sweet of you, George. Your softness has always been your greatest weakness."

Master George sat back in his chair as if slapped, but he quickly regained his composure. "Am I speaking with you, Reginald? Come to show me how low you've finally sunk, have you?"

"I know what you're doing," Chu said through Sato's mouth. Perhaps it was the eyes, or perhaps it was the unusual tone of his voice, but somehow it seemed like it really *was* Chu lying there, speaking.

"Quite smart, aren't you?" Master George replied.

A grin appeared on Sato's face, a grin so evil it made him look like a demon. "Yes, actually. I'm very, very smart, George. Which is why you'll never succeed in creating a cure for Dark Infinity."

"Who said anything about a cure?"

"Very well, George. Play your games, insult my intelligence. The day is coming, and very soon, when I will have an apprentice strong enough to make Dark Infinity fully functional. Everything will change, then. You'd be wise to consider your allegiances—I could use your help as well."

"What's your plan, Reginald?" Master George asked,

knowing he should just walk away but unable to. "Haven't you enough power? Why must you ruin so many lives? Why can't you use your skills to *better* the Realities? Still not powerful enough to wash away your pathetic loathing of yourself? Quite sad, really."

Sato's face tightened, reddened, any semblance of a smile gone. "What I do, I do for the good of all mankind, George. The Realities *need* me, and this is the only way to gain the power necessary to change things. In the end, you and everyone else will thank me."

Master George leaned forward, elbows on knees, his eyes narrowing. "That sounds quite familiar, Reginald. I've heard almost the exact same words come out of the mouth of Mistress Jane. The both of you have merely cloaked your evil with good intentions. We will win in the end, I assure you."

"You have—"

"Silence!" Master George yelled, standing up. "I will hear no more of your lies!"

He walked out of the holding cell immediately, slamming the door shut with every ounce of strength left in his old body.

⁓

"I've never seen such a thick forest before," Sofia said as they picked their way slowly—very slowly—through the thickly clustered trees. Hoots and howls rang through the air, as if every zoo in the world had released their animals into the woods surrounding them. Pungent smells of rotting foliage, leaves, and bark mixed with the pleasant scents of pine and wildflowers. Tick felt as if all five of his senses were overloaded.

He and Sofia walked alongside Paul, helping him as best they could when he needed an extra hand. Both of his were occupied—one useless because of his broken arm, the other busy holding the bad limb against his body.

"Dude, I know I sound like a sissy," Paul said through his pain. "But this is killing me, man. I want my mom."

"Unless your mom is a doctor," Sofia said, stooping under a massive, moss-covered limb, "I don't think she's the one you want right now."

"Maybe you're right," Paul replied. He struggled, doubling over to go under the same branch, his rear end and skinny legs the only way to balance himself with no arms to use. "I want a doctor. *Then* I want my mom."

"*My* mom would tell me to quit whining and put a bandage on it," Sofia said. "Frupey's the only one who'd care in my house."

Tick faltered for a second, almost tripping Paul, then kept walking as if nothing had happened. Paul's silence showed he must have felt the same way—awkward at yet another sad reference to Sofia's home life.

Despite the approaching noon hour, the forest was dark from the tall canopy of limbs and leaves overhead, everything masked in shadow. As Tick pushed through a thick tangle of brush, scratching his arms and legs, he couldn't help but feel a little desperation at their predicament. They had only a few hours to get back to Circle City, run to the intersection that represented five o'clock, and then find whatever talisman marked their way out of this Reality.

After exiting the crashed Portal Number Seven, they'd seen the huge swath of ruined forest they'd left behind them, a wide slice of knocked-down trees, many of them burning or smoking. Based on the direction of the fiery trail, they could only guess—and hope—that continuing in the direction the Portal *should* have been traveling would lead them to their destination. But with the towering trees and thick undergrowth, it was almost impossible to know if they were walking in a straight line or wandering in circles. Everything about the place looked the same.

"Any guesses on what happened?" Sofia said, practically pushing Paul over a boulder wedged between two trees. His only response was a grunt when he thudded back on the ground.

"A bomb or something," Tick said. "It's probably just another part of Chu's game. To see if we'd give up or not make it back on time."

Paul pushed past an outreaching limb with his shoulder, then let it fly backward to smack Sofia in the face.

"Hey!" she yelled.

"Sorry," Paul said, his pain-racked face somehow showing the slightest hint of amusement to Tick. "No arms, ya know—not much control."

"How'd you like to have *two* broken arms?" Sofia replied.

"Wouldn't be much worse than now."

They entered a short break in the trees and found a clearing about twenty feet across, covered in bright green ivy. Rays of sunlight broke through, glistening on the dew-blanketed leaves, still damp hours after dawn. Without discussion, all three of them sat down to take a short rest, each finding a fallen tree or rock on which to sit.

"This is kind of cool," Paul said, looking around at the border of trees, the green ivy, the cascading sun.

"Looks like something out of a fantasy book," Tick said.

Paul nodded, then winced as if the small movement had hurt his arm somehow. "Yeah," he said through a tight grin. "Maybe we'll see some elves."

"Or vicious, man-eating monkeys that glow in the dark," Sofia added.

Tick sniffed. "Way to look on the bright side of things."

"I just thought of something," Sofia said, ignoring his remark.

"What?" Tick asked.

"Chu wouldn't have any way of knowing we'd take that train today. How could this be part of his plan?"

Tick shrugged. "We know he's following us, spying on us. With all his freaky techno gadgets, I'm sure he could make a train crash whenever he wanted."

"I guess." She didn't sound convinced at all.

Paul stood after a few minutes of silence, his face wrinkling up like an old man's. "I can't take this much longer. We need to get back."

"Come on," Tick said, standing and pointing across the clearing. "I'm pretty sure we need to go that way." He walked in that direction, Paul and Sofia right behind him.

"We're getting close on the antidote." Master George leaned forward, resting his folded hands on the kitchen table. Mothball sat to his left, Rutger to his right, Sally across from him. Muffintops curled on his lap, sound asleep. "Rutger, why don't you give us a full report?"

The robust little man sat back in his chair, somehow resting one pudgy foot on his other knee—a feat that seemed impossible at first glance. "This plague is just about as fascinating a thing as I've ever seen. It's completely nanotechnology based, yet it shows qualities of an airborne virus, as well as some bacterial characteristics. It's basically an unprecedented mixture of biological manipulation, microarchitectural nanotech computer processing, and cellular airwave transmissions the likes of which we've never seen."

Sally slammed his thick-knuckled hands on the table. "George, what in tarnations is this fool-headed sack of pork-and-beans yappin' about?"

"Fool-headed?" Rutger countered. "Sally, you couldn't add five plus five using your fingers."

"So ya admit it, then?" Mothball said.

"What?" Rutger asked.

"That yer a sack of pork-and-beans? Only complained about the fool part, ya did."

"Ten!" Sally shouted out.

Everyone looked at Sally, who held up his hands, fingers outstretched. "Five plus five is ten."

"Well, I *do* apologize," Rutger said. "I've vastly underestimated your abilities to perform mathematical functions."

"Ain't nothin'," Sally replied. "I ain't never been

able to reckon how much food you can stuff down that there gully a'yorn."

Mothball snorted a laugh, then covered her face as her shoulders shook.

"All right," Master George said with a huff. "That's quite enough of this silly bickering. Rutger, I can only speak for myself when I say I had a bit of trouble following your analysis as well, and I've been working with you from the beginning. Please, tell us again, but this time don't try to sound so smart."

"*Try?* Master George, I—"

"Please, Rutger."

Rutger shot a nasty look at Sally, then composed himself, taking a deep breath, which resembled a beach ball inflating and deflating on the chair. "In simpler terms, so *all* of you can understand it—Sato has nanotechs inside his body that can take control of his brain functions—and therefore his whole body. It's a technologically created disease, a virus made completely of artificial materials. However, it spreads just like an airborne virus, and once the plague is inside you, the virus can be controlled from a centrally located command center, which happens to be inside the Fourth Reality."

Sally threw his arms up in the air. "Well, you done cleared it up, han't ya!"

"'Tis a robot germ," Mothball said. "A wee little

robot that makes ya do whatever that ruddy Chu tells ya. Spreads just like the flu, it does."

Sally looked over at Rutger, raising his eyebrows. "Now why on mama's grave couldn't you a-said it that simple-like?"

"Because I'm not used to speaking down to your level," Rutger replied, folding his short, fat arms.

Sally turned to Master George. "Why ain't *we* caught the sucker if it's liken the flu?"

"Because we've been extra careful," Master George replied. "We've worn gloves when we've had to handle Sato. We've fumigated his cell room on a regular basis. We've worn masks when necessary. It's a dangerous disease, dear Sally, but it's not invincible. Not yet, anyway."

"What about the antidote?" Mothball asked. "Methinks you've got news, ya do, or we wouldn't be sittin' 'ere tryin' to decide which of these two knuckleheads gots the smaller brain."

"We're very close to having it solved," Rutger said. "Since the whole power of this plague lies in its ability to be controlled from Chu's headquarters, we think we can kill it in one swift stroke. All we have to do is inject our antidote into the home source, whatever that may be."

"That easy, is it?" Mothball asked.

Master George cleared his throat. "Easy, Mothball? I'm afraid not. This . . . device, this *thing,* that controls those infected with the nanoplague will be well-protected. Ironically, its vulnerability will be the very thing that ensures its *in*vulnerability."

Sally merely blinked, and Master George had to suppress a smile.

"We can only assume that the device is what Reginald has referred to as Dark Infinity, and there's simply no hope or chance of us ever seeing it in person."

"Then what you figger we's gonna do?" Sally asked.

Master George paused, staring at Sally for a very long moment before finally speaking. "Our only hope is to get the antidote, once it's completed, to Tick and the others. Then they must win Chu's contest and get on the inside."

Mothball sniffed. Rutger coughed. Sally scratched his ear.

"Our only hope is for Reginald Chu to summon the very thing that will destroy him." Master George reached down and stroked the soft fur of his beloved cat, who was still snoozing. "But how we will do that without losing our dear young friends, I just don't know."

CHAPTER 32

MONKEYING AROUND

Paul was getting steadily worse. His arm had ballooned to twice its normal size, blue-purple streaks scratched across the tight skin. As bad as it looked, his moans of pain were worse; he sounded as if he were minutes away from dying. Whatever the case, his condition rattled Sofia's nerves.

"It can't be much farther," she said. "All that whining is only going to make it hurt more."

"Thanks for your concern, as usual," Paul replied, his voice strained. "Let me break *your* arm—see how you like it."

Sofia huffed. "I was in the train too." She held up

her hands, shook them. "Don't see anything wrong here, do you?"

"It's gotta be up there somewhere," Tick cut in, trying to prevent an all-out war between his two friends. "Just keep walking."

They did. Over huge roots, under branches as thick as three men, through thorn-spiked bushes, past swampy pools of sludge. Scraped and bruised, Tick felt his thin hopes vanishing altogether as trees gave way to nothing but more trees. The forest thickened; the animal hoots and howls increased in volume; the air darkened with shadows. Nothing gave the slightest hint they were approaching a city or any kind of civilization whatsoever.

All the while, Paul's grunts and groans made life miserable for everyone—worrying about his condition seemed almost as bad as being in the condition itself.

"Hey, something's up there!" Sofia shouted.

Tick stumbled on a rock hidden under a pile of wet, clumpy leaves. They'd gone so long without anyone speaking that Sofia's words startled him. He grabbed a thick vine, which saved him from hitting the ground, but rubbed a nasty sore spot on his palm as it slid through his fingers.

"What?" Paul asked through a tight breath, the one word taking all his effort.

"A light," Sofia answered, pointing, then moving in that direction, just slightly off the course they'd been following. "It's definitely a light—a couple of them. I think it's a building!"

Tick's heart soared, his weary pessimism from just seconds earlier vanishing. "Let's go!" he shouted, rather pointlessly. Even Paul's step quickened with renewed strength.

The three of them slipped past a thick wall of foliage and rounded a huge oak. Ahead of them, the trees thinned and signs of Circle City were everywhere. Tick could even see a couple of people walking along the great round road bordering the town.

"We did it!" Sofia said, then stepped forward, ready to start running. But something crashed down from the branches above, landing right in front of her. Sofia shrieked and jumped back, almost knocking Paul to the ground.

Tick stared ahead, his mind battling between fear and curiosity.

A thick, heavily furred animal crouched before them on all four legs, its slimy nostrils sniffing as it bared a mouth full of white fangs. Its body resembled a bear, but its face looked more like a wolf's, yellow eyes glaring from a narrow, elongated face. Drool dripped from its jaws and teeth; a low growl rumbled deep within its chest.

But what caught Tick's attention was how the creature *glowed*—a deep, eerie red that rippled along its fur like small waves on a pond. Each strand of hair shined, as if optical fibers charged with pulsing lava sprouted from the creature's skin.

"The glowing monkeys," Tick whispered.

"Radioactive demon bears," Paul replied, a little louder.

The animal took a step forward, its eyes focusing on Paul, then Sofia, then Tick. Its nonstop growl gurgled and grew louder; its mouth opened wider. The thing seemed to have a hundred teeth, all sharp and pointy.

Tick yelped when something crashed to the ground to the right of the animal, then another to its left. Two more creatures, looking as vicious and hungry as the first. But they all stayed where they'd landed, studying the three humans.

"What do we do?" Tick asked, not caring how shaky his voice sounded.

"If we run, they might pounce on us," Sofia said.

Paul didn't say anything, cradling his swollen arm, his tight face drenched in sweat.

"If we *don't* run, they might pounce on us," Tick replied.

The lead creature barked, a loud yelp that rang through the air like the sickening, desperate plea of an injured dog. In the distance, something called back, then another, then another—eerie, ringing wails echoing through the thick forest.

How smart are *these things?* Tick wondered as he felt his brief spurt of curiosity quickly igniting into all-out panic. There was nothing they could do—nothing!

Creaking and crashing sounded from behind them, twigs and branches breaking, leaves and foliage swishing as large things moved closer. More of the creatures.

"We have to do something," Tick said, not bothering to whisper anymore. "Before we're surrounded."

"Turn and run," Paul grunted.

"Can you do it?" Sofia asked.

"Got to," he replied.

"On the count of three," Tick said, "turn and go in a wide circle to the left. Head back around toward the city."

Sofia shook her head. "Maybe we should split up."

"No!" Tick said, surprised at how quickly the word came out. "On the count of three, together."

"Fine, to the left."

Heat surged through Tick's veins, his heart skittering. "One . . . two . . ."

"Three!" Paul screamed.

They turned in unison and broke into a run, back into the thicker forest, scurrying around a huge tree.

The three huge animals yelped their strange barks in response, and Tick could hear the heavy thumps of their footfalls in pursuit.

Sofia pushed into the lead, throwing herself forward through a tangled knot of bushes between two trees. Paul followed her, then Tick. He turned his head to see the first animal barrel around the wide trunk of the oak, slipping in the leaves as it tried to get its footing. Its yellow eyes flared, like two small suns buried in the dark red glow of its huge body.

Tick looked away, throwing his strength into his legs, running, ignoring the branches ripping at his clothes and skin. "Go, go, go!" he shouted.

They tore through the forest, Sofia dodging and sidestepping, finding the best route, slowly making her way in a wide arc to the left, back toward the city. Paul lumbered as he ran, gripping his hurt arm, leaning forward at a dangerous angle as he pushed ahead. Tick took up the rear, knowing the enormous monsters at his back could rip him to pieces at any second. He could hear their breath, their pounding footsteps, their steady growls.

More sounds entered the fray, crashing and breaking all around them, louder and closer than before. Tick didn't dare look, but it sounded like entire trees had been snapped in two. The ground trembled, as if dozens of the creatures had showed up to join the hunt,

flanking them, surrounding them—jumping through the branches *above* them.

"Faster!" he yelled.

The trees thinned again, signs of the city ahead jumping into view. They were only a few seconds from breaking through the forest edge and into the street. Tick suspected something prevented the glowing creatures from entering the town—he had no idea what, but he didn't care; they were almost safe.

They ran on, the deafening cacophony of sounds filling the air like a sonic whirlwind. Splitting wood, cracking, breaking, crashing. The roars and screams of the creatures pursuing them. The thumps of their footsteps. Above it all, a steady rumble shook the ground, as if lightning had struck nearby, thunder splintering the world around them. Tick didn't understand what was happening. Doubt filled him; how had they made it; how had they outrun the beasts?

Sofia broke past the last line of trees, Paul and Tick close behind. They didn't slow or look back, running at a full sprint until they had reached the far side of the wide road encircling the city. Once there, panting and heaving for breaths, hands on knees, Tick turned to make sure they were safe.

Despite his exhaustion, despite his racing heart, despite his need to suck in as much air as possible, his breath caught in his throat. He straightened, eyes widening.

"What . . . the . . ." Paul managed between gasps of air. "What . . . how . . ."

Across the street, past the narrow area of small trees leading to the thicker forest from which they'd just escaped, a huge bulk of mangled wood rose toward the sky, dozens of feet high, countless trees smashed into a coiled mass. It looked like a large section of the woods had been liquefied and squeezed together, *twisted* together, then frozen into a hideous swirl of matter. In several spots, some of the creatures that had chased them were trapped in the wall of wood, as if they'd been sealed in hardened tar right before escaping. One of the animals' legs twitched.

It was just like what they'd seen in the woods by Tick's home, right after the bizarre attack from Mr. Chu, when a deer had been trapped in the strangled structure of entwined trees.

Tick's mind emptied, void of thoughts. The two incidents had to be connected, but not even a hint of understanding cowered in the darkness of his head. Confused, he thought it must have something to do with Reginald Chu. Breathing heavily, relieved but uneasy, he turned away from the ugliness in the forest and looked at his friends.

"Someone please tell me what just happened," Paul

said, his eyes still glued to the massive lump across the street.

"Wish I could," Tick said.

"We have the weirdest lives in the universe," Sofia said.

Paul finally broke his gaze, lifting his broken arm a few inches, testing his injury. With a wince, he lowered his elbow back into the cradle of his other arm. "I've gotta get to a hospital."

"We don't have time," Sofia said.

Paul let out a bitter laugh, but didn't say anything.

"What do you mean?" Tick said. "We have to find him a doctor."

Sofia pointed to her watch. "It's already four-thirty. We only have thirty minutes left."

"But—"

"Tick," Paul cut in.

Tick looked at him. Paul's body was covered in sweat, his eyes so bloodshot they looked as if they'd been dipped in red paint. The scowl of pain on his face had created deep lines in his forehead, large cracks that seemed permanent. But somehow, despite everything, Paul smiled—a miserable grimace, but a smile all the same.

"She's right," he said. "Broken arm, broken leg, broken head—doesn't matter. Hungry, thirsty, ugly— doesn't matter. We've only got thirty minutes."

Tick paused, exchanging long glances with both of them. Finally, he nodded.

"Let's go," he said.

They took off, running along the wide arc of the border street.

CHAPTER 33

FIVE O'CLOCK

I t took fifteen minutes to find the intersection representing five o'clock. Luckily, their hotel, The Stroke of Midnight Inn, had been two streets down from where they'd exited the forest. Once there, Tick and the others ran with renewed strength, counting the times off as they sprinted toward their destination.

One o'clock. Two o'clock. Three, four, five.

Gasping each breath, Tick doubled over to rest, hands on his knees, while he scanned the area for any sign of what they were supposed to do to wink away. They had only ten minutes until the *real* five o'clock.

The thick forest hugged the outside curve of the main street, the line of massive trees looming like ancient wooden towers. Thankfully, there was no sign of any mutant radioactive demon monkey-bears. The road that led from the town square of Circle City to the woods was bordered with various buildings and shops, people bustling about with smiles on their faces but blank looks in their eyes, as if kindness had worn thin and they only wanted to get their next task done. The eerie opera-lady music blared from unseen speakers.

The "T" formed by the two-street intersection was mostly empty, the clean pavement unblemished from potholes or cracks. Tick couldn't see so much as a sewer grate, and wondered why everything about this Reality seemed simple but . . . *off* somehow.

I hope I never find out, he thought. *I want out of here.*

Paul zigzagged back and forth as he scanned the street for any sign or clue of a place in which they might need to stand at the appointed time. He clutched his arm and limped as if the pain had traveled through the rest of his body. Sofia searched as well, and Tick joined in. No one said a word, but worry and discouragement hung in the air like wilting clouds. Time was running out. Though confident they were in the right place, Tick didn't know if that was good enough.

```
It does not matter; I do not care.
Just make sure your feet find air.
```

"The word *air* has to be carved somewhere," Paul said.

"Yeah," Tick mumbled as he walked awkwardly along, bent over, searching the pavement.

Sofia had stopped, her arms folded. "I think we're thinking too much. Or maybe not enough."

Tick looked at his watch. Six minutes. "What do you mean?"

"I mean, I think all we need to do is jump," she replied. "Jump up at five o'clock, and our feet will be in the air."

Tick stood straight, stretched his back. "Hmm. Possible," he said. But something tickled the back of his brain. Something didn't seem right. "But what if that's not it?"

"Got any better ideas?"

Tick looked at Paul, who was still searching, still wincing with every step. His arm looked like a giant purple slug.

"What do you think?" Tick asked.

Paul answered without stopping his hunt. "I thought of that, but . . . I don't know, I guess there's nothing else to do. Just keep looking, and if we don't find anything by the one-minute mark, we'll stand in the middle of the road and jump at five o'clock."

"Sounds good," Tick said, resuming his search.

One minute passed. Two. No sign of anything, anywhere. Two minutes left. Nothing.

"Time's almost up," Sofia said, running toward the exact middle of the intersection. "Come on, hurry!"

Paul and Tick joined her. One minute to go. Then, like someone had dropped a water balloon on his head, a thought slammed into his mind. *Make sure your feet find air. Make sure your feet find* air!

"Your socks and shoes!" he screamed, reaching down before they could respond and ripping off his right shoe, not bothering to untie it. "Take off your shoes!" He pulled off his sock and then moved to his left foot.

Neither of them responded or argued—they did as they were told. Paul used his feet to kick off his shoes, then his one good arm to remove his socks. Anyone watching might have thought they'd gone nuts, or had ants crawling along their skin. But in a matter of twenty seconds, the three of them stood barefoot, the pavement warm on their feet, their shoes and socks gripped in their hands.

"Fifteen seconds," Sofia whispered through a big breath.

"You're a genius, Tick," Paul said, his shoes wedged under his armpit.

"Ten seconds," Sofia said.

"Maybe we should jump just in case," Paul blurted out.

"Do it," Tick agreed.

Sofia nodded as she counted the last five seconds. "Five, four, three, two, one—now!"

Tick had already bent his legs, and jumped into the air on her call.

When he came back down, the world around them had vanished, and his feet landed on something very cold.

⟿

"This is weird," Rutger said as he stared at the command center screen, his eyes glued to the tracking marks of Tick's Earwig Transponder. Master George, Sally, and Mothball stood behind him. They'd all come running when the chime had rung through the building, indicating Tick had winked to another location.

"Weird, indeed," Master George whispered.

"Whatcha two hanks goin' on 'bout?" Sally bellowed. "I ain't got nary a clue what that thing a'yorn's tellin' me." He pointed at the screen.

Rutger answered. "They just winked to a large plain in Reality Prime—but in the middle of nowhere. The far northern reaches of Canada, it looks like. Nothing for dozens of miles around them."

"Goodness gracious me," Master George whispered. "Chu's tests are getting way out of hand. The poor chaps and Sofia will freeze up there!"

"Mayhaps we need be rescuin' them," Mothball said.

Master George shook his head adamantly. "Absolutely not. The antidote is as complete as it'll ever get, and we have to get it where it needs to be. Let's just all pray it *works*. Sally."

The large man jumped, as if he'd been caught daydreaming. "Yessir?"

"This may be our best chance—our last chance. I want you to wink there right away and give them the antidote."

Sally's eyes grew wide. "But . . . I'm a-feared of the cold somethin' awful."

"No matter," Master George said over his shoulder as he walked briskly away, heading for the testing lab. "Come on, chop-chop!"

Rutger couldn't help but feel sorry for the big lug of a man. He reached up and tapped Sally on the elbow. "You'll be fine. Just wink in, wink out. No problem."

Sally laughed, his booming chortle echoing off the walls of the room. "You ain't got no thermal undies I could borry, do ya?"

"Hilarious," Rutger said, hopping down from his chair to follow Master George.

⁓

"Ah, dude, it's freezing here!" Paul said. He sat down on the hard ground and started struggling back into his shoes using only one arm. Sofia knelt down and helped him.

Although the bottoms of Tick's feet felt like they stood on ice, he turned in a slow circle, gawking at the new place they'd been winked to. It was a barren, miserable land, flat and gray in every direction, all the way to the horizon. Not a plant or tree or animal in sight. The sun poked through a brief break in a cloud-heavy sky, but it added no color to the bleakness, no warmth. There was no snow, but everything about the area looked cold and dreary.

Then he saw something that stopped him. A small building—a tiny, leaning wooden hut just a few hundred feet away.

"Just be glad it's not winter," Sofia said, tying her shoelaces. "Or we'd have already been frozen."

Tick snapped out of his daze and sat down, pulling on his first sock. "I wonder what that little shack is over there." He pointed.

Paul and Sofia glanced in that direction.

"Looks abandoned," Paul said. He grimaced as he lay back on his one good elbow, his injured arm resting on his ribs.

Tick finished tying his shoes. "I wonder where we are." He stood up, the ground too cold and hard.

Sofia joined him. "Who knows? Let's go check out that building."

Paul groaned. "Couldn't that jerk have sent us somewhere that has a hospital? I'd settle for a place that sells aspirin. But no—he had to send us to Pluto."

"Come on," Tick said, offering his hand to help him stand.

Paul shook his head. "It hurts too much. Got my own way of moving now." He pushed off with his elbow, then rolled to his knees. After taking a couple of deep breaths, he stumbled to his feet, a little off balance. Tears rimmed the bottom edges of his eyes; one escaped and trickled down his cheek.

Tick quickly looked away, pretending he hadn't noticed. *Oh, man,* he thought. *He's gonna die on us.*

Sofia wasn't as kind. "Are you *crying?* I thought you were a lot tougher than that."

Tick felt a shudder of anger wash through him; he had a sudden urge to punch Sofia in the arm, but quelled it. "I'd cry too if my arm was broken and I was stuck in the middle of nowhere. Come on." He started walking toward the small shack.

He didn't look back to see their response, but he heard them following. Paul's feet scraped the ground with every step, sounding like he dragged a dead body behind him.

As they approached the building, Tick noticed it was at least three times as big as he'd originally thought, and farther away. *There's something about a vast land of nothingness that messes up your senses,* he thought.

The building had only one story, its entire structure made from warped, sun-faded wooden boards with thousands of splinters poking out. The two-sided roof peaked in the middle, slanting steeply downward until it overhung the walls in eaves that almost touched the ground. *To handle all the snow in the winter,* Tick thought. The place had no windows, and its door was a simple slab of wood, the only thing on the shack that had ever been painted. Only a few streaks of dull red had survived the weather. A rusted doorknob hung loosely from the warped door.

"Looks just like Grandma's house," Paul said. His voice was so tight Tick couldn't tell if he was joking.

"I bet whoever lives here has never heard of Pacini spaghetti," Sofia said.

Tick was about to respond but stumbled on his first word. They were close enough for him to notice something creepy about the door. The red paint he'd seen wasn't the remnants of an age-old decorating scheme after all.

They were *words,* scrawled across the entire face of the wooden door from top to bottom.

"Look!" he shouted, already sprinting ahead to see what it said.

"What?" Sofia yelled from behind him. Tick ignored them, and soon they ran to catch up.

Tick stopped just a few feet in front of the door. At first, he couldn't make out the words of the message, the writing hasty and messy, some of the paint having run down like blood into the other letters. But there was no mistaking Tick's *name*, and soon everything else became clear.

He tried to speak, but his mouth had dried up and his tongue wouldn't move. He felt like someone had rammed a glob of cotton down his throat with a wooden spoon.

Sofia read the words out loud.

Only two people may enter this door.
Atticus Higginbottom and Mistress Jane.
All others will die a horrible death.
Do not test me on this.

CHAPTER 34

THE ANTIDOTE

Tick could only stare at the message, the world around him shrinking away. He felt like an entire hour had passed, but he knew it had only been a minute or two since Sofia had read the words aloud.

He could only stare.

"What's that supposed to mean?" Paul said, though his voice sounded to Tick like it came down a long tunnel.

"What do you think, Einstein?" Sofia replied, her tone full of anger. "Chu wants Tick to go in there, but not us!"

"I know, but what does that *mean?*"

"Looks like ya'll hain't got nuttin' but trouble comin' down dem gullets a'yorn."

The gruff voice from behind shook Tick out of his stupor. He whirled to see Sally standing there, arms folded, looking like he'd just lost that morning's grits and eggs. Face pale, beard scraggly, eyes bloodshot, the man didn't seem too happy to see them. He was dressed in his usual lumberjack garb—thick green-flannel shirt, dusty overalls, big brown work boots. A leather satchel hung loosely over his shoulder.

Paul let out a little yelp at Sally's surprise appearance. "Sa-Sally? Where'd you come from?"

"Where you think, boy?" He made an unpleasant sucking sound in his throat then spat on the ground. "Ol' George sent me after you rug rats."

"How'd you get here?" Sofia asked. "You can't tell me there's a cemetery nearby."

Sally turned and pointed at nothing in particular. "There's a might nice spat of his fancy kyoopy gobble-dygook back yonder ways. You three too busy starin' at that big pile of sticks to notice me comin' up on ya."

Tick shook his head, finally feeling like the world had solidified again around him. *That message on the door,* he thought. *That message!* "Why'd Master George send you back to us? I thought we were on our own."

Sally shrugged his bulky shoulders. "Still are, I 'spect. Just come to pass on a little somethin', that's all."

He slid the satchel off his shoulder and down his arm, then opened it up. After a few seconds of rummaging around, he pulled out a shiny silver cylinder, two inches in diameter and six inches long.

"This here whatchamacallit is for you whipsnaps," he said, holding the small rod out toward Sofia, who stood closest to him.

She shook her head. "If that's what I think it is, you better give it to Tick. We can't go with him anymore."

Sally's arm dropped to his side, the cylinder gripped in his hand; his eyes squinted in confusion. "What in the name of Mama's chitlins stew you talkin' 'bout? You ain't done forgot the plan, did ya?"

Tick wanted to say something, but the words stuck in his throat again.

"No, we didn't forget the *plan*," Sofia said with a sneer, then pointed toward the door with the creepy red letters scrawled across it. "But that stupid door says that only Tick can go through it. If Master George wants him to get close to Chu, looks like he's on his own."

"You don't know that," Tick said, forcing the words out through a cough that rubbed the back of his mouth raw. "Maybe I just need to go in, do something, and come right back out."

"Doubt it," Paul muttered.

"Why?" Tick asked.

"I just have a feeling it's done for us, dude. I think

Chu wanted you from the beginning because of your freak show back in the Thirteenth—winking us with a broken Barrier Wand and all. We're done—I know it."

Tick looked at Sofia, pleading with his eyes.

"I think he's right," she said, frowning.

Sally walked forward until he was close enough to read the message on the door. "Whoever wrote that nonsense ain't got a bit of learnin' in him, I can tell ya that. I can barely read dem chicken scratches."

Sofia raised her eyebrows at Tick as if to say, *When did Sally get so smart?*

"Messy or not," Paul said, "it doesn't beat around the bush. Only Tick can go in there. If we try, we'll die a, uh, horrible death."

"That's only half the problem I'm worried about," Tick said. "What does Mistress Jane have to do with it? Why just me and her?"

"Reckon you and that no-good tweety-bird's all Chu cares about," Sally said with a grumble. He spit again.

Tick squeezed his fists at his side, then rubbed them against his temples. "I can't do this," he whispered. "I can't go in there by myself." His insides churned with panic, as if internal wires had been crossed, messing up his whole organ system. He felt like a sissy, but the truth of it weighed on him like the chilly air had finally frozen solid around him. *I can't do it,* he thought. *I can't go in there without Paul and Sofia!*

"Ah, now," Sally said. "Ain't no time for that. You ain't got nuttin' but brave inside you, boy. Suck it on up, hear?" He held the shiny chrome cylinder out to Tick.

Tick stared at it, not moving a muscle.

Paul walked over and put his one good arm around Tick's shoulders, wincing with the effort. He leaned over and spoke close in Tick's ear. "You listen to me, bro. No way we're gonna let anything happen to you. You're the one with that transponder thingy in your ear—we'll go back with Sally and keep an eye on every move you make. We won't sleep, won't eat, until we can wink back to get you."

Tick nodded, then looked at Sofia. She stepped forward and grabbed the silver rod from Sally, then lightly shoved it against Tick's stomach.

"Paul's right," she said, trying her best to throw compassion into her voice. "The three of us will wink back to Master George and watch you like a hawk. First sign of trouble and we'll come help you."

Tick waited a few seconds, then finally took the cylinder from Sofia. It was cool to the touch and slippery in his sweaty hands. "I don't think you should do that. Follow me *or* come after me, I mean."

"Why?" Paul asked.

"Well, if Chu wants me alone—or . . . with Mistress Jane—then we better do things his way."

"For a while, maybe," Sofia said. She looked as if she might say more, but then closed her mouth.

Tick looked at Sally and held up the silver rod. "What am I supposed to do with this anyway?"

Sally grunted and rummaged through his leather pack again. "Ain't no way ol' George be lettin' *me* tell ya." He pulled out a wadded up piece of paper and handed it to Tick. "Read that, ain't too hard no-how."

Tick unfolded the paper with shaking hands then read it out loud:

```
Dear Master Atticus,
    You hold in your hands the
antidote to Reginald Chu's nanoplague,
which is causing people all through
the Realities to go insane. We
believe the plague can be destroyed
by injecting this silver rod and
its contents into the mechanism
that controls the virus-like
nanoparticles. You need simply to
smash the antidote against Chu's
device—Dark Infinity—and let Rutger's
brilliant engineering do the rest of
the work.
    I need not tell you the incredible
amount of danger you are about to
```

undertake. I daresay, I almost feel
tempted to abandon the whole thing.
But alas, I think you'd agree that we
have no choice. The fate of *all* the
Realities may hang in the balance.
Atticus, you must do this thing. You
must do it, no matter the cost.

Once we see sign of your success,
we will come and rescue you. This, my
good man, I swear to you.

> Your comrade in arms,
> Master George

Tick held up the cylinder, studied it closely, ignoring his surge of panic. The odd object had no blemishes, no scratches, no smudges—it was perfectly smooth, perfectly shiny.

"Piece of cake," he muttered with a pitiful attempt at a laugh. "Waltz into Chu's house and smash this against something. Piece of cake."

"Yeah, dude, piece of cake," Paul said. Tick couldn't help but wish he could trade places with Paul, broken arm and all.

"You heard him," Sofia said. "You heard Master George. We'll be watching your every move, and we'll come save you as soon as . . ." She trailed off, and Tick wished desperately that no one would say another word.

"I'm going," he said, pushing the fear away. *Now or never. Just move.* "I'm going right now. Sally, can I have that bag of yours?"

Sally nodded, then handed over the leather satchel. Tick put the cylinder and the message from Master George inside, zipped it up, then slung it over his shoulder. "I'm going right now," he said again.

Without waiting for a response, Tick turned and walked up to the dilapidated wooden door. As he reached down and twisted the loose handle, the others spoke from behind him.

"We'll be watching you, dude," Paul said.

"You'll be the only thing we care about until we're back together," Sofia blurted out.

"You be tough chickens, now, ya hear?" Sally shouted.

Tick pushed open the door and stepped inside. As he went through, a cold tingle shot down his back.

CHAPTER 35

BEAUTIFUL BLACK HAIR

The room was completely dark but strangely warm. Tick pulled the door closed behind him, fighting to calm his breath, standing still in the blackness. The floor beneath him was solid, smooth; the air smelled like . . . flowers. Like an old lady's perfume. He sniffed, then scratched his nose.

"Hello?" he called out. *Isn't that what they always say in the movies when they walk into a haunted house?* "Hello?" he repeated. His voice died as soon as it left his mouth, without even an echo.

The entire room abruptly flared with lights; Tick's hand shot up to shield his eyes.

It came from everywhere at once: the walls, floor,

and ceiling were made out of a rough material that glowed brightly. Tick turned around to see that the door had disappeared—and nothing looked anything like the inside of an old wooden shack.

Chu had already winked him to a new place.

The room was a perfect circle, thirty feet in diameter, bare of furniture except for several, almost invisible, clear plastic benches curving along the walls. That was it—no decorations, no signs, no light fixtures, nothing. Just glowing walls and invisible benches.

"Heaven's waiting room," Tick whispered.

"No, it's not," a soft voice said from his left.

Tick spun in that direction, stumbling backward two steps. Ten feet from him stood a tall woman, close to the wall, dressed in a tightly fitted yellow dress. Long, silky black hair hung from her head and framed a pale but perfect face; her red lips pulled tightly into a grim smile. Brilliant green eyes stared through horn-rimmed glasses. Tick was certain he couldn't have missed her before. She had appeared out of nowhere.

"Who . . . who are you?" he asked.

The woman ignored him, scanning the room around her with a disgusted look, as if it were full of snakes and lizards and frogs. "This place is about as far from heaven as you can get in the Realities." Despite her apparent anger, her voice still gave Tick goosebumps, as if he listened to someone playing the harp.

"Who are you?" he repeated. "Are you—"

"Yes," she replied, finally focusing her eyes on him. "I imagine you saw a message similar to mine. My name is Mistress Jane, as yours must be Atticus Higginbottom."

She walked over to him, her feet tap-tap-tapping as she did so. She stopped and held out a hand, which he took and shook quickly before letting go, a shudder of nausea trembling in his stomach. Master George's most hated enemy stood inches from him.

Tick cleared his throat. "I . . . I thought you were bald." He didn't know what else to say, what else to do.

Mistress Jane smiled, though it was empty of humor or kindness. "Yes, I was bald for a very long time. So very long." She stared past his shoulder as if remembering something sad from her past. "And it was quite . . . *painful* to grow it back so quickly. Painful, but sweet. That's how the Chi'karda works in the Thirteenth, after all."

Tick swallowed, fidgeted on his feet. He was so lost and confused and scared. His mind spun; his heart thumped.

Mistress Jane caught his eyes again, then continued. "So many things have changed, boy. *I've* changed. Do you understand?"

Tick couldn't speak. He slowly shook his head.

Jane nodded. "Yes, we have a lot to talk about. A

lot." She reached out and took his hand, squeezed it. "Reginald wanted me to kill you, you know? That was my task."

"Kill me?" Tick managed to say, almost a squeak.

Jane's eyes closed and opened in a long, drawn out blink. "Yes, I was supposed to kill you. And I could have, easily—I crashed your spintrain to make Chu think I was at least trying. But I knew you'd survive." She paused. "But you and I are going to turn the tables, Atticus."

"What do you mean?" Tick pulled his hand away from hers.

Jane paused again before answering. "As dangerous as you and that baboon George may think I am, Mr. Higginbottom, Reginald Chu is far, far worse. *Far* worse. And you and I are going to stop him. Forever."

⟨⟩

Paul stared at the door for a full two minutes after it closed behind Tick, tempted to rip it back open and chase after his friend. But after all they'd been through—after all the things they'd seen Chu do to them—he knew the warning scrawled across the wood was for real.

Finally, he looked away, turned his back to the building. A fresh burst of pain exploded up his arm and into his shoulders, making him cry out before he could stop himself. For the hundredth time that day, tears welled in his eyes.

"Best be gettin' on," Sally grunted, glancing one last time at the door. "Better get that little sack of taters Rutger workin' on dat nasty limb a'yorn." His eyes fell to Paul's swollen arm. "Dat don't look so good."

The lumberjack started walking away, making a straight line toward an area that looked just like the miles of dull nothingness in every other direction. "Come on, rug rats!" he yelled over his shoulder.

Sofia and Paul turned in unison to look at the door one last time.

"Wonder what he's doing now," Paul said.

Sofia touched Paul's shoulder. "We'll find him," she whispered, barely audible. "Master George'll help us find him." She nodded, then ran off toward Sally.

Paul followed; every step felt like a sledgehammer against his forearm. *My only hope now is a tiny, fat dude named Rutger. Great.*

They probably walked half a mile before Sally stopped and turned to face the kids behind him. "Right chere seems 'bout right. Scoot yer buns on over here."

Paul cradled his arm tightly against his body and stepped as close to Sally as he could. Sofia pressed in from the right until they were all squished together in a small circle.

"Great balls of turtle scat!" Sally bellowed. "You ain't gotta get so close I can smell yer pits, now do ya!"

Despite the pain, Paul snickered as he backed away a couple of steps. Sofia did the same, but her eyes kept flickering back to the wooden building.

Sally reached into the pocket of his flannel shirt, digging for a few seconds before he pulled it back out again with nothing in his hand. "Ol' George'll be winkin' us right directly."

"What did you just do?" Paul asked.

Sally scrunched up his forehead like Paul had just asked him what the color green looked like. "Triggered the nanobobbamajig, boy, what else?"

Before Paul could ask another question, he felt a quick chill flash across his shoulders and down his spine. The drab world around him vanished, replaced instantly by a room filled with leather couches and chairs, a warm fire crackling and spitting in a small brick fireplace. Master George stood in front of it, the Barrier Wand clasped in his hands and Muffintops the cat purring at his heels. Rutger perched on a floor pillow, leaning back against one of the sofas, his hands folded and resting on top of his huge belly.

"Quickly," Master George sputtered, throwing all greetings and formalities out the window. "Have a seat and tell us everything, and I mean everything!"

"My arm," Paul said, his voice breaking on the last

word. "My arm," he repeated. Now that help was so close, the pain seemed to intensify, flaring through his whole body as if more than one bone had been broken.

Master George looked down and noticed the ballooned arm, the skin stretched taut, bruised and bulging. "My goodness, man! Your arm is hurt!"

Paul said nothing, feebly attempting a smile.

"Rutger," Master George snapped. "Take Paul to the infirmary this instant. Then wink in Doctor Hillenstat from the Second and tell him to deaden the pain, set the bone, cast it—what have you. We'll follow you and have our discussion there. Chop-chop!"

Rutger rolled to his left, got stuck, then grunted as he tried rolling to his right. His body slipped off the pillow, his arms and legs flailing as he tried to find the leverage he needed to stand up. "Good grief, would someone *give me a hand,* please?"

Mothball entered the room, wiping her hands on her shirt and chewing on something. "What's this?" she asked. "There's a ruddy bowling ball loose, there is! Someone snatch it up before it breaks a vase!"

"Oh, go on and make jokes, then," Rutger said, lying on the floor as his body rolled back and forth. "Poor Master Paul only has a severely broken arm—no big deal."

Mothball's face melted into a frown as her eyes fell upon Paul's injury. "Oh, dear, terribly sorry. Quite nasty that, by the looks of it."

"Yeah," was all Paul managed to say. The room had started to pitch and spin in his vision.

"All right, then," Mothball said as she reached down and yanked Rutger to his feet with a big roar. "Get the lad the help he needs."

"Come on, Paul," Rutger said, swiping at the dust on his round bottom.

Paul nodded and followed him as he heard Master George speaking to the others.

"Sofia, Sally—I need to know everything."

CHAPTER 36

THE TALE OF
MISTRESS JANE

L et's have a seat," Mistress Jane said. "I'm sure Reginald will be here shortly to rant and rave his frustration that we both made it here alive."

She grabbed Tick's arm again, pulling him toward one of the impossibly clear benches lining the lighted walls. Once there, she let go and sat down, crossing her legs under the tight yellow material of her dress. She flicked her thick black hair across her shoulder then motioned for Tick to sit next to her.

Tick wanted to run. No, he wanted to yell and scream at Jane for the terrible things she'd done, including killing one of Mothball's closest friends, Annika. He wanted to rip her ridiculous glasses off, throw them on the ground, crush them with his shoe, then punch her right square between her flaming green eyes. He wanted to—

"Sit down!" she shouted, her voice echoing through the room as though a chorus of Janes had called out the two words.

Tick fell to the bench, his short burst of spirit crushed. He folded his hands in his lap, staring at the glowing floor below his feet.

Jane took a deep breath. "I'm . . . I'm very sorry, Atticus. I should not have spoken to you like that. I apologize."

Tick closed his eyes for a few seconds, then opened them again. He realized suddenly that the woman sitting next to him was crazy. Crazy and dangerous.

"Now," Jane said. "There are a lot of things I need to tell you. I'm sure George has made you think I'm a monster, a cruel and heartless devil who cares nothing for the Realities or their people. Nothing could be further from the truth."

Tick looked up. "How can you say that? I saw Annika die—killed by those disgusting monsters *you* created! Then you tried to have them kill me!"

Mistress Jane held up a finger to silence him. "I want you to be quiet. Do you understand this request?"

"Why should I—"

Jane flicked her finger. Something yanked Tick

from the bench and threw him three feet into the air, spinning his body in the middle of the room. He screamed, thrashing his arms and legs. He spun faster, the unseen force gripping him like invisible claws as it wheeled him about, pinching and battering him.

"Stop it!" he yelled. "Put me down!"

The force vanished in an instant, and he crashed to the floor, one leg bent awkwardly beneath his body. He cried out as he squirmed to the side and pulled it straight. Gasping for breath, he pushed himself to his knees and stared at Jane, his eyes on fire.

"Why would you—"

"Silence!" she screamed, cutting him off again as she stood up, her face flashing red. "You will come over here. You will sit. And you will listen. Do you understand?"

Tick felt as if his old nemesis, Billy "The Goat" Cooper, had just sucker punched him in the stomach three times. Fighting tears, he slowly got to his feet and walked back to the bench. Without looking at Mistress Jane, swearing to himself he would never look her in the eyes again, he sat down.

After a few seconds of silence, Jane sat as well, crossing her legs again.

"Atticus," she said, almost in a whisper, as if she hadn't spent the last minute torturing him. "This . . . these are the things about me I don't like. My temper, my impatience, my quickness to anger. I've tried very hard in recent weeks to better myself. To improve myself and be kinder to others."

Tick snorted with all the disgust he could muster. "Yeah, obviously."

Mistress Jane paused. "Think what you will. But know this—if Reginald had challenged me to kill you two months ago, perhaps even one month ago, your body would even now be rotting beneath several feet of earth. I have changed my ways as best I can, but my goal remains the same as it has always been—to save the Realities. I will never waver from it."

Tick clenched his hands together, still staring at the white floor. "I don't even know what you're talking about."

"Reginald needs us, Atticus. He needs someone very powerful to help him with his project. His Dark Infinity project. And the two of us were the only ones he deemed worthy enough for the test—you with your silly riddles and death-defying adventures, and me with the simple task of killing you. Only one winner. Only one apprentice for Chu."

Tick leaned back against the wall and looked at Jane, already breaking his vow. "How could he possibly think that killing me would be a challenge for you? That's the dumbest thing I've ever heard."

Jane smiled, her green eyes flickering with a dark flame. "Atticus. Boy. You have no idea what you've done these past days. What you're *capable* of doing. Though I don't yet understand it, I have no shame in admitting that *you* have more potential than even I do. And you've done it without the benefit of living in the Thirteenth and soaking in its quantum mutations."

Tick shook his head and leaned forward, his elbows on his knees, resuming his study of the floor. "You don't need to talk anymore—you've proven that you're crazy ten times already." From the corner of his eye, he noticed Jane's hands quiver. She folded them together and paused a long time before speaking again.

"I'm going to tell you a story, Atticus," she said in a calm, quiet voice. "I want to tell you so you'll understand me. I only ask that you listen without interrupting. Will you do that for me?"

Tick didn't say anything, but he couldn't help feeling a surge of curiosity. He finally nodded.

Mistress Jane began. "I'm a scientist, Atticus. I have been since my earliest memories, experimenting in the backyard and reading every book in the library on the laws of nature. I have lived it and breathed it, as they say. Twenty years ago I was recruited into the Realitants, in much the same way you were. It didn't take long for me to master the wonders of quantum physics and excel in my assigned missions to study and document the Realities. By my third year, I was the most powerful of all the Realitants, and everyone knew it."

She paused, as if her pride wanted to ensure Tick realized what she'd said. That *she* was the best of the best.

Tick didn't move or say a word, and Jane finally continued.

"But then something happened, Atticus. Something tragic that still wakes me in the night, haunting me with visions and memories. I fell in love."

Tick couldn't help but look up at her. He didn't know what he'd been expecting, but this surprised him.

Jane nodded. "I won't speak his name to you because your ears aren't worthy to hear it. And please"—she held out a hand and lightly caressed his arm then pulled back—"I don't mean that as an insult to you. It's just that . . . his name is sacred to me, and I've sworn to never say it aloud. I hope you understand."

"I don't care what his name was," Tick mumbled under his breath.

Jane's hands shook again, and Tick winced. *Shut up, Tick,* he thought. *Don't say another word or she might twist your head off!*

"He loved the color yellow." Jane laughed, a distant, surprisingly light-hearted chuckle that faded as quickly as it began. "It was strange how much he loved the color. Yellow shirts were his favorite; he painted the walls of his home yellow. And he always gave me daisies and daffodils. I asked him once why he loved it so much and he told me it was because yellow represented peace. And if anything described the life and purpose of that man, it was peace."

Tick rolled his eyes, quickly rubbing his face to hide it from Jane.

"I loved him, Atticus. I loved him so much. It hurt me when I had to say good-bye to him and attend to my Realitant missions and assignments. It hurt me when he kissed me good night, whenever his hand let go of mine. That's the only way I can truly describe how much he meant to me. I loved him so much, it *hurt*. I would have done anything to take away that pain, to be with him every second of every day. I loved him so much, I almost hated him."

A ball of sickness grew in Tick's belly. He didn't know why—and he certainly didn't understand all this lovey-dovey stuff Jane was talking about—but something about it made him ill. Something about it was *obsessive.*

"And then it happened," Jane said. "The tragedy that would serve as the changing point of my life, the moment that defined my purpose from that day forward."

After a long pause, Tick asked, "What happened?" He couldn't help it—he wanted to know.

"He was *murdered.*" She screeched the word, a raw squeal from the back of her throat. "Killed by inhuman slugs who'd only wanted money. Killed by slime and filth, left in his own blood, suffering as it leaked out drop by drop. Slaughtered like an animal *by* animals, and there was nothing I could do to save him. He was *taken* from me, Atticus. The only person I'd ever truly loved, and he was taken from me."

Jane took a deep breath, then spoke rapidly as she stared into space, as if in a trance. "I couldn't accept it, I just couldn't. I knew too much about the possibilities, the endless possibilities of life and the universe. I went to each known Reality, sought out his Alterants. I took them, captured them, tried to love them, tried to train them to love me. But they weren't him, they were different; they were disgusting and filthy and unworthy to bear his countenance. It taught me how disgusting and filthy and unworthy the Realities are—how wretched and *wrong* they are. It's not built right, Atticus, it's not *made* right. It's wrong, it's all wrong! We have to destroy it, fix it, rebuild it!"

Tick scooted away from her. She didn't seem to notice, barely pausing to breathe as she continued blurting out words.

"I devoted my life to him, to his memory, to making things right in the universe. He's out there, floating in the goop of quantum mechanics, waiting for me to find him and bring him back. But first I must remake the Realities, create the Utopia we all believe in. First I must make it right, make it right, make it right, *make it right!*"

She stopped, her chest heaving as she sucked in air. "I'm sorry . . . I'm sorry."

Tick's eyes were wide, his breath held somewhere inside his chest. He knew for certain he'd never seen someone completely wig out like Jane had just done. Not that he'd doubted it before, but she was now a certified nutso.

Jane pulled at her black hair. "It's why I cut it off, Atticus. I was ashamed of it. It's black, and I know that *he* always wished it had been blonde, to match his beloved color. Yellow. Dear, dear yellow . . ." She rubbed the dark strands between her fingers. "But not anymore. I've changed. I will change more. The goal is the same, but I've changed how—"

"What is this nonsense!"

Tick jumped so hard at the sudden, booming voice that he fell off the bench, his rear end slamming onto the floor. Even Jane sucked in a quick breath as Tick scrambled to his feet, his eyes darting directly to the source of the shout.

An Asian man with black hair stood in the middle of the room, dressed in a dark suit. A man Tick had always considered one of his best friends in the world, teacher or not. But even as he thought it, Tick knew this wasn't his Mr. Chu. This wasn't the kind, funny, humble science instructor of Jackson Middle School in Deer Park, Washington.

No, it was Reginald Chu. The *evil* Reginald Chu.

CHAPTER 37

TICK'S DARK SECRET

Tick backed against the wall, feeling the edge of the bench cut into the backs of his knees. Though Mistress Jane had obviously been as surprised by Chu's appearance as Tick, she'd recovered, sitting calmly and expressionless as she stared at their visitor.

Chu walked forward, his forehead wrinkled and eyes narrowed in anger, his pace brisk. He stopped ten feet in front of them, his eyes never leaving Jane.

"What is this?" he asked, scrunching up his face like he'd just spotted a rotting body. "I'm trying to find the one person in the Realities worthy enough to help me in the greatest scientific achievement of all time—and you two sit here chitchatting like old friends. All that's missing are the cups of tea."

"What did you expect us to do?" Jane asked, her voice calm. "There's not much here to keep us entertained. I guess we could've wrestled or played freeze tag." She nudged Tick with an elbow.

Chu folded his hands behind his back, smoothing the anger out of his face. "*Mistress* Jane, I don't care what powers you may think you have, but you'll be dead in an instant if I so wish it. Do you understand?"

Tick expected her to get defensive, but she merely nodded.

"I'm very disappointed to see both of you sitting here," Chu continued. "I'd expected at least one of you to have the vicious instinct of survival within you, the willingness to win my contest no matter the cost. Only one can win. Only one *will* win. One, or none—I can always scratch the two of you and start all over."

Tick couldn't take his eyes off Chu. It was unsettling how he looked *exactly* like his teacher back in Deer Park. And to see this mean, nasty personality stuffed inside the image of one of his favorite people in the world was very disturbing.

"Isn't it an even greater accomplishment that we *both* made it?" Jane asked. "That such bitter enemies could reconcile enough to work together for a common cause?"

"All I see is cowardice," Chu replied, wrinkling up

his nose as if such a notion disgusted him more than anything else. "If you don't have the strength, will, or ability to kill this young man, then I certainly don't want you by my side." He shifted his gaze to Tick. "And you—don't think you've accomplished anything great. Much tougher tests lie ahead."

Chu paused, looking back and forth between Tick and Jane. "Still . . . I need an apprentice, and my patience has run out. Like I said, one or none. You'll both come with me and settle the matter."

Tick finally found the voice that had been locked in a trap of panic inside him. "What do you mean? What are you going to do to us?"

Chu laughed, the humorless laugh of a man who just found out he has mere days to live. "I'm not going to do anything to you. You'll do it to each other."

"But what—" Tick stopped when Chu held up a hand.

"Don't say another word. You will follow me, both of you. And don't be stupid—I have more weapons hidden in this place than you could count in a week's time. Try anything against me, and you will die. If my sensors detect any spikes in Chi'karda levels within you, you will die. At least until we get to the chamber. Tonight, you'll sleep. I want you well-rested for the morning. Come."

He turned and walked toward the opposite side of

the room, though there was no sign of a door. "Now!" he shouted.

Mistress Jane stood up and motioned for Tick to come with her after Chu. Heart thumping, Tick fell in line beside her. His head swam with confusion. Both of these people were supposed to be his enemy!

He and Jane stayed twenty feet behind Chu, walking just fast enough to keep the distance consistent. Chu didn't slow when he came within a few paces of the curved wall, and just before he walked right into it, everything went pitch-black for a full three seconds. Tick almost stopped, but Jane grabbed his hand, pulling him along before letting him go.

Lights flickered above them, then ahead of them, flashing as if gaining power before finally shining at full strength. They strode down a long hallway with a carpeted floor of brown-and-black diamonds, the white walls lined with pictures of various instruments and odd scientific experiments—beakers and wires and microscopes and animals in small cages. It gave Tick the creeps.

He looked back and the hallway stretched just as far in that direction as it did before them, as if they'd never been inside the large, round room made of illuminated white material. It surprised him when he realized he *wasn't* surprised. He wondered if anything would seem crazy or magical to him ever again.

Jane reached over and grabbed his wrist. "Listen to me," she whispered.

Tick didn't want to trust her, but he nodded anyway, as slightly as he could in case they were being watched.

"When the time is right," she said, speaking so softly Tick had to strain his ears, "we'll strike. You and I together. Remember—no matter what you think of me, right here, right now, we have to stop him, or Dark Infinity will make every last Reality an insane asylum."

"*Strike?*" Tick whispered back. "What do you expect from *me?* I don't know what you guys think I can do, but I don't have any powers and I can barely lift fifty pounds."

Jane shook her head in anger. "Grow up, Atticus. Are you really that dense? Even I've noticed the things you've done the last couple of weeks."

Tick looked over at her. "What are you talking about?" He winced; his voice was way too loud.

"Just stay close. Trust me—your abilities will come out. And when they do, I'll channel them against Chu."

Tick almost stumbled. The floor seemed to bounce with ripples as he felt his head swim. "I don't get what you're—"

Jane held a finger to her lips and picked up the pace. The hallway stretched to infinity before them.

Tick kept walking.

For the first time in a long time, Paul felt like he might not die of pain after all. Doctor Hillenstat, a wiry old man with a droopy mustache and enormous teeth from the Second Reality, had barely said a word after Rutger had winked him in to work on Paul's arm. Paul had been grateful for the silence, because he'd been in no mood to talk.

The pain worsened before it got better, but once the medicine kicked in and the bone settled in the thin white cast, life became bliss. Despite everything—the near-death experiences and the disappearance of his good friend Tick—Paul felt on top of the world after having suffered for so long.

Now, still lying on the soft bed in the infirmary, he decided he better pay attention to the frantic discussions going on between the people sitting in chairs around him—Master George, Rutger, Mothball, Sally, Sofia, and Doctor Hillenstat, who'd insisted on staying around until he was sure Paul was on the mend.

"All right, Sofia," Master George said after shushing everyone from talking over each other. "The matter of greatest concern at the moment is this: the odd *melding* of materials you saw on several occasions these past weeks. I want you to take a minute now, think about it very hard, picture it in your mind exactly as it was, and tell us every detail. Can you do that for us?"

Sofia rolled her eyes. "How many times . . ." She didn't finish, Master George having given her his gentlemanly stare of death, eyebrows raised. "Fine, okay."

"Splendid," Master George whispered, rubbing his hands together as he leaned forward in his chair.

Sofia took a second before running through it all again. "The first time it happened was back at Tick's hometown. We were in the woods, and we met that psycho teacher of his, Mr. Chu. He strapped the things on our arms—"

Master George interrupted her. "I'm certain that was Reginald Chu from the Fourth, not Tick's science instructor. And the thing he put around your arm was a highly illegal device called a nanohijacker. If we ever catch Chu, he'll be punished severely and spend the rest of his days in a Realitant prison." His face reddened. "So sorry, please continue."

"The . . . nanohijacker hurt worse than anything I've felt in my entire life," Sofia said, her face grimacing at the memory. "We heard loud crashing sounds in the woods, and Chu told us something was coming to get us. Well, the pain made us all pass out and when we woke up, dozens of trees had been smashed together— almost like they'd melted. We even saw a couple of deer in the mess."

"Hope it wasn't the wee one I saw last year," Mothball said. "Sprightly little thing, it was."

Sofia gave her a confused look then continued. "In the weird underground place, a bunch of robot things called metaspides attacked us, but they all got melded together, too. There was a big tornado and they turned into one big heap of junk."

"That was the Industrial Barrens in the Seventh Reality," Master George said. "Miserable place. And those metaspides are Chu's security force. I didn't know he'd sent them to the Seventh. We've had trouble with those buggers before. Go on."

"It happened two more times," Sofia said. "In the desert, a huge beast catapulted through the tunnel right before it was going to kill us—and got trapped in a big chunk of melted glass. I think some of the glass might have been created from the super-heated sand. The last time was when we were running from the glowing . . . *monkeys* near Circle City and a bunch of trees smashed together again, killing a few of the animals. It looked just like it had back in Deer Park—like the wood had liquefied and twisted together, then solidified into one massive structure. Like it was something from a nightmare."

Sofia stopped and looked at the floor.

Master George patted her arm and leaned back in his chair. "Thank you, my dear. Yes, yes, I'm quite certain my suspicions are correct. Quite certain, indeed. I fear our problems are much deeper than we thought. Oh, goodness gracious me."

"What?" Paul said, his joy and relief from the vanished pain fading at the haunted look that crossed Master George's face. "How could it possibly be worse? What are you talking about?"

"It's Tick," Rutger grumbled. "It's Tick."

Sofia's head shot up. "What do you mean, *it's Tick?*"

Master George stood, any sign of the jolly old English gentleman gone, his face set in a stony expression of concern.

"Master Atticus is out of control," he said. "He's obviously not even aware of the power that's bursting from him. Tick's inexplicable abilities over the Chi'karda are completely and absolutely out of control. It appears he's *manipulating* matter on the quantum level—destroying it, reshaping it, restructuring it. It seems to be triggered when he is frightened or angry. I cannot stress enough the danger of such a thing."

Paul felt like someone had just ripped his brain out, stomped on it, then shoved it back in his skull. "You mean *Tick* did all that weird stuff with the trees . . . and the glass . . . ?"

"Quite right, Master Paul, quite right. Now imagine an out-of-control Atticus in the vicinity of Chu and his Dark Infinity device." Master George brought a hand to his chin and shuddered. "My fellow Realitants, we now have a new number-one priority. Tick must be stopped at all costs, or he might trigger a chain reaction that could destroy every last Reality. We need to bring him back here, where we can figure things out."

He paused. "Again, I can't stress it enough: Atticus Higginbottom must be stopped."

PART 4

✳

THE NEW
MISTRESS
JANE

CHAPTER 38

A TIME FOR SLUMBER

Tick was exhausted by the time Chu stopped and turned to face them. The hallway continued on for as far as Tick could see, but Chu opened a hidden passage to his right by placing the palm of his hand on a square section of a metal wall. A hissing noise sounded as the panel slid to the right and disappeared, revealing a long corridor with doors spaced at regular intervals on either side—maybe forty in all. The doors were made of wood but had no handles.

"It's late," Chu said, motioning the two of them to step into the new hallway. "You'll both be confined to a cell for the night, where I expect you to get sufficient rest for tomorrow's events. Much will be decided when the sun rises, and before it sets, one of you will be dead. Or both. Think on that as you sleep."

Tick fought the sudden urge to push Chu out of the way and run. Oddly, he wanted Mistress Jane to yell at Chu, to use her powers against the creepy man. With a lump in his throat, Tick realized that the woman Master George had deemed the most evil to ever live had become his ally and his only hope. It sickened him, and he didn't know how he could ever sleep.

"I could use a good night's rest," Jane said, stepping into the corridor as she ran a hand through her black hair. "Which one is my room?"

Chu made a quick gesture and a door on either side popped open, swinging outward. The hallway was narrow enough for him to reach out and grab both doors, holding them open. "The lady to my right, the boy to my left. You'll find food, a shower, fresh clothes—everything you need. But *rest* is your priority. In you go."

Tick looked at Mistress Jane, but she didn't return his glance. She simply nodded to Chu and entered her room. Chu slammed the door closed; it sealed with a hiss.

"In, boy," he said.

From somewhere within him, courage swelled in Tick's chest. "You won't win. The Realitants know everything, and they'll be coming for you."

Chu glanced at the leather satchel slung over Tick's shoulder, his eyes lingering.

Stupid! Tick thought. *You shouldn't have said anything!*

"*In,* boy," Chu repeated.

This time, Tick kept his mouth shut and quickly entered the room. He'd barely crossed the threshold when the door slammed shut behind him.

～⌒⌒⌒～

"It's very late," Master George said, walking at such a brisk pace down the dark hallway that Paul had to jog to keep up with him and the others. "But before we slumber, I must show you one last thing. Tomorrow is perhaps the biggest day any of us will ever face—and I want you to know exactly what's at stake."

He paused in front of a steel door with a heavy bolt thrust through its lock. He reached out and slid a small, two-inch peephole open, the scrape of metal piercing the air.

"I want each of you to look in here, for as long as you can stand it. Then we will speak one last time before we say good night."

Master George stepped aside and gestured for Sofia to go first.

As she peeked through the small slot, Paul saw her body go rigid, her hands clenched into tight fists.

She finally looked away after several seconds.

"Why didn't you tell us?" she yelled, looking accusingly at everyone in turn. "What's wrong with him?"

Paul pushed past her and looked through the hole in the door. His breath caught when he saw Sato, his arms and legs strapped to a bed in several places. Despite the number of constraints, he still thrashed about madly, ropes of veins bulging under his skin, his face red from the effort. Dark bruises and scrapes marked where he fought against the straps.

His lips moved as he screamed something, spit flying, but a wall of glass between the door and the bed trapped the sound in and Paul couldn't hear a word. Paul didn't know if he'd ever seen something so heartbreaking. He finally stepped back, wondering if the image would ever leave his mind.

"What's wrong with him?" he whispered.

"Yeah, what's wrong with him!" Sofia shouted.

Master George took a deep breath. "Sato was infected with the Dark Infinity plague—the very thing Tick has been sent to destroy with the antidote. You need to know that Sato displayed a supreme effort of sacrifice and courage to bring us the sample we required. But even more important, you need to know there are thousands, perhaps millions, who are in the same state as this poor boy."

Paul and Sofia locked eyes, not saying a word, but sharing the horror of what they'd just seen. *Sato,* Paul thought. *Oh, man, Sato.*

"As you can see," Master George said, "we have a lot of problems on our hands. We have sent in as our only hope a boy who has a power that could destroy everything around him if he loses control. We have a plague of insanity sweeping through the Realities. And it all could come to a head tomorrow."

"So what do we need to do?" Sofia said, not so much a question as a statement.

"Yeah," Paul said to show his support.

Rutger answered. "Tonight, we get some sleep— everyone needs rest. Plus, we're still waiting for some of the others to arrive."

"The others?" Paul asked.

Master George stepped forward and took a look through the peephole at Sato. After a long moment, he turned and faced the group, his face solemn.

"Tomorrow, we send an army of Realitants to the Fourth Reality."

~⁀∽

Tick lay in the small bed, the covers pulled up to his chin, staring at the ceiling he couldn't see because of the darkness. Full of delicious food, freshly showered, dressed in a nice set of flannel pajamas, he kept his eyes open, staring at the blackness hanging above him like the void of deep space.

Tears trickled down his temples, into his hair and ears. Never, not once in his entire life, had he felt so utterly alone. He finally squeezed his eyes shut, sending another surge of wetness across his skin. He concentrated, picturing each member of his family one by one. His dad, hooting and running in place as his guy scored a touchdown in Football 3000. His mom, baking cookies, tasting dough on her finger. Lisa, talking on the phone, sticking her tongue out. Kayla, her eyes glued to a Winnie the Pooh cartoon on TV.

Then he thought of Sofia. And Paul. Sato. Mothball and Rutger. Master George and Sally.

And then the image of Mr. Chu popped in his head. Not the evil one, not the one who looked at him like he was nothing but trash. The Mr. Chu in his mind was the good and kind one, the one who loved science like a kid loves candy. The man who'd devoted his life to helping students gain an understanding of the world and how it works, to help prepare them for life. To plant a seed in future doctors, engineers, chemists, biologists.

What happened to you? Tick thought. *What did . . .* he *do to you?*

Despite everything, Tick felt a little better. No matter what happened tomorrow, he would always have his friends and family in his heart and mind. And then a thought hit him: he should quit feeling sorry for himself—those people he'd just been thinking of *needed* him. Though he had no idea what to expect when morning came, he had to face it and do whatever it took to win. Everything depended on Tick.

Finally, the events of the day caught up to him. To think he'd awakened that morning in a place called Circle City, hoping to figure out a clue that seemed so silly now. Could this really have been only one day? It had to be the longest day of his life. And he felt it.

As exhaustion pulled him into sleep, he had one last coherent thought.

Tomorrow, I'm going to win.

CHAPTER 39

WEAPONRY

For some odd reason, Paul was dreaming he'd just been sworn in as President of the United States, but everyone in the huge crowd booed and threw rotten tomatoes at him. One hit him square in the face, wet and gooey.

He woke up to see yellow eyes and the flicker of a tongue. Muffintops had been sent to get him out of bed.

"Get off me, you furry rat," he said, pushing the cat aside. He groaned as he pulled himself to a sitting position—his casted arm almost felt stronger than the other one—and swung his legs to the floor. Muffintops glared at him, her yellow eyes regarding him with distaste.

"Sorry, dude," Paul said, reaching down to pet her.

"I'm grumpy when I wake up." He looked at his watch: 5:00 AM. "Ah, man, what's up with that? Muffins, go tell the old man I'm not ready to get up."

The cat hissed and clawed at Paul's foot.

"Holy lumps of stew," Paul whispered. "You are one smart kitty. Fine, I'll get up. Go scratch Sofia's face for a while."

They'd slept in a room similar to the one in the Bermuda Triangle complex—plain cots and blankets, no decorations. Mothball, Rutger, and Sally had slept there as well, but they were already out of bed and gone. While eating a scrumptious meal of pork chops and mashed potatoes the night before, Master George had told them he couldn't wait to move the main operations back to the ocean, but they still needed more time to make repairs and rebuild after Mistress Jane's attack back in May.

Paul stretched and yawned, then laughed when he heard Sofia yelling at the cat. He quickly ran to get in the shower before Sofia claimed it.

After breakfast, Master George summoned everyone to the meeting hall, where Paul was shocked to see dozens of people he'd never met before. He and Sofia took a seat while scanning the room, gaping at the strange visitors.

Tall people and short people, skinny people and muscled people. The clothing varied—everything from a large dude with a fancy robe containing every color possible to a slender woman with pale skin and red hair dressed head to toe in black. There was a guy with a turban, a woman with a baseball cap, another woman with a hat the size of a sombrero but decorated with tiny stuffed animals. Quite a few of the strangers wore what Paul considered normal clothes—jeans, flannel shirts, golf shirts, casual blouses, T-shirts—but the ones who didn't stood out like huge chunks of coal in a bowl of vanilla ice cream.

A tall man with night-dark skin had eyes so blue they seemed to pulse and glow. He wore a one-piece suit with shreds of cloth hanging off like mummy wrappings. A woman sat three chairs down from him with bleached-blonde hair, her face painted in the fanciest makeup job Paul had ever seen—bright red lips, purple eye shadow, lines of blue streaking across her temple like colored wrinkles. She'd drawn a star on one cheek and a crescent moon on the other. Next to her was a man almost as short as Rutger but not nearly so fat, wearing a white shirt, white pants, and white socks and shoes.

"Who are these people?" Sofia whispered to Paul.

"Other Realitants, I guess," he replied.

Sofia tapped the cast that covered his forearm from

just below his elbow to his wrist. "How's that broken bone of yours?"

"Feels great, actually." He held up his arm and punched the air a couple of times. "Especially compared to how I felt yesterday. Can't wait to whack Chu upside the head with this puppy."

"You think Master George will let you go?"

Paul glared at her. "I'd like to see him stop me."

Sofia rolled her eyes. "Ooh, you're such a tough guy."

"Tougher than you," Paul muttered, but flinched backward when Sofia made a fist to punch him. "Calm it, girl! You're the boss, you're the boss."

Sofia folded her arms and pouted. "We shouldn't be acting like idiots. Tick's in all kinds of trouble, I know it."

Paul felt his heart sink to the floor. "Yeah," was all he could get out. The room felt as if a dark cloud had formed on the ceiling, dimming everything to a dull gray.

"Can I sit next to ya knuckleheads?"

Paul looked up to see Sally. "Sure."

He and Sofia scooted over, letting him have the aisle seat.

"Thank ya much," Sally said with a grunt as he plopped down. "Gonna be one heckuva day, ain't it?"

"Guess so," Paul said.

"What's the plan?" Sofia asked.

Before Sally could reply, a door opened and Master George came marching through, Mothball and Rutger close behind. Both of them carried wooden boxes.

Master George stepped up to the small podium while his two assistants set their boxes down. Mothball's was the size of two coffins and looked like it weighed a thousand pounds. Rutger's was as small as a shoebox, but sweat poured down his red face and he sucked in two dramatic breaths when he dropped his box on the floor with a loud clonk.

Master George gave him a stern look, then turned toward the audience. "Good morning to you all, and thank you so much for being here. Coming on such extreme short notice mustn't have been easy, I'm sure. But a dreadful time has come upon us, and we must act quickly. We will need everyone in this room, without exception."

He took a breath, then folded his hands together on top of the podium. "You were all briefed on the circumstances in our message to you, but I want to stress the most important issues of the day. The Dark Infinity plague is wreaking havoc among the Realities as we speak, but we're very close to a solution. Realitant Second Class Atticus Higginbottom is armed with a powerful antidote that will shatter the source device and send out a cure through the quantum Chi'karda waves Chu has been using to control those he has infected. Thanks to Rutger's tireless work, I have no doubt it will be a success."

Several people in the room clapped, and Rutger did his best to bow, though it looked like a beach ball trying to bend in the middle.

"But unfortunately," Master George continued, "we have an even bigger problem. Master Atticus has a power over Chi'karda that is extraordinary—far greater than we'd first thought and far more complex and difficult to grasp. It's out of control, and the potential for disaster is extreme. It is vital that we find him, stop him, and bring him back here for a comprehensive study. I must say, as much as I admire the boy, he's frightened the dickens out of me, and I don't know what to think of it."

The man in the colorful robe raised his hand, and Master George pointed to him. "So what ye thinking on the plan? How do we make sure we flash out the plague and save the boy from killing us all?"

Master George nodded. "Yes, Master Hallenhafer, how indeed? Though we haven't had much time to prepare, we do have a plan. Rutger?"

The short fat man cleared his throat. "Tick's ear transponder confirms what we've guessed—he's been taken to the heart of Reginald Chu's business palace in the Fourth Reality. No doubt the Dark Infinity device is located there in his research and development chamber underground. We've had spies in the Chu complex for many years, saving them for the day we'd need them most. Today is that day."

"Sha people!" the dark-skinned man in the mummy suit shouted. "Sha to do such a linka?"

Paul exchanged a look with Sofia, having no idea what the guy was talking about.

"Yeah," a brown-haired woman said, dressed in a T-shirt and blue jeans. "What good are a few spies against Chu and all his weapons?"

Rutger held up his pudgy hands. "You're right, you're right. Our spies may only be good for opening a door here, smashing a window there, perhaps rearranging some schedules of workers if they can. No, we're not saying we're going to enter the heart of Chu's lair because of a few spies. But they *will* help."

"Then what's the plan?" Sofia yelled out, surprising Paul.

Rutger looked at her, then scanned the full audience. "We'll have to, I mean, all of *you* will have to *fight* your way in."

A small roar sounded from the crowd as everyone started talking at once. A couple of people stood up, shouting at Rutger.

Master George slammed a hand against the podium, sending a sharp crack of thunder echoing across the room, silencing the Realitants.

"Please, good people," Master George said. "Don't get in a tizzy before you've heard the entire plan. Many of us have spent our entire summer working on developing our weapons program, and we've come up with some dandies, I assure you."

Paul looked at Sofia. "Weapons? Sweet!"

Rutger spoke next. "In these boxes are samples of our latest inventions, most of them based on items taken from the Fourth. We have enough to equip an army of thirty-two Realitants, and we think that will be enough to get us to Tick and the Dark Infinity device. And, if I may be so bold as to express my professional opinion, these things are going to kick some serious . . . um . . . er . . ."

"Booty!" Paul shouted.

"Exactly!" Rutger pointed at Paul, grinning. "Now, shall we begin?" He plopped down onto his knees and opened the small shoebox. He reached in and pulled out a tiny, dark ball, about the size of a marble. He held it up between his thumb and forefinger. "This, my friends, is called a Static Rager, and it's not something you'd want to use for playing catch with little nephew Tommy."

"Unless you be wantin' little Tommy to be eaten by a forty-ton ball of dirt," Mothball added. "Nasty buggers, those are. Could've used 'em on the Bugaboo soldiers."

Paul leaned over to Sofia. "Now *this* is what I'm talking about!"

Mothball pulled a silver device from her bigger box. It was several inches thick, cylindrical, about two-and-a-half feet long, and had several tubes running down the sides, all coming together in a tapered point at the front; two straps of cloth hung from it.

"This 'ere's a Sonic Hurricaner," she said, hefting it up for everyone to get a good look. "Call 'em Shurrics for short. Makes the old Sound Slicer look like a BB gun, it does. Come on, 'ave a look."

"Yes, yes," Master George said. "Come up, gather round. We have much more to show you and not enough time. Demonstrations will take place at the canyon bottom shortly. Departure for the Fourth is in three hours. Chop-chop!" He waved his arm toward Mothball and Rutger's boxes.

Paul was the first one to get there.

CHAPTER 40

A THIN SHEET
OF PLASTIC

Tick's eyes snapped open.

He shot into a sitting position, wondering what had awakened him. Had it been a noise? Did something touch him? He scanned the small room but saw nothing out of place—except for the lamp shining brightly on the dresser. That was it. Someone had turned the light on.

Man, he thought. *My brain must still be asleep.*

A tiny closet offered the only hiding place, and it was barely large enough to fit a little kid. He kicked off his blankets and walked over to the closet, then ripped the door open. Nothing but a pile of his old clothes and a few fresh shirts and pants.

Sighing, he stumbled backward and flopped onto the bed. *Chu created something that controls people's minds in other Realities,* he thought. *Making a lamp turn on to wake me up is nothing.*

After another minute, he stood, rubbed his eyes and stretched, then started undressing to put on some of the fresh clothes in the closet. As he slipped into a long-sleeved gray shirt and black pants that were as comfortable as sweats, he felt an icy chill in his chest. He had absolutely no idea what to expect or what to do.

He put on his own tennis shoes, slung the leather satchel over his shoulder, and stepped up to the door. There was no handle, just a dull slab of smooth beige material. He reached out, but before his hand made contact, the door clicked and moved, swinging out into the narrow hall. Pale lights in the hall revealed that Mistress Jane's door was also open; her room was dark.

Tick wanted to say something, ask for help, run. He expected someone to come for him, to summon him to Chu. But as far as he could tell, the whole place was deserted.

He stepped out of his room, then peeked around the door. The main door leading into the long hallway was open. It was dark out there, too—darker than it had been last night. He walked into the hall and glanced in both directions. Small emergency lights cast pale semicircles of red that didn't even reach the floor—anything could be hiding in the shadows.

What's going on? he thought.

He started walking to the right, sliding the tips of his fingers along the wall. He heard a faint buzzing from the lights; the air smelled like plastic and computer machinery. He'd only made it a hundred steps or so when a shadow formed ahead of him, the figure of a person leaning against the wall.

"Who's there?" Tick asked.

"It's me," a female voice whispered. Mistress Jane.

Surprisingly, Tick felt a wave of relief splash over him. "What are you doing? What are we supposed to do?"

Jane pushed herself away from the wall and walked toward Tick, stopping beneath one of the emergency lights. It cast an eerie red glow on her black hair and down her face, creased with angled shadows under her eyes and nose and mouth. Tick pushed away the thought that she looked like she was covered in blood.

"What are we supposed to *do?*" she repeated. "We're supposed to kill each other."

Tick felt a chill at the simplicity of the statement, but he knew she was right. "That's it? He's just going to wait around until we follow his orders and fight to the death?"

"Looks like it," Jane said. She held out a piece of paper. "This was taped to the front of both of our doors—looks like you missed yours."

Tick took the note from her; the paper had an odd roughness to it. Jane tucked a strand of black hair behind her ear, staring at the floor. Tick's gaze lingered on her for a second—and he thought for the first time that she was one of the prettiest women he'd ever seen. He snapped his eyes away, focusing on the note in his hands.

She's evil, Tick, he told himself. *Evil people aren't supposed to be pretty.*

He could barely see the paper so he held it up closer to the light. To his surprise, he saw it wasn't paper at all, but rather an extremely thin piece of plastic. Electronic, glowing green letters scrawled across its face one by one, just like someone typing a message on a computer screen:

There are no instructions. No rules. Nothing is forbidden. When only one of you remains, please walk to the end of the hallway outside your dormitory. Go to the right. You have until noon, or you both die.

"We have three hours," Jane said when Tick looked up from the note.

"Someone's done lumped you over the 'ead with a teapot, they 'ave," Mothball said, glaring down at Paul with her thin arms folded. "You've got a ruddy broken arm."

"I don't care," Paul said. He flexed his fingers while moving his arm up and down. "It's set. It feels fine. I'm going."

They stood with Rutger and Sofia next to the armory door; the other Realitants going to the Fourth had already received all they needed.

"Now's not a time for false bravery," Rutger said. "This makes your trip to steal the Barrier Wand from Mistress Jane look like a nice stroll down a country lane. This is serious business, and it's highly doubtful everyone will return alive—if anyone does."

Paul opened his mouth then closed it, swallowing a sudden lump in his throat. He looked over at Sofia. "You're going, right?"

"Of course I am," she replied, looking awfully bored considering what was about to happen.

Paul turned back to Mothball and Rutger. "Then I'm going too."

Mothball surprised him with her booming laugh. "So be it, then. Won't be me goin' to tell yer mum you've been sliced to bits by one of Chu's nasties. Come on."

She stooped to enter the room; Rutger waved Paul and Sofia through before he followed.

The armory was large but cramped with several aisles of metal-grid shelves rising from floor to ceiling, packed with an odd assortment of menacing objects. Some looked like guns, but most resembled trinkets and gadgets from a futuristic toy store: metal shafts with glass spheres attached to one end; awkward chunks of machinery with no rhyme or reason, like 3-D puzzles; cool watches with all kinds of dials and switches, but no timepiece; countless small devices that gave no clue as to their purpose.

"Where was all this stuff when we went to the Thirteenth?" Sofia asked.

"Most of it's junk," Mothball replied. "Experiments and such that couldn't hurt a fly on a toad paddie. Sound Slicers were our best bet then."

"Over here," Rutger called from a couple of aisles down.

Paul almost stumbled over Sofia as they both hurried toward Rutger. The short man pointed up to a shelf holding the same large cylindrical objects Mothball had shown them earlier, with several tubes that tapered to a point on the end, straps hanging off both sides.

"Those are the Shurrics," Rutger said. "Sonic Hurricaners. Grab two of them, Paul."

Paul reached out—the shelf was at his eye level—

and pulled two of the weapons down. They were much lighter than he'd expected, and he handed one to Sofia before examining his own.

"The two straps go around your shoulders and across your back," Rutger explained. "It keeps the wide end flat against your chest while you activate the trigger mechanism in your hand." He pointed to a small plastic rod jutting from the bottom of the Shurric with a red button in the middle, just like a joystick. "It'll leave your other hand free to throw nasty horrible things at the enemy. This way."

He walked farther down the same aisle then turned left, where several large black boxes lined the bottom shelf. "Those little marbles are the Static Ragers. We just call them Ragers for short since Stragers is hard to say and sounds really stupid."

"What do they do?" Paul asked.

"You won't believe it until you see it," Rutger said with a huge smile of pride on his fat face. "They have static electricity compacted inside them under extreme pressure. After you squeeze the suckers with your fist, you have five seconds to throw them. Once unleashed, the Rager uses the lightning-strong static inside to gather hundreds of pounds of materials to it—dirt and rocks and plants, whatever—like the world's worst snowball as it rolls, growing larger and larger until it smashes into something."

"Nasty little things," Mothball muttered. She pointed at Rutger. "This little ball of lard just about smushed me into a hotcake, he did, testin' the buggers. Not much can stop 'em once they get movin' and such."

"How many times do I have to apologize!" Rutger said with a frown. "It wasn't *my* fault you decided to relieve yourself in the weeds, now was it?"

Mothball's face reddened, something Paul was sure he'd never seen before.

"What else do you have?" Sofia asked.

Rutger shook his head. "That's it, I'm afraid, at least for you two. Some of the others have more . . . *specialized* weapons, prototypes and such."

"Ah, dude, why can't I have one of those?" Paul asked. "Specialized weapons are my speciality." He grinned.

Mothball swatted Paul on the shoulder. "Zip it. You're lucky you're goin' at all."

"Before you leave," Rutger said, "we'll make sure the Shurrics get strapped on properly and give you a sturdy bag for your Ragers. But it's time to go down to the canyon floor—Master George wants everyone to test things out before leaving, which gives us just over an hour."

He started pushing past Paul to head out of the room, but stopped and looked up at Sofia. "Ah, I almost forgot. Master George has something very special he wants to give you. I have to admit I was surprised at his choice, but he said he felt strongly that you should be the one entrusted to use it."

Sofia's raised eyebrows, creased forehead, and greedy grin made her look half-shocked and half-thrilled. "What is it?"

Rutger exchanged a long look with Mothball, neither of them showing much expression or saying a word.

Finally, Rutger said, "On second thought, we better let Master George explain it to you. Come on, let's go down the elevator to the canyon floor."

CHAPTER 41

A CLOUD OF STARS

Do you trust me, Atticus?"

Tick looked at Mistress Jane, almost expecting her to laugh and say she was kidding. They'd been standing in silence for at least ten minutes since reading the Note of Doom. "What kind of stupid question is that? You're a traitor, and you really seem to like hurting and killing people. No, I don't trust you."

Jane scowled, the pale red light making her look like a devil. "Fair enough. Then answer this—do you trust Reginald Chu?"

That made Tick think. "Well, no. He's as bad as you."

"Listen to me," Jane said. "I know I can't convince you I'm a fairy godmother who loves to make cookies and play hide-and-seek with children. But you're a smart boy. Think about our situation. No matter the troubles between us—between me and the Realitants—we have a bigger problem, right here, right now. We have to stop Chu before he causes every last person in the Realities to go insane. And I need your help."

Tick threw his arms up in frustration. "Need my help? You keep saying that. Yeah, somehow I winked people out of the Thirteenth and—" He stopped, not wanting to tell her about how last spring he'd made the burned letter from Master George reappear. "But it was probably just a freak thing and will never happen again. Plus, what good will that do us? You want me to wink you somewhere like I'm some kind of human Barrier Wand?"

Mistress Jane grabbed her black hair that lay over her shoulder and gripped it in her fist like a ponytail. "Atticus, you're either a brilliant actor or not quite as wise as I thought."

"What are you talking about?"

Jane reached out and poked him in the chest. "Your whole body *exudes* Chi'karda. It practically glows on your skin. You're like a supercharged battery just waiting to unleash your power. I've never seen anything like it, and you can't tell me you don't feel it."

Tick suddenly felt very ill, and all he could do was shake his head.

"I visited some of the places Chu sent you to—after you were gone. Back when I was still deciding whether or not to kill you as he'd challenged me to do. How could you have done those terrible things and *not* realize you'd done it?"

"I have no idea what—"

"Please!" Jane shouted. "The twisted trees, the melted glass with a huge creature stuck in the middle—what do you think did that? A stiff hot wind? It was you!"

Tick felt too weak to stand anymore. He slid down the wall as his knees bent; his rear end thumped onto the hard floor. "What do you . . . I don't . . . you're nuts. That's not possible."

Jane crouched down until her face was level with his, reddish-green eyes shining through her glasses. "You really had no idea, did you? It was *you,* Atticus, it was you. Extreme amounts of Chi'karda are flowing through you like pulsing electricity, and you have no control over it."

Tick found he couldn't speak, his throat constricted. But he shook his head. Emotions swirled inside him— anger, confusion, disbelief. Panic. He'd done all those things? He didn't want to have some kind of weird power over Chi'karda, he didn't want the pressure, he didn't want to be *here.*

He felt hot, as if his heart pumped out boiling water. His mind *burned*.

Then everything seemed to go crazy at once.

A loud bang echoed down the hallway; the walls and floor shook as if a thousand pounds of dynamite had just been detonated below them. Mistress Jane cried out and fell backward, slamming her head against the wall. Tick sprawled across the floor, rolling as if the whole building had been tilted on its side. The floor gave way beneath him, dropping with another loud boom. Tick plummeted several feet and landed awkwardly on his arm. As he twisted it out from under his body, he looked up in time to see a wave ripple down the hallway like a massive mole burrowing its way underground.

As the ripple disappeared into the darkness, the building shook again, but this time constant and steady, rocking back and forth, an earthquake. Tick scooted back against the wall, looking around, not knowing what to do.

Jane got up on her hands and knees, shaking her head as she bounced up and down with the moving floor.

"What's happening?" Tick yelled.

Jane didn't answer, crawling toward him as best she could, getting back up each time she fell. A huge lurch sent her rocketing forward. She crashed into Tick and grabbed his arms to steady herself.

"What's happening?" Tick repeated.

Jane shifted until she was side by side with him, her back against the wall. She put her left arm around his shoulder and grabbed his hand with her right. She tilted his head toward her and started whispering in his ear, caressing his hair like a mother trying to console her child.

"Listen to me, Atticus, listen to me. Take a deep breath. Calm yourself. I promise you I won't let anything hurt you. Calm yourself, *breathe.*" She pulled his head down onto her shoulder. "Everything's okay, everything's okay. Close your eyes, breathe—everything's going to be okay."

Everything was a blur to Tick, shaking and rattling. He did as Jane told him, closing his eyes, sucking in deep breaths, surprised at the calm warmth that spread through him despite the chaos. Jane continued to stroke his hair, whispering words of safety in his ears.

As quickly as it had begun, the shaking stopped and all was silent except a creak or two as the building settled. Tick heard himself breathing, felt his chest rising and falling, felt the comforting touch of Jane. The thought repulsed him, but he didn't move.

"Open your eyes," Jane said, gently pushing his head off her shoulder.

Tick did, and gasped at what he saw in front of him.

A misty mass of bright orange sparkles floated in the air, a condensed cloud several feet wide, hovering and pulsating slightly as if it breathed. His eyes hurt, but he couldn't look away. It seemed as if he'd been transported to deep space, viewing a nebula or a swirling galaxy.

"What . . . what is that?" he whispered.

Jane's voice was soft. "It's your Chi'karda, Atticus. I told you I could channel it if you would only unleash it for me. I can't say I understand what's happening, but it seems that when you get angered or afraid, power bursts from you, completely out of control and dangerous. If I hadn't been able to calm you, I'm not sure I would've been able to harness it and form it before us. Now, don't worry, I'm about to do something. Trust me."

The cloud moved toward Tick, the shining particles dancing in the air, darting back and forth as they surrounded him, dissipating into the darkness. He felt a surge of warmth, like walking out of a freezer into the hot desert sunshine. For a few seconds, all he could see was light, a million bright stars, swirling around him. And then it was gone.

"It's flowed back into you," Jane whispered, her voice loud in the silence. "You may never see it in that form again, but now you know what sleeps inside you. I don't want to be your enemy the day you figure out how to control it."

Tick's mind spun in countless directions, too confused and overwhelmed to grasp what had just happened or even formulate a question. "I don't get it," he said.

Jane stood up. "Neither do I, and I suspect Master George is clueless as well." She held out a hand. "Come on."

Tick took it and let her pull him up. "I'm a freak."

Jane shook her head. "No, you're not. If you're a freak, then so am I."

Tick thought of all the things he could've said to that, but he stopped himself. Jane had probably just saved his life. "What now? Looks like we're not gonna try to kill each other, I guess."

Jane looked down the hallway in the direction they'd been ordered to go once things were settled. "No, we're not. And we're not waiting until noon, either. Come on." She grabbed his hand and pulled him along as she started walking.

"Wait!" Tick called out, snapping his hand back. He searched around until he spotted the leather satchel holding the antidote. He ran over and picked it up, then joined Jane again, still marching down the hallway. "Okay, what are we going to do?"

Jane paused before answering. "You and I are going to stop Chu. Right now."

CHAPTER 42

SOFIA'S TASK

Sofia stood by the small cave leading to the elevator shaft, leaning back against the warm stone of the dusty canyon wall. Master George had asked her to wait there until he could speak to her; at the moment, he was explaining to Paul how to use the Sonic Hurricaner, the Shurric. Sofia had picked it up easily and destroyed three huge boulders in quick succession.

The Static Ragers fascinated her, though. She watched as a Realitant woman threw one along the ground with a quick jerk of her arm. A sharp crack filled the air, then a low rumble of thunder as the Rager rolled forward, gaining speed and size with every passing second. Everything in its path—dirt, mud, rocks, bushes—compacted together in a huge chunky sphere, snowballing as it rolled. When the Rager finally smashed into a test boulder, both objects exploded in a spectacular display of earthy fireworks.

Awesome, Sofia thought. She couldn't wait to hurl one at Chu himself.

Master George was walking toward her, shouting at the Realitants scattered around the riverside. "Everyone! Back up we go. We can't spare another second!"

As the two dozen or so people gathered their weapons and headed for the elevator, Master George touched Sofia lightly on the arm, leading her out of earshot of the others.

"We must talk before you go," he said in a low voice.

"Rutger told me you had something special you wanted me to do."

Master George nodded, his mouth pursed with worry. "Indeed, my good Sofia, indeed."

When he didn't say anything more, Sofia said, "Well?"

"Ah, yes, sorry." He pulled a tiny silver pen out of his pocket and held it up for her to see. It had no distinguishing features other than a clicker at the top and a small black clasp on the side for attaching it to a shirt pocket or notebook. "I felt I must trust *you* with this. Please take it—but don't push the button."

Sofia took it from his hand and held it with only the tips of two fingers, as if its surface might contain some poison. "What is it?"

"Well, it's most certainly not a pen. Won't write a single letter, I assure you."

"I figured that much."

Master George looked troubled, his mouth opening and closing several times before he finally explained. "We expect things to be quite . . . chaotic once you get to Chu's industrial palace. Though you must do your part to fight whatever forces Chu might throw at you, I must ask you to consider that your second priority."

"And the first?"

"Yes, yes, it's difficult to say. Sofia, I need you to run through the chaos, get past Chu's forces, and enter the main complex at all costs. Our spies will do their best to ensure the locking mechanisms and sealants are sabotaged when I give the signal. I need you to get in, locate Chu's research and development laboratories, which is where I expect Master Atticus to be, and *find* our troubled friend."

"Why? What am I supposed to do?"

"I'm afraid Tick may lose control of his powers when he confronts whatever Chu has planned for him. I fear it will be worse, far worse than anything that has happened during your adventures these past days. He may do irreparable damage—damage that could grow and trigger chain reactions, doing very nasty things to matter both there and in the other Realities if it seeps through the borders."

Sofia felt a knot tighten in her stomach even before Master George said the next part.

"You need to find him, Sofia. You need to place the tip of that pen against his neck and push the button. It will traumatize his system terribly, sending him into a coma, but it will also block his body from his mind, his emotions, his anger and fear. That should cut him off from the massive surge of Chi'karda that I expect. But I promise you, Sofia, it will not kill him."

Sofia felt a cyclone of emotions storm inside her— pride at being chosen for a special mission, fear of doing it, concern for Tick and his out-of-control powers, sadness that she'd have to inject him with something horrible. Though she felt it in her nature to argue, to push back, she didn't. Master George was right. He *had* to be right.

"Okay," she said, feeling like she should say more but unable to find the words.

Master George nodded with a satisfied look, then reached out and squeezed her shoulder. "I debated this within my heart for many hours, Sofia, as well as with Rutger and Mothball. But in the end, I knew it had to be you. It must be you. I know you will succeed, as surely as I know Muffintops is up there"—he pointed to the complex above—"hissing at every Realitant who steps off the elevator who isn't me."

Sofia smiled, then looked at the dangerous pen. Finally, she slid it into her pocket.

"Let's go up now," Master George said. "It's time to send you off."

It made Tick's stomach turn to see the warped and twisted walls of the hallway. Some of the panels had melted completely into globs of metallic goo on the floor. *I did that,* he thought. *How is that possible?* He tried as best he could to quit looking and stared straight ahead at the never-ending corridor stretching before them.

He gripped the strap of his satchel. *I have to tell her. I have to.*

"Um, Mistress Jane?"

She'd been quiet while they'd been walking; she looked over at him. "Yes? Sorry, just planning things out in my mind."

"I need to tell you something."

Her eyebrows shot up, appearing above the rim of her glasses. "Oh?"

"There's something in this bag. Something I'm supposed to use against the Dark Infinity thing. An . . . antidote."

Jane stopped, turned toward him. "An *antidote?* How did . . ." She trailed off, as if not sure what to ask.

"Master George got a sample from one of the infected people. Then he and Rutger figured out what to do. He said if I smash it against the device that's sending out the nanowaves or whatever you call the stuff that's controlling people's minds, it'll work its magic and destroy it. Somehow send the cure out to everyone. No clue how it works, but that's what I was told."

"Hmm." Jane started walking again. Tick fell in line beside her. "Well, I guess that will make our task easier. But only a little—the hard part will be getting to Dark Infinity in the first place. There's no telling how Chu's going to react when he sees us both still alive, or what weapons he'll use against us. Prepare yourself— I'm going to need every ounce of your . . . *abilities.*"

Sofia stood next to Paul, both of them in the long, single-file line of Realitants about to be sent to the Fourth Reality. Mothball was with them; she said she wouldn't miss it if she had only one arm and leg. Rutger stood still and silent by the podium, looking somberly at the floor, while Master George paced back and forth, doing his best to give a pep talk.

"I needn't say much," he said, his hands clasped behind his back. "I know that all of you know the dire nature of the task ahead of you. Not only do we have a nanoplague running rampant through the Realities, but one of our own is on the verge of a catastrophic breakdown that could shatter the very substance of the Realities. Not to mention our dear friend, Sato, who is suffering so much in our own home. For them, for your families, for the people of your world and others, I ask you to do this thing."

He quit pacing and turned to face the group. "I do not ask it lightly. But I also ask that you do not *take* it lightly. I send you with my utmost confidence in your abilities and in your strengths. I send you in the good graces of Chi'karda itself. May it be strong within you on this terrible, terrible day."

He paused for a long moment, the room completely still. Then he turned and pulled his Barrier Wand off a shelf under the podium, its golden, cylindrical surface shining, the seven dials and switches preset and ready to go.

Rutger spoke. "Though it would be easier if you were all touching it, we have too many people for that, so it's been programmed accordingly. We've checked and rechecked all of your nanolocators, and replaced the hijacked ones inside Paul and Sofia. We'll be watching you closely."

Sofia closed her eyes and breathed deeply, trying to quell the sickening swarm of butterflies in her stomach. The tranquilizer pen in her pocket bulged, feeling twenty times bigger than it should be and weighing a hundred pounds. She fingered the strap of her bag holding the Ragers, tightened her grip on the handle of the Shurric, its straps slung over both shoulders.

I'm ready, she thought. *I can do this.*

"Are you scared?" Paul whispered.

"No," she replied, hating how shaky her voice sounded when it came out.

"Me too."

Master George held the Wand up high, then lowered it back to his eye level, holding his right index finger above the trigger on top. "My friends, we very much look forward to your safe return."

He pushed the button.

CHAPTER 43

THE DILEMMA
OF THE DOORS

Tick and Jane walked another twenty minutes before the long hallway finally came to an end. Large double doors marked an entrance to whatever lay beyond, heavily bolted slabs of steel with no handles or windows. A large blank square decorated one of the doors, black as pitch.

"What now?" Tick asked.

"I guess we knock," Jane responded. She stepped up and slammed the palm of her hand against the steel several times; the muted thumps barely registered through the thick doors.

The black square ignited with colors, swirling like mixed paint until the image of Reginald Chu's head

solidified, but in 3-D. His face jutted from the flat surface, every detail of his features perfectly clear. It was
almost indistinguishable from the real thing, and Tick
felt the sudden urge to reach out and smack it.

"You're trying my patience, both of you," he said,
the slight electronic static in his voice the only indica-
tion that what they saw before them was artificial. "I'm
almost ready to pull the plug on this sad experiment
and start anew. If neither of you have the guts to conquer the other, then you're of no use to me."

"What's beyond these doors?" Jane asked coolly.

Chu's recreated eyes glared at her. "You know how
to find the answer to that question. I gave you a simple
task. I watched your act of compassion when the boy
lost control again—and Atticus, I assure you, it was
an *act*. She knows she can't harm you, even though
you don't know what you're doing or how to ignite the
power within you. But if she struck, my guess is that
you would win—albeit with some serious collateral
damage to my facilities. That's why I put you in the
underground tunnel connecting Chu Industries to the
Winking Yard at Bale's Square."

"But we're *here* now, Reginald," Jane said, as though
speaking to a child. "I think I know what's beyond
these doors. Aren't you afraid of what the boy and I
can do now?"

Tick didn't like how things were going. Not at all.

Was it true what Chu had said about Jane? And how could they sit there and talk about him like he was just a tool, an object, a dangerous weapon?

"I'm not afraid at all, Jane," Chu said. "There is zero risk of Chi'karda levels spiking from you or the boy. Go ahead and try."

Jane's face whitened, the smirk vanishing from her face. Tick had no idea what she was doing, but a vein at her temple bulged and her fists tightened. "What did you do?" she asked, her voice tight.

Chu almost smiled, but it was more of a grimace. "Your mutated powers gained in the Thirteenth will never—and I mean *never*—come close to matching what I can do with technology. I've conquered the science of Chi'karda. You've merely captured a fleeting anomaly that will squeak its way out in the natural order of things. You should've done what I asked, Jane. You should have *done* what I *asked*. It's too late for you now."

Tick couldn't take it anymore, as scared and nervous as he was. "Would you two just shut up!" he yelled. "I'm a couple weeks short of fourteen—but I feel like I'm the only one around here who doesn't act like a snot-nosed brat trying to pick a fight."

Jane stared, unable to hide the shock at his outburst; Chu's face remained stoic. Tick felt like his mind had split in two—one side telling him to zip it, the other reminding him that Master George and the Realitants were relying on him to find and destroy Dark Infinity. And there was only one way to do it.

"I'll do it," Tick continued. "I *want* to be your apprentice, so tell me what to do."

"I already have," Chu said, his bizarre magical face turning to face him. "You have until noon to destroy Mistress Jane. If you do, you'll be allowed through the doors and we will begin our work together. If not, you will die. Both of you."

Tick looked at Jane, who returned his stare. *How could I possibly hurt her? I don't even know where to start. But I can't let Master George down!* He fingered the strap of the satchel on his shoulder.

He looked down at his watch. "We still have an hour."

"True," Chu said.

"Then leave us alone."

Chu laughed a mirthless chuckle. "If it makes you feel better, I'll remove myself from the Imager. But don't worry—I'll still be watching." His face disappeared and the screen returned to blackness.

"Atticus, I'm sorry," Jane whispered. "I've never heard of a technology that blocks someone from Chi'karda. Somehow he's kept that a secret—a formidable task, trust me."

"I don't get how it works," Tick said. "Normally,

can't you just fill up with Chi'karda and do all kinds of magical stuff? Like a wizard?"

Jane rolled her eyes. "Something like that. Perhaps all I need is a pointy hat with stars and moons sewn on it."

"And right now you can't do anything?"

Jane shook her head, squeezed her fists again. "It's gone, completely. I can't feel it, can't grasp it, can't do anything. It feels like my soul has been ripped from my body."

"I don't feel any different," Tick said.

"That's because you've never controlled it or understood it. You couldn't even tell when you'd used it before—which I still find hard to believe."

Tick looked at the floor. "I might've felt something. A . . . a burning."

"Well, it doesn't matter now. We need to make a decision."

Tick knew what she was going to say. "He's watching us, you know. I doubt it will count if one of us *volunteers* to die."

"That's not what I had in mind." She gave him a creepy look—a blank stare, her eyes glazed.

Tick took a step backward before he realized what he was doing.

"I have no choice," she said, taking one step toward

him. "But . . . it's for the best. Best for the Realities. I'm the only one who has a chance."

"What are you doing?" he asked, his back hitting the wall of the hallway.

Tears glistened in her eyes. One escaped and spilled down her cheek. "I'm sorry, Atticus. I'm so sorry. I have no choice but to kill you."

CHAPTER 44

FINGERS ON NECK

Sofia's breath stuck in her throat as she stared up at the humongous structure that was Chu's headquarters.

It rose from the ground like a mountain—with a pointed peak and everything—as tall as any building she'd ever seen, stretching to her left and right until it disappeared in a slew of other offices and complexes. There were no straight lines on the structure, nothing flat, nothing symmetrical. Countless odd-shaped windows were scattered across the building's surface, most of them with lights shining through, but others were filled with dark shadows. Chu's headquarters towered over her and the other Realitants like a natural formation, a manmade mountain of glistening black stone.

Spanning the several hundred yards between them and the building was a broad expanse of grass and trees. A nice park complete with little streams, bridges, benches, and sidewalks that couldn't possibly contrast any more with the massive thing that kept it half in shadow.

"That is one cool building," Paul said beside her.

Both of them were armed with Master George's strange weapons. The bulky body of the Shurrics were strapped on and pressed against their chest, joystick trigger clasped in their hands. Paul was using his broken arm for that, since all he needed was a finger to push the button. Each carried a leather bag tightly against their left sides, directly under their arm, with a small opening for retrieving the Static Ragers.

"Yeah, it's cool," Sofia said. "I can't wait to see it crash to the ground."

The Realitants stood in a rough formation, in lines of eight, all facing the mammoth mountain of black glass. Mothball was in front, her head tilted back as she gaped at the top of Chu's palace so far above. She finally turned to face them.

"Done with speeches, we are," she said, fingering her Shurric. "Master George got us quite nice and inspired, he did. Are we ready for a bit of battle? Ready to go in there and stop the monster named Chu once and for all?"

Several Realitants shouted their agreement.

"We all know the plan," Mothball continued. "Get inside and make our way to the studies. Third lower level, section eight. Seen the map, you 'ave."

Sofia felt a cold pit in her gut, her nerves jittery. An emptiness floated somewhere inside her; she knew what she had to do. *If* she could actually find Tick.

"I 'spect Chu'll be sendin' nasties after us before long," Mothball said. "Better get a move on."

Her last word still hung in the air when a great boom rolled across the park, shaking the leaves on the trees. Mothball turned around sharply and Sofia rose on her tiptoes to see what had happened. Another boom shot out, then another. Several more in rapid-fire succession. Soon they were almost indistinguishable from each other.

Sofia saw holes had opened up along the front of the mountain building, big circles that were black on black, barely visible. Silvery balls shot out of them, one after the other. After a very short flight, the things landed on the grass and started . . . *changing.* They reformed and reshaped themselves, twitching as objects twirled and spun on their bodies, long appendages protruding out and reaching for the ground. There were dozens of them. No, hundreds.

"Uh-oh," Paul said beside her.

As soon as he said it, Sofia realized what the things were.

Metaspides.

～～〇

Tick had to keep reminding himself to breathe.

A long, long moment passed, he and Jane staring at each other. Her eyes flickered away now and then, as if turmoil raged inside her as she thought about what she should do. Tick tried to think of his own options. *Run* seemed like a good one, but he couldn't move, as if his feet were riveted to the floor. Then Jane's eyes refocused on him, like she'd departed her own body for a few minutes and had finally returned.

She slowly walked forward, arms coming up, outstretched and reaching for Tick, her fingers curved like claws. Tick was so baffled by her sudden change, and the almost laughable Frankenstein gait she'd chosen, that at first he didn't react. When she came within a foot, though, he snapped out of it and dodged to his right, ready to run.

With shocking speed, Jane spun and kicked her right leg out, smacking him in both shins. Tick lost his balance and dove toward the ground, just getting his hands beneath him before he crunched his nose. He started scrambling, but Jane was on top of him, grabbing both his shoulders from behind. With a jerk of her surprisingly strong arms, she flopped him over and onto his back, gripping his torso with her legs like a vice.

She clutched his face with both hands and leaned forward, putting her mouth flush against his ear, her breath hot. She whispered so low Tick could barely hear her.

"*Listen* to me. I don't think Chu can stop the Chi'karda in you—it's too strong. But I need to draw it out. *Listen* to me. I'm going to strangle you, do you understand? I'm going to kill you unless you fight back. It's the only way, Atticus. Do you hear me? I will not stop until you die or until you let the Chi'karda explode out of you and it saves us both. *Listen* to me. I . . . am . . . going . . . to . . . kill . . . you. For your own good."

Jane pulled her face away, staring down at him with her green eyes aflame. She put both of her hands around his neck, squeezing. Panic flared inside Tick. He kicked out with his legs, beat on her arms with his fists, but she didn't budge.

"Let go of me!" he tried to yell, a guttural croak that barely came out.

Jane squeezed tighter. "Look at me, Chu!" she bellowed out, lunacy glazing her eyes. "I obeyed! I will be your apprentice!"

As pain enveloped him, as his breath left his body—

squeezed from him—Tick thought distantly that he couldn't tell her intentions. *Is she really going to kill me? Is she acting? Would she really* kill *me?*

Her fingers closed tighter, gripping his skin, pinching the tendons and nerves. Tighter still. Tick struggled, kicking, beating her arms, thrashing beneath her. She squeezed even harder. Tick couldn't breathe, couldn't find air.

"He's almost dead!" Jane yelled. "Chu! I've won your test!"

Tick's eyes bulged and he felt his face puffing up. He heard the choking sounds torn from his own throat. Black stars formed above him, swirling in the air, growing bigger until they blackened his vision. Darkness fell upon him, complete.

Images flashed across his mind's eye almost too fast to register: his family, Sofia, Paul, the library back home, Master George, snow, school, Mr. Chu at the chalkboard, the Barrier Wand, the Grand Canyon, Rutger, Mothball . . .

I don't want to die!

Something snapped inside Tick's mind. He felt it—he *heard* it, like a branch cracked by a bolt of lightning. Heat surged through him, first warm then hot, pulsing through his veins, as if his blood had combusted into lava, *burning* him.

A piercing scream rocked the air. He realized it

had come from him just as the blackness swept away, replaced by Jane's face, hovering above him as she kept trying to strangle him.

Tick screamed again.

Jane flew off him, catapulting across the hallway and slamming into the wall. An unseen force pinned her arms and legs flat as her head thrashed back and forth. The ground shook as Tick struggled for breath, gasping in air, fighting to get his arms and legs under him. Sounds of bending and breaking filled the air. He looked up to see the metal panels of the walls warping and cracking, bubbling and melting. Tremors rocked the floor, ripples surging back and forth like waves on water, crashing into each other as large cracks rent the hard material.

Jane hadn't moved, still pinned to the wall. The chaotic sounds of destruction hurt Tick's ears. Everything had gone crazy; he couldn't take it. Somewhere inside him, he knew it was coming from him, that it was all his fault. *I'm a freak. I'm a freak!* Knowing he had this power only made it worse, panicked him further, sent his mind and thoughts reeling.

I'm going crazy, he thought. *I can't do this. I can't control it! What have I done?*

Chu. Reginald Chu. This was all his fault. Everything was his fault.

Tick glared at the massive double doors, the black

square still blank. The world around him rocked back and forth, things breaking and crashing and melting. The heat within him intensified. He felt certain his organs were about to burn, fry to a crisp, leaving him dead.

Tick threw all of his anger and pain at the doors. At Chu.

With a terrible squeal, the doors wrenched to the sides, crunching into a mass of twisted steel, leaving a gaping, smoking hole behind. Tick caught movement out of the corner of his eye—Jane falling to the floor in a crumpled heap.

I can't do this, Tick thought. *I can't do this!*

Screaming, he got to his feet and ran through the twisted and broken doorway.

CHAPTER 45

THE SHOWER OF GOLD

A sea of metaspides littered the park outside Chu's artificial mountain, crawling along the ground with their creepy, jointed legs. Sofia found it hard to believe they were *machines* because they seemed so alive. They swarmed together in a tight pack, heading straight for the Realitants.

"Ready yourselves!" Mothball roared.

Sally stood a few people down from Sofia. He lifted his left hand into the air and shouted something completely unintelligible. But he looked ready to fight.

A small tremor abruptly shook the ground, making Sofia stumble backward a step. The Realitants looked around in confusion, Mothball in particular. Sofia looked up at the black mountain. It shook as well; in the distance, she heard the sounds of breaking glass and twisting metal.

"Need be keepin' our focus!" Mothball shouted. "Master Tick must be goin' about 'is business. On the count of three—we charge! *One!*"

Sofia nudged Paul in the arm with her elbow. "For Tick and Sato," she said, not caring if her voice betrayed how scared she felt.

"*Two!*"

Paul nodded without breaking his focused stare. "For Tick and Sato."

"*Three!*"

Sofia sprinted forward before anyone else, her body acting before her mind could talk her out of it. Pumping her fist in the air, she screamed out one word, louder than she'd ever shouted anything in her life, almost ripping her throat raw.

"REEEEAAAAALITAAAAAANTS!"

The thunder of footsteps and echoing calls of her rallying cry sounded from behind her.

Sofia ran straight for the closing pack of metaspides.

The world shook.

Tick felt as if his mind was detached from his body. He rotated in a circle, staring at the huge open chamber he'd run into. He saw a vast open space with an artificial sky above him, complete with stars and a moon. Half-completed machines and menacing structures covered the hundreds of square yards of floor space. Workers hung on for dear life as scaffolding fell apart beneath them. Large holograms of floor plans and complicated designs hung throughout the chamber like see-through kites, countless lifts constantly moving between them, hovering and flying as if by magic.

Tick saw it all, but still felt his mind slipping away from him, out of control, on the edge of insanity. He staggered back and forth, the ground shaking and cracking.

To his right stood a huge tower made of gold that rose at least ten stories into the air. Near the top, partially obscured by a metal-grid catwalk, two words were stamped into the shiny metal.

Dark Infinity.

At the bottom of the tower, a panel of gold slid to the side, revealing a bright interior. A man appeared, then ran straight for Tick.

Don't come near me, Tick thought. *Stay away!*

But then he saw it was Chu, and the anger and fear that had subsided flared anew.

"How!" Chu screamed, still running for Tick. "How could you possibly have done this?"

His words were distant, as if spoken through a wall. Splitting pain hammered in Tick's skull. He squeezed his hands into fists to stop them from trembling. Pressure mounted in his chest and it became difficult to breathe. He could feel heat scorching him from the inside out.

He felt that strange separation from his body. He knew he was losing control, completely—but he couldn't do anything to stop it. The chamber shook, the tremors increasing in magnitude. He stared at Chu and Dark Infinity and from the corner of his eye he saw things falling. Metallic crashes filled the air.

Chu stopped, his eyes darting around the complex. "How . . . what . . . stop this! Stop this right now!"

Tick could barely hear him. As if reaching through a bucket of mud, he grasped for and found a tiny glimmer of sanity in his mind. He'd been sent here for a purpose—to destroy Chu's plague. He held on to that one thought, forced his hand to steady, and reached inside the leather satchel at his side for the silvery cylinder that held the antidote to Dark Infinity. All he found was something hard and jagged, dusty and rough. Confused, he pulled it out and held it up to his eyes, squinting to see it through the blur of the chaos swimming around him.

It was a big rock. Frantic, he dug in the satchel again. Nothing. The bag was empty.

The antidote was gone.

Sofia did as she'd been instructed and threw a Rager toward the army of metaspides, never stopping her sprint. The little ball hit the ground and spun forward, ripping along with increasing speed as the static electricity erupted from it, gathering massive amounts of grass and dirt and rock. The weapon quickly grew into an earth-made bomb, a gigantic bowling ball of nature ready to destroy something. Sofia watched with elation as it crashed into the front line of the spidery robots and smashed a dozen of them into metallic shards.

To her left and right, other Ragers hit the metaspides, wiping out the first wave of their enemy. As soon as the dust settled, Sofia started firing her Shurric, pushing the trigger repeatedly as she swept the nozzle back and forth, pointing it at anything shiny and silver. With each shot, a muted clap of thunder shook the air, rolling forward in an invisible tidal wave until it slammed into its target. Metaspides flew through the air as if ropes yanked them backward, dozens of them catapulting toward the black mountain as more and more shots thumped from the Realitants.

Sofia kept running, reaching into her bag and grabbing another Rager. She spotted a thick cluster of robots and threw it in that direction, then ran after it. As soon as the massive ball of dirt and rock smashed another line of metaspides, she went in, firing.

She was almost starting to have fun.

Despite the whole world shaking around them, Chu laughed—a bitter, empty chortle. The man reached into his pocket and pulled out the silvery cylinder containing the antidote. He held it up above his head.

"Looking for this?" he shouted. "How many times are you people going to mistake me for an idiot?"

Tick ignored him, focusing his eyes on the shiny object, his heart sinking. If only he—

The antidote suddenly shot out of Chu's hand and flew through the air, turning end over end before it slammed into Tick's palm and stuck there, even before he closed his fingers around it. His breath caught in his throat as he stared at his hand in disbelief.

Chu couldn't hide the shock on his face, his eyes wide, his lower lip quivering. "How is this possible?" he whispered, too low to hear but his lips making the words obvious to Tick. The man's eyes shifted from the antidote to Tick's face.

"Listen to me!" Chu yelled, holding his hands palm out as if approaching someone about to jump from a bridge. "You don't understand! Dark Infinity is a giant Barrier Wand. It's powerful enough to control and shape the Realities. It's the greatest achievement in history! All I need is your help—and we can use it for good. You have to trust me. Give me a chance. Stop this madness!"

Tick stumbled about as the earthquake got worse, things crashing everywhere, the massive golden cylinder of Dark Infinity pitching dangerously from side to side. The black specks returned, swimming in front of Tick's eyes, but this time mixed with flashing colors, blinding lights. He felt as if his heart was a furnace, burning him from within.

"Atticus!" A female voice, barely audible, came from his right. "Atticus, you have to stop! You don't understand what you're doing!"

Jane. It was Mistress Jane. But he couldn't see her. The chamber shook and spun.

Tick screamed and threw the silver antidote in the general direction of Dark Infinity, the cylinder blurry and bouncing in his vision. He heard an ear-splitting crack, then the bubbling sound of sizzling acid eating at metal. His vision darkened until he could barely see. He fell to his knees, screaming, and grabbed his head with both hands, squeezing his eyes shut.

Then, though he would have thought it impossible, everything got worse. The pain, the sounds, the shaking, the spinning, the flashing lights. Tick didn't think he could survive another second.

A booming crack rocked the air, and his eyes snapped open. His vision cleared in time to see that Dark Infinity had exploded into countless tiny golden pieces, flying and swirling through the air like snowflakes in a blizzard. A sparkling tornado. It sounded like millions of killer bees swarming.

"Atticus!" Jane yelled again, somewhere closer to him. "You have to *stop!*"

Tick knew he wasn't thinking straight. His mind was a chaotic soup of jumbled memories and thoughts. He glanced to his right and saw Jane running for him; Chu had disappeared. A small part of his brain knew she was coming to help him, but all his eyes saw at that moment was the woman who had tried to kill him, to choke him to death in the hallway. The horrendous fear and rage he'd felt when he'd been so close to death returned full force.

He didn't know exactly what he did, but he knew he couldn't stop it. The swarming specks of metal that had been Dark Infinity flew at Mistress Jane, like flies descending on a feast, surrounding her in a blur of sparkling gold. The metallic tornado consumed her body, obscuring her from sight.

Somewhere deep inside of him, Tick knew he'd just done something terrible.

I didn't mean to, he thought. *I didn't mean to!*

In answer, Jane's screams erupted through the air.

CHAPTER 46

THE DRAG RACE

Paul threw a Rager at the only remaining metaspide close to him, watching with glee as it steamrolled into a massive ball of earth and wiped the machine out, sparks flying as pieces of crumpled metal flew in all directions.

"Yeah, ba—"

A hard claw grabbed his ankle from behind and lifted, slamming his body to the ground. Paul tried to scream but there was no breath left in his body. He looked up to see a metaspide staring down at him with glowing robotic eyes. He wanted to say something— spit, yell for help—but he could only open and close his mouth, fighting to get air back in his lungs.

Scissoring metal blades came out of a hidden compartment, snipping on its hinges as it moved toward Paul's face. But then the spider paused; its body rotated upward, as if it had spotted something behind them. Paul heard the glorious shouts of Mothball charging in to save him, when the metaspide took off on its spindly legs in the other direction, dragging Paul with it.

Paul's body finally let him suck in a huge gulp of fresh air. It was enough for him to shriek with pain as rocks and dirt scraped his back, ripping his clothes. He kicked with his free foot, tried to slow the metaspide down by clawing at the ground, but to no avail. A burst of pain exploded inside him when his casted arm smacked a stray piece of one of the creature's destroyed buddies.

"Mothball!" he shouted, trying without success to turn his head back to see if she was close. He kicked at the metaspide's body and legs, but it kept running, dragging him like a sack of trash.

❦

Enough of this ruddy nonsense, Mothball thought as she ran after Paul.

She lifted her Shurric, aiming more carefully than she'd ever done in her fighting life.

"Keep your legs down!" she shouted, still running, still aiming.

She pulled the trigger.

Paul came to a sudden stop, watching in disbelief as the body of the metaspide catapulted away from him and landed fifty feet away with a mechanical spurt of buzzes and sparks.

The thing's claw was still attached to Paul's ankle, the arm of it ending in a shredded clump of coppery wires. Paul reached down and easily separated the clawed metal fingers, then threw it far as he could.

Mothball ran up, towering over him as she sucked in gasps of air. "Ain't the first time I saved your life," she said.

Paul stood, wincing at the stings on his back from the cuts and scrapes. He didn't want to think about what his skin must look like. "You used your *Shurric!*"

"That I did," Mothball replied, calmly.

"You could've smashed me, too, ya know."

"Reckon you're right."

"Or the spider could've ripped my leg off when it went bye-bye."

"Reckon you're right."

Paul shook his head. "Well, thanks for saving me."

He scanned the dusty area around them. Not a single working metaspide was in sight, and he heard the muted thump of a Shurric in the distance and a couple of Ragers wreaking their havoc somewhere.

It's almost over, he thought. *We wiped them clean out!*

The ground shook worse than before, swiping away his extremely brief elation.

"Need to gather the others, we do," Mothball said. "Meet me at the entrance to Chu's mountain." She took off running without waiting for a reply.

Paul thought of Sofia. He turned in a circle, searching for her.

He ran in a stumble toward the dark shape of the mountain, the haze making it look even more sinister than before. The quaking ground was making him sick. He shouted Sofia's name, mad at himself for getting separated. As the dust settled, he finally caught a glimpse of her near the huge glass doors marking the entrance to Chu's palace. From the looks of it, the doors had been mostly obliterated by a full Rager, jagged shards of glass littering the ground.

"Sofia!" he shouted again, running toward her.

She spotted him and stared for a long moment, then turned her back to him. The earthquake made it appear as if she were jumping up and down.

"Sofia!" he called, but she ignored him, her attention focused on the gaping hole leading to Chu's palace.

What is she doing?

Without so much as a glance back at him, Sofia sprinted for the destroyed glass doors, disappearing into the darkness beyond.

What . . .

"Follow her!" he heard Mothball roar from a distance. "Everyone! We gotta get to Tick!"

Paul ran forward, but only made it two steps when the earthquake doubled in intensity, knocking him to the ground. He looked up just in time to see a huge section of the mountainous building crack and fall, exploding when it hit the ground, the sound of its crash splintering through the air.

"No!" he shouted.

The entrance was completely blocked off.

CHAPTER 47

PACINI

Sofia ran, her Shurric at the ready for anything that jumped out at her.

The building shook horribly around her; she heard a crash of breaking glass far behind. Around her, the walls and floor bent and rippled; chunks fell from the ceiling. Every step took her full concentration and balance to make sure she didn't fall down.

Tick is doing this, she thought. *I don't know how or why, but Tick is doing this.*

She pictured in her mind the map Master George had shown them—third lower level, section eight. Her legs already exhausted, she somehow kept going, winding her way through hall after hall, down staircases, through more halls. With every turn, she saw people running, heading in the opposite direction, fleeing the destruction.

She kept going forward.

～～○

Tick was lost.

The blackness killing his vision was complete now, which only escalated the sheer panic that surged through him, competing with the intense heat that still burned. He stumbled about, waving his arms, calling for help. Jane's screams still rocked the air, though they'd grown deeper, guttural, filled with gurgles and raw shrieks.

What did I do? he thought. *What did I do to her?*

And where had Chu gone?

All around him, the sounds of destruction penetrated the darkness of his sight, scaring him. Huge *things* crashed nearby; it was a wonder he hadn't been crushed yet by a falling object. He wanted to shrink to the ground and curl into a ball until it was all over. But he couldn't. He had to run. He had to get away.

He kept stumbling forward, searching for something, someone, anything.

～～○

When Sofia saw the big metal doors, she knew she'd arrived. Without pausing, she threw a Rager forward, then readied her Shurric. The Rager pulled the metal and plastic from the floor and ceiling as it rolled along, growing bigger and bigger. It crashed into the doors, bending them with a metallic squeal, but not breaking them open. Sofia fired repeatedly with the Shurric, its invisible thumps of sonic energy enough to finish the job. The doors parted to let her through.

She scrambled into a chamber as big as a football stadium, chaos reigning as things crashed and burned all around her. Most of the people had already fled, but she heard the skin-crawling screams of a woman in the distance.

"Tick!" Sofia shouted, getting no answer.

She ran forward, scanning her eyes left and right. *Tick—where are you?*

"Tick!" she yelled when she spotted him, sprinting toward her friend.

He looked terrible, sweaty and cut up, wandering around like a drunk man, feeling at the air with shaking hands, staring with blank eyes. His mouth opened and closed, but no sound came out. Every step he took sent a ripple surging through the floor away from him, like a stone dropped in water. Chunks of the ceiling fell and were whipped away just before crushing his body, as if a host of guardian angels hovered above him, protecting him.

"Tick!" she yelled again, but he didn't respond. He looked so awful, so . . . *crazy,* she could hardly believe it was the same boy she knew.

Sofia kept running, looking above to dodge falling objects, winding her way back and forth toward Tick. A few remaining workers pushed past her in the opposite direction, fleeing. A thick man with a spotty beard crashed into her, knocking her to the ground. Sofia screamed something rude in Italian as she scrambled to get back up.

She caught a flash out of the corner of her eye, looking up just in time to see a spinning rod of metal right before it slammed into her shoulder. She fell again, and a boxy contraption plummeted from the sky, landed on its corner, then fell over to pin her legs to the floor. She pushed at the smashed box with both hands, but couldn't move it off her feet.

The sounds of destruction intensified—crashing, banging, exploding, breaking. Objects of all sizes fell from the false sky like the world's worst hailstorm, smashing to pieces all around her. The volume of noise pierced her ears, threatening to break her eardrums.

Sofia saw the long rod of metal that had smacked her shoulder nearby. She squirmed awkwardly until she could reach it; she grabbed it, pulled it close. The rod was twisted and curved like a crowbar. Wedging one end under the clunky, destroyed box that used to be part of who-knew-what awful invention of Chu's empire, she pushed on the other end of the lever with both arms, gathering every ounce of strength left inside her. At first nothing moved, but she let out a scream of effort, throwing every part of her into getting that stupid thing off—

The metal box toppled over with a sound lost in the symphony of destruction filling the gigantic chamber.

Sofia got to her feet, ignoring the throbs of pain lancing through her legs. Half-limping, half-running, she went after Tick. He was so close, still spinning in circles, stumbling, shouting things Sofia didn't understand. He looked like a man who'd lost his mind. Falling objects from the ceiling were deflected at the last minute as though a shield protected him from harm. Sofia ran on, zigzagging and stumbling herself.

She reached Tick, tackling him to the ground. "Tick, what's wrong with you?"

"It burns!" he screamed. "Someone help me! I can't control it! Someone *help me!*"

Sofia didn't think he even knew she was there. She fumbled in her pocket, panic making her hands shake. She felt around, grasped the silver pen, pulled it out.

"My brain is splitting!" Tick screamed, thrashing around, hitting her.

Sofia didn't know exactly what the pen would do to him, or if it would hurt, or how long it would affect him. She didn't know anything for sure. But she had to do it.

"Tick, I'm sorry," she whispered.

She jabbed the end of the pen into Tick's neck and pushed the button. A quick hiss sounded as Tick's head jerked and hit the floor. His body went limp.

Everything went still—the shaking, the crashing, the ripping, the bending.

Everything stopped.

The only sound was a woman still screaming in the distance.

CHAPTER 48

OUT OF THE RUBBLE

Paul grunted as he moved another chunk of black glass off the pile.

"Isn't there another way in?" he asked.

"Ain't nary a one that ain't blocked!" Sally shouted, lifting a piece the size of a large suitcase. He threw it and Paul watched it split into several pieces upon landing.

Then Paul noticed the silence.

"Hey . . . *hey!*" he shouted.

Everyone else quit working, looking about.

"It's ruddy well stopped, it 'as," Mothball said, a crooked-toothed grin breaking across her face.

Paul ran away from the pile, craning his neck to

look up at the mountain as he got farther away. Though full of cracks and missing pieces, the building wasn't shaking or falling apart anymore. The ground wasn't trembling. The air had grown still and silent, the dust already settling to the ground.

"Sofia did it," Mothball said, waving Paul back over to help. "Come on, gotta clear this pile. Gotta find 'er and Master Tick."

Encouraged for the first time in a while, Paul sprinted back and started sorting through the rubble with renewed vigor, knowing his hurt arm would be some kind of sore tomorrow. Piece after piece, chunk after chunk, the Realitants worked together until a shaft of light escaped from within. They'd found a way through.

"We did it!" Paul shouted, grabbing more pieces. Soon they had a hole big enough for them to enter the damaged building.

Mothball went first, then Sally, then Paul and the other Realitants. They regrouped inside, sweeping their weapons back and forth in case of an attack. There wasn't a sign of anyone or anything dangerous, only dust and debris.

"Come on, let's—" Paul started to say, then stopped when he saw movement up ahead in the hallway. He couldn't make it out at first—it looked like an injured animal crawling along, slide-and-stop, slide-and-stop.

But then the dust settled and the figures came into the light. Everything became clear.

It was Sofia, her back to them, dragging Tick's battered body down the broken hallway.

⁓

Somehow, Jane finally quit screaming.

She lay on the floor, her mind trying to shut down in order to avoid the sheer agony of her pain. It filled every inch of her, every organ, every cell, every molecule. Her nerves bristled with it. The slightest movement of her ragged breathing sent fresh pinpricks shooting across her skin, *through* her skin, into her blood and muscles and bone. She hurt, she ached, she stung. The pain consumed her. The only thing that kept her from weeping was the promise of even more pain.

I tried to help him, she thought. *I was only trying to help him. How?* How *could he have done this to me?*

Her eyes had been closed for a long time, the prospect of seeing the damage to her body too horrific. But finally, she allowed her eyelids to slide up. The movement sent a new wave of agony across her face and through her head, as if needles had pierced her skull. But she kept her eyes open.

She did not, however, have the courage to move anything else. She saw only what she could from her current position, crumpled like a rag doll. But it was enough to let her know her life was over.

Shards of gold, small but jagged, covered every inch of her body, jutting from the skin at all kinds of angles. Blood was everywhere, seeping from the wounds. Her body was like a sea of red, a million tiny golden icebergs breaking the surface. Most of the shards appeared to be *fused* to her skin, impossible to remove. She could only imagine what her face must look like. A beast. A hideous beast.

A bit of the old Jane returned to her then. The one who'd been courageous and strong, unwilling to break under any task or trial. The one who'd fought on, no matter what.

Realities help me, I can do this. I will do this.

Bracing herself, Jane counted silently to three, readying her mind and soul for what she was about to do. Then, as quickly and as efficiently as she could, she pushed her arms below her and stood up.

The blood-curdling scream that erupted from her was inhuman—the terrified shriek of tortured demons. The sound tore through the air, filled the world around her, pierced her own ears until they bled. It seemed impossible that she didn't faint from the pain that had ruptured inside of her like the detonation of a nuclear bomb.

She stood still, enduring. Eventually, the pain lessened. Barely, but enough so that she had the awkward sensation of bliss, a warm calm.

All things are relative, she thought.

Then, a very strange thing occurred to her. She didn't understand it, didn't know how the thought formed in her mind or where it came from. Perhaps it had been something Reginald had said in the moments before he ran away, something he'd told the boy about Dark Infinity. No matter—she'd figure it out later. But regardless of *how* she knew, she *did* know.

She had changed forever. In the midst of all the horror, perhaps there was a silver lining after all. Yes, she knew. She *knew.*

Mistress Jane had no Barrier Wand within her reach. No one in her Reality had a Wand to pull her away from this place. No one, anywhere, had a lock on her nanolocator besides those who could do nothing about it. Yet, despite all that, Jane winked herself away, away from the Fourth Reality and back to the Thirteenth.

She did it by *thinking* it.

Yes, she had changed forever.

CHAPTER 49

AN UNFORTUNATE MEETING

Tick looked dead.

He lay flat on his back, his head cradled in Sofia's lap as every last Realitant stood in a group around them, staring down solemnly as if it were a funeral. Tick's face was pale, scratches and welts marring almost every inch of him. His clothes were ripped, bloodied, even melted in some places, attached to the skin. But he was breathing, marked by the slight rise and fall of his chest.

Man, Paul thought. *When that dude wakes up, he's gonna hurt something awful.*

They were gathered in an open grassy area of the ruined park, ignoring the hundreds of people who had evacuated Chu's mountain building. Most of them stood in silent huddles, staring back at the black structure, probably in shock at how close they'd come to dying.

"Gonna be just fine, he will," Mothball announced, kneeling next to Tick. "Sofia 'ere may ruddy well win a medal from the old man for this."

The crowd of Realitants broke into applause as Sally bellowed a long-winded cheer that echoed across the park but made absolutely no sense. Paul thought he caught the words "rabbit" and "coon dog." Sofia showed no reaction to anything, staring at a blank spot in front of her.

Mothball reached across Tick and grabbed him around the torso, lifting him up with a heavy grunt. His body flopped over her shoulder with no sign of life, his arms and legs dangling.

"Come on," she said. "Chi'karda spot's only a 'undred yards up yonder." She nodded her head in the direction away from the destruction.

As the others started following Mothball, Paul reached down and offered Sofia a hand. "Let's go, Miss Italy. Tick's gonna be fine, thanks to you. You can beg me for forgiveness later."

Sofia took his hand and pulled herself to her feet. "Forgiveness for what? Killing more spiders than you did?"

"*No.* For not telling me you had a super-secret mission to put Tick in a coma."

"Oh. Yeah. Sorry that Master George thinks I'm better than you."

Paul sighed. "You're forgiven."

A shout from behind turned both their heads. A dark-haired man, his clothes ripped to shreds, his body battered and bloody, was limping along as fast as he could, yelling something unintelligible. Sofia recognized him before Paul did.

"It's Chu!" she yelled. "Mothball! That's Reginald Chu!"

Mothball turned and ran back toward them, Tick still slung over her shoulder. "Right, you are. Reginald Chu! Sally! Grab the monster!"

Sally had barely taken a step before an even louder shout came from a cluster of trees to their right. *Another* dark-haired man bolted from the shadows, his fist raised in the air, screaming obscenities that made Paul wince. Then, in disbelief, he saw who it was. Paul looked back at the other man.

Two Reginald Chus were running straight for them.

"Whoa," he whispered.

"Oh, no," Mothball said, standing right next to Paul. "Oh, no!" she said louder. Then she screamed at the top of her lungs. "Run! Everyone *run!*"

Without waiting for a response, the tall lady sprinted for their Chi'karda launching point, Tick bouncing up and down on her shoulder, the other Realitants right behind her.

It took Paul a second to break his stare from the impossible sight of two identical men coming toward them—one limping, the other moving at full speed. Both seemed oblivious of the other, each wanting to reach the Realitants and unaware of his twin.

"Come on!" Sofia yelled, grabbing Paul by the arm and pulling him as they ran after Mothball. "I think I know—"

An ear-piercing noise cut her off just as a surge of blinding light flashed behind them. A terribly loud boom rattled the air, the sound of a million amplified horns going off at once. Paul had *heard* that sound before.

He'd barely had the thought when a rush of tornado-force wind hit them, knocking him and Sofia flat on the ground. The wind passed over them, a solid wave of air that was almost visible as it tore at trees and bushes and benches, traveling outward in a wide arc. It knocked over the other fleeing Realitants and kept moving along its destructive path.

All was still for a single moment. Then the ground started violently shaking, far worse than before. Trees crashed to the ground. Sounds of breaking glass and bending metal filled the air as the mountainous palace of Chu started collapsing all over again.

"Tick!" Paul yelled over the deafening noise. "He must've woke up!"

"No!" Sofia shouted back. "I think it has something to do with Chu meeting his Alterant."

Paul risked a glance over his shoulder and saw that only one Chu remained—the injured one. He limped toward them, struggling all the worse because of the earthquake.

Sally suddenly bolted past Paul and Sofia, running for the man. Like picking up a bag of sticks, Sally grabbed Chu and flopped him over his shoulder just like Mothball had done with Tick. He ran back toward them, stumbling left and right as the ground shook.

"Get up! Get up!" Sofia shouted, pulling on Paul's good arm.

He obeyed and ran after her, his mind twisting in a million different directions.

The earthquake worsened, throwing Sofia to the ground. Paul helped her up and they kept running, losing one step for every two they made forward. Sally caught up with them, moving as if Chu weighed only ten pounds.

Eventually, the Realitants gathered in the designated spot, every last one of them staring back toward Chu Industries in awe and fear. Mothball still held Tick, and she was shouting something over and over.

"Wink us out, George! Wink us out! Ruddy wink us out!"

Sounds of splitting and cracking and shattering glass rocked the air. A thunderous roar ripped across the ground, and Paul felt his heart wedge itself in his throat.

Chu's palace collapsed toward the ground, the whole thing at once. Paul threw his hands over his ears. The sounds of destruction were louder than anything he'd ever heard before as an entire building of metal and glass exploded nearby. He watched as a massive cloud of black dust rolled out of the falling ruins, billowing out and rushing toward them at an alarming speed.

"Now, Master George!" Mothball roared, barely audible over the sounds of the mountain collapsing. *"Now!"*

Like a fleet of starships zipping into hyperspace, the Realitants winked away in quick succession. Paul actually *tasted* the choking dust and saw the suffocating darkness before he felt the familiar tingle and was winked to safety.

CHAPTER 50

MUCH TO DISCUSS

No one did any celebrating.

After getting safely back to headquarters and undergoing full debriefings, most of the Realitants said their good-byes and winked back to their home Realities. Paul and Sofia stuck to Tick's side; except for the rise and fall of his chest, he seemed as dead as a corpse. Paul couldn't think of much to say as they followed Mothball to the infirmary, where Doctor Hillenstat hooked Tick up to several monitoring machines; an IV dripped a clear liquid into his veins. Rutger watched from the side, scrutinizing the doctor's every move as if waiting for him to make a mistake.

"How long will he be out?" Sofia asked. "Is he gonna be okay?"

Hillenstat frowned. "An hour. A day. A week. No telling."

"But will he be *okay?*" Paul said.

The doctor felt Tick's forehead. "Yes, he's fine for now. But in the long run?" He shrugged. "I think I'll let Master George be the judge of that."

Sofia huffed. "Aren't doctors supposed to make you feel better?"

Hillenstat smiled through his droopy mustache, the first time Paul had ever seen him do it. "Doctors are supposed to be honest. Now, I'll go and get Master George and you can bother *him* with your questions. I need a nap."

He wiped his hands together as if swiping away crumbs from dinner, gave one last look at Tick, then walked out of the infirmary.

Sofia looked at Rutger. "Nice guy you got there. I'm glad I'm not sick."

Rutger ignored them, looking over at a machine that monitored Tick's vitals, but Mothball spoke up. "Best doc in the Realities, he is. A bit snippy, though."

Master George walked in, Sally lumbering along behind him. They both pulled up chairs to the bed and sat down so the whole group was in a circle, looking solemnly at the comatose Tick.

"So what's the deal?" Paul asked.

"Yeah, what's wrong with him?" Sofia added.

Master George cleared his throat, not breaking his gaze from Tick's face. "Yes, yes, a very good question, my young friends. I certainly didn't expect things to go in this direction with the lad. Troubling, I tell you. Very troubling indeed."

He paused, and after a few moments of tense silence, Sofia threw her hands into the air, palms up. "Well?"

"Show some respect," Rutger growled.

"No, no," Master George said, throwing a quick glance in Rutger's direction. "We've seen a lot this past day, and answers are deserved. If everyone would give me a moment, I'll do my best to tell you what we know."

He took a deep breath, then began. "First of all, Sato is recovering nicely. The lunacy left him as soon as the trouble started with Tick in the Fourth—the antidote obviously found its target during all that chaos. But Sato's very battered and bruised from the abuse he gave himself while under the control of Dark Infinity. I'd encourage you all to visit him. He's back in his normal quarters—quite a relief, actually. It was very hard to see him locked up like that."

Master George pointed at Tick. "As for our young sleeping lad, here . . . goodness gracious me, what a turn of events. I believe I may have found a connection that explains what is happening."

Paul noticed everyone in the room leaned forward just a little, himself included.

"Entropy," Master George announced, looking around to see the reaction.

Paul squinted his eyes as if that would make his brain work better. "You used that word in the weird spinner movie you sent us."

"Quite right. It refers to the rule of nature that all things move toward eventual destruction. Entropy *accelerates* when a branched Reality begins fragmenting. The nuclear force holding matter together weakens, and things begin to break apart and dissolve—but at a pace millions of times faster than nature's course. A fragmented Reality can be gone—completely gone— in a matter of weeks or months."

"What does that have to do with Tick?" Paul asked.

The skin around Master George's eyes seemed to melt, sinking into a worried frown. "I fear that Master Atticus has no control whatsoever of the inexplicable amounts of Chi'karda stored within him. Where it comes from, and why it's there, I've yet to determine. But I do know what it's doing. It's unleashing itself on objects that frighten or threaten Tick. And when it does . . ."

He paused, as if expecting someone to call him crazy if he continued. "Well, it's *fragmenting* them. Tick is doing, on a very small scale, exactly what happens to a fragmented Reality. He's a catalyst—triggering a heightened state of entropy that dissolves the matter around him. But because it's so out of control, the matter slams back together, the quantum forces regaining their strength and forming the monstrosities you've seen along your latest journeys."

"Whoa," Paul whispered.

Sofia tried to sort it out. "So basically, if Tick freaks out, he can destroy and reform things, trapping whatever gets in his path."

Master George nodded. "Yes, and depending on how far along the entropy develops—how much matter is destroyed before it reforms—the objects may retain some of their old qualities and characteristics."

"We thought it was something Chu had done," Sofia said. "The trees by Tick's house, the spiders, the glass tunnel exploding and melting—all of it. We thought it was all part of the test."

Paul looked down at Tick's sleeping face. "Remind me not to make him mad."

Master George sighed. "I'm afraid Tick's life will have to move in a new direction. He'll have to stay at home, be monitored, watched over. We'll need an extraordinary amount of help from his parents—and we'll have to find ways of ensuring he doesn't have another . . . episode. At least until we sort things out."

"What about us?" Paul asked. "We can help. We can stay with him."

Master George shook his head. "No, no, Master Paul. I need you and Sofia to return to your homes right away and pick up on the rest of the school year. With Dark Infinity destroyed, I believe things will be quiet for a while, and I need both of you to live your normal lives for a bit."

Paul felt his stomach squeeze into a knot. Nothing, absolutely nothing, sounded worse than going back home and living a "normal" life.

"But," he said, searching for arguments, "we're Realitants. Why do we—"

Master George held up a hand. "All in its appointed time, lad. For now, you must go to school, learn, experience growing up. I promise it won't be long before we wink you in for further training or to help with whatever obstacle presents itself to deter our mission."

"What happened to Mistress Jane?" Rutger asked.

Master George looked at him sharply, then glanced away as if trying to hide his alarm at the question. "That, I don't know. We can only hope she's . . ." He didn't need to finish.

"Maybe when Sato's well enough—" Rutger began, but was cut off by Mothball.

"Pipe it for now, little man. One worry at a time."

Master George stood up. "Paul and Sofia, I need the two of you to prepare to return home. I'll send several specially prepared science books with you so that you can study beyond those things you'll learn in normal schooling. I need a little more time with Tick, and I need him to help me resolve the matter of"—he pointed a thumb over his shoulder in the direction of the holding cell—"our captive, Reginald Chu. Tick may be the only one who'll be able to tell *which* Chu it is."

Paul stood as well, trying to ignore the hurt growing inside him. He really didn't want to say good-bye to everyone. "Yeah, what's the deal with the Chu thing? What happened back there?"

Master George stared at him, his face serious. "Two Alterants *met,* lad, face to face. Such a thing is a disaster—a complete disaster, always."

"Why? What happens?" Paul asked.

"One survives, while the other is thrown into . . ." Master George looked about nervously. "Well, we don't know for sure. But Reginald himself always called it the Nonex, and it's something I hope to never encounter. Whenever Alterants meet like that, it causes a terrible disturbance in Chi'karda and the Realities. I wouldn't be surprised if an entirely *new* Reality, perhaps even solid enough to be a main branch, was formed from this. Dreadful, really."

Paul rubbed his eyes and temples. "My head hurts."

"Yes, yes, off you go," Master George said, shooing them away from Tick. "It's time for you to go home. Rutger, please fetch my Barrier Wand."

CHAPTER 51

AWAKENING

Tick didn't know how much time passed between the instant he grew aware of himself and the moment he opened his eyes. An hour maybe. Possibly two.

It was the pain that kept him hiding in his own darkness. Terrible, terrible pain, right in the middle of his skull, as if he'd spent the last week lending his head out as a neighborhood speed bump.

But he finally slid his eyelids open, scared the light would only make it worse but having no choice.

Master George sat in a chair to his left, leaning over him with a huge smile on his ruddy, puffy face. Sato sat to Tick's right, his face swollen but somehow cheerful—for him, anyway.

Tick started to get up, but only made it an inch before thumps of pain slammed his brain like hard fists.

"Now, now, Tick," Master George said, placing a hand on Tick's arm. "Let's not be hasty. You've been through quite an ordeal."

Tick had squeezed his eyes shut again, but forced them open. "What . . . what happened? Chu was there . . . and Mistress Jane . . . and a huge Barrier Wand—"

Master George patted his arm. "Yes, yes, we know much of what happened, thanks to Sofia. Though I'm quite anxious to debrief you about what happened from the time you left your two friends to the time Sofia knocked you senseless. Quite anxious indeed."

"Tick," Sato said, almost a whisper.

Tick tilted his head to the right, raised his eyebrows. "Yeah?"

"You've made me very unhappy. As soon as you're better, I'm going to punch you in the ear."

"Huh?"

Tick could only remember Sato smiling once during the few times they'd been together, but something close to a grin broke across the boy's face.

"Twice, now, you have saved me," Sato said. "You're making me look bad."

"I saved you?" Tick asked, then looked at Master George. "The antidote hit the thing? It worked? Last I remember, the whole place was about to fall down."

"Atticus," Master George said. "You're in no condition right now to learn the things you need to about what happened in Chu's black mountain. Just know that you're safe and Dark Infinity is destroyed, as are the nanoplague bugs it was controlling. Though things did get a bit hairy, it's all worked out in the end."

"Well, what about—"

Master George shushed him, then held up a thick, messy binder stuffed with papers, some folded, others ripped. "It's all been documented here for you to read while you recover. I'll also be sending you home with a big stack of Realitant textbooks and manuals. Now that you're a Realitant First Class, you can begin further study."

"First Class?"

"That's right, old chap." Master George held out a card, similar to the one Tick had been given in May, but dark red this time. Tick saw the words printed on it:

ATTICUS HIGGINBOTTOM
REALITANT FIRST CLASS

"I've already sent Rutger and Mothball ahead to have a very long discussion with your parents," Master George said after he placed the card in Tick's left hand.

"I'm afraid you'll need to be schooled at home now, and watched very closely—"

"What?" Tick tried to sit up again, but this time Sato pushed him back, gently. Pain throbbed through Tick's head.

Master George continued speaking. "No need to worry, good man, no need to worry. As you're well aware, you have an uncanny link to Chi'karda, and it appears capable of spinning completely out of control. But we'll all keep a close eye on you, and if anything troubling happens again, we'll wink you straight in and take care of it. It'll be quite simple, really, considering you'll have plenty of Chi'karda surrounding you wherever you go."

Tick groaned, so confused at the swirl of emotions inside him he didn't know if he felt sad, angry, hopeless, or happy. But suddenly, all he wanted in the world was to go home and see his family.

"Just wink me back," he said. "Please. We can figure it out later. Just send me home."

"An extraordinary idea, Master Tick! Exactly what I had in mind. Paul and Sofia have long since gone, and it's your turn. Don't worry"—Tick's mouth had opened at the mention of his friends—"they said they'd have e-mails waiting for you by the time you arrived in Deer Park. Muffintops, Sato, and I will miss you greatly, but I'm sure our next reunion will happen very soon."

Tick nodded, the pain in his head making him feel nauseated. "Where's your Barrier Wand? Can you wink me from here?"

Master George bit his lip. "Well . . . yes, yes, we can, but I need you to do one thing for me first."

"What?"

Master George looked across the bed. "Sato?"

Sato stood and walked out of the room, slightly limping. His arms were severely bruised, especially around his wrists.

A long minute passed. Muffintops wandered into the room and jumped up onto Tick's chest, purring as she settled into a comfy position, staring at him with her glowing eyes.

"You be good, cat," Tick said, wincing at how stupid it sounded. "Take care of the old man."

A sound at the door took Tick's attention away. Sato had returned and right behind him, looking even more disheveled and bruised than Sato or Tick, was Reginald Chu.

Tick sucked in a gasp of air, bolted into a sitting position, and squirmed backward until he hit the wall. Muffintops shrieked and jumped to the floor; Master George stood, trying to grab Tick's arm.

"Calm yourself!" the old man said. "Master Atticus, calm yourself!"

Tick ignored the pain that exploded inside him.

He noticed handcuffs on Chu's wrists, but that meant nothing. Nothing! The man had more tricks up his sleeve than—

"Tick." Chu said it, softly, calmly.

Tick ignored him, glaring back and forth between Master George and Sato. "How could you just let him walk around here?"

"Tick," Chu repeated. "Please. *Please*, look at me."

Finally, still breathing heavily, Tick did. An inexplicable warmth spread through him, and then a realization hit him. "What did you call me?" he whispered.

"Tick," Chu said, acting as if he hadn't heard. "Please tell these people who I am. I don't know anything about what's going on, or this other Reginald Chu they keep talking about. It's me, Tick—please, tell them!"

Thoughts churned inside Tick's mind. He remembered back in the woods by his house when Mr. Chu had appeared, looking haggard and desperate, acting like he wanted to help them. Something had seemed wrong then, something had been off. And now Tick knew what it was.

"That's my science teacher," he finally said, feeling so calm it seemed the pain had been cut in half. "That's Mr. Chu, not . . . Reginald Chu. Or . . . you know who I mean. This isn't the bad guy."

Master George gave a knowing look to Sato, the

slightest hint of a smile creasing his face. "I suspected as much, but wanted to be certain. Sorry to spring it on you like that, but I didn't want any chance of your having preconceptions."

"How do you know for sure?" Sato asked.

"Because he called me Tick. The evil Chu, back in Deer Park, kept calling me Atticus. My science teacher has called me Tick since the first day I met him. Never once has he called me Atticus. I can't believe I didn't think about that back then."

"No matter," Master George said. "I seriously doubted this could be the Reginald from the Fourth, but we had to be certain. Sato, please free the man."

Mr. Chu sighed, his shoulders sagging in relief as Sato took off the handcuffs.

"I'm sure the two of you will have much to discuss as you get caught up on things," Master George said. "Mr. Chu, I hope you'll serve as a tutor to our young friend back in Reality Prime, help him grasp the complexities of the science that is so closely linked to his welfare."

Mr. Chu didn't look much happier than he had when he'd first entered the room, but he tried his best to smile. "I think Tick has a lot to teach me first." He walked over and took Tick's hand, and squeezed it hard as he shook it. "I'll be expecting a full report, you hear me? And it'd better be good to explain everything

I just went through. I think I'll be avoiding dark streets and alleys for a while."

"Deal," Tick said. "As long as you give *me* a full report too. I don't even know why you're *here*."

Mr. Chu laughed, his face finally winning a victory and looking genuinely pleased, like the teacher Tick had always known. "Yeah, me neither."

"Very well, then," Master George said. "Sato, please take Mr. Chu and debrief him one last time. I'd also like to speak to him before we send him on his way."

"Follow me," Sato said curtly, standing at the door.

Mr. Chu patted Tick on the shoulder. "Real pleasant people you associate with, Tick. Can't wait to spend some more quality time with your friend Sato here."

"Could be worse—could be Billy 'The Goat' Cooper."

"Good point. See ya back in Deer Park. Take care, okay?"

"You, too."

Mr. Chu hesitated, sharing a long look with Tick, then left with Sato, who closed the door behind him.

"Right, then," Master George said, clapping his hands together. "Atticus, I'll put all of your study materials, this binder, and your other belongings in a suitcase of sorts and wink it straight to your room. I'm quite good at that by now. I promise not to destroy any more walls. As for you—your parents are waiting for you to appear in the forest near your home. Near the heavy Chi'karda spot we've used in the past."

Tick blinked. "Right now?"

The old man nodded. "Right now."

Despite everything, a laugh croaked out of Tick's parched throat. "Sweet. I'm ready."

Master George's face grew serious. He came closer and sat back down in his chair, leaning in toward Tick. "Atticus, my dear young friend. I just don't know what to think. There has to be some secret about you we've yet to discover, some . . . well, *something*, anyway. Your abilities and influence over Chi'karda are just mind-boggling, and there *has* to be an explanation. I give you my word, we'll not rest until we figure it out."

"I know what it is," Tick whispered. "I'm a freak. Mistress Jane only tried to help me because she wanted my freak-boy powers."

Master George's face reddened, his lips trembling. Then he composed himself before speaking again. "Listen to me, young man, and listen to me well. Though I fully expect to discover something uncanny about you and your relationship to Chi'karda, I also know this: a large part of it has to do with *you*, and the kind of person you are."

"What do you mean?"

Master George leaned forward even more. "You, my friend, have an incredible amount of conviction.

Courage. A sincerity of belief and principle. All of those things that make up the very essence of the power of Chi'karda. In other words, a considerable portion of your extraordinary gift comes from the simple fact that you very much want to do good. And for that, I'm proud to call you my friend."

Tick wasn't sure what he felt at that moment, but he knew if he tried to talk, it would come out sounding like a frog.

"And now," Master George said, patting Tick's hand, "off you go. I suspect your parents are quite anxious to have you home."

CHAPTER 52

ONE WEEK LATER

"Touchdown!"

Tick's dad leapt off the couch, dropping his game controller onto the floor as he started doing a horrific dance, waving one arm about like an elephant's trunk as he shimmied back and forth.

"Tippy toe left, tippy toe right," Dad sang. "Our team's the best, we're outta sight!"

"Dad," Tick groaned, not too happy about losing once again in Football 3000—in overtime, no less. The awful victory dance only made it worse, and the old man didn't show signs of stopping anytime soon, shaking his larger-than-usual rear end from side to side.

"Watermelon, watermelon, watermelon rind! Look at the scoreboard and see who's behind!"

"Dad, the neighbors might be watching through the window. Please stop."

"Two, four, six, eight . . . okay, that's enough." Dad flopped back onto the couch, breathing deeply as if he'd just run a six-minute mile. "Whew, all that celebratin' can really wear a man out. I wish you'd win more often and make it easier on me."

"Hilarious. One more game?"

Dad leaned over to pick up the controller. "You sure enjoy punishment, don't you?"

Just then, Tick's mom walked in, and without saying a word, she sat next to her husband. Tick felt his heart drop when he saw the look on her face, like she'd just been told she had cancer or lost a child.

"Mom, what's wrong?" Tick asked, feeling the controller slip out of his hands.

She didn't answer for a moment, staring at the floor. Finally, she looked up, her eyes haunted. "Atticus, I can't take it anymore. I have to tell you something. I told your dad several months ago—when he broke the news to me that you'd gone off to be recruited by the Realitants."

"Honey—" Dad began, but cut off at a sharp look from Mom. "Well, I guess he does deserve to know." He glanced over at Tick. "Don't worry—it's pretty neat, actually."

"Neat," Mom said in a deadpan voice. "Once again, Edgar, you've summed things up so eloquently." She reached over and squeezed Dad's hand. "Which is why I love you."

"What are you guys talking about?" Tick asked, much louder than he'd meant to.

"Watch your tone, young man," Mom said as she folded her hands in her lap. "It's just that, well, I feel so bad for not telling you before. I think it might have helped you a little, helped you feel more confident. But then again, if I'd known before you winked away that first time, I might have locked you up in a dog kennel."

"Uh . . . sweetie?" Dad said. "Maybe you should actually tell him what you're talking about."

Mom looked at Tick for several seconds without saying anything. Then, surprising him, she smiled. "I think the best way to tell you is to show you."

As Tick watched, he felt like the laws of gravity had just intensified, pressing him into his seat.

Through the neck of her red blouse, his mom pulled something out that was attached to a golden chain. A pendant. A Barrier Wand pendant, exactly like the one dangling against Tick's chest. He reached up and touched it through his shirt, his eyes stuck on the pendant in his mom's hand. His mouth opened, but no words came out.

"Now before you fall apart," she said, gripping her

pendant in her fist, "hear me out. I only kept this from you and your dad because I was under strict orders from Master George. He wanted to wait until you were old enough to accept it. Well, I think it's high time—especially now that he's sending Mothball and Rutger to us like ordinary mailmen."

"Mothball's a woman," Tick whispered, and somewhere deep down inside, he knew it was exactly the kind of ridiculous statement that pops out of someone who is in complete shock.

"Sorry," Mom said. "Mail *persons*. Anyway, yes, I was a Realitant recruit many years ago and earned my pendant. Back then, it was all about science—none of the dangerous things that are happening now. In fact, I left the group right after"—she paused, touching her lips as if holding back tears—"right after I met your dad. I wanted a normal family life, and Master George let me leave on amicable terms. I should have known that one day he'd go after one of my children."

"I can't believe it," Tick said.

His mom folded her arms defiantly. "Well, why *not?* I know more about science and quantum physics than most people, thank you very much. And now that all of this is out, I can tell you one more thing. I expect you to hit those books Master George sent with a passion, and I'll be on top of you every step of the way, quizzing and pushing. You've got a lot to learn, son. A lot."

"How did I end up with all these smart people?" Dad asked to no one in particular.

"Hush, Edgar," Mom whispered, patting him on the knee.

Dad looked at Tick. "I love when she says that."

Tick stood up, surprised he could do so—everything seemed to spin around him. "You've got . . . to be . . . *kidding* me."

"Now, look here—" his mom began.

"No, Mom, that's not what I mean."

"Then what *do* you mean?" Her eyebrows shot up when Tick laughed out loud.

"It's just . . . that's the coolest thing I've ever heard. *My* mom was a Realitant." He took a seat again on the couch. "I guess it's finally official where I got my brains from." He paused. "Uh, no offense, Dad."

⟶⟵

Later that night, Tick sat in front of the fireplace, staring into the flickering flames. Fall had settled in on Deer Park, making everything cool and crisp. Dad was too stubborn to turn the heater on just yet, so Tick warmed himself before heading up to bed.

As he sat there, almost in a daze, fingering the Barrier Wand pendant through his shirt, his thoughts spun. He'd be fourteen years old in a couple of weeks— hard to believe. How different his life had become in just one year. Not only was he a member of a group that studied and worked to protect alternate realities, he had some freaky power that was completely out of control. He'd been pulled from school to be taught full-time by his mom, with weekly lessons with Mr. Chu, and was monitored constantly for any signs of Chi'karda trouble. It wouldn't be proper to cause an earthquake and destroy half the town of Deer Park.

And always, always, there was the threat of a call for help from Master George. Who knew what waited on the other side of the horizon?

My mom was a Realitant, he thought. *Holy—*

A tap on his shoulder interrupted his thoughts. He turned to see Kayla, holding a teddy bear in one hand, a red-and-black scarf in the other. Her curly blonde hair brushed the shoulders of her pink pajamas.

"Well, what are *you* doing?" he asked, reaching out to ruffle her hair.

"This nasty old scarf was in my closet. Mommy said you lost your other ones."

Tick looked at the dusty scarf clutched in her hand. He had to admit he'd thought about the missing scarf and his birthmark a few times in the last few weeks. It still made him uncomfortable to think people might be gawking at the ugly red thing on his neck. But for all that, he realized he never cared about it much when it was just Paul and Sofia around.

ONE WEEK LATER

Kayla held out the scarf. "Want it?"

Tick took the scarf, then ran it through his hands, staring at the oh-so-familiar pattern of red and black. "Kayla, if I let you do something, do you *promise* not to tell Mom and Dad?"

"Will I get in trouble?"

"*No*—but I don't want you to tell them. Don't worry—this isn't a bad thing. It's a really good thing, actually. But we don't want them to worry, now do we?"

Kayla shook her head.

"I want you to throw this into the fire."

Her eyes lit up, almost as bright as the flames. She looked for all the world like he'd just offered her a lifetime pass to Disneyland. Burning things had always been the one no-no of which she was notoriously guilty.

"Really?" she asked, licking her lips.

"Really. But just this once, okay? You'd better not burn anything else. Promise?"

She nodded her head. "I promise."

Tick handed her the scarf and scooted out of the way. "Go for it."

Kayla wadded up the cloth into a ball, then stepped close to the fireplace. She looked one last time at Tick, as if she thought the opportunity had to be too good to be true. When he just nodded encouragingly, she turned back and threw the scarf into the fire. It took a second to catch, but then smoke billowed up as the flames began to eat away at the material. They both watched as it burned to ashes.

Tick stood up and gave her a hug. "Good job. You're the best pyro I've ever met."

"What's a pie-row?"

"Nothing. You better get up to bed or Mom will take that teddy bear away."

"'Kay. Good night." She turned and ran out of the room, shuffling along with her tiny footsteps.

Tick watched her go, then thought of the stack of Realitant and science books sitting on his desk upstairs. "I've got a lot of work to do," he said aloud to no one but himself.

He reached down and turned off the fire, then headed for his room.

EPILOGUE

YELLOW AND RED

Frazier Gunn hadn't spoken to Mistress Jane for more than two months.

As he stood in the dark stone corridor outside her room, he suddenly wished he had another two months. This summons had been unexpected, and he felt the uncomfortable sweat of fear slicking his palms. Everyone in the castle knew something horrible had happened to Jane; they'd all heard the screams coming from her chambers, often long into the night.

She'd gone through no less than eleven servants—only half of them surviving to tell about it, though it did Frazier little good, since they all had sworn a vow of silence, on penalty of death.

Frazier steeled himself, wiped his hands on his pants, and knocked on the door.

On the third thunk, the door swung open violently, slamming against the stone wall on the other side.

"Enter, Frazier."

It was a voice he barely recognized. Raw and scratchy—*weak,* as if Jane had swallowed a glass of lava, scorching her throat and vocal chords.

"Enter," she repeated.

Frazier couldn't see where she was in the room.

He stepped across the threshold, then closed the door. The only light in the room was a fire, burning hotly with several fresh logs, spitting and cracking. With a shudder, he remembered back to Jane's flying cinder display, and he hoped there'd be no repeat tonight.

"You called for me?" Frazier asked the darkness.

A figure stepped out of the shadows behind a deep wardrobe in the corner between the bed and a large open window, where curtains fluttered in the breeze. Though Frazier could not yet see any details, he knew it was his boss. But she appeared to have something draped over her head.

"It's good to see you again, Mistress Jane," he said, fighting to keep his voice steady.

"My dear Frazier," she said, her voice the sound of rocks rubbing on sandpaper. "You will never know how very good it is to see *you*."

For the first time, Frazier realized there was a slight hollowness to her voice, as if it were muffled by something over her mouth. Subtle, but there all the same.

"That means a lot to me," he finally said. And he meant it.

"I've often been . . . cruel to you," Jane said, taking a step forward. Though she was still mostly in shadow, Frazier could see that she wore a long, flowing robe, its hood pulled up over her head. Something glinted off her face, a flickering reflection from the fire.

Must be her glasses, Frazier thought.

"You've only ever done that which needed to be done," he said. "I know I'll have my reward some day, when we make the Realities as they were meant to be."

"Frazier," she whispered.

"Yes, Mistress Jane?"

"I want you to know that I love you as if you were my own brother. I promise never to be cruel to you again."

Frazier felt a strange mixture of elation and sick fear. "The feeling is mutual." His hands were sweating even worse than before. So was his face.

"That makes me happy, Frazier. Very, very happy."

Mistress Jane stepped out into the full light of the fire, and a puff of sharp air escaped Frazier's lips before he could stop it. He took a step backward, cursing himself silently as soon as he did.

The floor-length robe that draped over her head and shoulders and body was a brilliant yellow, glowing like molten gold in the flickering light of the flames. Where her face should have been, a red mask floated, bright as fresh blood. Though it sparkled like shiny metal, its surface moved and flowed, creating subtle facial expressions, alternating between anger, sadness, excitement, confusion, joy, pain. Small holes, as dark as the deepest depths of the ocean, made up her eyes, and somehow Frazier knew she was looking at him through the mask.

"Mistress Jane . . ." was all he could get out.

The flowing, red metal mask solidified into a stark expression of rage, eyebrows slanted up from the nose like a big V.

"*He* did this to me, Frazier," she said, her raspy voice bitter and tight. "I tried so hard to make him see—to work with him, to *help* him. But in the end, he looked at me and threw all of his powers against me. He *hurt* me, Frazier. I will always be in pain now."

"Who?" Frazier asked. "Who did this to you? What . . ." He almost asked her what was hidden beneath the yellow robe, but he knew better.

She turned her red mask to look at the fire as she continued speaking. "But perhaps it was for the best. I've been reminded of my life's duty. I've been reminded how cold and cruel the Realities can be. I've been reminded of the goals I set so many years ago. And I've been reminded of what kind of person it takes to accomplish . . . what we *need* to accomplish."

"Yes, Mistress Jane," he answered fervently. "I'll be by your side. Always."

"If I ever falter again, Frazier—if I ever doubt myself or doubt the things I need to do and the way in which I need to do them, I want you to do me a favor."

"Anything."

"I want you to say two words to me. Two words. It'll be all the reminder I ever need."

"What words, Mistress?" Frazier asked.

Jane looked back in his direction, the darkness of her eyeholes boring into him out of the shiny red mask of liquid metal. And then she told him.

"Atticus Higginbottom."

ACKNOWLEDGMENTS

✴

Somehow we made it to Book 2, so there must be a lot of people to thank.

I'm extremely grateful to my agent, Michael Bourret. He has single-handedly taken my career to an entirely new level. If it weren't for him, I'd never be doing what I love for a living. Thanks, Michael, and I look forward to more great things to come.

Just like last time, I owe a lot to Chris Schoebinger, Lisa Mangum, and everyone else at Shadow Mountain. It just baffles me how much hard work goes into getting a book in the hands of readers. Thank you all very, very much.

Thanks to Bryan Beus for his awesome artwork.

ACKNOWLEDGMENTS

You are one talented dude, and I'm honored to be partnered with you.

Thanks to those who read the manuscript and provided valuable feedback: My wife, Lynette, of course—she's always first. J. Scott Savage, friend, fellow author, and constant lunch partner. LuAnn Staheli and her incredible middle school class. Danyelle Ferguson, a very talented and up-and-coming writer. Heather Moore, good friend and brilliant editor, and her son, Kaelin. And probably others. If I forgot you, please forgive me and call me for a free dinner.

Thanks to Lisa Guerrero, a cancer research scientist from Chicago, for her services as a consultant and science genius. She's way smart, yo. Like, really, really smart.

Once again, thanks to the dude who invented football. I could never thank you enough. Oh, and I also really appreciate the guy who invented Tiger Woods.

Thanks to the cow that provided a very juicy steak at Hamilton's in Logan, Utah, in February of 2008. You will be missed.

Thanks to the mother of Christopher Nolan for going through the pain of birthing him. I never thought I would say this, but Christopher is now tied with Peter Jackson as my favorite directors. You are both geniuses.

Last but never least, *thank you* to my readers. You're what it's all about. I look forward to sharing stories with you for a very long time.

CONTINUE THE ADVENTURE IN

THE 13TH REALITY

BOOK 3

THE BLADE OF SHATTERED HOPE

———————✳———————

Sato shivered, then grimaced. He'd only stood in the open for a bare minute, trying to figure out where he'd arrived exactly. Already drenched, his rain-soaked clothes felt icky against his skin, as though an army of leeches clung to him for dear life.

The air had a feel of twilight, but he knew it was almost noon in this Reality. Massive, heavy clouds of gray-black floated far above him—though they seemed close enough to reach up and touch— emptying their contents on his sopping wet head.

George had said it rained constantly here, a dreary, dreadful place according to the old man. Sato couldn't have agreed more.

He'd supposedly been winked to a cemetery, though this looked nothing like one. He looked about, confused. There were no tombstones, no plaques planted in the ground to mark graves. In fact, he stood atop concrete—or something like it. Hard and flat, the surface was dotted with regular holes that drained away the water as quickly as it fell. Otherwise, he would have been standing in a deep pool. It looked more like a parking lot than a cemetery.

Why do I always get stuck with these jobs? Sato thought. Windy snow-swept mountains, insane asylums, rainy parking lots supposedly full of dead people. Fun stuff.

He noticed a small building about forty feet away, a scarce shadow in the wet darkness. It was more of a hut, square and small, without a glimmer of light from a window or an outdoor fixture. Seeing nothing else in any direction except the flat expanse of hole-dotted pavement, Sato walked toward the squat building.

As he sloshed his way across the ground, he wished he had a companion to whom he could grumble aloud. Why hadn't George at least given him an umbrella? Maybe next time the red-faced geezer would send Sato to the middle of the ocean without a boat, or maybe to the desert without any water. Maybe skydiving without a parachute.

Sato shivered and kept walking. He felt his socks soak through, the squishy chill feeling like he was smashing hundreds of iced shrimp below his feet. If no one answered at the building, he'd send the signal immediately for Rutger to wink him back. They might have found their first dead end in Sato's latest mission. A mission that creeped him out and left him in awe at the same time.

Tick, he thought. *Oh, man, Tick. What in the world does this all mean?*

As Sato got closer to the building, he noticed the walls were completely smooth—not a door or window, absolutely no markings of any kind. It was made up of the same drab, no-color material of the ground on which he walked, smooth and unblemished. The hut was a perfect cube, maybe ten feet in height and width.

He walked right up to it, put his hand out. Rain cascaded down the sides of the cube in sheets, and when his hand made contact with the cool, hard side of the building, the water parted and washed across his skin and down his arm, spilling to the ground in tiny twin falls. Sato pulled his hand back, shook it back and forth in a futile attempt to dry himself considering the pouring rain.

He was just about to call out the inevitable "Hello?" when he heard a loud thump and felt the ground tremble below his feet, as if some giant beast from the underworld was trying to break free from its lair with a massive hammer. It happened only once, but Sato's feet tingled from the vibration of the impact. Surprisingly, he didn't feel afraid. Not yet, anyway.

There was a loud hiss, muted by the pounding rain, and then the wall directly in front of him began to *move*. Outward, toward him.

Sato felt anxiety grip his heart for the first time since arriving, and he stepped back, almost turning to run. But he didn't run—George knew where he was sending him, after all. He had nothing to be afraid of.

He realized that the entire wall wasn't moving toward him, it was only the bottom edge that swung out and upward like an old-fashioned garage door. The left and right side walls were doing the same, the groan of metallic hinges a faint squeal in the background. A soft light shone from the center of the cube, turning the thousands of raindrops into silvery sparkles. Sato could see through the cube to the other side, where the fourth wall opposite him was lifting open like its counterparts. Seconds later all movement stopped with a loud *clank*—the four walls having reached a position parallel to the ground. Just a few feet above him, a wide shelter from the weather had formed, the doors and middle section now shaped like an overhead square cross, the entire structure now supported by four large metal pillars.

His fear vanished and Sato stepped forward out of the rain, toward the middle of what used to be a closed building and was now just a really fancy covered patio. He half expected to see a picnic table, maybe even a barbecue grill, but what he found instead surprised him greatly.

A hole.

A round hole, with a spiral set of stairs winding down into the depths. Sato saw an iron railing bolted to the side. The light he'd noticed came from somewhere at the bottom of the hole; everything in sight was surprisingly dry. A small metal sign was fixed into the floor next to the first step, words stamped onto the surface:

GRACE OF HER HEART CEMETERY

A prickle of fear raised bumps on Sato's flesh, but reason calmed his nerves as soon as it started. In a place like this, where rain was the norm, it made perfect sense for the dead to be buried in a vault or tomb instead of within the spongy, soaked, muddy earth. Otherwise, dead people would be floating all over the place. It was just a cemetery—a normal, peaceful, full-of-bodies graveyard.

And over the last few weeks, Sato had become very used to graveyards.

Blowing a breath through his lips, he squeezed as much water as possible out of his clothes and hair, then set off down the stairs. With each step an audible squish sounded through the air, inexplicably making him want to laugh. Step by step, round and round, he descended. With every full circuit he made, he saw a square light set into the wall, casting a warm glow—literally. Things heated up quickly and considerably.

After what felt like ten or so floors, he reached the bottom of the stairs and stepped through an open doorway in front of him into a massive chamber. Unable to hold back a gasp of wonder, he gaped at the rows upon rows of metal containers that stretched as far as he could see, fading away into a shadowy mist in the distance. Large pillars supported the roof thirty feet or so above him, standing like iron angels, guarding the dead.

For that's what filled the room, Sato realized. The dead. In metal caskets, stacked five high, with barely enough room between them in which to walk. Sato calculated there had to be thousands of deceased in the underground cemetery. Thousands upon thousands.

It took him exactly four hours and forty-five minutes to find what he was looking for.

The casket looked like every other one in the vast

tomb. Made from a dark steel, the slightest shade of silver prevented it from being utterly black. The final resting place of two other souls lay on top, two more beneath, hundreds to either side. The bronze plaque naming the person inside was tarnished and dirty. Sato reached forward and wiped away the dust, more out of respect for the dead than anything—he could read the words imprinted on the plaque just fine.

This was the seventh Reality in which he'd seen such words.

It was a casket for Atticus Higginbottom.